JOSIE AND NAT APPROACH BRADFORD LANE SURGERY

BRADFORD LANE

By Kay Frances

Facing Illustration BY JESSICA MACKINDER
Remaining Illustrations BY JIM MACKINDER

Bradford Lane

Trilogy Christian Publishers

A Wholly Owned Subsidiary of Trinity Broadcasting Network

2442 Michelle Drive, Tustin, CA 92780

Copyright © 2025 by Kay Frances

All rights reserved, including the right to reproduce this book or portions thereof in any form whatsoever.

For information, address Trilogy Christian Publishing

Rights Department, 2442 Michelle Drive, Tustin, Ca 92780.

Trilogy Christian Publishing/ TBN and colophon are trademarks of Trinity Broadcasting Network.

For information about special discounts for bulk purchases, please contact Trilogy Christian Publishing.

Trilogy Disclaimer: The views and content expressed in this book are those of the author and may not necessarily reflect the views and doctrine of Trilogy Christian Publishing or the Trinity Broadcasting Network.

10 9 8 7 6 5 4 3 2 1

Library of Congress Cataloging-in-Publication Data is available.

ISBN 979-8-89333-874-4

ISBN 979-8-89333-875-1 (ebook)

Table of Contents

Foreword..7

Prologue..9

Part I: *The Randolph Family*

1. Boston Massacre Remembered..........................13
2. A New Governor...25
3. Josephine Randolph..35
4. Tolerate No Uncleanliness................................53
5. Retreat to Stoughton..59
6. Mulberry Farm..73
7. Back to Work...105

Part II: *Mistaken Ideas and Expectations*

8. Confrontation at the Farm...............................117
9. Unforeseen Circumstances..............................121
10. Ethan's Rendezvous..133
11. Ambush at Dawn...147
12. Captain Ezekiel Penrose..................................163
13. Whales' Tale Tavern..169
14. Retaliation..187
15. Horse Sense...209

16. A Chance Meeting..................................217

17. Seeking Justice...................................235

Part III: *The Stowe Family*

18. Work Is Good for the Soul......................257

19. Lainey's Dilemma................................283

20. Tavern Talk......................................301

21. Dragon and Frederic............................319

22. New Haven......................................327

Part IV: *Do Good Where You Can*

23. Good Samaritan.................................351

24. The Way Home.................................377

25. Suffield, Connecticut Militia..................385

26. Stranger in the Woods.........................405

Part V: *Beat the Drums*

27. Travails of a Besieged Province (Boston).......429

28. Philadelphia....................................459

29. Either Way, It's Treason......................487

30. Lexington......................................509

Preview of Book Two...................................525

Map of New England and New York..................535

Foreword

Idle hands never made the corn grow. Such was the philosophy that drove my parents to rise before dawn to begin a new day of work. Their lives as farmers were dictated by earth's natural forces of the moon, the sun, the rain, and the wind. This was necessary work passed down to them by their ancestors. The smell of rich soil and the sight of sprouting seeds was a cherished miracle for my parents.

By this reasoning, Americans value work and the dignity of selecting an occupation that is unique to their God-given talents. Over two centuries have passed since risk-taking settlers crossed the Atlantic to a New World. Readers of the Bradford Lane story will sense a connection to the substance and toughness of those extraordinary settlers who taught us that work is a virtue.

Prologue

That predictable shelf of granite waited for me at the end of Bradford Lane. I stood on its mostly flat surface to view Hancock's long wharf jutting into the bay from Boston's solid precipice. My time of solitude to pay homage to my world—my home, my family, my neighbors, my bookstore, my apothecary, my work. All that I had loved for eighteen years was crowded into this small peninsula.

The gulls flew high above the trees and the bay, their wings flipping and flopping in the gusting March winds. Most gave up and walked close to the shoreline. Some screamed from hunger. The brave ones flew awkwardly with the remains of a codfish hanging from their beaks. My eyes moved to the tall spiral of Old North Church and the state house. I caught the smells of Fletcher's Livery and of lye soap wafting from wash tubs. "Some things will always remain the same," I whispered.

Shabbily dressed men passed off as pirates caught their orders and grumbled their replies as they stumbled along the dock, back and forth from the ships. Men pushed carts of boxes and burlap bags to house in Boston's warehouses—merchandise destined for shops and taverns to sell to Boston's inhabitants. Shopkeepers opened their stores. Delivery wagons journeyed up the middle of town, bringing milk and eggs and meat from the countryside farms. Hmm, how long will that last?

I sat atop the hard rock and spoke softly for the first time. "At present, I *am* satisfied with my world, but there *is* the future. Everything could change by the afternoon or tomorrow. 'Josie, it's happened before. It could happen again. There are no guarantees,' Auntie had reminded me." I gazed at the wayward gulls.

Josie's Commanding View of Boston Bay

Part I

The Randolph Family

Chapter 1

Boston Massacre Remembered

March 5, 1774

Boston had become the crowning glory of the wealthiest port in the colonies with its connection to the harbor, allowing merchants to ship their resources to Europe, the West Indies, and beyond. The common man who had a will to work and infinite courage sacrificed all they owned to travel across the sea to the New World. The small landmass, roughly seven hundred acres, was home to the colony's busiest and most prosperous shipping port. Men and women arriving in the New World had crushed the boundaries that, for centuries, had imprisoned them to live as peasants. American ingenuity had taken hold in this coastal province, promising extraordinary wealth and prosperity to New England. It also signaled that London's elite were anxious to get their hands on that wealth, but they were not going to get it without a fight.

The Randolph brothers woke early, long before Boston's church bells began tolling incessantly, commanding markets to open and merchants to attend their shops. Bostonians were fully aware when they blew out the last candle for the night that the following day would be devoted to Massacre Day.

It was a day of remembrance for five Boston citizens struck down by British soldiers outside the Boston Customs House. Their tragic deaths further galvanized the colony's indignation toward King George. His efforts to levy extreme taxes on men and women living in the thirteen coastal colonies had created the momentum for resistance among Boston citizens. It was a precarious time for thousands of self-reliant Patriots.

These were stubborn people who knew London's Parliament had meddled too far when their constitutional laws were violated. Rumors of closing Boston's port, the lifeblood of the province, had lit a fire under Provincials, realizing their survival was at stake. They were at a tipping point—willing to fight it out with the British or return to a meager existence in Europe. This day, farmers, blacksmiths, and merchants left their work and rowed their boats across the river to Boston to face the hard facts that could possibly result in disastrous consequences for their businesses and families.

Men came from the furthest western boundaries of Massachusetts Colony, riding in wagons and on horseback until reaching the Charles River. They traveled south from Charlestown and north from their farms located below the Boston Neck. They came with heavy hearts, fearing that King George III, ruler of the British Empire, would take command of the colonies with his huge army of soldiers, their warships, and sophisticated weaponry. They looked to Boston's leaders for answers.

"Merchant King" John Hancock was charged to pay tribute to the five victims who suffered their senseless deaths, making it the fourth year that Bostonians gathered for the service. The swelling crowds and the windy March day only intensified Jacob and Josiah Randolph's sense of urgency to depart the house on Bradford Lane and join in the procession toward Old South Meeting House. Their paltry breakfast—more like a soldiers' ration of a cold biscuit and a chunk of cheese—washed down with a mug of ale would have to serve their appetite until their return home.

Three months had passed since angry Boston Patriots, disguised as Mohawk Indians, had confiscated chests of East India tea that had been shipped three thousand miles to Boston Harbor. The tea was axed open and dumped into the harbor, displaying colonists' refusal to purchase it, much less pay taxes on it. The scheme to force Boston merchants to pay for the tea and the tariff had backfired. The chasm between the colonies and London grew deeper and wider. Tensions were high, and many spoke of war between the colonies and Great Britain. A time of reckoning was on the horizon.

"Ah, that's one thing I don't miss about living in Boston—actually, several." Jacob pulled his wool scarf downward to his chin to make clear his cynical comments directed to his younger brother.

"Only two. I'm sure there's a dozen or more," Josiah, choosing to keep his scarf in place to avoid breathing the fetid air, replied loudly to his brother, above the crowd's congested breathing and croup laden coughing, as the wild, sonorous ringing of church bells continued.

"It's the smells of baking bread, dead fish, stinking outhouses, livery, and distilleries all crowded in this, what, seven hundred acres?" Jacob extended his gloved hands to create the shape of an island, pulsating back and forth as if bulging outside of its boundaries of land into the ocean. "How can you stand the stench of this precipice overlooking the sea?"

The brothers continued walking uphill, finally getting a view of the front doors at the state house. Josiah rolled his eyes and responded to Jacob's mockery. "Exactly why I cover my nose and ears with a scarf. I'm not liking it any better than you are. I'm serving the community here, and as much as I love Stoughton, I'm not moving back to the farm anytime soon. The smell isn't that bad on Bradford Lane."

The pews were partially filled, as were the aisles, galleries, and stairways, packed with frenzied Patriots anticipating Mr. Hancock would share the latest news from London. The Randolphs arrived early to claim seats on a pew located midway into the room. Before either of the brothers could remove their hats and cloaks, Samuel Grimes tapped Josiah on the shoulder. "My gout's been ailing me fer two weeks now. Can I come by yer surgery today?" Josiah nodded and smiled in response. "Much obliged to ye, Doctor," and returned to his seat. Jacob cringed at the man's provincial slang.

Anxious people continued pouring into the room, looking for available spaces and a view of the speaker. Jacob and Josiah were wedged into their seats, regularly shifting their bodies at an angle to fit their wide shoulders and long legs amongst other hot bodies. The smells of sweat and ale polluting the air didn't help either. Even though it was bitter cold outside, the press of human bodies wearing heavy clothes made it uncomfortably hot.

Several men turned around in their seats, eyeing Josiah after overhearing Mr. Grimes' request for medical attention. This prompted a man to reach across Jacob to show Josiah his hand wrapped in a dirty rag, "Ken ye pull out a splinter? This here's a festering."

Josiah was quick to respond. "No need to remove the bandage. I'll take a look at it when we're finished here." Not recognizing the man, he added, "My surgery is on Bradford Lane." The man was a laborer. His calloused hands and fishy smell identified him as a longshoreman. He nodded and looked downward in humility, slowly leaning back into the pew, clearly embarrassed.

Accidents happened at Boston's docks every day, and this man was typical of the people Josiah served. He hesitantly glanced at his brother, recognizing that familiar, exasperated look, "I know what you're thinking," he shrugged. "I am a physician, after all. People need my services."

Jacob scoffed at his brother's response in a low voice, "We've been seated here for five minutes, and already, two strangers hire you as their physician. What are the—" Jacob's words trailed off as Mr. Hancock approached the podium, outfitted in stylishly tailored velvet breeches, a satin waistcoat, and a freshly coiffed wig. The room was hushed. Men sat poised in their seats, anxious to hear every word coming from the merchant's mouth.

John Hancock's demeanor reflected all that one of the wealthiest businessmen in the thirteen colonies and beyond could allow. The handsome and poised aristocratic figure of a man emanated education, wealth, intelligence, and sharp wit. All this attributable to his late uncle, Thomas Hancock, who had taken his young nephew under his wing and tutored him in the ways of business and civic responsibilities, indicative of the talents and genius of the senior merchant and landowner himself.

Hancock glanced at his notes and paused to take in the mass of Patriots assembled in the House, not yet opening his mouth to speak, more to get the measure of all those he was addressing. Farmers, doctors, merchants, craftsmen, shipwrights, lawyers, veterans of war, and any curious observer who sat on the fence regarding his allegiance—Loyalist or Patriot. Men who sensed the price that must be paid for their liberties and, above all, the independence they sought by cutting ties with England. The separation from the mother country would be an enormous undertaking that could take months or years. Did these men have the heart and the stamina for such a commitment? Mr. Hancock knew all that was at stake today. This could possibly be the final occasion for Bostonians to gather—legally.

John Hancock spoke as the leader he was to the silenced crowd. Lifting his voice, he reminded the audience of the brutality of the king and London's Parliament by imposing excessive taxes on consumables, the quartering of British soldiers in colonist's homes and taverns, the jeopardy of trade with Europe, the closing of ports, and the very reason they were assembled today: the massacre of innocent people, four years prior.

"These Intolerable Acts, created by London's ministers, are meant to punish us, enslave us, and force colonists to live under the rule of greedy Englishmen who believe they were born with a special privilege to govern us. This is the very reason our ancestors came to these shores—to escape the tyranny of England's kings and Europe's rulers and emperors.

"England means to inflict the same pain on these colonies as they have on certain other continents which, as you well know, have been reduced to total submission to Parliament, leaving them with mere crumbs! This is tyranny!" The audience stamped their feet and shook their fists in response. He continued with the demand for Bostonians and the other twelve colonies to abstain from buying British imports, and most definitely British tea. "Make your own!" he demanded.

"These colonies must unite to subvert and vanquish the corruptness of Britain's evil plots. In short, they intend to make us all paupers!" The audience roared, "Tyranny, tyranny!" as Mr. Hancock paused to wipe his brow. "I charge you, 'lovers of liberty,' arm yourselves and your families. Unite in our efforts by enlisting in the militias. Prepare yourselves to engage in battle against the thieves and murderers who seek to destroy what we have built. Alert your friends, neighbors, and adjoining colonies; this is our moment to defend all we have worked for. Our ancestors, who truly sacrificed in ways we could never comprehend, hoped to secure for their descendants a bright and freedom-filled future without the oppression of tyrannical kings." All eyes focused on the leader. "This army will surely arrive on our shores, and when they do, we must be prepared to protect our families and our homes!"

John Hancock stepped away from the podium, promptly surrounded by Patriot leaders who led him outside to his carriage amid the cheers and applause that erupted as he exited the meeting room. The spirit of hope in the room changed men and set them on fire to accept the challenge Mr. Hancock had put forth.

Jacob and Josiah sat spellbound, absorbing the urgent tasks descending on them like a load of bricks. Finally, Josiah murmured to his brother, "Let's take some air. The stench in this room is making me queasy." The weather remained freezing cold, even though the late morning sun shone brightly in the azure sky. The brothers walked around the crowds and the Saturday markets, taking long strides while the sonorous bells pealed the hour, bound for Josiah's home on Bradford Lane.

The modest, two-story, whitewashed, clapboard-sided, peaked roof house was purchased by Josiah as a gift to his bride, Josephine Harriet Spencer. The dooryard, surrounded by a white picket fence, was small but ample for two small crabapple trees that stood on either side of the walkway leading to the main entry. Lilacs, planted by the original owners, had grown immensely over the years, now dominating the drawing room side of the house. Jo had envisioned an herb garden for cooking and medicinal purposes on the opposite side of the dwelling designated as Josiah's surgery.

That life had begun twenty-four years ago. Through the years, nature had taken hold of the small garden where flowers and bushes had volunteered their beauty and usefulness. Josiah took a quick gaze at the gardens as he approached the front entry, where green sprouts promising cheerful yellow daffodils pushed through the cold, hard earth, ushering in a new season and a remembrance of his beloved Jo.

Jacob walked through the front hall of the house, stopped, and sniffed the pungent air. "My nose was expecting roast mutton. It is *now* betrayed by the smell of alcohol!" Josiah quickly stepped into his surgery and opened two windows, allowing the alcohol odor to escape.

Jacob made himself at home and walked to the back of the house, expecting to see his sister, "Minnie, we're home, and we're hungry. Minnie, where are you?" While walking to his brother's home on the chilly morning, he had visualized Minnie graciously welcoming her two brothers with a flavorful roast, vegetables, and freshly cooked bread, waiting for the brothers to sit and be fed.

Minnie was nowhere in sight. Instead, she had left a token pot of vegetable soup and leftover biscuits for her ravenous brothers, more a gesture of sisterly love. Jacob sighed and mumbled a few undesirable words aimed at his sister's obvious disregard. "It will have to do." He removed his cape and swung the pot to the side to kindle the smoldering fire. Upon adding two logs, a flame arose instantly, the crackling and popping sounds began, and heat filled the spacious fireplace.

"I can see your disappointment!" Josiah restrained the urge to laugh at his brother's irritation. "I should have warned you Saturday is shopping day for Minnie and Josie. Nothing short of a blizzard would keep them away from Boston's shops and markets. Regrettably, our dear sister's hospitality does not hold a candle to your sweet Lenora's genial nature.

"The alcohol scent is the work of my able assistant who never tarries from her responsibilities. Clean surgical instruments are vital to my work. Sorry, the smell is rather sharp at first. Oh, look, here's a note addressed to you."

A timely diversion, thought Josiah.

Jacob read the letter out loud. "'I pray this will not inconvenience you. It is my desire to visit your brother's home on Bradford Lane after today's meeting, with hopes that you will remain in Boston. A rather urgent matter needs our attention' signed 'John Adams.' As if we don't have enough urgent matters that need our attention," Jacob sighed.

A knock at the front entry door confirmed Mr. Adams was serious about his visit. Josiah and Jacob made their guest feel welcome with a smile and a slight bow. "Ah, Mr. Adams, welcome to my home. Join us for a bowl of hot soup," Josiah offered as he pointed Mr. Adams in the direction of the warm kitchen.

The fireplace had quickly removed the chill from the room. Jacob had closed the door leading to the scullery and the front entry to contain the heat in the kitchen and keeping room. Rays of sunshine poured through the big window, highlighting Minnie's flower and vegetable garden and adding more heat at the far end of the room.

John Adams' face was flushed from the cold, brisk walk from the state house, causing his nose to turn red and his eyes to water. He rubbed his cold hands together to generate more body heat.

The visitor from Braintree removed his cape, along with his leather shoulder bag, and stood toasting himself by the fire for a moment. He noticed the copper pot suspended from an iron hook in the enormous fireplace, stooping down to take a whiff, "a bowl of savory soup, just what the body needs on such a day," offering his thankfulness. "I barely had time to choke down the apple I picked up at the market. I was lucky to get that with the crowds pushing through with the same idea," he laughed. "So much tension in the air these days; it's dangerous to be on the streets!"

Jacob filled three mugs of beer from the keg he had brought from his home in Stoughton, and the men raised them in congratulations. "To John Hancock," cheered Jacob. Adams' eyes grew large after he took a sip, followed by a healthy swallow, ending with a pleasing sigh. The brothers watched the man's face light up with sheer delight. Jacob grinned broadly at his brother and jabbed his elbow into his brother's ribs in an amicable manner.

"I do relish a rich and flavorful beer! Such as the brew I've delighted in at a certain establishment down by way of Milton," Mr. Adams nodded his round face approvingly. "You don't mean to say that this was produced in your brewery! Congratulations on creating a most robust and aromatic brew. In my journeying across the colonies, I consume a good deal of beer, much to the chagrin of my wife. She laments my plumpness and claims I should temper my intake of the drink!"

"That certain establishment wouldn't be the Cackling Crow, by chance?" Jacob asked. This particular tavern had been serving Mulberry beer for over thirty years, long before Jacob had taken the helm of the family brewery. The favored tavern in Milton, boasting the same clientele who gathered evenings to drink beer and smoke their pipes while imparting the woes of Boston and oppressions caused by London's Parliament.

"So, what do you think?" Jacob looked seriously at Mr. Adams. "Do we take John Hancock at his word, or do we bow to Britain's demands? Are you as adamant about war as many are these days?"

Mr. Adams knew where this was headed. "I see you've been reading my cousin's circulars, Mr. Randolph. Sam has done an admirable job of organizing resistance against these royal governors who take their marching orders from Parliament. The colonies must unite, and his Committees of Correspondence have established communication so needed if we intend to work together to fight off Britain. He remains a steadfast ally to the cause of liberty."

"The problem remains with Lord North," Adams continued, "that pop-eyed, hard-headed prime minister who believes these Intolerable Acts he has concocted is the answer to Parliament's problems. If and when they are enforced, there will be more resistance from colonists than ever before. I'm afraid the stage has been set for conflict."

"There are many in Parliament who have no taste for war, believing colonists should devise their own system of taxing themselves," Jacob spoke, indicating that he had not given up hope that the problems with Britain could be hammered out. "Why not agree to negotiate our trade laws and stop meddling in the affairs of the colonies? War is inhumane and costly, after all."

"Spoken like a lawyer and business owner, Mr. Randolph. King George and his ministers apparently have not taken the prophet Jeremiah's lesson to heart, 'the pride of thine heart hath deceived thee,'" Mr. Adams declared assuredly.

"The king's subjects have been deceived, thinking he possesses a benevolent heart, but nothing could be further from the truth. He has been misadvised by those who whisper in his ear thoughts of deception advanced by his closest allies, 'the colonies' rich merchants are laughing behind your back; they are demanding their independence,'" John Adams mimicked London's ministers. "Those very words cause the king's hatred to grow. He feels ashamed that his authority is being compromised. With that state of mind, he will command his army and navy to crush these colonies. Blood will be shed." The brothers' pensive faces concurred.

Mr. Adams continued, "The colonies do an adequate job of mustering militias to mitigate local issues, but we need more men trained to fight the redcoats. This has been my purpose since January when the king began to talk of sending soldiers to Boston to quell the 'rabble-rousers' and of closing our ports. Naturally, we will need weapons, ammunition, and artillery to defend our colony, and that leads me to the purpose of my visit. I'm appealing to you, Jacob, if I may, to act as an agent in securing muskets and cannons for our soldiers in Milton, Stoughton, Roxbury, and Braintree. Of course, we will have the awesome task of caching these supplies until we need them."

Josiah considered the seriousness of Adam's predictions. "As I sat in the state house this morning contemplating the faces and reactions of those in attendance, I came to realize that the majority of the crowd had rowed across the river from Concord, Lexington, Acton, and Worcester. These areas may be looked upon as small towns and hamlets, but each has created their own political system. They elect representatives, conduct town meetings, muster militias, conduct church services, and print newspapers. They may gather to discuss local issues, and it's right that they should. But since Parliament has made such demands on collecting more taxes and creating more regulations, the topics of conversation in town meetings have drastically changed. These citizens have presented these issues as topics to deal with in their hometowns. The environment is ripe with talks of revolution and ways to secure their properties. They don't like outsiders meddling in their affairs. Mr. Hancock's words have catapulted these men to a new level of expectation. Their lives have been changed today. Mine has."

Jacob knew his brother had his hands full with organizing medical supplies and recruiting volunteers, so it came down to him. This was his time to step forward and commit to the work that every Patriot who valued his liberties should invest for the common good. He looked eye to eye with his brother Josiah, reading his thoughts: a familiar family strategy when critical decisions were in need of settling.

He turned toward Mr. Adams, "So, this is what resistance looks like? I'm not familiar with any ironworks in this area; I suppose you are. Who shall I contact?" Mr. Adams pushed a note in his direction—*Stowe Ironworks*, Suffield, Connecticut.

Chapter 2

A New Governor

May 17, 1774, Boston

Boston Loyalists welcomed the new Governor of Massachusetts and Commander in Chief of the Crown's forces in the colony, General Thomas Gage. Employed by King George III to replace Governor Hutchinson. He was authorized to quarter as many soldiers as necessary to suppress Boston's colonial rebels, particularly Sam Adams and John Hancock. Parliament allowed Gage four thousand troops. He had requested thousands more. Redcoats were scattered everywhere now, dribbling into Salem, Plymouth, and Marblehead, anywhere the regulars could set up camp and drill.

This was all well and good if you placed your loyalties with the king; naturally, you would welcome such fanfare despite the wet and windy day in May. British soldiers wearing their smart red jackets trimmed in gold demonstrated quite a show of force and superiority as General Gage was presented to the crowd of Tories and colonists. Loyalists (Tories) living in Boston, New York, and Philadelphia believed they needed the protection of the king, finding it difficult to separate themselves from the "mother country."

But not all in attendance were of like mind. In the last ten years, tensions had mounted between colonists and England's king and Parliament lords over excessive taxes and regulations. Their idea was of individual independence, remarkably different from the lives of common people in Europe.

The final straw came when colonists refused to buy British tea and pay the tax. England continued to meddle by laying siege to Boston. Now, their very presence posed a threat to the livelihood of Boston's residents: shipbuilders, craftsmen, merchants, and thousands of dock workers—the engine that made Boston's port the most prosperous in the thirteen colonies.

Traveling northward, up the mile-long Boston Neck, through the gates to the city, sat a row of fifteen houses beginning on the right side of Main Street. Each two-story clapboard residence was surrounded by a fence or a thick hedge for the owner's privacy. Also meant to discourage intruders and beggars and to keep out dogs, stray goats, and the occasional wild hog.

Josiah Randolph owned the end house on the corner of Main Street and Bradford Lane. A narrow cobbled lane ending at a cluster of craggy granite. One hefty step taken atop the rugged rocks assured one a view of the sea and crashing waves pounding the rocky shoreline. More importantly, the presence of Hancock's wharf extending into the harbor, soon to be the defunct workplace for Boston workers.

A tall, slender man wearing a dark cloak and a tricorn hat, Dr. Randolph strode single-mindedly down the lane across the way from his house on Bradford Lane, carrying a black doctor's bag intended as a ruse. With no evidence of daylight as yet, the town's lanterns on Main Street cast a dim glow in his direction. Having walked this route many dozens of times made him keenly aware of the path required to travel so as to avoid the narrow, wet, and slippery cobbled lane, keeping close to the side of the building. He relied on his sense of smell to point him toward his intended destination. The briny tang of Boston's harbor intensified as he drew closer to the print shop, noting the outline of the carved overhead sign board bearing the name,

The Boston Recorder
Stationer and Bookseller
Ezra Phillips, Proprietor

He walked to the back of the building and entered through the same door where printing supplies were delivered every other week. He approached the somber and pensive faces of the men standing at the fireplace, speaking in low voices. Josiah nodded and met the eyes of familiar Masons, who had been called to meet in the long room upstairs to discuss immediate plans for Boston's survival under the newly appointed governor.

He caught the eye of the tall, tawny-haired man standing at the front of the shop, Ezra Phillips, owner and operator, who agreed to host certain meetings when a time seemed prudent for the group to gather.

The pungent printer's ink was quite the contrast from the raw smells of the salty ocean air. The claustrophobic stuffiness of the room didn't help either. The long print shop presented an attractive entrance from the Main Street side, boasting an identical signboard hanging to the side of two twelve over twelve paned windows. Underneath sat a long table displaying books and small gifts meant to attract passersby. A solid wood door remained bolted, with a bell affixed to the top, built next to the windows. There were two small windows on the adjacent exterior wall that brought in more light on sunny days. But today, the sky was gray and drizzling rain. Over the windows hung dark curtains, closed now due to the nature of this morning's meeting upstairs and of certain people in attendance.

Ezra and his wife, Miranda, had invested the little money they had saved and a portion of her dowry to establish the print shop five years before. Together, they beat out the competition by putting their creative heads together: he worked the press and wrote the news of Boston while she produced relevant types meant to enhance Ezra's literary skills. Miranda's artful talent for drawing and painting gave rein to the carved sign boards she created. These picturesque elements of decoration, seen hanging from shops up and down Main Street and Bradford Lane, were a necessity that directed the public to various shops and taverns. Nowadays, Ezra was too busy to even think about profits. He and Miranda had turned their little enterprise into a booming success.

His part-time assistant, Herbie Connolly, set up lines of type and printed all the pamphlets, notifications, and broadsheets currently hanging to dry on the wooden bars attached to the walls. He rode horseback to deliver printed materials and *The Boston Recorder* from one end of Boston to the other and to the countryside on certain days.

Ezra worked from daylight to dusk, serving customers and conversing with Provincials about the present state of affairs in Boston. Some were certain men and women who worked under wealthy Tory employers. These reticent and dedicated employees served their masters well, but Boston's political climate was tense, and colonists had made their choice to either stay loyal to King George or join the army of resistance. This web of eyes and ears recognized their position as Patriots and hired help as being advantageous to the cause of liberty. These daring informers risked their jobs by delivering bits of information and tip-offs to the ears of Ezra Phillips. This intelligence would be sorted by the likes of Warren and Revere over a mug of ale at the Green Dragon Inn. Such critical news would become the secret weapon to control the provincial courts, militias, weapons, and Gage's Tory ideas of governing the province.

He knew full well why the meetings held in his upstairs storage room were kept secret. Loyalist spies were known to watch the comings and goings of his business. Ezra also knew that printing seditious materials could result in British soldiers seizing his property, making him a criminal who would be dealt with by the governor.

He paused when he considered the gumption of Samuel Adams, stating the obvious to some: "We can only have freedom by fighting for it, and that means war!" A few of the members were not ready to hear such blunt words, believing instead that colonists could hammer out their differences with Britain.

But Adams was a realist, having seen the handwriting on the wall for the last ten years. England would not stop in its attempt to drain the coffers of colonists and demand their weapons. Out of all of Britain's holdings in India and the Caribbean, none were as valuable as the colonies in North America.

Mr. Adams had made it his responsibility to inform all the colonies from Maine to Georgia of Britain's attempts to tighten their control over trade, taxes, and making royal appointments to govern towns and villages, including the General Courts. The objective of his Committees of Correspondence allowed the news to travel to duly elected government officials, bypassing governors appointed by the king.

Today, Britain's show of force was directed toward Boston's Patriots, as evidenced by the army of redcoats arriving this morning along with the new governor, Thomas Gage. What more evidence did one need? Weeks before, the British army had begun demonstrating their strength by setting up encampments in every direction of the crowded town of Boston and its nearby islands.

Ezra had set out five pewter candle holders on the desk where he received customers *and* informers. Knowing their time together was limited, Josiah Randolph picked up a candle, lit it from the whale oil lamp, and headed up the dark stairs to light the way for Messrs. Revere and Adams.

Other members followed, providing a dim light in the windowless and low-ceilinged room. Several chairs were arranged in a circle of sorts, and a small table placed nearby was intended for Sam Adams, who would preside over the meeting. Printing paper, ink, and typesetting trays were stored at the far end of the loft, where the ceiling nearly met the floor. Even though the uncomfortable conditions of the room were hot and stuffy, that was more to their advantage to keep the meeting brief.

Paul Revere needed no proof of what England's king had planned for the colonies. He had seen how Parliament had pressured the thirteen royal governors to impose exorbitant taxes upon men who owned land, purchased newspapers, glass, and paint, and everyday consumables.

Less than twenty years before, he had joined with family members and friends to fight alongside the British when they sought to ruin France's attempt to control the colonies, including western lands beyond the Appalachian Mountains. Colonists had sacrificed their businesses, and many lost their lives to do battle with the French and their Indian allies, the Hurons. At the end of the long seven years of fighting, the victorious British returned to their country, and the defeated French to theirs. Now, Britain expected the colonies to pay for the heavy financial burden incurred during that war. In Revere's mind, the high price had been paid in full.

Paul had spent much of his time with these same leaders he was addressing today, drinking ale at the Green Dragon Inn and discussing the details of how the events of the past ten years had come to be. Each man agreed that the time had come to unleash the kind of assault on Britain that would send them back across the sea.

"Some may argue that destroying that abominable tea six months ago was detrimental to our cause, but as I have traveled to New York and Philadelphia, many have celebrated our heroic and deceptive methods in executing that daring plan; hence, they have pledged their support." Mr. Revere stood in the center of the room where he could stand without stooping, assuring the members of his commitment to work for independence. "As long as I have a strong horse that's able to carry me over these coarse and inferior roads, I will deliver the news to draw men to our cause."

The thirty-three-year-old widower, Dr. Joseph Warren, residing president of the Committees of Safety, became enraged as he rose to speak, resulting in his fair complexion changing to scarlet. "Everyone in this room knows that London's lords have grown rich from these established colonies overflowing with natural resources. Certainly forsaking the men and women who have toiled to mine ore and fell trees for timber among the numerous resources exported to England. But they've gone too far, passing tax laws that overburden colonists. Do you realize we are restricted from importing products from other countries? These self-possessed elites seek to control these colonies from the comfort of their English estates, never intending to set foot on these shores."

"So many of us have struck out on our own, investing our capital not only to create our own wealth but investing in the people who desire to work. Why, we're not important enough to elect representatives to state our case in London, for they have rejected any representation from these colonies." Dr. Warren wiped the sweat from his brow and took a few swallows of ale. Other members nodded in agreement, whispering "hear, hear."

It had been nearly ten weeks since John Hancock had hit a proverbial nerve with colonists who gathered in the state house for the Massacre Day service. The prosperous merchant had charged farmers, merchants, tradesmen, doctors, and lawyers to "unite in our efforts by joining the militias; prepare yourselves to engage in battle against the thieves and murderers that they [the British] are!"

The crowd of men who assembled in the big hall had heard the rumors from London, and they came, in some sense, to receive permission from Mr. Hancock that it was time to take action, in whatever capacity they chose, to defend their homes and their way of life.

Since that day, and along with the valiant efforts of Sam Adams and Joseph Warren, the Committees of Correspondence and Committees of Safety, along with the express riders who delivered reports and news to surrounding colonies, and militia groups were organizing and swelling in great numbers throughout all thirteen colonies. In their minds, war had already begun with Britain.

"Within a matter of hours, this town will be filled with redcoat soldiers. Where they are to sleep and eat, I know not. I suppose we will learn the mettle of Governor Gage and how he intends to manage this colony in due course." The tall and fair-haired Dr. Warren spoke with intellect and authority. He was as committed to the cause of freedom as Sam Adams. He and John Adams had traveled the colonies, making arrangements to secure military supplies to store in various towns in the countryside across the Charles River. Warren looked in the direction of Josiah Randolph and nodded a signal for him to speak on the matter of defense.

Dr. Randolph stood to apprise the group of recent information he had acquired from John Adams, who chose not to attend this morning's meeting, nor did John Hancock. These two men were under heavy scrutiny by Loyalist spies who were itching to turn them over to the incoming governor. "My brother Jacob and I have met with John

Adams on two occasions now to discuss the manufacture of muskets, ammunition, and such," he continued, "at this very moment, we have contracted with the owners of several ironworks to build the weapons needed for militias and combat. Cannons and all its necessary equipage are under construction by two separate ironworks because of the time and materials needed to create the quality artillery needed."

A friend of Revere's and Randolph's quickly spoke, "Sirs, I just want to say that, well, some men are born rebels, and they don't mind getting their hands dirty." Thomas Crafts was massive in build and strong as an ox. He declined to stand, given the tight arrangement in the loft. "In other words, they don't shrink from danger. I've got some drinking mates who overheard Tories talking about a cache of muskets and gunpowder they aim to use on anybody who refuses to bow to the king. So these rebel friends of mine took a notion to ride over to where they were stashed, with a mind to collect it all and hide it in a more secure abode, if you know what I mean."

With the member's attention cast in Crafts' direction, anxious to hear the rest of the story, Dr. Randolph interrupted, captivated by the details of such intrigue, "I assume your friends stole the weapons and cached them, but where?"

Crafts responded casually, "Over Lexington way and thereabouts."

"Are you pointing to just this one occasion?" he addressed Crafts with suspicion, awaiting his answer. "I suppose you've kept track of the locations."

"To answer your question, Dr. Randolph, no, it is not the first time. It happens often," Crafts replied and shot a wink at Revere. "When the time comes, we know where to find them. We keep a guard on 'em at all times."

"Gentlemen, this is how the United Colonies will be victorious. When impassioned men and women take it upon themselves to use their talents to outwit the British. Mr. Crafts, I say hurrah to your spirited friends, and may God be with them. Remind them to be vigilant and do as I must do, keep a watch over your shoulder at all times." Sam Adams sat at a makeshift desk, making notes as each man delivered their message. Every few minutes, he would stop writing and attempt to relax his arm by dangling it in mid-air and wiggling his fingers. He suffered from palsy, and this exercise seemed to provide some relief. Josiah observed the involuntary tremors in his hands, considering the man's condition, *I wish I could find a way to give him some relief.*

This *provocateur*, Sam Adams, realized that the final success in the many struggles to obtain independence was due to the strength and support of ordinary men and women who were motivated by three powerful forces: personal freedom, self-government, and national unity.

Sam continued, "These so-called Intolerable Acts are meant to dominate our very lives by closing Boston's ports, putting thousands of men out of work. Gage intends to do away with the colony's legislature and enforce his own brand of governing just to prove he has the right to do it. You can be sure there will be backlash from hungry, unemployed men who will find ways to vent their anger. This day is the beginning of a new era when we will discover man's loyalty. I fear war is inevitable."

Adams' indefatigable pursuit to organize resistance and carry on the work of corresponding with the colonies proved to be a massive endeavor. "Britain's Lord North has assessed our rebellion as 'a handful of rebels without widespread support,' but he has failed to understand the situation in our colonies. Thousands of Patriots have come together for a common cause to consider ways to safeguard their liberties. Boycotting British goods is only the beginning.

"We will not permit the king to levy taxes against us. Virginia, South Carolina, and Pennsylvania are watching how we manage our affairs under Governor Gage's rule, knowing full well their time will surely come. Why, only a few weeks ago, New York boldly staged their own protests by sinking British tea chests into their waters. Resistance is taking hold in all the colonies."

Sam Adams' prowess as a quick-witted independent thinker urged him to rise above the typical frustrated Bostonians who spent their evenings at the fireside, swilling ale and anguishing over their plight under British control. All the more reason to establish the secret Committees of Correspondence as a shadow government to unify New England and the middle and southern colonies.

The members were given their orders to carry out over the weeks ahead, anything from communicating with friends and neighbors the necessity of owning a musket or a pistol, purchasing a bullet mold to make their own musket balls, and uniting with neighbors in defending their property.

Drs. Randolph and Warren were directed to recruit volunteers to quietly begin collecting medical supplies, lint, vinegar, alcohol, salves. Any provisions the two doctors would need to aid militiamen.

Mr. Adams closed the meeting and dismissed the members. "Gentlemen, keep your senses and remain vigilant. There are spies on every corner. God only knows when we will meet again."

The meeting lasted for less than an hour so members could take their leave before the sun rose. The gray sky showed signs of daylight, but today, the sun remained hidden, overcast with clouds settling over Boston, adding to the expectancy of gloomy days ahead. Seagulls were waking. Their sinister laughter seemed a warning to Patriots of the severity of their treasonous plans.

Before leaving the print shop, Paul Revere observed Dr. Randolph carrying his black bag and asked if he could walk with him to his house located on North Square. It seems his daughter had fallen out of a tree the evening before. He was worried she may have broken her arm.

"Certainly," he responded in a low voice, quickly calculating how to inform his family of his whereabouts, "I'll see that Ezra walks a message to my house."

The print shop owner wrapped the written message in a copy of the weekly newssheet and slipped it under the front door at the house on Bradford Lane. At the same time, Dr. Randolph walked through the front door of the Revere home on North Square.

Chapter 3

JOSEPHINE RANDOLPH

May 17, 1774, Boston

A devilish fiend had taken possession of my otherwise jubilant dreams of fair maidens searching for lovers, gossamer wings, and woven garlands of magical herbs, thrusting me into a revolting state of frightfulness that left my body trembling. I have tried desperately to make sense of a recurring dream where I am standing in front of Faneuil Hall with my wrists bound in manacles. A rather imposing figure of a man is wearing a red cape that balloons with each gust of wind, speaking in a grandiose manner, demanding the absolute attention of me, of all wonders. Thousands of people are in attendance, and seemingly, hundreds of British soldiers are carrying long guns with bayonets attached. Presently, the man points his chin at two grenadiers wearing those tall black hats, signaling they were to escort me to the edge of the wharf, which they did. He uttered some words that have since faded from my mind, and, at that, I boldly stated to his face that "you, the governor, and your boorish redcoats have no right to breathe the air of this city!" With those words, the soldiers pushed me off the wharf into Boston Bay.

A rapid succession of knocks on my door caused me to sit up in bed, half asleep. I was striving to determine where I was: falling off the wharf or sitting in my bedchamber in my nightgown? My muddled brain gave me no answer. I sat on the bedside, wondering if my feet would get wet if I touched my big toe to the wool carpet. My brain signaled to me that it was safe to stand. I was wobbly, dazed, and gaping as I stumbled toward the knocking sounds. Trembling, I opened the door. "Auntie, it's you!" I clutched the tall woman's slim shoulders. "It's really you, I uh…"

"Well, of course, it's me, Josie. Who else would come to rouse you from a nightmare, if that's what you call it? Here I am, frying ham and tolerating the never-ending beating drums… What of the screaming? Was it coming from your room? It has quite set my teeth on edge!"

"I was screaming? What do you mean beating drums?" I asked as I tried to get my bearings, fully aware that I should have made use of the chamber pot before opening the door.

Standing her tallest with head held high and her long arm stretched toward the ceiling, Auntie, striving to emulate royalty, announced, "A parade and reception in honor of the new governor is soon to commence." She bowed dramatically from the waist and swept her arm across the floor, mockingly showing her disapproval of the arrival of one of the king's finest.

I grinned at her dramatics. "Oh, I forgot that was today," I mumbled, remembering the wide-eyed soldiers pushing me into the bay. "In that case, I'd say this foul weather is perfect for such an occasion," I replied sardonically and set about dressing for the day. "Perhaps a cup of tea will wake me."

I grasped the reality of the day when I pulled the curtain aside at the front window of my chamber. Through heavy eyelids, I squinted at the overcast sky, then noticed the wet streets. My spirits were lifted when I realized today was an ordinary Boston morning happening before my eyes, despite the new governor's sham pageantry. So different from the terror of the nightmare that had left me feeling limp and tormented.

Gazing out the window, there stood my tall, graceful aunt Minnie, her dark and graying hair pulled back into a braided bun, conversing with Petey Harmon. They were likely disputing the hubbub at the state house today and the overall predicament Bostonians were facing. The two were carrying on quite a fiery discourse, obvious with their flailing arms and continual ranting as they took their turn expressing their opinions. But Petey had traveled from his family's farm, south of Boston and through the town gates, with a mission to proceed with his morning deliveries to customers. Auntie continued her rhetoric while he collected a jug of milk, a crock of butter, and a loaf of bread from his wagon and placed it all in her basket.

The two dray horses harnessed to the wagon were stamping and blustering, expressing their restlessness from standing on the wet cobblestone street, anxious to move on to the next house. Auntie waved her thanks to Petey as he climbed up onto the wagon seat and nodded to her a farewell.

Even though the calendar showed it was late spring, the weather had not quite caught up, judging from the movements of the front yard's crabapple trees. A gusty breeze from the east blew intermittently, compelling the tender green leaves to sway and flutter in one direction and then the other. While I stood barefoot on the cold floor next to the window, my feet felt like ice.

The smoldering remains in the fireplace produced barely enough fire to heat the kettle for my wash water. *So much for that*, I thought. *I'll take a hot bath in the afternoon.* I sat close to the fireplace, extending my legs to warm my feet before I slipped on my wool stockings and boots. I pulled a cotton chemise over my head, then stepped into a cotton petticoat to tie at my waist.

Examining the contents of the tall wardrobe for something heavy and serviceable for the day's work, I chose my gray twill skirt, suited with a heavy indigo bodice and a cotton neck scarf. When I stood in front of the tall mirror beside the window, a scowled and sleepless face stared back at me. *I'll have to change that before Auntie drills me about the screaming episode this morning.* I grabbed a ribbon and a comb and walked downstairs, stretching my eyes and facial muscles in hopes of transforming my countenance to a ready-to-receive-the-day look. There was no deceiving my aunt Minnie. She could be as shrewd as a fox.

Downstairs, the warmth of the kitchen and the fragrant smells of hot food helped to relieve some of the tension of the early morning. Auntie had laid the table with ham, stewed apples, along with fresh bread and butter from Petey's delivery this morning.

I took a sip of milk and asked the whereabouts of Father. "Oh, here's a note since I was still in bed when he left for his meeting. Something about one of Mr. Revere's sons and a fall out of a tree at his house in North Square," reported Auntie. "Also, you are to meet him at the Bignall's house on Salt Street and bring with you a small jug of vinegar and a jar of honey," she read from Father's note.

I nodded my head, mentally tracing the route to the Bignall's home to determine if I would have to pass by a tavern, considering the possibility of encountering redcoats hanging about harassing colonists, especially women. "And how do you plan to spend your day, Auntie?" I asked, knowing she was seldom idle. She always had a new pattern in mind for a quilt or a scarf to knit.

She placed her cup of tea on the saucer as she recalled her list. "After you leave, I have herbs to cut and hang for drying, I'm starting a pot of soup with the leftover ham, I'll be collecting our clothes to pack for the trip to the farm tomorrow, and I'm walking down to Mabel Foster's house to finish sewing the quilt we started. Frances Carter is coming over to help. She claims she has a new tea recipe made from strawberry leaves and currants that we should try because she thinks it tastes better than English tea. Hah, I'll be the judge of that!"

Auntie went about her morning routine, clearing away the breakfast trappings and making ready for the day's work while I stepped into the scullery for the vinegar and honey. Arranged on the floor were four buckets lined in a row. I decided at that moment that today certainly would be a fine day for a bath. I walked the fifty or so steps to the well while carrying two buckets at a time and filled them as much as I thought I could carry, setting them on the scullery floor in preparation for my soak in the tub after my day's work.

When water splashed on my shoes, my eyes became fixed on the dark water in the bucket. Captivated by its swirling movements, it brought to mind turbulent waves in the wild ocean. This morning's nightmare remained so present in me that I thought I felt someone push me into the deep waters as the redcoat soldiers had done so cruelly.

I looked up from the water and realized that Auntie was holding my arm to keep me from falling. "Josie, you've had a fright. Come and sit by the fire." It took me a moment to gauge my bearings. Her sympathetic eyes were locked on my face. She was clutching my hands.

"You are cold as ice and pale as a ghost. You're being tortured by this hideous dream. Please confide in me. It will help remove the burden that you alone are carrying. I will support you," her face showed such compassion, speaking from her caring heart. I nodded in response, knowing the time had come to release my pent-up fears. I felt childish for not discussing the matter with Auntie sooner but relieved that she demonstrated the courage to confront me.

Auntie passed me the cup of tea left over from my breakfast, and I managed a few sips. "I don't know what came over me when I set the buckets of water on the floor, but this abhorrent dream has consumed my mind and body. I do want to discuss it with you, but I'll have to postpone it for later today. I'm to meet Father at the Bignall's house within the hour."

Aunt Minnie adjusted my cloak and kissed me on the cheek. I walked out of the house to meet Father for our first appointment, grateful that Auntie boldly moved to intercede on my behalf, wondering why these mysterious nightmares had taken control of me. I at once called my senses to order and braced myself for a long day.

Sadly, the spirit and vitality that I loved so much about Boston was changing for the worse, and it was getting more noticeable every day. What was once a bustling and friendly town could now be characterized as one where its residents might be victims falling from the plague, confined to their homes. The aromas of baking bread, food vendors peddling their meat pies and pastries, shopkeepers opening their stores, and shouting a "good mornin'" were gradually disappearing. It seemed as if Bostonians had moved away and been replaced with foreigners. When, in fact, they had become prisoners in their own homes because their jobs were gone—or soon to be gone. With no money to buy fruits and vegetables or eggs and meat, there was no need for market days or food vendors.

The weather was cold, windy, and drizzling rain, much more than I anticipated, and it was getting late, so I walked briskly to Bignall's residence on Salt Street. I shrugged off the new governor's noisy reception as just another costly event that would place more debt and burdens on colonists. The ear-piercing clamor of church bells and drums welcoming the new governor sent a grim reminder that Boston's future was uncertain.

Despite the annoyances of the morning, I continued my schedule as promised: an appointment at the home of John and Sarah Bignall. Their three yellow-haired, blue-eyed, fair-skinned children, all under the age of ten, were suffering from a persistent sore throat, earache, and fever. When I knocked on their door, I heard the giddy sounds of children's laughter and running feet, which made me wonder if I was at the right house.

Mrs. Bignall met me at the door, her yellow hair escaping from under her linen coif, flushed cheeks, and the smells of this morning's breakfast, probably porridge and cornbread. She looked overworked and worried, sustaining her housewifery duties with limited sleep, no doubt, and the added work of tending sick children. Their symptoms were common but worrisome for parents of young ones, knowing the spread of smallpox and typhus was always a possibility in our crowded Boston community.

"Come in, Miss Randolph," she noticed my eyes following her active children playing in the front room. "John is working at the forge this morning. As you can see, the children are a little restless."

"Indeed they are," I stated, smiling. I removed my cloak and tied an apron over my skirt and bodice. The house was small but clean and uncluttered. With the springtime air so damp and chilly, I welcomed the blazing fireplace.

I made eye contact with Jonathan, the oldest Bignall child, who looked to be around age ten. "Good morning. How are you feeling today?" He answered with a cautious smile and a shrug. "Let's begin by washing our hands. Mrs. Bignall, may I trouble you for a basin of warm water and soap?" She invited me to follow her to the hot and fragrant kitchen, with Jonathan, Clara, and Samuel trailing behind us. I breathed with relief at their willingness to get started. I proceeded to wash my hands, and with surprising eagerness, each child took a turn with no prodding from me.

Presently, the children's attention was diverted to the bold knock coming from outside. Mrs. Bignall opened the door and welcomed my father, Dr. Josiah Randolph. His rain-spattered tricorn hat made him appear seven feet tall; six feet plus three or four inches was my estimation. Father, his brother, Jacob, and his sister, who was my aunt, Minnie, were tall people and were naturally accustomed to stooping as they passed through a doorway. I wasn't quite as tall as Auntie, but over the years, I had picked up the habit of tilting my head to the side as well.

We made eye contact and smiled a "good morning" to each other. He removed his black wool cloak, also dotted with raindrops, and proceeded to fold it when Mrs. Bignall interceded, "May I relieve you of your cloak?" She hung it over a hook near the front door. "We've all washed our hands, Dr. Randolph, uh…." She pointed her hand to the bowl of water in the kitchen, inviting Father to partake.

"Now that our hands are clean, Jonathan, tell me how you are feeling." Father surveyed the boy's face and looked into his eyes, awaiting an answer.

Without hesitation, Jonathan spoke up. "My throat hurts when I swallow, and my ears hurt too. Sometimes I cough, especially at nighttime." He looked at the doctor's face, nodding his head.

"I'll need to look at the back of your throat to see if it's red and blistered," Father responded.

Sarah Bignall took charge and suggested the best prospect for light would be in an adjacent room at the front window, a birthing room, I thought. Father walked into the small room, carrying his black doctor's bag, and positioned himself on a stool. With no prompting, Jonathan walked to the window, appearing ready and willing to follow the doctor's directions.

Father pulled a shiny spatula from his bag and showed it to Jonathan. "I use this instrument to hold your tongue in place so I can look at the back of your throat. Head back." Jonathan got the idea and opened his mouth wide and stuck out his tongue. "Jo," he instructed me, "light the candle and hold it close—yes, like that—so I can get a better look."

Clara and Samuel, proud of their clean hands, looked at each other with wide blue eyes while watching their brother from the doorway. Clearly, from their expressions, this was an exciting experience for three children who had been confined to their home during the chilly spring.

Father checked the throats of each of the children. There was the source of the problem: white sores and inflammation. It was a common seasonal problem due to the unpredictable weather, which could be warm one day and chilly the next.

Living in such confined quarters and few opportunities for fresh air allowed contagions to spread from person to person. Father turned his attention toward Mrs. Bignall and gave instructions to stir a teaspoon of vinegar in a cup of warm water. "If it's too strong, add a little honey and sip on it often throughout the day. It wouldn't hurt you and your husband to do the same."

Most importantly, I said to the children, "Keep your fingers out of your mouths and wash your hands often." I knew this would be added work for Mrs. Bignall, but I promised her I would look in on the children the next morning.

We said our goodbyes to the Bignalls and walked up the hill to Hanover Street to our next patient, Mrs. Flaudie Ellis. Her husband had spotted me at DeLaney's Mercantile two days ago and asked if Dr. Randolph would stop in to check a cankerous sore on the bottom of his wife's foot. This could be problematic and painful because the sore would have to be punctured and drained. More than likely, there would be infection and definitely inflammation.

Upon Father's examination and diagnosis, I removed a scalpel from his black bag and sterilized it with alcohol. I positioned myself at Mrs. Ellis' side, directing her to face me as Father quickly lanced the sore and drained the noxious fluids. Her face turned pale but showed some relief from the painful pressure she had endured for days. I demonstrated to her maid how to assemble an herb poultice, wrapping it around her foot and changing it daily. "Stay off your feet and keep them elevated for a few days," Father advised. "We'll look in on you tomorrow morning."

The Ellises were Tories, according to the gossip, and they were moderately wealthy. It was more than obvious to anyone who visited their home. So far, I had counted three different servants going about their household duties. But whether they thought we were Patriots or Tories did not concern me or Father. Mrs. Ellis required medical attention, as did so many Bostonians.

Mr. Ellis owned a warehouse on one of the wharves, which meant he bought and sold merchandise shipped in from other countries to local merchants. Even though Parliament had ordered Boston's ports closed by the end of the month, this would have little immediate effect on the Ellises' quality of life. He, of course, would have to lay off his warehouse workers who unloaded ships and kept inventories of merchandise. Nevertheless, we had a service to provide, and they were paying customers. Although Father had taken the Hippocratic oath—*to treat the sick to the best of one's ability*—and was passionate about attending to his patients. He also responsibly supported a family with his work as a physician.

Come June 1st, most of Boston's laborers would be thrown out of work since no ships would be allowed to dock at the wharves, per George the Third's decree. Parliament knew that when the ports closed, businesses would lapse into bankruptcy, bringing working men and women to their knees with the intent to make them starve. As Father said, "We cannot ignore the medical needs of our friends and neighbors, so our work must continue whether we are paid or not." Fortunately for us, many Tories and quite a few of Boston's Patriots were wealthy, and they had no intention of starving.

Father and I left the Ellis' home. We did not speak for several minutes as we walked toward our house on Bradford Lane. Perhaps the gray skies affected our mood. Perhaps Father heard my nightmare screaming in the early morning and was reluctant to confront me with it. The drizzling rain and the smells of filthy smoke swirling out of chimney pots left a feeling of dread hanging in the air.

My mouth watered when I thought of a cup of hot tea and a bowl of Auntie's hearty soup, warming and soothing my throat. I hoped I had not picked up the beginnings of a raw throat from the Bignall children. The drizzling rain was chilling me, and I pulled the hood over my head, hoping to warm my neck. *Burrr, wish I had brought along my wool scarf.* "Are you warm enough, Josie?" Father asked, wrapping his long arm around my shoulder for warmth. "You should have a hot bath this afternoon." I raised my brows at that, remembering the promise I had made to myself this morning.

"Hm, I thought the Revere children were all girls, and there's ten or maybe twelve of them," I stated as a matter of fact. "Is that the truth or just hearsay?"

"No, you're mostly right, although there's an older boy somewhere in the mix. All I can remember was a great many noisy females running hither and yon in the Revere house. It seems young Elizabeth fell out of a tree. She's badly bruised and scraped, but no broken bones nor damage to her head."

"I asked her about the fall, and she said, 'The kite got stuck in the tree.' She apparently lost her balance when she pulled it down, so says her sister Frances. I left some ointment for her scrapes and told Mr. Revere she needed rest. He expressed his gratitude, paid me in silver, and I took my leave."

Father gave me a sidelong glance. "Is there something else? You're giving me that look—like there's more to your question—but you'll have to wait on that. I think it's best to give you and Minnie information at the same time. You two have a knack for confusing the details." He gave my upper arm a tight squeeze and a big, reassuring smile. *Just what I needed*, I thought.

"Delicious meal. Did I smell tea brewing? Is it ready to pour?" Josiah asked curtly. With the tone of his voice, I knew he was preparing to share unsettling news. He stared at his steaming tea. I was well-acquainted with that agitated look of his. The show of force by Parliament transporting thousands of redcoats from England to take residence in our small Boston town of fifteen thousand was disconcerting for us all. The port of Boston had never been closed. The backlash from unemployed longshoremen and warehouse workers with too much time on their hands will be disastrous—fights and riots being two of the worst. The surgery located in our house on Bradford Lane had, for many years, seen the results of such tumultuous behavior of men who worked at the wharf.

Minnie set out a pitcher of milk for our steaming cups of tea. "We're getting dangerously low on English tea, so enjoy it now. It won't last through the summer. I suppose it's my job to create something equivalent to tea, although, at the moment, I'm not sure how to do that," she admitted. "Dreadful!"

"You could discuss that with Naomi while we're at the farm. She's handy that way." Father said as he massaged his temple. I could see he was getting frustrated. "Now, to my point. I was at the Reveres' home this morning to examine their daughter, Elizabeth, after her fall from a tree. She'll be fine. Mr. Revere told me the port will be closed to commerce indefinitely unless the tea tariffs are paid, which is not likely. I'm concerned about those in this town who will be unemployed; some of them are neighbors and patients. It is sure to be quite a devastating blow to families."

"I imagine Mr. Hancock is losing sleep over all his empty ships. That means merchants have nothing to sell in their shops." Auntie shook her head. "Nor is there anything for customers to buy!"

Father continued, "Many of our neighbors and patients are likely to remain unemployed if they remain in Boston. But they will not starve. Rhode Island, Connecticut, and colonies down the coast have acknowledged our plight. They're sending rice, cornmeal, flour, and beef, which will be arriving in carts and wagons up through the Neck. Boston will have access to food. For the time being, though, we should continue purchasing our food from the Harmon Farm and allow those in need to use the food brought in from the other colonies.

"Do you suppose they'll be sending tea to Boston?" I asked in a pitiful voice. Relaxing with a cup of imported tea was a pleasure I relished at the beginning and the end of the work day. The thought of living without it was something I would have to come to terms with. More to worry about.

Father shook his head and responded with a frown. "No, the other colonies refused to allow the tea mandate forced on them, so they staged their own boycotts, similar to the one in Boston Harbor. They dumped their tea chests in the ocean, and now the waves are pushing it all back to England! So, there's apt to be no tea for the colonies anytime soon, Jo. I'm sorry."

Auntie chimed in rather sharply. "Now that's a pretty kettle of fish! So, Governor Hutchinson, who I believed was a friend to Patriots and Tories alike, was too lenient in his directives to rebellious colonists, so he gets booted to London. Now we're stuck with these intolerable laws to be enforced by the new governor? What of the ships full of redcoat soldiers filling our streets, standing guard over the citizens of this colony? What if they decide they want to quarter in our house? What are we to do?"

"It wouldn't be the first time the king has sent soldiers upon our shores to keep an eye out for the comings and goings of certain people, harassing us with their threats and commands," Father sounded exasperated as he spoke the obvious. "Jacob and I will have more to share on the subject when we visit Mulberry Farm tomorrow."

"I mean, they've taken over the Common with their tents and horses to the point where it would be impossible to picnic or take a walk. I assume they will use the space for drills. I heard that Dr. Warren said the British have spies all over the city. Is that true?" I asked matter-of-factly.

"Uh, how did you come by that information? I mean, about spies?" Father's eyes narrowed and looked away to the window. I could tell he didn't favor that piece of gossip.

"Well, I'm sure most people know this already. I overheard a knot of customers whispering about it when I purchased some ribbon at DeLaney's Mercantile." I replied. "They said the Patriot rebellion was growing stronger by the day." Excited as I was about sharing secret information, I knew I was taking a risk with Father; I could see the disappointment on his face. I was no longer a child, after all. Was he trying to protect me from the ugly truth of it all?

Father groaned and rose from the table, quite shaken. He walked toward the big kitchen window, observing the gray sky. "For the time being, there will be no more discussion of spies and intolerable laws, please. Uncle Jacob and I will give you information about the current situation while the family is together at the farm. In the meantime, let's focus on tomorrow's ride to Stoughton. I'm sure you have clothes to pack. Also, please be mindful about where you walk in this town." He grimaced.

"Did your meeting go well this morning?" I was aiming to smooth over my earlier blunder regarding spies. Father still looked distraught.

"Yes, and we'll discuss that at the farm as well, Josie. I'll need my black bag refreshed and in good order for tomorrow morning's work. Right now, I have paperwork to complete. Also, I've arranged a meeting with Mr. Revere at his shop this afternoon. I want him to look over our scalpels, scissors, and tongs; some need to be replaced, and some need repair. Pack them in my black bag for him to examine. We will leave when I return from the livery stables. He exhaled a heavy breath in exhaustion, faintly smiled, and walked away. Auntie and I looked at each other, dismayed. We knew Father's overloaded schedule would leave him frazzled and in a foul mood by late afternoon. Best to move on with my tasks.

I remained at the table to finish my tea, pondering whether this could be the last cup of English tea I would ever drink. I was in a muddled state of mind, not sure where to settle my thoughts—preparations for tomorrow's trip, Father's surgery, or the British takeover of our lives. The scent of herbs suspended from the rafters, hanging to dry, drew my attention upwards. Medicines from Walden's Apothecary might not be so readily available during the coming siege. Auntie used them for cooking. I've read books on ways to make medicines. Maybe Aunt Lenora and Naomi could give us some ideas.

I continued my survey of the spaciousness of the room, with its heavy beams and support columns, thinking Mrs. Bignall would appreciate a space this size with her rambunctious youngsters. *What was it like at mealtime feeding three children?* I wondered. The long room accounted for practically the entire back of the house, including where I was presently seated in the keeping room.

The architecture allowed for a huge fireplace with a bread oven built on the end near the doorway to the scullery. Open cupboards held all sorts of crockery and utensils for cooking and serving, and my mother's china used for special occasions. In the center of it all sat a rectangular table with six chairs and a bench, all built by my grandsire, whom we called Poppi, a master carpenter.

A smaller fireplace at the opposite end, where two upholstered settles were arranged facing each other, sat a rectangular table sized to support a silver tea tray. This was a gift to my parents on the occasion of their marriage. A magnificent view of Auntie's flower and herb garden that was set just beyond the big window was like a giant-sized picture. Overall, a comfortable setting, making this my favorite spot for reading and sipping tea.

A nap to make up for lost sleep would have been perfect just now, but Auntie had other plans in mind when she called from upstairs, pulling me out of my tranquil state. I met Auntie standing in her bedchamber. She had pulled a handsome riding skirt and a matching red jacket from the trunk and spread them across her bed. "Hmm, what's this?" I asked curiously.

"They belonged to your mother, and I was wondering if they might fit you now that you've sprouted in the last two years. The waist might need to be taken in, but let's try them on anyway," she said in a persuading manner. "It looks to be about the right size in length." I stood at the mirror admiring the skirt, turning and twisting sideways, getting a glimpse of my brown hair that was extra wavy from walking home in the drizzle. "You're tall and slim like your mother. Ah, that looks right smart on you!"

I looked at Auntie and asked thoughtfully, "You knew Mother so well. How would she, if she were alive, handle this predicament we're facing? Would she be frightened? Would she lock the doors and never go outside? Tell me how she would manage her life under such circumstances."

Auntie had a faraway look about her as she spoke proudly of Mother. "She had a strong will about her, and she was forthright in her ideas and beliefs. Even with your father, she expressed what was on her mind, whether it was agreeable to him or not. Nevertheless, they worked well together, and she had a passion for caring for the sick, just as Josiah does. To answer your question, she would take one day at a time and adjust to the changes. Prudence would guide her through the day, and she most definitely would not lose herself in the commotion of the times. It's our Puritan blood, you know. Common sense and a level head always trump emotional decision-making."

I was thrilled about a new riding skirt; for that matter, anything that belonged to my mother was special. "Look, it does fit, and the length is perfect! This muted color brings out the red streaks in my hair." I picked up a dark green skirt still folded in the trunk. "What about this one?" as I shook out the wrinkles.

"Oh, that one belongs to me," she said. "I can't remember the last time I wore it. I so enjoyed riding when I was young and even when I was married. Your aunt Lenora enjoys riding. The thought came to me that riding alongside her would be a good time to catch up on the news and to clear my head while we're visiting Mulberry Farm if the sun is not too strong."

I smiled and nodded, "Yes, you should ride, and I wouldn't mind coming along with you and Aunt Lenora. Jake and Harry will want to ride in the Blue Hills, which I find interesting, but I don't want to risk running into a patrol of you know who.

"Auntie, on the subject of spies, I stand guilty of spying on Father," I confessed to her nonplussed face. "Not that I'm reporting information to the enemy or even to our side. I was awakened by a noise outside and walked to the window before dawn this morning. I saw Father walking close to the building where Mr. Phillips runs his printing business. If it had not been for the lantern casting a glow from Bradford Lane, I would not have recognized his tall stature and the shape of his medical bag. The interesting thing is, one by one, other men drifted through the back door of the building as Father had." I cast my eyes downward, feeling guilty that I may have betrayed Father, almost expecting Auntie to reproach me.

I glanced up at Auntie, who, for some reason now, saw a hint of humor in my confession, judging from her face that had turned comical.

"Fear not, Josie, the doctor has been making early morning house calls for a year now, all in the name of liberty, I can assure you!"

I walked downstairs to the front of the house, somewhat disconcerted but eager to spend some time alone, hoping to sort out Auntie's cryptic response. What does she mean "all in the cause of liberty"?

Father had left earlier to check on the carriage he had ordered two weeks ago for our trip to the farm. Miles Fletcher, part owner of Fletcher's Stables and Carriages and a longtime friend of Father's, had advised him to get his order in as soon as possible. Recalling the last time British soldiers had occupied the city, their high-ranking officers could be rather demanding.

Cleaning and organizing Father's medical bag, which he relied upon so greatly, was part of my job as his assistant. The curtains were pulled back in the surgery, giving my spirits a lift when beams of sunlight shone through the windows, warming the room.

Father thought highly of our two-story clapboard house surrounded by white-washed fencing. He called it handsome and distinguished. I believe he has always remained emotionally attached to our Bradford Lane dwelling. First and foremost, because he and my mother chose it as a perfect location for their surgery set on the corner of Main and Bradford. Second, because he would never betray his wife, Jo. His distinct memories of their lives and work here prevail. I don't believe he could ever separate himself from those few years of happiness imbued in every room, particularly the surgery room.

The busy traffic of carriages, horse riders, and carts on Main Street had begun to be a problem for patients entering through the front gate of the Randolph residence. To prevent potential accidents, it seemed a sensible plan to design a separate entrance for patients to enter the surgery through the Bradford Lane side of the house. A door replaced a window, and a spacious porch with handrails was constructed for patients who otherwise had difficulty navigating the narrow steps at the front door entrance. Miranda Phillips had designed, carved, and painted a handsome signboard, which we attached near the door jamb of the new side entrance: *Bradford Lane Surgery, Dr. Josiah Randolph.*

The surgery was located in a room off the front hallway, once designated as a library judging from the shelving that spread across an entire wall. Two tall casement windows covered the front exterior wall facing the street, and two half-sized windows were spaced on the rear wall to receive a partial view of the well and backyard. This arrangement allowed for an abundance of light needed for intricate work in either the morning or afternoon. Accidents occurred every day at the wharves, where workers used sharp knives and hooks, carelessly cutting themselves while preparing fish for the markets or opening crates of merchandise. Luckily, Father's surgery was within walking distance of the docks.

I believed the surgery was as much mine as it was Father's. I had actually spent the majority of my life in this room. Sometimes, while seated on the cushioned settle in front of the rear windows, I would turn around and face the back of the roomy seat so I could watch the seagulls soaring in all directions, squawking as they circled Boston Bay. I would listen to Father ask questions of his patients or watch him set a broken bone. It was fascinating to see Auntie clean a bloody wound as she talked to the patient, followed by Father stitching flesh together with his skilled hands. When it came down to it, my dream to be a physician, like Father's, was set in stone before I was ten years old.

When I grew older and learned to draw curves and circles, I sat at Father's desk with his human anatomy book opened to the page showing the heart, valves, and arteries. With chalk in hand, I would make a crude sketch of the drawing on parchment. Father and Auntie helped me label the parts, explaining how blood flows through different areas of the body. I was curious then, and I remain curious now as Father's assistant, about how the human body functions. Outside of reading books by DeFoe and Shakespeare, I remain captivated by all that I continue to learn from Father and his books.

I set about carefully removing the sharp surgery tools: tongs, scalpels, forceps, needles, small scissors, and lancets, each one in their designated space inside the thin wooden box. Father purchased these same instruments when he was studying at Edinburgh University. He took great pride in the expensive tools, keeping them clean to prevent corrosion. He had assigned the cleaning task to me when I turned age twelve, cleaning them with alcohol and laying them out to air dry.

I inventoried the medicines taken by mouth, which we purchased from Walden's Apothecary, followed by a collection of ointments, salves, and bandages for external use. I stared at the small cabinet filled with supplies, realizing we would not be able to purchase all that we required for the surgery while Boston endured under the control of the new governor. Our little world would soon come to a standstill. How would we treat our patient's medical needs? The idea of producing our own medicines remained with me. Yes, the scientist in me was anxious to grow the herbs and experiment with the leaves, stems, and flowers. Today, I was convinced it would truly be a necessity.

While my mind focused on surgery paraphernalia, I couldn't help thinking about Father and his furtive cronies exercising traitorous resistance to the king. I knew there were secret meetings held in taverns and homes, but what part was he playing in the defense of Boston colonists who called themselves Patriots? The only leaders I knew of were Mr. Revere and Mr. Adams—and possibly Mr. Hancock—but it was hard to imagine Father organizing protests and conspiring ways to defend Boston.

I was baffled and frightened that my father was involved in a web of illegal activities that could compromise our family's security. Were my nightmares a forewarning of things to come? I thought spending time at the family farm for the next few days was for relaxing and riding horses with my cousins. Presumably, it would be a time to learn about Boston's resistance efforts.

Chapter 4

Tolerate No Uncleanliness

May 17, 1774, Boston

Father entered the surgery while I was gathering surgical tools, carefully placing the sharp instruments in a wooden box for Mr. Revere's examination. His cautious demeanor sent the message that he regretted his stern tone earlier. "Hello, Josie. My, it smells clean in here. Glad the sun is shining. May I take the box?" he asked. He walked forward to open the door.

When we exited through the front, a gust of wind slapped a loose tendril across my face. Father grasped the hood of my cloak and secured it over my head. The wind blew fiercely. "It's not the best weather for walking to North Square," Father declared with uncertainty.

The gusty winds blew the apple trees chaotically along the route to North Square while brilliant rays of sun shone against an azure sky. The sun had begun sinking below the western hills. A perfect background for illuminating the spires rising from Boston's churches. We braved the turbulent winds and walked the distance toward Hancock's Wharf. We looked at each other and sighed. Father offered me his arm as we trudged uphill, wondering why we had waited so long to take care of this chore. We sensed an urgency to get our surgery in order before we left for the farm. We were not sure how the coming siege of our town would affect our ability to come and go as we pleased. We turned onto Fish Street to meet with Mr. Revere.

Paul Revere was a prosperous silversmith who had apprenticed under his father, Apollos Rivoire, an immigrant from France. The stocky, dark-complexioned, fortyish man was a paragon in the field of master craftsmen who served Boston. He glanced up from his work as we approached the front entry, setting down the silver pitcher handle he was crafting. The heat from the annealing furnace produced an unbearable smell of burning charcoal. The side windows were open to allow in cool air. The workers' faces revealed a florid look due to the intense heat. Their thin muslin shirts were covered with a heavy leather apron. Father and I removed our cloaks.

Revere's craftsmanship was well known to Bostonians, trusting Revere to repair their jewelry and spectacles. He understood how such items were assembled. His wealthy clientele desired an original silver piece meant to impress their guests. For over twenty years, he had designed ornate bowls, teapots, and candlesticks meant to satisfy the customer's desire no matter what the cost.

His copper engraving of the Boston Massacre was a popular artistic piece that hung in households all over Boston… It was important to Revere that colonists remember the lives that ended so cruelly at the hands of British soldiers. I moved in closer to examine the details of the famous engraving that caught my eye in the bright afternoon light.

At once, I felt Revere's light-hearted spirit that dominated his character.

"A good day to you, Dr. Randolph," he said, bowing to Father. He turned in my direction. "This must be your devoted colleague. I'm happy to meet you, Miss Randolph. I commend you and your father's eagerness to serve our community in a medical way. Your reputation precedes you."

"It's an honor to make your acquaintance, Mr. Revere." My eyes caught the assortment of silver articles housed in a large cabinet, giving customers ideas about pattern and size when choosing a silver piece. I was taken by the intricate detail worked into the handles of pitchers, spoons, displaying the skills of the shop's artisans.

Father opened the wooden box of clean, shiny instruments, infusing the hot air with alcohol fumes from their recent cleaning. He pointed out the nicks and rough edges that would require professional whetting and smoothing after many years of use.

Mr. Revere held one of the scalpels to catch the bright afternoon light from the window, studying its quality and shape. "How did you acquire these fine instruments?"

"I purchased them twenty-five years ago when I studied in Edinburgh. I'm in need of small scissors and tongs. If you're interested in crafting new tools from scratch, I can show you a diagram from a medical journal, or I can draw a sketch to give you the desired sizes." He gave Father parchment, quill, and ink to draw the shapes and measurements for each tool.

"The size will not be a problem for me," Mr. Revere observed. "Perhaps I could make the holes for your fingers a larger size. The scissors part will remain the same, which is what you need for navigating small spaces. For comparison, I'll show you the instruments I use for cleaning teeth. Give me a month to assemble everything. I'll send a message to your house when they're ready."

We said our goodbyes and emerged from the smothering heat of the shop, immediately met with a blast of refreshingly cool air. Main Street lanterns were lit when the late afternoon sun hung low in the sky, giving the street the eeriness of mixed shadows as we walked home. I searched Father's face. His forlorn countenance was worrisome. He had taken on too many of the world's problems today. I couldn't remember a time when he was so contrary and edgy. His tired body had taken over his mind and his disposition.

"Father, forgive my impertinence, but I believe you're overdue for a strong cup of chamomile tea and a good night's sleep!"

"That's the truth. How can you tell?" he chuckled. "I don't suppose it's because I've been overly demanding of the two people who love me the most?" he asked mockingly.

"Well, I'm not going to assault your peevish behavior tonight after the long day you've had. My suggestion is that you go straight to bed when we get home. Auntie and I are depending on you to be wide-eyed and of a sound mind when you drive us to Mulberry Farm tomorrow, and we'd like to arrive in one piece, please, sir."

The day had been hard on all of us, with the change in governors and the unknowns affecting our lives in Boston. What Auntie and I had suspected *was* going to happen *was* truly happening right before our eyes. I sighed, sustaining a queasy stomach.

On the other hand, we were the lucky ones because we could escape to the country to our Mulberry Farm, leaving Boston's problems behind for a few days. I think this trip was perfectly timed for us to clear our heads, to determine how we will conduct our lives for the next year. "She would take one day at a time and adjust to the changes," said Auntie of my mother. God help us!

It was late, nearly dark. The anticipation of a bath had darted in and out of my mind all day. Now that the surgery was clean and ready for patients and new instruments ordered, I reckoned that this was my time. I wanted to get a fresh start for tomorrow's trip, and a relaxing soak in a tub of hot water might relieve me of the mounting tensions in my mind and body.

Before I was born, my mother persuaded my father to create a bath area, such as she had experienced when they visited Paris. They decided the most practical place for a bathtub was in the corner of the room adjacent to the large fireplace in the kitchen. Heavy curtains on two sides hung from two brass rods attached to the ceiling rafters and two walls, creating a private space for bathing. This was the same arrangement that my grandmother had initiated at Mulberry Farm.

I poured two kettles of hot water into the copper tub, followed by two kettles of cold water, hoping to create a temperate bath for the hour in which I planned to transport myself to another world. My face felt flushed from the steamy water, and my limbs began to relax, knowing that I had needed this indulgence for several days. I gazed at the plaque hanging on the wall that Auntie had written in her sprawling handwriting: *Tolerate no uncleanliness in body, clothes, or habitation. B. Franklin.*

Reading those words, I closed my eyes and recalled an afternoon two months ago when the last of the winter rains had rolled in non-stop for several days. Auntie and I agreed that we could use a change of scenery.

We bundled up as best we could and walked to Folger's Books, keeping close to the building fronts to avoid the dripping awnings. Mr. Folger greeted us and expressed his joy for our company, as the shop was empty of customers. At my request, he escorted me to the fiction shelf, where I noticed ample collections by Defoe, Shakespeare, Swift, and Milton. I had spent many nights getting lost in the adversities and adventures of humankind, which these authors amply presented to the reader. On that particular day, I searched for something uplifting, whatever that might be.

Auntie got my attention with a loud whisper and directed me to a table and chairs in a reading section. She brought over another candle, and I saw the name Benjamin Franklin—the printer, philosopher, scientist, diplomat, and writer. Seeing the table full of pamphlets and booklets, my eyes were drawn to *Poor Richard's Almanack*. This was exactly the wit and wisdom I was looking for to boost my spirits during these dreary Boston times. We sat for two hours reading and laughing and finally decided to purchase a copy.

We walked to the front desk to pay Mr. Folger for our purchase when we almost bumped into a tall, fair-skinned Englishman, which I determined from his "fresh off the ship" accent. He was dressed in shades of pale blue, covered over with a silk red cloak. Instantly, I was offended by his vulgar garb.

It would be obvious to anyone with the slightest sense of color that a bright red cloak donned by a man with long, yellow curly hair and light blue eyes was totally incompatible. The outfit was for show, possibly imitating an actor in an English comedy play. Later, I thought it was a ploy to demonstrate his authority over not only women but the Provincials of Boston.

Auntie and I were put off by this costume, so we purposely walked around him while he was in the midst of a bow, intent on making our acquaintance. We paid for our purchase. I impulsively glanced back and noticed that he had stopped dead in his tracks, glaring at the two of us, wondering why anyone would shun him. This worried me at the time, but with the busyness of my life, it faded from my mind until just now.

I shook my wet head to recover from my lethargic state and muttered the words, "That's him." How long had I sat in the chilling bath water and recounted that rainy day? Covered in goosebumps, I stepped out of the tub to towel dry and slip on the dressing gown draped on the nearby bench.

I walked to the blazing fireplace. Auntie or Father had added on more logs, for the coolness of evening was drawing nigh. I rested on the settle to ponder my ghastly revelation. For two months, I had lain in bed at night, picturing myself standing on the edge of a cliff, looking down at the swirling dark water. Finally dozing off to sleep, only to be awakened when some unknown person gave me a push. Down I fell into the endless depths of water. Wide-eyed and scared, I could only see the darkness of my room. There's no telling the hours of sleep I've lost. This was maddening!

Auntie was now a part of my secret. She would not remind me that I promised to reveal to her the details of this horrible dream. Our connection was close and solid, and she would wait until I was ready to divulge my discovery. I was weary of carrying the burden of it all. At that moment, I chose to allow a measure of light to replace the darkness hiding in the crevices of my mind. It was time to discard this veil of secrecy and move on.

I found solace in staring at the fireplace, flames jumping and darting. Auntie knocked on the wall to announce her entrance to my sanctuary. "Would you like for me to brush your wet hair?"

I turned around and stared at her face, nodding slowly. A definite yes.

Chapter 5

Retreat to Stoughton

Final Week of May 1774

We rose early the next morning. The long-awaited day had arrived. Auntie and I dressed in our riding clothes and boots with the notion that we would tack our horses as soon as we arrived at the farm. Our enthusiasm for today's events was so beyond measure one would think that we were to board a ship to Paris. The world that lay south of Boston was so inconceivably counter to the problem-laden Boston. After a hasty breakfast, Father and I set out to fulfill our assignments before parting town, leaving Auntie to sort out the collection of bundles we planned to haul to the farm.

The gleeful, blue-eyed Bignall children opened the door when they saw us walk the brick path to their house, primed to receive the personal attention they knew was coming their way. We went through the hand-washing routine, with the children anxious to demonstrate their newfound responsibility of keeping clean. Clara and Samuel held up their clean hands for inspection. I nodded my approval.

We moved to a sunny window to check the children's throats with the metal spatula, and Father announced the white spots were in the process of vanishing. "I see you've followed my directions. Drinking the vinegar water helps sore throats disappear." The children's eyes widened with delight.

I started to suggest that Mrs. Bignall take the children out for a walk since it was a sunny morning, but I stopped short and commented on the pretty springtime day. Even though they could use the fresh air, she might not think it safe to be on the streets during this particular week.

When we said our goodbyes, Mrs. Bignall placed three shillings in Father's hand and offered her thanks. We stepped outside to hear the predictable sounds of the city in place of the throbbing tattoo of drums. One more stop to the Ellis' home near Beacon Hill and our morning commitments to patients would be concluded.

I cleaned the infected sore on Mrs. Ellis' foot and applied burdock salve that we had picked up at Walden's Apothecary on the way to her house. I wrapped her foot and advised her to stay off it as much as she could. Her maid looked on as I worked for the purpose of changing the bandage while we were away. I explained we would be away for seven days. We walked briskly for a half mile to Fletcher Livery and Stables.

Miles Fletcher was a heavyset man, broad through the chest, with a florid complexion, and stood about my height. His strong arms and hands demonstrated his competence in handling horses. His brother, Amos, owned the building next door, working in a similar capacity building wagons and carriages that could be rented or sold. It was a successful family enterprise created by their grandfather in the early 1700s. Their father, Miles Senior, apprenticed with his father, passing down the trade to Miles and Amos. It was a lucrative business, judging from the fact that the two brothers and their families lived in spacious homes on North Square.

Many Boston businessmen, not as affluent as the Miles brothers, operated their business from the street level first floor and made their home on the second and third levels. The expense of operating a business was costly, leaving few resources to maintain a separate residence. I predict these businesses will be the first to close once merchandise shipments cease.

"A pleasant morning to you, Mr. Randolph, and to you, Miss Randolph." Miles graciously bowed.

"Good morning, Miles. We're here for the carriage I ordered. Looking forward to a few days away in the country," Father added cheerfully.

"What about that big fire on the north end two nights ago? Do you know anything about it, Dr. Randolph? I wager you heard the bells ringing wildly, as I did."

"I did. We walked to that particular neighborhood around midnight, just as the house collapsed. The family escaped physical danger to themselves. It was the men who put out the fire who were badly burned," Father was plainly in no mood to discuss such devastation this morning, but he kindly afforded Mr. Fletcher a few germane facts and changed the subject.

The distant ringing of the fire bells had awakened us. "Fire, fire!" Auntie screamed. I hastily pulled on my clothes, throwing a shawl over any flaws appearance-wise; it would be dark, after all. The three of us hurried out the front door, carrying a bag of medical supplies we kept on the ready for such emergencies. As we walked, a chilly wind blew, strengthening the flames spiraling high in the dark sky.

The volunteer fire workers had pumped all the water stored in barrels on three wagons, hoping to salvage some of the house, but it was useless; the family was fortunate to get out with their lives.

Fires occurred frequently in Boston. Dwellings built with wood caused fires to spread quickly, mostly caused by carelessness. Maneuvering a wagon loaded with barrels of water pulled by a team of reluctant horses through the narrow streets made for great difficulty in reaching a building already gone up in flames.

After the fire had died down, Auntie and I assisted Father with cleaning and bandaging the burned faces and hands of the valiant men who came to the rescue in the pitch-black night. Auntie concluded that a scuffle by drunken ruffians collided with a lantern, causing the fire. The North End was home to hooligans and roughnecks, famous for riots and drunkenness. As I searched in Father's black bag for more salve, my fingers felt the handle of Father's pistol, which greatly reduced my distress of working in this part of town.

Father decided we had accomplished our mission, and we commenced the long walk home to Bradford Lane. One of the wagon drivers offered us a ride home. We were more than willing to cram our exhausted bodies amongst the empty water barrels. Auntie and I held on to each other and dozed as the wagon bumped along the cobbled street, finally coming to a halt.

"I envy ye, Mr. Randolph. We could all use some time away. What with this week's commotion? It seems like everyone's in a dither. Just look at them nervous horses!" I caught the circumspect look when Miles made eye contact with Father, discerning that the two men were like-minded regarding the dilemma the colony faced. The sting of hearing the brazen soldiers settling into our town yesterday was so fresh in our minds. Who could say how long this siege would last? I wondered if Mr. Fletcher was part of the same secret meetings as Father.

The covered carriage sat in front of the open building, ready to transport the three of us to our family farm in Stoughton, eighteen miles south of our home. Glad to be leaving Boston and all its problems behind us for the next seven days.

The voice of a young man caught my attention, and I turned around to see him walking in our direction—a stable groom, judging from the leather apron he was wearing. Miles Fletcher introduced us to his son, Davey. The four of us chatted and visited spur-of-the-moment for several minutes. Davey excused himself, saying, "I'll just check the harnesses." He returned a few minutes later, driving the shiny black carriage with Fletcher's Livery and Stables printed on the side doors. He introduced us to Herman and Chester. Two strong, handsome grays stood snorting and stamping, anxious to gallop and smell the country air. Father and I naturally strolled over to the horses, rubbing their necks and stroking their muzzles while speaking their names to become better acquainted.

We stopped by our house on Bradford Lane to collect Auntie and the numerous parcels she had organized for the trip. Father gave me a reassuring embrace. "It's going to be a beautiful morning for traveling," he said, smiling. He was right. The sky was a bright blue, layered with puffy white clouds, shining brilliantly on Auntie's flower garden. Nothing dreary about this day. We departed the busy city, heading southward to Stoughton.

We traveled over the mile of muddy flats of the Boston Neck, a narrow strip of land connecting the city to the mainland. The long-legged plovers were foraging. They ran a few feet, stopped, pecked at the ground, and then ran again to partake of their breakfast before waters rushed over the soggy land. We were mindful that in a few weeks, the trip we were making today would be impossible. Father's contacts had informed him that Gage had in mind to set up encampments in Roxbury, cutting off travel from Boston. A grim prospect.

I sat up front with Father to keep him company with hopes of diverting his attention toward the farm visit. Even though we worked together, most every day seeing patients, we seldom took the time to talk about the current state of affairs in Boston and his brother's family. His brother Jacob was a practicing lawyer as well as the manager of the brewery at Mulberry Farm.

Years of driving horses pulling a heavy dray full of beer kegs had awarded Father with extraordinary muscular strength, evidenced by the way he managed the reins and the horses. Aunt Minnie was settled in the rear of the carriage, engrossed in her knitting. I knew full well that she was too canny to miss any part of our conversation. She had keen hearing. I abstained from sharing any ideas with Father that might come close to a confidential nature.

The quality of the air had magically changed from smelly and stuffy to fresh and breathable as we traveled deeper into the countryside. I turned to Father. "Have you noticed when we visit the farm, we all seem to go our separate ways? Auntie and Lenora garden and play hostess. You and Uncle Jacob work at the brewery and drink beer."

He laughed. "We do drink a lot of beer *and* eat delicious food, thanks to Lenora. Jacob and I enjoy working together, reminiscing, and talking about the who's who in Boston. Nothing raises my spirits more than time spent in the countryside. You have the pleasure of riding Gertie and capering about with your cousins and Ethan."

"Well, I'm not sure about capering about, but my cousins are adventurous, besides being intelligent and full of wit. My favorite times are spent with Poppi, though. I look forward to hearing his tales about our family, how the farm was built, how the brewing business has progressed through the years. He showed me the books he studied to learn how to build the barns and the furniture for the house. The last time we visited, he showed me his father's journal writings. He wrote extensively about our ancestors. They certainly had quite the independent spirit!"

"Is it any wonder we want the king out of our lives? It's in our blood to be self-sufficient," Father glanced at me with raised eyebrows. "When they made up their minds to make something out of this poor and rocky land, our grandparents forged ahead until they made it work with the help of some friendly Indians. Their fingerprints are all over this land. Still, it remains to be hard work, but your uncle Jacob manages it well. We have all profited from your grandparents' hard work." He was referencing the privilege his parents allowed him to study medicine in Edinburgh.

My mind accustomed itself to the repetitive clip-clopping sounds of Herman's and Chester's hooves pounding the hard-packed road. I contemplated the English, French, Swedish, and German immigrants who sought a better life in the New World. My great-great-great-grandparents left Biddenton, England, mainly because of constraints when it came to religious freedom under the rule of Charles II.

Unlike others who made the arduous journey to the New World, they had sold their property and belongings, which allowed them to afford the ship's fare and money to purchase property when they settled in Plymouth.

That wasn't the case with many families who had no choice but to come as indentured servants, eager as they were to escape Europe. I wondered how these immigrants fared as they put their lives on hold to devote years in servitude to their masters. Could they ever totally release themselves from that bondage and become independent property owners?

We discussed the welfare of our patients and their various physical problems. Father offered some of the obvious reasons for their failing health, asserting that the food they consume is mostly limited to bread, mutton, and ale. Fresh fruits and vegetables are seldom a part of their meals, even though they are in abundant supply. I thought back to Mrs. Ellis' pallid face when I dressed her foot this morning, wondering about her diet and the last time she had taken a walk on a sunny day.

Unsanitary conditions and smoke inhalation from fireplaces in homes and taverns were most reprehensible, contributing to respiratory problems, sore throats, and coughs. We made it our mission to educate patients to the best of our ability. However, so many people turned to homemade medicines at the insistence of family members who swore by medieval remedies that were dangerous and even fatal. Old habits are hard to break.

We went back and forth about some of the obvious changes in Boston. British officers had begun dribbling in before the new governor's arrival. They had the authority to take up quarters wherever they desired. Naturally favoring homes owned by Tories. These loyalists wined and dined with their British protectors and felt less terrorized by attacks from riotous rebels. The Sons of Liberty, that elusive group of renegades whose mission it was to aggravate Tory citizens and government officials, boldly hung effigies of King George from trees on the Boston Common. London's excessive taxing and regulations continued to take its toll on working families, drawing men and women to join in protests against the demands made by Parliament.

Falling into the conversation, Auntie took a turn to pitch her versions of the gossip she chanced upon in her sewing circle. Recalling tales from previous years when redcoats had laid siege to Boston, referencing certain establishments that drew soldiers to engage in the "oldest profession" on the North End of town.

Prostitutes naturally flocked into areas where soldiers quartered, luring them like flies into a spider's web, dressed in their slapdash costumes, spewing forth their provocative invitations. Not that I was well versed in the workings of such a profession, but Auntie had acquired such knowledge years ago while traveling with her seafaring husband to ports in the southern colonies and the West Indies. According to Auntie, every port she and her now deceased husband had encountered beguiled soldiers and sailors with their rum and women for a price.

I reminded myself that my intent was to keep Father's mind occupied with a pleasant, healthy conversation to take his focus away from the politics of Boston. Last night, walking home from Mr. Revere's shop, he was so distraught that before he settled in bed, he drank only a cup of tea before retiring to his chamber. I was equally overwhelmed with the business of our day, but it ended well.

At dawn, he was a different person, running down the stairs like a schoolboy, planting a kiss on our heads before he sat down at the kitchen table to eat a bowl of porridge and apple slices. He was dressed for traveling and could not stop talking about the thrill of driving the carriage in such beautiful springtime weather. The man was transformed overnight.

By the time we drove through the Neck, the high tides had receded, and what remained was a soggy area of tidal flats, which Father navigated without incident as he manipulated the horses' reins. Herman and Chester, taking it in stride, headed toward their destination with confidence. The Blue Hills came into view, and I knew that, within the hour, we would be entering the gates of Mulberry Farm in time for a mid-day meal. I sat mesmerized by the springtime scents of hay, plowed fields, and fruit trees, intensifying as we moved along the dusty road. The desirable effect I had craved for months.

If only we could live in the country, life would be simpler, I thought. The well-known lawyer John Adams, who defended the British soldiers after the Boston Massacre, lived in the country. His wife and their brood worked a farm in Braintree, just east of Stoughton. Why couldn't Father and I treat patients in this area of the colony instead of Boston? It would surely be healthy, inhaling fresh country air instead of the dirty smoke from thousands of chimney pots. Even the water from the town pump was questionable.

Consumed with dolorous thoughts of why my life could not be different, Father nudged my arm. "When was the last time you've had an outing with your friends? It's been ages since I've seen the Mullins girls or Eleanor Cushman. Have they moved to the countryside?" Father asked me a question that I supposed was forthcoming. Frankly, I was hesitant to explain to him the reasons why they never visited me at Bradford Lane.

I cleared my throat and evoked a false laugh. I conceded that now was as good a time as any. "Father, there's one word that comes to mind when you speak of my so-called friends. That word being *priorities*." He glanced at me, thinking me absurd, and opened his mouth to speak, but to no avail. I don't think he could conjure the words to say.

Auntie and I had had this same conversation two weeks before. I felt confident that I could justify my current social standing with these affluent, unmarried women of Boston. But given that the most important decision my flighty friends were expected to make each morning was whether to consume their daily scone with or without cream. I had made up my mind long ago that my tolerance for such empty-headedness was beyond my scope of comprehension and patience.

"What if I told you that I was invited to a tea at Olivia Mullins' house for the purpose of mastering the art of employing a fan to allure a gentleman?"

He answered with a straight face, "I'm sure you're making this up. You've read this in a novel, perhaps." He turned to take in my wry expression, and I shook my head.

"No. I mean to say, I do read popular novels, and, so far, there is no mention of the art of using a fan," I replied doggedly. I turned toward Auntie, briefly exchanging glances. Clearly, she could not contain her snickering when reflecting on this bit of balderdash. Her knitting fingers moved in double time.

"What exactly would you do with a fan to invite a gentleman?" Father asked. "Indulge us."

I chuckled, wondering if he was serious. But then I thought, *Why not?* "Imagine my hat as a fan." I folded the floppy flaps together. "My fan is now closed. I point it at an admirer, then point it back toward me. Beckoning him to join me." Father produced a wry smile and shook his head. "Or if I desired to hint at my coquetry. I would open it and hold it like this, halfway up my face. My eyes, poised alluringly."

Father sighed, seeing as much fiction and guile as did I. He laughed embarrassingly.

I continued, "Truthfully, it was a choice between me assisting you while we worked almost a week picking the feathers off Mr. Gardner's body after he was tarred and feathered. Or having tea with Phoebe,

Marianne, and Eleanor at Olivia's home. Mind you, this would *not* be a casual affair."

I paused and took a deep breath, realizing I was becoming undone over this poppycock as I repeated it to Father. "You must understand, it would necessitate dressing in a fancy gown, renting a carriage from Fletcher's Livery, and traveling to the Mullins' home in Beacon Hill for a late afternoon tea while learning to master fan techniques." I could tell he was politely taking all this in while he concentrated on steering the horses.

"I, of course, declined the vapid invitation, viewing it as an extravagance and a monotonous waste of time. Days later, I encountered Mrs. Mullins and Olivia at Folger's Bookstore. I pursued them in order to offer my regrets once more. With an air of arrogance, they took no notice of me initially. After some persistence on my part, they coolly sneered and consented to hear my reason for declining the tea affair. Afterward, Olivia showed her deplorable self by stamping her feet and throwing a tantrum in front of the customers. She swore that I would never be invited as a guest in her home for all eternity! Which suited me fine."

"Eternity? That's a long time. How did you respond to that?" he asked nonchalantly. I considered my answer while watching the road.

"I explained the desperate situation of our patient, Mr. Gardner, as the reason for my absence. To which she replied, 'A young woman like you touching a grown man's unclothed body is reprehensible. It's shameful.' As you can imagine, they showed no concern that the man was in agonizing pain with his skin literally on fire and that he would be scarred for life. I was so put off by their indifference that I had nothing more to say. I walked away. I distinctly heard one of them mutter the word 'rebel,' to which I smiled and took my leave from the store."

"Bravo, Josie! I applaud your courage," exclaimed Auntie. "Now we know the Mullins are Tories, forever loyal to the king!"

A chill came over me when I was forced to concede that lines were actually being drawn between friends and neighbors, Patriots and Loyalists. Each man and woman would have to make a choice—a British colonist or an independent citizen of North America.

I considered the sacrifice of thousands of Patriots in Boston, Lexington, and Cambridge who were devoted to drilling and training at this very moment to repel the four thousand British regulars quartered in Boston. It was only a matter of time before conflicts would arise. Colonial soldiers would be in need of medical attention. Maybe this was a fitting time for Auntie and me to offer our assistance in a medical way. I recalled seeing books on botany in Father's library when I tidied the surgery yesterday.

Remembering the conversation at DeLaney's Mercantile about spies in Boston, someone had mentioned militias were being formed in Connecticut and Rhode Island. Coastal colonies like Boston, where British ships could unload soldiers, horses, and weapons to take over our lives and our homes. Eventually, all thirteen colonies could possibly be placed under British control within the year. No matter where we lived, the countryside or the city.

With that thought, I confessed to myself that the reason I preferred country life to Boston was that our city was under British siege. I despised the very thought of leaving Bradford Lane. My life would never have the order I was accustomed to. I was truly dreading the unknown.

Perhaps we are unruly Patriots, but we just didn't have it in us to surrender our liberties. There was plenty of fight in us. Now that I had dismissed my fleeting dream of country life, my thoughts returned to more practical matters. If independence meant making our own medicines, then Auntie and I would learn ways to do that. It would begin with Naomi and Lenora, the finest gardeners I knew.

I sat brooding over how to approach Father about a plan that I had contrived regarding ways to assist soldiers medically. It would be a huge endeavor on our part to create our own medicines, but we would have the assurance that our surgery would be stocked with fresh ointments, salves, and medicinal teas. No more dependence on Walden's Apothecary, which may or may not be in existence in a year's time.

He leaned his head in my direction while keeping his eyes on the road. "You do realize that I'm going to need your and Aunt Minnie's help creating supplies in the coming weeks. Have you thought about that?" No need to worry about Father's mental state. He was obviously a mind reader.

"Er, in what way are you speaking?" I asked expectantly.

"Governor Gage has no notion of crossing the Atlantic to settle thousands of soldiers in Boston for a holiday. They intend to put a halt to our rebellion by destroying our militias and our courts, thus taking control of the colony. We must be prepared to attend to our soldiers who fall in battle. Boston's physicians have been consulting for almost a year preparing for imminent conflicts," he explained.

"So, this is the purpose of the secret meetings, organizing ways to care for the wounded?" I asked, remembering our heated conversation yesterday about spies and covert activities. Now, I began putting the pieces together, a clearer description of what our jobs would be.

"Yes, mostly," he replied. "Of course, our local physicians have to work in harmony with Mr. Adams, Dr. Warren, and numerous others to review intelligence gathered from Boston and outlying areas."

I glanced back and caught Auntie's eyes. She noted my wry smile as an affirmation. Her eyes, brown and large, gazed at me accordingly, nodding her head. We could confidently move forward. Now, our planning officially begins. Our trip to Mulberry Farm was sizing up to be half pleasure and half work. Just as I figured, part of the new British resistance mindset.

The spring day offered us a refreshing landscape of verdant shapes and vivid colors that we had not seen for months. The warm spring breeze had changed to increasingly hot as we traveled south. Summer was in the air. I pulled the flap of my straw sun hat downward to protect my eyes.

Father slowed the team and pulled over to a shady area with a stream that was easily accessible for the horses. Herman and Chester stretched down their necks and lapped the water. I recognized the area from our previous trips. It was a good time to exercise our legs and wipe the sweat from our necks. Thankfully, we were just moments away from our destination.

"This trip could prove to be valuable for our new assignment," announced Auntie, directing her idea toward me. "Lenora and Naomi plant and replant herbs throughout the year. They both have a good head for medicinal plants." She elbowed me, "We've got lots to learn while we're here."

"My thoughts exactly," I replied. Something astir in the woods caught my attention, then stilled.

Father grinned at me as he guarded Herman and Chester. "So much for capering about with your cousins! Let's be on our way."

Chapter 6

Mulberry Farm

Mid-May 1774

Nothing felt more like home than when we entered through those Mulberry gates, each bearing an oval cut-out with the name Mulberry Farm carved around the top and a Mulberry tree fashioned below it. Father turned the horses to the left of the house in the direction of the stables. Although it was late spring, hundreds of white crocus dotted the sideyard, mixed among immense sycamores and evergreens, bordered by a stacked stone wall standing four feet high. It was quite a sight to see, the short-budded stems wrapped in green leaves *en masse* absorbing the sun's rays, a reminder of stability in the seasons. The grand scale of the Mulberry property came into view.

Ozzie MacClure stood outside the paddock, waving us up the drive, his thick gray hair blowing in the humid wind. He waved us to the huge two-story barn, practically the size of the family home. Ozzie was a permanent fixture on the farm. He had brilliantly managed the stable hands, the horses, and the building itself for thirty years.

"Good day to ye, Randolph family!" he bobbed his head and smiled at Auntie and me, exposing his crooked upper teeth, but none missing. He gave Father's hand a hard shake and spoke to Herman and Chester. "Some fine lookin' steeds ye got there, wantin' to throw off their tack, I reckon."

Aunt Lenora was a good four inches shorter than me, with sparkling blue eyes and yellow hair blowing. She hugged the three of us, as excited about our visit as we were. "We're happy you've come. Let's go in the house and get a cool drink. Poppi's been pacing the floor and checking the windows all morning for the sight of you." The flat stones led us to the front door, where lilac bushes filled with flowers stood at the entrance.

We entered the front hall, and I caught the aroma of cloves floating throughout the house. Aunt Lenora had placed the cuttings of dianthus in small vases throughout the lower floor. These pinks, as she called them, are like the Queen of Sheba of her garden. Auntie and I stood examining one dark pink variety sporting white spots when a voice behind us declared, "Gillyvors, that's what Shakespeare called them!" We walked into Poppi's open arms.

"Welcome, pretty ladies!" He held our hands to get a good look at us from our heads to our feet. "I see you're ready to put those steeds through their paces." We grinned at his enthusiasm. Auntie's riding skirt idea worked. I'd probably be wearing mine for the entire week. Poppi's strong hands led us to the kitchen, where the tempting smell of roasting meat and baking bread hit me hard.

"Yes, we've been counting the days, as anxious as we are to get away from the crowds and the stench of Boston, as you well know," Auntie remarked as she retrieved a package from her bag. "I've brought your tobacco from Abercrombie's."

"It's grand that you remembered. I'll enjoy it by the fire of the evening. How is the old curmudgeon? Still as tightfisted a Tory as ever?" grinning as he pictured the miserly old Moses Abercrombie, measuring pinches of tobacco into a drawstring pouch. Poppi, always a gracious host, "How does a cup of cider sound for our travel-worn guests?" His dark brown eyes sparkled with delight.

Naomi Asher had brought in cold cider from the spring house and set out toasted cinnamon biscuits leftover from breakfast. I was famished and gobbled down two biscuits without thinking. While the others visited, I sneaked to the front rooms to explore. It had been five months since our last visit in December.

There was nothing pretentious about our family home. It was simple and unfussy, more than adequate for a family with several children. The spacious central hallway allowed for a wide stairway ascending to the upstairs chambers and an additional hallway that led to the rear of the house.

I peeked into the drawing room to the right, and nothing had changed there. Still the same worn settees and chairs. A highlight of our visits included music and dancing in the spacious room—Lenora and Auntie at the piano and Poppi and Uncle Jacob on the violin.

I had always been drawn to the library across the hallway. Two walls were lined with shelves holding hundreds of books, a large, heavy desk, and comfortable leather chairs for lounging and reading. The furnishings, vases, and paintings, passed down through the years, were the same as I remembered. My mind escaped to the times Poppi would hold me on his lap, telling me stories about his father and mother and when they built this house in the early 1700s.

The sun's rays shone through the front window, catching the crystal prisms dangling from two candle holders casting rainbow colors across the creamy walls. I basked in the room's peacefulness, the smell of pipe tobacco, and treasured memories decorating the tables, like two giant arms embracing me.

Aunt Lenora entered the room. "Ahem, there you are! We're all headed to the barn. I believe there's a certain chestnut waiting for some special attention." Aunt Lenora's arms and face were browned from working in the garden. She walked up to my side and nodded in the direction of the side window, framing the stables and the paddock just beyond the drive.

"Oh, yes, of course, I'm coming. I was just caught up in the serenity of this room. I've looked forward to this visit for weeks!"

We headed to the barn. Ahh, I breathed in the smells of the stable: leather, horse, and hay. I have loved those smells forever, it seemed. I followed Ozzie to greet the sweetest and most gentle horse I have ever known: a chestnut with a white stripe marked her face, and a white sock covered her left back leg. Gertrude, or Gertie as I called her, shook her head up and down when I spoke her name. She stretched out her neck, inviting me to rub her muzzle.

Ozzie had outfitted the horses by the time I entered the barn. "I 'av your Gertie all curried and saddled," he said to me proudly in his heavy Scottish accent. "I was jes' sayin' to her this morn how she'd be in fer a treat with yon wee lass a takin' ye fer a gallop!"

Seated atop Gertie, I patted her neck and glanced at the paddock, watching Herman trotting after Chester, enjoying the fresh air and the freedom to run at will. Aunt Lenora and Auntie rode to the front of the property to catch sight of the impressive crocus display and the flowering mulberry trees.

Father and I cantered in the direction of the malting shed to meet up with Uncle Jacob and Harry. Our eyes were fixed on the beauty of trees bursting with springtime growth and the thick forest snugly surrounding the property. Today was perfect, with the sun high in the sky, playing hide and seek amid puffy white clouds. We smiled at each other, reading the other's thoughts, and galloped toward the expectant springtime sounds surging from the woods.

My cousin Harry was my age, tall and wide-shouldered, like all the men in our family, with a good-looking squarish face, dark brown eyes, and wavy auburn hair highlighted with yellow streaks. Today, he and Uncle Jacob were marking off an area for a new malting shed situated next to the current one, which was showing signs of decay in the wooden posts and flooring. He and Poppi had pored over sketches for weeks, intending to build a shed with a larger floor space and more substantial columns to support an enlarged roof.

Poppi had included many of the details of the new shed in his letters to us, and we shared his excitement over a new malt shed that would house a third more barley than the current one held. This was the only hindrance that kept Uncle Jacob from producing larger quantities of beer. The execution of this project would require the time and effort of Uncle Jacob, Harry, and Ethan, who was Naomi's son. The concept rested solely on the brains of Poppi and Harry, who designed the layout and figured the dimensions of the project.

The size of the property and the freshwater creek made it more than suitable for this industry. Uncle Jacob and Harry had spent the early morning hours tending to the brewing and discussing the new design. A shed built with deeper eaves to deter wind and rain from coming inside would keep the barley drier and keep the seed from ruining.

Since Harry had made the decision to leave Oxford and return home, he and Poppi, an accomplished builder himself, had spent weeks figuring the dimensions alone. The whole idea would require the support of Ethan, who had managed the workings of the shed since he was fourteen. Now, there was the worry of the unpredictable Governor Gage. He was sure to set up British encampments south of Boston, including Roxbury, located only two miles from Mulberry Farm.

Father trotted his tall gelding to the malting shed to meet up with Uncle Jacob and Harry. Anxious to move on, Harry caught my eye and tilted his head in the opposite direction toward the woods. We headed down a slope toward the creek and the shadowy forest beyond. Gertie made her way over slippery rocks and up the embankment. An immediate coolness settled over me.

The intermittent commands of bluebirds, brown thrashers, and thrush were overwhelming, giving me a sense of peace. I had not fully grasped how tense my state of mind had become, not fully comprehending the chaos and turmoil of the past months that had taken hold of my life. So absorbed in my thoughts, I didn't realize we were taking an unfamiliar course. With Harry in the lead, we climbed a higher embankment. Annoyed, I yelled to my fearless cousin, "Hey, this is a different path. Where are we headed?" On second thought, it wasn't a path. I kept running into briars.

"To visit the Ponkapoag, or what's left of them. It's an ancient burial ground I wanted to scout out. Are ye game?" He turned around and tossed me a sideways grin and raised eyebrows. "Of course, if it doesn't interest you, we can travel the same middling trail as always. Come on, let's give it a go!"

Not to be outdone, I made an effort to hide my trepidation. I forced a grin and pushed Gertie with a jab as we climbed the path, ducking under low-hanging limbs. I yelled, "Hey, I'm right behind you!"

My face was flushed and dripping sweat by the time Harry gave rein to Caesar. The big stallion showed no evidence of fatigue, unlike Gertie. We tethered the horses under a shade tree and sipped our water. The sun remained high and grew hotter by the moment. I wanted to sit on a nearby log, but Harry was on the move. I could see in the distance where we were headed. We would have to walk upwards a long way before getting close enough to the hillock.

I followed Harry to a thicket of tall holly trees encased with vines showing off a springtime growth of miniature white flowers. This copse of tall, thick shrubbery, tantamount to a square, was an enclosure for numerous platforms held up by tall, spindly posts on each corner. Each platform held spears, drums, feathered headdresses, and faded blankets. I determined what Harry's fascination was with the area. I could certainly depend on my cousin to pull me out of the doldrums of city life by leading me to the middle of nowhere.

I was pushing myself physically to keep up with my cousin, being unaccustomed to traveling up and down in thick woods on a horse, avoiding thickets where I could. My legs and hips would pay the price when I returned to level ground. "Uh, should we be this close to a burial site? Isn't this an Indian's sacred ground? How did you discover such a place, anyway?" I was reluctant about seeing some gruesome sight, but curiosity got the better of me.

"Yes, to answer all your questions, it is a burial site. It's safe. Ethan and I came across it last year when we were seeking shelter, trying to outrun a storm. We looked over the fifty or so burial platforms holding tattered Indian garments and found wampum beads that matched a belt and pouch that Ethan had seen his mother wear. Naturally, we were curious. Afterward, Ethan and I told his mother, you know, Mrs. Asher, about our discovery. That's when we learned her ancestors were buried in that same area many years ago. So, do you want to see their, um, bodies?" he asked with raised eyebrows, exposing a hint of gold in his big brown eyes.

"Well, of course not. I mean, that would be sacrilege, wouldn't it?" I exhaled deeply. "On second thought, I think I do. You do mean their skeletons, don't you?" I had seen expired bodies before lying on the surgery table at Bradford Lane. I'm not sure why I showed such resistance.

He laughed smartly, baring a mouthful of teeth, "I figured you would!"

My mind went back to a drawing mounted on the wall of Father's surgery that showed a human skeleton, including the names of bones. With a gentle feel of the shape of a skull through the thin blanket, I was satisfied that there was a skeleton underneath the tightly bound shroud. I declined Harry's invitation to uncover and view what was left of the bones. I could not bear the thought of disrespecting the Great Spirit dwelling among the proud Indians in their final resting place.

"Do you ever wonder what happened to Ethan's father, Eli? Do you believe he's really dead?" I asked Harry more out of compassion than curiosity. After all, we just encountered the burial site of Naomi's people. "Do you think it's possible that Eli's remains lie on one of these platforms? Naomi has a certain mystic aura about her that's difficult to describe. Just a feeling I have."

Harry nodded, looking at me warily as if he had always suspected some mystery about Eli Asher's disappearance. "Honestly, I believe there's more to the story than we've been told. They say he was shot by the French or a Huron, but his body was never found, according to the captain in his regiment." I nodded. Such tragedies happened to innocent people during wartime.

The heavily forested area was dark and cool, with barely a sliver of sun shining through the tall trees. The bird sounds had all but disappeared. I felt a chill and rubbed my arms. I glimpsed at Harry. "I'm ready to leave this place." He nodded in agreement.

We rode slowly downhill, stopping at the creek to give the horses a break for water. The disappearance of Eli Asher, after all these years, troubled me. "Where is Ethan today?" I asked Harry. "I miss his company."

"Well, I've been given orders not to divulge any details, so please don't ask, but he rode down to Connecticut several days ago on an errand for Father. I'm sure you'll hear more about that tonight after dinner." Harry wanted to tell me, but he stayed loyal to Uncle Jacob and remained mum.

I glanced at Harry and shook my head. "The British aren't leaving without a fight, are they? Our way of life is changing right before our eyes, and I should know Boston is becoming bleaker every day. So many of our patients barely survive on their paltry food as it is. Must London and their corrupt lords rule our lives? Has it come down to whether or not we can choose our own tea, for heaven's sake?" Harry nodded in agreement. It was disconcerting, never knowing what was happening from one day to the next.

We walked Caesar and Gertie to their stables and removed their saddles. Ozzie came over to assist, seeing that we were red-faced and famished. "I reckon you'll be wantin' yer supper. Go on, an' I'll be brushin' yer steeds." My legs felt weak for all the effort I exerted climbing that mountain.

We stopped by the scullery to wash off the dirt and sweat and met everyone gathered in the kitchen, chomping at the bit. The intense aroma of roasted meat engulfed the room. Harry kindly made our excuses and jokingly said, "We need to get Josie a faster horse," to which Father gave him a slap on the back, nodding in agreement.

Poppi blessed the food and took his place at the head of the long dining table. Auntie sat to his right with Uncle Jacob at the far end. There was a great deal to talk about and much family news to catch up on. The meal was beyond delicious. Naomi and Lenora had placed the food on large platters: roasted pork with a red wine sauce, sweet potatoes, braised cabbage, onion relish, and topped off with an apple strudel for dessert.

Lenora had become an expert at baking mainly Swedish pastries. Her family had crossed the ocean from Sweden last century and had settled in New Jersey for a time. Later, they moved west to make a farm outside of Philadelphia. Uncle Jacob teased her about the fancy bread and cakes she had been making since an oven had been installed in the huge fireplace. "Consuming all these fancy pastries every day is affecting my mid-section," as he patted his belly.

We all gathered in the library, continuing our noisy chatter. Father was busy assembling a tray of fancy glasses and a decanter of wine as a surprise. We all expressed oohs and ahhs as he served us and made a toast: "To our hostesses, Lenora and Naomi, to Jacob, Ethan, and Harry for brewing the best beer in all of Boston and beyond, to Jake laboring over his law books tonight, and to our esteemed father, our family treasure!"

Lenora sipped her wine, and her eyes widened, "Josiah, how did you come by such fine port? I can't remember when we've had such a luxury."

"We can thank Boston's prosperous merchant John Hancock for his well-stocked cellar and the expert captain and crew who artfully maneuvered their way around British ships to smuggle in this fine after-dinner spirit. In fact, this was payment for services rendered when he came to me seeking relief from a nagging headache!" To which everybody in the room cheered.

Harry shouted, "Long live Mr. Hancock!"

The room became unnaturally quiet when Uncle Jacob sat at the huge desk and affixed spectacles to his face. He referred to his notes and began. "When my brother and I attended the Massacre Day memorial in Boston, John Hancock delivered a speech after which we both concluded that any further attempt to patch up our differences with England had passed. We must learn to live independently. We simply can no longer survive under British domination.

"Parliament has no interest in allowing our independence as a nation. They expect Boston to pay not only for the East India tea they forced on us, including taxes, but every colony along the east coast will be forced to pay an increased tax on everything we import from the British Empire. If we bow to their authority, these exorbitant taxes will eat into our profits so much that farmers and craftsmen will lose their incentive to remain in business. Parliament has already voted to restrict us in every which way regarding trade with European countries. These Intolerable Acts will strangle Boston trade.

"As you know, Governor Hutchinson has been replaced by General Gage. Parliament believes the former governor was too soft on the rebels who were responsible for instigating mob rule. He turned his back on those who threw English tea overboard and allowed the perpetrators to walk free. Hence, the governor is on his way to London as we speak.

"In retaliation, Governor Gage has assembled four thousand British soldiers in and around Boston in an attempt to quell any uprising and armed rebellion from Bostonians. Each day, soldiers train and march, fill up our taverns, and do what they can to intimidate our people to the point where they stay confined to their homes for fear of being accosted by the enemy. Boston's port is gradually closing, which means no business will be conducted in our city come June 1st. Men's and women's jobs *will be* suspended. Laborers' families will go without food, necessities, and medical care. England means to starve us into submission," Jacob pounded his desk.

He continued, "Ten years ago, when Parliament began forcing taxes on colonists, Sam Adams organized the Committees of Correspondence. This was an effort to keep surrounding towns informed and to stay in touch in matters regarding British plans. The fruits of his labor have paid off. These thirteen colonies have never been as united as they are today. News is carried by messengers or so-called express riders—certain men who demonstrate good judgment and can be trusted to pass on accurate information to leaders in Philadelphia, New Haven, Providence, and New York. This effort has proved to be successful, aiding militias in ways to organize a resistance. Even trade between the colonies has expanded.

"Mind you, General Gage is a decent, respectable man who fought alongside colonists in the war against the French. But do not be deceived; he remains under the authority of King George. His orders demand him to cut off communications between the colonies and confiscate weapons that certain rebels have stored away. It is our duty to oppose the king's tyrannical practices. When the time comes, we must be prepared to protect ourselves."

"What do you mean when the time comes?" Auntie interrupted. "And how do we protect ourselves?"

Uncle Jacob reminded us, "Britain has inexhaustible resources. Her ships cover the oceans, and their armies are trained to be aggressive and organized. By comparison, our only resource is the resolve to preserve our freedoms.

"We Yankees have a reputation for being forceful and ingenious. But, in order to defend ourselves, provinces are encouraged to form their own militias, and that's exactly what's happening. Farmers, merchants, and anybody who is willing to serve and support the cause for liberty.

"It takes money to train these men and provide them with muskets and supplies, but the important point is colonists are willing to serve to protect their property. Fortunately, we do have some wealthy benefactors who have invested their capital to buy weapons and gunpowder. The biggest challenge is keeping it hidden from the British."

I stifled a yawn and glanced up at the oil-painted portraits of Poppi and Grandmother mounted on the wall behind the big desk. I remember when she died. It had been over ten years ago when Harry and I turned eight in the same year. It was an emotional time for all of us, losing the matriarch of the family. It was especially hard for Poppi. Anyone who knew them could tell they had an endearing love for each other, unlike many husbands and wives who are bound together in marriage because of convenience or an arrangement profitable for the family. If and when I marry, I pray it will be a mutual love for one another. I glanced over at Poppi, wide-eyed and absorbing Uncle Jacob's comments, knowing better than any of us that the tide had turned. A break from Britain was imminent.

I shook my head, trying to remember Auntie's questions and Uncle Jacob's answers. Oh well, I'm sure it will all be repeated in the following days. Aunt Lenora signaled Uncle Jacob with a glimpse, aware that everyone seemed to be in a somnolent state. She announced that coffee and breakfast would be ready at 7:00 the next morning. I stood up slowly from my seat, endeavoring to gracefully disguise my limping body. I said my good nights and ascended the stairs. It had been a tiresome day. I planned to sink into a feather mattress to ease my aching limbs.

Not long before dawn, the rich aroma of coffee reached my nose. In mere seconds, I was out of bed and in my riding clothes, following that mouthwatering scent as I descended the stairs. Having no idea where the family was at this time of day, I grabbed my coffee, sipping and walking toward the stables, anxious to greet Ozzie and Gertie. Much to my dismay, I was met with the sounds of splashing water and moaning sounds and the smell of blood.

I cautiously walked into a side room where tack and saddles were stored and discovered the source: Ethan Asher. He was slumped on the floor, visibly in pain from a wound dripping blood down his left arm. We made eye contact, and without a word spoken, I tore off a strip of muslin from his shirttail and wrapped it around his arm above the wound to stop the blood flow. "I'll get Father."

Doing all I could for Ethan, I ran to the house. I had gathered a bottle of rum, a jug of alcohol, and Father's black bag while I was practically dragging him out of the house, hoping these trappings would give him a clue of an indisputable emergency. He got the idea, and we made haste to the stables. Moments later, Ethan was lying on the floor while Father proceeded to remove the bullet from his arm. My heart began to beat again when I heard the ping of the bullet against a metal bowl. Father stitched the wound, and I offered more rum to Ethan's lips. We watched him for an hour, knowing that, inevitably, a fever would result. I patted his face and chest with rags soaked in cool water. He slept lightly as we comforted him as best we could.

When Uncle Jacob informed Naomi of her son's injury, she simply nodded, uttered not a word, and gathered the fixings she knew would be needed. Naomi Asher was, without a doubt, an original Stoic. Her cool aplomb allowed her to remain rational as she went about her duties: preparing an onion poultice to draw out the fever and brewing the bee balm tea to sustain Ethan during recovery. She was uniquely equipped to completely repress her feelings and endure the long hours of remaining by her son until his condition changed. A day had passed since Father and I had tended to Ethan's wound.

With Ethan in the care of his mother, everyone went about their chores and busyness. I planned to get some exercise in hopes of working out the soreness in my legs and other places. Ozzie was busy tending to the wagon horses and repairing tack, and I spent my time brushing and saddling Gertie. I noticed Harry at the front entrance sitting atop Caesar in conversation with a neighbor friend.

The man looked familiar, and I'm sure we had met on a different occasion. I recall Uncle Jacob's talk last night when he cautioned us to listen to others but to be careful about the information we share with anyone outside the family.

Mounted on a tall, black bay, the man looked to be Father's age, heavy set, and a farmer judging from his browned face and sweaty smell. I picked up on his countrified Yankee speech, hearing him respond to Harry's statements with a drawn-out "aya" for yes. He was bound for the blacksmiths in the nearby village to pick up some repaired bridle bits. When he saw me approaching the fence, he raised his slouch hat and offered a bow in my direction. "Good day to ye," he said.

"Who was he?" I asked as the man rode up the dusty road. "He looked familiar."

"Simon Grayson. He and his wife work a farm down the road. They have sons and daughters. I attended grammar school with two of his boys. They raise milk cows, goats, chickens—all sorts of farm animals. We purchase meat, eggs, milk, and cheese from them. You name it, they've got it, and the redcoats know it. In fact, they're hounding him for eggs and such to purchase whenever they set up camp in these parts. So far, he hasn't made any deals with them. He wants to discuss the matter with Father to determine what his legal rights are in case he is pressed to oblige them."

"That puts farmers in an awkward position, doesn't it? Then I assume the Graysons are Patriots, I mean, not Tories."

"Yes," he responded, "they are Patriots, and there are plenty of Tory farmers in these parts, so I'm curious about their insistence on offering to buy supplies from Mr. Grayson. Hey, let's ride down a ways, and I'll show you this side of the country."

I nodded and gave Gertie a nudge in her ribs, still needing to finish my point about the Graysons. "Perhaps the redcoats are drawing a dividing line between Patriots and Tories so they'll know who to harass or to pit one against the other. Hey, is this the route Ethan would have taken when he was riding home yesterday?" We passed two more farms, blackberry bushes escaping onto the riding path, and an odd apple tree here and there, the blossoms decorating the plainness of the dirt road.

"Yes, most likely. I'm hoping to talk to him about that later today if he's up to it. Of course, with Mrs. Asher's permission," he responded with an arched brow and a sideways smile. "Let's stop here to rest the horses." The opposite side of the road was lined with poplars and oaks, sufficient for shade.

We began riding along the dusty road, taking in the smells of freshly turned earth formed into neat rows now showing tiny green sprouts of corn and beans. Sitting on top of Gertie allowed me to see the tops of two corn cribs ready to receive whole ears of corn for drying, but not until late August.

There were two farms along the road that grew orchards of apple, pear, and peach trees. None of the fruit was ready for picking as yet, but the delicate blossoms promised peaches in the heat of August. Apples, pears, and quince would bear fruit in the cool of autumn. That's when the neighbors poured in to pick the fruit and make the cider to store in stone jugs. For two weeks, we would be buried in fresh-picked fruit, bees and flies enjoying their final hurrah before the first frost of the season.

Mulberry Farm grew a small apple orchard under the care of Naomi and Lenora. These apples were used throughout the year for pies, applesauce, and apple butter. Once the apples were harvested, the women put the men to work outside for several days of processing. Poppi and Harry had built long tables meant for outside jobs that required meat preparation and harvesting vegetables. Knives were sharpened, apples were cored and sliced, and some diced into quarter-inch chunks.

After that mass of work, Poppi would string the round shapes on linen thread to dry. Harry and I would hang the long, flimsy strings on rafters in the kitchen, scullery, bathhouse, even in the drawing room, wherever rafters held up the ceiling. These thin slices, bound for tall crocks, were placed in layers and covered with vinegar, preserved for untold desserts. Finally, apple chunks, copious amounts of sugar, lemon, and water were cooked in large kettles over an outside fire. All this work created crocks of applesauce to be stored in the cool cellar. It was a family affair, and we loved every minute of it. In due course, we grew sufficiently tired of the lingering smells of apples.

It couldn't have been a more glorious day, sunny and a slight breeze with chur-ree sounds of bluebirds busy flying back and forth to their nests. I thought I detected some movement, possibly a deer in the woods, when Harry and I dismounted and walked the horses down a shady embankment to cool down in the stream. I shook off that thought, curious to learn more about Harry's future education. We leaned against a large rock covered with moss. "Do you have plans to return to Oxford?"

"No, much to the regret of my parents. Two years of mathematics and physics were enough for me. I had no enthusiasm for chemistry. This is my home, and I want to use the knowledge I've acquired to make improvements on the property. When we do send the redcoats back to England, or whatever part of the world they wish to conquer, these colonies will expand and prosper. I want to have a hand in making it something more than producing rulers and kings. Every man and woman needs freedom to use their talents, and we can't have it with London breathing down our necks."

The horses were getting restless and needed to move out of the small stream area. "We should be getting home," I said. "I promised your mother I would help with weeding the garden this morning, and Poppi and I are playing chess after dinner."

Harry turned in my direction as I was leading Gertie up to the road. "Did I hear you correctly? You and our grandsire are playing chess today? Surely, you jest!"

"Yes, indeed, he's been showing me some of his winning strategies. I mean, I have a lot to learn since I'm not here that often… Hmm, did you say something?"

He answered, "I've never heard of, uh, a woman playing a game of chess. Do all the women in Boston participate in this man's sport? When did you start learning the game?"

"Well, I can't say what my neighbors do with their evenings. Perhaps some do play chess. Do you think it's strictly a man's sport? Auntie is learning as well; I mean, she's a very competitive player. Father and I often have a game going during those cold Boston nights as a way to relax. Poppi started teaching me last spring while you were away at Oxford." I grinned.

Harry did not answer my question and turned silent as we started down the road but managed a "hmm" as we picked up speed. Disconcerted that a female could have the brain to strategize over a game of chess, he changed the subject, "How do you assist Uncle Josiah in his physician's work?"

"We have patients who come to the surgery on Bradford Lane. There are occasions when Father and I treat patients in their homes. I welcome them as they arrive and determine the nature of their visit. I make notes in our patient journal to gain a history of their condition. I pass the journal to Father so he can determine how to treat the problem. He records notes about the patient as he learns them."

"So, you ask them questions about headaches or a nagging cough? I mean, do you find it difficult for a man to discuss a rash that covers his legs or some other place?" he cautiously asked.

"I've learned from Father how to extract information by asking detailed questions. I'm familiar with the surgical tools and medicines he uses. I'm competent in lancing boils, preparing poultices, stitching a wound, and evaluating symptoms for various diseases. Referring to your question, some men are more comfortable discussing their malady with the physician. Some have no qualms about showing me where it hurts," I said with raised eyebrows.

His face blushed, revealing more freckles. I pushed Gertie to move onward. Harry rode up to join me. "I'm interested in knowing how one recovers from being tarred and feathered. Surely, the tar is heated so it liquifies sufficiently to spread over one's skin. The agony of enduring such torment must scar the body forever." Harry looked at me through compassionate brown eyes.

"You are correct. The body is disfigured permanently. It is a gruesome sight to behold. One has to carefully remove the hardened tar from the skin with as much dexterity as possible. We give the patient laudanum to relieve their pain. Afterward comes the anguish of healing from the burns. Some men would prefer death over living with the horridness of such brutality."

"I'm amazed at how you can discuss such a ghastly undertaking and not become sick to your stomach. Just the thought of it makes me squeamish." Harry puffed out his cheeks, looking sickly.

"When people are screaming and in pain, we must rise to the occasion to give them the relief they are seeking. I have devoted myself to this task. Life is valuable. We must give of our talents in an uncommon way to attend to those in need. It will be more challenging when our soldiers fight it out with the British. I hope we will be ready when the time comes." He nodded in agreement.

The ride to the stables was tiring in the spring heat. One good thing is that I had not experienced any nightmares since arriving at the farm. The increased physical exertion could account for that. Also, Ethan's condition lay heavy on my mind. In any case, Gertie needed to be settled. I threw off her tack and wiped her down. Then led her to water.

I walked to the well and helped myself to a cup of cool water. I saw my aunts working in the kitchen garden. The space had grown bigger through the years due to Naomi and Aunt Lenora's propensity toward experimenting with plant cuttings from neighbors and friends. Corn was not part of the garden since the Morrison farm grew more than they could use. Lenora traded three kegs of beer for twenty bushels of yellow corn every summer.

I saw my straw hat hanging on the fence and opened the garden gate. Auntie escorted me to the squash rows and presented me with a hoe. I managed a smile. "At least it's in the shade." Aunt Lenora and Naomi had cultivated quite an herb garden over the years. In every direction, I picked up a different scent. My fellow gardeners were bantering back and forth about certain herbs that could treat this and that ailment. I was interested in learning about plants used to brew medicinal teas. This is where Naomi could be of help. I was lost when it came to determining which parts of a plant are the most beneficial.

I overheard Lenora suggesting ways to use ginger root to ease stomach distress and morning sickness. Once the root was pulled from the ground, how was it transformed into a medicine?

Purchasing medicine from Walden's Apothecary was easy, but now I was entering a whole new world of growing herbs and starting from scratch. I knew Auntie was intrigued with plants and as ambitious as I was to learn the beginning steps. Fortunately, we stood in the midst of the finest teachers.

I saw Naomi walking toward us from the farmhouse where she and Ethan had lived since he was an infant. Her grievous facial expressions had been unchanged since yesterday, but there was hope in her dark eyes when she approached us in the garden. "Come," she said. We dropped our garden tools and walked with Naomi. The sun was high, and I dabbed at the sweat running down my face. Lord, let it be good news. We walked up the porch steps into the house. There he sat on the side of his bed, smiling when he saw our faces. We all breathed a sigh of relief.

The heat of the day had taken its toll on my body, given its current exhausted state. I was considering a bath before my chess game with Poppi. As I prepared my bathwater, I recalled the bewildered look on Harry's face when he learned that Poppi and I planned to play a game of chess in the afternoon. His verbal reaction struck me as passe and old-worldish. If he truly believed that chess was a game for men only, Harry's limited knowledge of the aptitudes of women could use a quick brush-up. I considered that my responsibility, being that I'm a woman and his cousin after all.

My grandmother, being the pragmatic person she was, had complained to Poppi that filling a tub with water in her chamber upstairs did not make sense to her. To resolve the problem, he built an entire room behind the scullery with close access to well water.

I wondered how I could ever find a husband who loves me the way Poppi loved Grandmother. My marital chances seemed to be dwindling with so many men leaving Boston. I cringed at the thought of leaving Bradford Lane.

Relaxing in a tub of warm water did more than remove the grime from my body. I pondered the inevitable changes in the weeks ahead. The prospect of redcoat soldiers hanging about Boston's streets was frightening. But I could not—I would not—allow that to govern my life.

I resolved to stay true to my belief that colonists needed independence from England, but what preparations could I make for myself when an uncertain future lay on the horizon?

I walked outside, seeking a sunny spot to sit and dry my hair. Poppi sat on a bench facing the family's graveyard. I suspect he spent many days perched in his favorite spot to reminisce.

He looked up at me, and I smiled at his friendly and wrinkled face browned by the sun. His thin white hair blew in the breeze. "I'm visiting the family. Will you join me?"

I was in a noiseless world surrounded by a line of redbud trees and a huge elm tree where the limbs of new leaves draped over some of the headstones. I spotted my mother's grave. "Josephine Harriet Spencer Randolph, Cherished wife and mother, Born April 8, 1729, Died October 14, 1756" neatly carved in the granite headstone. I turned to Poppi. "Am I very much like my mother? I mean, her character and her temperament?"

Poppi took my hand and turned toward my face. "She was very comfortable with herself and was devoted to your father, especially in his work. I thought it a shame that she could not study medicine as Josiah had. She certainly had the mind for learning. She loved reading Shakespeare, and she would sometimes ask me, 'What do you think he meant with this line?' or 'How could anyone be as cruel as King Lear's daughters?' We would laugh. She had opinions, and she could impart them in a very spirited manner. She was not coy but a mature young woman who loved life. Now, does that sound like anybody you know? What say we go solve the world's problems over a game of chess?"

We had been at the game for an hour. We were seated next to the front window in the library, chatting back and forth about Father's work and certain diseases. I was determining which piece the rook could take while making conversation with Poppi. Then, out of the blue came the dreaded word "checkmate." He announced, "Josie, concentration *is* the key to winning."

The aromas of bread baking and roasting rosemary chicken drifting from the kitchen were not helping my ravenous appetite. I could tell

Poppi was experiencing the same distress. He politely spoke when he heard my growling stomach, "Are you as hungry as I am? Maybe the cooks will allow us a pinch of bread."

"Let's go," I said, "before I pass out from starvation!" Auntie buttered some bread for us, which we wasted no time gobbling down. Just then, I heard the men's excited voices coming from the scullery, washing up for dinner, accompanied by Ethan and Naomi.

Naomi managed a proud smile in contrast to Ethan's enthusiastic announcement, "I'm back, and I'm starving!" The hero stood amongst us with his arm across his chest, covered with a sling.

Like an animal released from its cage, he marched to the dining room ahead of everyone and took his place at the table, ready to return to the human race. We all joyfully followed him. There was no denying that Ethan's inherent leadership qualities had prepared him to manage the workings of the malting business, as evidenced by his enthusiasm to return to his work and his family. Uncle Jacob once commented, "He has the makings of a politician, but I'm not giving him any ideas!"

The techniques of making food tasty and hot by the time everyone had taken their place at the table struck me as a mystery. I suppose the key is timing and developing a sequence of cooking the meat first, the bread second, followed by the vegetables.

These two remarkable women, Auntie and Aunt Lenora, went from digging in the garden to cooking a splendid meal and then graciously took their seats, changing from cook to hostess. Poppi said grace, thanking the Lord for Ethan's recovery. We eagerly finished our soup and greens before loading our plates with rosemary chicken, vegetables, and buttered bread. It would have been wise for me to stop after the rich soup, but foolishly, I did not.

I paused and addressed Aunt Lenora across the table, "How do you make chicken taste so good? I'm enjoying every bite!" Her face lit up. "I wouldn't know where to begin making something that tastes this delicious and be brave enough to serve it to my family!"

Aunt Lenora's face beamed. Before she had a chance to respond, Ethan stopped stuffing his mouth long enough to interrupt, "Forgive me,

Aunt Lenora, but I must make a comment." He gazed in my direction. "Josie, I'll tell you something you are brave enough to do, and that is to rip the sleeve off a wounded man's shirt and see to the bullet hole in his arm. The action you took saved my life, and I'm grateful."

It was hard for me to respond to that. Harry broke the awkward silence by clapping and cheering in my direction, signaling everyone to join in the congratulations. I glanced over at Father clapping as well. My throat tightened when he flashed a wink and a smile in my direction.

We finished the main courses, and dessert was served—a vanilla pudding with ginger cakes and always a cup of ale to wash it all down. Ethan kept us entertained with stories of his trip to Suffield, Connecticut, where he was sent by Uncle Jacob on the advice of John Adams.

The purpose of the trip was to look over the workings of Stowe Ironworks, in particular, their gunsmithing manufacture. Nathan Stowe had come highly recommended by Mr. Adams, a trustworthy Patriot, and was eager to endorse the cause of independence. A hush-hush word that one was not permitted to voice but only think.

Naomi and I got no objections from the family when the two of us gathered the dirty dishes and carried them to the scullery. Harry brought in buckets of water from the well and filled a kettle with water to heat in the fireplace. Thankfully, he offered to pour the heavy bucket of water into the stone sink.

Another household installment of Poppi's, suggested by our late grandmother. He would say he copied the ingenious idea from the Romans, or perhaps it was the Egyptians. Auntie carried plates of leftover chicken and vegetables to the big kitchen table where Ozzie and today's stable helper would eat their dinner. There should be enough food left over for a light supper during the evening, but that all depended on the men's appetite. I seldom ate anything in the evening. On occasion, I would drink a cup of chocolate before bed. I hoped it would be an early night for me. I was famished.

The following day, the men headed to the library after our afternoon dinner to gather information from Ethan about the procurement of guns and powder from Stowe Ironworks. The dangerous undertaking of securing weapons to defend the colony against Britain was a treasonous crime. This was not going to be an easy operation to pull off, given that British troops were scattered around Boston and neighboring towns. Rebels had begun stashing guns and ammunition months ago. So far, they have not been discovered. I recalled our conversation about spies that had made Father cringe.

Jacob took out his notebook to begin recording ideas on how to proceed with plans, "Ethan, can you sketch the route you took from Stoughton to Suffield? Good thing you're right-handed." Harry entered the room and closed the door behind him.

The men huddled around the big desk to study the map. Josiah was the first to comment, "Where exactly were you set to a chase by a patrol of redcoats? Was it anywhere near the Stowe property?"

Ethan pointed to a town ten miles north of Suffield called West Springfield within the boundaries of the Massachusetts colony. "To set the record straight, there were only two soldiers, not a patrol, which I didn't think was unusual at the time, but now it is. After I left the Whales' Tale, I got on the road towards home, and I could hear a couple of riders trying to catch up with me. I caught a flash of scarlet and figured there were soldiers on my tail, so I tried to outrun them, but they were down for the chase. I rode as far as the Blue Hills. That's when I took the shot," as he looked down at his left arm in a sling.

"Do you recall seeing them in the taproom at the tavern," Harry asked, "or is it possible they started trailing you when you left the farm? If that's the case, then British spies are out in full force."

"I didn't see any redcoats at any tavern the entire time I was in Suffield," Ethan responded. "My thinking is they were riding from the east and spotted me on the road, noticed that I looked like a woodsman, wearing a buckskin jacket and all. Perhaps they were of a mind to run me down and beat in my head for sport. They got frustrated when they couldn't outrun old Comet and me, so they decided killing me would be more to their liking."

Josiah and Jacob glanced at each other, nodding and considering the account Ethan had communicated. "What time of day was it? Had the sun gone down?" Josiah asked.

"Daylight was fading, so the light was going fast. I approached the Blue Hills, thick and dark as they were, and rode in about a hundred yards. I settled in behind a thicket of cedars, and I never saw the buggers again. I was well-armed, though. I raised my rifle and aimed to shoot at anything that moved. Thank the Lord, I was carrying two pistols in my belt as well. I drank a long swallow of water and rum, and that's when I felt blood dripping down my arm. I did not realize I had taken a bullet until I made my way down the mountain toward home. Riding down the road would have been quicker, but I could not take any chances."

Everyone agreed with Ethan, considering all the trouble he had encountered. Poppi suggested taking a needed break, joining other family members outside to enjoy the rest of the sunny day.

While the men were in the library discussing Ethan's trip to Suffield, the women spent time outside to relax and enjoy the sunshine. Not a cloud in the sky, only a gentle breeze coming from the east, showering us with apple blossoms. We spread out a quilt across the bright green grass. I had enjoyed my time with Naomi during our dinner cleanups, so I felt inclined to perch beside her.

Ethan's temperament was quite the opposite of his mother's. He was outgoing and confident, whereas she was reserved and guarded in her conversation. I considered how Ethan must resemble his father in that respect. Ethan's hair and face truly were a representation of Naomi. The sun's rays danced across the crown of her black plaited hair, highlighting white strands. Her dark skin wrinkled at her mouth and eyes when she smiled.

"Ethan must take after his father with his tall and lanky build, but he resembles you in the face, except for his English nose." Knowing that her son meant the world to her, I was hoping to build on my relationship with Naomi. Her teeth gleamed when she smiled, emphasizing her dark skin.

She broke through her shyness and opened up. "Yes, and his blue eyes. Eli was strongly built. Very tall like the Randolph men and Minnie. That's one reason I was attracted to him and his agreeable spirit. So often, he would make me laugh when he told stories about hunting trips with my brother, Tall Tree, and with Chief Randolph, as he called your grandsire.

"They would come home with their kill, bear or deer, and the family would begin butchering, salting, and smoking the meat. Some of the neighbors would join us, and Mr. Randolph would say, 'Take what you can use.' Later, we celebrated with singing and dancing while the game was being roasted outside. Ethan and I have many fond memories of living here with such giving people. With the exception of a few cousins, the Randolphs are the only family we have now."

I listened attentively to Naomi as I lay on my side, propped up by my elbow, while she talked about Ethan's childhood and how she appreciated the family life offered by my grandparents since Eli had disappeared during the war.

I caught sight of someone, a long shadow hanging over me and something leafy brushing against my cheek. I kept waving it away and noticed Naomi grinning at someone behind me. Harry, always the tease, was pestering me for a chase. I appeased him by distracting his attention with a "Hey, there's a deer?" I was on my feet, running in the opposite direction. He gave chase and ran ahead of me, but still, my craftiness won over his tomfoolery.

As we walked back toward the house, I saw the women and Ethan chatting and lounging in the sun. A target had been set up on stacked bales of hay in front of a large oak tree, along with two bows and a dozen arrows. "What's this? Have you taken up archery?" I asked Harry.

"Ethan and I have been shooting a bow since we were kids, but it's probably the first time you've ever seen the target set up. I didn't think you would be interested before, but now that you've shown an unusual interest in manly sports, I thought you might want to give it a go," he said, shrugging his shoulders and grinning.

"Now you're poking fun at me. I've never used a bow, but it looks interesting," I said warily. He demonstrated how to hold the bow and insert the arrow. It looked simple enough, but once I tried it, I was surprised at the strength it took to pull the arrow back so it would hit the target. I shot three of the arrows, and they all landed somewhere in the woods beyond.

Harry moved behind me, taking hold of my shoulders, guiding my body and my feet to achieve the correct stance of a sideways position, and firmly grasping the bow with a straight arm. He pulled my shooting arm further back and said, "Let go of the arrow. Whew, almost a bullseye. I didn't realize you were so tall. Now, try it again and pay attention to maintaining a straight back and neck. Draw the string so it touches the tip of your nose. That looks good. Another good shot. Keep practicing. Uhmm, call of nature, be back shortly."

As he walked to the woods, I yelled, "Couldn't have anything to do with the three pints of ale you drank at dinner, would it?" He waved his arm as he moved toward a big oak tree. Must be the perpetual reek of the brewery that causes these men to drink ale so liberally!

I felt awkward picking up arrows and shooting them over and over, but I wanted to learn, and Harry was a good teacher. Before I knew it, Ethan had crept up behind me, holding arrows that had landed in the thicket behind the tree. "Align yourself with the target," he instructed, "and move in a little closer. Just relax your left arm and grasp the bow. Imagine the target as a red jacket, and you definitely want to shoot to kill. Get my point?"

"Speaking of a left arm, how is that wound doing today? Any pain?" I asked while looking at his left shoulder in a professional way. "It's only been four days since you were stitched. Although, it did appear to be healing well enough since I last changed your bandage."

"I'm in no pain, and I'm getting the rest I've been ordered to take by all you women attending to me. In fact, I don't recall the doctor checking my wound once since he stitched me," he said laughingly.

"Because he knew the women would check. We care about you, that's all," I said in a benevolent tone. "The first twenty-four hours can be risky. Besides, we can't afford to lose you. Who would manage the brewery? I noticed it hasn't affected your appetite!"

We turned toward the barn when we heard a voice yelling in our direction. Jake was as tall and broad-shouldered as Harry. He resembled his father with a head full of wavy dark hair and dark blue eyes. He walked towards us with a big smile, staring at Ethan's slinged arm. I was still holding the bow when he gave me a bear hug and casually asked, "How come you shot him in the arm?" He turned and shook Ethan's right hand. "What in the world happened to you? I could sure use something cool to drink." We walked toward the women, anxious to greet Jake.

Naomi and Aunt Minnie stopped by the spring house for some jugs of cider while the rest of us headed to the kitchen. Jake's arrival was unexpected, so I was thrilled to see him since we would be leaving for Boston in two days. He was exhausted from riding all the way from Cambridge, and it's quite possible that he had encountered some redcoat patrols en route. This was on all of our minds since Ethan's trouble on the road from Suffield. We all talked over each other, answered Jake's questions, and got the latest news from him. Poppi, disturbed from his rest with our loud voices, couldn't resist joining the welcoming party. "What's all the rumpus? Are we under attack?" he inquired laughingly.

When we were walking to the kitchen, I heard some hammering and racket coming from the wagon barn. I assumed Father and Jacob were repairing the wagons used to haul kegs of beer to taverns. Sturdy and well-maintained wagons were an absolute necessity in the beer-making industry. I left the family in the kitchen and walked up the hill past the stables with four bottles of cold apple cider. There they stood, the two brothers with their shirt sleeves rolled up and beads of sweat covering their foreheads, one holding a side rail while the other hammered a nail into place. Ozzie was busy digging nails from a bucket set on the work space. I made my presence known. "Ahem, a cool drink for the working men?" I offered with a smile.

The men grabbed a bottle, pulled the cork, and took a long swallow before any words were spoken. "Appreciate the drink, Jo. Your uncle's working me like a Trojan," as he wiped his neck and face with a handkerchief. "It will be a while before Ethan can use his left arm, so we thought of making some wagon repairs. Ozzie's giving us directions, but neither of us has the mechanical aptitude for this kind of work," he said with a grimace. I glanced at Ozzie. He nodded his head in agreement.

Looking around the barn, I never thought that it would require so many tools to fix a broken wagon. I wasn't sure if it was the efficiency of Ethan or Ozzie that each tool had its home all arranged on the three walls, creating an organized space for turning out a functional wagon.

Of course, without the ingenious skills of Poppi's father, the senior Randolph, the idea of creating an industry-producing beer and ale would never have happened. When Great Grandsire purchased Mulberry Farm, it was nothing more than a four-room farmhouse with some rundown outbuildings set on a generous size property, a hundred or more acres, at least. A large grove of mulberry trees planted along the front entrance and a kitchen garden produced their only sources of food.

The quality of beer and ale sold in and around Boston taverns at that time ranked far below Great Grandsire's standards. He claimed it was inferior to the rich stout beer he had come to love while growing up in Biddington. With ample land and a freshwater source, he began to formulate plans to build a malthouse and create a quality product to sell to local taverns. Boston was home to at least ninety taverns.

The excitement level steadily grew when we gathered in the dining room, drinking our late afternoon tea and hearing more of Jake's tales of news happening around Cambridge. "Yes," Jake informed us, "I can view the soldiers across the river from the Harvard Tower, setting up camp on Boston Common."

Father and Uncle Jacob walked in from the scullery and had changed into fresh shirts after they had struggled to make wagon repairs, which Ozzie would have to correct later.

Aunt Lenora grasped Jacob's hand as he stood beside her, showing her gratefulness for his hard work. "I raided the tea chest for a special occasion," she announced, pouring each of us a cup of the brew. Auntie passed around plates of sliced apple cake, making a real party out of the gathering.

"It won't be long before our black tea is depleted," Auntie said, shaking her head. "We're going to have to get creative and start making our own. But how?" She looked at Naomi for an answer.

"I can help you there. We'll experiment with some raspberry leaves and spices tomorrow." Naomi reassured her. It's true; Naomi had a tea concoction for every ache and pain imaginable, but it would take something magical to come close to English tea, in my opinion.

"It's more of a celebratory tea, really, since we're all sitting under the same roof at the same time. Ethan is back to being, well, Ethan again, in spite of his physical limitations, and Jake made a safe journey home. Even though we may face challenges in the days ahead, we still have the support of one another." It was apparent that Lenora's words were heartfelt, judging from my family's forlorn expressions. We all knew without saying that another visit would be impossible, at least for the next year.

"It's going to be a major challenge to rid our colony of four thousand British troops. We need an army to protect our property. We will more than likely be that army. Our days of being loyal English subjects are over. Men and women who desire to govern their own lives have separated from England. We're truly on the brink of revolution." Although the words Uncle Jacob spoke were somber, they were tinged with victory.

"All this talk about war makes me want to do something violent, being the rebel that I am," Jake stood up from the table. "Who fancies a hatchet toss?" Ethan, Harry, and I ran to the door, following Jake outdoors. "Don't worry, Uncle Josiah, we'll make sure Ethan uses his good arm!"

After an hour of sinking miniature axes in trees, I looked up and saw the sun lowering behind the tall alders on the mountain. Thank the Lord! I was wet with sweat, and my right arm was numb. We headed to the well for water. As competitive as always, Jake and Harry crowed about the accuracy of their tosses. Ethan and I rolled our eyes. He, with his lame arm, was as thankful as I was that daylight was disappearing. We stumbled to the well for a drink. We all perked up when we heard the sounds of dueling fiddles coming from inside the house.

We walked to the music-filled drawing room, where Poppi and Uncle Jacob were tapping their feet and picking their fiddles. Lenora and Auntie accompanied them at the piano. Father and Naomi, laughing and clapping, stood at the front window, catching the evening breeze. Ozzie was standing beside the fireplace and had just begun singing "The Sycamore Tree." The fiddlers played their instruments softly as he sang the ballad.

In his pleasing tenor voice, Ozzie sang the message of the tragedy that the Highlanders had lived in one form or another under the oppressive British. Easy to see from his watery eyes and sorrowful face that he had experienced it in a brutal fashion.

Once, he shared the story with me of his life as a fugitive, using only his wits and brawn to escape the soldiers and spies sent out by the Duke of Cumberland in the Scotland highlands in what was known as the Battle of the '45. Scottish Highlanders were stripped of their culture and their livelihood, leaving many to starve to death.

Ozzie didn't allow us time to become mournful. He swept up his fiddle and began playing "The Old Man Who Lived in the Woods," which was our cue to propel ourselves into reels and jigs. Poppi accompanied Ozzie on the fiddle, and the music and dancing stopped purposely. He stepped up with his fiddle under his arm and proceeded to sing out,

There was an old man who lived in the woods as you shall plainly see,
Who said he could do more work in a day than his wife could in three.

"With all my heart!" the old woman said. "But then you must allow,
That you must do my work for a day and I'll go follow the plow."

Ozzie plucked the fiddle and belted out the chorus, "There was an old man who lived in the woods…" while everyone danced. The fiddles were silent again. Harry, indulging in his amateurish dramatics, sang out in his most feminine voice,

> You must milk the tiny cow lest she should go quite dry,
> And you must feed the little pigs that live in yonder sty.

Again, the chorus and the dancing, and I picked up the second stanza. This went on until everyone had taken a turn singing a verse. Some of it being their own creative version. Finally, the song was exhausted. Aunt

Lenora and Uncle Jacob brought in cool water, and slowly, we exited the room to refresh ourselves outdoors. The sun was setting. Shades of orange and red splashed across the sky. We remained outside listening to the owls hoot until it was too dark to make out faces.

At dawn, I woke up to the sound of a crowing rooster. Today was Sunday, our last day at the farm. Our plan was to worship at the church in the village. It was time I dressed in something other than riding clothes. Descending the stairs, I smelled the coffee, and I heard an unrecognizable voice in the library in conversation with Father and Uncle Jacob.

On my way to the kitchen, Father motioned for me to enter the room, inviting me to join him. Little did I know that the entire family was assembled with the visitor. "Mr. Adams, I'd like to introduce you to Josie, my daughter."

"How do you do, Mr. Adams?" I smiled and nodded my head. "A pleasure to make your acquaintance." He was a popular lawyer in New England and a cousin to Samuel Adams. He and his wife and their children made their home in Braintree, located east of our farm.

The portly balding John Adams bowed graciously. "Lovely to meet you, Miss Randolph. I hear from your father that you assist him in his surgery on Bradford Lane. He has conveyed to me the ambitious plans you and your aunt are designing to aid our colony's militiamen. Very commendable."

Aunt Lenora poured me a cup of coffee, and I joined the others in a nearby chair. Mr. Adam's visit was unexpected but very much welcomed. He turned his attention to Uncle Jacob and Ethan, who were apprising Mr. Adams of the recent gun-buying trip to Stowe Ironworks in Suffield, Connecticut.

"The workings of the gun factory were uncommonly efficient," informed Ethan, "and in my estimation, met all the standards you discussed with me, Mr. Adams. Nat Stowe gave me a tour of the property and demonstrated how the muskets are assembled. He could see that I was impressed with the finished product, but he refused to take my order until I tested the gun's accuracy. After a brief target practice, I was persuaded and gave him an order for two hundred muskets."

Mr. Adams nodded and likely believed as we did that two hundred muskets were merely a drop in the bucket. He responded, "The requirements for Boston's militia are overwhelming, but the need for a reliable weapon is mandatory."

Oddly, I was overcome with distress. It had been easy enough to talk about spies and separation from England, but the reality of war, killing the enemy, hit me hard. I'm the one who's trained to remove bullets and clean up the messes created by riotous Bostonians. I closed my mind to "flintlocks, ramrods, gunpowder, attacks…" Not only a war fought between soldiers but a war that would soon bring heartache and peril to every home in Boston and beyond. I stared at the stables and dwelled on my rides with Gertie.

The unfairness of it all gripped my total being. My life was changed this morning—changed forever—this Sabbath morning at Mulberry Farm.

Chapter 7

Back to Work

Boston, End of May 1774

"We have patients to see today on Orange, School, and Pearl Streets. Let's try the new salve on Mr. Wilkerson's arms, the one Lenora gave us for burns. We'll need chickweed for a poultice." Father was ready for business this morning. I smiled and nodded, making mental notes. I reluctantly breathed in the swirling steam of a cup of strawberry leaf and currant tea.

"You're oddly silent this morning. Dreaming of horses and Swedish pastries?" Father commented, adjusting his taste to the new tea. Auntie had gone out front to clip some herbs for drying. Her creative side rarely involved anything having to do with cooking. Certainly not the type of cuisine we enjoyed at Mulberry Farm. Sewing a quilt and knitting a pair of stockings while in the company of her friends was her cup of tea. We were anxious to get started on our newfound knowledge of medicinal herbs. We brought home Lenora's books and Naomi's recipes to experiment with some new teas.

"Let's take our afternoon meal at Everly's when we finish our rounds. A bowl of chowder and fresh bread is something to look forward to." He raised his eyebrows, and I nodded in response. My mind was endeavoring to recall the last time I had seen a bottle of chickweed in the surgery.

We walked along Orange Street, passing taverns and shops, catching sight of church steeples silhouetted against a bright blue Boston sky.

The Hancock mansion, with its handsome chariot and horses parked at the front entrance, set atop Beacon Hill. It was a marvel, showing off the finest architecture and by far the most expensive in Boston. Harry mentioned to me that John Hancock's business relationships with British merchants and brokers would gradually be cut off. Apparently, he and Governor Gage had not gotten off to a good start.

Boston was filled with many fine taverns, but Father chose to dine at Everly's not only because it served the most delicious fare but also because it was a safe establishment. A place where rich merchants and lawyers dined each afternoon. A sailing ship adorned the swinging signboard with the name Everly's 1745 painted underneath. Undeniably, the best and most expensive food in Boston.

Father leaned across the table to make sure I heard him among the buzzing crowd of patrons. "Josie, I know we rarely dine out for dinner. I was hoping this diversion would bring a look of exhilaration to your face. So far, your despondent demeanor has not met my expectations." He grasped my hand and raised his eyebrows, expecting me to respond.

"I suppose my adjustment to the besieged Boston has taken the wind out of my sails. But you're very kind to treat me to a special meal. I promise I'll brighten up and give the appearance of cheerfulness. Look, I'm smiling." I tried for a big smile, showing lots of teeth.

Father pursed his lips and nodded his head suspiciously. "So far, I'm not convinced, but keep trying!" He jerked his head up from reading the menu. "Hello, Dr. Warren. It's been a while." He stood and nodded to the doctor. "You've met my daughter, Josie Randolph?"

"Good day, Miss Randolph. It has been several years." Joseph Warren bowed and flashed a friendly smile. "Your father regards you highly as his assistant. You are to be commended for your medical knowledge and service." I smiled, not having a chance to mutter a word. He was distracted by a waving hand at a nearby table. "I see my dining guest has arrived. Delighted to visit with you." He nodded his head in our direction and departed.

The young doctor, a widower in his thirties, tall and fair-complexioned, was popular among Patriots and devoted to our community. As head

of the Committees of Safety, he and Father collaborate closely, as I understood from Auntie.

"Didn't expect to see such a friendly face while on our excursion today. I wonder if we'll bump into Mr. Hancock or Mr. Adams. Here's our server. I'm starving." Father ordered a hearty meal. I meant to keep my selections to a minimum. Aunt Lenora had spoiled us with her Swedish foods during our stay. How she turned pickled fish into a delicacy was a mystery to me!

"I will have cod with onion sauce, bread with strawberry jam, and apple cider." At this time of the day, Father and I could eat enough for three people. Walking up and down hilly streets to patients' homes and tending to their needs was exhausting. We had worked up a robust appetite.

An attendant placed venison, parsnips, carrots, and bread with apple butter in front of Father and a mug of beer. Watching his big brown eyes dancing a jig in their sockets made me laugh. "Just what the doctor ordered? I'll have to push you home in a cart if you eat all that!"

"When have you heard from Anthony Archer, the aspiring physician? If you don't mind me prying into your personal life," Father asked conversationally. He was worried that my work was interfering with my social life.

I laughed. My relationship with Anthony was going nowhere romantically, which was fine with me. He definitely was not a prospect for marriage or a serious relationship. "I heard from him recently. Mr. Phillips brought a letter to the house. He plans to leave Edinburgh University and continue his studies in Philadelphia. I'm certain he is not interested in medicine. Doesn't have the aptitude for understanding human anatomy! He does not have the makings of a physician. He enjoys spending his father's money on fancy clothes and gambling. A dandy of sorts."

"I did not know. Do you think his father is aware of his behavior? The exorbitant cost of medical school and living in Edinburgh is more than any doctor that I know could afford. Of course, Mrs. Archer controls the money in that family, inheritance mostly, from what I've heard."

"His letters give the impression that he holds a rather high opinion of himself, boasting of his skill at cards and dice. I'll continue to write to him because I want us to remain friends. I treasure such fond memories from our youth. It's not my intent to discard our friendship. Regardless, his commitment to medicine is waning. With bad marks, he will surely be released from the university. Once his pockets are empty, he will return to Boston. Only time will tell." I was being kind to Anthony. Sadly, he would get caught up in the high life that Philadelphia had become famous for.

We were sufficiently stuffed and sat sipping on our drinks, recalling memories from our week at the farm when a tavern attendant visited our table. I was surprised when he placed a folded sheet of stationery on the table with my name printed on the front. Father and I looked at each other curiously. My initial thought was that my longtime friend, Eleanor Cushman, may have spotted Father and me from the other side of the dining room, asking us to join her at her table. Before that thought had a chance to register in my brain, I looked up, staring at the devil himself. I quaked with sudden anger, feeling my blood rise. My head began to itch. A sure sign that I was beyond self-control.

"You again. What is it you want?" I surprised myself when I raised my voice to such a demanding level to the intruder in a very public place.

Father cautioned me with an ahem, but I interrupted him. "No, Father, the arrogance of this person is intolerable!" Father resigned himself to folding his arms and waiting for the next blow. Nearby, customers ceased their conversation and gazed our way in wonder, not knowing what to make of the hubbub. "We're *all* awaiting your answer," I spoke mockingly to the evil man as I swept my arm across the room, inviting everyone to hear his response.

"Forgive me, mistress, for interrupting your dinner. I shall take my leave," frustrated and red-faced, the tall man bowed in my direction and strode toward the door, his red cape flying behind him.

I sat embarrassed by my unseemly outburst in a public dining room, fully aware that it had drawn the attention of diners nearby. I managed the courage to look at Father's face, which was expressionless. His words were brief. "I think we should walk home and enjoy the sunshine." I nodded and rose from my seat. I glanced at a woman dining at a table across from ours. She graciously smiled and winked at me as we departed.

Halfway home, in the distance, we heard the beat of drums and the shrilling fife sounds while British soldiers marched and trained on the Boston Common. With that, another surge of anger arrested my spirit, but I sought to dismiss it for the moment, knowing that I owed Father an explanation. I needed all the power I could muster to explain to him the anguish I had experienced for the past three months. Auntie knew of the man because I gave her the details before we left for Mulberry Farm. She honored my wishes by not telling Father about my nightmares or the encounter with the Big Englishman at Folger's Bookstore.

I told myself that experiencing the devil himself could be a small step toward dealing with the situation. The fact that Father had witnessed the entire affair at Everly's was proof that the Big Englishman was in pursuit of me when the time came to divulge the nefarious being's stalkings.

Father broke the silence between us. "You're awfully spirited today in spite of having the wind taken from your sails, as you mentioned. I'm curious as to why you demolished that brazen, intolerable Englishman. There is a story behind all this?"

We continued walking down the hill to Bradford Lane. I sighed and turned to Father. "Yes, there is quite a story, and I want to share it with you today. Alas, nature is calling, and I must quickly relieve myself of two mugs of cider. I'll meet you later, downstairs by the fireplace."

We walked speedily to the house. I ran upstairs to see to my needs. Father hurried to the privy. I changed into a looser-fitting skirt, thanks to the creamy onion sauce. I decided I had enough stress to manage when I laid out my story to Father. My nerves were at a point where I was beginning to doubt myself. Perhaps I was making too much of it all. However, the facts were there and could not be disputed. Why did he continue to stalk me, making a fool of himself in a public place? Perhaps Father had some explanation why men of that ilk were inclined to do such things.

I walked down the stairs and heard men's voices carrying in low, serious tones in the keeping room. I could feel the heat from my blushed face. My stomach was churning. I wanted to lock myself in my chamber. No, I had to face my transgression.

Standing by the fireside were Father and John Adams gazing out the large back window at Auntie's garden. The delicate, layered peonies always stole the show with their crimson beauty. "Mr. Adams, would you care for some tea?" I heard Auntie ask.

Both men turned toward me as I entered the room. "I'm just setting it on a tray, Josie," she smiled, meeting my eyes. She brought the tea to the end of the room where the three of us had gathered. Two upholstered settles were arranged on each side of the small fireplace with a tea table in the center, built for the large rectangular tray. She poured a cup for Mr. Adams and Father and asked if I cared for a cup, which I declined, nervous as I was.

Father opened the conversation. "We have the honor of Mr. Adams' presence this afternoon for the purpose of acquainting us with some particular details concerning our encounter at Everly's. Mr. Adams, will you be so kind?" Father cued him with his eyes.

"Please forgive my impertinence and my untimely visit. I felt inclined to impart information about the visitor who approached you and your Father an hour ago. I was seated within listening distance and heard the way you vocally 'tarred and feathered' the rascal. I applaud your courage, Miss Randolph. I was dining with a client, a merchant here in Boston who has business in London. He extended to me some timely accounts of the intruder's background. I wish to share them with you at this time, that is, with the consent of your father."

Aunt Minnie and Father returned their cups to the tray and leaned forward, ready to take in every detail that Mr. Adams commenced to share. "He is the only son of the Earl of Pinehurst, county of Kent, England. William Berkeley Granger left home several years ago, deserting the family estate and all its responsibilities to Pinehurst residents. Before he left home, he demanded from his father, Lord Granger, his promised inheritance and vowed he would never return to the county of Kent. He was never truly in a position to inherit his father's title. He deplored Pinehurst and sought to make his own way in Paris."

John Adams continued the Granger history. "While living in Paris, he ran up debts in brothels and saloons of such significance that the gendarmes posted broadsheets and came searching for him and his associate. Months passed as the two men concealed themselves from the authorities. They managed to escape to Boston six months ago. Dressing as he does in fine clothing and introducing himself as the Earl of Pinehurst and owner of Berkeley Castle in England, you would never suspect that he is a fortune-seeker."

Mr. Adams paused in his narrative and took a moment to sip his tea. Each of us sat, absorbing the facts and determining how our family fit into the picture. "Our family is common and certainly not wealthy. It sounds like this rogue is searching for wealth and position," Father explained in dismay. Mr. Adams nodded and continued.

"Miss Randolph, think back. Can you recollect the times and the circumstances in which you have encountered this man or noticed that he was stalking you? Forgive my bluntness, but I must have an accurate accounting," Mr. Adams asked me directly, revealing a compassionate face.

I glanced at Father and Auntie, and they looked at me with somber expressions. They trusted me to share detailed information so we could get to the bottom of this turmoil. That was not a problem for me, given that for the last three months, it had been constant on my mind. This was my time to impart the facts to Mr. Adams. I trusted him.

"The first time I encountered him was this past March on Massacre Day when Auntie and I were shopping at the markets." Mr. Adams wrote swiftly; his pen scratched across the paper. "I was speaking with Petey Harmon, who was helping me find a small roast for our dinner, when this man rudely interrupted our conversation. He pushed Petey aside and took his position. I was provoked by his unwanted presence and walked a distance away from him to continue my conversation with Petey and meet up with Auntie. The man vanished. I just assumed he did not want to make a show of himself in public. Of course, that did not stop him today.

"The next time was at the end of March when Auntie and I were shopping at Folger's Bookstore. We spent an hour reading together, and we made our selections. We walked to the front of the store to pay, and he blocked our way. Auntie and I were put off by his imposing manner coupled with that objectionable red cape he wore. When he bowed to introduce himself, we took the moment to escape to Mr. Folger's desk and promptly left." Auntie patted my hand and gave me a look of affirmation. Mr. Adams continued his writing, and Father poured out more tea.

I continued with my story. "I saw the back of him when Father and I were talking with Mr. Fletcher on the day we left for Stoughton." When we were leaving the livery stable in the carriage, he turned around and gazed in our direction. I quickly turned my head, not wanting to acknowledge his presence.

"He followed us to the farm because I spotted him atop his horse in the woods when Harry and I were riding toward the mountain. I should have mentioned it at the time it happened, but I did not want Harry to get involved by chasing after the man and possibly getting hurt. Ethan's accident was enough to worry about. My suspicions were growing.

"You can see how my frustration was building when he approached me at Everly's. I'm not the type of person who makes such public displays or accusations. I confess that I made some unladylike assertions, but I was angry and scared. I want to know why he is making such a nuisance of himself!"

"Now that we know who he is and his repugnant background, he could be a danger to our family and our neighbors. If he is the harpy you have described," predicted Auntie. We were silent for a few moments, which gave us time to absorb the details of the situation and determine how to approach the next step. I pondered the fortuitous timing of this gathering and was grateful for Mr. Adams' professional skillfulness in pointing us in the right direction. A knock at the front door brought us out of our speechlessness.

"That's likely my carriage. My family expects me home before dark," said Mr. Adams. He paused. "Dr. Randolph, you stated earlier that you are common and not wealthy, but in reality, your family has prospered for years in the brewing business. If this thief has been snooping around

Boston for these last few months, he may be on to learning your personal and business information. I think it prudent to begin devising some schemes of our own. Let's begin by alerting your brother and his family. My courier can deliver a message in the morning to his farm—with your permission."

Father escorted Mr. Adams to his carriage as the sun began sinking below the horizon. Since our return to Boston, I noticed that merchants were locking their shops earlier, and outdoor markets were becoming fewer each day. I wondered how farmers planned to sell their produce when their crops came in; after all, Boston Neck would be closed to wagon traffic. Church bells began tolling, sending a message for taverns to close up before nightfall. Lanterns were lit, giving patrons notice that curfew was nigh. The grimness of the day was wearing on my emotions, and I was not looking forward to tomorrow or, for that matter, the night ahead. Another sleepless night.

I was standing at the sink, washing the teacups, tears rolling down my face, feeling powerless. I heard Father close the front door and turn the lock. He came walking toward the kitchen, and I turned to face him. He opened his arms, and I rushed to him, accepting his embrace and sobbing into his shoulder. "What have I done but made a fool of myself? Our lives may be ruined for what I've done to this family!"

He gave me his handkerchief, took hold of my shoulders, and stared into my eyes. "Darling, Josie, you have done nothing wrong, and no one is blaming you. On the contrary, you showed great courage and independence today without leaning on me for support. This man expected you to concede to his wishes by trapping you in the midst of diners, expecting you to be stunned and meek, but instead, you placed him on the defensive. Auntie and I are proud of you. By your actions today, you have exposed this person as an outsider and a criminal, a menace to Boston. The word will spread like fire in this town, and he will be defeated."

I nodded to his kind face, too emotional to speak, feeling the respect and the love of the most important person in my life. "Our family will bond, and we will be drawn closer together. Yes, there will be fears and anxiety in the days ahead, but Mr. Adams knows the law, and he is a strong advocate for our cause. Heed my advice, remain vigilant, and do not leave this house unescorted. Actually, you and I have a full week of serving patients and stocking the surgery for future needs. Josie, pray for God's protection over our family and stay mindful of your personal safety."

His handsome face and his caring smile melted me. I stopped crying and managed a smile. "Speaking of the surgery," he said, "I received a new medical journal today from Edinburgh that I want to share with you." He led me to the front of the house to our Bradford Lane Surgery. We needed each other, especially during this critical time. Our common regard for practicing medicine and learning better ways to treat patients was our mission. Life goes on in spite of what the world throws at us.

Two days later, John Adams shared with us the letter he received from Uncle Jacob regarding the Big Englishman, as Auntie and I began referring to Mr. Granger. He apparently had made a call to Mulberry Farm, sort of.

Part 2

Mistaken Ideas and Expectations

Chapter 8

CONFRONTATION AT THE FARM

May 28, 1774, Stoughton, Massachusetts

Construction of a new malting house had begun at Mulberry Farm after Josiah, Minnie, and Josie had left for Boston. For two days, Harry, Ethan, and Jacob worked, taking down the old house, salvaging wood, shingles, and nails as much as possible. Ethan was strongly built, and despite his injured arm, the right side of his body showed matchless strength in prying off boards that would be used on the new house. Harry sat on the rooftop, removing shingles. Ozzie and Jacob gently pried out the nails and hammered them flat to be used again. Jake and Poppi sorted the boards according to size, sanding the rough edges and sawing off the rotted sections. The family did not shy away from hard work, especially when it meant saving money on building supplies. Two days later, a new foundation was completed, and new floorboards were measured and cut.

Now, a respite was needed from their back-breaking work. All the men had a sunny glow about their faces and upper bodies. The pain of blistered hands and sunburnt bodies was eased at the close of the fourth day when they stripped off their clothes and relaxed in the cool, rushing creek.

Knowing well the appetites of their men and proud of the work they had accomplished, Lenora and Naomi planned a special meal that was sure to appease the men's bellies. The two women had tended a side of pork at the barbecue pit since early morning. A haze of smoke hung heavily in one area of the yard and fanned out toward the new construction. A mixture of roasted pig and sawdust smells filled the air, conveying an expression of gratitude from the women and the personal fulfillment of creating a new malthouse so valuable to the future of the family business.

Harry walked through the scullery and heard water splash in the bathhouse. He peeked through the doorway and saw his father on his knees, scrubbing Poppi's back with soap and a brush as he sat slumped and closed to the world, relaxing in the copper tub. "Hey, just in time, Harry. Would you take the kettle off the stove and pour in some hot water?" Jacob asked. "It's getting a little cool for himself." Harry retrieved the kettle and poured while Poppi mixed the hot and cold water with his hand, uttering satisfying sounds of comfort.

Father and son helped their elder out of the tub and placed him on the cot set up next to a sunny window. "I'll be needing the liniment that Naomi mixed for my aching joints. Will you see to that, please?" Poppi asked Harry. He returned and began rubbing the minty-smelling liquid over Poppi's shoulders and limbs while Jacob stood and stretched the kinks out of his back.

"Let's take the day off tomorrow from building," announced Jacob. Poppi nodded his head affirmatively. "I've got paperwork to finish, and Jake is returning to Cambridge in the morning. Father and I have finished the keg order. It should be a good time for you and Ethan to make a trip to the cooper's in Springfield if you've got the strength to mount a horse!" The three men chuckled, even though Jacob felt the same pains while speaking the truth for everybody.

The following morning was a perfectly sunny and breezy day for the short trip to Springfield. Harry and Ethan were on horseback trotting toward the front entrance away from the house and stable. The ever-present smells emanating from the malting house and the charcoal smells from the pig roast saturated the air. The two men noticed some activity at the bulky front gates, clucked to their horses, and picked up speed, anxious to determine what could be amiss. The intruder had dismounted his horse and was fidgeting with the lock. Apparently with

I had finished my tea and told myself it was time to start the day. Aunt Minnie had been scurrying about making tea and our breakfast. I felt guilty that I wasn't being productive, but that changed quickly when there was quite a clamor at the surgery entrance. It brought me out of my melancholy as I walked toward the surgery, catching a piercing whiff of blood and sweaty bodies.

An associate of Father's, Thomas Crafts, was helping a man through the surgery doorway and was having a difficult time of it. The man insisted he did not need to see a doctor. He was a tall, beefy man with a thick neck, muscular shoulders, and a large head full of wavy dark brown hair. His right forearm was wrapped in a blood-soaked rag, apparently a gash of some sort. "Now, Leonard, Dr. Randolph is a friend of mine and a skilled surgeon." He guided his reluctant cousin into the surgery, where Auntie stood waiting, washed up and ready to assist.

She approached the injured man while holding a bowl of water in the crook of her left arm. "How do you do, sir? I'm Minnie MacPherson. It seems your arm needs attention." Leonard had declined Father's invitation to sit on the surgery table, but Auntie smiled and looked into his dark blue eyes, saying, "We wouldn't want this to turn to gangrene, would we?" He shook his head and sat on the table, motivated to cooperate.

Auntie got down to business. She removed the bloody rag and spoke encouragingly to her patient while dabbing cool water over and around the gash. Leonard closed his eyes and turned his head sideways while she worked.

When the alcohol fumes reached Leonard's nose, his eyes widened, and a pale look covered his face. He was sliding off the table. Mr. Crafts and Father came to his rescue and repositioned him in a supine position. "Much better." I heard Auntie mumbling. Father had assembled sutures, needles, and scissors in a pan, prepared to stitch while the man lay motionless. Thomas remained by his stubborn friend's side, knowing Leonard would likely jump and turn savage when the needle pierced his skin.

While Father and Auntie stitched Leonard, I prepared a medicinal infusion with a package of dried herbs to make a strong tea for Leonard.

Chapter 9

Unforeseen Circumstances

First Week of June 1774, Bradford Lane

Boston is a terribly overcrowded city with a population of over 15,000 people, adding to that the 4,000 or so redcoat soldiers who currently occupy the city. It makes me wonder just how we have managed to squeeze ourselves into such a small landmass almost completely surrounded by water. Taverns, shops, and several thousand small, two- and-three-story wooden houses fill the city. These facts lay heavily on my mind one morning while consuming my breakfast of raisin tart and a slice of ham when the thought occurred to me how quickly news travels in Boston.

It had only been a week after our unforgettable dinner at Everly's, but I knew tales would fly. Little gossipy tidbits dipped in and out of my mind while I sat drinking my tea, gazing out at the backyard garden. I laughed when I heard the morning birds chattering back and forth, telling their tales. Cardinals busily seeking their morning meal, hopping and pecking in the fertile ground while two bright red male cardinals stood guard over their female counterparts.

A sense of security and protection came over me as I sat in my little corner of Boston. The reality was that my work would begin soon, and I would cease to feel secure once I stepped through the front door and entered a world of unknowns. Father could not always be my protector, nor could Auntie.

Harry and Ethan watched the two men disappear into the woods, the red cape ballooning as his horse's pace increased. When they lost sight of the intruders, their plans to meet with the cooper were dismissed, thinking it necessary to alert Jacob to the potential danger in the making.

Trotting Caesar to the new malting house, Harry was filled with rage at the thought of the high and mighty Englishman's presumptuous remarks. "We live here because we've worked the land," he said to himself, "and paid the price with our blood and sweat. Work on the farm is never-ending. That popinjay looks like he's never turned a shovel of dirt. On top of the British occupation, now we have this rascal threatening he can confiscate our property. What next?"

"You two are back early. Did you forget something? I figured you would be gone until noon sampling Cyrus Floyd's whiskey after you ordered the kegs, of course." Harry and Ethan, looking pale and scared, remained unusually quiet while Jacob carried on with his inquisition. "What's the matter with you two?" he asked. "You look like you've just seen the devil." He walked closer to Harry and Ethan, looking them up and down and scowling. "Explain yourself."

the intent to enter through without any compunction of encroaching on private property. Harry and Ethan instinctively drew their pistols and found cover behind the numerous mulberry trees standing at the entrance. Their flying blossoms caused a slight whirlwind as they blew with the breeze. "Get back on your horse and explain your business. You're on private property," Harry uttered forcefully to the man.

Mr. Granger smiled, showing no remorse for his obvious intrusion. "No need for weapons, sirs. I only desire to speak with the proprietor of this estate. I have heard he produces a first-rate brew, if my friends in Boston speak the truth. I have a proposal to place before him, sir."

Neither Harry nor Ethan strayed from their protected position. Ethan, dressed in his usual buckskins and his long black hair draped down his back, detected an uneasy connection to the man and reflected on his red cape. His eyes scanned the woods beyond the road, partially obscured by the pale green growth of elms and oaks. "Who's your friend hiding back in the shadows?"

"Oh, yes, my associate and I were exploring the countryside," the miscreant lied. "He found a stream along the way to refresh his steed." Seeing no other option but to reveal himself, the unknown man, slightly built and half the size of the Big Englishman, stepped into view and touched the brim of his hat as a greeting.

Harry sensed that something was afoot and took no chances by demonstrating his refusal to converse with the man. "The owner has no business with you. Be off. You are wasting our time." Harry caught the same suspicions as Ethan. All the danger signs were there.

"I take that as a personal affront. You are addressing an English lord, you illiterate rabble-rouser. Your rudeness and disrespect are intolerable. The truth will reveal itself when I discover who owns this property. You and your commoners believe you can steal this land from the king to make your fortune. I'll have a thing to say about that when I meet with the new governor. Our soldiers will take charge of this property and toss you out on your heels. I shall take my leave." The Englishman looked back to cast a venomous look at Harry and thought, *I shall have my way if it takes destroying the lot of you!*

It would help with the pain and inflammation he would feel in a few moments. I was fairly new at preparing medicinal teas. My challenge was to not over-steep the brew, making it objectionable to drink. I remained hovering over the mug of tea, waiting and watching for the tea to turn the perfect color. I gave it a taste. My vigilance had paid off. Absolutely no trace of bitterness. I whispered a thank you to Lenora and Naomi. Our instruction time at the farm had paid off.

Leonard had moved to a comfortable chair by the surgery window and had propped his legs on a stool. "I need a mug of rum, if you please, ma'am," he said when he saw me coming through the doorway with a steaming cup of tea.

"No rum today. You need a restorative. Here, sip on this mug of tea." He raised a hand, rejecting the brew. I sat beside him to coax him to drink. He looked at Thomas, who gave him a nod. While Leonard sipped his tea, I got a close view of Father's fine stitching in closing up the three-inch gash. In spite of the yarrow tea, he would experience pain very soon.

Father leaned against the surgery table. "Thomas, tell me the details of the accident. Who slashed Leonard's arm?"

Thomas Crafts had a believable face, although animated. His blue eyes looked trusting as he moved them from Father to Minnie. Admittedly, he and his friends were daring risk-takers. At times, pushing the limits by staying out late after curfew. A true rebel indeed.

"We were on our way home. Leonard and I have families in Lexington. Yes, we had had our fill at Maurice's Tavern, but we could walk a straight line. We heard the curfew bells a-ringing and finished our rum. We were walking home, and we figured the cool night air would help us sober up before we reached our dooryard. Leonard's wife gets fairly wrought-up if we enter the house smelling 'of the drink,' ye know." He waved his hand sideways and grimaced.

"When we crossed the bridge, we were ambushed by a couple of blokes who came out of nowhere. They took us unawares and smashed us in the belly with an oar. We hit the ground, and before I knew it, Leonard and I were face to face with the point of a knife. They were

English, yelling in our faces, demanding our coins. But we had spent it all at Maurice's.

"I jabbed my knee hard in the Big Englishmen's middle," Thomas demonstrated by waving his hand in the vicinity of his groin. "His knife fell in the water. I smacked him a good one on his nose, and he fell over and screamed, powerless. Leonard wasn't so lucky. I could see the mugger was aiming to jab his neck, but I pushed my foot in his gut, and he rolled over. Cursing me as he was, he jabbed Leonard in the arm, rolled over to the edge of the bridge, and fell into the water. It sounded like he hit a rock. I believe it knocked him out, but I couldn't be sure about that.

"I tore off the bottom of my shirt and wrapped it around Leonard's arm. I've never seen so much blood oozing out of a man. We walked back to town by way of the Neck, trying to stay clear of the soldiers. We found your house, knowing where you lived and all. So we helped ourselves to some water from your well and sat outside until dawn. That's when we knocked on your door."

"You said they were Englishmen. Do you recall anything about the clothes they wore? How they smelled? Were they drinking?" asked Father.

I took note of Thomas Crafts, now seated, and Leonard Ledbetter, still sipping tea, wondering if they were cousins. They had similar features: over six feet tall, barrel chest and rotund middle, thick muscular shoulders, and a large, long face with small eyes. Mr. Crafts sported a head full of straw-colored hair, and his wavy tendrils tended to move down his forehead as he spoke with expression, more to make a point. Both men had a good-humored spirit about them, putting one to feel at ease in their presence.

Thomas nodded at Father, noticeably concentrating on last night's events. "They were Englishmen, alright, by the way they spoke with some authority, calling Leonard and me rebel trash. That's what got my dander up when I jabbed him in the middle. They smelled worse than myself—pardon me, ladies—like they had been living out in the wild for a spell. Ya know that rough, campfire smell after you've gutted a dozen trout and made your bed on wet leaves."

I grinned as he told his story. What a character! "Did you notice anything about their clothes or their boots?" I asked him.

"There was no moonlight—wicked dark. I didn't notice what they were wearing. They stunk, though. Just like Thomas said," Leonard managed to share his thoughts, seeking to be sociable, but he didn't have it in him. The trauma from losing blood and walking back to Boston had exhausted him. He needed rest before he could travel home.

Auntie observed the two men's conditions and spoke her mind, "I'd say you men need some food and rest. I can set out some cots in the next room. It would be wise to keep an eye on Leonard's arm for a while, which I don't mind doing." She looked at Father, and he nodded in agreement.

I escorted Mr. Crafts to the kitchen, offered him a seat at the table, and poured him a mug of cider. I pushed the platter of leftover raisin tart and a pot of tea from our breakfast in his direction while Auntie assisted Leonard. She settled him at the far end of the drawing room where he could not be easily disturbed. The cot was far too small for such a huge man, but in his exhausted state, he would have been content to rest on the floor. He fell asleep immediately and began to snore.

Father had left me a list of medicines to pack in his black bag along with a scribble at the bottom of the paper: "Don't be alarmed. The pistol will become a necessary element starting today." I felt nervous, but I decided to shake it off. With all that's going on in this city, we could use the protection of a weapon. Of course, if we truly needed to defend ourselves, there were at least ten sharp instruments that could do bodily harm to an assailant if we had the will to use them. I heard Father's footsteps. "Are we ready?" he asked. We left quietly through the surgery door.

Our first stop was at Ezra Phillips' print shop across the street from our house. I saw him looking out a side window as we passed. He met us as we approached the back door, which he unlocked first before opening. It felt odd, being so extra cautious these days. As soon as we stepped through the doorway, we saw Herbie Connolly, Eli's assistant, slumped on the floor. His shredded stockings were hanging around his ankles, and his leg was bloody. He managed a grunt as Father moved in closer to inspect his cut temple. It's going to be one of those bloody days, I decided.

Father kneeled over Herbie to take his pulse while running his other hand over his scalp to check for contusions. He glanced up at Ezra, questioning, "We came by to change the bandage on your hand, but it looks like there are more pressing matters. What happened, Herbie? Can you speak, man?"

I helped Father lay the injured man on the floor. He commenced to check the man's legs and arms for broken bones. Herbie was clearly shaken and in pain, judging from the sharp look on his face. His mouth moved to speak when suddenly his neck went limp, and his head fell to the side. I was kneeling on the floor beside him and picked up a thick bundle of parchment to place under his feet for elevation.

The young man's eyes popped wide open. "Welcome back to the world, Herbie," Father smiled at the young man as he spoke. "You've quite a cut on the side of your head. Appears you must have fallen and hit a rock or something as hard as a rock." Again, Father raked his fingers through the sticky, bloody hair to examine more of Herbie's head. "Just the one cut, and it doesn't feel that deep. I think we can get by with cleaning the wound and applying a bandage. Jo, dab on some of the yarrow ointment after cleaning," Father suggested. He was feeling rushed, and rightly so. We were late for our next appointment. We would have to change Ezra's bandage when we returned home. We continued walking to our other appointments throughout the morning and past the noon bells.

We walked with our eyes squinted into the bright sunlight, climbing the last hill before reaching Walden's Apothecary. There were no awnings here for shade. The late spring heat seemed unusually intense. We had exhausted our supply of quinine, a bitter liquid we gave patients suffering from malaria and tropical diseases. With so many of Boston's merchants traveling to the West Indies, the malady was easily contracted, given the mosquito-infested swamps.

"I just sold my last bottle to Dr. Crenshaw, and only God knows when we'll receive more, with all deliveries suspended," he said disappointedly, shrugging his shoulders. "I can sell you the cinchona bark to grind your own powder. It's simple to brew a tea." We took the package and left.

"No telling what we'll find when we get home. I'm concerned about Leonard's arm. That slash was deep. I felt guilty leaving Minnie with the two men, although she's well acquainted with Mr. Crafts. Sure hope she is still speaking to us, but she did offer to help," Father said matter-of-factly.

When we arrived at the walkway to the house, we heard music coming from the drawing room and men's voices singing a lively tune, sounding more like one of Auntie's sailing songs. Father and I looked at each other and burst out laughing. "Still worried about Auntie?" I asked.

The music was very loud when we opened the front door. Surprisingly, there were three men instead of the two we had left in Auntie's care. They were standing and singing around the piano. Minnie was all smiles, sitting on the bench while her fingers danced across the keys. I couldn't make out who the mystery man was, but he was as big and tall as Thomas and Leonard. The jaunty music ended, and the three men clapped and cheered for Auntie.

They turned around when they heard Father and me clapping and shouting hurrahs as we stood looking cheerful and surprised. Their sheepish faces gave them away. After all, Father and I had been at work all day, and they seemed to be engaged in a high old time! I must say, it had been a grueling day beginning at dawn with Leonard, then Herbie, and continuing to see patients without pause until our stop at the apothecary. My apron had never seen more blood or filth in its life.

Sometime between all the merrymaking, Minnie had squeezed in a pot of fish chowder and an apple cobbler for dinner. "Food smells good. Who picked up the fish?" Father asked when he checked the stewpot in the kitchen fireplace.

"Ah, yes, that was Mr. Crafts' contribution," Auntie replied. "I took care of Leonard while he made the chowder, start to finish. Let's all sit down and eat some dinner. I'm starving! By the way, I don't believe I've introduced Mr. Ledbetter, Leonard's father." He smiled and bowed to Father and me.

All three men favored each other in the shape of their heads and their tall, muscular bodies, which quickly filled up the small dining space.

I could tell they made their living using their hands, which were large and rough-looking, showing cuts and scrapes. They each had at least one bruised fingernail that had turned black. Predictably, their personalities were the same: congenial, talkative, and storytellers.

Taking a pause from sipping his chowder, Mr. Ledbetter spoke in the direction of Father and me, "I'd be honored if you called me Leo. I suppose you're wondering how the three of us gents availed ourselves of Mrs. MacPherson's hospitality today?"

"Yes, afford us with those details, won't you," suggested Father, grinning.

"Come morning, Leonard had not shown up for breakfast. I knew something was wrong. I didn't know it at the time, but his wife, Lucinda, had paced the floor all night long, not just because the baby was colicky but because she was worried that something bad had happened to her man. She was terribly upset this morning, so I set out searching in the direction of town, thinking he might have stopped at Maurice's place for a mug of rum on his way home last night. When I walked over the bridge, there was my first clue: his blue cap lying in the dirt and traces of blood like there had been a fight. There was no guessing about it. Leonard was in danger. When I walked into town, I started asking around when I came upon the lamplighter. I told him my story, and he suggested I try Bradford Lane's Surgery.

"I got to your place and saw this nice lady working in her garden in the dooryard. We commenced talking and came to find out he was stitched up and sleeping there in your front room. I've never had such a burden lifted off my shoulders as when Mrs. MacPherson took me to his bedside. Leonard lay there smiling like a baby, fast asleep! If that wasn't enough, there lay Thomas Crafts on his bed, dead to the world!" he laughed, shaking his head.

"More of this delicious chowder?" I interrupted. Leo passed his empty bowl to me.

"What about his family? I'm sure his wife must be worried sick by now," I asked the older man.

"Your aunt and I went back out to the garden, and she was giving me the details of Leonard's injured arm when a carriage pulled up. To my surprise, there was the lawyer, John Adams, walking in our direction, and we commenced talking. I told him about my son's misadventure. I've never known a man who listened as well as he, and all the questions he asked afterward! Guess that's the lawyer in him."

Auntie interrupted, "By the way, Josiah, there's a note on your desk, from Mr. Adams." She looked at him with raised brows.

Leo continued, "Anyway, I scribbled out a note for my daughter-in-law, and Mr. Adams offered to have it delivered to her. Poor girl's having a rough day of it. Leonard's got lots of explaining to do!

"Dr. Randolph, what do you think about my arm? I've got to get home to my family." Leonard was suddenly anxious to move on.

Auntie served the cobbler while Mr. Ledbetter talked. He had such a jovial disposition. I enjoyed his tales of fighting Indians. The irony of it all was that he offered the defeated Indians money to buy the property his farm sits on, which they gladly accepted. On top of this, they became friends.

Father and Leonard walked up front to the surgery. "You've improved one hundred times over since I first saw you this morning. Your arm is not as inflamed, which is a good sign, and the bleeding has stopped. Be careful not to stress it. It still needs to heal. No pitching hay or plowing. I noticed there's nothing wrong with your appetite, so that's not a worry," Father laughed and patted Leonard's shoulder. He cleaned around the stitching with some alcohol, dabbed on some yarrow ointment, and applied a new bandage. Leonard was ready to go.

"I came by this on the bridge." Leo showed a red cloth to us as he passed the knitted hat to his son. "Something I found while I was nosing around in the dirt." A piece of red silky fabric had fallen to the floor when he pulled the hat from his belt. He picked it up and showed it to Thomas Crafts.

"I can't tell by the color, but it feels silky, like something the Englishman was wearing. It must have ripped off his cape while we were tussling on the bridge."

KAY FRANCES

I glanced at Father. His eyes were focused on my face. He knew what was going through my mind. I shuddered and probably turned pale.

The front hall floor shook and creaked as the three heavy men walked across it to the front door. It took a while to finish our farewells. Thomas promised he would bring Leonard back to the surgery for a bandage change in two days.

You couldn't help but be in a happy mood around these men. The bantering between them was too hilarious for words! But we were ready for a break from the doings of the day, so I settled down by the big window next to the kitchen with the idea of getting lost in the beauty of Auntie's garden, all ablaze with the late afternoon sun.

I woke up with a start when I heard the front door close. Last I remember, I was relaxing on the settle, watching the birds pecking in the garden for the prized worm, which overlapped with the recollection of the tasty chowder from dinner. What was that distinct flavor that made it so unique? I yawned widely and shook my head, hoping for a nap.

Father and Annie were chattering away about a fence or something when they took a seat on the matching settle across from me. He was holding a letter and obviously wanted to share its contents.

"How long have I been asleep?" I shook my head, thinking it would help to bring me back to the world. "This must be the feeling you get when you're drugged."

"It's the sherry. Mr. Crafts poured an entire bottle of it into the stew," declared Auntie. "Had the same effect on me," she said while yawning.

Father laughed in agreement. "So, I've read the letters from Mr. Adams and my brother, and they are, in a word, formidable. Harry and Ethan caught Mr. Granger and his cohort breaking into the gate at the farm, attempting to pry open the lock. He demanded to meet the proprietor in hopes of purchasing the brewing business as well as the entire property, if you can believe that. He claimed he was an English lord who was interested in making an investment. Harry and Ethan, in typical fashion, chased them off with raised and cocked pistols. Jacob is enraged, as you might imagine. Most likely, they will lay low for a few days after the pounding they took from Thomas Crafts. Speaking

of which, Thomas and his rebel friends might be a good source of providing protection for Mulberry Farm, at least for a while," Father mused, thinking out loud.

I sat contemplating the color differences in Auntie's garden as the sun lowered and the late afternoon shadows moved across the bushes and flowers when Father announced that he had not looked in on Herbie Connolly as he had promised. I yielded to my calling, knowing two sets of hands would make short work. We were both fatigued from our day's work and our unexpected visitors.

I picked up two packages of the same herb tea that I had mixed for Leonard and another jar of the yarrow ointment we used for cuts and scrapes. His black bag in hand, Father was waiting by the surgery door when I arrived with my supplies. "This is a never-ending day, it seems," he stated with wide eyes. "Don't take this the wrong way, but have you considered a bath when we're done at the print shop?" I gave him a questionable look. "No, no, not that you smell bad or appear dirty. I've been meaning to tell you all day that you have a smear of blood just below your neckline." I tried to wipe it away with my hand. We burst out laughing! Both giddy from the tiring day, and it wasn't over yet.

"Doctor's orders, eh? Provided we don't have another arm to stitch or a broken leg to set, then yes, a bath awaits me!"

Chapter 10

Ethan's Rendezvous

June 1774, Stoughton, Massachusetts

A hundred thoughts swirled in his head as he lay wondering when to begin his day. He knew his body needed rest, but his mind was occupied with other matters. No matter that he faced a morning of packing and climbing the mountain that fortressed Mulberry Farm, his thoughts would not let go of the haughty Englishman who demanded a hostile takeover of the property. "My home," he muttered. The image of the tall, nose-in-the-air hellish creature perched on a fine steed soliciting a deal to take ownership was "in the offing," as the man put it, causing Ethan's blood to curdle.

He closed his eyes for a moment, thinking he could clear his mind of such grievous thoughts. He opened them just as quickly, distracted by the luster of the moon that flooded his bedroom. Father had a remedy for such self-important miscreants: a bullet through the head would put an end to this sorry plight, but Naomi would say, "Killing is not the answer to our problems." He put aside his illicit thoughts. Concluding that any attempt to sleep was fruitless, he rose from the comfort of his bed to attend to more practical matters.

The strong, earthy smells had drifted to the front of the house. He dreaded it, but he knew he had no choice but to walk to the kitchen where his mother worked, concocting the medicines that kept the family well. For that reason alone, he would endure the eye-watering, nose-tickling pungent smells. The long table where Naomi stood, surrounded by baskets of dandelion roots, nettle, chickweed, and goldenseal leaves and stems, sat parallel to the fireplace. Three iron pots hung suspended from hooks in the massive fireplace, along with two smaller pots with handles that sat on metal trivets, cooking the goodness out of the roots his mother used to create salves, liniments, and syrups. Ethan noticed the mortar, slightly concealed by the mounds of roots, holding the dried sage leaves she was grinding with the pestle. "You've got enough herbs and spices here to embalm a dead man," he laughed, attempting to bring some humor into the major dawn-to-dusk job Naomi faced ahead of her.

Naomi grinned and shrugged, "Yes, but you will thank me when the ague comes upon you, and the fever chills cause your teeth to rattle." She stopped her work and smiled at him. "I packed a sack of food to eat as you travel. When you return, the strong smells will be gone, and your face will no longer look sour." She felt Ethan's strength when he wrapped his long arm around his mother's shoulder.

He began his journey before dawn, walking toward the steep and rocky terrain of the mountain called Percy, so called by the Ponkapoag Indians for its wild persimmon trees that grew scattered about the landscape. Before leaving his house, Ethan tied the wampum belt that defined his mother's people around his green linen tunic, inserted his knife in the sheath sewn into his moccasin boots, and slung his bow crosswise over his right shoulder. He wore a weighty haversack packed with food and drinks and a scant supply of medical items that may or may not be needed. One could never be sure about the occasional bee sting or snake bite.

He chuckled when he recalled the time Tall Spruce was broiling trout for the cousin's afternoon meal on Percy Mountain. Without giving a thought, he leaned too close to the open fire, causing the feather hanging from his braided hair to catch fire. He danced around frantically, believing that flailing his arms and stomping his feet would somehow stamp out the flames, but to no avail. Gray Wolf had the good sense to pour a bucket of water over his head, which immediately doused the fire.

Not surprisingly, Tall Spruce's charred braid came detached from the right side of his scalp, next to his temple, and his right ear was blistered. Ethan lathered St. John's Wort salve over the burned spots. Since that little incident, Ethan wisely packed one of those necessary items that may or may not come in handy. The wounded feelings of the Indian were another matter that only Tall Spruce could sort out.

The smells of new wood and sawdust hung in the air of the recently built malting house, uncompleted at this stage. A hundred yards beyond, he caught a whiff of the fresh creek smells and heard the gushing sounds of water moving over the bulky rocks. From years of crossing the wide creek, his feet naturally carried him to the footlog that bridged one side of the creek bank to the other. Walking over the sandy entrance to the forest edge, he looked upwards into utter darkness, thankful for the coolness of the morning. He began his climb.

Ethan naturally walked briskly, taking long strides to the side of the mountain, as his father had shown him years ago, and angled upwards, allowing his moccasined feet to seek the hardened dark trail to avoid briars and vines. Falling from the trees came the morning mist, settling lightly on his head and face. The ghostly gray light replaced the darkness, inviting birds and creatures to begin their day.

Five moons had passed since the winter solstice when he last met with his cousins, Gray Wolf and Tall Spruce. He recalled the leafless trees, the absence of birds and tree critters, and the gray sky raining ice. With that came the occasional sounds of weak branches breaking under the weight of snow. Unlike his last trip up the mountain, today, the forest was alive with busy squirrels scurrying up trees, tapping woodpeckers, and noisy jays surveying nests for a stolen meal. Spring rains and warm weather had filled out the mountain's massive trees with greenery, protecting the new life, supplying creatures with their unending need for sustenance.

The three cousins met four times during the year for council to learn the news of neighboring tribes and to share the knowledge and experiences of their elders. The location had remained the same for the past six years. The plateau atop Percy Mountain was surrounded by huge granite rocks for sitting and standing and for protection. It seemed to them that they were the only two-legged animals that ever visited this part of the mountain, but no one could be sure. Today, it was their time to gather on this most propitious landing, affording them a view of the expansive valley below and the lake that lay at the foot of Wachusett Mountain. Mindful of the bond with their ancestors, their dependence on the land, wilderness, and sky, and the sense that this mountain was their domain.

Ethan had gathered the vegetables and salt as well as three bottles of hard cider from the pantry. His cousins always supplied the bass or trout. At this time of year, small animals and deer mated and raised their young in the spring and summer. There would be no fresh meat until late fall.

Ethan shook off thoughts of the new malting house and the work it required for completion. His wounded left arm limited his movements and caused him some minor pain. But the occupation of Boston with British redcoats and the visit to the farm by the Englishman and his companion were the most vexing thoughts of all. He was eager to discuss all these concerns with his cousins as they sat around the fire tonight. They would listen with great interest, asking questions, pondering, and sharing their thoughts.

A natural hunter, he purposely focused his mind on his surroundings, recalling the skills he had learned as a youngster—eyes roving in every direction and ears attuned to any unusual sounds. For some reason, today was different. It was difficult to focus on those skills. His mind kept jumping back to happier times when he and his father Eli had made this same journey.

He seated himself on the familiar resting rock, opening the packed haversack. He pulled out the leather pouch of ale for refreshment, sipping it slowly. His mouth watered when he caught the whiff of roasted venison wrapped in a Johnnycake. Before he took a bite, the explosion of the sun drew his attention upward and beyond, extending its red and orange rays across the horizon. He took a moment to gaze at the glory set before him, secluded among the trees and feeling the wonder of the new day.

A passing thought of his father swept through his mind: tall, blue eyes, fair-haired, and a bronze English nose. Perhaps it was because, years before, they had sat together on the same resting rock and eaten the same food before they climbed to the top of Percy Mountain. He desired that connection with his father today, suddenly feeling the ache of grief for his lost father. "He won't be gone forever," his mother Naomi had claimed that promise. *She believes in miracles*, he thought.

He leaned his head back to see the ridge of the mountain. "Halfway there," he muttered. His walking slowed. The rays of the sun were fierce, beating on his head, causing his mind to wander and to blame his slothfulness on his wounded arm. Slipping back to thoughts of the Englishman and the telling note written by Mr. Adams to Uncle Jacob, revealing an ugly mask of deceit by one man, aligned with equal deceit by the British army. He scolded himself for allowing his mind to drift. He returned to reality.

He continued up the steep trail, forcing himself to block out the dangers at Mulberry Farm. "Ooooo eeeee!" came the sudden sound from the top of the mountain. "That would be Tall Spruce," he muttered. Now, the woods were perfectly quiet. Creatures, stunned by the abrupt sound, had retreated to their hollow logs and treetops. The light blue sky was barely visible, given the thickness of the ancient oaks laced together at the tops and greened with new spring growth.

Ethan approached the landing and saw Tall Spruce nestled thirty feet high in the fork of an oak tree, one skinny leg swinging off the massive limb. He tossed down an apple core aimed for Ethan's head but missed—only because he cleverly stepped sideways.

"Too bad I'm not a black bear. You'd be scrambling to the tree top," Ethan chided Tall Spruce, who by this time had untangled his body from the limb and jumped to the ground, landing squarely on both feet.

"What took ye so long?" demanded Tall Spruce. "That there string of trout grow weary waiting on ye!" he answered amusingly while pointing to the basket of fish, still showing signs of life with their flipping tails. His cousins had done the work of pulling in the trout and striped bass at the river on the other side of Percy Mountain. Ethan inspected the landing where his cousin had laid the beginnings of a fire. His cousin's bow leaned against one of the boulders.

"Where's Gray Wolf?" Ethan asked while his searching eyes moved left and right beyond the boulders.

"Trailing a cat. He picked up the scent and followed its tracks in the direction of yon cavern before the mountain. I'm starting a fire. When Gray Wolf gets hungry, he'll come our way." Tall Spruce used his flint to spark dried leaves and sticks he had gathered earlier. He crouched on the ground, nursing a beginning flame, awaiting a blaze, munching on hazel nuts he had picked along the way.

Ethan busily gutted the fish while chatting with Tall Spruce. The arrival of spring meant an abundance of fish for Massachusetts Indians. After disassembling their wigwams and packing small tools, they moved to find natural food supplies. "When will your village move to the shore?"

"The women remain in the winter village. They have planted corn and squash. Now, some will move to the shore to feast on the cod and the mussels."

"What of Bright Sky? Has she made her choice?" Ethan was hesitant to ask Tall Spruce of his potential mate, but he was in a talkative mood.

"She chose Lone Hunter. She said I was too tall," Tall Spruce shook his head. "Who can know the mind of a woman?"

"There are others who think your climbing skills are worthy," Ethan smiled at his cousin, attempting to smooth over Tall Spruce's obvious disappointment.

Ethan wrapped the carrots, parsnips, and onions in large sycamore leaves, positioning them under the hot coals. It didn't take long before the intense heat allowed for the popping sounds as the vegetables blistered and roasted. While tending the food, it reminded him of the familiar aromas and delicacies of one of Aunt Lenora's dinners. The roasting smells permeated the air. His mouth watered.

He glimpsed the top of Gray Wolf's feathered head as he approached the protective granite boulders, dragging something heavy behind him, considering the bulk of a catamount. Noticeably exhausted from navigating the steep upgrade, his face was flushed, drenched in sweat. The cat was lying sideways on a crudely built liter, displaying a bloody gash in its chest. The struggle between man and beast showed in Gray Wolf's gouged face and neck. It wasn't the first time he had wrestled a cat. The animal was able to take a man down and was able to kill, but Gray Wolf defended his life with practiced skill and toughened limbs. He dropped the liter handles, staggered to the nearest rock, and collapsed to the ground. No talk was needed. Tall Spruce passed him a pouch of water and glanced back at the dead animal. An unnatural paleness wreathed the injured man's face. Heat and exhaustion consumed his body as he leaned close to the ground and vomited.

Gray Wolf lay against the granite, expecting his head to clear before he spoke. His back was stinging, and his muscles ached as if he had fallen off a cliff onto a massive rock. The back of his shirt was shredded, and remnants of blood had caked on his buckskin tunic. It was a gruesome sight. A slight smile lit his face when Ethan dabbed his bloody face with the warm water. "The varmint jumped me from behind and scratched the devil outta my back. How bad is it? Did he cut me up badly?" Gray Wolf managed to speak, grimacing as Ethan continued cleaning his face and neck with the intent to keep the flies at a distance before they caught the bloody scent.

Ethan ripped the mangled shirt back with his knife to get a look at the damage. The cat had pounced on his back with a fury and clawed it with a vengeance. He surveyed Gray Wolf's scratches and lightly doused them with alcohol. "This will sting," he warned. He smeared bear grease mixed with spearmint and yarrow oils on the cleaned scratches, silently praising his mother for the same medicine she had used on every member of the Randolph family, as well as he and his father.

"Whew, that stinks," as Tall Spruce covered his nose with his sleeve. "Got any spirits with ye?" he asked, hopeful. Ethan nodded his head toward his haversack.

The bear grease concoction was soothing and caused his back to quake, but Gray Wolf knew the price of taking down a cat. There was suffering on both sides. He rested and snoozed, hearing the sounds of voices coming from Ethan and Tall Spruce but not having the strength to make out their words. His body was aching and sweating. His sense of smell was aroused by the savor of broiled fish and onions, but he had no desire to eat.

Ethan ate chunks of trout while watching Gray Wolf attempting to rest his broken body, even though his mind was still wrestling the wild cat. Ethan figured his cousin would have a rough night ahead of him. He put the water pouch to the man's lips and encouraged him to sip. Beads of sweat were forming on his brow now, and he was flushed with fever. Ethan sat by his side, observing any possible changes. The chills began, and he covered Gray Wolf with his blanket.

"What of the coming invasion? I see more soldiers gather each day to set up camp," Tall Spruce informed Ethan. "They raise their tents, build their fires, and march with their muskets. Will we fight them when they seek their enemy?"

"The soldiers will stay in their camp. They are not hunters. When they run out of food, they will take it from the farms. Tell your people to stay out of their way. Keep watch from a distance. Chief Randolph says we must remain vigilant."

"What is *vigilant*?" inquired Tall Spruce.

"You must have the eyes of a hawk. You can see them, but they must not see you," replied Ethan.

"Such as when you and Harry held your guns on the man wearing the red cape?" asked Tall Spruce.

This took Ethan by surprise. "I believe you have eyes like a hawk since I never saw you." Ethan laughed at his cousin's candidness. "Were you sitting up in a tree while you were spying on us?"

"Oh yes, I saw it all. I heard it all. It sounded like a trick coming from the Englishman."

Ethan grinned at Tall Spruce's insight. "You are correct. He intends to set a snare and trick us as though we are a giant rabbit. But we must invent a trap for the varmint and become as cunning as a hawk. We are his rival."

"The Englishmen leave many footprints in the wilderness. They corrupt the land and lay in their own filth," Tall Spruce shook his head in dismay. His face showed contempt.

"Many times, Chief Randolph has removed the hardships of cold winters by giving our people blankets and medicines. He has shared his ways of salting the bounty of fish. When the snows fall, and while the deer hide deep in the wilderness, our bellies do not ache from hunger because we have stored away food. We remember your family's kindness. We will cast the English snakes from our land," Tall Spruce spoke favorably of Chief Randolph's generosity to his tribe.

Ethan nodded in approval of his cousin's proposal. He recalled the arrogance of the Englishman and the manner in which he had berated Harry and himself. Now, he sensed some relief from the anguish he had felt when he had studied the disheartened faces of his mother and each member of the Randolph family. The Englishman's visit was troubling. He and his cousin's scheme to drive away the English scoundrels will protect his family and the land.

Naomi and Eli had raised their son with the belief that they were blessed with a family who had given him a home, an education, and employment. He recalled his apprenticeship to the elder Randolph, who taught him the craft of producing the beer, the mistakes he made in his endeavors to learn the skills, and the trust the family placed in his abilities. All this, and they did not even share the same blood. *They treated me as an equal*, he reminded himself.

Gray Wolf was in a deep sleep. This heartened Ethan, knowing that his cousin was not suffering. He was in his own private world of healing. The slightly reddish color of the man's face had replaced his former drained and ashen look. Ethan assured himself that Gray Wolf would recover. The prospect of danger always lurked in the wilderness. *Expect the unexpected in the wilderness*, his father's voice echoed in his mind. Ethan kneeled over Gray Wolf's face, carefully mopping it with alcohol and water. He breathed through his mouth to avert the foul smell of the dead animal mixed with the man's sweat. He stood up and walked several yards away to catch some fresh air.

Tall Spruce had moved the litter holding the catamount out of the sun and set it under a shady tree. Its flesh was rotting, and it reeked. Hundreds of flies were drawn to the dead cat's body. With his hunting knife, he removed the animal's gray-yellow skin as best he could. For lack of the proper tools, he knew there was no way he could adequately scrape out the fat and tissue. He dug granite nuggets from the ground and used the sharp edges to remove what he could.

In the late afternoon sun, he and Ethan constructed a frame, crudely built, for stretching the animal's skin. As they worked, flies buzzed around their heads, attracted to their sweating faces and arms. The cat's skin looked rough, but he would scrape it thoroughly when he returned to his village. If Gray Wolf had the strength, he would have to soak the skin for several days and go through the process of smoking the skin while stretched on a sturdy frame. He looked over at Gray Wolf sleeping soundly and shook his head. "Had to run down that cat, did ye?" he jeered at his cousin.

They dug a hole with sticks and sharp rocks to bury the cat's remains. Anything to dispose of the rotted animal's body and to eliminate the source of the biting flies. The sun moved lower behind Wachusett Mountain, and a breeze rattled the leaves on the big oaks, providing a needed respite from the hot sun. Ethan pulled out the bottles of cider and offered one to Tall Spruce. "Take this. I believe you've earned some refreshment. I don't recall ever skinning a cat on Percy Mountain. Do you think it was worth the trouble?"

"I think it would be worth the trouble to throw it off the mountain," Tall Spruce replied emphatically.

While he slept with his back against the side of the cool granite boulder, Gray Wolf's cousins had built the sides and front of a lean-to out of sturdy saplings, topping the rudimentary structure with boughs of hemlock. It gave him some protection from the sun's rays and the coming night air and still allowed Gray Wolf to hear the voices of Ethan and Tall Spruce. "Bad omen," he replied weakly. "Did you bring more cider?"

"Only water and vinegar for you now. If you're hungry, I will give you some morsels of the trout," Ethan offered. "How is throwing the cat over the mountain a bad omen?" he asked Gray Wolf. "I've never heard of such."

"The old squaws predict fierce wind-driven snows if we kill a cat and do not bring its skin to the village," informed Gray Wolf.

Ethan glanced at Tall Spruce, who shrugged his shoulders and rolled his eyes. "I have lived twenty-one winters in this land. When have we *not* suffered through fierce wind-driven snows?"

Gray Wolf looked at his cousins, obviously disgruntled, then closed his eyes, pretending to sleep.

Ethan was getting anxious. He was tired of sitting, and he was bored with attending Gray Wolf. Regrettably, the day was turning into a disaster, and he had no enthusiasm to continue the evening with his cousins. He walked toward the cavern where his cousin had tracked the catamount. He followed the sand and rock path and relieved himself behind a wild persimmon tree. He paused to look upward when he heard the love song of a pileated woodpecker drumming on the tall, skinny pine tree in the distance. When his eyes drew downward, he caught sight of a narrow cave opening.

Out of curiosity, he walked up close to the portal and cautiously looked inside. The cooling breath of air swept across his face, inviting him to enter. One side of the cave's exterior was shaded by mature chestnut trees. A bar of late afternoon sunlight shone through to the inside wall, and he walked cautiously through the entrance. He heard water trickling way beyond where he was standing, but he deemed it too dark and risky to go any further.

He placed his hand on the sandstone wall and made out the imprints of carved animals: an elk, a catamount, a bird. His hand moved further up the wall, much higher than the animals searching for more engravings. This time, he traced straight lines going up and down, likely drawn with one of the infinite number of small granite rocks partially concealed in the sandy ground where he was standing. The impressions were undeniable when his right forefinger traced over the letters ELI. He shuddered from the chill that entered his being. *Could it be?* he thought. *Was this real?* A nervousness came over him that compelled him to search further back into the cave, totally filled with darkness now. A wistful feeling set upon him, but rather than caving to sorrowful emotions, he yearned to find out if there was any validity to his discovery.

He ran the dusty path toward the boulders and saw Gray Wolf comfortably resting under his lean-to. Tall Spruce lay snoozing by the flickering fire where the empty cider bottle had slipped from his hand. The aroma of broiled fish and onions lingered in the air. He felt relief that he would not have to explain his findings to Tall Spruce, allowing himself the freedom to continue with his venture.

He ripped off a generous strip of the bottom of his linen tunic, wrapped it around the top of one of the cut saplings, and sprinkled ale over the cloth. The torch caught fire when he put it to the coals. He hurried toward the cave, driven with one thought: his father had long ago tried to send a message to family members, but to no avail. With an aching heart, he discerned, *Father was attempting to escape from something or someone, but his plan had failed.*

There it was, the drawn letters indented in the stone, easily visible when he held the torch upwards, easily enough because they were lines instead of curves. They were drawn by a person with long arms, such as himself, who could reach high. Ethan began to doubt. *There are other men named Eli who are tall. You are too anxious. Forget this dream of finding your father.*

"No, I will not betray my father. I will continue searching," he whispered. It all sank in, and he somehow thought it possible that his father could be alive, convinced that he had carved his name in the rock.

The torch flame was fading as he cautiously walked further into the cave's darkness and closer to the sound and the damp smell of the water source. The stream of water trickled down the side of the cave and formed a pool in the sandy soil, keeping the soil wet and mushy but mostly absorbed into the sand.

Beyond the water trickle, the ceiling of the cave sloped. *The end of the cave*, he thought, *with no access to the outside.* He was trapped. Most likely surrounded by his predators, Ethan decided.

Leaning against the wall to consider all he had encountered, he knew this possibly could be the closest he would ever be to his father. He felt the presence of Eli in this dank cavern, dazed and muddled at the moment, not knowing his next step. He held the dimly lit torch at his side, close to the ground. He came out of his fog when he smelled the alcohol burning and knew it was time to leave the darkened space.

His eyes caught sight of what appeared to be the end of a leather lace as if it were the sprout of a plant seeking the energy of the sun pushing its way out of the sand floor, meeting the adjacent wall. With the edge of his moccasined foot, he gently nudged the incongruous object for further inspection. He brought the light closer, knelt, and pushed the sand away with his fingers, feeling more than seeing the leather piece strung with the disk and oval-shaped wampum. The same wampum used to make his belt and the purse that belonged to Naomi. All constructed with glass beads that belonged to his mother. The same wampum she had inherited from her family when she wed Eli.

At this moment, as he held the precious jewels in his hands while yearning for what was lost, he felt the spirits of his mother and father, as if they were all standing together with arms linked in the dark and musty cavern. Such an expression of love and family was overwhelming for Ethan—one he had felt as a youngster and now felt as a grown man. The wretched burden he and his mother carried every day of their lives, always wondering if Eli was killed or kidnapped. So much suffering he had endured.

He was certain his father had buried the wampum in this cavern on Percy Mountain for him to one day lay his hands upon. A token of hope that, ten years before, Eli had attempted to return home from the war against the French and their Huron allies. Regretfully, that attempt was intercepted by someone or something. Today, the veil was lifted. He could view the present and the near future clearly now. It was as if Eli had given his son permission to move on with his life; waiting for his father's return was not necessary.

He walked slowly back to the landing to his waiting cousins with a sense of raw courage and renewal. Prepared to create a strategy for eliminating the Englishmen. Prepared to work with Harry to complete the malting house. Prepared to drive the soldiers from Boston.

Chapter 11

Ambush at Dawn

First Week of June 1774, Mulberry Farm

If it hadn't been for Gray Wolf's determination to track a catamount, resulting in the fight between man and beast, which produced one dead cat and a wounded, feverish man, Ethan and his cousins would not be sitting on Naomi's front porch drinking a tankard of excellent beer and discussing plans to set a trap for the unfortunate sidekick of the Englishman. "Let's catch the Minnow before pulling in the Shark," Ethan suggested to his cousins.

The evening before had not been quite so hopeful. The sun had begun lowering in the late afternoon on Percy Mountain when the cousins' mood turned distressed. Gray Wolf's condition was declining, obvious to Ethan when fever and chills had returned to his cousin's body, causing him nightmares and out-of-his-head talk. He emptied the last of the alcohol and water mixture over his cousin's striped back, quickly bathing his wounds. The rawness of the wounds disturbed Ethan, admitting to himself that Gray Wolf's back could not heal with the paltry medical supplies contained in his pack. *So much redness and still the flow of blood*, he thought, shaking his head in dismay.

He saw Tall Spruce a distance away playing a makeshift game, striking a disk-like stone with a stick, hoping to cast off his late afternoon boredom. Ethan called Tall Spruce over to examine the open wounds.

He gazed worriedly at his cousin's back. "He needs strong medicine. We must take him to a safe place."

The dusk of evening was bringing on shadows that grew deeper around the base of the enormous oaks. What once had been a robust fire was nothing more than the light of a large candle now. Ethan raised his cousin's limp head, holding a flask of whiskey to the man's lips, encouraging him to take a few sips. Anything to rest his mind while he slept. Tall Spruce had spoken wisely; Gray Wolf needed special care—Naomi's care. A plan must be implemented to move his sick cousin to Mulberry Farm.

Ethan remained by his cousin's side, fully comprehending that the man's condition was hopeless; he could die from the seriousness of his wounds. There was nothing he could do to stop the fever or eliminate the poison in Gray Wolf's body. He stared at his sleeping cousin.

Falling into a stupor, Ethan recalled that dreadful night two weeks before when he was traveling from Suffield to Mulberry Farm. He was set to chase by highwaymen for reasons he could not determine: guns, gold coins, food, anything. The bullet had ripped through his upper left arm, but he was pushing his gelding, Comet, so hard up the Blue Hills, then down, that it never occurred to him that he had been shot. The pain intensified as he got closer to the farm, believing that if he could make it to the stables, he could rest and drink away the pain with whiskey. The stupidity of that very idea made him cringe now. He massaged his upper arm joint and gently shook his left arm; barely any pain, thanks to Josie and Uncle Josiah.

Working through the night, the cousins had made a litter for Gray Wolf, folded the smelly cat's skin, and packed their leftover food. Their night on Percy Mountain had ended. The next morning, they walked slowly in the gray light, dragging Gray Wolf behind them, down the steep, sandy track to Ethan's home. In the midst of the chaos, his mind turned to his peaceful spirit, so different now than when he had ascended the mountain the day before. He fingered the wampum necklace and smiled, thinking, *Best trip to Percy Mountain—ever*, then paused, *notwithstanding Gray Wolf's misadventure.*

Harry stood drawing a bucket of water from the well when he saw movement at the creek, obscured by the sun's haze. He walked closer, pulling his hat over his eyes to shade the brightness, realizing it was his cousins who were walking down the mountain, crossing the creek. The noticeably exhausted men staggered over the foot log, tugging and straining, sweat dripping down their faces, each struggling to manage the litter. The weight of which was making the contraption drag the ground. As Harry ran closer, it was as he had expected: Gray Wolf, apparently in distress, judging from the wretched look on his face. He was lying amongst bags, weapons, and a yellowish animal skin. "I pray he's not lame," mumbled Harry.

The sun illuminated their faces, giving the three men a ghastly, scarlet appearance. Their dry lips were parched white. Glossy black hair lay clinging to their water-soaked linen tunics. Harry shooed Ethan away from his end of the litter, grabbing hold of its handles and relieving his cousin of the heavy burden. Ethan paused to splash creek water over his head and face, relieved they had made the trip down the trail so quickly. He and Tall Spruce, drunk with fatigue, had pushed themselves to get their cousin to solid ground, never speaking to each other, never slowing their pace, moving like two scared horses. He wasn't even sure if Gray Wolf was still breathing. *Likely unconscious*, he thought.

Naomi stared at the distant movement. With her sunbonnet shading most of her face, she set the basket carrying her knife and herbs on the ground and ran close enough in the direction of the litter to evaluate the seriousness of Gray Wolf's condition. She motioned them to the house and directed the group to Ethan's bedroom. She set in motion the process of attending to her unconscious nephew, fully aware of the medicines required to pull him back from the darkness. It would take a few days to revive Gray Wolf, but she had the competence. She was fully able.

With Naomi in command, she had Tall Spruce and Ethan lay their cousin with his back exposed. She grimaced when she examined the deep scratches. The torn flesh was bloody and looked as if the man had been lashed with a whip. She poured cool water from the ewer into the bowl, soaking a towel for Ethan to press against Gray Wolf's parched lips and the sides of his face. "This will wake him. Talk to him. He needs to hear your voice. Tall Spruce, go draw water from the well. You need to drink. Bring a bucket of water to the kitchen fireplace." Naomi administered control over the emergency like a general commanding his troops. "There's soup in the stewpot. You need your strength today."

She made poultices from thin cloths containing goldenseal leaves, then dipped them in hot water. Throughout the morning, she applied the medicine to Gray Wolf's wounds, intending to thwart further infection. She left the room momentarily and returned with a cup of fragrant tea. Ethan recognized the familiar whiff of fever wort before Naomi entered the room. "How many times had his mother made him drink fever wort tea?" he muttered, feeling relief that there was hope for Gray Wolf. His cousin was showing some signs of life, making grunting sounds and shifting his back and shoulders. "Lie still, Gray Wolf. You're resting in my bed in my house. Naomi has put medicine on your back." His cousin grunted a sound of approval.

Naomi and Ethan had worked through the night attending Gray Wolf, sponging his face and arms and filling him with tea and broth. The following morning, while he slept, she walked outside to stretch her legs and back, feeling the sun's warmth on her skin. It had been constant work infusing herbs for tea and making a hearty broth, the medicines Gray Wolf needed to heal. She looked toward the woods at the towering beech tree. Her eyes caught the small green maple-shaped goldenseal leaves growing *en masse* under the shady tree. She cut enough for today's poultices, marveling at the healing power these medicinal leaves provided to fight infection.

Harry sat slouched on the porch floor, drinking a mug of ale with Ethan and Tall Spruce. "Did you say an ambush?" Harry asked laughingly to the cousins. "I don't believe I've ever ambushed a man—possibly a deer—if you want to call that an ambush. Can the three of us manage the minnow? What must we do to prepare for such a snare?" Harry and Tall Spruce had been working since dawn, hammering shingles to the roof of the new malting house. Their minds were ready for a distraction, and their stomachs ready for food.

At Lenora's insistence, the workers had sat down at her kitchen table, consuming enough flapjacks for a company of soldiers. Ethan spoke in a low voice when Lenora walked out to the pantry to replenish the supply of maple syrup, "This ambush plan does not leave this table." His eyes penetrated the faces of Tall Spruce and Harry. "You know, Uncle Jacob. He will put his foot down, forbidding such treachery, claiming that we're putting our lives at risk and breaking the law. Which we are."

"Yes, they are already discussing a plan with Mr. Adams, with the idea of allowing the authorities to handle the Englishmen," informed Harry. "It will never happen. Not with ports closing and men out of work, such as they are. There will be longshoremen and fish gutters committing looting and thieving such as Boston has never seen—certainly, more cases than the General Court can handle. These blokes will pull such stunts right under the nose of the redcoats and laugh about it later. It could take months or years before these two English rascals would be tried. If we don't protect our own property now, nobody will."

Tall Spruce continued eating flapjacks while Harry spoke but took the message to heart. Finally, he laid down his fork, "I don't know about longshoremen and the General Court. I do know about ambushes. We must choose which tribe to bargain with: the Mohawk, the Hurons, the Seneca. These tribes welcome such outsiders to their camps. They first must prove their worth. If not, they become slaves to the chiefs." Ethan and Harry looked at each other, like-minded, nodding their heads, considering Tall Spruce's plan.

Two days under the care of Naomi had ensured Gray Wolf's health was mending, but bed rest was essential in regaining his strength. He knew Naomi's ways, never doubting her plan for recovery, willing to yield to her authority. When he tried to stand, his head was dizzy, and his legs were wobbly. He needed a man's strength to hold him upright and usher him outside to relieve himself. There was no shortage of strong and willing men on hand to provide assistance to Gray Wolf.

Poppi had visited him at his bedside and delved into the past, recalling memories that he and his family had with Gray Wolf's Ponkapoag family. So many ways they had worked together long ago, anxious to learn each other's customs. Gray Wolf had little to say, but he was happy for the company of Chief Randolph. When the elder Randolph took his leave, he glanced at Ethan's desk containing writing materials, a copy of *Robinson Crusoe*, and Eli's wampum necklace. *I wonder where these glass beads came from*, he mumbled curiously.

Construction on the new malting house had tripled with the three men on the job at dawn, measuring, cutting, and hammering, putting out an extraordinary amount of work before the mid-day meal was set before them. Harry was betting on his father being impressed that the job was so close to completion. In his mind, even though the job had to be completed before August, his work was expedited for the distinct purpose of expelling one-half of the scoundrels who were attempting possession of Mulberry Farm, unbeknownst to his father.

The details of initiating the treacherous deed were crystal clear. But the location of where to dispose of the Minnow was still undetermined.

"A trip to the Mohawk camp will take more than a week," Harry declared. "I've constructed half a dozen stories to tell my parents, and they all sound like fairy tales. They would never believe such incomprehensible reasons why the three of us would need to leave the farm for a week while Gray Wolf is still healing."

"No, but Uncle Jacob would believe that we need new beer kegs for production this fall. We're getting dangerously low. That settles one piece of the puzzle. We'll have to travel south to collect the kegs and, in the meantime, dispatch our soon-to-be victim, but where?" Ethan was sitting on the creek bank with Harry and Tall Spruce. The three sipping bottles of stout, ruminating over their likely prospects, which seemed to be dwindling at every turn.

"The Englishmen keep goats in their camp—stolen, I'm sure. I smelled the roasted meat. The animals' bones are scattered for the wolves to gnaw. They have two horses, but one is lame. The Minnow fills his water pot from the creek at daylight." Tall Spruce claimed the Blue Hills as his territory. He protected it as Harry and Ethan protected Mulberry Farm. He guarded the hills in the evenings.

"If there's one thing I hate, it's a thief," Harry shook his head in disgust but marveled at Tall Spruce's tactics for gathering such information. The Indian moved like a ghost in the woods. He left no footprints. He became one with trees and creatures. He knew how to execute an ambush.

"We will need Naomi's strong medicine. The man must sleep deeply as we travel," Tall Spruce knew of the herbs he would need to make the potion. "Be mindful, the Minnow will sleep for only two days."

The idea came instantly to Ethan, wondering why he had not considered it before now. Ever since he descended Percy Mountain to settle Gray Wolf, he agonized over how to flush out the Englishmen. It seemed a mammoth task, replete with danger and uncertain outcomes, but to tarry would only prolong the grief the Randolph family and others had endured.

While lounging on the creek bank, feeling the sun's warmth as its rays slipped in and out of the leafy trees, Ethan recalled the hulking man at the Whales' Tale, always sharing a story about his whaling adventures in the North Atlantic. *I've traveled far and wide, but I n'er drank a brew that compares with the robust flavor of a Mulberry Farm beer.* The proprietor at the popular tavern in Enfield, Connecticut, had been purchasing Mulberry beer for ten years or more. Since Ethan had managed the brewing business, they had worked together agreeably, striking up a trusting friendship.

Ethan remained silent, turning over in his mind an idea that would separate the two Englishmen, causing each of them to be placed in a vulnerable position. Without saying a word, he quickly estimated the time factor in kidnapping the Minnow, traveling south to Enfield, explaining the idea to Captain Zeke of disposing of the Minnow in exchange for ten kegs of beer, picking up new kegs to use in the fall, and driving back to the farm before dusk. He looked at Harry and Tall Spruce, nodding his head in affirmation, displaying a canny smile, "Gentlemen, the solution to our problem is Captain Zeke."

"Never heard of him. Whoever he is, can we trust him?" Harry rinsed his empty bottle out in the creek water while he listened to Ethan describe Zeke's side business. A strategy was in the making. Outside of eating a hearty mid-day meal, the balance of the day would be spent working out the details and loading the kegs of beer bound for Captain Zeke's Whales' Tale.

Lenora had been working in the kitchen most of the morning, preparing food for the men. She could have easily made a pot of stew and a loaf of bread, but when Lenora's brain began thinking about food, her creative side got carried away. Besides, the men had poured their efforts into the new malting shed this week, and in her mind, they should be rewarded with special food.

She recruited Jacob to retrieve a ham from the smokehouse, then down the steps to the cellar for dried pumpkin and apples and a bag of currants. "What happened to this simple meal you were preparing today? You have the makings of a feast!"

"You're not complaining, are you? Since when have you turned down good food?" Lenora lifted her smiling face up to her husband as he took her into his arms. "Come on, I need your help getting the ham on the spit. You know full well how much food these young men put away?" Before long, the spacious fireplace was filled with an array of foods that only Lenora could swiftly assemble.

She considered Naomi, who had spent four days now cooped up in her house tending to Gray Wolf. At this time of the year, the two women worked as a team, gardening and preserving the early spring vegetables. What would she have done without Naomi's knowledge of herbs that had been so vital for making teas and medicines, not to mention the savory flavors that turned a tasteless capon into a delicacy equal to one served in the finest restaurants in Paris? "I do miss her company," she mumbled.

The men were washing up in the scullery before entering the dining room when the bell sounded at the entrance to the farm. Ethan looked around at hungry faces and determined it was his turn to walk the distance to the gates to greet the visitor. He slipped a loaded pistol under his belt and paused. "I want some of that pumpkin with cinnamon. Don't start eating without me!" he demanded as he walked quickly out the back door. In record time, he returned, red-faced and panting, to take his place at the table. He handed a sealed note to Jacob.

Before anyone took a bite, they all looked with anticipation at Jacob. "A note from Mr. Adams."

Interloper's list of transgressions is growing. Sending Th. C to your home immediately to explain and provide protection. J. Adams.

The somber diners interpreted the note as suggesting chicanery and evil doing on a level that not one person at the table could fully comprehend, possibly with the exception of Poppi. "Let's eat this delicious food while it's hot. We'll discuss this cryptic message in the library."

Lenora and Tall Spruce were just bringing in the quince pie and ale when the bell sounded again. Harry looked at Ethan, "It's my turn; I'll go." He picked up the spyglass and pistol before he left through the back door. He walked hurriedly toward the gates, recognizing from a distance the large brown mule, as well as the large man driving the wagon, Thomas Crafts. With a sigh of relief, he unlocked the new security lock from the inside and opened the wide gates, welcoming a friend of the Randolph's. His eyes scanned the dusty road and the woods across from Mulberry Farm, on the lookout for any unusual movement.

Ordinarily, the dining room appeared spacious, but it began to dwindle in size when Thomas Crafts entered the room, greeting familiar faces and enamored with the homelike feel of family and friends gathering for a mid-day meal. "If you're hungry, Mr. Crafts, we have plenty of leftovers," offered Lenora. "Sit here. I'll prepare a plate. Tall Spruce, would you bring Mr. Crafts a mug for ale?"

The guest was a tall, muscular man, and Lenora recalled from past visits that he could pack in the vittles, but she observed upon glancing at the man that he must have brushed the dust off his clothes and washed his face and hands before entering the house. "I don't believe we've met, Tall Spruce. I'm Thomas Crafts from Lexington."

Tall Spruce poured out the ale from a pitcher. "Good to meet you. I am glad you're here."

"I got the note from Mr. Adams while I was eating my breakfast—loaded my wagon, and we drove off. We did travel two miles out of the way to avoid the reds, and Flip naturally pulled me over to every stream he came across. Otherwise, we had no difficulties." Thomas was a talker, always saying what came to mind. "I hadn't had food like this in years, Mrs. Randolph. I'm a widower, you know. My cooking is barely passable, but I get by, as you can see." Lenora grinned when Thomas looked down and patted his bulging paunch.

"The food was outstanding, Lenora. You were right to prepare something special," Jacob smiled and winked at his pretty wife. "We're all meeting in the library when we're done here. Lenora and Father, you're going to need to hear the latest news, as well. You cousins get these dishes cleared away while I speak briefly with Mr. Crafts."

"A word with you, Mr. Randolph?" Thomas held up his finger as he walked toward Jacob. "I picked up some boxes of household goods from Bradford Lane at your sister's request." He reached in his shirt for Minnie's handwritten note to Jacob and Lenora.

Naomi heard Lenora walking up the steps. When she opened the front door, Lenora caught the heady scents of oregano and garlic, "Smells like you're making a pot of stew, or is it a poultice? I came to check on you and Gray Wolf and to bring you some dinner. How are you holding up?"

"Gray Wolf is much improved and is sitting in the parlor reading. Today, he began eating bread and butter and some meaty stew. You may visit him if you wish. The ham smells delicious," she smiled and took the tray from Lenora, setting it near the kitchen fire.

"Hello, you're looking more like the Gray Wolf that I remember. You have the best physician in these parts, of course," Lenora smiled encouragingly.

"My body is weak. I can walk and feed myself. If it had not been for my cousins and my aunt Naomi, I would be lying on a funeral pyre in the valley of death. Good friends are a blessing," Gray Wolf made eye contact with Lenora and spoke from his heart.

"I see you're reading *Robinson Crusoe*. It's a favorite of Ethan's. Chief Randolph has many books in his library that you are welcome to read when you're up to it."

Six tall men politely stood when Lenora entered the library. She seated herself in the small wooden armchair by Jacob's desk, then nodded her head and smiled in return. She caught the predominant smell of leather in the room mixed with the males' sweaty hair and bodies, which after all these years was second nature to her, being surrounded by males for the past twenty-four years.

"Gentlemen, may I begin by announcing that Gray Wolf is no longer bedridden and he is eating food. He sends his appreciation to you young men who saw to his needs, and he's sorry about his foolishness in tracking down the catamount. He is in good spirits and reading *Robinson Crusoe*." She looked at Ethan and smiled.

"Wonderful news," Jacob exclaimed. "Ethan, I want to put your mind at ease. Since Mr. Crafts has arrived here today to help look after the farm, you and your cousins will be traveling to Whales' Tale in Enfield tomorrow, as planned, to assess the captain's inventory and deliver his order. You are also picking up new kegs at Mr. Cyrus' in Thompsonville. This schedule should give you some time to sample a small amount of his whiskey and make the return trip home. You must leave before sunrise in the morning, so that means pulling out the wagon this afternoon and preparing it for travel." Jacob continued with his directions, "Weapons are essential, and by that, I mean pistols, rifles, and knives, which can be hidden out of sight in case you run into trouble. Ethan and Tall Spruce, you may leave your bows with Naomi." Jacob sighed with relief when Mr. Adams' note indicated that Thomas Crafts could help oversee the Mulberry Farm property. The visit from the Englishman worried Jacob, but the work of the brewery must continue. *Now, I can cross the trip to Enfield off my list*, he thought.

Thomas Crafts offered his comments to the group. "Gentlemen and Mrs. Randolph, these are two desperate men who will commit murder if it's to their advantage. The devils ambushed my friend Leonard and me when we walked across the bridge going into Lexington. For a moment, they had the advantage over us. We managed to push them off the bridge, which surprised them and fairly roughed them up. Dr. Randolph and his assistants mended our cuts and scratches, thank the Lord. These Englishmen mean to do harm as long as it gets them what they want. They're hungry and destitute.

"Mr. Adams asked me to share with you another episode. A week ago, young Herbie Connolly was riding his horse over the same bridge headed to Lexington to deliver newspapers. The devils had made it out of the creek from the night before, I reckon, and were hiding behind a boulder, making ready to accost Herbie. Seeing him atop his horse, they stood in the way of the rider and his mount, waving their arms and yelling to frighten them. Herbie was thrown to the ground, and they took possession of his horse, flying off to their camp or who knows where. They left the young man in bad shape, but he somehow stumbled back to the print shop on Bradford Lane. That's where Dr. Randolph examined his injuries and heard Herbie's story." After all that, Thomas took a swallow of his ale and sat back in his chair, shaking his head in disgust.

"I assume they have made camp in this area?" inquired Jacob as he looked around at the indignant faces in the room. "Tall Spruce, you're often in the Blue Hills. Have you seen evidence of these outlaws?"

Ethan and Harry froze, wondering how their cousin would respond. "I have smelled the roasted meat from their fires, sir."

Jacob pondered Tall Spruce's answer and shrugged his shoulders. "Probably raiding the surrounding farms—chickens and goats, I imagine. I'll talk to Ozzie and the stable hand to be on the lookout. Lenora and Father, I think it best you stay in the house for the next few days and lock all the doors, with the exception of the scullery. Keep a pistol close at hand, please. Thomas and I will stay outside tomorrow to patrol the front and back yards. I'll check on Naomi and Gray Wolf and advise them on the situation. You cousins should get set for your early morning trip."

"This would not be the first time we've fought off interlopers. It's a dangerous business," Poppi added in his two cents worth, emphasizing the seriousness of the predicament.

The cousins thought it best to stay overnight in Naomi's house, located close to the stables, where the packed wagon remained behind locked doors. Harry and Ethan chose the four strongest and most reliable horses to pull the heavy load of beer kegs and the weight of four people. These particular horses had been disciplined to pull heavy loads, to halt, and to advance when the driver spoke with authority in his voice. No need to worry about their dependability.

The Mulberry Men had calculated every minute of their kidnapping plan. They depended on Tall Spruce's commentary acquired through his spying efforts, which began in the late winter months when the Englishmen set up their campsite at the foot of the Blue Hills. The same woods that Tall Spruce and Gray Wolf had used for a hunting ground since they were old enough to shoot an arrow from a bow.

The two Indians were keenly aware of the Englishmen's daily schedule. The Minnow rose before sunrise from his lean-to, carrying a metal pot to fetch water for coffee, then built a fire for warmth and cooking. The Shark rose from his rudimentary bed when his nose inhaled the rich coffee aroma. The Englishmen never deviated from their early morning habits. With these detailed certainties, the Mulberry Men developed their plan.

Food was the last thing on the Mulberry Men's minds before they settled down for the night. Nerves, most likely. Three bottles of ale and dried apples would have to sustain them until they reached the Whales' Tale. Naomi placed the special tea for the Minnow in Tall Spruce's hands.

They tossed and turned on their pallets in the parlor while Gray Wolf slept comfortably in Ethan's bed, as he had for almost a week now. Their sleep came in intervals throughout the night when the ever-present details of their plan to kidnap the Minnow ran through their minds, causing them to wonder if they had plenty of shot and powder or if the pouch of tea contained enough drugs to keep the Minnow sleeping for two days. Ethan offered his father's war club to Tall Spruce. He planned to whack the base of the Minnow's skull with the club while he crouched down to fill the metal pot with water. More assurance that the man would not make a sound for three solid days.

The Mulberry Men rose when it was pitch dark, departed Naomi's house, and walked to the stables. A sliver of moon was hardly sufficient light for walking the path to the barn, much less hitching the horses to their harnesses. But their well-trained moccasined feet calculated the distance.

Gray Wolf was no fool. He knew there was some scheming involved in the trip to Whales' Tale, which he envied, but he was in no condition to partake in the kidnapping. He could scarcely stand up without support. The lesson he had learned on Percy Mountain would be a reminder to him for many years. He pushed the curtain aside and watched as Harry drove the wagon toward the property gate, bound for the Minnow's camp.

The moon was sitting low. The sky remained gray when Harry guided the horses to the designated spot. Tall Spruce had watched the comings and goings of the Englishmen for two months now. He knew the exact distance from the road to the creek. He knew the time of morning when the Minnow would be crouched on the ground collecting water in the pot, albeit in a most vulnerable position. All this was stamped in his brain. He knew within a foot where the wagon should be parked: beside the wild holly bushes drooping from the weight of its red berries, shaded by the mature elm trees.

With the sounds of water flowing over rocks in the creek, birds twitching in the hollies, and deer snorting in the woods, no human could hear the wagon wheels turning or the horses snuffling. Ethan and Tall Spruce moved from behind the trees to approach the back of the man. He never heard a sound. The tall Indian swung the club perfectly. The man fell sideways, never twitching. The cousins bound the Minnow's legs and arms, then wrapped his entire body in a canvas shroud.

The moon had disappeared, and the darkness now turned to light. The two cousins carefully dumped the man in the wagon, and Ethan sat beside him. The Minnow was out cold. Tall Spruce grabbed a leafy tree branch and jogged behind the bumping and rattling wagon for the next quarter mile, sweeping away any sign of wheels and hooves headed in the direction of Whales' Tale.

Ethan knew well that nervous feeling in his gut. That same nervousness he felt when he and Tall Spruce hastily descended Percy Mountain a few days before. He was confident his plan would work. Captain Zeke and his brothers were businessmen. They were risk takers, not about to allow two thieving Englishmen to horn in on the production of Mulberry beer that had kept customers returning every day to his famous Whales' Tale tavern.

Ethan attached his rolled-up whip to his right side. Secured with a wide belt. His knife was strapped to the outside of his right boot. He laid the pistol beside him and placed his hand on top. He knew Tall Spruce would not take his eyes off the canvas bag. This was his prize. He had scrutinized the Minnow for two months now, deeming the foreigner an invader of his lifelong domain. Thomas Crafts' description of the man's crimes only added to the loathing he felt towards the Minnow and the Shark. So far, the plan had worked, or at least the first part. Now Ethan could sleep, immersing himself in the satisfaction of a successful mission.

A strip of red lined the edge of the clouds. The sun was rising, welcoming the new day. The wagon bore down the dusty road to the next stop, Whales' Tale. Harry was as proficient in driving a team of horses pulling a heavy load as Ethan, Jacob, or Josiah, but he couldn't help but be nervous. Besides, his stomach was growling, and he needed to relieve himself. No time for that now. "Something wicked this way comes," Harry kept repeating the verse to himself as a distraction. "Uh, what comes next? *When the hurly-burly's done*—no, that's not it. *When shall we three meet again? In lightning...* Forget it. I'll ask Josie. She knows Macbeth better than anyone I know."

Chapter 12

Captain Ezekiel Penrose

Cornwall, England The Year of Our Lord 1725

Jeremiah and Dorcas Penrose raised their sons in a three-room cottage in Ruan Minor Village in the county of Cornwall, England, barely a mile in walking distance from the coast. The stone cottage, topped with a thatched roof, was built in 1725 on the lush pasture land given to Jeremiah and Dorcas as a wedding gift by his father. The beauty of the coastline, the blue horizon, camellias and palms, and the mild climate made up for the deficit of trees and the barren landscape. Sheep, chickens, and pigs were purchased with gold from Dorcas' mediocre dowry. Pieces of furniture for the cottage were castoffs donated by her mother, with the exception of a newly built settle for the fireplace, given by her father as a wedding gift.

Jeremiah and his three hulkish, rugged brothers spent weeks digging the stones from the ground, then began the work of stacking and mortaring them in the shape of a dwelling. After three months of building the properly raftered and thatched cottage, the banns were formally posted in the village. Now, the couple set their sights on a new beginning as husband and wife.

A year later, Dorcas gave birth to Ezekial, their firstborn named after the Old Testament prophet. He had his father's light brown hair and powerful build and his mother's dark blue eyes. Another year passed, and Joel was born into the world, robustly built like his father, with straw-colored hair and blue eyes like his mother. Right on schedule, one year later came Micah, just as brawny as his two older brothers and bearing his father's dark brown eyes and hair.

Dorcas was proud of her husband. He labored each day, beginning before dawn and ending after sundown, tending to the pigs and chickens, moving the sheep to the next pasture, bringing in buckets of milk for his growing sons. When will they grow big enough to milk the cow and feed the pigs, he wondered. When his day was done, he sat down to a hearty meal, followed by wrestling on the floor with his active boys. He smiled at Dorcas, proud of the family they had created. She put their sons to bed and turned her attention to her handsome husband, sponging the dirt off his neck and his back and washing his feet in a basin of soapy water. She fell asleep in Jeremiah's arms, content and at peace in their happy home.

Each morning, Dorcas took the boys outside to throw out the dried corn to the chickens, to plant seeds in the kitchen garden, and to leisurely walk through the pink primroses and blue cornflowers scattered across the fields. She marveled at the way her sons were sprouting, their muscular size constantly changing, and the questions they asked about the farm, including the mysterious far-off sound in the distance that never stopped.

She held a stick in her hand and drew the word *ocean* in the dirt, then pointed toward the sound in the distance. She laughed when they pointed as she did, and then each put their hands over their ears to block out the endless sound of crashing waves. "What is the ocean, Mummy? When can I look at it? Who lives there?" Ezekiel questioned her. She was anxious to answer her son's curious questions.

"The ocean is more water than you have ever seen. It is as deep as a mountain is tall. There are small and large animals that live in the ocean. Most of them are called fish, and some are called whales." She wrote the words *fish* and *whales* in the sand with a stick. "When you are seven years old, you may watch the ocean with your papa." The boy took the stick and drew the words while his brothers watched. Then, he pointed the stick toward the ocean.

Ezekiel had finished feeding the pigs, milking the cow, and filling the barn stalls with hay. "Papa, may I see the ocean now? I have finished my work."

"You may stand on the cliff and watch the ocean as I have shown you," Jeremiah consented. "You must return home when the sun looks as if it is touching the water." Ezekiel ran toward high cliffs and the boisterous noise of the ocean. He picked up a stick and beat it against the gorse as he moved across the bright green peaty landscape, closer to the cliff's edge.

The wind came in gusts, blowing his hair and his tunic, bringing the sound of breakers booming up on the beach below. Sometimes, he felt a spray of water across his face if he stood at the edge of the cliff. He saw the waves crash against the jagged cliffs. He watched for an hour or more, his eyes peeled toward the distant sea, straining to catch a glimpse of tall ships. Nothing invigorated him more than watching the actions of the ocean as he stood a hundred feet above. He smelled the tang of seaweed in the air and knew he was close to the beach.

His mornings, as well as his brothers, were filled with reading, writing, and ciphering, all due to Dorcas' efforts. Then, on to their chores, which they diligently performed in hopes they would be permitted to watch the fishing boats arriving with their catch for the day. Perhaps Jeremiah would allow them to borrow his spyglass to watch for whales and the huge ships far out to sea.

The Penrose boys, so enchanted by the activity of the sea with its ships, screaming gulls, and occasional sea animals that surfaced now and again, never missed a day of watching the ocean. They were convinced they would not be satisfied with anything but going to sea someday. When they turned older and stronger, they scrambled down the rocky cliffs to the water's edge, exploring the coves, captivated by the cool sprays of water drenching their body. Their cheeks reddened from the chilly air as they chased each other through the moors. There was the romance of the sea: dreaming of how they might one day command a tall-masted schooner, trim the sails to catch the wind, explore new worlds, and search the nighttime sky for directions.

When he turned twelve, Dorcas would send him to the village to pick up oranges and limes, food items that could not be grown on the farm. He always stopped to shake hands with Ole Tom, who was sitting on a wooden bench outside Whales' Tale tavern. The watering hole where seamen came to drink their ale and share the day's activity of fishing and pulling in "the haul" to sell at the market.

Every day, Ole Tom sat with his right hand curled around the top of his crutch. His aged hand showed blue spider-like veins under his thin, weathered skin. The gold ring pierced through the sailor's earlobe brought Ezekial's attention to Tom's leathery, wrinkled face and neck. He used the stick often as a pointer—to the sky, to the ocean, to the fishing boat—as he spun his stories. His story details worked in symphony with the direction his crutch moved. His clear blue eyes moved with his mouth when he spun a yarn of torrential rains threatening their survival on the open sea. "Nary star nor moon to light our way o'er them steely ocean depths, hopin' and prayin' fer a fair wind and a speck o' sunshine." Ole Tom bowed his head in remembrance of the violent gales he endured at sea.

He had lost part of his left leg above the knee when he worked on a whaling ship sailing around the North Atlantic. But that little accident, as he called it, didn't end his career as a sailor. He worked thirty years more on a whaling ship as a carpenter and made music for the crew each evening with his fiddle. He told the best tales because he had sailed the seas, thousands of miles from Cornwall, to search for the biggest and most profitable catch of all, the sperm whale.

Ezekial could listen to Ole Tom and his mates talk for hours about when a school of sperm whales was spotted. "Thar she blows," he would cry, then proceed to tell how the dangerous work of the sailors in their small boats worked to spear a whale and bring it alongside the ship for capture.

The same stories were shared every day. Ezekiel had heard them all, but he had his favorites. He had learned the timing of Ole Tom's tales and would make it back in time from his shopping to hear the best parts. As Ole Tom talked, he could visualize a school of whales in the distance spouting, throwing the white water up high as the sky. Ezekiel knew without a doubt that this would be his life's work.

Ezekiel's day came when he was sixteen. He had walked to the village one late afternoon, leaving his brothers to tend the sheep, moving the noisy animals back to the paddock close to the cottage. He had woken early with an anxious feeling that the day would be different somehow, anticipating a change but not quite knowing how it would play out.

As he moved closer to the village markets, he caught a whiff of spices, cinnamon for sure, and nutmeg, which brought to mind the apple pies his mum would often bake. In the distance, he heard the hubbub just outside the tavern, the one with the whale on the signboard. Whales' Tale, it said. He saw the man sitting at the table, and the weathered seafaring man saw him. "You're a big feller, full-limbed and a strong-looking lad. Do you have an interest in whaling?"

He had seen the man writing something as he talked to others who appeared to be his age, not quite his height, but they didn't look as though they could manage a bale of hay in each arm. He'd been doing that since he was twelve. "I don't know anything about whaling, sir, except the big ships I see in the distance and Ole Tom's stories. I would think it hard work pulling in a whale. What does it pay?" Ezekiel had never been shy about asking questions nor about looking a man in the eyes and expecting an answer. He had watched his papa do that often.

He knew he was taking a risk by committing himself to work on a ship for a year. He thought he might never get another chance to see what was beyond the horizon, but his mind was made, and he signed his name. He walked home feeling an energy that he had never experienced. His world had already changed by the time he walked to the cottage. "No more of the tiresome farm chores," he muttered. Today, he became a man of the sea.

He saw the back of the small woman adding a tray of vegetables to the big pot at the fireplace, feeling a tug at his heart, knowing he would miss her most of all. Before she turned around to greet him, she said, "You remembered the cinnamon and nutmeg." She turned and looked at him with tears in her eyes. She recognized the change in his countenance. He gave her a peck on the cheek. Something had changed in Ezekiel today. She knew it was his time.

Ezekiel realized, on the morning he sat in the small boat, ready to be rowed to the huge ship, which lay in the distance, that he would be gone for a year's time. He knew in his heart when he said his farewells to his family that he would see them again, and when that time came, he would tell them the great stories of pulling in a whale. Beyond that, he had no comprehension of how it was to be done, but he knew he would learn the captain's expectations soon enough. He had prepared himself for that when he had first stood on the cliffs, imagining himself part of a ship's crew.

After a year's stint at sea, Joel and Micah were full of questions for their brother: how tall is a sperm whale, what happens to the blubber, how much oil goes in the barrels, what does Nantucket look like? Ezekiel told the stories of pulling in the whales, which seemed very dangerous to Jeremiah and Dorcas, but they were satisfied that he had fallen in love with whaling. Now, the time had come for his second ocean voyage. Before he left home, he handed over the majority of his earnings to his parents. He was off to a distant ocean, the North Atlantic. He would stay away twice as long this time.

Weeks went by. Jeremiah and Dorcas realized the impression their son had left on Joel and Micah. They spoke in secret of Ezekial's sea adventures as they went about their work, yearning to leave the farm and pining for a different life. Jeremiah and Dorcas recognized the same look in Joel and Micah as they had seen in their son Ezekiel. The sea was calling their sons, and there would be no stopping them. They were not selfish parents. They had taught their sons to give great ponderance to their decision-making. They knew the time would come when Ezekiel, Joel, and Micah would leave Ruan Minor to realize their dreams. They were destined for the sea.

Chapter 13

WHALES' TALE TAVERN

Enfield, Connecticut, 1762

Ezekial Penrose had spent twenty years of his life roaming the seas of the North Atlantic and Newfoundland, chasing the prized sperm whales. Spending a good portion of those years managing his own crew from his ship's home port in Nantucket, realizing his dream and working toward his fortune. Loathe as he was to give up the seaman's life, reality had set in. Being sober-minded, a new life must be established. His mother was alone now, and his brothers were settled and prosperous in the New World. The family had lived apart for twenty years. Dorcas was anxious to reunite with her sons. Jeremiah had died suddenly. Losing her husband unexpectedly, she knew now was the time for the family to settle in the same place. Dorcas did not care which part of the world it was as long as they were together.

Ezekiel sold the family's farm in Cornwall. With no ties to bind him to Ruan Minor, he set his sights on New England. The Massachusetts colony was too political for his taste. If the family were to reconnect, Connecticut was the place. It was not as close to the sea as he preferred, but he was accustomed to adapting to new customs and new people. Joel and Micah Penrose had learned the business of privateering, settling along the Connecticut River. They each owned their own sailing vessel. The time had come for Ezekiel to acquaint himself with his two younger brothers' occupations.

Dorcas needed no prodding from her oldest son to move to Connecticut. She trusted his judgment. Even though she sensed her heart stirring at the prospect of a different life in a distant land, she did not want to tempt fate by getting her hopes too built up. Today, as she journeyed to the ship, she was at peace with Jeremiah's passing. Dorcas was satisfied her life had come to an end at Ruan Minor County, Cornwall. Her husband was buried alongside his parents and brothers in the Penrose burial ground by the sea. She turned her back on the only life she had ever known, bound to discover a different world and a new life with her sons that would keep her happy for a long time to come.

"I lament crossing that wicked sea to enter this wretched place," Dorcas Penrose exclaimed bitterly to Ezekial as she staggered down the gangplank at Boston Harbor. "I must sleep in a bed tonight that stays in one place and food to eat other than bread and peas!" The terrors of sea travel were like nothing she had ever experienced. For all her life, she had never left Cornwall. Her life was her family and her home. Now, in two months' time, she had traveled three thousand miles, crammed in the bottom of a ship with strangers, finally landing in the New World. No wonder her legs were shaky as she limped along Boston's cobblestone streets, clasping her son's trusting arm to guide her to safety and a familiar cup of hot tea to soothe her nerves.

"Yes, Mum, I will seek out a comfortable bed," Ezekiel promised. "You have suffered much on that monstrous ship and the desolate ocean. Storms and stiff winds a-blowing are part of sea travel," he grimaced. "You wouldn't know these things as I do." A sense of urgency had descended on him when he realized that his mum was beyond exhaustion, needing time to rest and to eat palatable food. The tables had turned. She had devoted her life to him for sixteen years, and now it was Ezekiel's turn to see that his mum was provided for during the latter stages of her life.

He strolled over the Boston Common, gazing at the opulence before him. In the distance set the estates on prime property in the exclusive Beacon Hill. Homes of Boston's wealthiest stood like castles against the bright blue sky. He took note of the most striking features of the edifices: cut stone, brick chimneys, numerous windows and dormers, balconies, fences, gardens, orchards, and even ponds with ducks and swans. His mouth watered, envious of the well-kept landscapes surrounding the mansions. It was a picture he committed to memory. He was now more convinced than ever that his life as a seaman had ended, a landowner and business owner he would become.

Ezekiel and his mother sat down to dine at Everly's, one of Boston's fine establishments. Ezekiel savored oysters swimming in a creamy sauce and ham steak topped with a sweet raisin glaze. Staring out the window, his gaze focused on Main Street lined with blossoming apple trees and black metal lanterns, giving beauty and light to residents as they strolled to the many shops and churches. The very sight of it set his heart to flutter.

His mind was exploding with the possibilities of operating an inn, a tavern, or an establishment that served fine food such as he was devouring at the moment. He knew he had to settle on one idea, but at the moment, those ideas were jumbled in his head. Drinking the rich claret did not make the decision any easier. He desired to live in a fine place in the style of Mr. Hancock's mansion, but he questioned the reality of servants running hither and yon and a fine carriage to drive him where? And to what purpose? He contemplated the wealth and status of Boston's merchant king.

In contrast, Ezekiel was a man of the sea, accustomed to sharing bawdy tales whilst drinking ale with his mates, correcting the work of an incompetent sailor, and living sea-bound for months at a time. He examined his coarse, large hands that had pulled ropes to raise and lower sails to catch the wind in the middle of the ocean. Steering a bowing and plunging ship through gray seas and gusts of wind that forced the schooner to dip under, drowning the deck with seawater and working through the night until the storm had blown itself out.

He settled Dorcas in her room, certain that the accommodations were to her liking. Her mood had changed for the better since the day after she had arrived in Boston. Now, his petite mother was her old self, relating stories she remembered from Joel and Micah's letters and their adventurous life working along the Connecticut River. Ezekiel loved hearing her laugh again and watching her delicate hands wave back and forth, adding to the drama as she spoke about her sons.

Good food and rest made the difference in her demeanor. After twenty years away from the farm and his family, Ezekial still could not believe he and his mother were within arm's reach of each other. He loved the sound of her gentle voice, giving him practical advice about the future. She listened to Ezekial's ideas about the new life he had in mind for the family, nodding her head and smiling as he spoke. Tonight, his heart was content and full of joy. He was a happy man.

Upon entrance to his room, he was drawn to the window where the light of the moon cast its silvery shadows across the bed and furnishings, exhausted as he was from exploring Boston's sites and walking amongst the crowds of people on narrow streets and alleys. He lay on a soft feathered mattress with a belly full of rich food, pondering the differences between his life experiences and those of the wealthy Beacon Hill residents. His mind was moving closer to a more realistic path to go forward with his new life. He was as confident now as when he signed the papers at Whales' Tale tavern in Cornwall as a sixteen-year-old young man, leaving his family home to become a seaman. Tonight, he felt prepared to pursue the next chapter in his life. He would have a peaceful night's sleep.

Ezekiel visualized a new tavern on the corner where two roads intersected—Hartford to the west and Boston to the north. Ezekiel knew this was prime real estate and planned to purchase one hundred acres upon his arrival in Enfield, Connecticut, which was within throwing distance of the Connecticut River. He was not sure at the time how he would use all the property to his financial advantage, but in time, it became clear.

Vigilant as he was, he observed the area's traffic when riders and horse-drawn carriages traveled past the large section of property to head north. Men and women would surely stop for refreshment at a certain popular tavern within two miles of travel in Springfield, Massachusetts. The idea of building a tavern facing the Connecticut River with access to the Boston Post Road would bring in customers from New Haven,

Weathersfield, Suffield, and Hartford. The probability for business would appear more inviting as the communities around Enfield began to flourish. When he observed the water traffic and activity along the massive river, he was most assuredly convinced that building a tavern on this particular corner was where he and his mum would settle.

Whales' Tale tavern looked more like a whaling ship than a public house serving customers food and drink. If you were acquainted with Captain Zeke's passion for the sea, you would understand its unconventional decor. The oddities and curiosities on the exterior of the structure were certainly an inducement to draw patrons to sample more of what awaited inside. At least, that was the thinking of the eccentric Captain Zeke.

The two-story structure was clad in cut stone, such as he had seen on the mansions in Beacon Hill. Small pediments, each the width of the second-floor dormers, hung over each window, identical to the larger triangular architectural feature defining the front door entrance. A massive weather vane, crafted in the shape of a whale, was perched in the center of the shingled rooftop, taking precedence over the tall smoking chimneys. When the mammoth whale was spotted from a distance, patrons knew they had arrived at the most distinctive tavern in all of northern Connecticut, the Whales' Tale.

Curious patrons entered the property through an iron gate, then walked the brick path ending at the front door of the tavern. Painted carvings of a merman and mermaid attached to each side of the entrance greeted customers, giving one the impression that a magical nautical experience awaited them. Once inside, customers were amused at the sight of these mythical creatures adorning the walls and doorways, lending sailors occasions to spin seafaring tales of those underwater denizens of the deep sea. To Captain Zeke's way of thinking, the more stories shared, the more beer and food were consumed, awarding visitors unique entertainment and the captain a fatter purse.

June 7, 1774

"How's the Minnow?" asked Harry as he slowly drove the horses off the dusty road, steering them to the back of the tavern. "This heat is unbearable!" He turned around to see for himself how they were managing in the crowded wagon bed. Tall Spruce sat beside the shrouded rascal, gripping Eli's war club, ready for action should he observe any movement coming from inside the canvas. Ethan had curled up in a small space at the end of the wagon bed, aiming to catch a few winks, separating him from the beer kegs, Tall Spruce, and the Minnow.

"Have you given him a drink of your special potion yet? He should be getting thirsty by now, judging from this heat. I see you've loosened the canvas covering his head. The varmint must be roasting!"

"He appears calm. He will wake soon. The potion sits next to me." He tapped the pouch at his side. Tall Spruce sat unperturbed. His placid state of mind confirmed his purpose and stability.

Harry removed the horses' harnesses and walked the thirsty animals two at a time to the water trough. Ethan, half sleeping, sensed they had arrived at the tavern. The acrid smells of beer and horses drifted to his nose, pulling him out of his languid state. He stretched his eyes wide, catching a view of the underside of the leafy shade trees. He exhaled heavily. "Now the work begins," he muttered.

"How's he doing? Any trouble?" he glanced at Tall Spruce, who shook his head, still holding on to the club, eyes glued to the canvas. Ethan jumped down from the wagon back and walked to the remaining horses, leading them to the water source. He turned toward the familiar bold voice behind him.

"Barmy, mate. I had a feelin' in me bones ye'd be comin' this way." Captain Ezekial Penrose stood just under six feet, his limbs large and muscular, and a head full of light brown and gray curls long enough to cover his short neck. "Looks like ye brought venison fer roastin'," he said, spying the hump under the canvas cover. "Will ye be stayin' a day er two?" he asked Ethan. "Ah, this must be yer cousin ye go a-huntin' with." The garrulous captain, reverting to the common speech of sailors, dominated the moment with Ethan. He doffed a small cap he wore on the crown of his head as a welcome to the tall Indian. Tall Spruce gently smiled and nodded.

"Yes, this is my cousin, Tall Spruce," Ethan introduced the two men. "He is from the Ponkapoag tribe, as is my mother. He brings honor to my family with his excellent hunting skills. Ahem, about the deer under the canvas, Captain, we wish to discuss with you a trade when my cousin returns." Harry was busily tethering two of the horses to a shade tree, where they ravenously began cropping the weeds. He had brought along bags of oats and carrots from the stables, intending to feed to the horses before they began the return trip home.

Harry strolled toward the wagon to join the men, looking exhausted with his sweaty hair falling around his face, loosened from its leather thong. The sun's glow highlighted the red and blond streaks in his auburn hair. His face flushed from settling the horses. Harry extended his hand and flashed a smile to Captain Zeke. "I'm pleased to meet you. It has been a while since I've traveled to this part of Connecticut."

"Oh, yonder comes my brother," Ezekiel called to his brother Joel, stepping from Dorcas' cottage onto the brick path edged with foxglove and primrose. He concealed the lit pipe in his bear paw of a hand, knowing his mother absolutely forbade smoking in her cottage, chancing several puffs when he turned his back to her.

He saw the strangers talking to his brother under a shady elm, then walked their way. Joel was as tall as Captain Zeke and as robustly built. His straw-colored hair picked up the sunlight, revealing strands of white running through his thick curls. The gregarious brothers radiated a special charm and wit that drew the attention of patrons and friends, particularly Ethan Asher and his Mulberry Men.

Before Joel allowed himself to be introduced, he pointed to the kegs still loaded on the wagon. "Haha, the famous Mulberry beer, delivered to our door!" Curious as he was, he stepped in for a closer inspection. "Pardon, sirs, for my impertinence. I'm Joel Penrose, brother to this old sea dog and son to Mrs. Penrose." He doffed his cap and bowed to the grinning Mulberry Men.

Captain Zeke made further introductions to his brother, along with praising the attributes of the beer and its popularity with Whales' Tale customers. As he stood boasting, he inadvertently placed his hand on the canvas-covered lump, causing its contents to jump. "What's this? Is it alive?" he asked, which drew the wide-eyed attention of his brother Joel.

Tall Spruce, alarmed at the danger that might possibly ensue, commenced to pull the knife from his boot but thought better of it when he heard Harry clear his throat, followed by moving his right hand in a swift sideways motion. Tall Spruce got the message.

Ethan stepped in closer, making eye contact, and spoke without hesitation, "Yes, Captain, it is alive. This is the trade I spoke of earlier." Ethan commenced the story of the nefarious Englishmen who had threatened to forcefully take possession of Mulberry Farm brewery by inveigling the assistance of the British army. Meanwhile, piling on more of their malevolent crimes against Boston citizens. "My thinking was to transfer the canvas-covered lout to a certain sloop docked yonder ways in exchange for ten kegs of Mulberry beer." Ethan obligingly paused, giving the brothers a moment for his plan to sink in.

Joel shrugged his shoulders and nodded at the captain, anticipating the outcome of Ethan's scheme. "I suppose you have in mind to have him delivered to my brother's schooner near the Long Island Sound. His final destination being some faraway location such as Jamaica. Am I correct?" Joel's eyebrows raised at his own assumption.

The Mulberry Men nodded in affirmation, uncertain whether Joel would be agreeable to accept the bargain. Their faces showed a degree of dismay. Ethan made the effort to stand firm, knowing the colonies would be far better off with the stalking Englishmen shipped off and out of the way, preferably to another continent. He felt confident that the Penrose brothers were of like mind in that decision.

"I'd like to take a gander at the devil, do ye mind?" the captain asked Ethan's permission, who nodded his head in agreement. Tall Spruce responded by pulling back the canvas hood displaying the devil's face, drugged and in a deep sleep. The brothers gasped in unison.

"Do you know this man?" Harry asked, seeing their surprise.

"We know him *and* his partner in crime. Why, if they'd been on my ship out in the middle of the ocean, I'd have shown no restraint in casting them into a bevy of sharks," Zeke answered Harry's question. "Only last week, the filthy buggers showed up here, drinking yon fine stout, and the big'un pulled a knife on the serving maid. He smuggled her out the back, forcing her into the woods over yon ways. If it hadn't been for my doorkeeper, Big Ham, who was answering the call to nature out back, the lass would have had her throat slit. As it were, before the barbarian got his breeches down, Ham lashed his whip around the big'un's neck, confusing the lout so that he had time to wallop his ugly English face." Big Ham took his job seriously when it came to protecting Captain Zeke's property.

Hearing this account, Ethan recalled the night he was given chase by two unidentifiable horsemen and ended up hiding in the Blue Hills with a bullet in his arm. It made sense now that it could not have been the work of British redcoats since they had not yet entered this part of the colony. He had a strong feeling the "big'un" and his punky mate, who at the moment lay out of touch with the world, were the true culprits.

With the realization that this part of Enfield, Connecticut, would be a safer place without the kind of human debris presently snoozing in the wagon, Joel Penrose was more than willing to accept Ethan's plan to make the transport within the hour. Such opportunities had arisen in the past when Joel had taken on special cargo of this sort. He was positive that when it was all said and done, the citizens of Enfield would appreciate his contribution toward the welfare of their town.

Of course, he was reluctant to share any details of the outcome of the poor man's life. He would leave that up to his brother Micah. These delicate matters were not for just anybody's ears; such gossip could ruin a man's reputation and his business. Micah would manage the task of holding the man prisoner until their arrival in Jamaica or Antigua. Truly, Micah Penrose stood to gain a healthy profit when the unfortunate soul was sold into servitude. Wealthy plantation owners throughout the West Indies were always in the market for English-speaking captives to cut sugar cane.

"Care to stretch your legs? You've been guarding the prisoner since dawn," Harry offered to Tall Spruce, who nodded in agreement. He eagerly jumped out of the wagon. There was a cool breeze under the big shady trees, but the sun was rising higher, signaling a scorching day approaching.

Harry retrieved bottles of ale he had stashed in front of the kegs the day before and passed one to Tall Spruce, who was walking behind the tavern, stretching the kinks out of his legs. The four heavy dray horses were content to munch grass, raising their heads occasionally at the comings and goings of patrons rushing to the nearby woods to relieve themselves. Ethan and the Penrose brothers stood clustered under a tree, finalizing the details of the trade and discussing the miscellaneous cargo items Joel would be transporting today to his brother Micah in New Haven.

Tall Spruce's back was turned to the villainous man staggering toward him, who, judging from his ornery expression, appeared highly offended that an Indian had the nerve to trespass on a white man's property, on top of which, indulging in his spirits. Since a youngster, Tall Spruce, who had spent every day of his life tracking forest animals for his daily sustenance, was nobody's fool. The rancid smell of the man's clothing and the heavy breathing of the drunken man's presence gave him away.

The man's vengeful mind controlled his will and his movements, swaying and reeling in the direction of the tall Indian, intent on a surprise attack. Tall Spruce keenly took one long step sideways, allowing the idiot a clear path to slam into the back of the wagon. All eyes and ears shifted to the wagon, where loud profanity and threats flowed from the drunken man's mouth as he fell to the ground. Ethan and the Penrose men ceased their conversation. Harry grinned, predicting how the scene would likely unfold. Tall Spruce anticipated the man's next move, fully aware that he was the intended target.

It's been said a drunken man has more courage than should be allowed when he's challenged with the impossible. False courage, that is. "Yonder comes that McGinty feller with a mind to whoop that big Indian," warned Captain Zeke. He yelled for Big Ham to come and haul the drunkard on his horse while, at the same time, McGinty's drunken mates staggered out the tavern's back door to investigate the racket. Squinching their eyes in the bright sun and seeing McGinty's predicament as he was on all fours now, groveling in the dirt, attempting to raise himself from the ground, the two lanky mates weaved toward Tall Spruce. All the while seeing double and full of hatred of all Indians, never imagining the hornet's nest they were soon to encounter.

Judging from their size and stature, the heads of the skinny scoundrels did not quite make it to the tall Indian's shoulders. All things considered, Tall Spruce heartily demonstrated his advantage when he extended his apish arms, his hands taking hold of either side of the devils' heads and banging them together like two coconuts. A defense mechanism he had used often with his tribal brothers.

Furious that his woeful rescuers lay crumpled on the ground, McGinty set out toward Tall Spruce in retaliation, swearing, as he stumbled along, that Tall Spruce was a dead man. Harry was on guard when he intercepted the drunken man by extending his long leg at the appropriate moment, causing the idiot to fall face down in a pile of horse dung. Needless to say, the drunkard was down for good and not apt to indulge himself for a second round with Tall Spruce.

Big Ham finally made his appearance, assessed the scene, and took note that not one ounce of blood had been spilled. Disappointed, he announced in his booming voice, "I missed all the hurly-burly!" Ham was taller than the Penrose brothers, wide through the shoulders, with thick muscular arms and a head as big as a ham. A powerfully built Scot.

He surveyed the yard, shaking his head at the human debris scattered about. "These drunken brutes deserve all the whacks they get and more!" He pushed each one of them onto their backs with the toe of his heavy boot, then reached down with his large hands to take possession of their money pouches. "Can't have them leave without paying!" he announced to everyone. He pulled a handkerchief from his back pocket and swabbed his face of dirt and sweat. Making himself presentable, he walked to the tavern door, smiling and greeting customers as they walked inside. Big Ham took care of maintaining a proper business demeanor and protecting his boss' property.

Dorcas Penrose, naturally hospitable and oblivious to the tumult in her dooryard, stepped outside the cottage and called to Ezekial, "Come get this basket of nibbles I've made for your friends. Surely, they're starving by this time of morning."

Nine years ago, at his mother's request, Captain Zeke had built a replica of the thatch-roofed cottage his little mum had lived in all her married life in Cornwall. She made it clear to her son that she could never live in anything as fancy as the dwellings in Beacon Hill. She desired the same size and likeness of the cottage her husband Jeremiah had built when they were wed. She kept a vegetable patch, an apple orchard, chickens, and goats. All of which sufficiently met her needs and kept her busy maintaining the property. This was her domain in the New World. She was in a fine fettle now. Having her sons nearby made all the difference in her happiness.

Joel, like his brothers, had come from humble beginnings, learning the satisfaction of completing a day's work and pushing himself to finish his tasks in the allotted time, which always meant before the day turned dark. Managing the care of the farm animals in his boyhood home in Ruan Minor, Cornwall, was a priority. This meant food for the family along with a few coins from the sale of sheep's wool.

Growing up, the strenuous work of farm life kept the Penrose boys busy from dawn till dusk. It was also an education, developing their character and working out their problems together. This was not just a happenstance. It fell back on their father, Jeremiah, who expected his boys to perform their tasks to his satisfaction but also allowed them to make mistakes. All in an effort to promote respect and confidence, guiding them to accept responsibility and paving the way for them to stand on their own two feet.

A hundred years prior, when New World colonists traveled south from Boston to make their homes in the Connecticut River Valley, they discovered fertile soil for agriculture. More than enough for their own needs, they profited by selling produce and meat to Boston and the coastal cities. Trade flourished and created wealth for merchants, farmers, and artisans.

Joel and Micah had heard talk from sailors that there was work available to experienced seamen. The widespread commerce that presently existed along the Connecticut River, along with hauling that commerce to various outlets in the West Indies, helped them solidify the idea of purchasing sailing vessels to transport exports and imports. The brothers made the decision that this was their time to settle down after years of pulling in whales from the icy waters of Nova Scotia. Creating work in the New World was the envy of thousands. Those who had the work experience, the brains, and the cash could make it a reality, and they did just that.

The morning was slipping away, and there was still so much to settle before leaving Whales' Tale tavern. The heat was rising, but some relief came with a slight breeze, causing elm leaves to twist and move like tiny fans and the ever-present squirrels skittering back and forth between connecting trees. "Let's move these kegs to the cellar," directed Ethan to Harry and Tall Spruce. "I'll hand them down to you while keeping an eye on the Minnow." He glanced over at the canvas covering, wondering if the culprit was truly asleep or so thoroughly drugged that no amount of noise could rouse the man.

While keeping an eye on the prisoner, Ethan noticed Captain Zeke and Joel arranging certain cargo in the wagon, walking back and forth, carrying packages from a storage room in the back of the tavern. It occurred to Ethan that the Whales' Tale property was more than a tavern. He considered its various functions: taproom, dining room, inn, the Penrose home, Dorcas' farm, warehouse, cargo drop off, and business office. He began to understand why Big Ham was such a valuable employee. He had identified himself as "protector of the property," which could mean more than tossing out the riff-raff. *I hope they pay him well*, Ethan thought.

Joel would be driving the loaded wagon the short distance to his anchored sloop, The Jeremiah, named after his father. This was standard practice in Joel's business to collect items from farmers, artisans, and weavers. Really, any businessman who had previously made arrangements to have his merchandise shipped to vendors in the West

Indies. The Jeremiah was small, but it was the fastest and most reliable in transporting small cargo to Micah's schooner in Long Island Sound. Joel was acquainted with every vessel that traveled down the river; some were larger sloops carrying heavier cargo, but only Joel made daily deliveries down the busy Connecticut River.

Ethan was acquainted with the financial details of Joel's business techniques, which were clear-cut and made sense to him. All shipping costs were paid up front, meaning before any cargo was delivered to The Jeremiah, these fees were paid to Joel. Cash on delivery was the rule when the merchandise was transferred from the customer to Joel's hands. This was no problem for the wealthy merchants who owned shops along the river. They appreciated the speedy deliveries handled by Joel and his capable crew. It kept their merchandise moving and their cash flow sustainable.

"What's going down the river today? I mean, besides our minnow, er, cargo," Ethan inquired of Joel with a mischievous look in his eyes.

"Looks like boxes of hats and wigs, bundles of furs, pots and small tools from the ironmongers in Suffield, some unidentified packages wrapped in oilcloth, probably clothing, boxes of flatware from the silversmith's, and four barrels of crockery." Joel approached the wagon and explained the procedure in place for handing off the cargo by workers employed by the numerous transporters, discharging the merchandise bound for Long Island Sound, as well as allowing room for the obscure contents of the canvas sack. Thankfully, the Minnow was of slight build, which meant finding a space for him to continue his repose on the sloop was not a problem.

"Tall Spruce dosed the Minnow while you were talking to Joel," Harry informed Ethan. "The kegs are safely stored in the captain's cellar. What other loose ends do we need to tie up?" Tall Spruce never missed any part of a conversation. Literal-minded as he was, his head shot up at Harry at the thought of something that needed to be tied. Always willing to help, his eyes instantly surveyed the wagon bed for a rope.

"Sorry, Tall Spruce, it was only a figure of speech. I was asking Ethan if there were any other jobs to complete before we left for the river." The

Indian gave Harry a queer look and shook his head at the strange way of communicating. "Barmy, the horses," Harry said, smacking his forehead with the palm of his hand. "Another idiotic gesture that must surely seem odd to my Ponkapoag friend," he muttered.

Harry and Tall Spruce walked in the direction of the horses. The four weary drays snorted and shook their heads, communicating that a change of environment would be to their liking. They guided the horses to the watering troughs, then walked them to the wagon, noting that McGinty and his toadies remained sprawled in the dirt, never budging at the racket that came from hitching the horses. "Should we throw a bucket of water on them or leave them to roast in the sun?" asked Ethan, not knowing that Big Ham had the same idea as he came around with a bucket.

"Might make us look like an unsociable sort if customers come upon drunkards lying about. This is a respectable establishment, after all," claimed Big Ham, jokingly, looking around for a temporary lodging for the boozehounds.

"You fellers better be on yer way. Joel has the wagon filled to the brim. Best make hay whilst the sun's a shinin'," Captain Zeke advised the Mulberry Men. "Don't you have a care o'er yer minnow? He's in good hands with my brothers," he laughed, wiping the sweat from his face. As a farewell gesture, he turned toward the wagon, removed his hat, and bowed, then walked to Dorcas' cottage.

Tall Spruce resumed his position at the front of the wagon, checking the canvas bag for any movement, while Ethan remained cautious and sat next to the wagon gate just in case the Minnow might play them for a fool by pretending to sleep. Some of the burden he was carrying was beginning to feel lighter, but not until he was positive the Minnow was tucked into a safe spot on the sloop would the pressure be lifted. He carried the responsibility of this entire scheme. Should anything go awry, he would face repercussions. Harry called out a giddy-up to the team of anxious horses, ready to gallop, happy to kick up some dust on the road to the river.

The Connecticut River was the lifeblood of the towns of Enfield, Suffield, and Bloomfield, among other towns, giving landowners, merchants, and artisans the opportunity to develop their wealth due not only to the river's resources but to the rich and fertile lands stretching for miles on either side. Transportation along the river allowed for an assortment of vessels to ship their products north to Quebec and south to the Long Island Sound by schooners and ships belonging to merchants who traded back and forth to colonies in the West Indies. With all the wealth came mansions and plantations built along the riverfront and towns full of specialty shops, apothecaries, shipyards, churches, and schools.

Harry slowed the horses as he approached the river, awestruck at the scene before him; a virtual mecca of grandeur lay in the distance. When he studied at Oxford, he had a taste of the grandness of the fashionable addresses while visiting London and Westminster, where homes of the royal family stood. Although the mansions standing along the immense river did not, by any means, come close to the architectural styles of Hampton Court or Burghley House, he was more impressed that such structures even existed, having never visited this area of Connecticut River Valley.

Ethan stood in the wagon bed shielding his eyes from the bright skylight with his hand, capturing the same view as Harry of miniature palaces surrounded by neat green lawns and orchards, but he focused particularly on the anchored sloops, one being The Jeremiah. There he stood, the big, proud seaman looking toward Ethan and Tall Spruce, waving his captain's hat, inviting them to drive to his dock.

It was a simple boat supporting one mast with one mainsail and one jib sail, *the fastest boat on the water*, as was rumored. A crew of six men was hauling the merchandise from the wagon to the twenty-foot sloop's hold while Joel ordered specific directions on how to carefully stack the cargo. He was very particular about the handling of his customer's merchandise, making sure it was delivered in excellent condition. He staked his reputation on keeping the customer satisfied. He and his brother Micah were sticklers at that point. Reliable service made it easier to charge slightly more above the going rate.

Harry hoped this would be the final encounter with the Minnow, thinking at the moment about the man's fate, recognizing the authority he and Ethan had discharged in assigning the man to a life of penury. *If Father discovers my part in this, would he ever forgive me?* he thought.

He heard a faint rumble of thunder and glanced upward at a mostly blue sky speckled with puffy white clouds, with the exception of the gray-rimmed cloud that his eyes fixed on for a moment. *Could it be an omen?* he wondered gloomily. Now, he felt nauseous, doubting his decision to go forward with the plan. *Was it right for me to be the judge of right and wrong, to play God?*

On the other hand, was it wrong to defend his property? How about the victims who have suffered from the scurrilous actions of the Minnow and the Shark: threats made toward his family during these precarious times with the British, the near-death attacks on Boston citizens, the stalking and brashness perpetrated on his cousin Josie?

Tall Spruce spoke of the way the two had ravaged the forest, broken crockery lying about, the disrespect for the game evidenced by the brutal ways they slaughtered their food, and the thievery of chickens, goats, and produce from his neighbor's farms. Where is the law that would prohibit such actions of two men who sought to lay waste to the land, then move on to other areas to play havoc with people's lives? Is this what the British were about, controlling the lives of hardworking men and women with the aim to reduce them to peasants? His grandsire had expounded for years to him and his brother Jake a few history lessons of the suffering caused by monarchies to its people. Millions of whom were seeking refuge at this very moment in these colonies, separated by the sea.

Harry searched the sky for the gray-rimmed cloud, replaced now by a puffy white cloud, while he was occupied with reorganizing all the reasons for banishing the Minnow from the colonies. More convinced than ever, he had made the right decision.

Tall Spruce slipped the potion bottle to Joel, giving terse instructions on mixing it with a cup of ale. One more dose would guarantee the Minnow's unconscious state of mind and body until he was transported to Micah's schooner in Long Island Sound. The Indian had completed his mission, and he was satisfied with the results. Now, he was ready to move on with the next part of the journey, and a little sleep wouldn't hurt either.

The Mulberry Men shook hands with Joel and expressed their thanks to him as he stood on the deck of The Jeremiah. Just like his brother, Captain Zeke, always good-natured, tending to business in a responsible way and confident in the tasks he was proud to accept. His sloop was a tribute to his teacher, Jeremiah Penrose.

Chapter 14

Retaliation

June 7, 1774, Mulberry Farm

The Big Englishman lay in his usual warm dug-out dirt bed under a huge elm tree, sleeping soundly. Dreams scattered through his head of a more indulgent and civilized time—goose on a spit, roasted potatoes, brandied peaches, cups of chocolate, violins playing while he delighted in the comfort of flavorful food and the pleasure of a beautiful woman sitting across the table from him.

The constant sound of water rushing through the stream nearby reminded him of the narrow creek that flowed through the property called Pinehurst, his home in Kent, England. Thoughts of his childhood entered his dreamlike sleep, recalling times when he was in the care of the estate's butler, Thadeus Thorndike.

The estate's butler wore many hats, being the caretaker of the property that afforded the services of a cook and a housekeeper. Additionally, he managed the daily routines of the Earl of Pinehurst's only child, William Berkeley Granger, who, on most days when the weather permitted, accompanied young William to the creek that gave him many hours of discovery and satisfaction—fishing, searching for frogs, and throwing pebbles.

Half asleep now, his mouth watered for the bass he and Thadeus would often grill while on the bank of the creek, enjoying the informalness of the adventure. He smiled, thinking of the more pleasant times of his life while under the butler's care.

His back began to ache as he lay in the scooped-out dirt and leaf bed, built purposely close to the creek for cooking, cleaning, and watering his horse. William raised his head, wondering if the horse had remained tethered to a tree in the distance. The beast was definitely incapacitated. The last time he rode the reddish brown horse, he noticed a halting in its gait, thinking it best not to push his luck. He allowed the bay to rest, lacking any knowledge of how to prepare the horse's leg to heal.

It was the second horse he had stolen since he arrived in Boston, this one belonging to an unfortunate young man who appeared to be delivering circulars on his route into Lexington. The horse reared and threw the man when he was spooked by the red flowing cape William wore as he jumped from behind a boulder. He briefly thought the delivery man might have hit his head on a rock, but his main concern was hightailing it before anything about him could be identified.

The man and his companion's escape to the Blue Hills was their only possible way to stay alive if they could endure rough living through the icy rains of late winter and early spring. They had no choice since they had no money and few provisions. Having worn out their welcome in Boston taverns, making their bed under hay stacks on Lexington farms, and stealing hams from smokehouses. Word had traveled fast in the small town about the vagrants. Truly, they were outlaws.

William and his traveling companion, Henry Wyatt, quickly exited the crowded Boston to abide deep in the woods. Although frustrating in the beginning, it became a matter of survival. Their refined tastes for rich delicacies experienced in Paris were now limited to their dreams. They had not a single shilling between them.

Under gray winter skies, leafless trees filled the forest. Squirrels and rabbits remained hidden in their shelters, making do with their stored-up morsels. There were plenty of farms in Stoughton. Hunger pushed the men to doggedly survey the livestock of certain vulnerable farms with the intent to bag two or three chickens at a time and perhaps cart off a goat on those wintry days. With little effort, their bellies remained full. "All that's missing is a stout to wash it down," Henry said to his partner, who, with a malicious grin, nodded in response.

The warmth of the spring season brought on a more promising landscape. As a boy, William had learned how to create snares for trapping small animals, thanks to Thadeus, who had taken an interest in teaching the boy skills for survival. The forests in Stoughton were no different from those surrounding Pinehurst estate in Kent. Rabbits, squirrels, and wild turkeys were easy to trap. "If we had some powder and shot, we could use that musket to shoot a deer. At times, when I'm sleeping, I'm certain there's a deer eating berries in yon thicket," William said, looking uncertain. "Perhaps it's all in my dreams, Henry."

On that springtime morning, when pesky squirrels twitching their gray tails sat on the top of the big elm, dropping hazelnut shells, he was satisfied that his morning dreams had concluded. Reluctantly, he pulled his heavy body out of the rutted ground that he called his bed and walked to the creek to wash the sleep from his face. William was positive he smelled coffee cooking, so he called out to Henry, believing he had started a fire and begun the breakfast meal, subconsciously reliving his morning dream. No answer came.

He scoped out the serene landscape—the stolen horse remained tethered to the same tree, munching what little grass he could find. The ashes from last night's fire were cold and undisturbed. Henry's bedding under his lean-to lay in an unkempt fashion, which was out of form for the man.

William called out for him. "Perhaps he's at one of the farms, lifting a chicken or, better yet, stealing a side of salt pork from some rebel farmer's smokehouse," he muttered. Remembering happier times when the cook at Pinehurst prepared smoked bacon along with a plate of eggs to satisfy his hefty appetite.

He started the fire. A mug of coffee would wake him and clear his mind enough to focus on the day's problems. Not having a horse was his latest irritation. His scheme for taking over the Mulberry Farm property showed little promise at this time.

He looked around for the familiar metal pot Henry had used to collect water. *He must have left it at the creek*, William thought as he walked toward the rushing water. Smelling the coffee in his mind took him back to the day he and Henry had ridden their stolen horses south of Boston to Stoughton in the early spring. The March winds carried the invigorating scent of roasted barley mixed with the tang of hops to their heads. The Boston tavern keeper had said, "You won't find a better-tasting beer than Mulberry Farm's." To his surprise, they passed by the very farm that brewed the famous beer. The wheels in the black-hearted men's minds began turning. They were just low-down and desperate enough to eliminate the Randolph family, even if it meant murder or an accidental conflagration.

Since the two were wanted by the law in certain counties in England and the city of Paris, they had little choice but to remain in the colonies. What was left of their money was a few coins won from dice games, enough to buy a haunch of venison, coffee, and corn meal from a street vendor in the city. The two rode their stolen horses carrying packs loaded with the bare essentials to Stoughton, intending to set up camp and live rough while they finalized their plans to shanghai the owners of the brewery.

The metal pot was revealed when a ray of sun flashed upon the silver metal, causing William to pause and blink. The force from the rushing water had caused it to become wedged between two rocks. His little inside voice spoke clearly: *Henry is gone. He's disappeared. He's not returning.* William returned to the lean-to, searching for evidence. Henry's brown leather bag containing his shirt and breeches lay hidden under the blanket, his cloak tossed to the side. *Why would he leave and not take this?* his persistent little voice asked.

Seeking more proof, William climbed the hill to the road and spotted the red berries on the holly bushes, the sounds of birds tittering about in the vines. He saw no signs of wagon tracks or horses' hooves. The truth came to the Shark. *They've taken him away*, he thought. He recalled the two men at the Mulberry entrance gates, sitting atop their fine horses, holding pistols over their laps and barely revealing themselves amongst the leafy mulberry trees. "They attacked Henry while he was filling the pot for morning coffee," he said loudly, causing the birds to go quiet. He searched for footprints but to no avail. A wave of nausea engulfed him. He staggered down the hill.

It didn't matter that his stomach was empty. His urgent desire for coffee vanished. He desired answers and revenge more than sustenance. This recent calamity was the biggest blow to his plans since his arrival at Boston Harbor and would prove to be his ruin. Disbelief enveloped him.

He looked down at the knife in his boot. His only weapon besides his body's savage strength. He yearned to hurt the first person he encountered. His sinewy form had placed him in a separate class from small, lanky, thin-faced Henry. William had always been amazed at his own strength, attributing it to his Viking bloodline. He was confident he could pit himself against two large men and come out on top, particularly the two colonial rebels he had encountered at Mulberry Farm.

He cursed the Randolphs and their high-minded methods of operating a brewing business on property that he believed belonged to the British government, allowing them the same standard of wealth afforded by Parliament's lords. "We have no business with you," the rebel had stated. *You'll have business with me today*, thought William, staring into nothingness. *You are nothing more than swine, just like Hancock and Adams and all the other high-minded rabble.*

Sitting on a dead log in his usual place by the diminished fire, a steely glitter came into his eyes, seeing the face of the Earl of Pinehurst—his father, the drunkard, the cheater, the most despicable person he had ever known. The derelict condition of the estate, the physical and mental abuse he had cast upon his frail mother, putting her through the torment that ended in her death. The accident that had taken Thadeus from him. "When I needed him the most!" he cried. His father's refusal to summon a physician who could have saved the butler's life, choosing instead to abandon him by escaping to the woods on the pretense of hunting game. William's rage boiled, strong and out of control. His light blue eyes stared at his strong hands. He clinched them into fists, and his arm muscles flexed. He sat on the tree stump, devising his plan of attack.

June 7, 1774

Lenora had risen at dawn. Gazing out the window of her upstairs chamber, she had a distant view of the malting house to the northeast, which remained unfinished, but she was hopeful. Thomas Crafts had arrived the day before to help Jacob keep an eye on the property. But Thomas wasn't one to stand about and wait on intruders. He promised he would finish hammering in the shingles today.

The day before and out of necessity, Harry, Ethan, and Tall Spruce had changed course, switching from their part of the construction work to prepare for the trip to Enfield and afterward to Springfield. Thomas assured them he would start work on the shed the following morning. With that decision made, the Mulberry Men spent what was left of the day preparing for their journey to Enfield, Connecticut.

The three men left before daybreak to make their way to Whales' Tale. *No telling how long that delivery will take*, Lenora thought. Ethan had described to her the unusual tavern and its proprietor, leaving her shaking her head in disbelief. "Captain Zeke always has just one more story to tell," Ethan said, explaining why he allowed extra time to visit when he made deliveries to the Whales' Tale.

The sun peeked through the thick, lush trees on the mountainside just beyond the creek. She caught a glance of the apple orchard now showing its bright green colors; the white blossoms spent, blowing where the winds scattered them. Hundreds of apples would grow through the summer, ripening and ready to be harvested in the fall. She shook her head, bringing her mind to the present. The desire for coffee and corncakes with pear marmalade urged her downstairs.

She heard Jacob's footsteps toward the library. He had complained to her about the nagging mountain of paperwork stacked on his desk. Even though working on the malting shed in the cool morning was a temptation, he resigned himself to join Thomas later. At the moment, he was nervous about some pressing deadlines. Thankfully, the musket and ammunition order was settled.

"Coffee with cream?" The rich aroma instantly filled the air, mixed with the leather smells, creating the ambient effect she desired. She stood in the doorway of the library, waiting for a response from Jacob, then set the steaming mug of coffee in the safest spot she could find on the desk.

"What do you think our young men are doing at this moment?" she asked, with eyebrows raised along with a mischievous smile, her blue eyes sparkling.

"Ha-ha, I can only imagine," Jacob responded, thinking back to their disastrous nightmare of a trip to Percy Mountain. "It will do them good to get away from the farm. The Whales' Tale offers an uncommon sort of entertainment; those Penrose boys are sailors, after all! Just sorry Gray Wolf couldn't join them."

"I'm sure they will have stories to tell. As for Gray Wolf, he's better off staying close to Naomi, and he knows it. She was in a panic for a while. Not positive he would survive." Lenora shared her sorrow with Jacob and shook her head in dismay. "I'm off to the garden if you need me."

"I thought we agreed that you and Naomi would remain inside today? These Englishmen are outlaws, desperate men who don't mind shedding blood," Jacob looked at his pretty wife, cocking his head to the side, anticipating her response.

She walked to his side, laying her arm across his shoulders, pressing the side of her face against his. "Thomas has a view of the garden while he's atop the malting shed, and I'll keep a loaded pistol nearby. Naomi is sure to be in possession of a knife. That should ensure my protection. What do you think?" She asked with raised brows.

Jacob shook his head, then shrugged his shoulders. "I think you're taking a risk, but I'm just a husband who cares about his wife."

She kissed his cheek and walked out of the room.

Lenora walked to the end of the scullery where drying baskets and small ladles, made to her requirements by the blacksmith in Stoughton, hung on the wall. Shelves, built by Poppi ages ago, lined part of the wall, holding small glass jars and crockery of various sizes ordered from

England and Holland. Most were treasured vessels handed down by family members. These were used for liniments, syrups, salves, dried herbs, and spices. She took a mental inventory of the well-stocked pantry, tied on her sun bonnet, and walked through the dewy grass to the garden, now awash with the morning sun.

She immediately got a sense of the work ahead of her—digging out weeds and managing the slug population would be her biggest challenges, as it was for all gardeners, she asserted. She loosened the damp soil with the hoe, catching the fresh smells of earth.

Naomi had mapped out the timeline with Lenora for harvesting certain herbs to preserve their full value. She would kick herself if she missed the opportunity to gather St. John's Wort at its peak. Of all the herbs she grew, this one was the most useable. The relief it gave from muscle and joint pain was beyond measure when it was made into a liniment. For the inevitable cuts, burns, and wounds, her family relied on the salve made from this particular herb. She had sent Josie and Minnie home with a full basket.

Rays of sunshine highlighted the bright yellow buds and flowers of the precious herb, clearly standing the tallest and showiest among the oregano and parsley. She pinched the fully ripened and freshly opened flowers and buds with her thumb and forefinger. The verdict lay in the red stain on her fingers. She knew today was the best day to harvest the all-important St. John's Wort.

In the distance, she saw Naomi walking off her front porch towards the garden, adjusting her sun bonnet. "Time to get to work—we have a long day ahead of us."

Gray Wolf smelled dawn before he saw any light. He awoke feeling some purpose, but his brain had not yet discerned what that purpose entailed or which direction he should take. *No reason to brood over it*, he thought. It would happen naturally. The morning mist settled on his hair and skin as he walked to the creek, casting his eyes toward the dark woods. He marveled at the obscurity of the forest before it became alive with the sounds of birds and animals. The sky had turned a slight gray, showing a sketchy outline of potential clouds waiting for the morning sun to display its fullness.

He had relished the comfort of a soft bed, hot tea, and his aunt's hearty food, sometimes feeling like an old chief who expected to be served. Indeed, the nurturing he received from Naomi was the only reason he could walk outside on his own this morning, starting to feel human again.

His body was mending, giving him the freedom to begin considering the first action he could legally attempt, as long as it was approved by his aunt Naomi. She had been the master of his life for *how long has it been now?* He tried to calculate the days. His mind recalled the fierce eyes of the cat that caused the predicament he had sustained. He shook his head to remove the depressing thoughts. *I wonder if my cousins have clubbed the English varmint as yet*, rubbing the back of his neck, knowing full well the strength of his cousin Tall Spruce's right arm.

Gray Wolf walked around to the front porch and sat down with his back supported by the outside wall of the front room belonging to Ethan. He recalled moments when he hated the room. Yes, it had been his sanctuary, his healing space, his place to stare at the moon through the tall window. When he could sleep no more, he pondered his life, losing himself in the traditions of his people, matters of right versus wrong, the restlessness he felt because he was too weak to stand without support. Some nights when he woke, he tried to remember the details of how he had arrived at this place surrounded by walls and the smells of liniment and teas. He yearned to sleep under a star-filled sky, breathing the earthy smells.

He picked up the bow lying under the window. The same bow Tall Spruce set on top of his wounded body as he and Ethan carried him down the mountain. The quiver holding the ten arrows he always carried. One by one, he placed them on the porch floor, examining each arrow's pointed end. He removed the flat oblong stone that fit securely in his left hand, running his thumb over the smooth surface. He began sharpening the arrowheads. It was an action Aunt Naomi would approve, he thought.

Enjoying the peaceful sounds coming from the tall elm trees shading the side of the house, relishing the slight breeze across his face as he went about his task. He felt a sting of jealousy hearing the predictable sounds of Thomas Crafts hammering nails into the rooftop shingles. He longed to feel the satisfaction of the work he would like to be doing at this very moment.

Naomi stepped up to the porch, smiled, and nodded at him, satisfied that he was interested in accomplishing something useful. "Beautiful morning. Just going in to start a pot of stew. I left Lenora in the hot sun digging herbs," she reported.

His body was getting stiff, and his back and neck ached from hunching over his work. He carefully stood, his hand using the window ledge for support. "Wouldn't hurt to give the arrows a test," he said as he grabbed his bow and two arrows, walking slowly toward the yard in front of the house.

Gray Wolf heard the words coming from an unfamiliar voice. Instinct prompted him to stop, looking from side to side regarding the sounds coming from the garden ahead of him. "Where are the Randolph men? They know the whereabouts of my associate." The big man demanded with a strong English accent. "I'll cut your throat if you scream. I have no patience for the likes of you." Gray Wolf's heightened sense of danger identified this man as the Shark.

He saw the wide back of the tall blond-haired man, who was wearing filthy breeches and a grayish linen shirt. The man's sleeves were rolled up, showing his bronzed left arm wrapped around the front of Lenora's neck, his mouth at her ear. His right hand held a knife pointed at the right side of her lower back.

Her heart was pounding. "I've been working in the garden all—" she said as the fiend tightened his hold around her neck. "Who are you, and what do you want?" *Where did I lay that pistol?* she asked herself.

Without hesitation, Gray Wolf crouched as far as his body would allow. He moved into position on his side of the well to shield himself if the arrow missed; otherwise, if his aim was accurate, it would pierce the man's right buttock. He had not raised his bow for the last two weeks, uncertain if he had the strength to pull the arrow back with enough force for it to enter the man's flesh. He stood, using the well house to steady himself, wiping his sweating right hand on the side of his buckskin pants.

Possessing the desire to save a good friend from a gruesome death along with the same physical strength he exerted when he killed the catamount, he aimed and pulled back the arrow, familiarly brushing the right side of his calm face. He let the arrow fly. The devil yelled, "AARRGG!!!" as he collapsed to the ground. His knife dropped from his hand. The Shark lay moaning face down on the freshly loosened dirt. The rising sun's rays shone down on the defeated man.

Gray Wolf walked cautiously towards the garden to move Lenora to a safer place. Lenora, shock filling her perspiring, reddened face, reached for Gray Wolf's hand as she pulled herself up. They stumbled out of the garden together holding each other for support.

Jacob, antsy to be outside working with Thomas on the malting shed, plopped a slouch hat on his head before he walked out the back door from the kitchen. He immediately caught the most unusual sight of his wife and their infirmed friend clutching one another, intent on settling themselves on the bench, seeking shade under the elm tree. Fear struck his mind and body. Realizing they were both in distress, he ran to their aide. "What's amiss? You're hurt!"

The two survivors shook their heads and remained unable to speak to Jacob's question. Gray Wolf answered by tilting his head in the direction of the garden. Jacob touched Lenora's face and quickly appraised her condition, searching for blood or a wound. Assured that Lenora was not in any immediate danger, he ran towards the garden, intersecting with Thomas Crafts, who was following Jacob's lead.

The two men arrived at the garden to witness the hulkish man walking slowly and painfully to the area where he had entered the property: a clearing where the mulberry trees ended and the forest began. Thomas gestured a move to pursue the Big Englishman, but Jacob held up his hand to stop him and said, "No, let him go. I do not want a confrontation with the man. He created this conflict. Let him reckon with it." Thomas Crafts pursed his lips and nodded his head in agreement. The two men stopped by the well, pulled up a bucket of fresh water, and picked up two ladles, then walked to the bench under the elm tree, overcome with concern and questions.

Jacob ushered Lenora to the *chaise longue* in the drawing room by the front window. A place where, under normal circumstances, she would often relax by the front window to savor the cool breeze, read, and catch a nap. Naomi placed a pillow under her feet, thinking Lenora might feel faint, but more so she could look over her upper body for cuts and bruises. She smiled at Lenora and patted her arm, reassuring their close bond. "Don't worry about the St. John's herb. There is still time to make our medicines," promised Naomi.

Gray Wolf sat in a chair close to Lenora, occasionally looking her way, keenly aware of how close she had come to a horrible death. The intense emotion he felt when he saw what the powerful man could have done to the small, innocent woman made him shudder. *What if I had remained on the porch sharpening arrows?* he thought. *She would be dead at this moment.*

Naomi gave Gray Wolf a wet towel to cool his face and arms, discerning the physical and mental stress it had taken on his body and mind.

"Can either of you talk about what happened, or would you rather we discuss it later?" Jacob stooped down to meet Lenora's eyes, hoping to read an honest answer, then looked at Gray Wolf's face.

Lenora spoke, "At this moment, I am overwhelmed with so many emotions." She turned her head to Gray Wolf. "You saved my life today. I have no idea why you were near the well and, more than that, why you carried your bow. I recall feeling so isolated in the garden, knowing I was trapped and fearing I would never see my family again." Tears came to Jacob's eyes as he held her hand, garden dirt caked under her fingernails. "I will speak to more of the details when I have the presence of mind. Still, it all remains veiled in obscurity."

Lenora knew she would work through her emotions in the days ahead, calculating how she might have prevented such an incident or if it was even possible to do so. Thankful to be alive. She blotted the dirt and sweat off her face and neck with Naomi's wet towel. At that moment, her thoughts turned to her garden, wondering if the big monster had trampled over her prized herbs. That would set her teeth on edge. *I hope*

I have enough glass bottles for the liniment, she thought. Looking at her fingers, still showing the red juice from St. John's Wort, she managed a smile.

Poppi's eyes puddled with tears as he sat watching his daughter-in-law. "We will wait, Lenora. Let's be thankful that our dear friend Gray Wolf's natural inclination to shoot his bow happened at this most critical time. Through the years, we have seen several attempts to confiscate Mulberry Farm, some ending in loss of life, unfortunately. The Lord above has certainly preserved us today."

Gray Wolf's reticence would only permit him to communicate the obvious to Poppi, known to him as Chief Randolph. "I believed I was able to walk the distance to the trees and try my strength with the bow. I heard the Englishman's death words to Aunt Lenora. He meant to shed blood."

The family's eyes turned toward the doorway, hearing heavy footsteps and cups clinking against one another. "I thought we could do with some tea." Thomas Crafts glanced toward Lenora, who smiled and nodded her head in consent while thinking it comical that this bear of a man had no qualms serving tea to a roomful of men and women.

The affable Thomas served Lenora and Naomi first, followed by a fragrant cup of English tea to Gray Wolf. "Friend, I would like to commend you on your excellent bow shot, given your weakened condition. It takes a high degree of accuracy to shoot an arrow into the meaty part of a man's leg!"

Gray Wolf groaned inwardly, sipped his tea, and sneered into his cup. *I'm sure I aimed at the man's right buttock!* A feeling of gloom settled over him, wondering how long it would take for his strength to return to its fullness.

Ethan's attempt to sleep was useless. He closed his eyes instead, reliving the events of the morning. The excitement of accomplishing the mammoth task of deporting the Minnow dominated his thoughts. He smiled. "It helps to know the right people."

The wagon joggled up the dusty road toward Springfield, the sun gradually reaching its full height, strongly bearing down on the

Mulberry Men. Before they left Whales' Tale, Harry suggested they stop at a tavern in Springfield. They had eaten the ginger cakes and salty ham prepared by Mrs. Penrose and washed it down with the last of the cider. Now, their bellies craved something hearty and filling. Their day wasn't over yet. They had been pushing themselves since before dawn to complete their tasks.

A plate of roasted chicken and corn pones with honey had been on Harry's mind since early morning. Of course, they would have to eat in the wagon since Indians were barred from any establishment serving beer and ale. Even though Ethan was half-Indian, it was hard to identify him as one. With his pointed English nose and brown skin, he could pass for a farmer who worked in the fields. His thoughts turned suddenly to the fight behind Whales' Tale earlier, provoked by the three churlish yokels who thought they could whip Tall Spruce. He wondered if they had ever done a day's work.

They sat outside the Howling Hound tavern, finishing off three chickens and a bag of corn pones, washed down with several pints of ale. Although inferior to Mulberry ale, it slaked their thirst. "This drink is sour," announced Tall Spruce. Tired of the taste, he spewed the drink in the dirt. "I prefer barley water over such."

"Uh-huh, they failed to roast the barley seed to the proper temperature," Ethan spoke casually with knowledge of his profession, busily gnawing the remaining flesh off a chicken bone. Harry and Tall Spruce, enamored with his instant reply, stared at him in wonder. "Chief Randolph has taught me well," he spoke confidently with a shrug of his right shoulder.

A cool breeze stirred the trees, offering the Mulberry Men some relief from the muggy day. The pressure of the morning's ventures was behind them now, relishing the freedom to move on to the next chore at the cooper's and direct their thoughts on the malting shed construction.

Tall Spruce spoke his mind, "The Shark, as you say, will be cross when he finds the Minnow has fled. Will he make trouble for your family?"

"To be honest, I think he will try anything. He's a desperate man," Harry offered. "There are various ways he could enter Mulberry Farm and take any one of us hostage to get what he wants. Two things are certain: he will not set fire to the property, as that would defeat his purpose, and the idea of him colluding with the British army is a lie. He is a man wanted by the law for crimes committed in Boston and England. The army will dismiss him as a joker. He could potentially be sent to London to be tried as a criminal. John Adams has advised Father on the matter."

"We're not exactly without sin," Ethan exclaimed. "Heaven forbid that Uncle Jacob and Aunt Lenora discover that we just sent the Minnow down the river. He deserved it the more I think about it." He pondered that thought for a moment. "Who knows, they might praise us for our transgressions!"

While the Mulberry Men filled their bellies with hot food, the four gray horses were not without a meal. They stood expectantly, stamping their hooves as Harry readied their feed bags and fastened them over the horses' muzzles, giving them the grain they desired. Now they were rested and strong, ready to continue the journey up the road to collect the newly built Mulberry kegs from Cyrus Floyd.

One could smell Cyrus Floyd's barrel-making business half a mile before viewing the giant sign advertising the various wooden vessels he constructed on his property. The heavy smell of fresh-cut ash and hickory wood strips penetrated the air as they set soaking in massive water troughs under a pole barn, waiting to be processed as barrel staves. This, coupled with the dizzying aroma of whiskey, caused the team of horses to snort and whinny; the unfamiliar, pungent smells made them anxious.

Harry drove the wagon toward a stand of elm trees and drew the horses to a halt, then pulled up the brake, figuring the wind would blow the acrid smells in the opposite direction. Seeing their agitation, Ethan and Tall Spruce jumped hastily out of the wagon, placed their hands under the horses' noses, and spoke to them in low voices, hoping the technique would serve to calm their nerves.

Ethan opened the heavy door constructed of thick-cut vertical timbers, bolted together with horizontal boards that held the solid thing together. Cyrus was at his work table, attaching handles to an assortment of wooden pails. "You driving some excitable horses today? Sounds as if they're spooked!" The cooper was a heavy-set man, sporting a neatly trimmed gray beard, making up for the loss of hair on his bald head. The senior Mr. Floyd sat on a stool at the table, trimming barrel staves, helping his son as he could regardless of his bent fingers and frail arms.

Cyrus' son, a young man about Ethan's age, stood at another work table stationed at the opposite end of the rectangular room, pounding the softened wood strips with a mallet. The smell of wood and tar was overwhelming. Which would explain why the back door stood open, allowing the breeze to soften the thick air. He held up his hand as Ethan caught his eye and walked toward him. "Your oak kegs are ready; same ones we use for whiskey, as you requested. I drank some of your prime stout at Whales' Tale last evening. Fine taste. Goes down smoothly."

"I see you've installed some heavy doors on the building. Have a break-in, did you?" Ethan changed the subject, directing his observation to the three men.

Cyrus glanced at his son. "We have since the last time you stopped in. A big fair-haired feller broke down the door while we were in here, working. He and his skinny mate pulled their knives on us, swearing they would slit my father's gullet if I didn't give them all the whiskey I had. Said he smelled it coming down the road." He pointed his thumb toward the empty cabinet where he usually kept his home brew and shrugged his shoulders in regret. "Mean folks all around looking fer trouble, and it ain't gonna get any better from what I see." He sighed heavily and shook his head. "I've started keeping a loaded pistol nearby, kinda out of sight," he said.

Ethan chose not to reply to the man's unfortunate break-in, knowing it was probably the work of the Shark and the Minnow. He had had his fill of the two outlaws for today.

Ethan and young Cyrus carried the kegs toward the wagon where the horses had quieted now, feeling safe with the Mulberry Men rubbing their necks. Tall Spruce met the men halfway, grabbing up four of the heavy kegs at a time, placing them in the same racks that had held the full kegs for the Penrose brothers. He looked up at the deep blue sky, quickly filling with white clouds, some rimmed with gray edges, predicting rain before they would enter the Mulberry Farm gates late in the day. He jumped up in the wagon, taking his same place in the back.

Worn out and anxious to get home to put the four horses to pasture, Harry seized the reins and shouted a hiya and a resounding, "Let's get outta here!" Ethan assumed a reclining position in the wagon's back, fully expecting to nap now with his mission accomplished, knowing for certain Stoughton would be the next stop. The end of a precarious journey.

The rain began with little dots sprinkling Ethan's face. Moving his head from side to side, thinking he was under attack by flies, the aggravation eventually pulled him out of his deep sleep. The wagon and horses kicked up the dry dust now, causing both men to choke and sneeze. Tall Spruce, always observant, sat in his corner and stared at the wooded surroundings as the wagon bumped along the rutted road, jiggling his body and the long skinny braids hanging around his face. The sun peeked around the puffy white clouds, dismissing the prospect of pouring rain for the time being.

As they approached Stoughton's farms, Ethan breathed in the familiar fecund earth smells, anticipating a dip in the deep end of the creek behind the house as he noticed the brown dust collecting on his tunic. The Grimes boys always planted corn in the fields at the front of their property, which seemed odd to him. Their house and outbuildings could vaguely be detected as Harry slowed the wagon driving around the curve. The neat furrowed field showed tiny green spikes of sprouted corn against the dark brown dirt. Ethan recalled how Naomi always raved about the fine taste of corn the Grimes' farm produced. Summer solstice was drawing near, he reckoned.

The Mulberry Men removed the anxious horses' tack and released them to the paddock. Ozzie was busy filling the water troughs. "A bonny June day," he announced to the men. "I'll give the beasts their rub downs once they run out their kinks. Ye men look lak yer ready fer a dip in the creek."

They walked to the well for a ladle of water to drink and another to pour over their dusty heads. As Harry drank the cool water, he looked askance at the unkempt garden, giving Ethan's side a jab with his elbow.

"Something's amiss here," Harry said, pointing to the crushed plants and the broken garden gate. Unknown to the Mulberry Men, the Englishman's presence had startled Lenora as she had begun clearing her weedy garden.

"A bear searching for food, perhaps?" Tall Spruce asked assumingly.

Harry felt fear rushing through his body, sensing there had been trouble, almost sure it wasn't caused by a bear. He rushed through the scullery, then through the kitchen, and caught the smell of cold ashes in the kitchen fireplace. No evidence that food had been cooked during the day. "Och," he groaned. "What's happened here? Father, Mother, where are you?" he yelled, panic-stricken.

"We're in the drawing room," Jacob spoke loudly, knowing Harry would think it strange since the room was seldom used but on special occasions and Lenora's late afternoon sanctuary.

He saw Lenora lounging on the chaise by the open window. "Mother, are you alright?" he asked nervously. The air in the room was warm but tolerable. She held out her hand to him as he bent down to kiss her cheek. "Have you seen the condition of the garden? I thought you may have suffered an accident with the gate door broken as it is." Jacob watched the scene from his chair, between mother and son, aware of a certain harmonious understanding they shared. He did not interfere. Confident that Lenora would convey to her son the explanation she desired.

"I'm fine, maybe a little shaken. We have had some excitement today," she said assertively. Seeing the alarm in his face, she cupped his freckled cheek with her hand. "Mr. Adams was right. The Englishman came here with threats, intending to harm anyone who stood in his way. He used me as his hostage." Harry closed his eyes, consumed with regret for his part in the kidnapping. He squeezed his mother's hand with affection.

"If it had not been for Gray Wolf, I would not be sitting here feeling the love and security of my family. The man claimed we knew the whereabouts of his associate. I tried to explain that I knew nothing, but he would not listen. He continued to swear that we were thieves, building on stolen land. Then, by the grace of God, he dropped his knife and fell to the ground. Gray Wolf rescued me. He saved my life!"

"Is the man dead?" Harry asked, hoping her answer was yes. She shook her head no. *In that case, he's held up in the woods nursing his wound, planning his next attack*, thought Harry.

Jacob reassured Lenora and Harry, "I don't know how far he could have made it into the woods. Gray Wolf's arrow went in deep. He's going to have the devil of a time removing it from the back of his leg, his upper thigh, that is." *Wait til Josiah hears about this*, he thought.

Lenora sat up on the chaise. "I have to get up and get busy. Since I cannot work in the garden, I will make a pie or a cake, anything to take my mind off this horrid person. Help me up, Harry."

"You should take care, Lenora. I'm not expecting you to pick up where you left off this morning," Jacob gently squeezed her arm, looking at her with caring eyes.

"I cannot allow this murderous fiend to take possession of my world, and neither should you," Lenora demanded to Jacob as she walked out of her safe spot in the drawing room. "Harry, would you be a dear and bring me a crock of cream from the springhouse?"

Jacob shook his head at his feisty wife and closed the window, quickly scanning the front of the property. "I guess I'll get the coffee started."

Ethan caught up with Harry when he saw him walking to the springhouse. "Gray Wolf told me the story, and Naomi added in her two cents worth, as you might expect. How is Aunt Lenora?"

"A Stoic, if there ever was one. She said she won't allow the Englishman to control her life, so she's proving her point by stirring together a cake."

"Tall Spruce wants to search the forest tomorrow morning, hoping to find the man dead, which I would like as well. We'll get an early start. Smells like rain tonight. Be over directly for cake," Ethan added as he walked toward the malting house to check on Thomas Crafts' progress. Harry grinned at Ethan's never-ending appetite for cake.

Walking in the direction of the springhouse gave Harry some brief moments to take in the beauty of the farm—the mountain, the creek, the orchards, even the original farmhouse, all extending across the spacious property, attributable to his visionary ancestors who had long since passed. A gift to their descendants to carry on the family's traditions and to remember the toil and industry of providing a family home and maintaining their enterprising brewery. *Our way of life*, he thought.

He considered the British soldiers setting up their camps in the Boston Common, Salem, Castle Island, and soon in Roxbury, no more than ten miles from Stoughton. If Parliament was not satisfied that the siege in Boston accomplished the desired effect, the reimbursement of the destroyed tea by the colony's rebels, Governor Gage would resort to capturing certain leaders, holding them accountable for their actions. This could mean a trial, possibly in London, and most likely a march to the gallows.

From discussions with his father, Harry learned the new governor was attempting to take over Boston's government affairs and retire the General Court and its officials. Of course, John Hancock secretly continued his work as president of that court, and Sam Adams continued his correspondence to New York, New Hampshire, and all of New England. All these colonies conducted their own Sons of Liberty meetings. All due to Sam Adams' management of unifying the separate colonies.

Now, talk from the neighboring farmers gave way to concerns that we would need protection from soldiers encamped below Boston Neck. Transports were regularly bringing in British soldiers, which meant Connecticut and Rhode Island would be subjected to the same sort of siege.

Harry believed it was time to set up their own militia. He heard Lexington had set up a system for mustering troops. The time had come for his Stoughton neighbors to organize. He knew he could count on Ethan but wasn't sure how his father would react to such a proposal.

His eyes looked upward, gazing at the setting sun. Harry would gladly welcome the dark sky sprinkled with millions of stars when he would finally sink into his feather mattress, closing out the events of the day. *That's just it*, he thought. The events would never end. Sooner or later, he would have to spill the beans to his parents: he colluded in drugging and kidnapping the Minnow, sorry as he was. Then sold the man to a privateer. While unbeknownst to him, his mother was being held for ransom due to his part in the shenanigans. *My mother, the most important person in my life, could have died today.*

He shuddered when he saw her garden in disarray. Twice in the same day, he regretted his part in the trip to Whales' Tale. *For all I know, the Shark may be curled up under a tree, dead to the world. He's not seeking vengeance tonight,* Harry calculated when he looked upward for the second time. Dark gray covered the sky. The bottom's about to fall out! He hurried to the house, taking care the crock of cream made it safely in the hands of his waiting mother.

When the house was finally empty and the cake demolished, leaving behind the aroma of freshly cooked coffee and the ambrosial scent of baked deliciousness, Lenora believed the day had culminated on a high note. She had welcomed Naomi and her family of tall men to her dining room because she believed she needed the diversion of playing hostess and chef. An art form she was more than capable of executing. Now, the day's events left her feeling spent and anxious for solitude. Naomi's keen perception of Lenora's perilous day had her shooing the men out the door in the pouring rain.

Harry, still feeling cautious and guilty, thought it wise to clear out the dishes and then heat water for his mother's bath, which he had promised to prepare for her when their company departed. Jacob observed his wife gazing thoughtfully suspiciously at her dutiful son, astonished at such unusual attention, but he shrugged it off as kindly gestures of care resulting from today's unusual circumstances.

When Jacob escorted her to the bathhouse and closed the door, she smiled, no longer concealing her astonishment, "I haven't received this much attention since I gave birth to Harry." She sat down on the bench, reaching down to remove her shoes and stockings, when Jacob kneeled on the floor and took hold of her hand. She got the message that Jacob was not going to allow her to turn a hand. "I'll just relax and allow you to control the rest of the bath."

He helped her into the copper tub of hot, perfumed water, allowing her the comfort of soaking while he scrubbed and massaged her small feet. Jacob gazed at Lenora's contented face and the glister of her light blue eyes—the enchantingly beautiful woman who inspired him over twenty years ago, clueless that the promise of marriage was a consideration. She stole a glance at her husband and smiled, relishing the tranquility of a hot bath and the safekeeping of her trusting husband. The burdens of the day were now relinquished to some unknown domain that Jacob would sort out. "How do you make all this work?" He asked her, catching the enticing scents of lavender. "I mean the garden, the house, and the amazing food creations?"

Enraptured by the hot, perfumed water spilling over her body, she lay in the tub soaking her long hair, recalling their trip to Paris when she and Jacob were wed, experiencing the same sensations. "Did you say something about work? I have no intention of working today, or is it night? Anyway, do you remember Paris and the little snails in the wine sauce?"

Jacob laughed. "How could I forget Paris? I do remember. But you promised we would never talk about those vile slugs again. Particularly in its edible form. I believe you called it a culinary adventure." He soaped her hair, massaging her scalp, enjoying the feel of soapy water oozing through his fingers. She slid under the bath water and rinsed. He finished by scrubbing her back with a sponge, then held out his hands to her. "Parisians indulge in some unusual fetishes," he conjectured, inspecting her freckled face.

She kissed his mouth. "Indulge me with your favorite fetish." He helped her out of the tub and wrapped her in a towel.

At that moment, he deemed her to be the most precious possession in the world.

Chapter 15

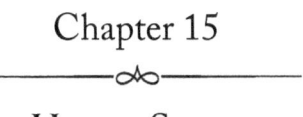

Horse Sense

June 8, 1774. Morning After the Shark

The reddish brown bay had his fill of water at the creek before he progressed slowly down the muddy road, visibly drained from hunger and heat, searching at the moment for a stand of grass to munch, preferably under a shade tree. The horse craved a sack of grain, but that had given out the week before. Nothing was more satisfying to the horse than dry oats and barley.

During the previous night's raging storm, the racket of thunder and bright streaks of lightning scared him so that he forced the rope off the tree trunk after a desperate struggle. Now, he was free to wander slowly in the early morning light and feel the cool breeze ruffle his mane. Limping down the wet road, favoring his front left leg, was all he could manage. He paused when he felt the need to rest, staring at the rows of young corn sprouts and bright green leaves twisting around wooden stakes in the nearby field. Calculating how he could manage the sloping path to get a sniff of the farmer's crops.

Before dawn, Ethan and Tall Spruce set out on foot in the direction where the Shark had exited Lenora's garden the day before. Ethan recalled Uncle Jacob saying the big man staggered to the end of the mulberry trees where a thicket of gooseberry vines began, headed in the direction of the woods across the road.

Two of the four Mulberry Men were obliged to seek out the wounded Shark and report their findings to the family. Under the circumstances, they blamed themselves for the attack on Aunt Lenora. Indeed, they were curious to see if he was dead or suffering from the arrow wound. The man deserved both punishments, but they were careful to make such judgment calls after yesterday's events.

Harry, filled with grief and guilt over the incident, slept badly during the night. He would rest later, hopefully, if his conscience would allow it. This morning, he felt compelled to make the necessary repairs to his mother's garden, particularly the broken gate. Lenora and Naomi had begun the previous morning with serious gardening plans in mind, all thwarted by the Shark's vengeful arrival.

Harry would do anything to please his mother today, handing her the moon if he could reach it. The thought of telling his parents the truth of all the reasons for traveling to Whales' Tale tavern the day before made him sick to his stomach.

Gray Wolf felt some guilt. Had he not been recovering from wounds inflicted on him by that wicked catamount two weeks prior, he would have joined the group in their shenanigans as well.

The heavy rain beating down the night before had washed away any sign of footprints the Shark would have made on the dusty road, now replaced with muddy ruts and furrows. "Reckon he walked to his camp to be close to water." Tall Spruce observed as he and Ethan continued down the road.

The bay stood in the middle of the lonesome road, eyeing the two Mulberry Men, turning his attention away from the fields. The frayed rope remained tied around his neck. Tall Spruce remembered the horse when he had seen him tethered to the tree, feeling grateful that the animal was freed to move at will. "Wise animal," noted Tall Spruce to Ethan as they walked closer to the horse.

The bay greeted the men, shaking his head up and down, then plodded feebly toward them, looking sad-eyed. Recognizing the horse's downcast spirit, the tall Indian pulled out some dried apple slices from his buckskin bag. Holding out in his hand, the horse sniffed and grasped them eagerly with his big yellow teeth, enjoying the tartness of something he had longed for. Ethan motioned Tall Spruce toward the woods. The bay nosed around the side of the road until he found a patch of grass to nibble.

The ground was perfect for a campsite. Heavily wooded at one end, looming dark and shadowed, sloping down to a grove of elms and oaks. Dark purple leaves thickly covered several clusters of wild plum trees, giving protection to springtime birds. A shallow rocky creek flowed below a hillside of thickets and saplings, deep enough in some places to immerse oneself in its coolness. Ethan and Tall Spruce crouched behind thick, spicy-smelling cedars, giving the Mulberry Men a straight-on view of the creek and access to the road. Woodland sounds permeated the cove-like hideaway.

A slight movement guided their eyes to the creek. Morning mist had gradually burned away with the onset of daylight growing brighter, revealing a lean-to and bedding, soaked through from the overnight rain, and a deserted campfire ringed with stones. The men's eyes grew wide, focused on the arrow that stood straight up from the back of the Shark's meaty thigh. They heard curses from the Shark as he belly-crawled his body to the edge of the creek's bed, dipping his hand in the water, bringing coolness to his face and mouth.

A flutter drew the Mulberry Men's attention to the woods in the distance to their right, moving cautiously through the darkness between the trees. *Probably a deer edging toward the creek*, thought Ethan. Birds and animals had remained unusually quiet this morning, sensing the presence of strangers. "That's not a deer, something taller," he whispered to Tall Spruce. "Should have brought a spyglass." He felt the outside of his pack for the shape of the spyglass to satisfy his doubt. No luck.

Emerging from the woods crept two wretched-looking Indians, shabbily dressed. The new morning light accentuated their black glossy hair. They each held a long spear, eyes drifting around the site, taking in their surroundings. They moved hesitantly down the sloping hill to flat, shady ground, hearing the sound of rushing water. *Trout*, thought the first Indian. Their nostrils caught the smell of horse dung. Trading a horse for coins or food entered their thoughts. Thieving chickens from nearby farms had become risky in the days past. Digging and eating roots sustained them. Acorns were too much trouble.

Fearing they could be trapped with no outlet for escape, one Indian crouched his body and advanced toward the lean-to while the second Indian stood guard, watching from behind a huge elm. He lifted the soaked bedding with his spear, then turned to the leather bag, hoping for anything to eat or trade. The sight of shirt and breeches whet his appetite. He hung the bag over his shoulder. He moved forward to crouch behind a rock, adjusting his eyes to the light reflecting off the water, unable to make out the hulkish object ahead. He motioned with his head to the second Indian.

Ethan and Tall Spruce remained low behind the spicy, dewy cedars, eyes set on each move the Indians made, intrigued with the drama playing out before them. Anticipating how the next scene would unfold when the curious Indians discovered the big bulk was not an animal for roasting and eating but the body of a man. Such unparalleled entertainment could never quite reach the level of the fight in the backyard of Whales' Tale tavern, but it could add up to a close second.

The Englishman's languid body lay next to the rushing creek where he had collapsed, partially obstructed by boulders large enough to sit atop. Feverish, sweating, his mind in disarray, he lay sleeping off and on, unaware that two inquisitive Indians would momentarily invade his world. Cunning as they were, they considered the opportunity that lay ten yards ahead of them.

The first Indian crouched and walked toward the man, examining the protruding arrow. His sidekick moved to a closer position, guarding and attending the surroundings, still wondering about the missing horse.

"Yenguese," said the Indian, jabbing the Shark's side with his moccasin. "Yenguese!" He sprinkled water over the big man's head, watching as it dripped down his face and in his eyes, anticipating a response. He continued the dripping process, then cautiously stepped out of the man's reach. The Shark moved his wounded leg and swept his hand over his face, getting a close look at worn-out moccasins and buckskin pants. He let out an enraged groan, compelling the Indians to take another step back. Even though the hulk could not move, his powerful-looking sinews could not be overlooked.

He wondered why the Indian hadn't jabbed him with the spear he was holding. *Perhaps all Indians don't mean to kill*, he thought. "Help," he cried, propping up the left side of his body with his arm, pointing to the arrow in his leg. He dropped back to a flat position, his energy depleted.

Ethan and Tall Spruce got the story they were after and more, with all they witnessed at the creek. But the morning heat was rising. It was time to leave. They grew tired of slapping at mosquitoes. The second Indian walked into the creek and pulled out the metal pot, indicating he would start a fire to heat water. He would make medicine for the Shark.

The search for roots and plants to make a poultice would not be a problem; the creek bed offered mud and various medicinal plants. Ethan had already spotted mustard and ginger roots growing among the trees. The Indians would find them, too. Judging from their posture as they gazed and gestured around the landscape, the two Indians had noticeably devised a plan to help the Shark. The Mulberry Men chose not to interfere. The work on the malting shed was calling them home.

The Mulberry Men walked down the embankment to the road, expecting to run across the neglected bay before reaching the farm. Ethan spoke first to Tall Spruce, "What did you make of the two Indians? They appeared desperate and starving to me."

"As far as I could see, they carried no provisions. They appeared lazy. One of them has in mind to raid a farm, I believe," Tall Spruce spoke with assurance. He had studied their faces.

"Yes, they must eat soon. It didn't appear they had much success in tracking game. As you say, 'they are lazy.' I saw the gainful look on the man's face when he discovered the Shark, like someone handed him a bag of gold coins."

Some Indian tribes would look upon the Big Englishman as a prize and would pay handsomely for a man of his size and his fierceness. Even though Ethan had never lived in a tribe, his mother had talked of how such an outsider could make a tribe appear powerful to their enemies. As if they were favored by their gods.

"Hauling him to a tribe will be the problem." Tall Spruce pictured the Big Englishman lying across the back of the lame horse they encountered on the road. "If the Indians can't feed themselves and the big man, how would they feed and care for the lame beast?"

"I expect the threesome will be forming an alliance in the days ahead. I want to see them gone from this colony for all the damage the Shark has done to people's lives and properties." Ethan wished the man had died from the arrow wound.

"Come the winter, they could sled him to the nearest tribe," Tall Spruce said, grinning.

"Too far into the future. They don't appear to be the industrious sort." Ethan shook his head.

The heat was stifling, the sun just barely peeking over the mountain, shining in their faces while they walked. Ethan's stomach growled. "I haven't had a bite to eat today." *Wonder if Aunt Lenora made corncakes for breakfast*, he thought. *What would we do without her? What if she had been hurt yesterday? Mulberry Farm would never be the same.* He pondered these thoughts that caused him anguish over his aunt's welfare. *Life is so precious*, he mused.

"I have Gray Wolf on my mind. He's eating better, although he's not fit to travel in the heat." Tall Spruce was worried they couldn't travel to their people until the cool weather.

"There's plenty of work to be done on the malting shed that would keep both of you occupied—if you don't mind staying longer." Ethan was thankful that Thomas Crafts had finished installing the roof shingles. But he had business in Lexington. He will be leaving today.

They approached the fence and big gates where honeysuckle vines curled around rails and posts; its red berries consumed by the birds in mid-spring, now replaced with tiny pink flowers. Predictably, there stood the bay, enjoying the sweet scent of honeysuckle, swishing flies with his tail, snorting a hello. Tall Spruce looked at the horse and shook his head. He couldn't help himself. He rubbed the horse's neck and peered into the horse's eager eyes. Clutching the dangling rope, he guided the woeful horse through Mulberry Farm gates.

The morning had brought many surprises to the Mulberry Men. The sun was barely up, and along came a stranger. They heard hooves pounding the road from the south. They naturally paused to see who would come riding at such a clip so early in the day. The outline of the tall man seemed familiar, but Ethan couldn't place him in the hazy distance. "What in the world? Surely that's not...."

"Morning, gentlemen." Nat Stowe stepped off the horse and took a swig of watered-down ale, sweat dripping down his red face. "I have some news for you concerning Eli Asher."

The depressions in the road were unmistakable this morning. Tall Spruce's curious nature had pulled him back to the road the following morning, searching for signs. Recalling the sight of the two Indians, their faces had changed from hopelessness to jubilance at their first sight of the Shark.

That picture played on his mind. Denying the Indians an unforeseen fortune was pure guile in his mind. Taking possession of the stray horse was his unexpected prize. Tall Spruce smiled at that.

The campsite appeared deserted. Ashes cold and wet from morning dew, and no sight of the metal pot and the leather bag. All this had settled in Tall Spruce's mind when he crouched to the ground. He ran his hands over two perfectly formed ruts in the soft earth. "Perhaps the two Indians demonstrated more promise than I gave them credit for," he muttered. He followed the tracks of the travois and footprints leading to the road, making the turn south toward Connecticut. He glanced at the cedar tree grove where he and Ethan had sat, watching the two Indians devise a plan that could possibly mean their fortune. Most assuredly, a second chance for the Shark.

A ray of sunlight beamed down on something metal, catching his eye and causing him to take two steps toward an incongruous bulk sparingly covered with cedar branches. He instinctively looked around in all directions in the closed space. No one in sight, he decided. The panicked sound of a blue jay chased by a hawk made him jump. The pounding in his chest slowed when he heard the natural flitting and twittering of birds in the plum trees. He drew his knife from the side of his boot and poked at the branches, moving them aside. "The bay's saddle," he muttered. He stared at the harness and gear and made a decision. The horse had shown good sense to escape this corrupt place, he concluded. He picked up the saddle and walked to Mulberry Farm.

Chapter 16

A Chance Meeting

June 8, 1774, Beacon Hill

"Are you sure the invitation included my name? Who is he?" I asked Auntie as we sat eating our dinner. She passed the invitation to me as evidence. My name was included, along with Mrs. Minerva MacPherson and Dr. Josiah Randolph. "Father, do you know this family?" He was finishing off the last of the mulberry preserves and herby goat cheese. Lenora had sent us home with a basket containing confections, jams, and cheeses, anticipating that Saturday markets may never set up shop again with British troops occupying the city.

Hard to believe it had been over two weeks since our return to the gloomiest province in the colonies. Boston's ports were officially closed on June 1, 1774. No more lemons and limes and sugar loaves from the West Indies until we ostensibly got on our knees to beg forgiveness for our sins perpetrated against King George and present him with a wagon load of gold coins.

"I've known Jerome Pierpoint since my final year at the Boston Latin School. I worked as his apprentice in his surgery. I had an uncommon interest in science and anatomy. I started out sweeping the floors and keeping the fireplaces going. He showed me how to boil and scrub his surgical instruments. He's a stickler for cleanliness. I observed how he cleaned and stitched patient wounds and set broken bones. I asked questions, and he explained the procedures. He insisted I study his medical books. Three years later, I boarded a ship to Edinburgh University to study medicine." Father recounted with that far-off look in his eyes.

"Josie, I'm surprised you want to attend such an affair after you turned down the fan party at Olivia Mullin's home," Auntie grinned and winked at Father.

"I think this will be different. On the other hand, maybe I shouldn't be quite so willing to accept until I discover who the invited guests are. Any ideas?" I asked, hoping Father would mention names.

"I should preface my answer by informing you that our host is neither a Patriot nor a Tory. He shares sentiments for both sides, according to Dr. Warren," Father said, making it clear that even though our family believed independence from England was the only way to safeguard our liberties, there was no point in making it the major topic of conversation. It was considered treason.

The mere suggestion of cutting ties with the mother country sent most people, even Patriots, into a tailspin. "Those are seditious words," they would say. We stood firm in our decision as Patriots, but it was still early. Only time and events would tell when it would become obvious to our friends and patients.

"I hope it's not a bunch of stodgy physicians bragging about their relationships with the wealthy Bostonians they *pamper*." I was bent on determining whether there might be someone, male or female, who would be inclined to share an intellectual conversation.

Most women my age fell into two categories: they were either on the lookout for marriage material, such as a gentleman with status, financially and socially, believing that it would behoove them to hide their intellect by smiling behind their fan. Or someone like me or my longtime friend Eleanor Cushman, with whom I shared a kindred intellect. Our favorite times were spent reading Socrates and Shakespeare and discussing the histories of the world's cultures. We were of the same mind when it came to marriage and children, allowing it to happen naturally—when and if the time came.

"Probably, the Archers, Dr. Warren, and likely some family members. Actually, I'm not privy to the guest list, so we'll find out this coming

Saturday," Father predicted upon rising from his chair and giving me a peck on the top of my head. "I'll be in the surgery if anyone needs me."

Auntie and I sipped our homemade tea. Our stock of English tea was officially depleted. We accepted our plight and humbly began brewing a tea recipe with raspberry leaves and currants that Naomi shared with us. After several attempts at getting the measurements right and the brewing time perfect, our palates became accustomed to the medium-strong brew with the addition of cream. I persistently tricked my brain by not thinking about the black tea flavor we had sipped for years. Auntie and I took turns crushing the herbs and leaves, resigning ourselves that this would be the least of our worries once Governor Gage began enforcing the new Intolerable Laws in Massachusetts.

"Have you considered which gown you would like to wear to the dinner party, that is, if you decide to accept?" Auntie asked, knowing my collection of formal wear was limited to three choices.

"I'm not wearing the red one, even though it's a dull shade. I'm repulsed by all things red." I was in a stew that was boiling gradually, and I was not holding back my wrath.

"What's got you so worked up all of a sudden?" Auntie was not one to tiptoe around my feelings, pretending there was nothing wrong.

"It's Anthony Archer, 'future physician to Boston's elite.' He has been a friend of mine since we were children, playing hide and seek in this very yard. I cannot bear the thought of the way he has thrown away his life while in Edinburgh, flitting around brothels and gambling, pretending to be serious about his medical education."

"How do you know he's not serious? He's lived there for at least four years. He's had plenty of opportunities to be educated. Do his parents know about his behavior?" Auntie asked. I had not shared this piece of information with my aunt, which I had known for months. She is a close acquaintance of Mrs. Archer. Auntie's tongue tends to loosen after a mug of blackberry wine.

"It bothers me that professional physicians, like Father and Dr. Pierpoint, could possibly be called upon to endorse a reference to Anthony's abilities and his character, recommending him as a candidate at Philadelphia's medical school. They would be clueless about his past behavior in Edinburgh and his future intentions. Frankly, his money and his time are spent with trollops and gamblers."

"Pity. You're not jealous, are you?" Auntie hit a nerve. "Josie, you've been preparing yourself to be a doctor since you could talk. Your medical knowledge far exceeds many physicians I've encountered in Boston. Your compassion to serve others in a medical way demonstrates how much you care about your fellow man. Educated and uneducated doctors will challenge your knowledge and your ability because you're a female, but you've pledged to heal others regardless of their social status. Our work is not for the faint-hearted, and we're not in business to become rich. Don't underestimate yourself. I would trust you to stitch a wound on my body much as I would trust Josiah Randolph."

Bells tolled, announcing dusk on the day of the party. Street lanterns were lit one hour prior to the sun setting in Boston. The familiar sound of horses' hooves pulling a carriage large enough for four adults signaled it was time for us to meet in the downstairs front entrance hall. Upstairs, I took a final appraisal of my dress and hair, twisting around to get as much a view as possible in the full-length mirror in my chamber.

Father had reserved a carriage for our threesome to travel to the dinner party in Beacon Hill. Still not privy to the other guests attending, we were clearly excited and nervous. Father assured us the Pierpoints were gracious hosts, and a spirited conversation was a certainty.

Three days before the Pierpoint party, Auntie came to my aid with a gown that I never knew existed. The shiny mass of teal satin that lay on my bed was stunning. Tears came to my eyes when I thought I knew who it had belonged to—my mother. The three-quarter-length sleeves were edged with pleated netting and tiny beads. Simply appealing, I decided.

"I thought this would bring out the lighter highlights in your dark hair," Auntie surprised me when she walked into the room. She held up a dark pink rosette to the side of her head, made with pearls and ivory ribbon. "What if you wore your hair long with one side pulled back?" she demonstrated as I stood at the mirror. "Or we could build a chignon and randomly add in the pearls and ribbons. It's up to you."

We settled on a portion of my hair turned under and pinned with the rosettes just below the crown of my head while the balance of long tendrils draped down in the back. It suited my wavy hair already holding moisture due to the immense heat of the day.

The driver pulled into the circular drive of the modest mansion, adequately illuminated with lanterns lined along the front and the porch entrance. The house's architecture was built in the French chateau style, covered in off-white cut stones with twenty well-lit Palladian windows in the front and a mansard roof covered in gray slate shingles. I wondered if this was Pierpoint's creation or that of the previous owner. Rest assured, by the time the party concluded, Auntie would learn when the Pierpoint family arrived in Boston, why they preferred French architecture, and how the couple acquired their wealth.

The butler welcomed our arrival, opening the front door widely and leading us through a spacious white-marbled floor entry. Walls were painted with pastoral scenes of vineyards and countryside, which came to life with the glow of enormous chandeliers scattered throughout the never-ending entrance. This sight transported me to a world of splendor and opulence. The veined marble floor continued, ending at a wall of Palladian windows and doors connected to a terrace surrounded by gardens of roses, hedges, and vegetable plants.

I stepped onto the terrace, enthralled with a view of Boston from the highest point of Beacon Hill. The prospect made a display of church belfries, spires, and stately buildings in the gray light. I remained mesmerized by the sunset and the sound of ocean waves crashing along the seashores and the wharves. The air was sweet and moist. Hundreds of tiny lanterns glowed and twinkled, illuminating the perfectly trimmed trees and grass mixed in with flowers of all kinds. "I know a bank where the wild thyme blows, where oxlips and the nodding violet grows…"

"Quite overcanopied with luscious woodbine, with sweet musk-roses and with eglantine." A man's voice completed Shakespeare's couplet, compelling me to turn around. He walked in my direction along the path of stones that ended at the arbor of roses where I stood. "Welcome. I'm Nat Stowe. You must be Josie Randolph." The stranger announced.

"Pardon, my ma'ma is beckoning from the salon. I shall return." He was gone.

The man named Nat Stowe had made his appearance in the secluded rose garden while I was bent over examining the layered petals of yellow roses. My nose was buried in the intoxicating flowers. Hearing footsteps, I turned to view the outline of the stranger once more. This time, carrying a bottle of wine and two empty glasses.

I liked the sound of his voice. I had paused momentarily, then turned and smiled at the dark-haired man, tall and slim-bodied, with wide shoulders and olive skin. Difficult to tell in the dim light. I caught a hint of a mischievous smile and then a flash of teeth as he approached me while I stood cornered inside the arbor, ensconced under hundreds of tiny yellow roses.

"Made from Chardonnay grapes grown in my family's vineyard," he said after passing the open bottle under his nose and proceeded to pour out a glass of the liquid. "What shall we drink to—faithful privateers risking their lives to smuggle in the treasures of Europe or a glorious nighttime sky soon to be filled with twinkling stars?"

"You don't sound French," I spoke jokingly. I took the glass of wine he offered, holding it up to toast. "I should think a toast would be in order for your gardener!" Waving my other arm through the air, indicating the expanse of the garden. The wine, a buttery, honey flavor, went down smooth. Between the mix of French wine and the perfumed scent of roses settling in my head, I was in a dizzying state, feeling slightly off balance as dusk eased into nighttime.

"*C'est bon!*"[1] he confessed. "My ma'ma was raised in the village of Chardonnay in southern France, making her proud of the native grape. Naturally, there's a cellar full *de vin blanc*."[2]

"Looks as if we've been discovered," I said, moving away from the yellow roses onto the illuminated stone path. Father and Auntie, escorted by our host, I assumed, walked in our direction.

"Dr. Randolph and Mrs. MacPherson, it's been too long," the doctors bowed and smiled, each with a familiar twinkle in their eyes.

1. That's right!
2. ...of white wine.

Auntie clasped each side of her azure silk skirt, and with head bowed, she curtseyed graciously, smiling her prettiest. Earlier in the day, she had arranged her dark brown hair, graying hair into a chignon, pinned at the nape of her neck, surrounded by a strand of pinkish-colored pearls. Her tall frame and straight nose made her appear queenly even though her style of clothes remained simple. She looked beautiful tonight.

"I see my grandson is showing a young lady my yellow roses. Is she your daughter, perchance?" Dr. Pierpoint asked as the threesome turned in the direction of the glowing lanterns exposing the arbor covered in tiny yellow roses.

"She *is* the one and only Josie Randolph," Josiah said, slightly smiling yet embarrassed that she had so quickly been pursued by a young gentleman. *I hope Anthony Archer was not invited to this shindig*, he thought, knowing it would throw Josie into a sullen mood.

"I say we should become better acquainted," Aunt Minnie chimed in, with eyebrows raised, taking another sip of the light Chardonnay. They moved closer to the arbor.

"Pa'pa, have you met Josie Randolph?" Nat Stowe inquired enthusiastically, holding his glass of wine in my direction as if I were a famous dignitary. "Ah, Ma'ma is signaling for me once again." Nat left me standing with Father and Auntie to become acquainted with Dr. Pierpoint.

"You must forgive Nat," the doctor explained. "His ma'ma is putting him through his paces tonight!" As we chatted on the terrace, sufficient gray light remained, with the aid of lantern lights, to get a clear visual of the property overall. Tall, thick spruce trees surrounded three sides, filling in as a palisade for privacy and protection. A welcomed sea breeze swept across my face and neck to temper the heat of June's humid air.

So often, I took books off the shelves at Folger's Bookstore featuring French history and architecture with sketches of small and large edifices that showed the connection between the indoor and the outdoor with expansive portals. A dream world of gardens filled with flowers and vegetable plants seemed to be connected as if they were part of the living quarters. The Pierpoints had created such an atmosphere of intimacy and seclusion at their Beacon Hill mansion. I was enjoying every part of it all, wondering how the romance and mystery I felt at the moment were any comparison to a visit to the Palace of Versailles.

The guests had assembled in the salon, and we followed inside. The room was completely French with its Prussian blue furnishings, gilded mirrors, paintings, and brass sconces, Aubusson carpets, crystal chandeliers. Numerous uniformed servants were busy, rushing in and out of the kitchen carrying trays and filling cups with punch. I wondered how all this opulence was possible on a doctor's salary. Mrs. Pierpoint must have brought a hefty dowry into the marriage, or could the wealth have stemmed from the doctor's family?

The soft strum of harp music emanated from one corner of the room while Auntie and I stood in an adjacent corner swooning over a table laid with melon balls and cheese savories circling a large wedge of Roquefort cheese sitting so prettily on a platter of salad greens and berries.

Our biggest challenge was tempering our intake of Chardonnay to wash down the salty *hors d'oeuvres*.[3] I giggled over Auntie's stumbling speech when she attempted to pronounce Pierpoint's name; all the while, I expelled a noticeable hiccup. Hopefully, my one and only *faux pas*[4] for the evening, but who could say in this crowd of unknowns in such a lavish setting?

My nervousness was tempered when Nat Stowe appeared at the small table of refreshments, offering Auntie and me more wine, which I graciously refused. His urbane manner became more evident when he made inquiries about Father's medical practice. "I understand from my grandsire that you apprenticed under Dr. Randolph. How did you assume such a role, if I may ask?"

At first, I hesitated, then decided there was no reason for secrets. "It seems I've always been a part of Father's surgery, but realistically, since I was mature enough to follow his directions." I glanced at Auntie for confirmation, of which she smiled approvingly and winked. I nibbled sparingly at a stuffed mushroom as Nat sipped Chardonnay.

---

3. Appetizers.
4. Misstep.

"I fear that in the not-so-distant future, we will need all the physicians that can be mustered during..." he said when he was unexpectedly approached by one of the servants. Nat excused himself.

"Well, that's the first evidence of a Patriot that I've seen thus far. What do you think?" I directed my whispered question to Auntie as I contemplated the platter of melon and cheese. She apparently had walked away.

"No Patriots in this house," came the answer from a familiarly dreaded voice.

I dismissed the urge for melon and looked over the man's shoulder, feeling deserted and wondering which direction Auntie had gone. She had taken more than her limit of wine, so the idea that she may appear glassy-eyed and besotted made my blood freeze. My eyes quickly returned to the gentleman who took the liberty to move close to my face. I picked up a more-than-ample whiff of strong drink and took a step back, smiling smartly. "Anthony, you've returned to Boston, I see."

"Yes, I have for many reasons." The tall, fair-haired man grasped my hand and bowed.

"Oh, I didn't know you would be at the party tonight. Are your parents with you?" I asked.

Either he did not grasp my question, or he dismissed it. "I came home to protect my parents from these nasty, violent rebels who believe they have control of this city. The governor should escort them all to the gallows. To the king!" Anthony held up his glass as a salute.

He pointed his finger at me, stressing his point. I tried to back away, but I was wedged between Anthony, a couple behind me, and the table of food to my left, trapped like a rabbit in a snare, not daring to take a step in any direction to escape. He continued to imbibe as he ranted.

Anthony's speech was slurred now, and I detected a sway in his stance. I looked across the room and saw the back of a woman with black hair coiffed similar to mine, with dazzling pink flowers trailing down the back. She was holding a glass of the famous Chardonnay while in conversation with Father. He looked rather handsome in his dark blue embroidered waistcoat. I thought he looked unusually relaxed as he focused on the woman's face as she talked.

I set my eyes on Father, hoping he would sense my dismay and come to my rescue while I occasioned to switch back to Anthony's face. He kept rambling on about our duty to the king and uneducated ruffians who sought to control Boston Harbor, intermittently gulping down something that I knew was not wine.

Finally, an older gentleman with gray wavy hair took his place beside the woman, and Father excused himself. Relieved, he glanced my way. I tilted my head and widened my eyes as an invitation to rescue me, which he did, immediately determining my predicament with the inebriated Anthony.

"Greetings to you, Mr. Archer," Father spoke to Anthony, nodding slightly and thankfully coming to my aid by securing a spot by my side. "Are you taking a break from your studies in Edinburgh?" Auntie, seated on an upholstered settle covered in the exquisite Prussian blue silk, turned around and smiled at the three of us. I drew a breath of relief at seeing her sip a cup of tea while conversing with Nat Stowe. I endured Anthony's ramblings as background chatter.

"I have recently withdrawn from the university's medical school, believing it prudent to continue my education in Philadelphia, what with the recent uprisings. On behalf of my parents, considering their requirements, I would be well disposed to reside in closer proximity to attend to their needs if necessary." Anthony lied with a straight face, forgetting that, months ago, he spelled out very clearly in his letters to me that his grades were failing and he had squandered his allowance.

"That's a noble gesture, Mr. Archer," Father replied, showing a strained smile, totally unimpressed with the man's manufactured story. He took me by the arm, and we excused ourselves, abandoning Anthony and his lying tongue. "Stay as far away from that man as you can, Josie. I mean it, beginning this evening!" he whispered distinctly in my ear. I nodded.

I walked where Auntie and Nat Stowe sat in deep conversation, as Father branched off in a different direction when Dr. Pierpoint motioned him to join his little clique of guests. The doctor stood under six feet next to Father's taller frame. His receding salt and pepper hair was pulled back with a ribbon, exposing a squarish jaw, sun-browned skin, and dark blue eyes.

Frequent exchanges in French and English were made by Mrs. Pierpoint, who, like a butterfly, flitted amongst her guests to chat and make merry, making them feel welcome in her little chateau. I noticed her skin was bronzed like her husband's. *They spend time enjoying their gardens*, I thought. It was truly a paradise that Auntie could get lost in. If only she could view it in the daytime. Gardening was her pastime and diversion. I praised her skills, which enhanced the character of our Bradford Lane home.

All my family had traveled to France except for me, so they had the advantage of speaking the language, as well as familiarity with the customs and the cuisine. I had no hesitation being among guests who were far more acquainted with French traditions than me. The harp music ceased, and the room quieted. All eyes turned in the direction of the grand gold-trimmed French doors, opened by the butler announcing, "Dinner is served."

Our hosts took their places behind two footmen who led our group of twenty guests across the marble-floored entry into a regal dining room, walls covered in maroon silk outlined with gilded panels and illuminated with brass sconces. Three chandeliers suspended from the tall ceiling lit a long table set with gleaming silverware and crystal goblets.

The Pierpoints stood at their seats in the middle of the table while footmen seated guests at their designated places as we entered the dining room. The process took less than two minutes to accomplish. I'm sure they were tutored in advance to learn the names and faces of the guests, familiarizing themselves further during the pre-dinner affair in the salon.

Nat Stowe and Father were seated directly across from me. It wasn't until after the soup course, *vichyssoise*, that I thought of Anthony. I resisted any attempt to allow my searching eyes to be discovered by other guests, thinking I might have some interest in the besotted popinjay. I was delighted to be seated next to Father's unknown female acquaintance, anticipating some interesting conversation and, most importantly, the connection between her and Father. She turned to me purposely to initiate a formal introduction. My eyes couldn't get enough of her creamy white skin and shiny black hair. Her bright blue eyes sparkled when she smiled. "I hoped we could get better acquainted," her blue eyes sparkled when she introduced herself as Elise Beaumont.

Footed silver platters stood in a line along the tabletop, artfully stacked with colorful fruit and flowers, making it tempting not to sample the juicy plums and apricots. I hesitated, considering it might be a decoration. I had read that the French cleaned their palate by eating fruit between courses. But still, no more *faux pas* this evening, I cautioned myself.

"Is this your first time visiting the Pierpoints' home? The gardens could easily compare with those at Versailles. Have you seen them?" she asked exuberantly, eager to hear my opinion.

"This is my first occasion to visit their home. I chanced to encounter the miniature rose garden earlier. The fragrance was dizzying." I absentmindedly looked across the table at Nat Stowe, who caught my eyes and smiled. He continued his conversation with Father.

"My father," Elise nodded in the direction of the older man who had stood by her side in the salon, "is brother to Eloise Pierpoint. They were raised in the south of France. They created the arbor of roses and the entirety of the gardens. I regret you could not view them when the sun's rays highlight such rare beauty and color. Perhaps a daytime visit could be arranged." Cucumber salad dotted with a vinaigrette, goat cheese, and crusty bread took the place of the tasty potato and leek soup.

A different white wine replaced the first-course wine, leaving a fruity lime taste so different from the Chardonnay. If I even dared to drink the entire glass, I was sure to take on flushed cheeks and that tipsy, out-of-control aura that I was hoping to avoid. I hoped Auntie remained conscious of her intake. Each time I looked her way, she and Mrs. Pierpoint were busily discussing their gardens.

"How thoughtful. I would enjoy the gardens, as would my aunt Minnie." Elise gave me a generous smile, displaying her pretty teeth, her blue eyes still sparkled. "You may not know that most days I assist Father in his surgery, but I'm sure we could allow time for a visit."

"*C'est bon*.⁵ I'll have a courier deliver a note to your home."

The entrée replaced the *concombre salade*.⁶ Beef topped with mushroom and onion sauce, string beans and braised carrots were offered on trays by footmen, allowing guests to serve themselves. A third-course red wine replaced the salad wine, which I had sipped only twice.

Conversations became noticeably livelier as the dinner progressed. Across the table, Nat engaged Elise and me in stories of supply wagons he had encountered while driving up through Boston Neck carrying bags of rice and grains, sheep and chickens, and produce from other colonies.

Since Britain had seized control of Boston's ports, food and supplies were donated by neighboring colonies, intended for distribution to families whose breadwinners had lost their jobs at the wharves. Nat was quite passionate, talking about the current plight of Boston's families, adding in humorous tidbits, which seemed natural to his outgoing character. I was attracted to his genuine smile and his non-existent egotistical manner, as far as I could detect. He could definitely hold his alcohol. Just the opposite of Anthony Archer.

The three of us were so absorbed in our cozy little clique that, at first, we didn't hear the disturbance at the far end of the table. I glanced to the right in search of the rowdy noise. I took a double take at a young woman's tawny-colored hair stacked unusually high on top of her head, poked with colorful butterflies and flowers. Of all things, she was holding a fan in front of her face, showing only her big blue eyes. I laughed to myself, remembering the fan party frivolity I had rejected months ago, then wondered if she was one of the featherheads who had attended the affair. I dismissed the notion and determined the inexcusable boisterousness came from Mr. and Mrs. Archer sitting at the other end of the table. Anthony was drunk and had lost total control of his speech.

Nat and Father looked in the direction of the Archer family and stood up from the table at the same time, rushing toward the commotion along with two footmen. Mr. Archer, rightly enough, had taken hold of

5. That's good.
6. Cucumber salad.

his son's arm to lead him out of the dining room. The move was harshly rejected by Anthony, causing him to continue shouting profanities and casting some toward his parents. Nat and Father quickly took hold of the young man's arms and literally dragged him from the dining room to the outside dooryard, screaming indecent words as if he were being arrested by a constable.

In the meantime, Dr. and Mrs. Pierpoint politely excused themselves from the table and approached the embarrassed Mr. and Mrs. Archer, offering them the services of a footman to bring their carriage to the front. They were compassionate and responsible hosts. I could not hear all the words spoken, but I saw the caring smiles and concern on their faces as they escorted the Archers from the dining room through the marble-floored foyer, handing them over to the footmen's care.

"Apparently, a disagreement with their son. They are on their way home now. Let us continue with our dinner," Dr. Pierpoint announced. The remaining guests applauded our hosts, who, by this time, were grinning and bowing. Their plan to continue the evening was evident when they seated themselves.

Presently, cheers of "here, here" and applause followed when dinner guests toasted the return of Father and Nat to the dining room, leaving them surprised at the guests' gratitude. The two rescuers took an exaggerated bow and returned to their seats, where fresh plates awaited them. Guests respectfully took up their conversations and sipped their wine as though nothing had happened.

I caught Father's eye when he raised a fork of beef to his mouth, acknowledging his heroics. He flashed a grin and shrugged his left shoulder. Elise leaned over to me and whispered, "Our champions!" *Who in the world is this woman?* I wondered.

The dessert wine was poured, followed by a colorful dessert featuring red and blue berries mixed in a sugary wine sauce atop a thin pancake roll stuffed with whipped cheese and cinnamon. A footman stood beside each guest with a bowl of whipped cream peaked high in a bowl with a silver spoon for self-serve. I spooned on a mere fraction of the fluff. My stays were already pinching my sides, and the waist of my gown was wet from the humid heat. I was literally stuffed. One more bite, and I imagined the seams popping on my bodice. I took two bites of the rich dessert and called it quits.

When I looked up from my plate to take a sip of wine, Nat's eyes were keenly fastened on my face, regarding me carefully. I smiled politely. Elise and Father were engrossed in their own conversation. I tried to hide my disconcerted smile by showing interest in my abandoned dessert. The courage came for me to take a quick examination of Nat's handsome, tanned face—wide forehead, black hair, high cheekbones, and dark brown eyes. The sides of his mouth turned up naturally with a perpetual smile.

I initiated a conversation with him, wondering how I had missed his long black eyelashes. Anthony Archer was equally as handsome, but his pompous demeanor made me cringe. "Do you plan to return to your home soon? Connecticut, is it?" I inquired of Nat as he emptied his wine glass.

"Yes, Suffield on the west side of the Connecticut River. I plan to leave in a week's time unless my pa'pa gives me more work. He writes medical journals now that he has retired. He requires my services to do his research. His library is quite extensive." I mentally checked off two marks in favor of Nat Stowe: a grasp of medical knowledge and a devotion to his family.

We walked through the marbled foyer toward the salon, giving me another occasion to view the detailed mural. The entire wall of muted colors depicted the simple life of people who savored the seasons and the earth so vital for the vineyards growing on the mountains and the families working the land. It paralleled the labor contained in the creation of the Pierpoints' gardens, a place of solitude where one's worries were displaced by the sweetness of flowers and the tang of herbs.

I followed the whiff of rich coffee and the delicate thrums of the harp to the salon. Guests were assembled around what was formerly the fruit and cheese table, magically transformed into a coffee service. A tall silver urn and a collection of delicate china cups drew my attention. I was glad to get a reprieve from wine and cordials. The night of fabulous

French food and wine had educated me far beyond what a trip to Folger's Bookstore could do. Amazing how our senses incorporate so much understanding of people and cultures.

I joined Auntie and Elise on the terrace to catch a breath of fresh air. I gazed upward at the clear sky with thousands of glittering stars. The night's breeze caused a stand of bamboo to sway to one side, its shaking leaves sending forth a rattling sound. The sea breeze sent pungent tobacco smoke in our direction from a cluster of male guests smoking pipes. I heard Governor Gage's name mentioned several times, but all else was indistinguishable amidst the scraping of crickets in the garden and the splash of frogs in the pond in a distant part of the garden.

Nat joined us on the terrace, empty-handed this time. I guessed he had had his limit of wine and brandy for the evening. "Are you acquainted with Mr. Archer—I mean, the younger?"

"Anthony Archer and I have been friends since I could walk. He, along with several other Boston friends, were my playmates as children. We chased each other to the harbor; we played tag in my backyard; we drank lemonade; we counted the stars. All those activities that interest children. Then, one day, we grew up and went our separate ways. We've exchanged letters since he's been away in Edinburgh, so I had not seen him in four years."

"Your father said Mr. Archer is studying medicine. Forgive my impertinence; he doesn't seem well-suited to the medical profession. What do you believe are his prospects?" Nat seemed interested in Anthony's welfare. I wasn't prepared to convey what I knew about his personal life communicated to me through his letters; hence, I was cautious as I spoke.

"Anthony had the best intentions when he began university, but he has seemed misguided and led astray in recent months. I'm worried about him and his parents. I'd like to continue my friendship with him, but I'm not sure the Anthony I once knew still exists."

"'A true friend is one who is faithful even in adversity,' that's a quote from something I've read somewhere along the way," Nat said with sympathetic eyes. "We all go through difficult times. Perhaps, in time, you will have occasion to extend your friendship... Ah, I see I'm being summoned by my pa'pa. I heard a rumor that you have accepted an invitation to visit Ma'ma's garden. I hope we can visit once more before I leave for Connecticut. In the meantime, it has been my pleasure. *Bonsoir, mademoiselle!*"[7] Nat bowed and returned to his duties inside.

I turned around to join Auntie and Elise, who were staring wide-eyed at our farewell scene. I simply smiled and fluttered my eyelashes. They raised their cups and cheered me with a "Hurrah!"

Right on cue, Father appeared on the terrace. "Our coach is ready," he announced.

---

7. Good evening, miss!

Chapter 17

Seeking Justice

June 8, 1774, Bradford Lane

Four days later, I was standing in the Pierpoints' garden. Before dawn, Auntie and I had dressed in our work clothes and old shoes, expecting to be covered in garden soil by the time we returned home. Father was adamant that we travel in a carriage to the little chateau, where he had promptly ordered our transportation from Fletcher's. In his words, "You cannot walk anywhere in this town without a chaperone, and that includes your aunt Minnie!"

We gobbled a cup of cider and buttered bread and gathered our baskets and sunbonnets by the time Father called from the front entry. He was wary about walking in the dim light of the early morning. I noticed the handle of his pistol beneath his coat when he raised his arm to open the door, barking and motioning us with a "shoo, shoo" to hurry outside.

He was right to be worried. There were redcoat soldiers standing along the storefronts and under the lanterns as the carriage moved toward the Pierpoints. Reports of looting had been rumored since the ports closed—out-of-work men looking for ways to vent their anger. I heard a bugle call from the direction of the Common, ordering soldiers to ready themselves for the next shift.

The driver drove to the iron gates, depositing Auntie and me in our ragamuffin outfits at the front steps where the butler, Gaston

LeBlanc, was waiting with a smile. The coolness of the early morning was invigorating. The scorching sun would rise soon enough to sap our energy. We followed Gaston closer to another set of iron gates, inviting my eyes and nose to get a hint of the garden's beauty.

"*Bonjour, madames.*[8] Welcome to our garden," Eloise Pierpoint's friendly voice reached us, catching a glimpse of her straw bonnet before we saw her face. "I was snipping some herbs for our *le petit déjeuner*.[9] Are you acquainted with the *Quiche Lorraine*?" Auntie and I shook our heads. "It is a tart made with eggs, ham, and cheese. It is light but filling." She smiled, flashing her big brown eyes. I did not recall an invitation for a morning meal, but I knew it would be a welcome delight coming from the Pierpoints' kitchen.

I saw the excitement in Auntie's eyes as she took in the neat rows of herbs intermingled with sweet alyssum, candy tufts, and marigolds. Tall and leggy against the white fence stood phlox, baby's breath, and delphinium, so pleasing to the eye. "Dig up a sampling of each plant if you like. If they are not thinned out soon, Henri will throw them in the compost pile," Eloise recommended. Our baskets were filling quickly.

A generous garden section was planted in lettuces, wild dandelions, cucumbers, and peppers. Squash, beans, and peas were planted around obelisk-shaped wooden structures where the vines were trained to trail upwards, making it easy to stand and harvest without kneeling or bending. Clever idea for Eloise and Henri.

Pumpkins planted in with the corn for fall harvesting were located toward the rear of the garden. Carrots, beets, parsnips, and turnips— those plants that would not be harvested until winter were planted in their own special section. I was impressed with the garden's structure and tidy rows. Eloise's brother had created the walking paths out of stone pavers within the garden, all surrounded by short picket fencing.

A profusion of flowers covered each garden section, giving me a surprise at every turn. The recurring spicy scent of boxwood kept calling my attention. My curiosity got the best of me when I stood on tiptoes

---

8. Greetings, ladies.
9. …breakfast.

to view something I had only seen in books—a parterre, boxwoods trimmed to form small and large circular shapes or any shape really.

"Would you like a closer look?" Nat asked. I turned and laughed nervously, then nodded. I clasped my hands at my back in hopes he wouldn't notice my dirty hands. He pointed his hand in the direction of the lower level. I began walking down the granite steps.

"How is the research coming?" I asked, wondering if he was truly working on a medical journal. My eyes scanned the neatly trimmed boxwoods and walkways, trimmed perfectly by the hands of the gardener. I didn't give Nat a chance to answer. "Do I hear chickens?" I chuckled at the thought.

"Yes, do you want to see them? There are numerous hens and one lonely rooster, obediently carrying out his duty to keep the kitchen supplied with eggs," he answered. I couldn't tell if he was being silly or serious. We continued walking.

"I'm aware of the chicken and rooster relationship." I didn't want to appear ungrateful. "Does your ma'ma have a hand in gardening? She seems very capable." I wasn't just making conversation; her skills in gardening far exceeded anyone I had ever met.

I could see the shapes in the parterre now. It reminded me of a pie sliced into six wedges, each slice planted with a different flower within the boundaries of a separate section of boxwood. In the center of the circle stood a statue of a Greek goddess surrounded by purple lobelia. Diana or Athena? I wasn't sure. We strolled through each pie wedge, admiring the differences in each flower, and settled on a bench perched on a small hill beyond the parterre. From this point, we could see the entire garden.

A chickadee flew from a dead tree lying on the ground, left there purposely for all kinds of small birds to nest and feed. The black-capped bird landed atop the goddess' head and looked around until a big red cardinal squawked and took her place. "Father says you're a Patriot. How did that happen in the midst of all the Tories I met the other evening?"

"Let's move under some shade. The sun is cooking us," he suggested. I followed him to a bench with a back, positioned under a large elm beyond the pond. "My family are ironworkers and have been for over a hundred years. The mountains in Connecticut have enormous supplies of iron ore. My ancestors purchased hundreds of acres of land from the Indians, which they meant to farm. Instead, my four-times great-grandsire decided to dig ore and build a forge. Am I boring you yet? I will get to my point soon.

"He was educated enough to know that when iron ore is smelted in a forge, it has the potential to become a high-quality iron once it is processed. Naturally, the British government placed restrictions on how much iron could be produced in the colonies as well as the degree to which we could make a satisfactory profit. Here, take my handkerchief. You have dirt and sweat rolling down your face." I accepted his offer, removed my bonnet, and wiped my face and neck. Finally, a welcoming breeze settled over us.

"We were never allowed to make a finished product such as a pot or kettle—if you can believe that. Our smelted ore was shipped to England, where it was refined and manufactured into household supplies. These products were shipped back to the colonies to be purchased in shops. It didn't take long for colonial ironworkers to catch on to the game that London's Parliament was playing. Being the rebellious colonists that we are, we did away with the middleman, in this case, England, when we began refining our own iron and producing our own firearms and kettles. To answer your original question, the Stowe family are Patriots, as are the workers my father employs. My grandparents, not so much, but I wouldn't call them Tories either."

I looked up and away. "It seems as though we're being summoned to the terrace," I said to Nat. Eloise motioned for us to join the group on the upper level. Elise and Auntie were chattering away in the yellow rose garden, which took on a different appearance in the bright sunlight.

As we strolled around the parterre, breathing in the spicy boxwood, I glanced to my right, where a small cottage sat concealed in a nook of dark green hemlock trees with hundreds of miniature cones hanging delicately off each branch. I knew it would take more trips to the Pierpoints' property to get the full measure of its splendid gardens and unexpected adornments. I wouldn't mind an occasion to visit inside one more time. I knew Auntie would.

My eyes shifted toward the prepared table intended for ladies only. Nat excused himself and wished our family well. He planned to return to his home in Suffield within the next week, having performed his duties as dinner host and medical assistant. I was delighted that we had become friends during our short time together, but what were the prospects of our building a relationship in today's risky times?

The Pierpoint family offered Auntie and me a world of discovery and solitude—friendship as well. Perhaps it was Eloise's innate sense of the lives of doctors, always on call for emergencies, patients depending on you to repair their bodies, or just making their pain disappear. It was a tremendous responsibility that affected our emotions, sometimes believing we stood between the patient and the healing power of the Almighty. Yes, I believe she was aware of the needed diversion of caring for sick and wounded Bostonians, notwithstanding the daily frustrations of waking each day to the sound of drums and bugles, anticipating another round of punishments perpetuated by the king to inflict on us naughty colonists.

The Pierpoints' butler, Gaston LeBlanc, was our server today. He thoughtfully set up a hand-washing area on the terrace for a quick cleanup. With the exception of Elise, our hands and faces were quite nasty. There was nothing we could do about our soiled bodice and skirts but brush off the dirt. The lingering lavender scent of the French milled soap made me anxious for a soak in the bathtub when we returned home. Mosquitoes had already made a meal of my legs!

The first thing I noticed as I took my seat at the table was a bowl of tiny yellow roses perched on a silver platter, causing me to forget about itchy legs and unkempt hair. The savory aroma of a baked pie crust holding together a mixture of eggs and ham with rosemary and assorted herbs attacked my olfactory sense. My long-ago meager breakfast had vanished. Humidity hung in the air, causing everything about me to droop. Gaston served each of us a tasty meal of fresh greens and strawberries with the *Quiche Lorraine*. "Let us celebrate our friendship and our bounty," cheered Eloise. As I raised my glass, bright light shone through the golden liquid mixture of ginger, lemon, and honey tea, just the refreshment we all needed to rejuvenate our bodies.

Elise appeared as a China doll compared to us working-since-dawn-gardeners. Her black hair glistened in the sun, and her white skin set off quite a contrast with our sunburned faces. "I understand that you make your own medicines. Did you find the plants you needed in the garden today?"

Auntie turned toward Elise to answer her question, "Yes, we found many plants that we had only read about, never believing we could find them in Boston. We're so thrilled with Eloise's generosity."

"Do you generally purchase medicines from the apothecary?" she asked. I thought to answer, "Not since soldiers lay siege to Boston." Truthfully, our only source of medicines had been Mr. Walden's apothecary. He packed up his store and moved out of Boston to the countryside, unwilling to transact business with British soldiers.

"We have in the past, but lately, Josie and I have worked unceasingly to create the medicines Dr. Randolph likes to use with his patients. We're anxious to start grinding away on today's supply of plants. I just hope we can collect an ample supply of jars to fill with all the medicines we create."

Auntie was right; we were dangerously low on containers. We had discussed the idea of ordering glass jars from a manufacturer in Holland and having them shipped to Connecticut. The part we had not worked out was transporting them to Boston, something we had intended to discuss with Father.

"I daresay that could be a problem," Elise replied. A tone of nonchalance rang clearly.

A silence settled over the table. Eloise and I chatted as we consumed our *Quiche*. Auntie and Elise shared stories about their times in France. I had become acquainted with Suki shortly after I sat down for our meal. I allowed the big yellow tabby to brush against my leg, letting him know we were a friendly sort. It was his domain, after all.

Seated as we were, facing the yellow rose arbor, I noticed the lazy cat squinting his eyes in a drowsy state. A large dragonfly appeared on the scene, flitting amongst the roses and the neighboring purple lilacs, compelling Suki to come out of his languid state. Mr. Dragonfly began to play dangerously, swooping in lower, permitting the cat to bat at him with its paw.

"You're welcome to the jars stored in the potting shed. My brother and I concoct *some* medicines, but only enough to suit our needs. I'll give that job to my brother. He has lately shown frustration at my hoarding *mes petites*[10] treasures!" Eloise laughed. "Oh look, Suki seems to have captured a dragonfly. *Coup de maître*,"[11] she clapped her hands, celebrating his triumph. The gratified cat pranced confidently toward the table with gossamer wings hanging from his mouth.

Proud of his catch, Suki deposited the dead insect next to my dirty shoes, looking up at me for approval. I got his message. I held out my hand, offering him a bit of *Quiche*, which he licked and then swallowed, expressing his appreciation with a "meow."

I detected familiar voices coming from the vegetable garden quadrant. All four of us looked up to see Gaston escorting Father to our table. We had left the arrival and departure times of the coach to Father's discretion, never occurring to me that he would take the time to retrieve Auntie and me so soon. "Father, what a surprise. I never thought you would come for us at this hour. There's no emergency, is there?" His face looked troubled.

"There certainly is. We need to leave quickly for the surgery. I'm sorry for the interruption, Madame Pierpoint and Madame Beaumont." He bowed and stepped away. "Do these baskets go home with us?" Not waiting for an answer, he picked them up, catching sight of Dr. Pierpoint and Nat advancing hurriedly toward him.

"There's been an explosion at the ironworks. I've been working on a badly burned patient for the last hour, lying in my surgery at this very moment. His wife is treating him now, but I'll need the help of my

---
10. …my little…
11. Masterstroke.

assistants here." We followed behind Father, recognizing his haggard demeanor I had seen so often when life and death hung in the balance.

"You go ahead, Josiah. Nat and I will follow in my carriage." Dr. Pierpoint suggested.

We entered our house. Sarah Bignall stood at the surgery table where her husband lay, dabbing cold water from a pan onto his burned face. His wide eyes were filled with fear. Trauma, I observed. The rest of his body was a different story—blisters covered his arms, hands, and body. Father had covered his torso with linen sheeting and wrapped his arms and hands with bandages in an effort to keep impurities from the air from reaching the blisters, which could erupt and become open wounds. This was Father's biggest worry.

Auntie poured a cup of water for Mr. Bignall. His wife, Sarah, raised his head to help him drink a few sips. I knew he worked at a forge near his home on Salt Street. I guessed we would hear the details of the accident later. The patient was in no condition to talk.

"Who's minding the children?" I asked Mrs. Bignall. She wiped the tears from her face at the mention of them. A small woman with a fair complexion and freckles dotting the top of her nose, she attempted to smile, but she was too upset over her husband's critical condition.

"Miss Randolph, I'm happy you're here." Her lips quivered as she spoke. She pushed her straw-colored hair off her face. "I left the children in your backyard when I brought my husband to your surgery. I hope you don't mind."

"No, you were right to do that. I'll see to their needs." I nodded to Father and Auntie, who were removing the man's boots and stockings, checking his legs for blisters. I spotted the playful children chasing one another outside as I walked through the kitchen to the backyard. Matthew's hands were placed over his eyes, and I heard him counting to ten. His brother and sister were scrambling to find a place to hide.

"Ready or not, here I come," Matthew announced loudly, searching for them as he ran from tree to tree. He recognized my face and stopped when he saw me. "Wha…I know you. Do you live here?" he asked. "Clara, Samuel, come see Miss Randolph!" They ran toward me, blushed and sweaty faces looking curious, and then remembered me when they walked closer. "Can Dr. Randolph make my father well?" asked Matthew. "I helped Mother walk him to your house." The children stared at me, waiting for an answer that was hopeful.

"Dr. Randolph will do his best to heal your father. Your mother is helping too. In the meantime, let's drink some cool cider to refresh ourselves." They sat on the bench under the big oak tree. It was shortly after the noon hour, and the sun was piercingly hot. My clothes were soaked with sweat and dirt from the morning's garden work, but there was nothing to do about it now. The children needed my attention. Auntie opened the kitchen door and motioned me to come over.

"Sarah said there are two more workers who are injured. The Pierpoints should be here soon. Can you continue with the children? I've set up two beds in the surgery and am searching for more linens." Auntie's report was not encouraging. I wondered about the extent of their burns. *We'll have a long day ahead of us, I'm sure.*

I resolved to stay calm and not involve myself with the patients. They were in good hands with two doctors and two assistants. I glanced at the children, viewing them from the big window. Nothing urgent concerning them, just a little row beginning about who gets the best seat under the oak tree. I set the cups of cider on a tray and headed outside, chuckling at their eagerness to get situated on the bench.

Nat called to me while the children and I sipped our drinks, "Your aunt said you have more bandages in storage. Where would I find them?" I left the children and walked inside to the scullery pantry, half filled with bandages, the other half was filled with jars of crushed herbs, syrups, and liniments. Auntie and her sewing group had spent days cutting strips of linen in three different sizes, placing them in large sacks to keep them dust-free.

"Nothing like being prepared for accidents," Nat commented, impressed with our readiness for the unexpected. "You have enough supplies for an army!" *Probably not*, I thought. Especially after wrapping the men's burned bodies lying in the surgery. He walked toward the surgery with the bundle.

Father had persuaded Sarah Bignall to go home and get some rest; she had been standing by her husband's side since late morning. Daylight was waning, and the children were asking for food, so I assumed they had not eaten since breakfast. I did slip in some buttered bread with their cider earlier. Dr. Pierpoint thoughtfully offered his carriage to Mrs. Bignall. She reluctantly gathered her three children, and Gaston LeBlanc whisked them away to their house on Salt Street.

Mr. Bignall was sleeping now, although restless and in pain. His face and neck did not look anywhere near as bad as his body. After his face had been bathed and covered with cool compresses, Auntie came back with some St. John's Wort ointment, dabbing it lightly over the red spots.

The two new patients were in the same shape as Mr. Bignall, with blistered skin and shallow breathing. Apparently, they had walked to our house and collapsed in the front yard. Dr. Pierpoint and Nat discovered them when they arrived by carriage. They examined the men and determined the degree of their blisters and lacerations, immediately settling the burn victims on the surgery beds.

The patients were stripped of their homespun shirts and wrapped in sheets and bandages, looking like mummies ready for burial. While wrapping their arms and hands, I choked when I smelled scorched cloth and burned flesh. The oldest man looked to be about Father's age. His dark hair was singed above his forehead, and there were blisters on the top of his right ear. The younger of the two did not appear as serious… More like a sunburn on his face and neck. All three men sustained blisters on their arms, hands, and torso, needing to be wrapped with bandages. It was a grim process.

They were all in pain—groaning and asking for water. As we had done with Mr. Bignall, Auntie and I began a regiment of warm water and honey to hydrate their bodies and quench their thirst. I was confident their bodies would respond in time. The healing process had now begun and would continue for several days. Proper care and constant attention were mandatory at this stage.

Auntie began heating kettles of water. Our well water always tasted brackish. It had been a habit of ours to boil the water before using it to rid it of impurities. That process would continue throughout the night. Auntie consigned the job of drawing water from the well to Nat. He filled kettles to boil, then poured it in dishpans to cool down. Bathing the patient's burned necks and faces with cool water was essential to prevent blisters from developing.

Auntie and I glanced at each other in awe of Nat's willing spirit. He had no apprehensions about taking orders from Auntie and me nor in attending to the patients. An extra set of hands took a load of work off us. I leaned over to Auntie and whispered. "How do you think Mr. Archer would manage a room of burn patients?" I asked her, having an idea of how she would respond.

"By getting drunk!" she replied. We laughed, aware that Anthony Archer could not stand the sight of blood or vomit.

Father and Dr. Pierpoint had stepped outside to take a break from the patients. The air was marginally cooler but still heavy with moisture. The gulls had stopped their circling and squawking, now hunched on their roosts after a day of scavenging dead fish. The street lanterns were lit. Soldiers stood posted in front of businesses along Main Street, which were ordered closed when the sun went down and the evening bells tolled. "Do you know the owner of the forge?" I heard Dr. Pierpoint ask Father. "There was definitely an explosion from a furnace, judging from all the cuts and bruises on the men's bodies. The owner should be responsible for the family's financial maintenance."

"Oh, that's my carriage," the doctor remarked. Anxious to return to his home, I'm sure.

I looked out the front window to see the driver stop in front of our house and then step down from his seat. He proceeded to open the door for Mrs. Pierpoint, who stepped to the ground and spoke to the doctors.

"Good evening. I understand you're running a hospital here," she chuckled as the two doctors walked to greet her at the walkway. The driver had pulled out two baskets, hopefully food. I was starving. Out of respect for the patients, we declined to speak of food in their presence.

"The cooks and I assembled some food to satisfy the belly and your spirits," she said, smiling. "I know it will be a long evening." Dr. Pierpoint kissed her cheek, and Father bowed and smiled. To my surprise, Dr. Pierpoint and Nat would remain in the surgery to help with the patients.

I watched the carriage pull away in the dark. *So sweet*, I muttered. My eyes teared up. I turned around to see Nat faithfully dabbing water on the new patient's face. He glanced up at me and smiled.

Auntie set the basket of food on the table, laying it out banquet style. While two of us tended patients in the surgery, the other three sat at the table eating cold chicken, cheese and herb bread and strawberry tarts. Father set up a keg of ale he gathered from the cellar, always available.

We worked throughout the night. Dr. Pierpoint and Nat took the first four-hour shift. Father, Auntie, and I took the next four hours. Trying to sleep in between as much as we could, but it was a challenge. When I thought I had gotten two hours of sleep, it turned out to be only thirty minutes. The anticipation of rising at four in the morning played tricks on my brain. At least I was off my feet and resting my body. Giving my mind a rest was a different story.

Nat never faltered in delivering fresh water to the three patient's sides, placing cold compresses on the face and neck, wherever the skin was burned, avoiding any blistered spots. Auntie and I continued our honey water concoctions, feeding them by teaspoons regularly to each patient. Dr. Pierpoint sat at Father's desk, writing journal entries on the conditions of each patient and their treatments, rarely leaving the surgery.

He had cause for alarm when Nat noticed some oozing through the bandage on the older man's left hand. The only remedy for that was to carefully remove the dressing and replace a new bandage strip over the wound promptly to avoid any poisons from entering.

In the kitchen the next day, Minnie had begun organizing the plants we had gathered from the Pierpoints' gardens, giving immediate attention to bee balm to make a tincture for fighting toxins in the digestive and respiratory tracts. The good thing is, it has a long shelf life.

When Eloise offered her supply of glass bottles for medicines, I had no idea she would have her maid clean and boil them in water, making them ready to fill. Gaston brought them to our house the day after we received the burn patients. This family's generosity was beyond belief. We were so thankful.

Dr. Randolph recruited Nat to walk with him to Sarah Bignall's house to give a report on her husband's condition. She was very worried but knew he was in good hands. "Can you give me information about the other workers?" he asked. "Two of them walked to my surgery, badly burned and cut up, although their condition is stable at the moment. Do you know anything about their families?" She gave Josiah the men's names.

"Forgive my manners. This is Nat Stowe, my assistant." Nat nodded his head and smiled at Mrs. Bignall and her children. They remembered Nat from the day they played games in the Randolph's backyard.

"When is my father coming home?" asked Matthew. "We miss him."

"It should be several days. His skin was very burned. At this time, he needs to be doctored." Josiah gave the most literal and truthful answer he could give to a ten-year-old and his younger siblings, not wanting to build up the family's hopes to no purpose. The children looked up at the two men, thoughtfully nodding their heads. Still, it was difficult for them to understand.

Nat and Josiah walked two streets over to Ledbetter's Forge. This was Nat's line of work. He had learned the fundamentals of running a foundry by the time he was twelve years old. Stowe Ironworks was one of the largest in Connecticut, shipping many of its products to Europe and the Caribbean.

The furnaces spewed smoke from charcoal fires that burned continuously, blackening the landscape and rooftops of nearby buildings. The forge was small, housing three stone smelters where workers stood in protective apparel, heating ore at high temperatures to create pig iron. Then, it is forged into various shapes and sizes, resulting in a high-quality iron that can be shaped with hammers and tongs. Local blacksmiths depended on wrought iron to manufacture small products such as nails, household goods, bits, and bridles.

Mr. Ledbetter was apparently absent from the building. Nat and Josiah took the liberty of walking further into the forge to get a close look at one of the stone smelters. No doubt, this was where the accident occurred. Some of the stones had become overheated and crumbled, causing the smelter to collapse to one side, exposing the combustion chamber to full fire, which caused the explosion.

In the ensuing chaos, bits of super-heated stone and iron ore flew indiscriminately. Nat looked around for leather aprons and gloves, but none were to be found. "This was no small accident. I'm surprised those three men are still alive. The owner of this place has no business running a foundry if he does not maintain the smelters." Nat examined the stonework closely. It was literally crumbling at its base.

Nat and Josiah turned toward the door when a burly man, covered in charcoal dust, walked in carrying a pair of metal tongs. "If you're looking for Mr. Ledbetter, he's at the tavern drowning his sorrows." He took note of the fine clothes and shoes Nat and Josiah wore, determining they weren't looking for a job. "I've got work to do. Three of the workers walked out this week and left me to do the smelting. What's your business here?"

"I'm Dr. Randolph, and this is my assistant, Nat. The workers you mentioned are confined to my surgery at the moment, unable to walk or use their hands. They're badly burned and cut up. Where were you when the explosion occurred here?"

"I don't know nothing about an explosion. If you're here to cast blame on the owner, I guarantee you'll regret making such trouble." The man took a step toward Dr. Randolph to show he meant business.

Dr. Randolph stared at the man's grimy face while pointing to the crumbling smelter. "There's been an explosion here, and you know it has. Three of your co-workers are in critical condition and in need of constant medical care. There will be restitution."

The burly man turned back to his work. Nat and Josiah departed the premises.

"How would your father handle a situation like this, Nat? Surely there have been accidents at your ironworks?" Josiah asked while the two men walked toward Bradford Lane. He had no desire to take matters into his own hands, but as a doctor, he knew these men would be out of work for several months. "What about their families? How would they survive?"

"In all the years I've worked with my father, nothing as serious as an explosion has ever occurred. Yes, sometimes workers suffer minor burns and heat exhaustion. Nothing like the blisters on the patients in your surgery. Operating a forge with stone furnaces is a huge financial investment, and the furnaces and tools of the trade require maintenance, even replacement, when necessary. We invest more in worker's safety than in profit. We close down our forges during the hot summer months to make repairs and improvements. This closure gives our laborers time to work their farms and spend time with their families."

No wonder their business is successful, Josiah thought. *It takes money to make money, just like the brewing business. There's got to be a way to hold Ledbetter responsible,* he pondered as he and Nat walked to Bradford Lane.

Dr. Randolph walked inside Ezra Phillips' print shop. "Good day, Mr. Phillips. I have some news for you!" He recited the events of the past two days—the details of his patient's conditions, the plight of their families, the explosion of the furnaces, the neglect he had seen firsthand, the desertion of Mr. Ledbetter, and the irresponsibility of his conniving employee. He knew Bostonians would be roused, given the current hostile environment.

"This is front page news, Dr. Randolph. How does this headline sound?" Ezra Phillips dictated:

EXPLOSION AT LEDBETTER FOUNDRY
THREE WORKERS IN CRITICAL CONDITION

"That should start some talk in the taverns." Josiah saw no other alternative. It was obvious the ironworker who threatened him was covering up the explosion and protecting his boss, but for what purpose, he did not know. One day is all it took for the news to settle in on the unemployed dock workers and merchants in Boston, itching for a way to vent their anger.

Meanwhile, Mr. Bignall had improved enough to recall the events at Ledbetter Foundry four days prior, confirming Nat's detailed account of how he believed the explosion occurred. The faulty condition of the stone smelter was proof of Mr. Ledbetter's negligence.

Before Nat and Dr. Pierpoint left the surgery and the three burn patients in the hands of Father, they had helped the patients become mobile insofar as standing with assistance, walking to the kitchen and back to bed. It was exhausting work, but it was exercise that helped their blood circulate, and their limbs became stronger as a result.

Eloise Pierpoint continued to supply fresh food as Gaston delivered mid-day meals to Bradford Lane. The "new patients," as they were called until Sarah Bignall furnished their names, were Aaron Watters and his son, Malcomb, who resided in their family's home in Lexington.

There wasn't a man or woman living in Boston who did not know about the ironworks explosion. The Ledbetter family members, which were many, felt shame and embarrassment that one of their own was so low down to allow his business to fall into disarray. It didn't take long for Thomas Crafts and Leonard Ledbetter to corral their corpulent cousin, Felix Ledbetter, continuously sousing himself at Maurice's Tavern to either sell his family home or the foundry. He swore he would do neither. He felt no responsibility toward his employee's crisis.

Under any other circumstances, Boston's General Court would take up the matter of settling the dispute between Ledbetter Foundry and our three burn patients. Upon Governor Gage's arrival on Boston's shore, he dismissed our form of self-government and the selectmen who evaluated and settled such legalities. At present, Parliament's Intolerable Acts allowed only British rule in such matters.

Thomas and Leonard were beside themselves, learning that a member of their family possessed no scruples in ruining people's lives. They recoiled at the thought of allowing the British government to intervene in their personal affairs. "Over my dead body," Thomas Crafts asserted.

It seemed there would be no justice for our burn patients. Not until we received a visit from two strangers. One was an older man, short and small framed with thinning gray hair pulled back with a leather thong and wearing a linen shirt already soaked with moisture. It was still early morning, but the heat was stifling. He escorted a young woman who looked like she could be his daughter, having the same small oval face with barely a chin to speak of and thin lips. Father invited them into the house, believing they needed medical care. "Good morning, Doctor. My name is Curtis Phelps, and this is my daughter, Lillian Ledbetter. This appears to be your surgery," the visitor spoke softly, nodding his head to the left of the entry hall. "May I inquire about the three patients you're treating? I mean, as to their current condition?" He looked up at Father, waiting for his permission.

"My patients and their families require their rights to privacy in these matters," Father answered.

"I trust my impertinence will not offend you, but there is a matter I would like to discuss with you concerning my daughter's husband. He is the owner of Ledbetter Foundry." Mr. Phelps' statement changed Father's demeanor from suspicion to intrigue.

I offered our visitors a seat in the drawing room and a cool drink of water.

"You've read the newspaper account, I assume?" Father asked, not wanting to add fresh details about his patient's current conditions. He had picked up a few nuggets of the law from Uncle Jacob. "Mr. Ledbetter's workers suffered serious wounds from the explosion in the foundry. They remain in my care at the insistence of their families."

"I am grateful for all you have done to preserve these men's lives. I fear the defective conditions of the smelters were the fault of Mr. Ledbetter. Legally, he does not own the building, nor does he own the house where he and my daughter reside. I hold the deeds to both of the properties. I am in a position to sue Felix Ledbetter. I daresay he has the resources to make financial settlements with his employees." Mr. Phelps suddenly shone a bright light on the perplexity of the situation.

"Have you discussed this with a lawyer?" Father asked. He had no desire to involve himself in legal matters.

"I have retained the best there is in Boston," Mr. Phelps stated with confidence. "My lawyer will pay you a visit at the noon hour to explain the details. We shall take our leave now."

An associate from John Adams' law office brought the legal papers by our house for Father to study and sign. According to the decree, Mr. Bignall, Mr. Waters, and his son, Malcomb, would receive compensation for missed wages and additional funds for a time to convalesce in their homes. In addition, a generous sum was allowed for Dr. Randolph and his assistants, as well as the use of Bradford Lane Surgery.

We all breathed a sigh of relief, never anticipating the benevolence of Mr. Phelps. I wondered how this would settle with Felix Ledbetter now that his foundry was closed. He stayed drunk all the time. Hopefully, he would move to a different part of the colony or just leave altogether—hard to tell.

It had been over a week since the foundry explosion; our patients were in their final phase of healing, thanks to Dr. and Mrs. Pierpoint and Nat Stowe's attentive care. Their determined spirit to relieve us of the impossible task of doctoring three critically ill patients simultaneously ensured the burn victim's survival and allowed the three of us to maintain our sanity through it all.

It made me wonder, what if we had *not* been invited to the Pierpoints' dinner party? "God works in mysterious ways," Auntie maintained. We stood in the kitchen at the long table, pouring precious herbal liquids into small glass bottles, some to be stored in the cool pantry. Others would require the sun's heat for several weeks of infusion. We had been on our feet since early morning, chopping and mashing plants from Eloise's garden. Our hands were numb and stiff, and our backs ached.

With each of us grinding herbs with the help of mortars and pestles, Auntie and I put our heads together and got down to the business of creating medicines. Father would be so proud of our work. Yet, I noticed he hadn't stepped foot in the kitchen all morning. Perhaps he thought we would try to solicit his help. Auntie was apt to run him out. Once she began a project, she worked it through to completion, adamantly opposing interference by anyone, including her brother.

These were lifesaving medicines derived from roots, leaves, and flowers. Essential to our work as healers. Auntie and I depended on Lenora, Naomi, and Eloise's infinite knowledge in concocting all these potions as they had shared their receipts for syrups, tonics, and teas. Three women who believed ancient medicines were the key to help fight diseases and cure common medical problems. They made it their business to cultivate the plants and share their knowledge. This was new territory for us, but we had no choice but to create our own medicines. We would make it work.

Father was in the surgery enjoying conversations with our three patients, never mentioning burns and blisters or work at the foundry; just men talk. Their bodies and minds needed to convalesce. I was sipping a cup of tea when I walked in to say hello and congratulate them on their clearly improved condition. My eyes teared up when I saw them propped in their chairs, talking and laughing with Father.

The noise coming from the kitchen—filling kettles, chopping and grinding herbs—was increasing every second. Auntie's way of beckoning me back to work, I suppose. It was going to be another long night for us. I paused in the hallway to finish my cup of Liberty tea when there was a knock on the front door. It was the Pierpoints' butler, Gaston, delivering our afternoon meal, dependable as always, carrying a wooden box of fine cuisine. Father and I followed the aroma of fresh bread wafting in our direction and into the kitchen.

Father began unpacking the box. "Look, Josie, these flowers are for you," he announced. "Here's a note marked with your name." He gave me a bundle of yellow roses wrapped in a linen cloth and tied with a yellow ribbon. The heavy rose scent and the fragile petals took my breath away.

I read the front of the note. I felt my face blush under Father and Auntie's gaze, waiting anxiously for me to respond.

Part III

THE STOWE FAMILY

Chapter 18

Work Is Good for the Soul

Late April 1774, Suffield, Connecticut

Emmaline Stowe stepped outside her warm kitchen into the cool, damp spring morning, clutching her pewter mug filled mostly with her special home-brewed tea. Special because she had poured the hot liquid over a teaspoon of brandy. Wearing a light blue knitted shawl and sipping her hot tea, she walked through the gray light with the assurance that the sun would slowly rise over the mountain and burn off the mist and the chill of the new day.

Her aunt Mae had slipped a hot biscuit filled with ham into her satchel, as she always did, giving her the sustenance for a busy morning of teaching youngsters in the one-room schoolhouse. The faithful drink was a pleasure and a fortification she allowed herself, fully aware that in a half hour, her mind, body, and spirit would be totally dedicated to the eight boys and four girls whom she had committed her mornings to since last September.

While walking the quarter mile toward the school building, common sense ruled, and she stopped at the privy. A naggingly full bladder was the last thing she needed to interfere with the precious time she planned to devote to each child. Emma had learned during the last five years of teaching that possessing a good-hearted disposition was the key to building a relationship with each child. Giving her pupils a good experience in her classroom just might instill in them a lifelong desire to learn; at least, it had worked for her and her sister, Maddie.

Teaching her collection of sprightly students to become proficient readers was her primary aim, for she perceived the obstacles of illiteracy among the adults living in the community of Suffield, especially women. The few engaging hours she spent with each child each morning, five mornings a week, were targeted toward embedding in them a love of reading and discovery. For that reason, she began each morning with a Bible story or sometimes a fairy tale, which at its core taught grammar and lessons in everyday life coupled with adventure and, sometimes, make-believe.

She smiled when she saw the swirl rising from the school building's chimney. Nathan never let her down. She hailed him as he walked across the property from the direction of the foundry, "I'm grateful for the fire. I'm freezing!"

He turned around and walked over to her before she climbed the porch steps. They kissed each other, followed by a long embrace. "Your face is cold, and you have a red nose," he wrapped his arms around her shoulders. "There's a mystery solved. Now I know who's draining the brandy bottle," he looked at her face and smiled accusingly, eyebrows raised. "You looked terribly engrossed in something from a distance. Expecting any problems with the children this morning?"

"None that I know of at the moment. Just recalling the fairy tale I'm planning to impart to my students. Getting all the phrases established in my mind," Emma replied. She was a storyteller at heart and a stickler for details.

"I wish I had had a spirited teacher to tell me stories. The only tales I heard from Mr. Gutfield was the one about a certain student who could not recite his Latin lessons," he laughed. "I'm sure you can imagine the outcome of that episode!"

"I certainly can, but, after all, how often do you use Latin with your employees?" Emma laughed. "By the way, you can be assured we have a plentiful store of spirits in the cupboard and other places." She sighed and smiled. "Today, I have three reasons to be happy: a touch of brandy to warm my belly, a blazing fire to warm my nose, and a loving embrace from the man I love. Surely, that will carry me until noon time," she whispered in his ear.

"Yes, well, my body's heat is suddenly rising, and it's not from 'a touch of brandy', as you say. I have plenty of work to tend to at the forge." A quick goodbye kiss and he was gone. He contemplated as he walked along the damp trail, breathing in the smells of burning charcoal and hot metal. How does she manage a room full of other people's children and our own five?

Emma laughed at her husband's eagerness to take his leave and entered the warm classroom to start her day. This was the work she loved: teaching children about the world outside of their small Connecticut town and instilling in them the confidence to face the challenges of life.

Looking at the property from the road, you wouldn't know there was a house set a great distance back, large enough for a family of eight—and more if the occasion presented itself. Fenced-in pasture land, a quarter mile in length, ran from the road up to the Stowe dwelling. Fencing on the front roadside of the property was lined with dark green cedar trees with a wide drive cut straight through the middle.

Fencing on either side of the drive had corralled various large beasts through the years, mostly mules and oxen. Only recently, its inhabitants were horses and ponies, along with numerous mules for transporting wagons filled with iron products produced for shipping down the Connecticut River.

Crabapple trees, first planted as seedlings, were purposely spaced at twelve-foot intervals along the fence line to allow the miniature trees sufficient room to grow and mature. As an added benefit, it gave the animals a window of sorts between the trees to view anything or anybody moving down the drive toward the big house. Aunt Mae valued the tart crabapples for the jelly she created in late summer.

On her initial visit to the Stowe house as a new bride-to-be, Emma was impressed with the simple style of the two-storied stone edifice—the symmetry of the front windows arranged around a solid timber door barred with a substantial crossbar, a fan light perched above gave it an English look. The impressive stables matched the house with the same uncut stone inside and out, supported by post and beam timbers cut and milled on the Stowe property. Adequate fencing enclosed the pastures, providing the rustic look Emma always loved when she visited her father's country homeplace in England.

The French-inspired chateau her parents had planned and built as their home in Beacon Hill was as different as night and day compared to this charming country home. Curved windows and doors and gilded mirrors were a thing of the past for Emma. Starting her new life as wife to Nathan, she preferred a simple architectural style, straight lines, and less fuss, where she could initiate her own ideas.

She was well-disposed to accepting the noticeable changes of farm life, becoming accustomed to the constant malodorous smells of farm animals mixed with the verdant country air, so different from the dead fish and sewage smells of Boston. It was the journey up the mountain that inspired Emma's decision to embrace all that the landscape offered. Not just the beauty of the thickets of hardwood trees and pines and spruce but the rocky creek beds overgrown with useful herbs and multitudes of wild berry vines shooting up from the fertile wet earth. The silence and seclusion of the forests kindled a vitality within her soul that caused her destination to radically change from city life to country life.

At present, the house was a hodgepodge of add-ons to the original structure built in the early 1700s by Nathan's grandfather, Nathaniel Stowe. The steep slate shingle roof allowed for stone chimneys attached on either side of the building and a large one in the back for the kitchen. After Nat and Lainey were born, they built an addition for a music room and a larger dining room. Above that was Nat's new room. It wasn't long before Lizzy, Dory, and Debby came along. Now, an addition was built to the right side of the house for more bedrooms and an office for Nathan on the main floor.

She loved the steep roofs with layered shingles. When the two additions were added, she and Nathan thought to copy the same roof lines, looking like three separate triangular roofs reaching toward the sky. It reminded her of a castle built in the classical architectural tradition of

England. Much like homes that have stood for centuries surrounded by mountains, pastures, meadows, and farmland.

Each time Emma rode down the long path to the house, she felt as if she was passing through an avenue of magical trees that sensed her fears and her shortcomings. She imagined that something hidden inside those leafy facades knew her struggles in raising her five children in this secluded part of the world. The care they needed and deserved, the dreams she had for each one, guiding them toward excellence in their attitudes, their God-given talents, and their love for each other.

Every day for the past twenty-one years, she saw to each child's needs. It was her life, and she accepted the challenge of it. In fact, she reveled in the satisfaction that problems, if handled properly, have solutions. That philosophy made her a strong advocate for her own children and those she taught. "They don't stay at home forever," she recalled her father expressing that reality to her mother.

"Nat Stowe, you come back here this very minute. Simon McGinty is not a lout nor a lush!" The raging voice called after him as his long legs carried him swiftly down the dirt path towards the forge. There was no need for him to turn his head around to see who was responsible for the yelling. While it could have come from any one of his four sisters, he knew the source of the hysterical shouting came from Lainey, two years his junior. He jumped over a puddle of water left over from last night's rain.

Lainey had turned eighteen the week before, and she was in a dither, for she had no likely suitor whom she considered marriage material. Lately, she was prone to worry about her future, trapped under the same roof with her parents and younger sisters, envisioning the possibility of life as a spinster music teacher terrified her.

Nat and Emma Stowe had cautioned their daughter that it takes time to develop the kind of trust and friendship required for a husband-and-wife relationship. "Time is not on my side," she stated tearfully. "Surely, this would not take years," she grimaced as she passed by the kitchen mirror. She stared momentarily at her scowling pink face.

Truthfully, if her friend Glenda Berkman had not made such a racket over her recent engagement to Calvin Whitney, this conversation would have never taken place. Jealousy and irrational thinking had taken hold of her, causing tension in the family. She knew, without a doubt, that her parents would not allow her to marry Simon McGinty. He had never worked a day in his life. That alone would repulse her parents.

Nat ran about halfway toward the forge, slipping on wet leaves left over from the previous rainfall, not knowing the degree to which Lainey would take out her angst. He stood up and looked behind him, doing what he could to brush away the wet leaves, managing a reprieve from his sister this time and being thankful for it. With that hot temper of hers, Lainey, without considering the consequences, could turn a piece of crockery into a weapon. He temporarily dismissed the hostilities of the morning, knowing full well that the matter would surely pick up where it left off following the family's mid-day dinner. Aunt Mae, who governed over matters of discipline and the Stowe children's conflicts in the household, would see to that.

Nat hesitated ten steps before he entered through the double doors of the main forge. He took a deep breath and smoothed his black hair back from his sweating forehead. He could feel his face flushed after running the distance from the kitchen, fleeing his sister's fury. His father would likely give him a scowling look and ask questions later.

Nathan Stowe stood talking to a young man in an uncluttered area of the foundry with a view of the refinery in the distance, away from the deafening sounds of workers hammering hot metal. Nat joined the two men as his father acquainted the stranger with the different operations of the establishment. He looked up at Nat and smiled, making no mention of his disheveled appearance, sweeping a wet leaf off his son's shirt while handing him some paperwork. "Examine this order we received from Jacob Randolph, and let's meet in my office later to discuss the details."

Nat smiled and nodded at the young man standing at his father's side. "Welcome to our world, John. That is your mule tied up in the front pasture, isn't it?" Nat was sure the animal belonged to the new worker, but he wanted to give him an opportunity to answer.

"*Oui, monsieur, pardon, c'est mon beast,*"[12] John corrected himself. "It is true. I believe you and Frederic have met. How did you know it was mine?"

"He's the only animal I've ever met that heehaws in French," answered Nat, laughing at himself. "I'm sure he'll feel more at home in the paddock with the other mules as long as he's not too pig-headed." His mouth took on a distorted look at the thought of Lainey, meaning to brain him with a flying coffee mug. "Feel free to move him when you can. He'll need water and hay."

A large portion of Nat's work in the forge was training new recruits, such as the new man standing before him, John Dupre. He seemed like an affable sort, but so had all the other prospective apprentices. They would work long enough to earn a week's wage, but they never returned. Working in the forge meant standing on your feet all day, heating iron rods to make them malleable enough to be hammered and shaped into a finished product. Not every man had the manual strength or an inclination toward learning the trade. Nat wondered if it was not more like strength of character that induced men to persevere, denouncing the adversities of the physically demanding foundry work.

John gazed upwards eight feet above him at the double-chambered bellows suspended from the rafters, intrigued that each time the operator pulled the connected rope, the fat end of the bellows deflated and inflated. This simple technique blew air through the bellow's nose, then through a pipe that continuously fed oxygen to the rapidly burning coal in the fire pit. John's eyes followed the procedure downward to the fire pit's base, where a worker stood heating iron bars in preparation for hammering into desired shapes once it was placed on the anvil positioned no more than three feet beyond the pit.

Nat smiled at John's interest in the operation. "I gather you've never been inside a forge this size or one with an open hearth furnace."

"*Non, mon ami.*[13] You are correct. I regret to say I have never had the opportunity. What will become of the bars once they are hammered into shapes?" John asked. His interest grew as he observed each step.

---

12. Yes, sir, excuse me, it's my beast.
13. No, my friend.

Nat began with his detailed explanation, "You have seen two, four, or six horses pulling a wagon or a carriage, I presume?" He spoke loudly, realizing that he would have to repeat everything he said to John. "Er, step this way to the desk, *monsieur*, and I will draw a model on parchment instead."

"Consider the harnesses that the horses wear. The harness begins with a leather collar attached to leather straps held together by metal rings and buckles." Nat drew a crude flatbed wagon with a wooden pole extending forward from the underside to wooden crossbars. "The horse harnesses are attached to the cross bars with leather straps and metal rings which are attached to the center pole with metal rings, hooks, and center pin. This contraption allows the horses to move freely while pulling the wagon and allows it to turn the wagon as the driver pulls the reins attached to the horse's bridle and bits that are made of metal parts."

"The wagon itself is mostly wood held together with metal nails. The wheel's metal axle, the steel band around the wooden wheels, and the metal pin that allows the front axle to pivot so the wagon can turn. These are all parts that are made from the metal bars we produce," Nat laughed at John's overwhelmed reaction to his detailed description. But impressed that John took such interest.

So their morning work began just as it had for the last five generations of the Stowe family. An establishment that began when the family moved from Roxbury, Massachusetts, to the new colony of Connecticut in the late 1600s. A native Algonquin tribe offered to sell John Stowe a portion of land in Suffield. They hunted, fished, and farmed together with the notion of enjoying a peaceful life in the wilderness and learning each other's ways, even their respective language.

The timing of the land offer could not have come at a more advantageous time for the Stowes and the peace-loving Algonquin tribe. King Philip's bloody war with the settlers had run its course, and peaceful times lay on the horizon in 1665. Philip, the son of Massasoit, who had greeted the Mayflower Pilgrims in the 1620s, had waged war against New England settlers after his father's passing. For almost fifty years, Philip and his warriors burned colonists' towns and murdered families as a consequence of building their homes and farms in Massachusetts, Connecticut, and Rhode Island.

Serving a meal at the Stowe home every day for a family of eight was indeed an accomplishment, but, nevertheless, it occurred each day precisely on schedule when the clock struck three. Aunt Mae embraced the responsibilities of running the Stowe household, which involved managing the gardening and the chickens, the marketing, the meal planning, the laundry, and the delegation of tasks to the four daughters. No homestead could have run more efficiently than the home that Aunt Mae commanded and held so dear to her heart.

She had delivered Emma's five babies into the world and helped raise the healthy infants in such a way as if they were her own. Gone were the days of toddling babies scooting across the floor and their chattering sounds as if they were a talking bird. Now, the four daughters were growing toward adulthood and had assumed personal and household responsibilities that grounded them to embody the self-discipline needed to make capable decisions.

Aunt Mae knew these things in her heart, and while she went about her morning's work, her thoughts kept coming back to the aspirations of honor and preparedness she believed she had instilled in the four daughters. So, why did she feel deflated and disheartened on this beautiful spring day in April? She recalled the snarling looks Lainey had flashed at her brother earlier. So much divisiveness bothered Aunt Mae, causing her to lose faith in her ability to manage the children.

Emma's work in the classroom was finished for the day. The work was draining, but she was heartened when Isaiah successfully read a story out loud, pronouncing each word correctly. His face beamed when he returned to his desk. The female students even clapped their hands.

When Emma entered the house through the kitchen door, she found Aunt Mae seated at the work table with a hanky to her eyes. She dropped her bag on the table and came immediately to the gray-haired, plump woman. Emma embraced her shoulders and bent her head to Aunt Mae's temple. "Whatever is the matter, have you been hurt, or is there some bad news?"

Aunt Mae looked up at Emma with such affection and sniffled, "I'm not hurt, in the physical sense, but my spirit is low today, and I believe I have failed you and Nathan in the nurturing of our, I mean your daughters. I have always believed that since they came into the world, God intended for me to raise them and love them as if they were my own."

Emma sat in the chair beside her and held her hand. "Of course, Nathan and I believe you have been a mother to them as well, and we would never think it any different. Aunt Mae, you brought me up since I was a baby, and you never left my side. I will always love you for raising me and the thousand ways you guided me and prepared me to be a married woman."

Aunt Mae gazed at Emma's pretty face with its sharp little nose and bright blue eyes. "Oh darling, you were such a joy to raise. A sweet baby you were, enjoying your playful times, and as you grew, you never faltered in your lessons. Ah, the enthusiasm you showed for playing the piano! You cheered my emotions so, and I believed I had been faithful in raising you to be the woman you have become."

Emma's demeanor changed from happy eyes and a smile to a confused and serious look. "But your emotions are not cheered today, so it has to be a problem with the children, hopefully not all of them."

Aunt Mae's blue eyes were pouring tears now as she bent her head toward her folded hands. "Oh fie, it's Lainey. She has been in her room all day, and she will not speak to me in a polite manner, but rather a 'go away, don't bother me' manner! She's star-crossed, I tell you!"

"What makes you think she's lovesick? I've not heard her speak of any young man with whom she holds any affection! Who could it possibly be, Aunt Mae?"

"You were gone by the time the explosion happened between Lainey and Nat this morning," Aunt Mae began her tale. "I stood back in horror while she was throwing food and screaming all sorts of horrid expressions at him as he was backing out the door just there. He took off running like a hound chasing a fox, and she commenced to hurl the coffee mugs at him as he fled. She slammed the door and hastened off upstairs in such a crying fit, all her red hair flying behind her! She doesn't exactly hold back her emotions. She called the young man's name. I don't remember." She fidgeted with her apron, tears rolled down her flushed face.

Emma recalled a conversation with Lainey last week in the barn when they were saddling their horses for a ride to the meadow. She had seen Lainey's disappointment when she told her mother about Glenda Berkman's engagement. Lainey's unusually quiet demeanor should have signaled a warning to Emma. *A missed opportunity on my part*, she told herself.

Emma needed a distraction to rekindle her thoughts. She took a deep breath, removed herself from the work table, and walked to the cupboard that held the spirits. Pushing the applejack and blackberry wine aside, her hand searched in the back of the cabinet for the familiar shape of the brandy bottle. *French cognac will do nicely*, she muttered. She poured the amber liquid into two glasses and moved one of them in Aunt Mae's direction, which she eagerly accepted and commenced to imbibe. The two women sat talking over the situation and decided that this heartthrob better be worth the anguish suffered by their oldest daughter. Aunt Mae dried her tears, now managing to speak coherently.

Hearing the clock chime, she was prompted to get a move on to finish dinner. The family would be expecting their meal in two hours. She needed to hasten the preparations. Solving Lainey's problems would have to wait.

Emma offered her help. "I see you have some chickens roasting on the spit and a cobbler in the oven. Oh, there's sweet potatoes roasting on the side. You've got a good start on the meal, Aunt Mae, even though the day's been exhausting and unpredictable for you. It takes a while to peel apples, after all!" There was no need for concern. Emma knew full well her aunt had pulled off meals under the worst of circumstances. She was an organized whirlwind in the kitchen!

"Oh no, that was Deborah's doing. She finished her lessons and came to keep me company while I was lacing up the chickens. She offered to make an apple cobbler; made the whole pie by herself! What a delight she was, chattering about a tale she read of a boy and a girl lost in the woods, rescued by a witch," Aunt Mae's face beamed as she unfolded the tale, at least the parts she remembered, knowing in her heart that little Deborah's story had helped to relieve her tension.

Their heads shot up, and their mouths flew open when through the kitchen door walked a dusty figure wearing a ragged oversized jacket and a slouch hat with the brim partially missing. Strands of light brown hair hung over most of Dory's face. "I snatched three rabbits from the snares I set yesterday, and here's the bag of peas you wanted. Is there anything you want from the garden or the springhouse?" Aunt Mae stood looking aghast at the child, slowly shaking her head in reply.

Father and son, ravenous as they were, came through the scullery to wash the charcoal dust from their face and hands, then changed into fresh shirts. Their work at the forge had ended for the day as it had for all the workers. Ideally, Nathan employed a minimum of forty men to manufacture the iron products needed to fulfill contracts for customers, not only in Connecticut but in Massachusetts and Rhode Island. The superior quality of products Stowe Ironworks generated was recognized by many in the industry. The need for good men who were serious about learning the trade kept Nathan and his son busy training them. Workers who were skilled and dependable were paid well. Some of those men had begun an apprenticeship with Nathan's father twenty years ago or more.

Nathan observed Aunt Mae stacking roasted chicken pieces on a platter; the juicy, roasted meat smell filled his head, tempting him to snatch a crunchy morsel that fell to the side. He managed restraint by extending his long arm around her shoulders, giving her a gentle squeeze, remembering how her face tended to scowl if itchy fingers interfered with the masterpiece she spent hours creating. "As always, you've outdone yourself," he said, looking over the work table filled with vegetables, sweet potatoes, bread, and a crusty apple cobbler. He shook his head in disbelief. She stood a little taller at his compliment, wondering herself how in the world it all came together after the craziness of the morning. Nathan caught a whiff of brandy, pondering why women in this house began imbibing unusually early in the day.

The dining room housed a long table with room for a dozen chairs. Years before, during one of the renovations, Emma insisted on two large chandeliers to hang from the ten-foot ceiling to adequately illuminate the expansive table. Nathan thought it was a waste of money, insisting that he could easily build two fixtures of her design at the forge after working hours. One, two, three years passed, and still no fixtures. Plenty of light shone through the windows facing the back of the property while they ate their mid-day meal. Hence, in the evening, they sat at the table with candlesticks scattered about, drinking their coffee and chocolate.

With Nathan dragging his feet on the chandeliers, Emma was at an impasse. She was seven months pregnant with Lizzy, and her parents would be visiting in two months to welcome the new baby. To save Nathan embarrassment, Aunt Mae drove the carriage into Suffield along with Nat so Emma could order the fixtures she had in mind. To top it off, and in light of the three-year wait time, she asserted that beeswax candles would complete the look she imagined for the simple but elegant wrought iron chandeliers. She had the clerk send the bill to Emma Pierpoint, never making reference that her husband owned and managed Stowe Ironworks. Nathan paid the bill, and his only response after they were installed was, "You have such magnificent taste in decorating, Emma. Beautiful!"

Today, with rays of sun streaming in and the gentle sounds of ale poured in cups and silver flatware gently resting on plates, Emma still delighted in the rustic feel of her dining room. So proud of her chandeliers.

"Am I the only one who's noticed that Lainey is not present?" Nathan looked first at Emma and exchanged eye contact with Dory, then Lizzy. "She's not ill, is she?" All three waited on the others to answer his question. Aunt Mae exempted herself by focusing her eyes on her plate and stuffing her mouth with sweet potato. The tension in the air could be cut with a knife.

Emma and Lizzy began speaking at the same time, but Lizzy was quicker to the draw. "Yes, Lainey is definitely sick, but not the sort of sick that requires medicine. The person most qualified to answer that question would be the only other male at the table. Isn't that correct, Nat?"

Nat gave Lizzy an exasperated look. "Yes, I'm qualified to answer that question, but out of respect for Lainey, I'm inclined to speak privately with her along with Mother and Father, that is, if they are agreeable," Nat, thinking back to this morning when he dashed out the door to save his head, decided to table the discussion for later. At that, Lizzy was notably dejected that Nat and Lainey were getting off the hook so easily. She wrinkled her nose at her brother, which he ignored.

Emma showed her approval by nodding her head toward Nat. "That's very kind of you to consider your sister. Don't you agree, Nathan?" Purposely changing the subject, "Debby, this cobbler is delicious!"

Nathan yielded his assent. "Perhaps we'll discuss this with Lainey later in the day." Turning his attention toward his other daughters, "Dory, I see you've been trapping this morning. Any good hunting in the woods?"

"Yes, but you're not going to like it," she focused serious eyes on her father and replied regretfully. "I followed a set of footprints all the way up to the ridge, but they weren't made by moccasins. Redcoat boot heels perfectly pressed into mud and the outline of the shoe, along with this." She pulled a piece of red lint from her shirt pocket that she had found on a briar bush. "Could be from a redcoat jacket, I don't know." She placed it beside her father's plate, and Nathan noticed her dirty and ragged fingernails. She peered directly at his face. "Did you trade for a new mule? He stared me down when I walked past the paddock this morning." Dory spent most days outside if the weather cooperated.

Nathan looked to his son for the answer. "The strange mule in question is French, and he belongs to our new worker, John Dupre," Nat announced.

Typically, Lainey was in charge of cleanup after the mid-day dinner. In the early morning, she had confined herself to her room, being either too embarrassed to face her brother or made the decision that today was an off day for her. Emma placed Lizzy in charge of Dory and Debby's part of the cleanup. "It's your responsibility to see that everything is clean and stored properly," she reminded Lizzy. "Work in cooperation with each other. No cross words between you!" Emma admonished.

Such an exalted position endorsed Lizzy as competent and appreciated. This is where Lizzy bloomed. Her eagerness to command her sisters was her primary delight, but she yearned for notice and praise from Emma and Aunt Mae. That was her motivation to see the job performed as her mother directed. Not dispelling the fact that today, she felt superior to her older sister, Lainey.

Nat carried the kitchen fireplace utensils and pots outside for cleanup next to the well near the scullery. Aunt Mae went from the table to her room to recover from the morning's work. This had been mandated by Nathan long ago in an effort to guard the woman's health and mind. He recognized Aunt Mae's physical and mental limits, so he protected her. No need to jeopardize the daily meal preparations. She was an excellent cook. Emma was a talented woman, and thank the Lord she was, but she lacked the knack for preparing a satisfying meal. They were both mum on that subject.

With the children involved in kitchen cleanup, this signaled a retreat from the family and the house for Nathan and Emma to take their afternoon constitutions. Intending to exercise their body and calm their mind. Freeing themselves from listening to the indignant comments amongst their daughters. Each bragging about some superior attribute they just happened to be born with because they were born uncommonly smart.

Walking down the long drive and past the green pastures toward the road lifted their spirits, putting aside the flurry of their occupations. The spring day brought dry air and warm weather, with a slight breeze blowing crabapple blossoms in their direction. The smell of new spring grass was invigorating as they strolled down the length of the driveway and then down the road to the meadow. "What's going on with Lainey? She's barely spoken to me in the past week." Nathan wasn't going to let the mealtime conflict between Nat and Lizzy pass.

Emma looked straight ahead, avoiding his eyes. "It seems Lainey took great offense to Nat's comment about a certain young man she met at the Brookings' barn dance recently. I'm told there was a goodly amount of crockery thrown in the direction of Nat's back this morning as he ran to the forge. It's Lainey demonstrating her frustrations with her brother's comments. That innate fury takes hold of her." She turned her head toward Nathan's face, taking note of his scowling forehead and an unidentified gravelly groan coming from his throat. "Nathan, I'm giving you all the details passed on to me by Aunt Mae. We won't get the truth until we speak with Nat and Lainey, which I hope will be today."

"It sounds more serious than a typical skirmish to me. When I came upon Nat first thing this morning, he was sweating like a racehorse, his hair falling in his face, looking like he was running for his life! It's not like Lainey to stay in her room during dinner." He was perplexed. He dropped the matter for the time being.

Nathan had been at the foundry since before daylight. After each day's work was completed, he looked forward to spending time with Emma. She was beautiful. Her golden hair glistening in the sun and her bright blue friendly eyes, she was smart and full of life. Sometimes, it was hard for him to believe she was really his wife. He glanced down at his hands, regretting that his fingernails were black from today's work, but she didn't mind. She held it anyway.

They had worked up a thirst and got a drink of water at the well. She turned to him, "Don't worry. We will work this out with Lainey, but remember, she wants her independence just like we did when we were eighteen." She gave him a hug. "I just hope she finds a husband like I did, who truly loves her." They parted. She walked to the house to help Dory and Debby with their violin lessons.

Nathan retreated to his office, sitting behind his desk as he usually did to study contracts and schedule future work. The quill scratched across pages in the record book as he ciphered the financial accounts of the foundry. Payday for his employees came around each Saturday.

The summer foundry schedule was approaching, beginning the fifteenth of June. The ironworks would continue its operations but with a skeleton crew. Most of his workers lived on small farms, were married, and were raising children. The planting season had begun, their farms needed work, and families needed time to be together. This was Nathan's father's doing, beginning when he managed the forge; a few of the same men hired by his father now worked under Nathan. He was against making drastic changes that might cause employees to seek work elsewhere. These veteran employees were the backbone of his business. In his mind, they were indispensable.

Nat assisted his father by defining which workers would best manage certain jobs. He recognized particular skills and attitudes in workers that guided him in selecting the right man for the job. Some of the stone forges needed repair, which fell under the heading of summertime work. Nathan had a good head for determining the length of time needed to complete certain jobs, so he maintained his own ledgers of accounts, recording dates and deadlines. At times, he believed his life was ruled by the demands of the ledger. For all that, the business end ran smoothly, although not perfectly.

A large sheet of parchment caught his attention, lying halfway under the book of John Milton's poems. A broadsheet advertising the call for counties in northern Connecticut to "form militia groups for the defense of property and businesses to thwart the tyranny of King George III." The words fell hard on him, causing a queasiness in his gut. *This abominable British government*, he muttered. *Has it come to this?* He poured himself a whiskey, seeking to relieve the built-up tension.

He walked toward the front window of his office, watching the horses. Some foraging for new green grass; some gazing in between the crabapple trees at the mules in the paddock across the drive. His inherited property from five generations of running the ironworks was the livelihood for his family and his forty devoted workers.

His eye caught the brown leather book on the shelf, a journal authored by his great, great grandfather. It was so ancient, with its torn parchment pages and slanted handwriting, some words were barely legible. He forbade his children from picking it up and reading without his assistance. It was a family treasure, giving an account of the first Stowe family having the courage to cross the sea to make a start in the New World.

An account of the Stowe family, written by Nathaniel Giles Stowe, November 1710, as declared to me by my father, born 1630.

The first Stowe to emigrate from England, Hawkhurst, county of Kent, to the Massachusetts colony, settled with his wife and ten children in Roxbury in 1634. My father, John Stowe, was a school teacher and a landowner of over two hundred acres of property, including an estate and farm animals. He was twice elected as one of eighteen assistants serving under an elected governor and deputy governor. These officials, called selectmen of the General Court, as it was named, were empowered to make laws for the colony and defend against land and sea attacks.

As a young man, he had dreamed of owning property and having an influence in society, but English laws were strict and confining for such a man as John Stowe. He settled his family in the New World, where the rolling hills, the flatlands, and the river valleys were reminiscent of his home in Hawkhurst. In a matter of time, my father realized that his convictions concerning religion, economics, and independence corresponded with those of the colonists in Massachusetts.

Because of New England's long, harsh winters, the growing season was short, providing only an adequate amount of food for our family. We mostly relied on small game and deer from the woods. The sea provided some livelihood in fishing and whaling. But John knew his financial security lay in owning property. He purchased as much as came available and at a price he could afford. For settlers like us living in Roxbury, protecting our property and homes from Indian attacks was a constant test of survival.

I, being Nathaniel Giles Stowe, ambitiously purchased one thousand acres from an Algonquin tribe in Suffield, Connecticut, near the wide river in 1665. As the fifth son of John Stowe, I received a small inheritance upon my father's death, a portion of which was remitted to the Indian tribal chief in the amount of eight pounds, in addition to three metal stew pots, twenty beaver pelts, fifty blankets and two sacks of tobacco.

What was left from the inheritance money went to purchase hogs, oxen, mules, chickens, and a milk cow. Also, the required tools needed to dig out the rocks in the land were intended for building a small house for my family—my wife, Dorothy, and our four children, Nathan, Samuel, Katherine, and Margaret.

I had invested my inheritance money in the land, hoping to create a farm for my family to thrive and to earn a profit from the sale of barley, corn, and animal products. The acreage not used for farming would benefit my children when the time came for them to leave home.

Isaac Thomas, Dorothy's widowed father, came to live in our house. He obligingly helped with the daily chores as much as his health would allow. He was uncommonly suited to making hand tools and furniture pieces for the house. He built a square stone forge a hundred yards thereabout from the creek bank. This proved handy for forming horseshoes and mending bridles.

Isaac had learned the iron-making skill as a young man when he lived in Cranbrook of county Kent, England. He knew the work well—creating the charcoal from the property's timber, smelting the ore he dug out from the nearby mountains, repeatedly heating and hammering to produce the tools the farm needed. It seemed interesting to me, but I had no time to spare for the additional work.

When the house was completed, it boasted a front room with an ample fireplace, two rooms off to the side for sleeping, a sleeping loft above for Nathan and Samuel, and a long kitchen for cooking and dining. Out to the side was the scullery and the well.

My loving wife, Dorothy, tended to the management of the household affairs and educating our four children. I began my work each morning while it was still dark, came inside to eat my mid-day meal, then returned outside to manage the animals and the crops until sundown.

In the beginning, I proposed to farm only a portion of the land. The terrific labor of carving fields out of dense woods and rocky terrain took over two years. Working the fields was strenuous. Breeding and caring for the animal's needs required several strong men, which I could not afford. The work was backbreaking and never-ending. Were it not for the kitchen garden planted and maintained by my wife's father, we would have starved.

Three years had passed. I scarcely produced ten barrels of barley and the same of corn to sell to local merchants for shipment to the islands. So little return on my investment was disappointing.

I thought it foolish to place the strains of farm life on Dorothy and the children. My vision of owning the mass of acreage was weakening, causing me to consider selling a portion.

It was autumn, and cool weather urged me to the woods to hunt. I was hoping for a deer, for Isaac was well established in the methods of butchering the animal and proper storage of the meat in the smokehouse. I gathered my bow, a pack of food, and ale and headed toward the mountain.

I walked through the wilderness to a granite shelf jutting out from a rocky summit, settling myself to rest. I gazed at the valley below, thick with mature trees and a wide creek twisting through the landscape. I acquainted myself with the land I owned, having never traveled beyond the creek.

I navigated my way down the mountain to the flatland, where I walked a mile alongside the creek. Less than twenty miles to the east was the Connecticut River. To the west stood the mountains. Something stirred in me when I reminded myself that this land belonged to me. This was my security, as his father knew so well. Why am I confining myself to a mere portion of the land to live and grow food when I have all this, I asked myself?

I left the mountaintop, almost forgetting the purpose of my trip. Halfway down the mountain, movement through the trees caught my attention. I raised the bow to let loose an arrow and heard the animal fall. My intended purpose. I draped the heavy deer over my shoulders and walked to the farm, laying it on the table in the butchering shed. Isaac stood waiting with a wooden bucket of salt and a leather bag holding the meat cleavers and saws. The old man tied on his heavy apron and smiled at my sweating face, noticing something different about me, a sense of renewal, possibly.

In the evenings, it was my habit to sit by the fireplace recounting the day's events, enjoying the company of my wife and father-in-law, drinking a hot rum. With chalk and a piece of cloth, I sketched a map of my property: the front pastures surrounded by crabapple trees, the homestead, the barn and fencing for the animals, and the fields of barley, corn, and vegetables and set it aside on the hearth.

I brought out a different cloth on which I had crudely drawn another sketch of the property with no fields and no farm animals. With chalk, I drew arrows in a southeast direction of the property, ending at three crudely drawn stone furnaces, earth mound kilns, the mountain, the valley of hardwood trees, and the Connecticut River in the distance. Dorothy and Isaac studied the sketch. His wife sat speechless and bewildered. His father-in-law nodded that he understood. He reached toward his son-in-law to shake his hand. Resin from a log in the fireplace popped, then spewed a speck of hot ash on the hearth, catching a corner of the first sketch; together, we watched it shrivel and burn. A sign that my life had changed within a day's time. Soon to move forward on a different path.

I began slowly, under the apprenticeship of Isaac: mining, then smelting iron ore, converting timber to charcoal, and hammering iron into bars to sell to local blacksmiths. In a year's time, we were shipping iron down the Connecticut River headed to England. Stowe Ironworks now beat out some of its competitors in Windsor, New London, and Essex. Maybe it was the foundry's prime location, the distance being within twenty miles of the river. Maybe it was because this was the work I was meant to learn and manage. Maybe it was because my kinsman came to me in a time of need, understanding my struggles.

Half a century had passed. In an act of rebellion, colonists, including the Stowe family, built their own refinery forges and furnaces, ending Britain's control over colonists who desired to manufacture their own finished products, opening up business ventures directly with Europe. This took England out of the picture. It wasn't long before colonies in the New World became one of the top producers of iron products in the world—because of the abundant natural resources found in Connecticut's mountains.

Thanks to Nathaniel Stowe's investment in land, furnaces, and labor, it became one of the most productive ironworks in the colonies, providing a steady income to his workers and remarkable prosperity for his family. The production of iron paved the way for progress in the colonies and the world. The Stowes were like so many who had a dream when they entered the New World. The shackles of dependence on England were released when they experienced the freedom of standing on their own two feet.

Suffield, Connecticut, had been home to five generations of Stowes. The sprawling acreage was mostly wilderness, some pastureland, ample creeks and tributaries running off the Connecticut River—all necessities for building the ironworks that brought prosperity to the Stowe descendants, its workers, and all who profited from the manufactured products generated by the three furnaces operating on Stowe property.

Nathan placed the journal on the shelf. "A vision. A purpose. Honorable work. His ancestor, Nathaniel, was a visionary, willing to sacrifice and willing to take risks," he said of his great, great grandsire. He cleared this land, rejected all the odds by going forward with his expectations, building something from nothing because he valued his liberty and the mark it would make on his descendants.

Reality hit Nathan hard. "If they can demand closure of Mr. Hancock's wharf, they can do the same to Stowe Ironworks. That puts forty stouthearted men out of work. Where does that leave my family and their families?" He held the broadsheet in his hand.

His solitude and concentration were broken by a knock at the office door. Nat walked into the gloomy, cheerless room. "I see I'm interrupting." He turned to leave, reading his father's face—worried, pale, sorrowful. *Maybe he's worried about Lainey*, he thought.

"I'd rather you stay. We need to talk," Nathan said, still holding the parchment in his hand. "Have you seen any of these at the tavern?" he asked, passing it to his son.

Nat scanned the broadsheet. With a grimace, he shook his head and sighed deeply. He stared at his father's face. "We knew it was coming." Like so many men in Suffield, he would, on occasion, ride to the Black Rooster to drink a mug of beer, more for social reasons than the drink itself. Crossing the paths of familiar faces was part of the delight in visiting the tavern, giving way to discussions of business and of local news. He knew all of the families in Suffield. Most managed a business or a farm that had been established in the last century. Carrying on the work their ancestors had created and providing for their families. "These broadsheets are posted in every business in town."

Lately, the talk of revolution consumed the majority of their discussions. Tensions in the colonies were mounting as more talk of Britain's frustration with the colonies was high on the list of conversational topics—many were enraged about the prospects of British soldiers quartering in villages and towns, amounting to a loss of their personal freedoms. "To what purpose has Parliament permitted their soldiers to violate the peace and welfare of colonists?" Nathan asked.

"I encountered Ben Abbott at Whales' Tale recently. He's starting a militia for his area in Enfield. He's been recruiting men for a month now and will begin training the first of June." Nat informed his father, his lips pursed, and his head nodded in a matter-of-fact way. "Father, Patriots all over Connecticut are itching for a fight. Revolution has been in the minds of men for years now."

"Fight, fight! Do you mean engaging in war with the best-trained, best-equipped military in the world?" Nathan paused. "I've denied this was even a prospect, choosing instead to tend to my own small world. You know more of what's going on in the colonies than I do. I could kick myself!" Nathan's face reddened from the explosion going on in his head. Nat had smelled whiskey when he entered the room. There sat the cup. Very unusual for Father to drink at this time of day, he thought. "Any other significant happenings in your life you would care to share with me?" Nathan, plainly flustered, asked with a smirk and bulging eyes.

As usual, Nat remained calm. "You do remember I'm visiting Pa'pa and Ma'ma the first of June? Something to do with publishing a medical journal. Anyway, I'll find out more when we get to it. I'm interested in seeing what all is involved for a city under siege. Do you think Pa'pa even knows what's going on outside of Beacon Hill?" Nat laughed. His mother's parents lived a secluded life amongst a small circle of friends in the wealthiest area of Boston.

"By the way, Father, we do have the advantage over the redcoats. We fight differently than them. They line up on a green field so they can shoot us down one by one like we're a passel of stunned possums. We prefer to attack them from behind trees and boulders. Frontier style. I'm proposing that all the women on Stowe property learn how to shoot a musket and a pistol and make their own bullets. As it happens, I know just the person to put in charge since I will soon be leaving for Boston." His father questioned him with a lifted brow. "John Dupre."

Nathan Stowe was in the habit of coming out of sleep during the darkness of a new day with only the embers of the fire and sometimes the glow from the moon giving off light. While he lay in bed, he could make out shapes of familiar fixtures in the bedchamber: the rectangular lines of the oil painting mounted over the fireplace, the circular shapes of the vases perched on each end of the mantel, the triangular lines at the top of the corner cabinet giving protection to Emma's porcelain objects displayed behind glass doors. He looked at his wife lying on her left side, sound asleep, his eyes tracing the outline of her chin and nose.

He raised his arms and stretched his fingers apart, examining what he could see of his exaggerated joints, knowing his strong and toughened hands were a product of the work of pounding and shaping iron. *Since I was ten years old*, he reminded himself. Sometimes, he worried how many more years he could continue the foundry work. Would Nat want to take my place, he wondered.

He glanced at the shape of Emma's right hand lying delicately on her pillow beside her face. A talented musician who had given endless hours of her life teaching their children the violin and piano, how to thread a needle, and how to hold a piece of chalk to write their name. *My wife, full of expectations for her family*. His eyes misted when he considered his parents, who had not lived long enough to experience their grandchildren.

When Nat was ten, he came to the forge to observe until his father allowed him to use the smallest size tongs to hold an iron bar, anxious to craft a horseshoe, his first project. *Nat was anxious to experience everything*, Nathan contemplated. He was naturally drawn to driving a team of mules and riding horses. By the time he was four, Emma had stirred his interest in books and music, singing ballads and encouraging him to pick out familiar tunes on the piano. His education came naturally as he grew and prepared him for higher learning. *Ready to leave home*, Nathan lamented.

Lainey was born a teacher like her mother. She pondered the lives of people who lived centuries before and dreamed of traveling and exploring the world. *What kind of man would desire a woman with such varied interests? I hope he has plenty of money*, he mused.

Lizzy was unpredictable and a fibber, seeking to impress her older brother and sister but never reaching a mark that was believable. She pushes herself to outperform Lainey as a musician. Maybe that's why she and her mother play duets together. *Emma understands Lizzy's character*, he surmised.

If ever there was a horse of a different color, it was Dory Stowe, short for Dorothy. Nathan considered the few times he had seen her wearing a dress and leather shoes, preferring buckskin trousers and moccasin boots. *My little hunter*, he thought. *With keen instincts of her surroundings and two steps ahead of what others were thinking, she'll probably never marry. The little mind reader. Surely, she would never consider joining the militia.* He chuckled at the outrageous thought.

"Ten-year-old Debby, so eager to please the family, my baby," he confessed. "What joy this happy child brings to us with her made-up stories. I wonder if she's going to be as pretty as Emma. She's got the golden hair and blue eyes like her mother."

"The glue that holds this family together—Aunt Mae. O Lord, preserve her strength and will to serve this family," he prayed. "Our work is our life," he summarized. "Work is good for the soul!"

Nathan closed his eyes, knowing in his heart that nothing happens by chance; there is purpose in the ways of life. This habit of reviewing his family gave him stability and appreciation, drawing his attention to the uniqueness of each family member. Now, he was ready to tackle a new day. His attention was drawn to a long streak of light barely showing in the gray dawn sky.

Emma spoke, "You're thinking out loud again, Nathan. I'll go start the coffee."

Nathan scoffed, "My intuitive mate!" He pushed away the covers, walked across the cold floor, stirred the embers in the fireplace, and added logs to get some heat in the chilly room.

Chapter 19

Lainey's Dilemma

First day of May 1774, Suffield, Connecticut

It couldn't have been a more pleasant day to lay in the new green grass, losing oneself while deciphering the shapes of clouds in the brilliant blue sky. Lilacs showed their first blooms in early spring, now bursting with lavender flowers, orchard trees flaunting white blossoms emerging forth from green leafy trees. The sound of a woodpecker drilling the bark of tall trees at work close by, concealed within the dark forest. Spring was exploding all around.

"Hail, bounteous May, that doth inspire mirth and youth, and warm desire," muttered Lainey, quoting Milton with as much enthusiasm as the lazy fat cat snoozing beside her.

The late afternoon sun was bearing down. Long leafy branches from the oaks shadowed the granite shelf, Lainey's place. She claimed the seat years ago when she would climb the steep hill behind the house, seeking the solitude of big shady trees and chirping birds. Enthralled in the adventurous tales of King Arthur and Sir Galahad, she imagined the wizard Merlin in the forest lying beyond, teaching young Arthur wood lore and the ways of a would-be king. But those were the illusions of a child, the wonder of such stories now tucked away in her mind. Today, she gazed at the same mysterious woods, trees blurred through her tears, facing the reality of heartbreak and indecision, not sure of how to move her life forward.

Emma had delayed the inevitable as long as she could. There was more to the story than all she had heard from Aunt Mae and Lizzy, and she meant to get to the bottom of it. She climbed the stairs to check on Lainey, naturally assuming she was in her room. Her heart stopped when there was no sign of her. Glancing out the window, she caught sight of the back of her daughter's strawberry blonde hair, red strands glistening in the bright sun. An open book lay beside her as she gazed at the mountains.

"Good place to dry your hair," Emma surprised Lainey as she approached her from behind. She glanced at the book of Shakespeare plays opened to *The Tempest*. Her heart quenched when she saw the bookmark Lainey had stitched with her name when she turned eight. "Feeling like *Miranda*, a castaway on a lonely little island?" Emma asked as she stroked her daughter's wet hair.

Lainey laughed half-heartedly. "Not quite a castaway, more like a prisoner of the mountains." The reality of the day was coming back to her. "Mother, I do want to marry someday. I want my husband to be handsome, kind, and responsible, like Father. It might be a long time before that someone drops into my life. I don't believe he lives in Suffield, Connecticut."

"That's true, maybe he doesn't, but neither did *Miranda* have any thought that her future husband would be caught in a tempest, drifting in the sea, desperately seeking refuge," Emma reminded her of the story.

Lainey's solemn gaze remained on the mountains ahead. "Maybe I'm not expecting *Prince Ferdinand* to make his appearance today. To be honest, I'm searching for a change, a person, or even an idea. Does that sound ridiculous and unrealistic to you, Mother?" she asked, brushing her wet hair away from her pinkish face.

Emma watched her daughter's sweet and innocent countenance, remembering her as attentive and obedient, mimicking her and Aunt Mae's ways, gravitating toward the piano to discover her musical inclinations. Now, Emma comprehended her daughter's grown-up words. Her maturity had never been more evident than just now. Lainey's time had come, just as Nat's, to break away from the family. This is the place in time her parents had guided her since she arrived in the world.

Her scowled forehead and sad eyes revealed a hurt and a heavy heart. "I'm aware of what you're feeling. No, darling, it sounds perfectly normal, and I can see you're ready to make some changes. You look spent. These last few days have been difficult for you, but it's been an important day for your future. I hope you'll trust me when I say that marriage is not always the answer, and nor is living with your aunt and uncle in Paris. I pray that you never have any thoughts of living in Boston with your grandparents. The turmoil in a city like Boston would be disastrous for you... You remind me so much of me when I turned eighteen. I wanted to be independent, but I didn't know the first step to take. That's why you have parents—to help you get started—and we will help." They embraced, and tears flowed. Emma assured her daughter that she would speak with Nathan, and together, they would sort it out. At the moment, her mind was drawing a blank, but Emma was confident the answer would come.

Lainey was a natural-born teacher, particularly musical. She had mastered her scales, arpeggios, and chords before she was twelve, opening the door for her to play fluently and with expertise. With Emma's help, she developed a guidebook for teaching lessons to her students by taking a step-by-step approach to learning the fundamentals. Her students were neighbors, church friends, and foundry worker's children. She patiently guided her younger sister, Lizzy, through the beginning process. Her mother never vocalized comparisons involving strengths and weaknesses among her children, but truthfully, Lizzy was as proficient as Lainey. A testament to Lainey's eagerness to teach music to anyone who showed an aptitude for learning.

Music and books were her best friends. With so few schools, it would be next to impossible for her to find a teaching position anywhere close to home. Moving to a more populated area is what Lainey really wanted, but where? Fine time to send your daughter off on her own with the colonies in the precarious position of battling out their problems with Britain. Boston was expected to be under siege by George the Third's army any day. Connecticut could be next.

"You're telling me our daughter, our Lainey, wants to move out of this house to a faraway city, to live amongst strangers, people we've never met. I guess she wants to leave as soon as possible," he retorted in an elevated tone. "Where is this kind of thinking coming from? Is this the sickness that Lizzy was speaking of at dinner? Why aren't you as upset about this as I am?"

Too many questions and very few answers were dizzying for Emma, but her attention was drawn to a knock at their bedroom door. "May I come in for a moment?" It was Nat's voice.

Emma was sitting on the bed in her shift, brushing her long golden hair, when she looked up at Nathan. He scanned the room for her dressing gown draped on a nearby chair and tossed it to her. Wide-eyed and flushed-faced, he walked to open the door enough for his son to enter, hoping he looked composed but knew he didn't. "Come in, Nat. What's on your mind?"

He walked into his parent's room confidently. More than ready to give the details of his sister's explosive reaction to what he knew fueled her behavior. Lainey had moped around for days.

"I'm responsible. I called Simon McGinty a lush and a lout. She asked for my opinion, and I told her what I knew of him, just as I'm imparting to you now. I've witnessed his drunken behavior at the Black Rooster and the Whales' Tale, drinking copious quantities of rum while he speaks coarsely of women. Pardon my language, Mother. Everyone knows he's never worked a day in his life. He claims it's not necessary, given that his father has enough wealth to meet his financial needs, including his alcohol consumption.

"I could no longer permit Lainey to be deceived about the unseemly man, knowing full well that his intentions would be the downfall of her. I thought it best to be truthful, but perhaps I overstepped my boundaries. She accepted my apologies, and we are on speaking terms again. I'm fairly well talked out for now. I should leave. I'll bid you goodnight."

He left their room, leaving his stunned, disheartened parents staring into nothingness. No words were spoken between them. They knew from past experience not to draw hasty conclusions. The matter would have to wait until tensions eased. Still, Nathan agonized over why his daughter would give a second thought to Simon McGinty.

"We have to stop meeting like this," Emma said as she approached the classroom steps, holding out her hand for Nathan to clasp. He pulled her down beside him and kissed her warm brandy mouth. The smell of chimney smoke made her cough.

"I'm becoming accustomed to it, but all good things must come to an end," he said regretfully. "In four days, you'll have four daughters to teach, or will it be the other way around?" He grinned. Then spoke his mind. "You've brought up Lainey to be a lady. Now, she wants to bring home trash for a husband who can't stay sober. It's hard to figure. We've never faced a challenge such as this. How shall we approach it?"

Emma sighed. "You didn't get much sleep last night. You flipped from one side to the other like a giant fish stranded on a beach. I gave up and slept downstairs," Emma teased. Nathan nodded his head in agreement and yawned.

He was weary and frightened over the prospect of losing his daughter to something out of his realm of comprehension. His only choice was to turn to his wife. But hearing her ideas scared him sometimes. What if he didn't agree with her plans? He hated that he was so vulnerable. That out-of-control feeling was eating him alive.

Emma gazed at her husband with hopeful eyes. "I haven't thought through all the details yet, but hear me out. This morning, when I walked to the kitchen, I stopped short at the whiff of coffee. Wonder of wonders, there was Lainey, wearing a work dress and an apron, kneading bread at the table, singing like a lark. Can you imagine the smidgeon of sunshine working its way into my spirit? Quite a transformation from yesterday!

"Then I was struck with an idea: why not offer her an opportunity to work? Something to give her a different purpose and some independence? Set her on a new path. Do you recall when Nat attended Yale and lived at the Peevy farm? He worked as a stable hand to pay for his food and upkeep. What do you think about Lainey living at their home, instructing their children in music and academics, like a governess? They have three little ones now. It would definitely be a change of scenery for her. She's so anxious to see what's beyond her world in Suffield. Her words!"

Nathan thought for a moment, "'Ay, there's the rub,' says Hamlet. We won't allow her to marry you know who, so instead, we send her hundreds of miles away to live with a family I barely know. Either way, we lose her." Nathan stared at the orchard of peach trees, considering how the blooms last for such a short time, then the wind blows them in all directions. He had no choice but to listen to Emma.

"That's asking a lot of them, don't you think? Taking in another child of ours, like the Peevy home, is a repository for young adults who want to run away from home or their parents. I'm not convinced that sending her away will make her a more responsible person. Her sisters may get the idea they can leave home when they turn eighteen. What do we do but ship them away to some far away home to be educated in the ways of the world? Anyway, what's to become of her music students?"

"Nathan, she is going to be miserable if she remains under our roof. It is her time to spread her wings and experience life as an adult—away from her parents. She will make mistakes and learn from them as you and I did. Clive and Susannah own a huge house. They entertain university associates, students, and friends. You remember Clive is a professor at Yale? Why are you sneering at me?"

"That's just it. I'm thinking about all those young men from Yale who will attend those entertaining affairs at the Peevy home," Nathan said. He was not keen on his daughter living on her own in a faraway place. It brought to mind a family trip to Boston three years before to visit Emma's parents, Dr. and Mrs. Pierpoint. The family was strolling around Boston Common, enjoying the springtime trees and the distant sound of ocean waves crashing upon the shoreline. He became wary when he heard voices of workers coming off the wharves after a day's work of unloading ships, rough-sounding blokes who headed to the numerous taverns along Main Street. He quickly gathered his family into the carriage and returned to the safety of the family home in Beacon Hill.

Nathan tried to justify the similarities of Boston with its busy seaport to New Haven's location on the coast, but Emma was not having it.

"Nathan, you forget I grew up in Boston. I'm familiar with the street gangs and taverns full of roughnecks. It's different in New Haven. The town has turned out brilliant lawyers and businessmen all because of Yale's excellent educational opportunities. The townspeople are totally separated from the shipping port. I know because I've visited there."

The Stowes lived secluded from the world. Everything they needed was available on the thousand acres of land the family-owned. They had neighbors and friends in Suffield. The workers at the foundry lived within walking distance. It all seemed so perfect and safe to have access to his family any time of the day. Too much talk of war with England had placed him in an extremely protective disposition concerning his family and property.

"Has it occurred to you that all Lainey can see is the excitement of making her own decisions, meeting new people, and living away from her sisters?" Nathan asked.

"She should be excited! She has to learn sometime, and she's ready to start making her own way, but it doesn't happen instantly. Lainey will be under Susannah's authority while she's living in New Haven. She will be on a short leash." Emma's students were arriving for class. "It's going to work out, Nathan." She smiled confidently.

It was difficult for Nathan to accept the inevitable. "What comes easy for you is a mystery to me! My work is stacking up, and you have a class to teach. We'll meet again for dinner!" They parted, and he walked toward his work. The emotional weight of losing his daughter was tearing him to pieces. *This is only the beginning*, he contemplated. *Nat will be gone next. What about the other three?*

Nathan and Emma sat in silence on the bench underneath an arbor, surrounded by dark green jasmine leaves bursting with tiny white flowers. They remained at a stalemate, digesting previous discussion points over the possibility of their daughter's move to New Haven. The noise of fluttering birds caring for their young gave Emma a moment to consider the difference between parents and birds. The concern for their children is never-ending.

"Realistically, children are in our care for such a short time. They reach a certain age, and they want to make their own decisions; at least, they think they can," Emma stared into her mug of lemonade, pondering the discussions she and Nathan had begun two days before. *Like a little fledgling, finally getting its feathers, then fearlessly leaping into midair, attempting to go on its own, ready to fly. I wonder if we have given her all she needs to leave the nest?*

They knew their quiet time had ended when Dory approached them from behind like a prowling cat ready to ambush its prey. She was dressed in buckskin clothes, her braided hair trailed down her back. Nathan turned to Emma, both knowing that Dory was sneaking up behind the bench. "I'm getting a faint hint of bacon and a foul smell of hunting clothes. What do you think?"

Dory walked closer, carrying her bow, hatchet, and a knife exposed in her moccasin boot. "Didn't mean to disturb you. I'm headed to the woods. I'll be back before dinner time. Another thing, Lainey and Lizzy are at it again."

"What do you mean?" Nathan asked, his face scowling. "Are they fighting or yelling at each other?" Lizzy had a habit of snatching books and clothes from Lainey's bedroom and never returning them. A constant complaint of Lainey's that never seemed to be resolved.

Lainey was aware she was off limits when she searched Lizzy's room for her treasured medieval book currently missing from her bookshelf. "Lizzy walked up behind Lainey, pulled her braid, and dragged her out of her room. Lainey slapped her. That's all. I'm leaving now." She walked up the hill toward Lainey's seat, then slid down the other side to a thicket of saplings. She had promised Nathan she would not venture up the mountain, fearing more evidence of soldiers. Truly, she didn't want to be anywhere near the house when her parents confronted her two sisters.

"Nathan and Emma sprung off the bench and walked swiftly to the girls' chambers upstairs, where a great deal of name-calling and slamming doors was percolating. Nathan took charge of the situation. "Lainey and Lizzy, meet me in the hallway—now," he demanded loudly. Emma stood behind him with her arms crossed and a quirky smile on her face.

The two sisters came quickly at their father's command, surprised their parents knew a row was going on. "Lainey, how often do you find personal items missing from your chamber?" Nathan asked, gazing at his daughter's flushed face.

"Father, I'm embarrassed to say it happens every day," Lainey answered politely.

He turned to Lizzy. Her dark brown hair was partially wet, in the process of drying after her bath. She was biting her lip and on the verge of crying, hoping it would help her case. She remembered times when her father would become so incensed at her and Lainey's behavior he would remove his belt and smack them each a half dozen times. Not that it hurt that much, physically. The real pain came when they saw their father's disappointment in their bad behavior. "Lizzy, tell me what you know about Lainey's missing books and her, um, other things. Do you know where they could be hiding?" Now, Emma drew in her lips, holding back a snicker she felt coming on.

A tear rolled down Lizzy's face. "I wanted to wear the heart-shaped necklace you and Mother gave Lainey for her birthday. I didn't plan to keep it. I just wanted to wear it when I was alone in my room. As for the shoes and the books, I guess I forgot to return them." Regret and anger choked her remarks. "Lainey has nicer clothes than I do, and she has more hair combs and pins than me. Why can't I have as much?" she stomped her feet and yelled. She knew her sins had caught up with her.

Nathan turned to Emma for an answer. "I gave you the same opportunity to buy the same nice clothes as Lainey. But, you'll recall, the last time we traveled to Hartford, you chose to spend your money on paints and chalk. I tried to talk you out of it, but you refused to listen."

Nathan considered how the effects of the row could quickly transcend to an uproarious rage if he remained confined to the hallway as referee. Peacemaker, he was not. Without comment, he moved past his wife and daughters, descending down the stairs in the direction of his office to protect his sanity. *Why can't they get along?* he wondered.

Lizzy stood with her arms folded. Her entire body, from head to toe, was cloaked in pronounced fury. She fled to her room, slamming the door. Lainey retreated to the kitchen.

Emma escaped to her chamber for a lie-down and some solitude. She needed time to think through a strategy she could implement to turn the friction that existed between her daughters into a situation where they could help each other, learning to work together to resolve their differences. *But how?* she thought. *Is it even possible?* She pondered the dispositions of each daughter.

Lainey seemed to always have everything under control; her ideas were more accepted by Dory and Debby, and even Nat. Emma knew Lizzy was as smart as her older sister, but that wasn't the problem. Now, she recalled Lizzy's dejected demeanor, feeling as if she never had a worthy thought. This left her feeling unimportant, believing Lainey was too aggressive and overbearing, causing permanent resentment.

Emma chose a more tolerant view of the conflict at hand versus handing out threats and ridicule, which would leave Lizzy feeling shamed and unloved. Maybe this morning's row was the tipping point. She pulled out her handkerchief and patted her tearing eyes. She took a deep breath and coughed. The spicy aroma of rosemary and peppercorns saturating the kitchen had floated to the upstairs chambers. She rose to open her window for some fresh air.

She was heartened when she saw Nat and John Dupre walking from the foundry engaged in a lively dialogue, both speaking French mixed with English. Just what Nat needed since he returned from Yale, someone his own age who was detached from family obligations.

Her thoughts turned to her daughter's predicament: would Lainey and Lizzy ever be inclined to share in such an exchange? Inevitably, if the two were in the same room, the air seemed to boil around them. Possibilities began swirling in her head as she watched the two young men. Suddenly, her appetite for whatever Aunt Mae was preparing for dinner was front and center of her mind.

She walked to the kitchen, feeling jubilant that maybe life in the Stowe house was about to change for the better. The security of her family seemed more in check now. Emma was under no illusions that Nathan would agree to her New Haven proposal, but he didn't have any choice. Either his daughters remain under the same roof, fighting like two feral cats and continuing to cause tension in the family, or somebody moves out of the house. Changes were on the horizon.

Around noon time, Dory brought in a bag of gooseberries she had picked while tracking game earlier in the morning. She washed them in a pail of water she pulled up from the well, proud to contribute something special to the afternoon meal. Lainey met her outside. "Better wash off and change clothes before dinner is served. Father's in a foul mood."

Dory looked at her sister and grinned. "Guess it has something to do with all the yelling coming from you and Lizzy. Has she been stealing from you again? I knew it would get her in trouble someday!"

Lainey laughed, not knowing Dory had any idea about Lizzy's pilfering. "Books, clothes, jewelry," she shrugged. "What has she stolen from you?"

Dory stood with her hand on her hip, the sun catching the red strands in her light brown hair, "Seriously, why would Lizzy be interested in my hunting clothes? She's not the type to go after my deer antlers and bear skin." Dory looked at her sister with raised eyebrows. They laughed at the idea that Lizzy would be disposed to stealing Dory's wall decorations.

Aunt Mae and Debby set the dining table as they did every day for the mid-day meal. China and silver flatware was spread across a white tablecloth for eight people. Salted venison was cut into chunks and made into a stew with potatoes, carrots, and onions in a wine sauce.

Ten-year-old Debby, Aunt Mae's "little helper," was oblivious to the pandemonium going on upstairs between her sisters. She was no fool and was just as clever as her sister Dory, pledging never to interfere in her oldest sister's affairs. Today, she styled her golden tendrils away from her face, pulled back with a blue ribbon, showing off a pretty bronzed forehead.

Debby started early before breakfast, assembling the dough makings, dividing the yeast mixture between the two bowls, and covering them with towels to begin the rising process. When she formed the loaves to her liking, she slid the pans of dough into the outdoor oven with a long wooden paddle. She loved her new responsibility of making the bread from start to finish. It gave her great satisfaction. She was at an age where she wasn't treated like a baby anymore. She loved to read and recite stories to Aunt Mae, play the piano and cello, and now she could make bread for the family. Such domestic accomplishments made her proud.

Lainey cooked the gooseberries with sugar and spices, boiling them sufficiently down to pour into pie crusts. Aunt Mae had taught her to cook when she was younger than Debby. She loved the creativity of it all, never considering it a chore. Under the circumstances, it was more restorative today, a change of setting from the morning's tumult.

"Aunt Mae, this is a feast for a king!" Nathan exclaimed. "Lainey, it's your turn to bless the food." Lizzy refused to come to the table after Nathan sent her to clean the horse's stalls as punishment for stealing and pouting over her misconduct. She was grubby and smelled like a sweating horse when she finished her work, which meant she would have to take another bath and wash her hair again. The intense heat inside the barn, slinging shovels of horse dung, adding in the biting horse flies put her in a foul mood. Lainey's going to pay for this, she promised herself.

Lizzy came to the table with wet hair. She smelled like rose petals, which did not exactly match her irreverent mood. The rest of the family was happily chattering away, which enraged her even more. She felt cut off from the family today, and she was in no mood for polite conversation. She excused herself before the gooseberry pie was served.

Debby's sad eyes followed her sister as she walked away from the table and up the stairs. She shook her head and pursed her lips at her sister's indignant mood. "Lizzy broke the eighth commandment," Debby announced with all the soberness of a clergyman. "When will she ever learn? May I eat her pie?" Nathan and Emma stared at their plates, aiming to hide their reaction to Debby's cleverness, holding back their laughter.

After dinner and a sufficient cleanup, Nat and Lainey saddled their horses. They galloped down the long drive, stirring up fallen white blossoms as they moved swiftly past the line of crabapple trees. The blinding afternoon sun caused their faces to pour sweat, but an occasional breeze passed across them, persuading the two to continue in spite of the heat. They led their mounts down a mile of the dry, dusty road, then branched off down a hill to a meadow with rows of hedges, which Nat occasionally used as jumps. Both needed time away from their duties at home and time to talk. Their riding time ended with a race back to the stables to unload and wipe down their horses, then lead them to water.

Aunt Mae settled in her room on the main floor as she did every day to rest her back after the non-stop morning's work. It didn't take long for her body to relax sufficiently to fall into a deep sleep. She woke when she heard the violin teetering for the right note, halting any further dozing. Well-rested, ambitious energy swept over her, calling her to consider all the tasks that had popped into her mind while she prepared today's meal. Bake a cake, take a walk to stretch her legs, or trim the out-of-control rose bush outside her window. Unconsciously, she picked up Debby's unfinished dress to turn up the hem. Decision made. She took her work outside to make use of what light was left of daylight.

Dory and Debby took to their cello and violin in the music room, where Emma accompanied them on the piano with a complicated Vivaldi piece. Looking out the window, they saw the sun lowering, urging the girls to explore the garden to check on the seedlings they planted the week before. "They need water. They haven't grown any taller!" Debby exclaimed. Convinced that it would take longer for their plants to grow than anticipated, they brushed the dirt off their clothes and closed the garden gate. Debby ran ahead of Dory, shouting, "You count to ten while I hide."

Lizzy had secluded herself in her room. Typically, it took two days of fuming and stewing while she alienated herself from the family to recover from her misdeeds. Finally, resolving that she and the family would, in kind, forgive one another, eventually returning to normal conversations and activities.

The sun had dropped behind the mountains. Slowly, the sky turned from a red glow to a pale pink as twilight approached. Nathan and Emma sat on the garden bench, absorbed in the mountains beyond, staring upward at shades of blues and pinks. Marveling at the vastness of the ever-changing sky.

They talked about the day's events and the new worker, John Dupre, circling warily around the subject each one knew was coming. They were at odds in deciding their daughter's future, but after today's fracas, a change could be on the horizon. Emma's challenge would be convincing Nathan that whatever decision was made about Lainey would affect Lizzy. *It's complicated*, she thought, sipping her mug of cider, but it must be done.

"Lizzy is envious of Lainey," Emma began. "I don't mean material possessions like we saw today. She envies the position of her sister. I'm referring to hierarchy." Nathan stared at his wife's face, wondering how she had arrived at this conclusion. "Think about Lizzy for a moment. Intellectually, she's at the same level as Lainey, musically speaking. Precocious, she is. She strives to do things differently than her sister, hoping to be recognized. She wants to strike out on her own. I can't recall the last time she asked for my help in mathematics and science. Just the other day, I saw her reading one of Nat's architectural books from Yale. She has great confidence in her innate abilities."

"Are you saying she wants to dethrone Lainey?" Nathan asked, recalling the explosion in the upstairs hallway. "So your next assumption will be that the degree of competition between our daughters has reached an intolerable point that precludes them from living under the same roof?"

Emma nodded in agreement. "They are both maturing, and they want their independence from their parents and each other, just like Nat did. If you will recall, I was anxious to make my own way twenty-four years ago when a certain man convinced me to move from Boston to this little place in the country." Her eyes were glued to Nathan's, and that familiar over-confident smile across Emma's face told him she had made her decision.

"Stand down! The wrath of Lizzy Stowe is to be feared!" Nathan shouted. He walked nervously across the garden, feeling resentful, as if someone were pushing him off a shelf of rock to the valley below. The light was dimming, and the noise from the trees had quieted to whispers. A rumble of thunder was heard in the distance. "This move to New

Haven is not what I imagined for my daughter," he signed. "We should discuss this with Lainey tomorrow morning." Emma stretched out her hands to him, unsmiling, gazing into his eyes, giving him a slow nod of agreement.

Lainey believed her Dragon to be magical—like Pegasus. "The fastest runner of all our steeds, he must have wings," her father had often said. Today, Lainey was feeling spirited after she had emptied her heart to her mother, expressing her desire for a different life to be lived in a different place. The impetuous, quick-tempered Lainey was fading, replaced with a clear head and hopeful expectations, still wary of her parent's intent. She was confident her mother accepted this new stage in her life.

There was no pretense on Emma's part. She was a doer, not a talker nor a "let's wait and see." Her father saw things from a different perspective—hesitant and protective of his children, placing limitations on what he viewed as potentially dangerous to their mind and body.

Such was the invitation that came to Lainey to accompany her father on the journey to the meadow, so familiar to the Stowe family as a place of solitude when one needed a retreat from the grind of work and troublesome problems. A haven of natural beauty to refresh the mind and soothe the soul.

Father and daughter walked their horses across the grassy meadowland to the noisy creek, spilling water continuously over large rocks, locating a deep rivulet for the horses to drink their fill. They led Dragon and Captain to a shady area to graze, tethering their reins to a sycamore tree. Nathan and Lainey sat next to a row of hedges, refreshing themselves with a drink from their leather pouches. The sky was overcast, and a breeze swept across the trees, making it a tolerable day for an outside talk. "Are you disappointed in me, Father?" Lainey said, gazing at his dark face, hoping to read his thoughts.

"I'm not disappointed in you. I just don't want to lose you to the world. I fear for your safety, with you living hundreds of miles from home. It's like Dragon and Captain over there connected to that big tree, in the same sense that you've been connected to your family for eighteen years. I don't remember a time when we've spent more than three days apart. That sense of connection will be gone forever." Lainey saw so much goodness in her father's countenance as he spoke. *No wonder mother loves him so*, she thought.

"Yes, the study of music has given me the joy and appreciation of learning and teaching it to others. I'm thankful to you and Mother for that opportunity. Imagine all the books that have taught me lessons from the past, playing out the dramas of kings and queens and knights, sword fighting with Lizzy and Nat. Aunt Mae taught me how to stitch when I was eight and helped me make a pie when I was ten. I love making pies!" she exclaimed with laughter. Nathan grinned.

She looked at Dragon, his coat black as night, dazzling where the sun cast its rays. "Remember the first time I sat on one of the ponies? Of course, I fell off, but you helped me get back on the saddle." Nathan nodded. "Then you gave me Dragon to raise when he was a colt. He was my responsibility. All the nastiness of cleaning the stalls, feeding and tacking, cleaning his hooves. I first rejected the notion that I should have to care for him. That was the job of the stable hand. You were adamant: 'If you ride a horse, it's your job to care for him.' Those were your words. I have not forgotten them."

"Whew, if you keep this up, I'll get dewy-eyed," he laughed. "I can see you have so much to offer three young children. Tell me about your dreams, Lainey."

"I yearn to travel away from the mountains. To visit other societies—east, west, south—all that I've read about in books. New Englanders have a certain industriousness about them. I came by it honestly." She smiled. "Most are content to operate their entire lives within a twenty-mile radius from where they reside. Still, I'm hopeful to visit new worlds as you and Mother have. Beyond that, I desire to settle down and marry, not out of convenience or necessity, but to experience a special love between a man and a woman.

"Now, Father, I am mindful of your circumspection. There will be dangers and obstacles wherever I live, but I'll always be chaperoned. If Mrs. Peevy is in any way like Mother, she will steer me from harm.

"In regards to Simon McGinty, I acknowledge that he was misrepresented at the Brooking's party. I saw him as a gentleman, never once smelling of rum. He was handsome and gentlemanlike and a good dance partner. How was I to know he lived a dual life as an abhorrent drunkard? Thankfully, I have a judicious brother who revealed to me the repulsive side of Mr. McGinty. A lesson learned for a country girl like me. Otherwise, you and I would not be engaged in such a conversation pertinent to my future prospects this morning." She gazed at her father, feeling self-assured, believing she had stated her case in a self-controlled manner.

Nathan squeezed Lainey's hand and smiled, feeling love and pride for his daughter. "You've given me much to consider." Captain and Dragon were getting antsy—snorting and stamping, raising their heads to pull their reins away from the tree. "They're trying to tell us something," he grinned, nodding his head toward the horses. He looked upward, squinting. "The sun's moving higher. We should go home." Lainey walked to her father and kissed him on the cheek. Neither said a word riding to the stables. Nathan sensed relief that they could discuss the details of Lainey's departure.

Chapter 20

Tavern Talk

First Week of May 1774, Suffield, Connecticut

If all Nathan wanted to do was drink a beer, he would have walked to his office and filled his tankard from a keg as many times as he liked. However, there came times during his busy workday when a ride to the Black Rooster tavern suited his purpose. Occasionally, Nathan worked at a distance from the forge when he met with clients at the local tavern. Smoking his pipe and engaging in conversation in a casual setting suited his needs. Nowadays, the talk was London's Parliament taking siege of Boston, eventual closing of ports, out-of-work merchants and yeomen, *and* revolution. Travelers brought news from Hartford, New Haven, Boston, and New York, settling themselves in a comfortable inn and indulging in a refreshing drink.

As daylight came to an end, the red signboard swinging from its black hinges, secured to the whitewashed clapboard building, beckoned weary travelers to stop and ease their bodies and minds before darkness fell. The familiar image of a crowing black rooster assured patrons of a respite—a good fire and hot food lay ahead. Lodgers had a choice of a soft feather bed or ticking stuffed with husks, depending on how many shillings one desired to lay out.

Nathan had never stayed overnight in the tavern. For him, it was an afternoon getaway from the constraints of work and the dirty smoke that spewed from the forges at the foundry. When the family's mealtime concluded and he and Emma had walked their two miles, she encouraged him to sequester at the Black Rooster. "It does your disposition a world of good to engage in society." He agreed with her. He saddled Captain and headed for the Black Rooster tavern, leaving his cares behind.

What was once wilderness had been transformed into farms, industries, and towns engaging in commerce between settlers, other colonies, and Great Britain. The most expedient route for Nathan and his neighbors to travel was Boston Post Road. The more than two hundred fifty mile stretch of narrow Indian trails ran from New York to New Haven, located at the southwestern coast of Connecticut, and extended north to Hartford and on to Springfield, Massachusetts. The gates of Boston lay twenty-five miles north. The Black Rooster was part of the Suffield community, set between Stowe Ironworks and Springfield.

Sloops and schooners navigating up the Connecticut River brought merchandise from the West Indies and Europe, keeping the provincial shops well-stocked in Suffield's small town. Not quite the selections in the capital city that Hartford offered, but it was adequate for the county's colonists.

Suffield did not lack for public buildings. Those who could afford it had donated money to build a congregational church topped with a belfry and a tall spire, giving it prominence. A pole barn had been erected for dances, weddings, and concerts. An outdoor market was arranged on the main thoroughfare on Saturdays, offering meats, cheese, mead, dried fruits, and bargain-priced dry goods.

Emma and her four daughters rarely missed a Saturday of shopping, meeting neighbors and friends to visit and share news. The bookshop, coffee house, millinery, and general merchandise store offered anything from needles and fabric to kitchen utensils. Mothers and their children fawned over new fashions and perused books and pamphlets, some written in French and German.

Emma and Nathan realized the expense of feeding and clothing five children. Substantiated by insisting their daughters wear hand-me-down dresses and bodices. Lainey and Debby were keen on sewing a skirt and knitting a shawl. Their shopping consisted of selecting fabrics and trim, stockings, hats, and ribbons. Merchandise that suited the tastes and needs of the Stowe females.

They shopped for sheet music, garden seeds and bulbs to plant, pewter and silver tankards and platters, vases, and tea sets, especially books about world travel and marvels not seen on this side of the Atlantic. Aunt Mae was the more practical shopper, purchasing tools for garden work, smoked meat, chocolate, and fruits for the following week's meals.

All sorts of business was transacted on Saturday's market day. At the popular Black Rooster, tables were arranged outside under trees where customers bought cakes and meat pies prepared by women and their daughters. Husbands and wives sat drinking a cup of chocolate while they gave the pharmacist time to mix a bottle of elixir or wait on their horse's bridle bit to be repaired.

Some men segregated to their own area, where they played checkers, drank beer, and discussed politics. Talk of Boston's latest woes never ceased. Every Saturday brought a different event to discuss. It was on everyone's mind, and some were more eager than others to express their opinion, "I say we defend what we have. What's to keep the king's men from taking over my horses and oxen, even burning down my house if they have a mind to? I'm keeping a musket by every door in my house."

The front passage of the Black Rooster tavern was busy and noisy during the day and night, with people arriving and departing. Some came to pick up mail and packages; some came to play billiards, cards, and dice. But Nathan enjoyed the relaxed atmosphere of the taproom where good-tasting beer was served, and the conversation was lively, especially when the impetuous Colonel Israel Putnam dropped by to wash the dust from his mouth and argue local politics. His courage and fighting spirit during the French and Indian War had branded him a well-known hero among Connecticut colonists. At present, "Old Put" traveled across the state recruiting young men to join the militia in defending the colonies from Britain.

Aside from hearing tales of Colonel Putnam eluding the Huron and the French during the last war, Nathan was equally fascinated with John

Adams, attorney and farmer, who made his home in Braintree, a town south of Boston. Adams journeyed throughout the colonies' countryside in all sorts of weather as a circuit lawyer, attending to problems encountered by men and women of settling debts and disputes, writing wills, and transferring deeds as he interpreted the law.

This morning's early visit to the Black Rooster was far removed from listening to war stories or solving the problems between colonists and the king. The friction between Lainey and Lizzy weighed heavy on Nathan's mind, compelling him to seek a quiet recluse to ruminate and sort out the family issue. *I've got a revolution going on under my own roof,* he thought as he and Captain plodded down the drive. His eyes clouded over, never noticing the beauty of the flowering crabapple trees.

He had left the forge only an hour after he unlocked its doors, welcoming his employees as they entered, soon realizing his distraught emotions placed him in no position to manage the work scheduled for the morning. He gathered paperwork into his satchel and proceeded to put Nat and his four supervisors in charge. He settled Captain with the tavern's stable hand and walked into the warmth of the Black Rooster. His head was instantly filled with the rich smells of tobacco and beer. Nathan's mood changed, and his nerves began to settle as he pulled a chair close to the fire, knocking the early morning chill off his face and hands.

The reality of Lainey moving away from the family home had set his mind reeling for the last four days. He could not escape the black cloud hovering over him. He blamed Emma—only because she came to terms with Lainey's situation before he did. At first, he rejected her plan of sending Lainey to New Haven, but to keep peace in the family, he thought it best to let her go. Emma always seemed to have an answer for everything concerning the children. He shook his head in resignation. *Why can't I see the benefits of my daughter leaving home?* He emptied his pipe and packed it with tobacco, lit it with a tender from the fire, then inhaled the soothing smoke. Immediately gratified, he sat down in his usual chair and stared at the dancing flames. Nathan was now ready to put his daughter's move to New Haven in a sensible order.

The bell over the tavern door rang, in walked Clarence Tatum. He turned toward the bar area. "Good morning, Horace. Too early for a mug of ale?" He laid down a pence and walked toward the fire. "I haven't seen you in months, Nathan. You're probably covered up in work." Charles was older than Nathan by ten years. His wavy white hair contrasted his browned face and light blue eyes. Nathan observed the glow of the man's sunburned nose and forehead. He and his wife Constance spent much of their time outside exercising and maintaining their stable full of horses. They were horsey people and talked about them constantly, as if they were their children. In unison with other business ventures, the Tatums had achieved a portion of their wealth by raising some of the finest thoroughbreds on this side of the river.

"Yes, I've been busy with work and family. Had to get away to settle my nerves this morning. How's your family?" He moved a chair closer to the fire, inviting Clarence to join him.

"Our family is doing well. Constance and I are traveling to New Haven today to visit with the twins and their families. I left her at the store to buy gifts for the girls." The Tatums have five daughters and no sons.

Nathan had no idea his daughters lived on the coast. "What was their attraction to New Haven?"

"They grew weary of country life. *Marooned in the wilderness*, as my Lynnette used to say. After one visit to my sister and her husband's estate. They were quickly spoiled with city life, the theater, and society in general. It is a clean and beautiful town. They met their husbands at a dance, and it turned out they were brothers. Now we have six grandchildren, three lassies, and three lads—hard to believe sometimes! They're always asking us to come visit." The excitement showed in his face. It actually made Nathan envious of Clarence Tatum's family situation.

"Congratulations, Clarence. I'm happy for your family. Our oldest daughter is moving to New Haven soon. Did you have any regrets when they moved so far away?" Nathan picked Mr. Tatum's brain. Hoping his face showed genuine interest instead of a bewildered countenance.

"At the beginning, we were out of our minds with fear and grief, like they were deserting us. We believed we were losing our daughters forever. Not so after, we visited them in my sister's home. In three months, they had matured, actually carrying on an adult conversation with us. It was the best move for them, and we've not looked back." The clock struck the hour. "Well, I must be off. Constance is expecting me now. We're catching the riverboat in an hour," he spoke enthusiastically. Clarence and his wife had accepted what Nathan was reluctant to acknowledge.

Nathan walked with Clarence to the porch. They shook hands. "You've given me much to think about, helping me more than you know. Safe journey to you and Mrs. Tatum." Clarence left in their carriage, loaded with baggage strapped to the top. Standing on the porch of the tavern, Nathan puffed his pipe, visualizing himself and his girls taking a trip on the riverboat to New Haven. *If I resist letting her go, she may never speak to me again.* He shivered at the prospect of marriage and grandchildren, wondering how the time had arrived so quickly. He walked inside, settling himself at the fireplace.

Nathan continued his work by the fire, drinking his beer and smoking his pipe as he read one contract after another, writing instructions and assigning projects until he finished his work. The clock struck noon. His back and neck ached from sitting too long in the tall chair. Anxious to stretch his legs, he walked to the porch for some air. When he looked down the street at the line of shops, a signboard caught his eye: *Shaws, French Imports*. Clarence's words came to him—"I left Constance at the store to buy gifts for the girls."

He stuffed his satchel with papers, quills, and ink, bade a farewell to Horace, and walked in the direction of *Shaws*. *Definitely not a store that fit in Suffield*, he thought. He consciously pulled his hat down on his forehead before he entered the store, diverting his eyes from the clientele and the delicate merchandise displayed.

He stood face to face with a stylishly dressed clerk standing at the front desk. She sensed Nathan's apprehension and spoke first, "*Bonjour, monsieur. Peut-être que je peux vous aider?*"[14] The woman smiled, waiting for his reply.

---

14. Perhaps I can help you?

"*Oui, mademoiselle. Je voudrais un savon parfumé pour ma femme,*"[15] Nathan asked, hoping his French was correct.

The petite woman looked upward at Nathan's nervous face and spoke assuringly, "*Oui, je comprends. Un instant, sil vous plait.*"[16] She walked to a tall cupboard containing small packages of wrapped bars of soap tied with ribbons and shapely bottles of perfumed bath crystals.

Nathan waited patiently, staring out the front window, confident that she understood his requests. She returned in less than five minutes, carrying a basket containing small wrapped packages tied with pink ribbons, smelling of lavender and verbena. "*Voici. Est-ce que vous approuvez?*"[17] she asked in a soft voice.

Nathan caught the familiar whiff of lavender and smiled, "*Oui, madame.*"[18] He laid two shillings on the desk. "*Très bien. Merci, mademoiselle.*"[19] He placed the package in his satchel and departed.

He trotted Captain down the road. His thoughts drifted back to the fortuitous conversation with Mr. Tatum, giving him assurance that Lainey's move was for the best. The gift for Emma was his way of saying, "I'm sorry; you were right." He had questioned her decisions, showing a lack of trust on his part.

The following morning, Nathan met Emma in the warm kitchen, where she sat at the work table, drinking her coffee. "Where have you been? It's still dark outside." She squinted her eyes. "Your forehead is wet with sweat, or is it raining?" Nathan's improved disposition made it easier to have an easy-going conversation this morning, even though Emma was half awake. She smiled when he pushed a stray lock of hair behind her ear.

"I couldn't sleep, so I dressed and walked to the forge," he shrugged. "Any more coffee?" Emma poured a mug of the steamy liquid. He drank a sip, and his eyes widened at the savory taste. "Did Nat pick up the list

---

15. I would like some perfumed soap for my wife.
16. Yes, I understand. One moment, please.
17. Here it is. Do you approve?
18. Yes, ma'am.
19. Very well. Thanks, miss.

of instructions I left for him and John?" Nathan studied her weary face. She gave a nod.

Nathan sighed. "Pardon me while I read your mind." He began, "For your information, I've reconciled that Lainey is leaving home for New Haven. No more indignant words, no more slamming doors, no more cross looks. Let's get her safely to her new home. I'm confident that you can manage it all. I'll be in my office if you need me." Nathan gave her a peck on the top of her disheveled head of hair and left the kitchen with his coffee.

Emma had slept very little the night before. Too many details crowded her brain. She took a deep breath, then exhaled. *I'm confident you can manage it all*, she repeated Nathan's words to herself. If he only knew all it takes to run this place. She pulled a list from her pocket to cross off the completed chores and added two more. In truth, there was nothing she could cross off with completion, which only added to her dismay. She pushed it aside and poured more coffee.

Minutes later, Nathan returned to the kitchen, holding Emma's gift from *Shaws*. In the dim kitchen light, he stared at her head full of golden hair spread across her arms. He wondered if she might be ill. He looked closer to see the familiar little smile on her sleeping face. He shook his head, wondering how she could go to sleep so quickly. He placed the package close by and walked quietly back to his office.

Nearly noon, still endeavoring to finish his work, Nathan had had his fill of interruptions. He loved his daughters, but they had their out-of-control moments. It was the constant running up and down stairs, piano playing, and Aunt Mae ordering Debby and Lainey in the kitchen. He acquiesced. Concentrating on the business of the foundry proved impossible this morning. He went searching for Emma to no avail. *I hope she's resting*, he thought. *She's worn out.*

He walked to the stables and saw John filling the water trough. "Please inform Mrs. Stowe that I'm going to the tavern." He saddled Captain and trotted him to the Black Rooster, his satchel strapped to the horse's side. After two hours of organizing projects and studying contracts. He lit his pipe and ordered another beer, ready for a break. He stood and stretched his back. He turned around when the door opened at the sound of the bell. "Mr. Adams, good day to you."

Adams walked to the fireplace, joining Nathan. He glimpsed Adam's hands, holding his tankard of beer, large and rough like his own. Outside of reading the law and appearing in courtrooms, he and his wife farmed the family's land in Braintree. Pruning trees and pushing a plow was similar to forging iron products. It was dirty, strenuous work that built strong hands and arms.

"Doing any business in this part of Connecticut?" Nathan knew he traveled from New York to Maine riding the circuit. He would stop at the Black Rooster on his way home to Braintree, depending on the time of day.

"I dare say my business is slowing, soon coming to a halt." Adams' round, pinkish face showed distress when he looked up at Nathan. "This state of emergency declared by Britain has upended everyone's life. Business has all but disappeared in Boston. I'm on my way home to farm my land so my family will have food to eat next winter."

"You've got the weather for it today," Nathan said. John and Abigail Adams were brought up in farm families, ambitiously training their children to employ the work of a farmer. It was during these slow times he remained in Braintree to dig stumps, chop wood, and tend the orchards. Jobs he would usually hire out to workers under normal circumstances.

They smoked their pipes by the tavern fireplace, discussing the tax burdens imposed on colonists. "If Parliament had not broken their own constitutional rule concerning taxation, we would not be discussing this feeble situation. Only assemblies elected by the colonists themselves have the right to decide how much money should be raised by taxation and how it should be spent. I'm certain London's demands placed on working men and women have created such division and resistance that colonists will never be placated. And so the boycotts and propaganda begin."

John Adams spoke as an orator, then dramatically threw up his arms in disgust. He understood the natural rights of men and could sit for hours discussing them. He also understood that Parliament had betrayed the colonies by insisting they should be forced to exist under British rule in whatever method the king chose. George the Third's threats had become realities.

"I'm surprised Sam Adams hasn't rallied certain leaders in Boston to write a petition of grievances to the king and his Parliament with the intent to create a compromise." Nathan was familiar with Sam's genius concept of corresponding with towns across the colonies.

John Adams moved his head in the direction of Nathan, speaking *sotto voce*, "It's in the works. Delegates have been elected by colonial legislatures to meet privately in an undisclosed location." This was unexpected news for Nathan. He nodded slowly in agreement.

"Now, Mr. Stowe, I know you operate an ironworks business," again, Adams spoke in a hushed voice. Pipe smoke encircled his head.

Nathan stood, his head bent forward, nodded at the unexpected statement, and looked around the room for listening ears. He had a hunch about where this discourse was going. "Shall we retreat to the dooryard, Mr. Adams?" They stooped over the fireplace hearth to empty their pipes.

Once settled under a shady apple tree, breathing in the fresh spring air, John Adams commenced to explain, "In my travels, I have learned of craftsmen such as yourself who manufacture iron products. The land in this colony is overflowing with high-grade iron ore. Now that owners of forges have ceased to bow to England's demands, colonial refinery forges are capable of producing cannons and muskets. I ask you, Mr. Stowe, are you outfitted in such a way to take on the extra work of supplying additional arms for our defense?" Mr. Adams asked this question to Nathan in such a direct way their eyes became locked.

Nathan sat speechless for the moment, aware that Mr. Adams expected an immediate answer from him. He mentally reviewed his production schedule. "Yes, we can manage such work. I'll have to hire additional workers to build the muskets. Exactly how many more did you have in mind?"

"I believe you have met Jacob Randolph's agent, Mr. Asher from Stoughton, of Mulberry beer reputation. Mr. Randolph is financing this venture for militias in his area."

"Yes, we have met, and that work is in its initial stages." Nat had recently worked out those details.

Speaking candidly, "I am merely the messenger seeking prospective craftsmen who have the time and the will to provide our militias with the thousands of weapons they will need for their fall and winter training. I'll leave it to you to determine the additional quantity you can provide."

"I'm sure you are aware that, at this very moment, British ships are en route to Boston's port loaded with soldiers, horses, cannons, and weapons intending to take siege of that province. General Thomas Gage has been appointed by King George to replace the current Governor Hutchinson. We shall see how he governs. Nevertheless, patriots must be prepared to protect their property. For that reason, caches of muskets and ammunition are being distributed secretly throughout the Massachusetts countryside as we speak, hidden in the most unthinkable places. Still, muskets remain in short supply."

In Nathan's mind, this is the point in time when the revolution began for him, during this impromptu meeting with John Adams outside the Black Rooster tavern on a springtime day in April. Boston's port was projected to close at noon on June 1, 1774. Only weeks away. The gravity of the situation was intense as he began to feel the heat rise up within him and the notion that the defense of this part of the world rested on his shoulders.

Mr. Adams mounted his horse and proceeded down the dusty road—to where? Possibly to the next tavern to engage in the same conversation with another owner of an ironworks. Nathan discerned the man appeared weary and exhausted, wondering how many days or weeks he had spent in the saddle. That idea made him feel ashamed that he was not doing his part in the defense of his homeland. There was no time to waste. Nathan watched as the man galloped away, recalling bits of their conversation. Mr. Adams was persuasive and spoke with authority. "The time has come for colonists to make a choice: remain in the crosshairs of Parliament's whims or chop off the head of the snake?" Nathan favored the latter.

Less than a week after his conversation with Adams, Nathan was back at his favorite tavern, sitting by the fire, mulling over his work schedule. There was plenty of work to keep his employees busy for the next year; delegating the jobs was the most challenging. The skills of one worker did not mean that another worker could accomplish the same quality work in the same amount of time. So many variables to consider.

Who would be the most competent workers to build the 200 or more muskets for the militias, plus the order given by Mr. Asher? The summer recess at the foundry was quickly approaching, beginning the middle of June. Most of his workers would be on summer break to work their farms. He began writing a list of certain furnaces within the forges that needed repairs.

While Nathan sat deep in thought, contemplating his schedule, he heard bits and pieces of a conversation between a patron and the tavern keeper, Horace Foster. The unfamiliar voice paused at intervals, searching for the correct word to make his point. He spoke French.

Curious to get a visual of the young man, Nathan looked up from his papers and viewed the tall, slim traveler standing in his dusty clothes and wearing a bulging leather bag strapped across his shoulder. Seeing the young man's strained face, he was growing increasingly frustrated with Mr. Foster. A language barrier was ensuing.

From the tone of his mulish voice, it was obvious that Horace was on the verge of booting the traveler out the door. *This is probably a mistake to interfere*, but Nathan did it anyway. Meaning to get the attention of both men, he bowed and caught the weary eyes of the traveler. "*Excusez-moi, est-ce que je peux vous aider?*"[20]

The young Frenchman's face relaxed when he heard Nathan speak in a language he understood. "*Je voudrais une chambre, s'il vous plaît. Je m'appelle John Dupre. Et vous?*"[21]

Nathan took a chance and spoke English, "I'm happy to meet you, Mr. Dupre. My name is Nathan Stowe." He turned toward Horace Foster, aiming to ease the man's frustration. "This gentleman would

---

20. Excuse me. Can I help you?
21. I would like a chamber, thank you. I am John Dupre. And you?

like a room." Horace smiled reluctantly and introduced himself to the traveler. Nathan saw the tension drain from John Dupre's face, sensing the man could use a friend just now. He extended an invitation to the traveler to join him by the fire. "A mug of ale?" Nathan pointed to his mug. John nodded.

The clothes he wore had seen better days. His breeches and tunic were buckskin, cinched at his waist with a piece of rope. He removed his slouch hat revealing dark brown wavy hair that came to his shoulders. His face was handsome, even with a scar below his left temple, drawing one's attention to his large brown eyes. They were friendly eyes, moving expressively as he talked. His rough hands were large and cut up, and one fingernail was missing.

"Have you always lived on the coast of Maine?" Nathan asked. During the half hour, he and John sat at the fireplace drinking ale and conversing. John said he had traveled for two months working his way southwest to avoid Boston, not sure when British soldiers were expected to arrive on its shore.

"*Non, Monsieur Stowe. J'arrive de l'île Saint-Pierre près de Terre-Neuve.*"[22]

John continued talking of his life in the small fishing village in St. Pierre. He spoke affectionately of his parents as he stared into the fire, sharing the trials of their work as fishers, living in a cabin on a hilltop next to the ocean. He regretted his move from Newfoundland. "*Ma mère et mon père sont morts.*"[23] He slowly shook his head at the obvious grief he was suffering. His eyes appeared remote, and he remained silent. Nathan believed it took all the strength the young man had to speak of his parents' deaths.

Horace had taken on a despondent appearance as he listened to bits and pieces of John Dupre's story between assisting customers and sweeping the floor. Realizing the young, shabbily dressed man was in search of shelter and a new life. He approached John and Nathan. "I can offer you, gents, a plate of hot food if you're hungry."

---

22. No, Mister Stowe. I arrived from the island of St. Pierre near Newfoundland.
23. My mother and my father are dead.

The two men sat next to the window, getting a view of horses and carriages traveling down the potholed Boston Post Road. A plate of venison stew with carrots and onions and a loaf of bread was far beyond what John had imagined for a mid-day meal. Nathan spent his time talking about Suffield while John ate two plates of food.

John Dupre had left in a hurry when he departed his uncle's cabin in Newfoundland, but he managed to cram his satchel full of potatoes and turnips, not taking time to think how he and his mule would survive on his journey south. Nathan could see how the two-month trip had taken its toll on John physically. The man needed time to sort out his life.

Nathan took his leave feeling confident that John was settled and in an improved state of mind. He approached the bar where Horace stood, wiping out the tankards for later use. "Here's five shillings for the refreshments and a chamber for our friend. You're a good man, Horace." He grinned at the tavern keeper and departed.

He walked to the stables to retrieve Captain. A big mule stopped chomping on hay and looked at Nathan when he asked the stable hand for his mount. "Does this mule belong to the Frenchman?" Nathan asked. "Will two shillings cover his board?" The young man nodded.

He trotted Captain toward home in the warm sunshine, giving him time to think about the morning's doings which set heavy on his mind. What compelled this young Frenchman to travel hundreds of miles from his home? Possibly seeking refuge from his noxious uncle or escaping the memories of his deceased parents, whom he clearly loved and respected?

Nathan's mind was filled with a multitude of scenarios as to what could have happened in John's short life to cause him to land at the Black Rooster. *He's running away from something*, he pondered John's words and his sense of remorse, although he did not seem bitter. *He was not seeking revenge. He once had a pleasant life, but now he was alone in the world, except for his mule, whom he seemed very attached to.* The day's events had sapped Nathan's energy.

He thought of Nat. There were not enough hours in the day for Nat—anxious to experience so many things in the world, most of which lay outside the boundaries of Suffield. He smiled at Nat's infatuation with horseracing. When his four years at Yale were over, Nat showed interest in the foundry work, especially at the management end. Now, he was more like a partner.

The mundane job of managing the stables and looking after the horses and mules were Nat's responsibility, some of which his sisters shared in. Nat loved and respected his sisters, offering his help in their education. His lighthearted disposition kept his relationship with his sisters unbroken and solid. *Thank God he's dependable*, Nathan thought.

If he joins the militia, they'll make a captain out of him for sure. That was a depressing thought. He knew that time was approaching soon. Nat would be reporting for militia duty in the coming summer months. He turned his mind back to John Dupre's plight, wishing he could help but not sure how without showing impertinence. John was grieving over his parents. He had burdens to bear that Nat had never shouldered, such as survival. He seemed self-reliant. *Uncommonly self-reliant. I'll talk to Nat.*

The following afternoon, Nathan and Nat rode to the Black Rooster. Nat gazed upward. The sun hid behind the clouds. The cool air breezed over their faces. The early April rains would pour in soon. They entered the dark barn, catching the scent of sweet-smelling hay. The front and back doors were wide open, bringing in fresh air. "*Bonjour, mon ami,*"[24] came John Dupre's voice as father and son tied their horses to the posts and walked toward the Frenchman. Nathan introduced Nat to John.

John stood in a stall toward the back of the barn with his mule, giving the animal a well-deserved brushing, cleaning more than two months of collected filth from its dark brown coat. The mule was in a languid state, judging from his half-closed eyes and his relaxed neck, enjoying the massaging strokes John made with the curry brush.

Nathan leaned against the rails of the stall across from the mule's, considering John, still wearing the same dirty buckskins from the day before but with a cleaner face and neck. He watched him brush the mule and converse naturally with Nat. John attempted to speak in English more than Nathan had remembered from the day before. All in all, he seemed more refreshed and energetic.

---

24. Hello, my friend.

Gathered at a table in the taproom, they continued their visit for the purpose of learning more about John's life without probing too deeply into his grim past. He spoke in great detail about his parent's fishing vessel, the quantity of cod they would catch each day, and the process of preparing the fish to dry, salt, and pack in barrels for shipping to England and the Caribbean. This was their industry where money was exchanged for a product.

John's family came from meager beginnings. They risked their time, their health, and the little money they had to create a fishing business out of nothing. In the end, it took knuckling down each day to perform the necessary work, sometimes forgoing immediate gratification. His mind flashed back to his great grandsire's journal. It gave him chills to read the story of building a foundry from scratch. Pondering the progress of the current Stowe Ironworks.

"What are your future plans, John? I'm sure you are aware the fishing industry will soon be cut off when Britain's ships stop up the harbor." Colonists had known since January that this action was imminent.

"*J'ai besoin de travail,*"[25] John said, shaking his head with doubt.

"Would you have an interest in working with horses?" Nathan asked. He and Nat had discussed this possibility when they were en route to the tavern. Now they were sitting across the table from each other, with Nat sitting by John's right side. He poised a wry smile in his father's direction, not believing he had just offered this stranger employment.

"*Oui, monsieur. J'aimerais travailler avec les chevaux.*"[26] John was as surprised as Nat with Nathan's sudden proposal. A look of relief covered his face.

"I will make the necessary arrangements," Nathan said, smiling confidently. The men stood and shook hands, indicating an agreement and a farewell for the time being.

The noticeable silence was out of character for Nat while he and Nathan trotted down the road. He was naturally quick to voice his opinion when a decision about the foundry and the stables was in the making. Then it came. "When we were discussing the help required in

25. I am in need of work.
26. Yes, monsieur, I would like to work with horses.

the stables, I never expected you to make an offer so quickly, especially to a man you only met yesterday. What do we know about the man's skills? Is he capable?"

Nathan's face underwent a sudden change at Nat's question. "Are you in doubt of me possessing the ability to examine a man's words to determine if he is qualified to manage the work we would require of him? Are there not certain elements of a man's disposition that we expect to stand as a marker to judge whether he has the ability to achieve the level of work expected of him? Why, he saw to the duty of cleaning his mule before he cleaned himself!

"I can say in retrospect that I have spent but a mere portion of time with our current workers in comparison to my time with John Dupre, listening for hours to his recollections of his family and their work. All of which are indicators of his past. Finally concluding that he is a man of honorable character who recognizes that work is good for the soul.

"When you shook John's hand today, did you not feel the calluses and the strength of one who has performed a yeoman's daily labor of pulling in nets overflowing with fish, then on to gutting and drying and salting and packing the product in barrels? All accomplished to meet the demands of the merchants who hired him. That is evidence to me that he spoke the truth of an honest day's labor.

"His steadfastness in preparing his boat before the sun rises, taking it out to sea, searching the grounds for the catch he plans to pull in. He has been trained, and he's not afraid of hard work. He learned his lessons well at his parent's insistence. He learned the skills of a working man able to stand on his own two feet to make a living. If it wasn't his parents, he learned the job from someone who cared for him.

"What prompts a man to travel by mule hundreds of miles from his home, enduring the hardships of surviving in the wilderness during the cold winter months, foraging for food for himself and his beast? Whatever obstacles he encountered, he fought on with determination and would not accept defeat. He was rewarded by finding a safe haven, as it happened here yesterday. It is true; I do not understand why he hurriedly left his home. Perhaps it will be revealed to us. Perhaps not."

They were halfway home. Traveling was easy in the cool spring weather. Nat glanced at his father, glimpsing silver strands mixed with his black hair, then visualizing the wheels turning in his father's mind. How to make the best use of John Dupre's talents. Nat grasped the meaning of his father's words. Of course, he was right about John Dupre.

Nathan owned and managed the ironworks, but he seldom picked up a pair of tongs to heat a bar of iron to fifteen hundred degrees. Nathan's job was working out problems. Mainly people's problems. Stowe Ironworks doesn't just happen every day. It takes well-trained workers to produce anchors for ships and steel to build equipment. Nathan Stowe guides his workers to understand their strengths and weaknesses, working alongside them until their confidence is built.

This is my father, he thought, *always looking for the good in people.* Something he learned from his father, no doubt. He found the good in John Dupre in only one afternoon. "We could use a strong man, an honest man, to manage the horses and mules. I saw the care he took with his animal when we met in the stables. Perhaps I can help him with his English," Nat offered to his father.

"If John Dupre accepts my offer, he could begin work this week. He'll need some time to learn about hauling the mules and the horses. Keep in mind, Nat, soon, you will travel to your grandsire's house for ten days or more, then back to work. With all that's going on at home, I cannot run this place without you. Another reason for hiring John." Nathan was getting anxious about all the comings and goings during the fast-approaching months.

"We'll work it out, Father. I understand why you believe John will be a good worker. So, when did you become an authority on seafaring and pulling in a catch?" Nat asked. "A part of your life you're keeping a secret?"

Nathan chuckled. "Books mainly. An occasional trip to the Whales' Tale can be entertaining and educational," Nathan said, grinning. "There's more to Captain Zeke's stories than harpooning whales and singing mermaids, the enchanted ones, of course!"

Chapter 21

Dragon and Frederic

First Week in May 1774, Suffield, Connecticut

"May I be of service, mademoiselle?" asked John Dupre when he noticed Lainey struggling to lift the saddle off Dragon's back. He had entered the barn for a bucket of oats for his mule when he noticed she was experiencing difficulty separating the saddle from the horse. He could plainly see she was becoming agitated as her face was reddening with every second that passed. The horse was having a time of it as well, shifting nervously and shaking his head.

Lainey heard the heavy French accent, but she never bothered to turn around to notice the person offering help. "For some reason, it won't budge. Would you check the band closure on the other side? Oh, that worked." She slid the saddle off easily now and hauled it to the saddle rack, her body slumping over from its heavy weight. Her red hair, pulled back in a neat braid, dulled with color in the dark barn. She walked toward Dragon to remove the remaining tack and met John's dark brown eyes and his wavy brown hair, getting a close-up view of his face for the first time. *I didn't realize he was so handsome*, she thought.

"You will want this, I trust, mademoiselle?" He offered her Dragon's blanket, and she nodded, accepting it and holding it in her arms as she stared at him. "Your horse will need refreshing. May I assist you by walking him to the water trough?"

"Why, yes, of course. Um, where are my manners?" She smiled, showing her pretty teeth and friendly blue eyes. "My name is Lainey Stowe. I live here. Well, I assume you already know that, and this is Dragon," she said as she proudly stroked the horse's neck.

"*Je m'appelle John Dupre*,[27]" he caught her eyes and bowed. "It is a pleasure to make your acquaintance—and your horse, as well." He took hold of Dragon's reins and walked him outside to the water barrel. Lainey followed, carrying a curry brush and a towel. "Monsieur Stowe has been so kind to allow me hay and shelter for my Frederic, who, as you can see, looks quite confused at the moment."

The mule stood under an area of shady elms in the paddock, seemingly content with eating his oats. His ears stood up straight when he lifted his head upon hearing his name. "Haha, maybe Frederic is jealous of all the attention you're giving Dragon," Lainey concluded.

"That is possible. Frederic has been my only true friend—and I his—since we were both quite young, so he could be jealous. We have traveled for many months and a great distance, enduring much hardship together, and as you can see, he is content to feel the warmth of the sun and the pleasure of a full belly."

John smiled. "*Excusez-moi, Mademoiselle Lainey*,[28] I must complete my work in the stables as I have promised Monsieur Stowe. *Au revoir*.[29]" John bowed slightly and departed for the barn.

Lainey stopped brushing Dragon for the moment and watched as he walked away, thinking out loud. "Actually, I'm the one who is jealous. I want to travel to a new place like Mr. Dupre. Where did he come from anyway?"

After a quick wash-up, she changed into a clean skirt and bodice to prepare for Glennie and Josh Fowler, who would be arriving any minute for their music lessons. Their father, Robert Fowler, worked as a manager at the foundry, having been a dependable employee at Stowe Ironworks for twenty years or more. He chauffeured his children to the Stowe home this afternoon for their violin and cello lessons taught by Lainey.

---

27. My name is John Dupre.
28. Excuse me, Miss Lainey…
29. Goodbye.

Afternoon rays of sunshine bathed the room with brilliant light but, at the same time, made it uncomfortably hot. Nathan had opened the front windows to allow some cool air into the room. The big tabby cat lounged on a cushion at the music room window, observing the natural back-and-forth movements of twittering birds, flying insects, and a frisky squirrel whenever he opened his eyes.

The big ball of yellow fur suffused with a tint of orange woke and stretched its legs and feet when Mr. Fowler opened the front door, then darted outside through the opening. "There goes Peaches," cautioned Josh. The cat knew what was coming: the screeching, rasping violin and cello sounds that disturbed his *milieu*.[30] He preferred the sounds of chirping birds, buzzing insects, and horses snorting in the pasture. His natural instincts took over when he spotted the red-tailed squirrel he had watched all morning from the window, running up, over, and down the big oak. Peaches sat crouched halfway under a quince bush in front of the house, awaiting the perfect time to pounce.

Mail and parcel deliveries arrived slowly in the town of Suffield, being so isolated from the larger towns. Today, Robert Fowler felt obliged to pick up the Stowe's mail as well as his own from the Black Rooster tavern. He escorted his children, along with their bulky instruments, to the music room where Lainey stood ready to greet her students and help them get settled. Mr. Fowler placed the letters and packages labeled with the Stowe name on a nearby table.

Nathan walked from his office to the front of the house when he heard the children's excited voices. "Greetings. Must be music lessons today. The only time that lazy cat moves from its perch!" He welcomed Robert Fowler, acknowledged the mail delivery, and caught sight of the envelope from New Haven. "News I'd rather not see," he speculated. "John, before you head out, may I speak with you outside? It's business related—if you don't mind?"

The warm-up sounds of violin and cello followed the two men out the front door, catching sight of the horses and the French mule in the front pasture. Butterflies darted around the Sweet William, bordering the

---

30. ...environment.

large quince bush full of scarlet flowers. Nathan began the conversation with Mr. Fowler as they walked in the direction of the foundry. "I'm interested in hearing your assessment of our new worker, Mr. Dupre, since he has worked with us for almost a month now. What do you make of his work ethic?" John's main job was managing the stables. Of late, Nat had been training him in the foundry work for a short time each day, hammering bars into various shapes to sell to local blacksmiths. If John developed an aptitude for foundry work, Nat had in mind for him to assist in the manufacture of muskets.

Because of Robert Fowler's tenure and his dedication to his work, he had seniority at Stowe Ironworks. It was common for Nathan to discuss certain employees' standings with him to gain an understanding of their willingness to learn the trade. Robert pondered the question for a moment with the intent to give the most truthful evaluation. "I've observed him. He keeps to his work and follows directions as he has been taught by Nat. Mind you, Nat stays close by to guide his hand and answer his questions. He is not distracted by the other workers or their comments, and he has a pleasing temperament. I believe he's ready to move on to more complex work than pounding iron bars. More responsible tasks. Where did you find him, anyway?"

Nathan looked at him and laughed. "I met him at the Black Rooster over a mug of ale." Robert's eyes widened, chuckling in response.

Emma and Nathan walked to the stone terrace to settle themselves on the bench in the cool shade of the jasmine arbor, giving them a clear view of their four daughters running barefoot in the new spring grass, playing a game of hide and seek. It was nearing the end of an unusually cool day in May, perfect for watching the setting sun, showing off the purples and pinks in the fading blue sky.

Nat and John Dupre had ridden to the meadow to put their horses through their paces at a course the two men had constructed for the purpose of training Captain and Bouncer. To Nat's way of thinking, if he was serious about joining the Suffield Militia, improved skills in jumping, cantering, and galloping at his command would be to his advantage.

"You've read the letter from the Peevy's, I assume?" asked Emma. She paused and waited for some indication that Nathan was listening.

"I have," he answered tersely. Nathan waved Lainey over to the terrace. He pulled the letter from his shirt and passed it to his daughter, now red-faced and breathless from running. She seemed so young and carefree to him, with her hair sweaty and unkempt, barefoot, and wearing a plain muslin dress. Lainey stared at the return address, then held it to her chest, eyes closed, making a wish. As she read, her eyes widened. She danced a jig, stamped her bare feet, round and round in a circle, shouting a hallelujah! Never believing that her life was actually taking a new direction.

Nathan took Emma's hand, looked into her teary eyes, and smiled. He was satisfied this was the right direction for his daughter, even though he truly never wanted her to leave home. It was time to cut the strings.

"Father, Mother, I am so happy. May I tell them?" She pointed toward her sisters. Nathan nodded. Her jubilance caught the attention of her sisters, excitedly running to hug her but leaving her puzzled as to why. "Let's celebrate! Follow me!" Off to the kitchen, she led her sisters, finally free to divulge the specifics of her future home—her new life in New Haven. They drank apple cider and ate tea biscuits. The girls attacked Lainey with multiple questions, commencing to talk over one another until their questions became a jumble of sounds.

She raised both her hands, patting the air. "I do not have answers to your questions. The note is brief, only confirming that I will be employed as an instructor for their three children and an approximate date for my arrival." Lainey turned to her mother for answers.

"Yes, there are stables with horses and ponies. Yes, they have servants. Yes, they have a piano and violins. Yes, they live in a big house in a city. Yes, they have neighbors." Emma spent the next hour giving details of what she remembered about life in New Haven. She looked around for Nathan. He had left the room without her knowing. A wave of sadness fell over her, realizing their daughters had shown more interest in city life than a quiet rural life. A life that Nathan was proud to provide for his children.

Emma could read her children like a book—Nathan included. Lizzy's "why her, not me" envious disposition had turned her mood from elated to morose during their spur-of-the-moment kitchen celebration while all attention was focused on Lainey. *Time to divide and conquer*, she reckoned.

While the men were outside drinking ale, she ended the party by sending Dory and Debby to the music room for their afternoon violin practice. Now that the cat was out of the bag regarding Lainey, this was her time to discuss future plans with her oldest daughters. She had to get this right or pay for it in the long run.

"Lainey, discuss with Lizzy and me your plans for your music students. We've not talked about that because we did not yet know Mrs. Peevy's response to our proposal." Emma smiled at her in a familiar way, requiring Lainey to answer.

"I was hoping my sister would take on my role as teacher. Lizzy is an accomplished musician." Lainey paused, looking back and forth between Lizzy and her mother. At that, Lizzy's countenance now changed from dispirited to overjoyed. Her eyes sparkled, and her face blushed. She was more than overcome with joy and surprised by her sister's recommendation, never realizing that Lainey had taken note of her talent for teaching.

Emma's heart jumped with elation. The burden of her two daughters' irascible relationship was lifted off her heart in a matter of seconds. If only Nathan could be here to experience how the world had suddenly changed for her and the entire family.

All eyes were on Lizzy. "I, uh, don't know what to say. I'll need help from you, Lainey. I wouldn't know how to start." Lainey walked to her sister's side, holding out her hand, expecting Lizzy to accept it. They walked together to the music room, talking in a most civil tone as they went.

Nathan walked to the kitchen table where he had left the celebration over an hour before. "Where's our gaggle of squawking geese?" he asked Emma. Her back was turned, and she was gathering the empty mugs. "I guess I deserted you, sorry."

"You want to know where our girls are? Take a peek in the music room," she said hesitantly to Nathan, her back still turned towards him while she stood, washing the mugs. He walked to the front of the house. Emma's eyes filled with tears when she looked back at Lainey, extending her hand to her sister, all forgiven. "They're growing up," she whispered.

Emma sat at her vanity table dressed in her night clothes, cleaning her teeth, and readying herself for bed when Nathan opened the door. He walked to her side, watching her in the mirror, brushing her long golden hair, more yellowish in the candlelight. Her blue eyes noticed the complacent look on his face, opposite to his worried, scowling forehead from the past week. He stood behind her now with his hands cupping her shoulders, taking in the lavender scent emitted each time she brushed her hair.

"I wanted to tell you you were right." She glanced in the mirror, watching him exhale. "Everything you said about Lizzy standing in Lainey's shadow is true. I watched them from a distance, making plans for Lizzy to take over her music students. I don't deny that I will miss my daughter. My gut is still aching over that. But to see the two of them working together conveyed to me their maturity and their willingness to forgive. It's nothing short of a miracle!" Nathan continued, "It comes down to parenting. They're well-mannered and educated girls; nothing foolish or silly about them. We haven't pampered them or caused them to be irresponsible. We cannot comprehend this yet, but they are each on their private mission to do something good in the world. We have to help them open the right doors and then get out of their way. Do you think we can do that? It's the hardest thing in the world to give them their independence."

He took Emma's hand and walked her to the window. A sea of dazzling stars filled the sky. The lustrous moon radiated its beams on two dedicated parents who had given so much of themselves to their children. "Three more to go. Do you think we can manage it? It's hard work, but we can't stop yet." She gave his hand a squeeze and nodded, endorsing all he said as truth.

Chapter 22

NEW HAVEN

May 20, 1774, Suffield, Connecticut

"Make sure you place my list of spices in a safe place," Aunt Mae cautioned. She had Lainey and Debby running crazy—checking inventory in the pantry, making an account of all the spices she knew were running low. Twenty loaves of sugar, fifty pounds of coffee beans, a barrel each of limes and lemons, another of oranges.

"The peaches won't wait. If I'm to make pickled peaches and peach jam, I'll need more cloves, cinnamon, nutmeg, and more sugar than you could imagine. Your father will be crowing for apple pies, and I cannot do them justice without spices. Have Captain Joel bring the lot of it from the coast. He'll store it for me. He's paid well enough for all his trouble. Nat can pick it up in Enfield on his way home from Boston."

Aunt Mae had turned weepy at the news of Lainey's move to New Haven. She set herself to stay busier than ever, guarding her mind and her words to control her emotions. Otherwise, tears would flow. Besides her kitchen duties, she and Lainey were planning to devote an entire day to washing, drying, and folding her clothes to pack. She reminded herself there are three other daughters who could take on some of her work. She dreaded the long summer ahead without Lainey.

Everyone under the Stowe roof was in a dither the week before Lainey and Nat were to leave for New Haven. Everyone except Nathan. He spent his days at the foundry, then off to the safe haven of the Black

Rooster to smoke a pipe and hear the latest news. The details of the inane fanfare put on by the Tories welcoming the new Governor Gage seemed idiotic to Nathan. It was the governor's intent to force Boston's workers into a desperate situation. "These thirteen colonies have made London's elite wealthy, and now the king wants to halt all commerce, making us all paupers," Nathan deduced.

He hesitated to think of what his life would be like with Lainey living with another family, learning their ways, and meeting new people whom he might not approve of. He recalled when Emma left Boston. Did his father-in-law feel the same when he carried Emma off to Connecticut?

Nathan was in distress. After a full day of strenuous work, he was anxious to rest his body and mind. But his sleep was now reduced to two hours at the most, waking with troubled thoughts of Lainey never returning to her family home. With no expectations of sleep, he retired to his office to read, whatever it took to take his mind off the emptiness of Lainey's eventual absence. One night, Emma joined him. "I don't recall you grieving for Nat when he moved to New Haven." Nathan looked at Emma with clouded eyes and a strained face.

Emma had no regrets in her decision; this was an opportunity for Lainey. But since it was her idea, she felt compelled to pull her husband out of his gloom. She was suffering through grievous moments as well. "I get teary-eyed when she and I are in the same room! But I have resolved to stay busy, to lose myself in preparing for Nat and Lainey's departure. It's going to take some doing to get them on the road. Between Aunt Mae and the girls, we will manage."

Determined to pull her husband from his bottomless pit, Emma offered her idea as a solution. "Hey, we're two tied-up-in-knots night owls in need of a particular potion to clear away the cobwebs. Follow me." She held out her hand for Nathan to grasp, then tilted her head toward the kitchen.

"This isn't one of your ma'ma's fiery potions that will keep me making tracks to the privy all night, is it?" He made a vexing growl as he reluctantly rose from his chair, trudging behind Emma for one of her brandied concoctions. An hour later, they were sound asleep on their goose feather mattress.

Aunt Mae watched the golden sun slowly climbing above the mountains, pouring in through the dining room windows as she stood finishing her coffee. Lainey walked in, giving her great-aunt a kiss on the cheek. *Looks like a perfect day for washing clothes*, Aunt Mae mused. *Never thought I would hear that from a Stowe female.*

Lainey dressed in a thin muslin skirt, the hem striking her midway between knees and ankles. She tied a sash around a muslin tunic, reaching halfway over the skirt. Oddly enough, she felt not one degree of antipathy knowing she would be arms deep in a steaming tub of sudsy water scrubbing and rinsing her clothes. She and her aunt walked inside, feeling the coolness of the stone laundry house. Lainey pulled a cart filled with her clothes. Her silk gowns would need a sponge cleaning on another day.

Washing clothes was the least desirable job among the Stowe daughters. When it was their turn to help Aunt Mae in the laundry house, they would make their excuses or hide out on the farm. Better to be chastened later and pay in turn by shoveling out the stables than to wash clothes.

The job was different today for Lainey. She was too busy chattering about her new job of teaching the Peevy children. Aunt Mae answered her questions about New Haven, adding in her own experiences when she had visited the coastal province years before with Emma and Maddy.

"I wonder who built the fires and filled the tubs?" Lainey asked Aunt Mae. "That will save us some time—and backache. Will I have to wash my clothes at the Peevy's?"

"I shouldn't think so," she laughed. "The Peevy's have servants who take care of the kitchen, the laundry, the housework, the gardens. The lord and lady have their own personal servants." At this new bit of information, Lainey's head popped up from stirring the clothes.

"Are they aristocrats?" Lainey asked. Something her mother had never mentioned.

"I doubt they rub shoulders with the king and queen. Mr. Peevy is the second son of the Earl of Orangeburg. He took his share of the family wealth and moved to New Haven. Of course, he was educated at Oxford. He's a professor at Yale. I wouldn't think there was much money in teaching. It's his thoroughbred racehorses where his time and money are spent.

"They live in a beautiful stately home, light and bright, with windows in every direction and the finest of furnishings and chandeliers. It's dizzying to see all the estates built along the coast and the miles of fencing with the horses running freely. You'll find the lord and lady very accommodating and a pure delight with their jolly nature. You will so enjoy it, I assure you!"

Aunt Mae looked longingly at Lainey's freckled face, wondering how she had gotten so tall and grown up so quickly. But Aunt Mae had worked through all that, grieving that their time together would soon end. Lainey was preparing to leave home, and it was Aunt Mae's job to see that she got on that riverboat in a fine fashion.

Hairpins loosened and fell from Lainey's limp hair as she pushed the long paddle round and round in the laundry tub, then jostled it up and down to clean between the folds of clothes. Strands of long curls straggled down the front of her face, wet from the steam rising from the tub. She blew the pesky tendrils off her mouth. The labor was intense, causing her arm muscles to ache—to sweat. She persisted. Her mission was to accomplish the laundry work and pack it all in her mother's big trunk. She wondered if she even had enough clothes to fill it.

Without a conscious thought, Lainey had been humming Handel's "Arrival of the Queen of Sheba" throughout the morning. The music was stuck in her head. She continued humming when her conversations with Aunt Mae tapered off. Her paddle stirred in sync with the music. She was suddenly interrupted by a loud knock on the door.

Nat and John Dupre stood slouching over the bottom section of the Dutch door, drinking a tankard of ale, watching the women at work. She looked up from her scrubbing, embarrassed as she stood barefoot in her thin muslin skirt and tunic, dripping with wash water. It seemed to

Lainey every time she and John were within ten feet of each other, she was wearing worn-out dresses or riding breeches, giving her a churlish appearance. Nat and John surveyed the wet clothes hanging about. "Ahem, pardon, ladies. Are you ready for some buckets of fresh water?"

Lainey nodded. "Do we have you to thank for filling the tubs this morning?"

"Yes, we're here to help! Your shoulders are going to be sore tonight, sis. You'll need a hot soak at the end of the day!" Nat laughed. His unrestrained advice was a normal reaction. Lainey sneered.

"Thank you for speaking so candidly, brother!" Lainey snapped, pushing a loose tendril behind her ear. "Two buckets will be sufficient." She turned to stirring her clothes, anxious for the men to leave.

There was no time for Emma to show an ounce of heartbreak in her daughters' presence. Her tears flowed when the business of the day was done and her head hit the pillow. She slept nonetheless. She aimed to have Lainey packed and ready to leave in seven days. It seemed an impossible task, but it wouldn't be the first time she had moved a mountain.

The women had made their Saturday trip into town to purchase the necessities—and a new summer straw hat. The May sun played havoc on Lainey's fair complexion, causing freckles to pop up on any exposed skin, which was very disconcerting for her. A wide-brim hat would be her best protection as she traveled by carriage to Enfield, then by riverboat to New Haven.

She would need at least two party dresses, but time would not allow her to have anything custom-made in Suffield. "I'm leaving that chore to Mrs. Peevy," Emma told Lainey. "You'll find more fabric choices and styles in the New Haven dress shops. Twenty pounds should cover it." She gave Lainey a purse holding the silver coins, relinquishing the task to Lainey and Susannah Peevy.

"I sent a note to your aunt Maddy explaining your move to New Haven, of which she is very jealous. She insisted on purchasing a chemise, stays, silk stockings, and pantalettes for you as a gift. Just know, it won't arrive for six weeks on the slow boat from Paris." Lainey could hear the excitement in her mother's voice as she shared details of the move.

"You'll find the shopping in New Haven to be *très magnifique*![31] It's a temptation to get carried away buying things you may never use. The town of New Haven is laid out in nine squares similar to those in European cities, filled with shops, businesses, and stately homes. So different from Suffield and Hartford." Emma was getting puzzling looks from Lainey from too much information. "Let's get back to more pressing matters."

Aunt Mae and Emma entered Lainey's chamber, expecting her trunk to be packed with nightgowns and muslin skirts. Instead, they were blinded by the sunlight reflecting off the shiny silk gowns spread over her bed. "That's my blue gown!" cried Emma. "That's not going to New Haven! Besides, it wouldn't reach down to your ankles." She removed it from the bed. "You're not going to need a gown for every day of the week, darling. There will be a few occasions to dress formally, to be sure."

"But Mother, what about the university parties and the afternoon teas? I can't wear the same gown to every event." The color rose in Lainey's face. "I don't want to look like a country bumpkin in this gown with all the lace and ruffles." She frowned at the pink satin dress she wore to a dance at the Tatums two years before.

"Lainey, we want to pack practical items for everyday wear. Think of the purpose of your work with the children. Simple, lightweight bodices to wear for outside games. Riding skirts when you help the children with the ponies. New Haven's hot summers extend through September. The moist air can become very uncomfortable near the coast. You'll need at least two riding outfits. Pack one formal gown and accessories—your choice." Emma gazed at her aunt. "A cup of tea would be perfect right now." Aunt Mae nodded. Anxious to leave the hot room, feeling the twinge of a headache coming on.

The wagon barn was an amazing piece of architecture situated fifty yards behind the present horse and mule barn. Fifty years prior, it was built to house the horses and mules, a room for the milk cow, and a workroom for storing and repairing the tack. A loft situated on one end

---

31. …so magnificent!

of the barn was quarters for the stable hands. Hay was stored on the opposite end. Three sections of thirty-foot-long beams supported the roof of the ninety-foot-long barn.

The timber was cut from the Stowe property. The thirty-foot beams were dragged by oxen to the building site. He hired the work out to his ironworkers, who were interested in earning extra money and didn't mind working from the tall scaffolding.

As Stowe Ironworks grew, the need for wagons, mules, and oxen was required to move finished iron products to the Connecticut River for shipping to the coast. The wagons and tools required for repairs took over the barn, leaving no room for the animals. That resulted in a new barn construction for horses, ponies, and mules, as well as a loft for stable hands, the current home for John Dupre.

It had taken two days to get the barn ready for Lainey's farewell party. Not a small chore. Nat and John moved the twenty wagons and tools to a not-so-distant location but definitely out of the way of guests attending the event. Now, the emptied building became a blank canvas for which the Stowe daughters could create a party atmosphere.

Nat climbed the ladder to the hayloft and leaned over the rail to look down below at the expanse of the room. The floor was packed down with dirt. Everything and everybody would have a fine dusting of dirt on their clothes and shoes by the end of the party, but it couldn't be helped. With forty or fifty guests attending, this was the most logical space to gather for dancing and entertaining. He looked up at the massive ceiling beams forming an upside-down V-shape from the sides to the center, the length of the barn. It was a thing of beauty and wonder to Nat, with heavy beams supported by massive posts, seeming more like a cathedral, he thought.

His eyes roved around the barn, remembering times when he and Lainey played in the wagons, hiding from each other and Aunt Mae. He cupped his hands around his mouth and yelled to John, "I'm headed to the creek to cool down." They took off running in the May sunshine, two days of work behind them.

Food for the party was getting more complicated as each of the daughters demanded certain must-haves, then came the disagreements. Anything but civil tongues filled the kitchen. That's when an exhausted Lainey escaped to her granite shelf overlooking the valley. "What's wrong with bread and butter and a keg of beer?" Nat asked laughingly, overhearing his sister's bantering back and forth. Unexpectedly, Lizzy threw a handful of pastry dough at his head. "You don't have to get violent," he shouted, flying out the back door.

Lizzy, in her new hierarchy position, decided on a workable strategy. "Debby and Dory, would you like to bake the pies? You can bake any kind you like. You must put them together tomorrow, so you can cook them the next day. It's an important job. Everyone likes pies!"

"I can pick some gooseberries today." Dory was anxious to get outside. "I may need some help rolling the dough. Mine never turns out as good as Debby's."

"I can help you with the dough. Apple with raisins is my favorite. We have lots of apples in the cellar, but I need help bringing them up the stairs," Debby said with a sad face. Her sisters knew she was afraid of going to the cellar by herself, believing there could be a witch hiding in the dark.

Dory sympathized with Debby, wanting to protect her. "Let's get a basket and go now."

The kitchen door slammed, and in walked Nat and Emma, chatting about tables and benches to set up in the barn. "What happened to everybody? I don't smell anything baking."

Lizzy spoke up, "We've settled on pie making—I mean, with Dory and Debby. Aunt Mae gave me this list of her ideas." At that moment, Emma knew Lizzy had taken command, just as she expected.

"Lizzy, let's work on the party list. I want you and Nat to go to Suffield and pick up fruit and cheese. What's the status of the punch-making?" Lizzy was ready. She proudly mapped out the strategy for the food detail with her mother.

"Aunt Mae made the punch after breakfast. We stored it in the springhouse. I'll help her with the savories tomorrow morning." Lizzy was feeling emboldened these days with her new responsibilities, seeming happier and more confident than Emma had ever seen her.

Emma had Nat and John at her beck and call, bribing them with time off in the afternoon to go fishing was her suggestion. She knew John had missed living near the water. The big creek on Stowe property was no comparison to the wild ocean in Maine, but she believed having a friend like Nat was more important to John. Nathan had shared with Emma about John's past life in Newfoundland.

Lainey walked through the door after taking a break from the craziness in the kitchen. "Is it possible to find some pineapples in town?" That took everybody by surprise. In some comical way, it released mounting tensions with the load of work yet to be accomplished.

"Nat, check on your father. I'm sure he's escaped to the Black Rooster again." Emma shooed her children out of the kitchen, sending them on their way. "No dallying while you're in town. We still have lots to do for the party."

Good food and music promised a well-attended party, believed Emma Stowe. She took her cues from her mother, Eloise Pierpoint, who knew the ingredients of a successful celebration. Her Boston residence had been the location for formal and informal get-togethers since Emma was a child.

Perhaps it was the casual style of their home where the gardens connected with the indoor salon, allowing guests to congregate inside or outside at their leisure. Perhaps it was the cleverness of transforming simple foods into cuisine fit for a king. Perhaps it was the charm and hospitality that radiated from their hosts, giving their honorable guests a pleasurable evening. Such were the ingredients that compelled friends and neighbors in Suffield to eagerly attend parties given by the Stowe Family.

Emma allowed Lizzy, Dory, and Debby to decorate the tables in such a manner to pay tribute to Lainey's musical talent and her fondness for literature. Many of her students and their families were among her invited guests. Some of those same students would provide the entertainment during the festivities. Lainey had taught violin, cello, and piano to neighbors and friends since she was fourteen, most of whom resided in Suffield. Naturally, they desired to be a part of Lainey's send-off to New Haven. "But Lainey likes horses too, like Dragon," said Debby, "and cats like Peaches."

Lizzy looked with surprise at her little sister. "I believe you may have hit on an idea for decorations, Debby!" So, the ideas began to flow, and together, they made a plan to celebrate their sister Lainey.

"Here they come!" yelled Nat to John. The last rain had fallen five days before the party, giving the sun time to dry out the packed dirt road leading to the Stowe entrance and the avenue of crabapple trees lining the driveway. Most of the white blossoms had scattered to the winds, but the new green leaves gave a sense of fullness, replacing the harsh dark limbs of the cold winter. Trotting horses kicked up dust, causing it to swirl around, finally settling on the fine attire worn by the arriving guests. It was expected, of course. Prudent and thrifty as New Englanders were, a handy brush was part of the traveling paraphernalia, as well as hats and shawls for the women. Fresh as a daisy and nothing less.

Nat stood at the top of the driveway to greet and welcome guests. John led the horse riders to unsaddle their mounts to get them settled in the paddock. Once the guests alighted, John directed them to the party, where the lively music was going strong. Carriages and wagons were a different story. Nathan had hired two of his foundry workers, Jeremy and Jason, to tend the horses that pulled the wagons and carriages. Two men who had a keen respect for the differing temperaments of horses.

That morning, Nat and John had moved the Stowe mules, including Frederic, to a separate pasture, knowing how cantankerous mules can become when their territory is invaded. They weren't taking any chances. The warm day had begun with the sun hiding mostly behind white clouds. Now, a cool breeze rustled the trees, making the work of steering horses in the right direction a little less unnerving.

The double doors, fully opened at the back of the barn, framed a showy view of the mountains, thick with shades of green; some trees, especially the showy Queen Anne's Lace, were in full bloom. Nearby, sycamore leaves rustled softly, bringing a fresh breeze through the barn.

"Beautiful day for a party," Nathan said to Emma. They stood expectantly at the barn entrance when the approaching sound of carriages and wagons reached their ears, catching a whiff of cedar from the swags hanging on the big doors.

He walked beside her and took her hand. In Nathan's mind, she would be the prettiest female among all the party guests. At the rear of the barn, two violins and a cello sounded out a vibrant Corelli piece, creating an atmosphere of happiness and celebration. "Your yellow gown is dazzling. Is it new? It highlights your pink cheeks."

"This gown is new for me," Emma answered Nathan. "It's actually a hand-me-down from our daughter." She chuckled. "Aunt Mae put in a new hem. Seems Lainey takes her height from your side of the family. You look very handsome today in your snowy white shirt and blue waistcoat, and you're smiling!" She stood on her toes and gave him a peck. "I hope I can keep from breaking down tonight!"

Chattering guests walked through, greeted by Nathan, Emma, and Lainey. Some brought small gifts or a posy for Lainey; some brought a confection to add to the overflowing tables. Then streamed the jubilant cortege of mothers and daughters dressed in bright springtime gowns made of silk and satin, with colorful ribbons for sashes and bows. Some wore lacy shawls and carried hand-painted fans.

Aunt Mae and the three sisters had taken full control of the party decorations, informing Lainey that she was not to take a peek in the barn until she was escorted into the vast space to view their masterpiece. The sisters were beyond giddy, knowing their work of art fulfilled their purpose to pay homage to Lainey's singular style regarding her musical achievements, her love of horses, and her penchant for mythical characters from medieval times.

Dory and John had spent half a day cutting pine boughs from the mountains, each dragging burlap sacks of the spicy and sappy greenery to the barn. They made twine hangers to twist around each bough, suspending them from a nail at every other vertical post. The contrast of dark brown wood and the dark green pine swags was reminiscent of a natural woodsy setting, perfect for the milieu the sisters were bent on creating.

Nat found a supply of handheld tin lanterns in the loft storage. Once he brushed away the dirt and the cobwebs, they would work fine for a soft glowing light. Attaching the big rings at the top to a hook hammered into each alternating beam would give enough illumination to keep the barn from feeling like a cave when the sun set.

Emma was adamant that tallow candles were not to be used; the smell was repugnant, clashing with the sweet flower and forest scents and the savory food smells. The main purpose for Nat and his sister's shopping trip to town was to purchase as many spermaceti candles as were available. "They give off three times as much light and a bigger flame," Emma was quick to state her case. "The inside of the barn gets very dark when the sun starts coming down." Nat nodded. More work for him, but his mother was very convincing, and she *had* given a few parties in her lifetime.

Lainey gazed at the surrounding tables laid out with vases of pink and red roses, ivy artfully strewn across the food tables in a crisscross fashion, fitting in large bowls with each holding a stately pineapple surrounded by grapes, individual fruit tarts, sweetmeats, and black walnut crisps.

A small wooden platform took center stage on the table, holding a rectangle-shaped silver tray boasting four whimsical Italian porcelain figurines of cats. The tallest of which stood eight inches high on its hind legs while its front paws held a violin under its chin as if strumming to make music. The remaining three cats held their own instruments, playing an accordion, piano, and flute. The figurines were wedding presents to Nathan and Emma twenty-four years before. The delicate porcelains remained behind the glass doors of a small cabinet in her bedchamber to be admired from a view.

The second table was of a horse theme, covered in brilliant pink satin, flanked at both ends with a collection of silver bowls filled with dried apricots, figs, and dates. Large platters held horse-shaped cookies iced with a vanilla glaze and decorated with raisins and seeds. In the center of the table stood a large oval-shaped metal bucket turned upside down. The flat metal surface was covered in green sod, which John had meticulously trimmed from the landscape and cut to fit inside the oval space meant to give the impression of grazing horses.

For several days, the three sisters had labored tirelessly in the kitchen, cutting horse shapes out of gingerbread dough while Lainey and Aunt Mae were confined to packing clothes. The gingerbread was baked in the outside oven and set to cool, resulting in a thick, hard-surface cookie. The sisters were so pleased with the appearance of the horses they couldn't wait to spread a glaze over each one, decorating them with features of their own imaginative style.

Lainey bent over the table, glowing with heartfelt joy while breathing in scents of confections, fruits, and flowers. She inspected each decorative horse through misty eyes as it stood independently in the sod, reflecting her love of horses, one of which was sporting wings. "What do you think?" Lizzy asked when she walked to Lainey's side.

"I feel more love for my sisters than I ever have! Who decorated the winged horse?" she asked.

"That was me," exclaimed Debby. "His name is Pasasus. He can fly!"

"Debby, that's Pegasus." Lizzy corrected her. "A Greek mythology horse."

Lainey laughed. "Come here, you two." She hugged her sisters. Nathan and Emma watched the scene from a distance, adding to their high emotional state.

Dory was busy at the third table, arranging the wooden deer figures around a replica of a tall gray stone castle sitting amongst small hemlock branches, creating a version of any one of a hundred medieval stories. "Dory, how did you create such an imaginative scene?" Lainey asked, giving her sister a hug. "You know my fondness for all things medieval!" She looked at the wooden trenchers overflowing with special foods, imagining all the work her family had devoted to this celebration. *A celebration for me*, she thought.

"It's not my work," Dory answered truthfully. "Debby and I baked the pies and helped Aunt Mae with the little mushroom pastry pillows and the biscuits for the cheese. But the creator of the castle and the deer asked not to be revealed. It will have to remain a mystery, I think." Dory shrugged her shoulders, knowing full well that John Dupre had built the castle.

Punch and cider tables were set against the two side walls, adorned with ivy cuttings, pine boughs, and a tin lantern in between, setting off the splendor of the huge silver punch bowls containing Aunt Mae's sweet-tart citrus punch—*sans*[32] rum or wine. Both tables were under the supervision of Aunt Mae and Lizzy. Once the dancing and reeling began, guests would naturally swarm to the tables for a drink.

Nathan stood by Emma at the food table, serving guests pie and savories. "It's hard to fathom that, less than a week ago, this barn was filled with wagons and all manner of filth. How did you get our young'uns settled down long enough to make this place look like a grand party hall?"

"Like I always say, you have to divide and conquer if you want to get anything done!" Emma smiled.

"I've never actually heard you say that. Is it anything like dangling a few carrots?" asked Nathan.

"They're not mules! I take that back. Sometimes they are. With hard work comes reward."

The musicians changed to one of Lainey's favorite Handel compositions, "The Queen of Sheba." This cued the sisters to begin their march from the entrance doors to the rear of the barn where the orchestra platform sat. Guests stood to the side expectantly, applauding. Nat followed, escorting Lainey, prompting guests to cheer and whistle as they walked front and center until the music faded away.

Emma had made each of her daughters a floral wreath headpiece, giving the appearance of a handmaiden, and Nat wore an impressive embroidered waistcoat. He placed a bouquet of flowers in Lainey's arms and kissed her cheek. "It's all yours, sister!" He walked away.

"Welcome, friends, family, and neighbors. Thank you for joining in our celebration. As you know, soon I will be leaving Suffield to assume a position as governess to a family in New Haven." Lainey stood tall and confident, smiling and meeting the eyes of friends she had known since

---

32. —without…

she could walk. The soft candlelight played on her strawberry blond hair, bringing out highlights of red as she moved her head speaking to guests.

"You have been an encouragement to me through the years by allowing me to teach many of you how to make music. Tonight, let's celebrate together by dancing, making it a real party. Form your circles while the musicians are tuning their instruments!" The guests cheered. She caught the gaze of her smiling parents, feeling a tear slide down her freckled face as she walked to the punch bowl.

This was the country dance that Lainey had envisioned, with lively music and a variety of reels mostly among the younger guests while their parents looked on, visiting and eating with friends. Lainey had spoken earlier to her mother that she expected to see the older folks engage in a waltz. Emma promised her it would happen.

"A splendid celebration, Nathan." The tall, barrel-chested Clarence Tatum put out his hand. His deep voice resonated, competing with the orchestra sounds. "The time has come. How are you and Emma handling it? It's nerve-wracking in the beginning, but things will settle down when Lainey gets situated."

"Glad you're here, Clarence." Nathan shook his hand. "We've been going back and forth for several weeks making the arrangements. Our daughter knows what she wants, and she isn't shy about speaking her mind. I just hope she will be happy in New Haven."

"That's the way it is with so many females living under the same roof. They get competitive, sometimes feral, if you know what I mean." Clarence laughed guardedly. He and his wife, Constance, had raised five daughters. "What's her destination once she gets there?"

"I'm sure you've met Clive and Susannah Peevy. Emma and Susannah grew up as neighbors in Boston. Lainey has been hired to teach their three children." Nathan showed no enthusiasm, and Clarence noticed.

"It's hard to come to grips with it all when your oldest decides to leave the nest—as if you've been betrayed—but you will recover. Somehow, it gives the younger ones some space to sprout their wings." Clarence was speaking from experience. He gazed toward the dance floor where two of his youngest daughters were having the time of their lives, reeling and dancing.

"I have to say, Clive Peevy owns some of the finest thoroughbreds in this colony. If Lainey loves to ride, she's headed to a prime location." Clarence got a smile from Nathan on that note.

"Here lately, I've been more concerned about what's happening in Boston. This siege is not going away anytime soon. Which brings me to another topic. I've offered my property for drilling purposes to Charles Talbot, who's forming a militia for Suffield. I mentioned it to Nat; I hope you don't mind." Clarence started to share more information but was interrupted by an announcement.

"Ladies and gentlemen, after a pause for the musicians, you're invited to the dance floor for a waltz," announced the conductor. At that, guests flooded the food and drink tables. Suddenly, the barn was filled with talking and laughter, reminiscent of a sky full of Canada geese flying south to warm weather.

Men and women escaped outside for some much-needed cool air, aiming to experience twilight as the orange light of the sun slowly disappeared, replaced with purples and pinks in a darkening sky. John and Nat were in the process of lighting the wrought iron cressets with a flaming torch, placed where they would do the most good, at the side of the barn and along the path to the stables and paddock. "So, what do you think of our country dance, John?" asked Nat. The music kept the party lively, and the time flew by with dancing and conversations. This is what the people of Suffield loved: the enthusiasm of visiting with friends and neighbors, putting away their work for a few hours to enjoy life.

"I take great pleasure in the music and dancing, and the *jeunes filles*[33] in their colorful gowns are quite extraordinaire," he answered Nat. At that moment, John had a vision of Lainey's demeanor, expressing such happiness when she stared into his eyes and held his hands during the reels.

"Yes, well, maybe you haven't noticed there are several of those *jeunes filles* who have whispered of your *débonnaireté*[34] and your elegant dancing," Nat said, grinning, curious as to John's reaction.

---

33. …young girls…
34. …good nature…

"Haha, *mon ami, naturellement!*"[35]

The orchestra was tuning when Nat and John came inside, meandering their way to the big silver punch bowl, still under Aunt Mae's guard. Lainey and Lizzy took their seats on the platform, holding their violins in ready position, while bass and cello players settled their bulky instruments. Younger guests took time out to drink their punch and watch their parents and grandparents waltz, sure to jeer and make comments they could not hold back.

Nat and John moved close to the front entrance to catch the evening breeze and sample some of the cheese and fruit. Jeremy and Jason had left their positions as purveyors of the horses to grab food to take back to the stables. Nat noticed how John was thoroughly mesmerized by the music, moving his head slightly to the tempo and, in particular, watching Lainey play the violin.

The peculiar noises outside the barn went unnoticed until Jeremy jabbed his elbow into Nat's side. "Look behind you," Jeremy whispered loudly. "We've got company."

Nat set his plate of food aside and went searching for any uninvited guests in the darkening shadows. Any guests who might be brandishing knives and pistols with the intent to spoil the party. No worries there. He spotted Simon McGinty and his toadies staggering around the grounds, sucking on their stinking flasks of rum.

"Drunken skunks," he muttered. As usual, it was the three village idiots: scrawny, filthy excuses for humans, oily hair falling over their faces, glassy-eyed. They probably had not eaten in a week. One of the lizards attempted to make his appearance known but had trouble spitting out the words, discharging only grunts and slurs. The popular Suffield ruffians who thought it their duty to crash parties they weren't invited to and doing their best to make sure the host knew their purpose. A typical drunkard attitude: believing they were never treated with respect and nobody liked them.

There is no point in trying to reason with them, thought Nat. *They'll get loud and ruin Lainey's party. It would be fruitless to begin slugging at them.*

---

35. Haha, my friend, naturally!

They can't defend themselves. Nat signaled Jeremy and Jason, forgetting about John for the moment. His eyes were closed, absorbing the music, obviously in another world.

"Here's the plan; there's three of us and three of them. Choose your victim and run toward him like you're going to punch him in the face with the hope of scaring them off the property. Pick up some rocks to use if they don't budge," Nat started toward the ringleader, Simon McGinty.

The surprised drunkard moved in the direction of the stables when he saw Nat's stern face. "Hey, we just wanted to see…" Simon managed to eke out the words while walking speedily as Nat took long strides toward him, never saying a word to the skunk.

Jeremy and Jason followed Nat's lead, picking up rocks and pelting Simon's drunken pals as they staggered and ran into each other down the dusty driveway.

One of the slimy men attempted to reach down and pick up a few rocks to defend himself but instead lost his balance and fell to the ground. His hand raised as he grasped, seeking support, but grabbed a handful of air instead. His pouch of rum lay on the ground, dribbling its contents. Simon and his toady proceeded to run toward the paddock but were more concerned with shielding their backs from the oncoming rocks raining down on them.

Nat and his men continued pursuing them as they closed in on the road, the slimy man stumbling behind, trying to catch up. "Let their horses loose," hollered Nat to Jeremy. The horses, anxious for their freedom, ran down the road past their riders, the ruffians yelling for them to stop, but to no avail.

"That should keep them busy for a while," laughed Jason. Nat joined Jeremy and Jason at the well to get a drink and wash their faces, attempting to recover from the ruckus and hoping the music and dancing were not disturbed. Nat thought It would be very unlikely that Nathan hadn't heard the ruckus.

It was early evening, and the party was dying down. Aunt Mae had resigned herself to a chair but remained glued by the punch table, having a fine time herself visiting with friends and neighbors. The musicians packed their instruments, and final goodbyes were made to Lainey with Lizzy at her side. Any hint of rivalry had dissipated as the sisters stood together on a level playing ground.

Nat, John, and the daughters packed leftover food in baskets, loading up a wagon with fruits, cakes, and punch to be deposited in the spring house. Nathan and Emma stood at the barn entrance, bidding guests farewell as another memorable barn dance came to a close. Jason and Jeremy managed the line of carriages and wagons down the driveway while a half-moon peeked in and out from behind the clouds, providing light for the drivers. They strapped a sack of party food across their saddles along with a purse of coins in payment for their part in the event. The daughters escaped to the house, full of merriment, talking over each other, asserting their preferences for the most fashionable and stylish gowns worn by their peers.

The cresset fires had burned down sufficiently. Nat doused the flames with a bucket of water and checked on John, snuffing out the lanterns and closing the back barn doors. "Do you need help with closing up? Better get some sleep. We have a big day tomorrow, filling this place with the mule wagons. Not looking forward to that!" Nat walked toward the front entrance. "I'll say good night."

"Yes, *et bonsoir*,"[36] John replied as he stood in front of a chair on the musician's platform meant to conceal Lainey's violin, which she had mistakenly left in all the excitement of the evening. He continued with his lantern work, nervously debating whether he should take a chance on playing the instrument.

He found himself humming the same Italian pieces the musicians had played, which only intensified his appetite and yearning to play the instrument. He closed the front doors and walked toward the instrument, feeling it in his hands, plucking its strings, then placing it under his chin. Quietly, he played Vivaldi's "La Notte," becoming lost in the concerto. He played it as he knew it should be played, with gusto and passion as he remembered his father played.

---

36. ...and good evening.

Lainey lay in bed gazing at the starless nighttime sky, recounting the details of the day: the guests, the music, the lavishly laid tables, the flowers, and the smiling faces of her parents. Remembering the music pieces made her replay them in her mind. A thought struck her: *I don't recall bringing in my violin or even storing it in its case. Where could it be? I don't think it was in my hands when I walked to the house.* "No reason to worry," she muttered. "I'll check the music room."

She put on her dressing gown and fetched a lantern, fleeing downstairs to the music room first. No violin. She walked through the house, stopping to retrace her steps until she reached the back kitchen door. Stopping in her tracks, she caught the sounds coming from the wagon barn, wondering if she should move forward. The what-ifs made her pause. Hearing clearer sounds, she knew it must be Nat, finally picking up the violin after all these years, she mused.

She walked to the barn with the help of the waning moonlight, enough light along with the lantern to guide her steps. She stood listening at the door. Nudging it gently, she caught a glimpse of John's back, his muscles flexing as he took control of the violin. She gasped and walked in quietly to listen, totally mystified at what was taking place before her, fully aware that John was putting his entire body and soul into the workout he was giving her violin. It brought tears to her eyes.

He moved the bow gently over the strings for the last time, ending Vivaldi's beloved concerto. His neck muscles relaxed, causing his chin to collapse to his chest, feeling more fulfillment mixed with joy than he believed was possible.

He sensed movement behind him and froze, discerning it was Lainey coming to retrieve her violin. "Mademoiselle, I…" With nothing more to say, he laid the instrument on the chair and walked to her. He bowed, catching only a dim view of her pretty face from the glow of the lantern.

"That was very beautiful," she said in a whispered tone, her eyes filled with tears. "How do you know? I'm overcome with awe and thrill at your talent!" She looked into his brown eyes, searching for answers, knowing that the entire truth could not be conveyed so easily.

"I'm honored to play your fine violin. Forgive me for… I was very much overcome with the music during your celebration. I could not help myself. *Mon père*[37] was my instructor. It is late. I must finish my work here." He bowed again, hesitating and wanting to say more to Lainey, but instead walked away.

"Perhaps we can talk another time. I must go now." She picked up her violin and turned to him. "As wonderful as you played 'La Notte,' it's most beautiful when accompanied by the flute. My mother knows the concerto well," she informed him with piercing eye contact and raised eyebrows. "It is one of her favorites!" She left the barn, and her white muslin gown flowed as she walked. Tears rolled down her cheeks.

John heard the back door to the kitchen close. He sat down in a chair, full of more emotion than he had felt since leaving his home. His head bowed, and his tears began to flow uncontrollably.

---

37. My father…

Part IV

Do Good Where You Can

Chapter 23

Good Samaritan

Last Week of May 1774, New Haven, Connecticut

Micah Penrose stood on the upper deck of The Dorcas, hunched over the rail, gazing over the calm waters of Long Island Sound, smoking his pipe. He sailed his schooner to New Haven's wharf less than an hour before. He stood motionless while his crew went about their work of unloading barrels and boxes, the bosun shouting orders and curses at mates scurrying back and forth while their mouths thirsted for that first sip of ale at Sailor's Grog.

The trip to the Indies was routine for this time of year. The winds were astern, blowing steadily. The sailors steered, and the crew trimmed sails and wound ropes. Cargo moved down the Connecticut River, was transferred to The Dorcas, and delivered to Jamaica's port. The return trip was the same; Jamaica's cargo was stowed on The Dorcas at New Haven's port to be stored in warehouses until customers claimed it.

Micah was a master at solving problems: managing crew members and the mechanics of his ship and navigating The Dorcas in mild and stormy conditions. Today, he was suffering from a different kind of problem that had begun three days before. A crewman had collapsed in his bunk, consumed with fever, chills, and delirium. Seeing the man in such agony nagged Micah, for he was at a loss for how to help him. He had wondered if the ailment was cholera or dysentery. It was certainly not contagious, judging from what he had seen of the crew still eating heartily and tending to their work.

The sick man's life lay mostly in the hands of Johnson, the cook. A chilling prospect for Micah. He heard only complaints from the cook and a constant clanging and slamming of pots and kettles. Was he to heal the sick or cook the captain's meals?

Apparently, the ship's physician had involved himself in a card game on the final day of their stay in Jamaica's port. The doctor had wagered and lost his personal belongings, with the exception of a case of rum. He had disappeared and could not be located on the day of departure to New Haven.

Nat walked briskly across the wharf toward The Dorcas. As the light breeze refreshed his face, Nat was anxious to settle any particulars about Aunt Mae's mandated fruit and spice order with the captain. His eyes squinted from the smoke expelled from Micah's pipe and the reflected sunlight coming off the water. From twenty yards away, he recognized the man's stature, brawny back and arms, and a head of curly brown hair, unmistakably a Penrose brother. When Micah turned toward Nat, his lack of a capricious spirit was uncharacteristic. Not the smiling, shake your hand, pat you on the back sort of greeting he was accustomed to from a garrulous Penrose brother. Micah met Nat with a worried face.

Nat went straight to the matter. "Micah, what's all this about? Has there been an accident?"

"Let's move out of this hot sun," Micah sighed, leading Nat to a covered spot on the deck. "One of the crewmen is seriously ill. He appears on the verge of death. For three days, he's been out of his head, his flesh as hot as a kettle. We mopped his brow with cold water and tried to feed him. I'm at a loss for how to go on with him. My physician jumped ship. My doctor is the ship's cook. He's done all he knows to do. Nothing seems to work."

"What does the cook think? Take me to him. Maybe I can help," Nat insisted. Micah led him down the stairs to a tiny cabin serving as the sick room.

The room reeked of sweat and urine, prompting Nat to hold a kerchief over his nose and mouth. He pulled up the man's soaked shirt, searching for sores. Nothing. He searched for a heartbeat. "Rapid," he muttered. "Do you know if this was the man's first trip to the tropics?" He turned to Micah for an answer.

"I hired him six weeks ago. He called himself Eli Asher. I don't know many details, but he came off a British vessel. He was a good worker. This was his third trip." Micah swallowed hard as he stood staring at the sick man, believing the worst. Judging from the man's soaked body and chattering teeth, he was freezing to death.

Nat spotted a blood-stained lancet lying beside a bowl on a table. "Bloodletting is mostly overused by doctors"—his grandsire's words rang in his ears. "We will need more blankets and another pillow to warm his feet. "Do you store quinine powder amongst your medicines?" he asked Micah. "He could have yellow fever or malaria. Has he complained about a headache?"

Micah nodded to Nat's questions, then dashed from the room to search for the powder in a locked cabinet. He returned with a bottle of ground feverwort leaves. Nat pulled out the stopper and took a whiff. "This is something we can use." Nat turned to Micah. "Tell the cook to bring a pan of water and some clean cloths and heat a kettle of water for the tea."

He wasn't the cleanest looking cook, noticing his dirty fingernails and his blood-stained apron. The unsmiling man nodded at Micah, likely thinking his job as doctor might soon come to an end.

"One would think it necessary to swab a feverish man's face constantly with cool water," he muttered under his breath. Nat leaned over the man's ear. "Sir, Eli, can you hear me? Squeeze my hand if you can hear my voice." He clutched the man's clammy hand more to give the patient some reassurance. Surprisingly, Nat felt pressure on his palm.

In a few minutes, the sick man was covered in blankets, tucked in and around his slim body. Nat slipped a pillow under his head and mopped his face again with the wet cloth, speaking to him as he worked. Johnson brought in a steaming mug of feverwort tea, emitting a familiar sharp herbish smell. At least it was a start, but only if Eli accepted enough of the liquid to make a difference. The man could die if he doesn't take some fluids. No telling how long that's been.

Nat sat on a stool next to the bunk that supported a straw-stuffed pallet, spooning a tiny drop of the concoction to the man's lips in between bouts of chattering teeth. Eli's throat moved after each drop, giving Nat some assurance the man swallowed the medicine.

The small cabin was dark and windowless, making it difficult for Nat to make a determination about Eli's skin color. He passed a lantern holding a stub of a candle over the man's chest, which cast a yellowish light over him. He could be jaundiced, or it could be the glow from the candle.

Nat continued spooning Eli the liquid, scowling at the man's extreme condition. Nat felt overcome by the heat and removed his stock and waistcoat. The air dripped with steamy heat. He looked at Micah's tense face. "This will take some work, but Eli would be better off if we moved him to sunlight and open air." Nat was hoping to get a good look at the sick man's skin in the bright light. "Surely, it's not measles or smallpox, but it's hard to tell in this dim light. No evidence of a rash on his chest or throat."

Micah walked to the upper deck and loudly called two of the workers unloading cargo. "Abe, I need some help. We need to bring Eli up on deck and bring your brother with you."

It took two crewmen, in addition to Micah and Nat, to carry Eli's limp body up the narrow stairs to get him situated on the upper deck. "Fetch his pallet and blankets," ordered the captain to Grif, the youngest crew member. Eli's teeth began chattering. His eyes squinted in the bright light.

They worked quickly to settle Eli. His new helper mimicked Nat's ways of tucking the blankets and settling the pillows. "Will this 'ere do ye good?" Grif asked Nat. "Cap'n sez to stay close by ye for a time. I'm called Grif, at yer service, sir. Not my real name; it's what me brother calls me."

"This will do fine. At least I can get a look at him in this light." Nat adjusted his eyes to the brightness, immediately inhaling a needed gulp of fresh air. "Hot as Hades down there. How do you stand it? My name is Nat Stowe. I'm thankful for your help."

"Bring up the mug of tea from the cabin and tell the cook to prepare a pan of fresh water," Nat ordered. Grif was slightly built. His oily, tawny hair was pulled back in a tail. A smattering of stubbled whiskers covered the chin of his young face. His clothes and his body smelled nasty, as did all the crew, but he was friendly and eager to help.

Nat estimated that Eli Asher was taller than himself, judging from his long neck and lanky arms and legs. His big hands were calloused, and his head full of whitish hair shone in the sunshine. Nat had cut the man's shirt off and proceeded to sponge off filth and stinking sweat. The name "Asher" stuck in his head. *Where have I heard that name?* he asked himself. Nat allowed the sun to heat the man's body while he spooned more of the tea to Eli's lips. The chattering of his teeth seemed to lessen now.

"Do you think this will improve his condition?" Micah's face was less strained when he stared down at Eli. "You're giving him the sort of attention I didn't know to give. The shipmates are scrubbing that filthy cabin. What can I do to help?"

"He's responding well to the tea. That's a good sign. Where's the nearest apothecary? I want to get some quinine in him when he wakes and observe how he reacts to it." Nat remembered he had plans to ride with Lainey at noon at Excalibur farm. That trip could be delayed depending on Eli's condition. "The man's in bad shape. I don't want to see him slip away. Continue administering the tea. His body needs liquids to survive. Can you remain on deck until I return?"

Micah nodded in response, relieved that Nat was willing to attend to Eli's needs. "You'll find a shop well stocked with medicines and herbs on Water Street, owned by a chap named Arnold; you'll see it on the sign. Next door to that is a tavern if you want to wet your whistle. That's where most of my crew are at the moment. Do you think the quinine will help?"

"I'm making no promises. We must try." Nat looked soberly at Micah. "I'll return as soon as possible." Nat walked across the wharf, feeling revived each time a balmy breeze blew across his face, in search of a chap named Arnold.

The paned windows across the front on either side of the door showcased an assortment of cosmetics, medicines, ribbons, stationery, books, and maps. *Fancier than any apothecary than I have ever seen*, Nat thought. The signboard hanging from the rafter read: *B. Arnold Druggist and Bookseller.*

Nat stepped inside the shop and moved to one section advertising herbs, the most likely place to find quinine powder. His eyes and nose were quickly overpowered by peppermint, rosemary, and bergamot. He escaped to the book area.

He did a double take when his eyes caught the name "Dr. Jerome Pierpoint." He stopped at the cabinet to withdraw a book titled *Causes and Treatments for Tropical Diseases.* "Will wonders ever cease?" he gasped. He quickly thumbed through the pages until he saw the word "malaria." He scanned it to learn other methods of treatment besides quinine. His uncanny discovery revealed a victorious smile and a noisy gasp that couldn't be helped. He saw the sales clerk approaching.

"Excuse me, sir, I did not realize our medical books could bring such entertainment," sneered the tall, handsome woman, searching his face for an answer.

"You are correct. Such an inane expression does warrant an apology and an explanation from me. My mission upon visiting your excellent shop was to obtain a bottle of quinine. I was overwhelmed with relief when I came upon this informative booklet on the treatment of tropical diseases." *Can I help how my face appears when I'm overjoyed?* Nat mused with disgust.

The clerk thought it best to proceed with caution, believing she had encountered an insolent Yale student intent on making her look foolish. "The quinine can be found in the direction of the herbal section. Allow me." Nat followed at the clerk's behest, still in possession of the booklet, bracing himself for the pungent smells and burning eyes he would soon encounter.

Anxious to conclude his business at B. Arnold's, Nat assumed an amicable manner while waiting for the clerk to bag his purchases. "May I be so bold to ask if you can recommend anything in addition to quinine to treat my associate? At this point, my only option has been to administer feverwort tea," Nat asked the clerk, looking as grim as he thought plausible.

Surprisingly, the clerk smiled at him, realizing his predicament. She took the liberty of opening the booklet to a page titled *Treatments for Malaria*. 'I've read that Dr. Pierpoint recommends strong black coffee, not as a cure, but to give the patient some relief and to act as a deterrent. Do you own a coffee grinder?"

"I never thought of coffee. That might help his headache," he said. "Well, if that's the case, may I trouble you for a bag of coffee beans?" Nat asked her, thinking an additional purchase might help soothe her ruffled feathers. He anxiously produced five shillings for his purchase.

Nat left the shop, satisfied that the unbelieving clerk's first impression of him was assuaged after he shared his desperate plight. *Whew, it's likely I'll need to purchase more quinine and coffee beans*, he contemplated. *Definitely not a job for the cabin boy, Grif!*

Considering the time, he gulped a beer at Sailor's Grog and dashed back to The Dorcas, anxious to make a cup of quinine tea for his patient. Moments later, he noticed the mug of feverwort tea was empty, thanks to Micah's persistent care. *Either this man is very thirsty, or he's anxious to recover*, Nat mused. All in all, it was a good sign. Eli was responsive. He hailed over Grif. "Tell the cook to prepare a kettle of hot water."

While the aromatic tea steeped, Nat shared with Micah his blunder at B. Arnold's with the clerk and showed him the booklet about tropical diseases. "In my conversation with the pub keeper, he said the beer was produced at a brewery in Stoughton, Massachusetts, not far from where I live. Reminds me of the beer from Whales' Tale."

"It's one and the same. My brother Joel barters a keg with me when he needs a favor. Brings it down on his sloop," Micah stated casually, unaware that the ailing man lying on his deck had any connection to the family brewing business at Mulberry Farm.

Eli's pulse had slowed, to Nat's relief, and he hadn't heard his teeth chatter since his return. He cautiously spooned the concoction between Eli's lips. Eli's face turned sour at the foul-smelling brew. His eyes flew open. Nat and Micah looked at each other astounded, harkened by this human display of resistance, to which Nat responded, "I suppose it's very bitter, is it not, Eli?"

"Och. Who are you?" the sick man demanded.

"I am a friend of Micah's. My name is Nat Stowe. You have been feverish and out of your head for three days. I believe you are suffering from malaria. The bitter tonic I gave you will help relieve your symptoms."

Through watery blue eyes, he squinted, attempting to focus on Micah's face. "I'm freezing, and my head aches. Where am I? At the islands?" Eli mumbled faintly.

"Be assured, Eli, we are many miles from the islands. We are docked in New Haven, Connecticut. Nat is assisting you medically. We should stop talking so you can drink more of the tea. It will help shed the fever and relieve your symptoms," Micah said with certainty.

Eli sipped the tea without complaint. Somehow, the process seemed familiar to him: the acrid aroma, the feel of hot liquid sliding down his throat, some person leaning over to feed him because they cared. At the moment, no faces or voices came to mind. Only moments mattered. There was no thought of tonight or tomorrow. He moved his head to the side. Sleep overtook him.

While Eli slept, Nat sat reading the malaria booklet, discerning treatments that he could actually employ when the patient woke. He remained struck with wonder that he had come upon such helpful information at such a fortuitous moment. He recalled times past when he had assisted his grandsire in producing medical booklets, never thinking he would be in a situation where such valuable information could save a man's life.

Nat walked to the ship's bow and rested his arms on the rail, pondering Eli's situation just as Micah had done earlier that morning. He had heard the noon bell toll. "But how long ago was that?" he muttered. He thought of the plans he and Lainey had made the night before of riding horses on the beach and his familial obligations to Clive and Susannah. *I'm a guest in their home. I'm sure they expect me for dinner.* He stared at Eli stretched out on the pallet, his feet dangling off its end. His stomach turned nervous with indecision. "There is no way I can desert this man," he decided.

The sun had reached its zenith; the hottest part of the day was soon approaching. Nat deemed it necessary to move his patient to an accommodation where he could receive care at a moment's notice. But where and with who? The deck of The Dorcas was not a suitable location for a man in his condition, and I'm certainly not leaving Micah's cabin boy to be responsible for the man's health. He thought of the dankness of the cabin below and how he would feel if that was his only option.

Micah walked to the deck to speak to Nat. "Since it is getting on in the day, I've made arrangements for Eli to stay in my cottage for tonight. My housekeeper has agreed to remain with him to give him a better night and see to his needs. I'm in your debt, and I cannot expect you to adjust your plans to doctor him. We will need your guidance in preparing the brews and additional treatments. If only Eli could think clearly and talk to us. I seem to remember him saying he has family in these parts, but where, I cannot say." Micah was in a tight spot. His schedule called for another run to Jamaica in five days.

"You are correct, Micah. My time in New Haven is short. When your brother Joel arrives, my plan is to sail on his sloop up the Connecticut River with my aunt's purchases. She would be mad as an old wet hen if I do not see to her spices and citrus order. From Whales' Tale, I travel on to Boston."

Micah nodded, recalling the occasion he had met Nathan Stowe several years prior. His father had sailed with Nat on Joel's sloop to New Haven, escorting Nat to his first year attending Yale University. "I suppose your father's foundry continues to manufacture heavy equipment. Has he considered building muskets? We're going to be in a desperate fix if colonists cannot defend themselves." Micah was right, of course. Every ironmaker in Connecticut should be in the business of manufacturing weapons.

"I dare say militias are forming all over this colony, even in Suffield." At that moment, Nat knocked the palm of his hand against his head, recalling Ethan Asher's musket order. "The man from Stoughton!" Nat exclaimed.

"I know this man, Eli Asher, or I believe I know his relation. An uncommon tall, slim man interested in examining the muskets we produce." With that thought, Nat gazed at the supine figure in front of him—slim and tall, the long, straight nose, he was sure. "He searched us out on the advice of a lawyer well-known in Boston. I wouldn't allow him to place an order until he tested the weapon we manufactured. We spent some time together in target practice, of which I was immensely impressed with his marksmanship. He ordered several cases to be ready for pickup in August. He was an Indian—half-Indian, really—with that same long nose."

Micah reflected on Nat's discovery, thinking back on previous conversations he had had with Eli. "At the moment, all that comes to mind is his unfaltering work ethic, putting out twice as much work as the other crew members. He appeared to be educated. He seldom spoke in the beginning but loosened up in time with the other crew. Never complained about anything."

"He must have been hiding out; God only knows how long. One day, he showed up starved and filthy. He said he came to Haiti on a British vessel, the Starr Jones. He was anxious to jump ship to escape the vile ways of the captain. I was familiar with that captain's *peculiarities*, according to crew members I had hired from that ship. I had been searching for a steady worker, so I took a chance and stowed him away until we loaded our cargo and departed Haiti."

Nat nudged Micah with his elbow. "Look," he said. Eli had raised his hand to his eyes, rubbing them as if to remove some dirt. Tears rolled down his cheeks. Nat felt Eli's forehead for fever. "That's a good sign. Your fever is lessening." Nat paused, considering whether the man had absorbed the details of his conversation with Micah. He cautiously proceeded, "Is it true? Do you have a son named Ethan?"

The word came faintly from Eli's mouth. "Yes." He closed his eyes and wept.

Micah placed a handkerchief in Eli's hand, then walked down the stairs to the galley. He returned later with a steaming cup of coffee.

Nat had propped Eli to a sitting position in the bed situated in the corner of the cottage's front room. A large mahogany bedstead made up with a goose feather mattress, pillows, linens, and blankets. An improvement over the child-sized bunk and thin straw pallet he had endured for days.

Considering the cottage's front room, Nat became aware of certain amenities one could potentially possess as owner and captain of his own ship: damask-covered chairs, polished furniture, fine crockery, two brass sconces attached to each wall, more than adequately illuminating the spacious room. A pretty housekeeper to boot.

Nat stood at the fireplace demonstrating to Micah and his housekeeper, named Lynette Pomme, the particulars of brewing and administering the quinine drink. "Give it to him slowly with a teaspoon. He may prefer to drink it from the cup. He will signal when he's ready. The brew is strong and bitter, but don't let that deter you."

Nat was gratified when Madame Pomme took an interest in their overnight patient. She leaned into the conversation, absorbing his instructions. Her facial features were striking as the afternoon light streamed through the front windows, accentuating her oval, unblemished face and creamy skin. Her deep brown eyes and scowled forehead assured Nat of her concern for a person who would be dependent on her care.

"Should we offer him some broth?" Madame Pomme, her eyebrows raised. "Perhaps it might upset his stomach. What do ye think?" The answer came before Nat spoke when Eli raised his arm and nodded. Lynette's eyes caught Micah's spirited face, indicating progress was finally happening.

Micah breathed a sigh of relief. "I say that should restore some life to him. Good man!" He gently patted Eli's arm. His body was worn out from the ravages of fever and bone-breaking chills. He closed his eyes.

It was an encouraging sign for Nat and an approbation that now was the time to leave the care of Eli in the hands of the captain and his housekeeper for the evening. He said his farewells. "If you need me, I'm staying at the Peevy estate across from the university."

As he walked to Excalibur, his mind reflected on the bulk of the day in which he had stretched his mental capacity and his endurance for a person he had only known for several hours, notwithstanding the remarkable experience at B. Arnold apothecary. If he had his way, he would slip to his room at the Peevy house and take a long nap. That would be difficult to explain to Lainey, regretfully.

"Where have you been all day? It's two o'clock?" Lainey stood in the barn, tacking up her new bay, Merlin, named after the famous soothsayer. She was not exactly upset with her brother. He *had* made it possible for her to be standing in the most incredible stable she had ever encountered. She was dressed in riding breeches and a lightweight tunic belted with a purple sash, her hair pulled back in a braid, topped with her reliable straw hat. It had spared her fair complexion from the sun's rays while on the boat trip to Whales' Tale three days prior.

She played it safe with Nat by refusing to appear distraught. Instead, she offered a degree of concern as he was soon to embark on another leg of the journey to Boston. "I hope there was no problem in arranging shipment for Aunt Mae's citrus order." She feigned a disappointed expression.

"There's no problem," he lied, remembering he had not discussed the order with Micah. "Some other matters came up. I'll tell you later."

"Has it occurred to you that the Penrose brothers are named after Old Testament prophets Ezekiel, Joel, and Micah?" she chuckled. "Just curious if there is some special reason his parents chose illustrious biblical figures. Are they endowed with the ability to forewarn, prognosticators predicting the future?"

Nat shook his head in disbelief. "You read too many medieval books." He walked his mount to the drive, with Lainey catching up from behind. "Mother was right. You do need a change of scenery."

"I'm ready if you're ready," Lainey said. Nat took the lead, trotting toward a stretch of beach east of the farm. The wind in his face and the salty air were invigorating, and he was more than happy for fresh air.

They left the earthy smells of kitchen gardens and horse dung behind them, breathing in the spray from the whitecaps crashing upon the shore. They became lost in a world of sunshine, blue skies, distant sounds of gulls, and the never-ending sounds of the ocean's movements. Escaping the cares of their world for a few brief moments. Cutting loose and letting go to absorb the marvels of a natural phenomenon never to be changed by mankind.

They rode their horses through the sand and water, laughing and ignoring the whitecaps, playing keep away when the high surf threatened to drench them. They slowed their horses to a trot when the stretch of beach disappeared, replaced by a mountainous conglomeration of rough, craggy rocks.

Breathless and giddy, they dismounted to recover from their jaunty excursion. Nat passed his sister a pouch of water. "Hey, you're wet and covered in mud. Look, yonder's your hat being pecked to shreds by a nosy seagull. Oops, there it goes, never to be seen again!"

"Won't he be disappointed when he discovers it's not edible? I mean, not a fish," she laughed, shaking her fist at the noisy thief. As if the gull understood Lainey's response, it swooped down and screamed its rebuttal. They looked at each other and erupted into uncontrollable laughter.

Eager to collapse as they walked their steeds to the barn, the stable hand looked them over and grasped the horses' reins. Nat and Lainey stood in soaked boots, covered in wet sand, with their bedraggled hair hanging down their neck and face.

He turned toward his sister. "Wait, I'm going to show you a backway up the stairs to the chambers. It's Phineas, the butler. He gives nasty looks at visitors like us when we come in from riding because we're covered in sand. He hates the extra work. Put your wet boots in this room." A side room off the back hallway was filled with riding paraphernalia and dirty boots waiting to be cleaned by the footmen.

As the afternoon tea hour approached, Nat and Lainey bathed and dressed and met Clive and Susannah in the drawing room, where they gathered to enjoy refreshments. It was an informal family affair offering cake and biscuits, hot tea and lemonade, and nepus, wine, sugar, nutmeg, and lemon juice concoction. This casual hour marked the end of the day's work, meant to refresh and catch up on the day's events.

"I gather you've discovered the thrill of riding along the shore," Susannah said to Lainey. "I see your nose is glowing pink, much like my fair skin. You're welcome to my toilette table to dab on face cream. It *will* take time to accustom yourself to the intensity of the sun in this climate, being so near to the ocean." Lainey gazed at Susannah's coppery autumn hair pulled around in a braid at her nape.

Before Lainey could respond, she heard the children's voices as they scrambled into the room. Nanny was in tow with the youngest, two-year-old Walt. He wiggled his chubby body from the woman's clutches, proceeding to run with arms open wide to embrace Nat's knees. Nat bent down to the floor to meet Walt's blue eyes and big grin, welcoming him to afternoon tea. The giggling child was irresistible, his yellow curls bouncing as he moved, straddling Nat's leg for a horsey ride. An exercise that had begun the day Nat and Lainey arrived in New Haven.

Soon, the room was filled with laughter and whoops from the children and adults. Clive was on all fours, waiting for Charles to climb aboard for a ride around the room. "Go faster, Papa, like Sir Kay, run faster." Clive gave it all he could until he eased himself to a prostrate position on the carpet, pretending to play dead. Charles, with energy to spare, jumped off his papa and waved his arms at Nat, shouting, "My turn, my turn!" His little brother, Walt, familiar with the switch-off, ran to Clive for his horsey ride.

All this while Susannah and Lainey stood clapping their hands and shouting, encouraging the game until the men simultaneously heaved a giant sigh. Clive checked the knot in his stock and ran his fingers through his curly brown hair, rearranging it as best he could. He came up off his knees, standing tall, breathlessly announcing, "The horsey race is finished!"

Nine-year-old Patrice had long ago given up the childish game, preferring to engage the family's pet schnauzer by training him to stand on his hind feet for a treat—tidbits of biscuit from the tea table. Distracted as Felix was with the commotion of the horsey rides, the dog managed to grab a few bites of biscuit. This was new training for the dog that Patrice had begun the week before.

She was the oldest child, leaving her younger brothers to develop their own playtime sports. Her interest in drawing and music had lately flourished. For three days now, Lainey had spent time with her, learning her daily schedule, her moods, and her relationship with Clive and Susannah.

Lainey thought it best to allow Patrice to take the lead in developing their relationship, particularly while the two rode horses on the estate property. All the while, Lainey was evaluating the girl's skills and how keenly she accepted her responsibilities. *Formal academics could wait a couple of months. Besides*, Lainey thought, *I need time to create a suitable course of study.*

Walt observed some movement at the tall front windows, showing off a flower garden brimming with Sweet William, foxgloves, and Canterbury bells. He toddled over to get a closer view. "Ook, ook, wumbabee, wumbabee," his finger pointed to the bee dipping in and around the flowers. Everyone in the room crowded at the window. "Ook, ook," he continued. He proceeded to smack the window with his biscuit in hopes of drawing the bee's attention.

It didn't take long for his older brother to correct him. "It's called a *bumblebee*, Walt." Charles looked up at Lainey's face, his sparkling dark blue eyes seeking confirmation. She nodded and smiled. "We saw a picture of one in the book Miss Lainey read… Look, the sun is shining on that spiderweb. What do spiders like to eat, Walt?" His little brother's pudgy cheeked face looked up at Charles, followed by pouty lips and a back-and-forth movement of his head. "Insects!" Charles shouted. "Flies and mosquitoes!" Uninterested in Charles' unusual words, Walt returned to the window to pound his biscuit at the bee.

In walked Nanny to escort the two boys upstairs for their baths, leaving Patrice to visit with the adults. The room had turned silent now that the entertainment had vacated the premises. Nat stared heavy-lidded down at Felix, jealous of the gray-haired dog lying on Patrice's feet sound asleep. Clearly worn out from jumping up and down for biscuit treats.

Nat was inclined to lean his head on the chair back and close his eyes, fatigue getting the best of him. He thought better of it when Phineas stood bent over his chair, tempting him with a tray of biscuits and cake. "May I have…" Too late. Before Nat could say a cup of coffee, Phineas had returned to the tea table, standing at attention as butlers do, with his hands clasped behind his back. The bright light highlighted the silver strands in his dark hair, pulled tightly around into a short plait.

Same trick he tried on me last time I was here, Nat thought. Deciding instead to see the humor in the servant who sought to mimic a statue.

"Sorry, Nat, I'll speak to him privately about his conduct. You're looking unusually droopy-eyed and wearisome. You should go to your chamber and relax before dinner. The stress you've experienced today at the Sound has been dizzying for you, I'm sure." His gracious host encouraged him quietly. "I'll keep the ladies company."

Nat woke wide-eyed when a rooster crowed in the distance. He had slept like a rock during the night, missing dinner. Now in a fine fettle to prepare for the day, whatever it might bring. Still, his mind was shrouded in concern for Eli, not knowing what to expect when he would enter the cottage in a short while. "What if the fever came back stronger?" he muttered. "What if Madame Pomm had not fed him the quinine drink?" He shook his head, frustrated that he was creating an illusion that didn't exist. "Give Micah some credit," he said out loud. "If he didn't care about his crewman, he wouldn't have extended his hospitality to the man."

He knocked on Lainey's door but got no answer. At the stables, he decided. The smell of frying ham caused his stomach to rumble. He turned toward the kitchen and spoke with a familiar cook. After a brief conversation, he exited the kitchen and headed to the stables.

"Good morning, nice looking pony, Patrice." Lainey stood assisting Patrice, demonstrating how to brush a horse's coat. *One thing about my sister*, he thought, *she's serious about teaching what she knows*. He turned to Lainey to relay his whereabouts and a brief explanation of the ailing crewman now recuperating in Micah's cottage. "I informed the dining room servant that I would have to miss breakfast, but would you give Susannah my regrets?"

"Won't you get hungry, or are you stopping by a tavern?" Lainey asked. "Perhaps you can tell me more of the story later. The man is not contagious, is he?" she asked, her forehead scowled, knowing something was seriously amiss. Knowing Nat, he had everything under control.

"Luckily, the kitchen maid wrapped up some biscuits with ham," he laughed, patting his satchel. "Maybe I'll see you at luncheon, and no, the man is not contagious!" he shouted as he walked toward the wharf.

The brightness of the clear blue sky made his eyes squint as he walked into the brightness of the clear blue sky. He looked up and saw *B. Arnold's* signboard; the light from lanterns glowing inside showed customers milling around. He crossed the narrow street where food vendors pushed their carts of meat pies and fruits. He ate his own breakfast as soon as he left Lainey and Patrice. His mouth was watering for a mug of coffee, but that would have to wait.

He never noticed the sounds of seabirds squawking at each other or The Dorcas docked in the same position as the day before. His mind dwelt solely on Eli. He turned to the right after stepping off the wharf, where Micah's cottage came into view. He considered the house as he walked toward the small wooden structure painted gray, thinking it handsome and spacious enough for two people. After all, Micah spent most of his days and nights on the open sea. *No reason for anything larger than a cottage*, he reasoned.

Nat approached the front porch, craning his neck as if spying through the large front window before he made his presence known. He saw the light of the blazing fire with a copper kettle perched on top of a trivet to the side, a good sign that quinine tea was brewing. His eyes settled on the corner next to the fireplace, viewing the back of Micah, sitting in a chair, holding something in his hands. Nat rang the bell at the front door.

Lynette opened the door wide, inviting him to the fire. "Good morning, Madame Pomme," Nat announced. "Feels toasty in here!" He loosened his stock.

"Nat, please call me Lynette. Would you care for a mug of coffee?" She flashed a pretty smile.

Micah stood then turned toward Nat, smiling graciously, pausing to shake hands. His left hand held a book he was reading to Eli. He removed his spectacles. "We've had a tolerable night, I'm pleased to report." Eli was sitting up with three pillows behind him and an extra one set up high to relax his neck while he clutched a mug of his special tea. "Lynette and I took turns feeding him broth and brew throughout the night. He has asked for some bread. Probably to remove the bitter taste from his mouth," chuckled Micah.

Nat chuckled, astonished at the improved condition of Eli. He was mindful that the easygoing, affable nature of Micah Penrose had returned. He felt more than relieved when the nervousness in his throat vanished. Moving to Eli's side, he placed two fingers on the side of his neck, searching for a steady pulse, then placed the underside of his wrist on the man's forehead. The pallor of Eli's face had changed from a yellowish tone to a healthy-looking pink. "Quite an improvement from yesterday morning." Nat noticed a cautious smile forming on Eli's lips. He turned around to acknowledge the hosts, standing arm in arm, their faces glowing with delight.

"If this is malaria, the symptoms of fever and exhaustion will return. It is a disease you will have to learn to live with. The quinine powder is the medicine required for treating this disease; it is the remedy. Although, at times, it can be difficult to find at the apothecary. Eli, I'm concerned. Do you have family members who can help you through these recurring times of fever and exhaustion?" Nat had puzzled over how to transfer Eli to his home, not being sure of where or how to get him to Stoughton.

Micah searched Eli's face for affirmation, hoping he had the strength to talk about the events of his past and why he had traveled on a British vessel to Haiti. "I have family in Massachusetts. I have not seen them for more than ten years. Naomi is my wife. I have a son named Ethan." He looked straight ahead; tears filled his eyes. "My story is complicated. I will reveal it as long as I have the strength… My home was on Mulberry Farm in Stoughton. I managed the brewery there until I joined the militia to fight against the French. My downfall occurred when a British captain took me under his wing. He taught me how to defend myself. I am, or I was an excellent marksman, but there were other factors to consider when fighting against savages." He took a sip of cold coffee.

"On our way home from Quebec, we marched for weeks. I became acquainted with a man from my regiment who lived in western Massachusetts. His name was Barnard. His surname has faded from my mind. We talked for hours on our way home. We discussed farming. He raised hogs and cut timber for export. He was interested in my work as a brewer. He asked very specific questions about managing the brewery, which at the time seemed like conversation to pass the time of day.

"My shoes were worn out from walking. The British captain named Cyrus gave me a pair of extra shoes in return for hunting and preparing our food. The final week of the journey home, I noticed an Indian now and again speaking with the captain in the evenings and then returning the following night. I didn't think much about it. The closer I marched toward Stoughton, all I could think about was my home, my family. I split off from the soldiers as they walked to their farms scattered along the way. Earlier, I had said my farewells to Captain Cyrus and Barnard, believing they were marching toward Boston while I walked southward.

"I was about a day's walk from Mulberry Farm, struggling to stand up and walk. I made camp and built a fire, ready to rest and sleep. I woke to the sound of a turkey perched in a tree, not twenty yards from where I lay, thinking this could be the sustenance I craved. I took aim and brought the bird down. Before long, I had devoured half of it. Adequately stuffed, I sat against a granite boulder and dozed. Again, I woke to the sound of what I thought was a bear on the prowl looking for a meal. The beast was welcome to it. I threw sand on the fire, grabbed my musket and pouch, and moved eastwardly.

"Dusk was coming on, and I was ready to settle down, but my instincts told me I was being followed. I continued on when I approached Percy Mountain, believing I had lost the varmint as I climbed the familiar mountain. The footsteps behind me continued. I was convinced that I was being tracked. The thought of the big Indian talking with the captain came to mind. I knew of a cave on top of Percy Mountain, so I proposed to trick the Indian by allowing him to see the few footprints I made at the entrance of the cave. Then, I backed out and took cover behind the cave, where I lay low in a thicket of holly bushes.

"It was coming on dark, and I was anxious to escape down the mountain, knowing I was close to my home. Hearing no further footsteps after an ample amount of time had passed, I exited the thicket without cutting myself to pieces with thorns. I had no choice but to walk close by the side of the cave and then proceed downward. In moments, I realized my fate was sealed when the canny bloodhound seized me from behind and held a knife to my throat.

"Moments later, I awoke with a blinding headache apparently brought on by a blow to the back of my head. I was lying on the ground, squinting at two men perched on a log, their eyes fastened upon me. When I looked upward, there stood the big Indian. From the light of the moon, I could see I was in the presence of Captain Cyrus and Barnard.

"The Indian, whom they called Many Lives, stared at Cyrus until he shoved a leather pouch of coins in my captor's direction. The Indian returned to the woods. They gagged me and bound my wrists and ankles in chains. I was identified as a prisoner of the British army. They dragged me onto a British ship, where I was hauled to the brig." Eli paused, reliving the nightmare that forever changed him and his family. He felt ill from recalling what his mind and soul had endured, never knowing from one day to the next where his fate lay. "I must stop talking." He lay his head back and closed his eyes.

Lynette kept the fireplace in the front room stoked for Eli's comfort, but the other men were roasting. Nat and Micah stepped outside to absorb Eli's unsettling story, eager to catch a cool breeze and a change of scenery. They sipped their mug of ale on the porch, gazing out at the Sound. Micah's schooner was docked in clear view of his cottage. He stood watching his crewmen engaged in ropework and sail mending, mates swabbing the deck, whistling as they worked.

Grif walked off the ship carrying a load of the crew's hammocks, laying them across the dock to air and sun. The cabin boy looked up when he heard the men's voices, waving and shouting a good morning. Then, he turned back to the ship for another load.

Nat stood facing The Dorcas, never quite experiencing the majesty of the schooner as he did at this moment, yielding gently as waves moved the immense structure. He felt a pang of regret that his father couldn't be there to share the moment with him. Nat took in the vessel's hulking length and width, its protruding bowsprit, and its towering intricate rigging, wondering how Micah's crewmen could tell one mast from another within the giant web of ropes.

Micah broke his train of thought. "I expect Joel's sloop to arrive from Whales' Tale tomorrow morning. Let's see—that would be Wednesday. The Dorcas departs for Jamaica on Friday morning. Do you think Eli will have the strength to board the sloop on Thursday?" Micah asked. Nat shrugged.

Micah turned toward the cottage, confident that Lynette was ready to serve breakfast. "Let's walk back. Lynette is expecting us. I don't know about you, but after listening to Eli's story, it turned my stomach so that I thought I couldn't eat for the rest of the day. Now I'm ravenous." Nat laughed at Micah's confession, never being one to turn down a good meal.

"It's hard to say what this new governor has... Will wonders never cease?" Walking through the doorway, Nat looked twice at the specter sitting in the corner of the front room. He switched from political chatter to encountering the new version of Eli Asher.

Eli's skinny legs dangled off the side of the bed, toes barely touching the floor. The strain in his face was gone. His fever was gone. His body was relaxed. A dramatic change had occurred to Eli during the short time Nat and Micah stood outside reviewing his tragic story and formulating decisions for a man who lacked the stamina to change into a clean nightshirt. Perhaps telling his story to people who cared about him opened his mind to the prospect of returning to his home. Giving him hope that his life as a prisoner had come to an end. Nobody cared a whit about him until Micah had given him safe shelter.

It came down to Lynette. She had coaxed him with a mug of ale and the prospect of a hot bath at the kitchen fireplace after breakfast. Eli had been more than eager to dispatch the ragged remains of his filthy breeches and his thin homespun shirt to the dustbin along with their haunting memories. "Mulberry Farm," he said. "This ale is from

Mulberry Farm. There's none any better," he said, gazing into Lynette's caring eyes, believing it all to be a dream.

Nat and Micah helped Eli off the bed and moved him to a big leather chair set at the kitchen table. "What is it about French food?" Nat asked Lynette. "Who would have thought mushrooms and onions stirred into eggs could taste so delicious?" He noticed Eli putting away eggs, potatoes, and the thinnest pancakes he ever tasted. "What do you think, Eli?"

"Today, I'm the luckiest man alive. It's the most delicious food I've put in my mouth since I left Mulberry Farm." He stared into nothingness, not quite sure he was living in real time.

Micah broached the subject of Eli leaving New Haven. "Nat believes you will be able to travel soon. We want you to reconnect with your family in Stoughton. You have today and tomorrow to prepare for the journey. My brother Joel is sailing his sloop down the river to deliver his cargo from Whales' Tale tavern in Enfield. Nat will travel with you."

Eli studied Micah's face, recollecting the time he had trusted Cyrus and Barnard. He felt a twinge in his gut. More than ten years had passed since he had been forced to board a ship and thrown into a dark cell to barely exist for six weeks. He had never forgotten that devastating feeling of losing his freedom to move and speak as he pleased. The same feeling descended on him at this very moment, changing his countenance and sending a chill up his spine. *How can I trust anybody?* he thought. He pushed his breakfast away, then dropped his head to his chest in dismay.

Lynette eyed Micah and shook her head hesitantly. The conversation ceased. She saw what Micah and Nat could not: a reticent, grim-faced man who had lost all hope and trust in humanity. Eli's glazed-over eyes and grievous demeanor revealed a fear that he could be caught up in another scheme that could enslave him, carrying with it too many horrors.

Perhaps Eli has misread Micah's arrangements for returning home, Lynette brooded. She broke the silence. "Eli, do you think you need a lie-down? You have not experienced this much activity in a week's time." He felt light-headed, but his body made the move to stand anyway.

Micah and Nat saw his intentions and grasped Eli under each of his arms to help him stand, wavering on his long legs.

Lynette stared at the backs of the men as they helped Eli to his bed, considering the man's plight. Disconcerted at Eli's situation, they walked out the front door, leaving Lynette to take the next step. Nat walked in the direction of Excalibur, and Micah walked toward The Dorcas.

Lynette stood at the window overlooking the Sound, knowing she had her work cut out for her. She deemed it necessary to trust her instincts. She was struck with an idea of how to help Eli move forward with the departure plan. It's a matter of getting him to talk about his life before and after the war.

What of his family? Lynette wondered. He had not talked much of his wife and his son and his work on Mulberry Farm. She brought along a basket of sewing and sat beside his bed, a silent message to Eli that she wanted to talk. His eyes studied the ceiling rafters. "There's so much evil in the world."

"There always has been. It never ends." Lynette paused, measuring what to say next. "There's a lot of good in the world also. You're in a fragile state. You've been abused by someone you thought you could trust. If you cling to your past, you will torment yourself."

"I've slept with one eye open for so long. I've learned not to trust anybody. How can I move past the torture of beatings and starvation? Slaving for a black-hearted person until I nearly dropped dead."

She considered the unfairness of it all. "Eli, I know you want a better life. You escaped from England by using your wits, and you made it to Haiti. Out of mercy, Micah rescued you when you were desperately seeking freedom. It's obvious to me that you have a desire to live!"

"My family won't know me. They've moved on with their lives. They believe I'm dead after all these years."

"Your family thinks of you every day. Imagine their pain of never knowing if you are dead or alive. Imagine the homecoming of reuniting with your wife and getting to know your son now that he has grown. The only way to restore your relationship is to talk it through and live your life, even if it's a struggle in the beginning, I know."

"How do you know?" Eli asked her.

"My family lived in France as Protestants. The terror for Huguenots started up again under the rule of Louis XIV. My parents and their business were seized by the authorities. They were imprisoned and tortured, but they refused to convert to Catholicism. They escaped to London only because a bribe was paid by my mother's cousin, who was a government official. We lived in London for three years, then moved to New Rochelle to live with relatives. My parents worked and raised their children and made a new life for themselves. You can do the same."

Her outstretched hand felt Eli's forehead and the side of his face for fever. He opened his eyes and smiled. "How can you stand so close to me? I smell like a horse."

"I've smelled worse," she said. "When Micah sails home from his trips to the Indies, I send him straight to the kitchen for a soak in the tub," her eyebrows raised, hoping he would be receptive to the idea of a bath when Micah returned. She grinned at him and handed over a mug of his quinine tea.

Eli made a repulsive face but accepted it anyway. "Raising your eyebrows the way you did seems very familiar. It reminded me of Naomi," he smiled. "At the end of the day, when I came close to her, she would push me away. 'You stink of hops and sweat. Go wash.' She was Indian, you know. Such a kind face." He stared at the fire, dreaming of their life. "My life was so perfect with her."

"It could be perfect again. I understand from Nat that Mulberry Farm has expanded its business to taverns in New York and Connecticut. Your family must have a good deal of business sense and a fine-tasting beer to be so successful."

"I keep hearing the name Whales' Tale. I don't recall making deliveries to such a place. The furthest I delivered to was a tavern in Suffield called the Black Rooster. I wonder if it's still there. Suffield and Enfield were two towns I remember on either side of the river."

She laughed. "Whales' Tale is the epitome of eccentricity, owned and operated by Ezekial Penrose, Micah's oldest brother. I don't want to give too much away, but Captain Zeke made his fortune in whaling.

He moved to Connecticut from Cornwall and built a tavern next to the river, along with various outbuildings and a cottage for his mother. If you fancy mermaid yarns and whaling adventures, and the finest beer in the colonies, that's the place to stop when you're tired and hungry. Just ask your son when you see him."

Eli felt a tightening in his throat. "Ethan, my son," he exhaled a nervous gasp. "What will he be like after all these years?"

"The person who can answer that question will be arriving tomorrow—Joel Penrose," Lynette said with certainty. They looked up when Micah came through the door. "I believe Eli is ready for a bath." A faint smile flitted across Eli's face. Micah took that for a yes.

Chapter 24

The Way Home

Last Week of May 1774, Enfield, Connecticut

The back-and-forth work of loading the cargo on The Jeremiah was complete, and the canvas bag stuffed with the Minnow was gently placed in the hold guarded by Angus Marsh, a small stout man who worked double duty serving beer for Captain Zeke and, when necessary, protected special cargo on The Jeremiah. He was a wounded veteran of the French and Indian War and walked with a limp, which was not a problem for the Penrose brothers. They had experienced their share of sailors who had lost limbs, eyes, and fingers in the dangerous work of sailing ships. In fact, such men were held in high regard by the brothers as long as they were honest and aimed to follow orders.

Joel stood at the wheel, packing tobacco in his pipe, waiting for Israel's signal. It wasn't a long journey to The Long Island Sound, and there was still plenty of daylight left. The sun sparkled on the flat surface of the water, and the glare came. The sloop was not overloaded, judging from the water line. The sky was clear. *Favorable*, he thought, as he pulled the bill of his hat a little lower on his forehead.

Israel Patton looked upwards, examining the sky, calculating the wind, the absence of clouds, and the time of day at departure, which was definitely in their favor. He was nervous and agitated that it had taken so long to get the boat loaded and to break the captain away from his family and friends. What of this canvas-wrapped package? He made an effort to conceal his dismay. "No point in gettin' riled over details," he muttered. "It's not my sloop."

The mainsail was hoisted by second mate, Ned Jenkins, another veteran of Joel's whaling days. Israel then disconnected the fore and aft rope loops from their pilings. He jumped on board The Jeremiah, giving Captain Joel the nod he was waiting for: "Let's be off." Joel steered away from the mooring, maneuvering the craft with the current. In no time, the sails began to draw, giving the sloop its power. It was up to Israel and Ned to operate the sails until they reached the Sound.

"If fair winds hold for the day and the sky remains clear, we might pull into the Sound around midnight," Joel directed his prediction to Israel in hopes the sailor would look past his dereliction of tardiness that had caused such anguish for the man. "A stickler for keeping to schedule—a good reason to respect him and his work ethic," Joel admitted to himself. No better sailor did he know than Israel Patton, an expert at manning the sails. He puffed on his pipe, satisfied the boat was in a fine fettle.

Joel steered the craft masterfully down the crooked river, sailing as close to the wind as possible to maintain the high speed he desired. "We'll be staying overnight at the Sailor's Grog," he addressed Israel and Ned, "in case you were wondering." Israel was busy managing the sails, but he got the message. He'd never known the captain to jilt him and his sea mates out of a good night's sleep. "I'll tend to the special package for the night."

Angus had a knack for reading people's minds. He would listen to people talk, but he knew what came out of their mouths did not always match their intentions. An experienced seaman with such a canny gift could be valuable to Captain Joel's business of trading. At the moment, he had a sharp eye cast on his canvas-wrapped prisoner, recalling times when he and the Big Englishman would stop in for a mug of ale at Whales' Tale.

He recalled how the Big Englishman had bragged about his life in England as the son of a wealthy earl and all the important people he knew. To further his self-importance, he identified himself as the agent representing certain English lords, the Earls of Beaufort and Halleck, whom he named for the purpose of purchasing properties in the colonies as investments. "If you're so rich, why not lay out two pence for the mug of ale you're swilling?" He was tempted to ask.

The Big Englishman was putting on airs, and Angus knew it, but he played along with him just for the sport of it. When it came time for the scoundrel to pay, he and his sidekick would sneak away from the premises when Angus had his back turned. A few drops of flaxseed oil in his ale might keep the Englishman away for a few days, but when he attempted rape on Lottie, that did it for Angus. "You deserve everything that's comin' to ye vile self," Angus preached to the knocked-out scoundrel in the canvas bag.

The sun was lowering, and the heat of the day was replaced by cool breezes, giving the crewmen's eyes some relief from squinting. Ned and Israel kept their eyes peeled on the sails and the river current to determine the change in wind, in strength and direction, tacking as was necessary to catch the wind. "Holler when you're wanting me to steer," Israel shouted to the captain, noticing Joel shifting his weight from one leg to the other. It was time for a switch off, judging from the pink and purple lines in the sky indicating a halfway mark to the Sound. Lynch should be bringing up mugs of ale directly, he hoped.

Captain Joel heard some commotion below where he had situated Angus and the special cargo in a nook of sorts next to the galley. He knew that Angus wouldn't last long—what with the stuffiness of the hidey-hole, in addition to the problem with his leg. During the war, he caught a musket ball in his hip, causing a persistent limp in his right leg. The ball had remained lodged in the same spot for fifteen years. Joel heard the man shuffling around in the galley.

"I'll be needin' a cup of ale for the varmint, Lynch." Angus knew this wouldn't set well with the cook, but he also knew better than to get in his way. "Got to mix his poison to keep him snug like, ye know."

The last thing Lynch was interested in was preparing a cup of ale for an additional passenger. "The captain and his men'll be 'specting their tea and biscuits at the moment. You'll 'ave to wait ye turn," came Lynch's reply.

Angus expected such indignation from the man who resented his status of cook. "I take me orders from the captain only" was his snappy comeback. Lynch carried out the captain's orders and returned to the galley from amidship with an empty tray. "Yer tea and the varmint's cup of ale is waitin' on ye," he yelled to Angus.

It was early evening. As the moon began to rise, Joel put away his pipe, steering one-handed while sipping his tea. He glanced in the distance toward the western shore, spying a blue heron. The bird was huge, standing four feet tall, poised in the shallow moonlit water, confidently searching along the shore for its dinner of fish and frogs. Beyond the heron, he sighted the town of Meriden. *More than halfway there*, he thought.

He wasn't too concerned about dumping the responsibility of the varmint on Micah's shoulders; admittedly, it would come as a surprise to his brother. After all, he only learned about it not even an hour before he left Whales' Tale. Once Micah heard the story behind the miscreant's plan to sabotage Mulberry Farm brewery, his surprise would be tempered, Joel decided. Of course, it would be extra work to keep the man drugged, but Micah had pulled his share of shockers on Joel. *We're all seamen here; no voyage or cargo is ever the same*, he convinced himself.

What a relief to the crew when Captain Joel steered The Jeremiah into the Sound. It was like having a heavy weight lifted off each sailor's shoulder. The hard part of the journey had ended. Alas, feelings of joy and relief filled each man when they heard the wild surf rushing to the shore and viewed the faithful moonlight that had guided them to New Haven. Israel looked upwards and paused, giving a salute to the Lord above, who made it happen. He walked along with his sea mates to Sailor's Grog, confident that a soft bed awaited him. He raised his chin at the innkeeper as he walked through the door, receiving a nod in return. Tom Canton never disappointed Captain Joel's crew.

Earlier, Lynch had prepared a hearty supper of pigeon pie and neeps in the Whales' Tale kitchen and provided the men with plenty of hot coffee to wash it down. He served the food on deck so the men could eat in shifts, knowing they could not desert their tasks for long. Captain Joel had kept the vessel steady. The wind remained favorable, so there was no worry in steering. The moon shone its glow adequately across the deck of The Dorcas, just as the captain had hoped.

Israel had taken over the wheel while Captain Joel walked down to the galley to eat his meal and discuss a plan with Lynch. He sent Angus up to assist Ned with the sails, then peeked in the hidey-hole, taking notice of the canvas-wrapped cargo. "Lynch, how would you like to earn some extra shillings for the night?" That got the little cook's attention when he met the captain's eyes and nodded. Joel knew the man to be hot-tempered and had no trust in any of the crew, even himself. "I promise it won't have anything to do with the rigging, to be sure." Lynch was scared of heights.

Joel's plan was for Lynch to guard the varmint for half the night. That would give him time to visit with his brother Micah and relay the particulars of the canvas package. Joel would relieve Lynch in four hours' time. He knew he wouldn't get much sleep, seeing as how, in the shadow of darkness, his special package would have to be delivered to Micah's hold while Micah's crew would deliver The Dorcas' cargo to The Jeremiah. Sleep would be postponed until the following evening when they would finally dock in Enfield. Seamen were accustomed to the irregularities of their work; therefore, they made allowances for such times when sleep was not possible.

Micah and Lynette sat by the bright fire, drinking a cup of mint tea while Eli sipped on a mug of quinine tea. Eli was in a talkative mood; maybe it was because he was leaving the next morning that he felt compelled to talk about more of his life as a prisoner in England. Talking about his misadventures was hard emotionally, but it seemed to take a load off his mind with the more he shared.

They knew Joel would be arriving at any time, so they weren't surprised when he came through the door with a big cheer. He hugged his brother. "Good to see ya. You little sea pup!" Lynette set down her tea and went to Joel's arms, thrilled he had arrived, and offered him coffee or whiskey. Eli rose slowly and held onto the back of the chair, still a bit wobbly but anxious to present himself as best he could.

"I didn't know you had a guest." Joel extended his hand and shook Eli's calloused hand, examining the tall man's weak eyes. "I'm Joel Penrose, just now arrived from Enfield. Happy to meet you."

"Glad you've arrived safely. I'm Eli Asher. We've been expecting you."

"As it happens, I know a man named Ethan Asher. Would you be related to him by chance?" Joel and Captain Zeke never missed an opportunity to make connections with anybody they met for the first time, particularly at the Whales' Tale. At the moment, his mind was racing, wondering why this stranger was sitting at the fire in Micah's house at this time of the night.

He thought it odd when he caught Eli giving Micah an unexpected nod. Joel stood agog at this exchange, anxiously awaiting Micah to begin his explanation. Lynette wanted to laugh out loud at the oddities of the scene but thought it best to control the urge. Instead, she invited Joel to take a seat, and she poured him a whiskey.

Micah began, "You have just met Ethan's father." Joel's mouth flew open, and he started to speak, but his brother was quick to continue with more introductory information. "He was a sailor on The Dorcas and is now recovering from a bout of malaria. Long before that, he was a prisoner of a British captain whom he served under in the war with the French." Micah paused, giving his brother a chance to absorb it all. Especially the fact that the war ended in 1763, over ten years ago.

"For the past five days, he has been Lynette's patient and my guest. We've actually had a jolly time telling stories and reading books. I should also mention our mutual friend, Nat Stowe, who is the real hero in this story. He analyzed Eli's condition from the very beginning and began pouring quinine down his gullet while he was wrought with fever and delirium. It's a miracle that he's sitting in a chair drinking the nasty concoction at this very moment, but it works."

"Well, cat on the moon!" Joel looked at Eli, seeing tears poured down his face onto his new shirt. "Brother, I'd say you've been to hell and back this week. It's time we get you home to Mulberry Farm! I suppose this all needs to happen in the morning?"

Joel walked across the wharf toward The Jeremiah with a spring in his step, gladdened and proud that this voyage would be historic in bringing the Asher family together after so many years. He shook his head, grieving over Ethan's pain of losing his father at such a young age, believing he was dead. He yawned widely as he walked in the coolness of the morning hours before dusk. Lack of sleep caught up with him when he felt a twinge in his low back. The urge to lie down to rest himself settled over him. *Two hours will do*, he decided.

He stumbled down the stairs, noticing a lantern aglow in the galley. "Oh, Lynch arranging charcoal in the brazier," he muttered. He smiled and nodded at the cook, turned into his cabin, and crashed on the bunk. Lynch settled a blanket over him and went back to his work.

Captain Joel woke to the smell of sausages and coffee wafting tantalizing smells down the short companionway, giving him a reason to come out of his dreams and begin a new day. He took a deep breath and exhaled heavily, recalling parts of his visit with Micah and Lynette and the tall, lanky stranger named Eli. Good sense took over Joel when Angus brought him a cup of coffee. "Heard about your short night. We've loaded six barrels in the hold and several boxes, and the varmint's been drugged and moved to a locked cell on The Dorcas. Ready for your breakfast, sir?"

The idea was to have the sloop loaded and all hands on deck before the sun rose. Traveling up the river would take half again as much time as moving downstream with the current. Joel would prefer to settle Nat and Eli into his mother's cottage at a decent hour, but such as it was, arrival time would fall around midnight in Enfield. He was being considerate of Eli, knowing the man was nervous about traveling to a new place and meeting new people, including his son. *Best to follow Nat's lead*, he thought. *Eli trusts him as he does Micah and Lynette.*

Joel passed by Nat as he was on his way to the privy. "Will ye see that Eli makes a stop here before we board? I want him to be comfortable or as comfortable as he can on a boat. I'm worried about him."

"Yes, all taken care of. He's in the cottage," answered Nat. "Just going to say my farewells to Micah and Lynette." Nat was more than ready to leave New Haven, fully aware that, in two days, the port of Boston would be shut down. He was anxious to settle himself at his grandsire's home in Beacon Hill.

Nat had informed Eli that he would remain with him at the Whales' Tale for one night, leaving early the next morning to ride to Mulberry

Farm to give his family the details of his return, then on to Boston. It was a monumental task. Nat tried not to ponder too heavily on the prospect that Eli's family might not believe the remarkable story of the man's return to humanity. *Actually, the only link I have with the family is when I met Ethan that one time at Stowe Ironworks, where he inspected their musket order.*

Israel let go the ropes off the pilings, then gave the official nod to his boss—"Let's be off." Gulls were flying all around, squawking as they fought for crumbs scattered on the wharf. Joel steered the sloop in the gray light of the morning. Reds and pinks bordered the horizon, promising a burst of the sun's rays to their back as they would travel upriver. He stood at peace, hands on the wheel, drawing on his pipe, watching a puff of smoke vanish in the wind. He glanced over the deck at Nat and Eli playing a game of whist. *No voyage on The Jeremiah is ever the same*, he reminded himself.

Chapter 25

SUFFIELD, CONNECTICUT MILITIA

Mid July, 1774

Nat had been awake for an hour, judging from the time his eyes popped open in total darkness. The waning moon had edged its way to the left side of the window, offering a smidgeon of pale light. It made no difference. He stared at the ceiling, allowing his overworked brain to recall the details of the trip to New Haven: chaperoning Lainey on the riverboat, getting her settled at Excalibur, sorting out Aunt Mae's citrus order, returning to Whales' Tale with Eli, riding to Mulberry Farm, finally settling at Beacon Hill. *I'm lucky I got back in one piece*, he concluded.

Excursions are full of traps, he thought. *Not traps, really, but incidentals, some good and some bad. Josie Randolph was a good incidental. Some of the circumstances were bad. I wonder if I'll ever see her again. Boston is not that far from Suffield. Again, it's the circumstances—the entire province under siege by British soldiers. That was definitely a trap.*

He laughed, recalling his grandparents. *They had me coming and going with that dinner party. More incidentals, like Josie Randolph—tall, pretty, and smart.* Her confident face flashed through his head. *No beating around the bush with her; she had more medical expertise than I'll ever have.*

What about the note of instructions for the tall man in New Haven? I'm sure I gave it to Captain Zeke. Another incidental. They seemed to rain from the sky the moment we arrived at the Whales' Tale. John and Lainey were more than intrigued with the place. *Perhaps I should take my cue from Captain Zeke and open a tavern. He doesn't seem to take life's incidentals so seriously!* His mind wandered back to his note to Josie and the yellow roses.

He got out of bed and walked to the window. The mountains were barely visible through the mist. *I'll store the traps and incidentals for later*, he decided. The smell of coffee had reached his nose, calling him to the kitchen. He could depend on a cup of his mother's strong brew to clear his head and move him in the right direction. Militia training would begin in an hour.

The house was still cool inside, thanks to the huge oak trees that surrounded it. Not only that, the house was quieter since he had returned from his month of travels. His mind returned to Lainey when he escorted her to Excalibur. "All the beautiful horses!" she exclaimed.

Nat stepped outside. The mist was fading over the mountains. His forehead broke out in a sweat as he walked toward the barn. July's heat was ruthless. "Better take water," mumbling as he walked. He checked the paddock for a good riding horse, hopefully Captain, maybe Dragon. It struck him that his choices would be limited this morning at the sight of empty stables, only the two mules munching on hay. Not a good way to start the first day of militia.

"Good day, *mon ami*. Will you require a mount this morning?" Nat saw John Dupre walking from the barn holding the reins of the dapple gray, leading him to join Frederic and the other two mules, Nutmeg and Raisin. "If so, the selection may not be to your liking. *Le farrier*[38] is attending all horses with the exception of Twister."

Nat craned his neck toward the bright sky and shook his fists. "*No*," he groaned loudly, aggravated that this dimwit of a horse was even taking up space in the paddock. He stopped before he got to the barn, turned around, and mumbled a string of profanities. John joined in force.

"*Cheval sans cervelle!*"[39] Twister responded by raising her head at the sound of irate voices, nonplused, then continued her breakfast.

---

38. The farrier...
39. Horse with no brains!

Twister, like all horses, had certain mannerisms that characterized her behavior. Some horses shy away from climbing mountains; some are frightened at the sound of a hawk. Sometimes, the rider can allay these fears by whispering gentle words of consolation or rubbing the horse's neck. Nat had tried his best to lure Twister with apples, carrots, or sugar to encourage her to follow his commands. She wasn't having it.

Twister would gallop at a satisfactory clip, get distracted, and take a sudden notion to make an unexpected turn. There was no stopping her. She was the opposite of reliable.

Distracted by twittering birds and scurrying squirrels, she steered into brambles and low-hanging limbs. Gee and haw meant nothing, no matter which direction the reins were pulled. John and Nat swore they would never put a saddle on Twister again.

Nat had no choice today but to ride the scatterbrained horse to his first day of militia training. Three miles down a flat road with no mountains but no promise that a hawk might swoop over unexpectedly. Nat reviewed the militia's rules of conduct book he had started. Twister's erratic behavior nagged at him. He urged the feathers-for-brains horse to a slow trot.

The sun moved higher, beating on his back. His dark hair, pulled back in a neat tail, was soaked with moisture, dripping down the back of his shirt. Certain faces came to mind, wondering which of the neighbors and locals would attend this morning. This was a newly formed regiment gathering at Clarence Tatum's farm for drilling and training "in defense of Connecticut Colony," stated the broadsheet.

At least the musket-making at the forge was in good hands. After two months of training John Dupre several hours each day, Nat believed he could continue investing his time in the man. His skill in handling the long iron bars, hammering, and filing had far exceeded his and his father's expectations. The large order from Jacob Randolph was complete. Only the building and installation of the gun stocks remained. John was the right man who came on the scene at the right time.

The meticulous work of shaping wood to fit the musket barrel and trigger was given to Daniel Taylor, an expert craftsman whose woodworking skills had taken years to develop.

Nat had read John Hancock's speech given on the occasion of the Boston Massacre memorial event in March, invoking able-bodied men who "loved their liberties" to lay down their plows, close their shops, and take up arms against the "murderers and thieves" who demanded colonists to yield to King George's demands. Nat had decided that he could not live under such subservience. "I could be wrong, but I don't believe Parliament and the king grasp the vast power of the colonies," he muttered, momentarily forgetting about Twister.

He dismounted the horse and rubbed her muzzle, complimenting her. "You were a good girl for not running me into a tree, and for that, you have earned a carrot." He led Twister to a nearby stream to stand in the cool water and slake her thirst. Nat took a long draw on his pouch of watered-down ale as he stood listening. In the distance, he heard men and horses gathering, not knowing what the day held for them.

Horse and rider plodded along, finally reaching the property. Nat hobbled Twister under a shady tree, unsaddled her, and rubbed down her back. He left his musket and ammunition box attached to the saddle, figuring that today Captain Talbot would instruct them more on marching and drills. Most of these men were born holding a musket anyway. Nat touched the right side of his belt where his hatchet hung and walked to the sign-in table.

The Tatums were one of the few Puritan families who settled in Connecticut in 1636. After living in Massachusetts for six years, some colonists fell out with Governor Winthrop's austere governing, believing it limited their freedom to speak their mind. The exodus to Connecticut began under Thomas Hooker, a minister who, with his supporters, would seek to limit the new government's power.

Land was purchased from an Algonquin tribe with the plan to farm and produce corn, wheat, and barley to supply the family's needs and sell the remainder to local millers. Looking over the thick forests, Mr. Tatum had comprehended the wealth that could be acquired by cutting timber and selling it to English shipyards. Two years later, when the profits began to roll in, investments were made in other commodities—rum, horses, barrels, and grains.

Generations of Tatums carried on the family tradition of expanding their businesses and becoming wealthy landowners. Employing men and women who desired to raise families and build their own dwellings, depending on fertile land for food.

Now, the subtle changes made by the British through taxation and restrictions in the past ten years were becoming an irritant to the Tatums and other Connecticut businessmen. When Britain shipped thousands of redcoat soldiers to suppress rebellious Bostonians and replace the governor with a British general, it could only spell one thing for colonists—war. Militia groups began forming all over Connecticut…

"State your name, please. Is that Stowe spelled with an 'e'? Oh, morning, Nat. I didn't recognize your voice. I've been sitting at this table all morning, writing names of strangers, attempting to answer their questions. It's a tiring job," Micah Grayson offered wearily. He wore a floppy leather hat to shade his face from the bright light. "Got seventy-five signed in. Most carrying a fowling piece, knife, and a hatchet."

Nat chuckled. "Hey, better you than me." He walked a ways to settle under a shady oak. The sun was blistering. He looked around to see what kind of a man would come out on a scorching day to take orders from an unknown. He spotted Charles Talbot, the man who put the regiment together, standing in the shade, talking to the farm's owner, Clarence Tatum.

Charles stood six feet tall, with lean shoulders and a slight roundness to his chest and midsection. He spoke loudly and exactly in a commanding voice. The men took that as a signal to refrain from talking and moved in his direction.

Nat had met Charles at his father's favorite watering hole, joined by Israel Putnam, who was working double time to find men interested in leading a militia group. Nat and his father drank ale and visited with Charles and Israel while sitting on benches under a big oak tree in the front yard of the Black Rooster tavern.

Charles was a lawyer who practiced out of his home in the town of Suffield, settling cases involving assault and battery, horse thievery, trespass, debts, and virtually any case that involved reading and understanding the law. He had achieved a successful practice and made a good living. He chose not to ride the circuit to drum up business, knowing it would take him away from his wife and their four children. He was a patriot, a rebel, and, according to the king, a traitor. He knew what was at stake for the colonies. He committed himself to learning what he could from the French and Indian War veterans Israel Putnam and Clarence Tatum. Charles pledged his time and money to not only train volunteers but to purchase muskets and ammunition.

Charles learned from Putnam that Nat and his father had some medical training. When Nathan's employees suffered accidents at the forge, he and Nat examined the problem and provided needed care. Aunt Mae maintained a cabinet in the scullery dedicated to an array of bottled medicines and salves that she concocted during the spring and summer months when her herb garden produced the freshest and most available plants, stems, roots, and flowers.

"Can you remove a bullet, stitch a gash, set a broken arm? What is the extent of your training? Who was your teacher? I mean, you are two men who make kettles and muskets for a living, after all," Charles asked with a sense of disbelief.

Nathan and Nat looked at each other and grinned. Nathan said with some hesitation, "My father-in-law instructed me in the basics of medicine when I lived in Boston. He is a surgeon and earned his medical degree in Edinburgh. He was of the opinion that if I was going to marry his daughter and live in the country, I needed to know how to deliver a baby and mend a wound. I spent a year in his so-called training program. I earned permission to marry his daughter… That was twenty-four years ago."

"I learned from the same man after I finished my education at Yale," Nat chimed in. "I lived with my grandparents for a year in Boston, studying, observing, and practicing surgeon skills. To answer your question, I'm not married." They all laughed at that. A thought ran through Nat's mind. *I'm not about to mention that my grandsire is a fence sitter, intending to remain loyal to the king but remain living in Boston under a provincial government.* He considered the implications of releasing such information in the present company.

"Attention, men! I would like to introduce our host, Clarence Tatum. He has generously offered his property on which to drill and train. Water and refreshments will be supplied during our break times. The necessary is located to your left," he pointed in that direction. "Mr. Tatum served alongside the British during the war against the French, so he can speak to you about his personal experiences and how we can prepare ourselves to defend our communities. Mr. Tatum, please."

"Gentlemen, we're here to defend our property and our families during a critical time in history. Our aim is to oust the British from our shores. We would like to come to a reconciliation with the king and Parliament. We're landowners—all established in our farms and businesses. We don't like outsiders telling us how to run our lives or keeping track of the number of horses and mules we own.

"We've had the privilege of militia units serving our colonies since the 1630s. Ever since our families came upon these shores, we've had cause to defend our land and communities from hostiles, English soldiers, French soldiers, and even pirates. Now, we're met with this most recent challenge of threats from Britain regarding taxes, regulations, confiscation of property, and dissolving our local governments.

"If you're going to be part of a militia, you must learn to take orders from your commanding officer, Captain Charles Talbot, and his assistant, Lieutenant Micah Grayson. They have recently trained under the command of Captain Israel Putnam, who, as you know, is a Patriot leader and a veteran soldier. You'll learn how to push yourself to march a little further each day, go without food and drink a little longer, and find ways to defend yourself against the enemy. The discipline you learn from this training will aid you for the rest of your lives. Let's get started." Mr. Tatum hoped to instill in these young men the importance of loyalty to the causes he set forth.

Captain Talbot had not expected such a large turnout of young men to show up for training on a hot day in July. He divided the men in his company between himself and Lieutenant Grayson. They moved out about fifty yards from each other to allow space to march.

You could tell that many of the men had been up since before dawn by the way they were yawning. Farm work could not be put on hold; animals required attention before the sun rose. The beginning date for training had been set for the middle of July, anticipating crops would not be harvested for another month or the hay cut and baled.

Lieutenant Grayson ordered his men to form up in three columns. He watched as the men scrambled to be near familiar faces. He smoothed out the line by adjusting each body an arm's length directly behind the man in front of him and an arm's width between each column. He demonstrated how to stand. "A-tten-tion! Shoulders back, arms by your sides, legs together, look straight ahead, now march by taking small steps, and begin with your left foot. Left, right, left, (pause), left, right, left, (pause), watch and follow me," he continued the cadence. "Company halt!" he bellowed with his arm raised. "Let's try that again. Keep lined up in straight columns and rows. Company march! Left, right, left, (pause)…"

The marching continued for an hour. The men moved in and out of the sun's rays and the shadows from the big oaks, breathing the tang of mature summer grass and the reeking smells of mules and horses grazing in the pasture. Most of them came with the purpose of learning what they would be up against in the coming weeks. They had considered the consequences of the British army encroaching on their properties, learning the particulars of how a farmer made his money. This was confidential business information that farmers were not willing to share with anyone.

Others were the more high-spirited type, attending out of curiosity, measuring their decision to stay or leave depending on whether they had a liking for the men in charge. Later, some would gather at a tavern to express their opinion of the training, making their preliminary decision at that time.

Captain Talbot dismissed his men and led them to the shade of a big oak. The men wore either long linen tunics or homespun shirts, which had now turned gray with sweat and dust. The shirts were gathered at the waist with a belt, worn over a pair of breeches which reached to just below the knees. Some wore shoes or moccasins; some were barefoot.

Nat was drinking well water from his leather flask when the captain called him over. "Do you know Jed Morgan?" He jerked his head in the direction of the lanky young man with the bleeding foot. "He cut his foot on a rock, and..." Nat didn't give Talbot time to finish. He saw blood dripping from the man's foot as he leaned against his brother to steady himself. Nat grabbed his satchel and hurried to him.

Jed was seated on the ground against a tree trunk with Ted at his side, both looking nervous and disappointed. Sweat streamed down their look-alike freckled faces. With no coaxing from Nat, Jed stretched his long, skinny leg over a fallen limb, giving the impression that a cut foot was a natural occurrence for someone who never wore shoes. The bottom of his foot was caked with black dirt. Nat saw where blood was pouring from the foot's arch. He gently pressed a cloth dripping with water against the gash to get a measure of the damage. He estimated the gash to be two inches in length. Nat doused another cloth with alcohol and water and pressed the wound again, causing Jed to wince and suck air through his teeth.

The jagged, dangling flap of thin skin worried Nat. "Have you ever had a wound stitched? It will not heal unless the skin is pulled together and stitched." Jed and Ted looked at each other, perplexed.

Ted handed his brother a flask of water. "Did I hear ye right, sir? Ye want to stitch my brother's skin together like my ma stitches my breeches? If you're thinking of using a needle, won't that hurt?" That answered Nat's question. He considered an alternate plan.

Recruits had gathered at the scene, curious about Jed's injury. Captain Talbot ordered them to pick up refreshments and move under a tree further away. Jed was in pain and bleeding, already feeling like a spectacle, which caused talk among the other men.

Nat held Jed's heel in one hand while he applied pressure to the bloody wound with the other. The brothers exhaled nervously in frustration when they saw Nat pull another bandage from his satchel to replace the bloody one. Jed's face turned pale at the sight of dripping blood. "Do you live close by?" Nat asked Jed. "We'll need to get you home so we can apply a poultice."

Ted helped his brother with more water and spoke up. "Our family works a farm up the road apiece. It's in walkin' distance. I surely hope this little scrape won't deny us the right to join this here militia. Me and Jed ha' been looking forward to it all summer."

Nat thought for a moment, considering how to respond to Ted. "The bleeding has stopped for now." He dotted a clean bandage with some comfrey oil to start the healing process. "I'm going to apply this bandage to the wound, wrap it around, then tie it at the top to hold it in place," Nat said. Jed and Ted stared at Nat, wondering why a man his age understood the same healing methods as their mother.

"With your permission, Captain, I will see them home. Jed can ride my horse."

The captain nodded in agreement and offered his regrets to Jed. "You're in good hands with Nat, I can assure you. Our next training will be this Saturday at dawn."

"Captain Talbot told me to bring some bread and cheese over." The young man set the food on the ground next to Ted. "I'm Tom McLain. I'm sure sorry you messed up your foot on the first day of training. I'll bring you some mugs of ale." Nat nodded thanks to Tom and tied Jed's bandage in place.

Nat stood up to stretch his back and introduced himself to Tom. "Good to meet you. I'm Nat Stowe, and this is Ted and Jed Morgan. We're mighty thirsty. Ale would be fine. Appreciate the food." When Tom turned toward the drink table, the brothers dove for the food, cramming big pieces of bread into their mouths like they had not eaten in a while. Without saying anything, Nat walked to the table to get food for himself, feeling obliged to pick up a large helping for the brothers.

At the moment, they had their eyes fastened on Captain Talbot standing in the distance, demonstrating the workings of a musket to his company of volunteers. The brothers glanced at each other with regret, knowing they would miss the best part of today's training.

It took some doing to get Jed on his feet. He stretched his arms over the shoulders of Nat and Ted, hobbling with care, favoring his foot by walking on his heel over to where Twister stood, contentedly cropping grass.

Nat contemplated how this brainless animal would behave among two strangers, one of them reeking of blood. As the men approached the horse, they leaned Jed against a tree, where he placed the heel of his damaged foot on the ground. Nat held a carrot in his hand for Twister to munch and was surprised she didn't gobble the food, nor did she nip at Nat's hand as he fed her. "Some strange horse," he mumbled and rubbed her muzzle. "Twister, I want you to meet Ted and Jed. We're going to need your help seeing them home," he looked at the brothers and winked.

Nat assumed Jed and Ted were twins, even though he hadn't mentioned it to them. Their height and build were identical: lanky body, narrow shoulders, and a long, skinny neck supported a head covered in thick, straight, auburn hair. They both grinned a lot, making their freckles seem somehow more pronounced. More than that, they were likable. Nat was drawn to their plain and easy manner.

Twister walked along the road confidently. "Ye fish much," Ted asked out of the blue. "If ye do, I know of a prime spot fer pulling in a mess of trout. Ye gotta walk a ways to find it, but it's worth the trouble!" The words flowing from his mouth were simple but genuine. Maybe this was Ted's way of thanking Nat for the care he had shown his brother and the likelihood of a friendship to come.

The day was passing quickly as the threesome traveled to the Morgan property. Ted did most of the talking as Twister plodded forward while Nat attended the reins, keeping the fickle beast in check. Jed seemed neither troubled nor let down with the way his first militia experience had ended. He remained quiet, clutching the saddle horn tightly as if he feared falling off the horse. Nat remained ready to catch him if he began to swoon and keel over.

Riding down the long entrance to the Morgan's house, the big oaks, poplars, and birch trees provided some needed shade and a slight breeze occasioned by fluttering leaves. Sunlight peeked through now and again. The ground cover encroaching on the narrow and dusty lane was mostly brambles, berry briars, and saplings scattered throughout, struggling for a piece of the sun. Towhees inhabited the thickets, twitching for insects and berries. Their chew-wink bird chatter gave the entrance to the farm a motionless and peaceable character in contrast with the goose pimples popping up on Nat's arms.

The derelict state of the property worsened as they edged closer to the house. A massive tree had fallen into one section of what was once a sizable barn, judging from several posts that remained standing. The other end had survived the crash, and a lonely milk cow made its home there amidst the fragrant hay, a three-legged stool, and several buckets. The beast raised her head and glared at Nat and the brothers when they passed.

A gray mule got their attention with a hee-haw greeting. Ted responded with, "Af'noon, Lightnin'." The mule stood watching as they helped Jed dismount Twister and walk him to the porch, which hung off the back of the kitchen. Two cots and a table were the only furnishings in the small outdoor room. Exhausted, Jed collapsed on the bed and closed his eyes. "I'll get a bucket of water from the well," Ted offered.

The hot air was sweet and spicy with the scent of honeysuckle and cedar, interspersed with whiffs of manure and animal skins, stretched and tied to posts sunk in the ground. Nat noticed beads of sweat popping up on Jed's pale face as he helped him with a cup of water. He mumbled, "It needs a poultice to draw out the inflammation, hmm."

Nat looked around and saw a tall woman standing in the palisaded garden, leaning on the handle of a hoe and observing the activity on the porch. She came walking towards Jed and Nat with two young girls tagging along behind her, all wearing sunbonnets.

"What happened to my boy? H'aint been shot, had he?" said the woman, moving to Jed's cot. "Where ye hurt son?" Jed pointed to his foot. His ma eyed the bandage. "Right, fine job on the wrappin'. You mind if I take a look?" she asked Nat without looking at him. She had her hand on the bandage, ready to untie the knot. "Ahem, Ruby, you go heat up the kettle. Amy, you bring me them rags over yonder in that bucket." Mrs. Morgan removed her bonnet, revealing the familiar coppery auburn hair of her sons, pulled back in a tight bun at the nape of her neck. Nothing was more important to her at the moment than doctoring her son's foot.

Within ten minutes, Mrs. Morgan had rags soaking in a pan, emitting a combination of alcohol and herbs, which she squeezed out gently, folding the wet and smelly poultice to fit Jed's foot. Ruby and Amy caught wind of the noxious fumes, looked at each other with sour facial expressions, and stepped backward from the cot. Nat smiled at them, and they laughed, one showing permanent molars halfway growing in to replace baby teeth. The younger one was missing her two front teeth. They both gave off the same characteristic grin just like their brothers', amplifying their freckled faces, an adoring inherited family trait. "Got anything in that bag to make a tea?" Mrs. Morgan asked Nat, adjusting the poultice.

Thankfully, he had packed his mother's cure-any-ailment tea in his satchel, so he offered it to Mrs. Morgan. "Go yonder to the fire and make Jed a mug of that tea fer his fever. Ye'll find all ye need at the hearth." Nat took a few steps to the kitchen to do as she instructed. He was taken aback when he noticed how clean and orderly the long room was maintained, quite a contrast to the disorderly yard. Nat refused to judge but to assist Mrs. Morgan for Jed's sake. The mother's affection for her son was so clearly demonstrated when she knelt beside the cot, held his head against her bosom, and guided the mug to his lips. After consuming a portion, she gently placed his head on the cot. "Now you get some rest, sweet."

She directed Ruby and Amy to their chores in the garden and motioned for Nat and Ted to step out to the yard. She cast a stern and demanding look at her boy Ted. "Did it cross yer mind to wear a pair of shoes this morning before ye went traipsing off to learn soldiering? What was ye thinking? It ain't lak you don't have none!" She paused, arms folded, and waited for some indication that her son was listening. Nat was embarrassed for Ted, but he respectfully stayed by his side, remaining quiet. He looked askance at the back of a tall, skinny man just to his left working in a shed of sorts.

"Ah maw, we jest had our mind set on gettin' to Mr. Tatums, 'fraid we might miss sumpin'. Ye know we go barefoot all the time, it dint make no never mind to us. I promise we'll wear shoes next time." Ted glanced from his ma to Nat. "Much obliged to ya, man. I don't know where we'd be now if it weren't for yore help."

"Jes now, ya go down to the waterin' hole and clean yerself; ya smell lak a horse. Use soap!" Ted walked to the creek with his head bowed. She turned to Nat, her fair-skinned face pink as a peach from working in the sun. "I'm grateful to ye," she smiled. "I'm Esther. Will ye come meet Mr. Morgan?" They walked toward the hammering sound in the small shed. In the distance, Nat saw a field of waving corn with pumpkin vines crawling up the stalks. The corn's bright green blades and glossy silk tassels were a beautiful sight in the hot July sun. The corn would be ready for harvest in four weeks, he estimated.

Mr. Morgan, absorbed in his work, stood at the work table fitting buckskin over the carved wooden shoe form, unaware that he had visitors until Esther called his name. He took two steps toward them while steadying himself, clasping the edge of the table. Like a flash, Nat realized the family's plight. Mr. Morgan was crippled. The deer skins stretched across the poles, the barn demolished by a fallen tree, the unkempt property, and an empty pig pen were all signs that the owner was incapable of swinging an ax or plowing a field.

His sons kept the family fed by hunting and fishing. The women kept the kitchen garden. From where he stood, Nat saw that half of it was planted in herbs, the other half in peas, squash, beans, and peppers. There was no sign of an apple or peach orchard, another sign that the farm was in disrepair. All farms maintained orchards. Perhaps disease took over their fruit trees. A common problem if they were plagued by insects.

He reached out his hand to Nat. "Good day to ye. I'm Matthew Morgan," he said, smiling. A tall man with long arms and narrow shoulders, he offered his big, coarse hand to Nat, demonstrating a strong grip. "I understand you rescued my son this morning. Little Amy gave me the story… Those two refuse to wear shoes! It's shameful, and with me being a cobbler." His amiable nature seemed contrary to what Nat would expect of a man with his infirmity. Visibly, an impaired leg with the way he limped. "I could see how my boys were set on joining the militia, so they bargained to help their brother hoe the corn and gather the hay. I didn't have the heart to turn 'em down." Mrs. Morgan made a groaning sound of disapproval. "Now, Esther, they grow weary of working in the fields and hunting our food."

Nat and Esther departed the small shop, relieved of the intense odor of animal skins and grateful for a breath of fresh air. Before Nat left, he checked on the patient, who lay sleeping soundly on the cot. He caught a whiff of the herbal poultice and felt confident Jed was in good hands with Esther Morgan. Judging from the numerous herb plants in the garden, she was a healer who concocted her own medicines. Considering the brother's untamed spirit for running barefoot in the woods, keeping a check on the condition of her son's feet was an everyday necessity. He set the bag of Emma's tea on the rough table and said his goodbyes to Esther and her two giggling daughters.

Nat walked around the chickens, pecking dried corn out in the hot sun. Twister blustered as Nat approached her, ready for a change of scenery and expecting a carrot for good behavior. From inside the house, he heard the faint sounds of someone playing the piano, and he smiled. *Must be one of the daughters*, he thought, hearing the slow, hesitating tempo. *This family is quite an enigma*, he thought. *Just gets more interesting by the minute!*

He trotted Twister down the dusty lane, enjoying the quietness of the burgeoning forest on either side, looking forward to reflecting on the day's unanticipated events. Just as he reached the road toward home, he looked to his right and caught a glimpse of the back of a figure sitting on a low summit holding a large board on his lap, his right hand presumably drawing on parchment. He tried for a closer look by reining in Twister, detecting the figure's head looking away for a moment, then down at his lap while his hand moved across the board. *I guess this is the other son Mr. Morgan mentioned.*

He laughed, shaking his head at the curious bunch of people he had met today. Clearly, an industrious and devoted mother who has spent the better part of her life raising three boys and two girls on a broken-down farm. Before Matthew Morgan's accident, he had taught his boys to hunt and trap and raise corn, bringing food to the table every day.

With the kitchen garden managed by Esther and her two daughters, there was enough food to feed their flock. It appeared they carried on their small farm operation with only one mule to pull the plow. The land provided all they needed. I wonder to whom Mr. Morgan sells the shoes he makes. *That will be a question for later*, Nat decided, too exhausted at the moment to delve into problem-solving.

The brothers were another matter. They had spent their entire lives outdoors. Proud hunters alert to all the goings on in their little world in Suffield.

Nat mopped away another trickle of sweat rolling down the side of his face. He was looking forward to a splash in the creek and a mug of cool cider as soon as he tended to Twister. Judging the intensity of the sun's rays, Nat slowed the horse to a trot, careful that she did not overheat. She had shown no inclination to return to her wicked ways. *Perhaps she was holding out for a rub down and some oats*, he thought, bumfuzzled by this horse's state of mind.

It was best to keep Twister under the shade of the trees and continue the slow trot. This easy ride accorded Nat the pleasure of taking in the tree-filled landscape lining the dirt road. A dozen or so well-aged sycamore maples with their coarse-toothed leaves woke his memory to the numerous times he had traveled this way to the Tatum property for barn dances.

Nat looked upwards, catching sight of a skeleton tree, its dead limbs distinctly outlined against the canvas of white puffy clouds. On its highest limb set a hawk evidenced by its shape, for there was not a twitch or movement. Its harsh, piercing sound came without warning, followed by the hawk's gliding sweep across the sky, diving to pluck up its prey in one swift motion.

Ordinarily, Nat would have sat up in his saddle to gauge where and what the hawk had pursued. Instead, he shook his head to wake from his listless state. Twister made nare a twitch. They turned homeward to a needed wash and a cool drink.

Saturday morning brought Nat to Twister's stable again. The horse was balky at the beginning of the trip to the Tatum farm, giving Nat the idea that Twister was testing him. He stopped the horse in the road and gave her half a carrot. "If that's what it takes to keep your temper in check, you can eat the other half later." He submitted his deal plain enough to the testy animal. Nat relaxed in his saddle and trotted down the road, humming a soothing tune.

Nat led Twister into the paddock upon Mr. Tatum's invitation and offered the half carrot to the horse. Now, he was able to focus his mind on militia training. Nat's eyes narrowed at the distant movement he saw coming slowly up the drive. It resembled a sapling topped with bushy leaves. Nat chuckled when, upon closer inspection, he made out the ears of a mule standing straight up. It was Jed Morgan riding atop Lightnin', the Morgan's only source of transportation.

Nat walked toward Jed and Ted to make them feel welcome. "A good morn' to ye both. Would you like to settle Lightnin' in the paddock? Some fine green grass for chompin'."

"That'd be jes fine. He could use some waterin'," Ted offered, "looks like another scorcher day. Look, yonder stands Captain Talbot."

"Good to see you've returned. How's that foot coming along, Jed?" The captain looked downward, noticing that the brothers were wearing moccasin boots today.

"It's a healin', thanks to Nat Stowe. Jes need to take my time with the marchin', if ye don't mind, sir." Jed spoke the truth, not wanting to give the impression his foot was in fine fettle, knowing there was more to learn in militia training than marching.

"Be careful with that foot. Don't push yourself today. We all have lots to learn about serving in the militia. Do you recognize that man riding through the entrance?"

Jed shook his head. "That would be Rufus McGinty," Nat answered, watching Captain Talbot's face. "Should I tell him to put his mule in the paddock, Captain?"

"Yes, by all means, and then direct him to Lieutenant Grayson."

Rufus stood as tall as Nat, with wide shoulders, long, brawny arms, and a bulging belly that jostled when he walked. He held out his strong, calloused hand. "Nat Stowe, I never expected to see you here. Are you part of this militia?" Rufus asked, walking his mule to the water trough.

"It's only my second time here. Mr. Tatum offered his paddock for our mounts today. If you want to get your mule settled, I'll show you where to sign in."

Captain Talbot nodded to Clarence Tatum, who had agreed to observe the volunteers as they marched and received orders from the captain. He was truly the sole military veteran within twenty miles who could qualify men with leadership abilities and who demonstrated serious respect for soldiering. Captain Talbot and Lieutenant Grayson made their announcements. "A-tten-tion! Form up in twos in two lines, shoulders back, arms by your sides, eyes straight ahead, pick up your feet, march by taking small steps, begin with your left foot. March! Left, right, left, (pause), watch and follow me, company halt." Earlier, the captain had pulled Nat aside and assigned him the task of shadowing Rufus, catching him up on the maneuvers learned on the Wednesday before.

The July morning was heating up quickly. No chance of a breeze. Not a single leaf moved in any of the big oaks. Nat watched Rufus. His face was red and sweating as much as the other men, even with the extra weight he carried. "Please, Lord, don't let him collapse from heat exposure."

"Go easy on the water. Don't overfill, or you'll get a bellyache." Captain Talbot gathered his men and Lieutenant Grayson's men in a grove of sycamore trees out of the sun's heat. He motioned his head for Clarence Tatum to talk to the seated volunteers.

"Men, you're here today to become part of an army. I'm talking about an army of men who can protect Suffield when and if British soldiers are ordered to take control of our town, our roads, our river, our businesses, and our farms. Don't take for granted that Gage will look past our province because it is small and of no consequence. That kind of thinking will come back to bite you. If British soldiers are ordered by their commanding officer to burn houses and fields in Suffield, they will either obey their captain's orders or die by firing squad.

"Speaking of orders, because you have agreed to sign on as a volunteer, you will be expected to follow orders from your commanding officer, such as drilling, using a weapon properly, and working with people you may not like. You will learn to comport yourself with respect and discipline in the presence of fellow soldiers. Following directions is key to doing the job correctly and protecting your life."

After Mr. Tatum's talk to the recruits, Captain Talbot fell easily into identifying details of proper conduct, which he had learned from Colonel Putnam and Clarence Tatum. If men were serious about joining Suffield's militia, they would be required to sign an agreement that forbade profanity, gambling, and drunkenness. The captain had already detected rum on the breath of some of the volunteers. Profanity was so commonplace it was ingrained in regular conversations amongst the men.

Volunteers were required to participate in twelve militia trainings. Lieutenant Grayson made his living as an accountant for a shipping firm, which qualified him to maintain perfect records. His sign-in sheet was proof that a volunteer attended militia training two days per week. Whether they signed their name or made their mark, the lieutenant kept track of each man and could identify his handwriting. Nat noticed him in possession of his militia book at all times except when he was directing drills.

"How are you holding up?" Nat asked Rufus. "This heat can surely drain you of energy."

Rufus mopped his face with a handkerchief. "The heat don't bother me since I work in it from sunup to sundown," he said. "I'm not one to sit on my haunches like them three over yonder behind that oak."

Nat chuckled. "Just something to remember. Captain Talbot won't take kindly to you mixing with that crowd. If you expect to get paid for your work, you come under the captain's authority," Nat advised Rufus. He didn't want to give him the impression that he had some position of leadership in the militia, coming off as a know-it-all.

"Are you saying that any man who signs Lieutenant Grayson's book earns a wage? How much do ye think it is?" Nat was taken aback by Rufus' question. *Perhaps he didn't read the same broadsheet I did*, he speculated. *Can he even read? I'm sure he can write his name because I saw him do it.*

"Every time you show up for work and follow the manual rules, you're paid two shillings," Nat said.

"Don't that beat all? I thought I was coming here to learn soldiering, and now you tell me I'm gonna collect a wage. Where can I find this manual? I want to know more about how it works."

Chapter 26

STRANGER IN THE WOODS

Mid-July 1774, Stowe Property

There was a time when Nat thought he would never have any inclination to ride Twister again, but after a month of militia training, he realized her worth. He was now disposed to believe that he and the quirky horse might have a future together. "Perhaps I should spend some time brushing and trimming her mane. The Lord knows I've done everything I could think of, from re-shoeing her hooves to adjusting her saddle. Whatever it takes to improve her attentiveness and her wandering disposition," he muttered. Nat was riding home from militia, pondering Twister's accomplishments.

It had taken some time and patience for Twister to prove herself. Nat was satisfied that the horse was due a second chance after his first experience at militia training. He believed Twister deserved a congratulatory carrot for hauling the wounded and bleeding Jed Morgan to his home with all its strange animal and poultice-making smells.

She had not changed overnight, for her petulance had shown through a time or two when riding toward Mr. Tatum's farm. Some rustling in a thicket had caused her to chase a young deer, judging from the pounding of its hooves. But the horse recovered herself when Nat reined her in and spoke to her gently. Thinking back, he couldn't recall a time when the dapple gray had bucked when she heard a musket fired or smelled its resulting sulfur smoke.

While Twister might prove herself to be reliable, Nat was not prepared to make any formal declarations to John about her improving temperament. She still had a ways to go before she showed the maturity of a well-bred, dependable horse.

At the moment, and in this summer heat, the animal needed a good deal of water. Nat's clothes were soaked. He literally slid off the wet saddle and led Twister to the water trough while he took a pull on the leather water pouch of warm liquid. The dinner smells, wafting from the kitchen, sent a message to his growling stomach, causing him to reconsider the length of time he could realistically spend with Twister today. *All I can manage is a quick brush and a bucket of oats. Pampering will have to wait.*

He stumbled from the barn toward the house. He saw someone running toward him, calling, "Nat, help, help!" The sun was in his face. A blurred figure continued running toward him, yelling his name. *Must be Dory*, he thought when he saw the hat flopping up and down as she ran. He moved inside the shadow of a tree and caught Dory's frantic voice. "Nat, you must come. Bring your medicine bag—now!" The knapsack was his medicine bag, which hung from his shoulder.

He followed Dory to the woods, passing by his mother's schoolroom on the right and smelling the smoke from the forge on the left. His sister was running on nerves and fright. Nat's energy had been expended for the day. Barely keeping up. Clearly, his fatigued body had been pushed to its limit today.

"Nothing could be more important than my stomach at the moment," he yelled at his sister when he heard the dinner bell and more stomach growling. "Whatever the emergency, it better not be a wounded deer or rabbit that Dory doesn't have the heart to watch suffer. What a conundrum. She's all about eating roasted venison for dinner, but she becomes unnerved when a wounded animal is left writhing in pain," he muttered, knowing she could not hear his reproach.

There it lay, face down in a thicket of hawthorn bushes, with an arrow protruding from its left shoulder. The two-legged animal wearing buff-colored breeches and black knee-high boots was groaning with pain; no blood showed as yet. Dory's pitiful face was colorless when she looked up at her brother. "I thought I was aiming at a deer," she burst into tears—uncommon behavior for Dory.

The woods were quiet. Squirrels had scampered to the safety of tall, dense trees, and birds had escaped to deeper woods. Nat loosened the man's collar and placed two fingers on his neck, feeling for a pulse. "Rapid but regular," he muttered softly. He spoke to the young man. "My name is Nat, and I want to help you. We're going to move you out of these woods to a safe location. Don't waste your strength by attempting to sit up."

Nat yelled at his sister, "Run, and bring Father quickly!" She took off in the direction of the forge, knowing that Father was likely washing soot and dirt from his face and arms by now after a day of work. She had heard the dinner bell earlier but could not fathom how much time had passed. *No matter*, she thought. *Just hurry.*

Nat knew she was scared, but so was he. The day had turned into a most unordinary day, testing his limits and pressuring him to make spur-of-the-moment decisions that left him flustered. The scorching heat and hunger were exhausting his body even more. He crouched over the injured man, dabbing water over his forehead and his right cheek. He began considering ways to transport the man out of the woods, knowing a litter was the only answer. He scanned his surroundings, looking for construction materials. He lashed limbs together with vines trailing from the huge trees, not even bothering to strip off the leaves, thankful that he was in the habit of keeping a sharp knife in his boot.

Nat heard footsteps and limbs break when he caught a glimpse of his father and Dory scrambling up the embankment, muttering to himself, "Thank the Lord," feeling tension escape his body. He flapped his hand back and forth over the man's head to shoo away the predictable arrival of flies attracted by blood and sweat.

Seeing the man lying face down in the leaves, Nathan searched for a pulse. He closed his eyes to avoid any distractions and voiced the same conclusion Nat had had. "Rapid but regular. Let's lay him face down on the litter. Dory, you pick up his legs. Nat, brace his back and right arm and keep him still. I'll support the injured shoulder and his head." Finally, the man was arranged on the litter. Nathan slowly led the trio down the leafy bank, the most arduous part of the journey leading to the schoolroom.

The wounded man was scared out of his head and in great pain, shouting "No, no, no!" attempting to free himself from strangers, but to no avail. He was conscious, at least. Nathan placed his hand on the man's back and stooped down to make contact with the man's eyes, reassuring him that he was in a safe place and would be cared for. Lamenting the grievous situation, Dory stored away her emotions and ran outside to ring the school bell.

Emma ran toward the sound, seeing Dory furiously pulling the rope to get her mother's attention. "There's been an accident. I shot an arrow at a man in the woods. Father and Nat are in the schoolhouse with him now." Dory was on the verge of tears but managed to blink them away.

"John is shaking the crabapple trees out front. Run and tell him we need help." Emma maintained her calm and headed to the scullery for the surgery bag.

By this time, Aunt Mae and Debby showed up wearing their aprons and smelling like cinnamon and pungent spices. Emma rattled off the news to her aunt, "I'm gathering surgical supplies for Nat and Nathan. A man has been shot. John is on his way. I'll need a camp stove, charcoal, pans, and a kettle for making infusions. You know what I'll need. Help him put everything together along with my medicine box." She ran to the schoolhouse carrying a sack of supplies, confident that Aunt Mae would see to the other paraphernalia. Emma's aunt knew more about surgery preparations than the entire family.

Emma stepped into her hot, stuffy schoolroom, shaking her head and breathing through her mouth to avoid inhaling the smells of filthy clothes, urine, and sweat. She opened a window and stuck her head outside to catch a breath of air. Moist air had already caused droplets of water to slide down the men's faces. She hurriedly opened the windows, eager to catch a breeze, then pulled a handkerchief from her sleeve to mop the faces of Nathan and

Nat, wondering how they could abide the stench wafting from the victim's body.

The tricky part for Nathan would be getting the stubborn man to move his head in a sideways position to swallow the dose of laudanum, essential to ease the forthcoming pain. Nat carried him up the steps and placed him on a table at Nathan's direction. He rolled him on his right side, then stretched his arms across the soldier's back and legs to keep him still while Nathan cut off the protruding arrow as close as possible to the entry point of his shoulder. The man continued to fight his losing battle by yelling obscenities. Nathan held the wounded man's neck and head in a solid hold against his legs. Emma passed the bottle of laudanum to her husband.

Assured of the man's bear-hugged position, he forced the bitter liquid down the man's throat in two small separate doses, no more than two thimbles full. The soldier wiggled his head away from Nathan and let out a gagging sound that made his face cringe, repulsed by the taste. The turbulent nature of the young man hogtied by two large strange men forcing him to swallow a nasty liquid was expected.

Looking at the victim's boyish face and slight build, Nathan thought he couldn't be more than fourteen years old. He fought the darkness enveloping him by shaking his head, adamantly refusing to surrender his trust to the giant strangers standing at his side. He slowly slipped into a semi-conscious state, hearing only twittering bird sounds flowing in through the open window. The opium mixture was taking effect. "Let's give him a few minutes before we start," said Nathan.

Aunt Mae sent Debby back to the kitchen to finish the conserve mixture. "Just follow the receipt while I'm gone. I'll return soon." She and John loaded a cart with the necessary supplies, running on adrenaline, making record time to the schoolhouse.

John took his orders from Aunt Mae regarding the camp stove set up on the porch. He loaded it with charcoal to get a fire started and a kettle of water heated. Arrangement of the surgical instruments was another story that she had no time to explain to a novice like John. She took charge, using Emma's desk to spread out the instruments in the order that she was well-acquainted with, judging from what she could see of the young man's wound. She listened to Dory explain the incident as she worked. "I've never spoken to the man. I thought it was a deer!" Dory exclaimed defensively, meeting three sets of anxious eyes while giving an account to her parents and her brother.

"When I climbed the slope this morning to the woods, there were deer tracks in the muddy part, so I followed them up to the big rocks, and I sat down and waited. I heard what I thought was an animal moving around a stand of saplings. When I stood up, it looked like the color of a deer. I aligned my bow, took a step forward, and let go of the arrow as the sun shone in through the leaves. I was blinded by the light, and then I heard a grunt that sounded more like a person than a deer, so I rushed over, and there he lay, face down in the leaves."

Tears mixed with sweat were falling down her dirty face now. Dory tried to talk and cry at the same time, her shoulders trembling. She began gagging and stepped outside behind a tree to vomit.

Nathan glanced at Emma, nodding his head toward the door. "Take her to the house." Dory was in turmoil. Emma led her to the scullery, cleaned her face and hands, and gave her a cup of water while her tears flowed.

Hearing the sounds coming from the drawing room, Lizzy was helping one of her students with a violin lesson. The way was clear for Emma to quietly seclude Dory upstairs in her room with no interruptions from her sister. Lizzy was older and was prone to be blatantly cruel to Dory, believing she merited oldest sister status now that Lainey had moved out of the house. *Debby would just ask lots of questions*, she decided.

Emma removed Dory's floppy hat and smiled at her freckled face and brown eyes. "You've been through so much today, and your body needs rest. You did the right thing by calling on your family to help. Your aggressive actions may have saved this young man's life. I'll bring you some morsels to nibble on." She closed the bedroom door and prayed, "Lord, may the young man survive?"

Emma returned to the schoolhouse and regarded the severity of the situation, aware that it would take two people to assist Nathan. She advised Aunt Mae to return to the house to check on Dory. Emma washed her hands with soap, followed by dipping them in an alcohol and water solution. She took a moment to admire Aunt Mae's efficient instrument setup. "Exactly the way Father taught me," she muttered. She took her place at the surgery table.

Her aunt had spread a large square of clean linen on the schoolroom desk, then arranged two bowls of solution: alcohol and water, vinegar and water. She checked the surgical instrument list: probes, incision knife, scalpel, forceps, crooked needles, and pins. Followed by the implement list: lint, linen for compresses, sponge, bandages, wax thread, and tourniquet.

The smell of burning charcoal wafted through the open windows. She checked on John, following orders per Aunt Mae: a kettle of water was heating on the broiler rack to be used for infusions and poultice-making. Clean cups were arranged to the side, ready to fill with medicinal teas. John was dependable and efficient, prepared to assist at a moment's notice.

It was sad to watch the wounded man overcome with insufferable pain brought about by a loose flying arrow. All the while, Nat wondered what the man was doing in the mountains anyway. The arrow had impacted the muscle on his left side, just missing his shoulder blade. Nathan knew he had one chance to push with all his strength to thrust the arrow through to the front, slashing the tendon as it cut through flesh, leaving a minimum two-inch gash in the indentation under the front shoulder.

The patient made a movement, and his face grimaced while Nat and John held him still on the table. Nathan took the probe from Emma to search for dirt and leaves in and around the wound. She handed him the forceps to pick out any debris that would cause infection, followed by dabbing the surrounding area with alcohol. To prevent any possibility of infection, she cleansed the used surgical instrument with the alcohol solution.

The threesome communicated with their eyes and nodding heads. Nat held the patient's shoulder perfectly still as his father operated with precision. The slightest movement from the patient could cause a slip of a knife or needle, endangering the surgical process and creating additional tears. He watched his father now as he had watched him work for years as a craftsman, forming delicate iron pieces with small tools that gave him the practice and agility necessary for handling surgical instruments.

Nathan stopped the blood flow with lint compressions. He examined the wound, searching for foreign matter or lacerations to veins and small blood vessels. Emma stood by with more lint as the old ones filled with blood. If she had not seen the soldier's chest rise and fall, she would have assumed the man was dead. The opium was doing its job. The patient had drifted off to a world of dreams; his tranquil face showed the evidence.

Next came the stitching. He pushed the lips of the wound together with his left-hand fingers. Emma handed him a threaded needle, puncturing the skin on either side of the wound, and sewed as if he were repairing a hole in his pants. Emma dabbed the area with alcohol. Inflammation and swelling were inevitable.

He had done all he knew to do, wondering if his father-in-law would have treated it any differently. He looked up at Nat, who had stood no more than twelve inches from Nathan's hands the entire time, keeping the patient still. "What else can I do?" Nathan asked his son.

"I believe you have done all that can be done. Pa'pa would approve," Nat said honestly.

"Emma, do you have your magic potions ready?" Nathan asked facetiously. John chuckled.

Aunt Mae, in all her wisdom, had brought in several tinctures, one of them made from Goldenseal, which grew prolifically in the shade of the forest. Knowing the bitterness of the tincture, Emma used less than a teaspoon of the liquid in a cup of hot water to make a tolerable tea. If that didn't work, she could use a tincture of yarrow. She looked them over and decided to try the Goldenseal first.

Emma turned toward her supplies and created two poultices containing yarrow and elderflowers. She consulted her receipts for other herbs to add. She kept receipts for poultices and teas like Aunt Mae kept receipts for sauces and cakes. She had watched her mother make the same poultice for her father's patients, so she felt confident it would work. Anything to begin the healing process of the wound and stave off as much inflammation as possible.

"Nathan, you should take a break after stitching. His face was strained, and his shoulders slumped. Beads of sweat had formed on his forehead, if not from the heat, more from the tension of performing delicate surgery after a day of hard work at the foundry.

She stood gazing at the pale, slightly built patient, no bigger than Dory, expecting inflammation and fever to come. *Always is*, she thought.

"Nathan, go to the house and rest. You've had a long day. I want to show Nat and John how to create my magic potions. We'll have to doctor in shifts."

Lizzy had been occupied in the music room, preparing lessons for her students, when she heard the screams echo across the property, all the way to the front of the house. She had shed tears for the injured man when Aunt Mae told her of the accident. Now, she found herself shedding tears for her sister, Dory.

A change in her character had begun before Lainey left for New Haven. Part of that change was loving her family in such a way where she aptly displayed physical affection with smiles and hugs when she deemed it appropriate. This was new behavior for Lizzy. A side of her that developed naturally since she had allowed her wall of resentment and insecurity to crumble down.

She walked upstairs to Dory's room, finding her sister curled up under her bed in an uncontrollable state. Lizzy lay on the floor next to the bed and placed her hand on her sister's back. "I'm sorry, Dory, I am so sorry."

Less than a day after the shooting incident, John was charged with combing the woods to search for possessions belonging to the wounded man. *The slightest clue would help*, he thought. Nathan warned him to be on his guard when advancing deep into the woods. The possibility that their patient could be a deserter was real. British soldiers could be on the hunt for the man the family had rescued.

For his protection, John wore buckskins, moccasins, and a fur hat—a loan from Dory. The idea was to disguise himself as a hunter armed to the hilt with a musket, pistol, hatchet, and knife, just in case he should run into a patrol of soldiers.

John had spent most of his youth in Maine's wilderness, hunting for game alongside his father and uncle. He was trained by accomplished woodsmen in the mandatory rules of conduct: keep a keen eye roving as you walk, learn the habits of wild animals, and remain mindful of your bearings. *You must keep with your purpose when you are hunting. Wandering thoughts are a distraction, and it can mean your life. Only you control your thoughts*, his father's words reminded him.

John left at dawn to proceed across the creek and up the embankment, following the trail left by the litter's tracks. The steep, sloped course was clear of brambles and vines. Beech trees provided shade. Saplings and adult trees and shrubs were crowded on the left and right sides of the trail.

His skill as a hunter would have allowed him to detect the acrid remains of a charred campfire, but there was no evidence of any. *The man had to have eaten something*, John thought. *You can only survive for so long on hickory nuts and roots.*

Sweat streamed down his face as he walked upward toward the peak of the embankment. He grew tiresome and began to stumble over bare roots and slippery rocks. Thoughts of his hunting days in Maine tried to steal his concentration. He shook his head, aiming to store the memories for another time. *Only you control your thoughts*, he reminded himself.

He got his bearings and felt the heat of the sun on his right side. If he walked another hundred feet, he would get a view of the blue mountains in the distance, set against the bright sky. *Not today*, he decided. *They are extraordinaire, but it will wait.*

His body was sweating, and he was in need of refreshment. He sat down under a shady elm and took his fill of honeyed water while enjoying the scents of spruce and pine in the distance.

From the angle where he was seated and across the trail, he spotted some either roughly cut or broken ends of pine branches. This gave him the notion that a makeshift pallet may have been hurriedly constructed, probably something he would consider doing if he was tired and on the run…

He looked up, around and behind, memorizing his surroundings and remaining alert to the sounds of footsteps and dry twigs breaking. He cautiously moved to the opposite side of the trail. Crouching down with the whole back of his body against a bulky tree for protection. He tossed a stone into the pine boughs. No movement. He crouched-walked around a granite boulder to look over and into the hovel. It was empty. Using the musket's barrel to poke around inside the stacked branches, he determined it safe to crawl around to view the rudimentary encampment.

Crouching as low as his body would allow, he pushed aside the tree branches, noticing a dug-out grave of sorts. He swallowed hard and looked around for anything, animal or human. His curiosity getting the better of him, he vigorously dug out the loose dirt with his bare hands.

He spotted something red. No, it wasn't blood. He removed a knapsack, holding a red waistcoat, and muttered, *"Mon soldat."*[40] He returned the loose dirt to the hole and pressed down to pack it in with the idea that an observant British soldier may be as suspicious as himself. He brought along pine boughs to sweep over any noticeable footprints.

The heat in the woods was smothering, and he was anxious to strip out of the hot buckskins and relax in the cool creek. The triumphant joy of unearthing evidence that could potentially have jeopardized the soldier's life and the Stowe family's livelihood was now dispelled. The rapid, downhill pace toward the creek eased his anxiety, and the knot in his belly disappeared.

"Will you take water, *mon ami?*"[41] John Dupre was taking his shift to attend to the wounded soldier, now resting on a pallet on the schoolroom floor. The young man burned with fever, groaned with pain, and suffered unimaginable nightmares of wicked men swearing and swinging whips, causing the soldier to scream while cursing the devils.

---

40. My soldier.
41. …my friend?

John soothed the man's face and neck with cool water, helped him walk to the privy, and even sang French ballads to him, mindful that the soldier needed comfort and constant care. He had seen the lash marks across the young soldier's back, wondering how often the young man had risked the desertion scheme.

The family took turns brewing tea and making poultices for healing and reducing swelling and inflammation. Four days after surgery, a white pus had formed in the wound, a good sign that healing was taking place. Emma insisted that the soldier remain in the schoolroom and continue with the doctoring, feeding him broth and stressing rest for continued healing.

Dory and Lizzy visited the soldier together at Nathan and Emma's insistence. They brought him biscuits to eat with his tea, which was all he could stomach. They tried to entertain him with card games and reading books, but he tired out easily.

He never asked about his injury or how it happened. It seemed that he did not care about recovering; he was in a safe place, and that's all that mattered. John had a gut feeling that nothing added up with this soldier. But he does talk in his sleep. *I shall become a better listener*, he decided.

Two weeks had passed since Nathan, Nat, and Dory had rescued Private George Winslow from the woods. "This man, this soldier, has deserted from the British army, and you think we should allow him to live on our property and eat our food? I understand his predicament, but what about our predicament if the word gets out that we are harboring a deserter? We could be imprisoned in one of those filthy ships stationed in the Boston harbor. I've never heard such crazy talk from you!" Nathan spoke sharply when Emma offered her suggestion, allowing Private Winslow the safety and protection of their home until other arrangements could be made. Nathan was slow to anger, but this made it for him.

"You are shouting on the Sabbath!" Emma exclaimed. "You know full well we cannot turn that boy out so he can be arrested and possibly stand before a firing squad because we did not have the courage to protect him. Now, do you honestly have such an uncaring heart?" Emma defended her position, even though she knew it was risky.

"I know the game you're playing, Emma, and it will not work. There's too much at stake here. We don't have many choices. And since when is it a sin to shout on Sunday? The Lord shouted at Moses and Jonah no matter the day, right?" he said, shoring up his defense.

She came back at him, laughing and shaking her head in disbelief. "You're making things up now, Nathan. The Lord says to help those in need, your fellow man! I do recall a certain Frenchman who was seeking food and shelter one day when you just happened to be in the right place at the right time to come to his aid. Tell me, Nathan, how did that work out?"

"How did it turn out, you ask? Beyond my expectations. John is smart and has quickly learned his responsibilities. That does not mean this deserter has the same work ethic and willingness to pull his weight on this property. He could be a spy, for that matter. Whatever your ideas are, we must discuss them with the entire family, including John," Nathan shrugged, shaking his head in disagreement. Now, he was backed into a corner. He would have preferred escaping to the Black Rooster, but the taproom was closed on the Sabbath. Instead, he remained in his office until dinner was served.

Emma walked the path to the schoolroom to assume her shift with the patient. She carried two different books with her to read aloud in hopes of keeping the young man's mind centered on something other than his pain and boredom. Ordinarily, when she looked up from reading to see the man's reaction to a particular scene in the book, Emma found him staring at the wall or pretending to sleep. *Very frustrating*, she thought as she gazed at his sullen demeanor.

Besides reading or doctoring his wound, she would talk to him about her trips to England when she was much younger. The grand castles, the busyness of London, the countryside, hoping to generate some conversation. Asking him questions about his home in county Kent, expecting a reply. The young man would smile reservedly or reply with a yes or no.

But something in his face and his eyes gave her reason to think he was troubled and was inclined to shield his emotions and his private life.

She was as suspicious as John and Nat concerning his past. He's not just a young man who was pressed into service. He may have joined the army to escape England. *Possibly a bad home situation*, she conjectured.

Relieved to see his mother coming through the door, Nat gave Emma a peck on the cheek and took his leave from the scorching classroom. He stood on the porch for a moment, watching the sun slowly slip down behind the mountains, spreading purple and red flames across the horizon. *A cool breeze would certainly make the schoolroom more tolerable*, he thought as he walked down the steps. *Mother's compassionate spirit for the soldier seems excessive. It's a combination of motherly love and her desire to nurture young people*, he brooded.

John spied Nat leaving the schoolroom, and they stopped to chat. "Any difference with our patient?" John asked, as frustrated as Nat about the patient's tacit demeanor. Nat shook his head in response.

"I have made much effort to discuss subjects of interest to him, but *pas du tout*.[42] I serve him his tea and broth, and he sleeps." John shrugged.

John switched to a different subject. "*Comment était votre sortie avec la jeune fille, Lillian? Comment Lillian a-t-elle trouvé le pré pour monter à cheval?*"[43] John asked Nat.

"It was enjoyable. Lillian knows quite a lot about horses, which, unfortunately, is the substance of our conversations. She's a talented horseman, er, horsewoman, I'll give her that." He laughed at his awkward remark. "I'm very fond of horses and desire to be a more astute rider, but I don't live and breathe the art of horsemanship. She must take after Mr. Tatum, her father. No matter what subject we discuss, it always comes back to horses. Very tiresome."

"Does she not favor art or music as your sisters?" John asked, befuddled that horses were her only interest.

"No, she does not. She's a jolly dancer, but what kind of a conversation can you have with *la jeune fille*[44] when you're dancing a reel? You're

---

42. …to no avail.
43. How was your outing with the young girl, Lillian? How did Lillian find the meadow for riding?
44. …the young girl…

moving the entire time! I admit my heart skipped a few beats when I saw her beauty up close, her hair bouncing, and her pretty teeth when she laughed at my mistakes, mostly!" A picture of Josie Randolph flitted through his mind. She could talk about anything.

John grimaced, then shrugged. "*C'est la vie!*[45] Your visit to New Haven was enjoyable, I trust?"

"Mostly. There were some surprises. Of course, I enjoyed my visits with Micah Penrose and his housekeeper." He smiled, recalling Lynette. John's eyes went wide. "The more time I spent with them, the more I realized she was more than a housekeeper. Talk about beauty! Her big brown eyes, her friendly smile, and she's French—what a cook!"

"What of your sister, Lainey? Was she pleased with the journey downriver and her new accommodations?" John missed her and was reluctant to ask, but he couldn't help himself.

"Yes. She remarked that Whales' Tale was the most romantic and unusual place she had ever encountered. She enjoyed the entertainment—some of it bawdy. Mother and Father need not know, of course. She sang along with musicians playing their fiddles and flutes and, of course, the storytelling and ballads—such merriment!

"The following morning, we traveled by riverboat down the Connecticut River to New Haven. She was taken with the beautiful mansions and farms along the way. It was a new experience for her, moving languidly along the flat, watery surface, mesmerized by the endless sky and the water birds.

"I believe the most wonderful experience for her was the day we rode our horses to the ocean. The freedom of riding on the wet sand, feeling engulfed with the wind in your face and the crashing sounds of the ocean. She was drunk with laughter." Nat stared at the mountains, breathing deeply, smiling, and remembering the experience. He glanced at John, who nodded and smiled as though he were imagining the thrills of a journey taken with friends and family. Musing that someday it would be a reality for him.

---

45. That's life!

Emma stood by the window, inhaling a cool breeze, sending the sweet scent of jasmine in her direction, watching the soldier while he slept deeply. She overheard John and Nat's conversation about women and exciting adventures that young men delight in, causing her to laugh.

Listening to Nat speak of their journey to New Haven, tears of thankfulness rolled down her face. All that her heart and mind had led her to believe about Lainey's dilemma two months prior had come to fruition. "Thank You, God," Emma whispered.

Lainey's big brother saw his sister's need to assume independence from her parents and sisters. Her desire to experience a life that she had only read about in books began when they crossed the river to Whales' Tale. He had ungrudgingly guided his sister to a different world outside of Suffield, Connecticut, protecting her along the way. "Bless you, Nat."

Nathan and Emma had kept a close check on the soldier, observing his pallor fade from gray to healthy pink tones peeking through his fair English skin. They checked his wound. They breathed relief when they observed a scab had formed over the wound, revealing the advance of the healing process.

In their unprofessional but experienced opinion, the man was in no pain, in spite of the sling he insisted on wearing to immobilize the wounded arm. They sought the medical wisdom of Aunt Mae, who concurred with their prognosis. She had assisted her brother, Dr. Pierpoint, since she was a young girl of twelve, trained to recognize certain evidence of progress, particularly the sparkle in his eyes.

"What's amiss with the soldier? I can't budge a word out of him. He lies in that hot room like he's got a fatal disease!" Nathan was put off by the man's taciturn manner, swearing to confront the man's pretense. "I've a good mind to drug him and send him sailing down the river as your friends from Stoughton were forced to do," he said to Nat. "He is a threat to our family's security and to Stowe Ironworks!"

"There's no complaint about his appetite; he eats like a horse—so says Aunt Mae!" Nat was as protective of his great-aunt as his father was. Preparing additional food each day for an outsider was getting under her skin. Her goodwill was coming to a halt, and she made sure everyone knew it.

"If he thinks he can hide from the redcoats in my schoolroom and eat Aunt Mae's cooking until he finds something better, he has another thing coming. I don't care for his stubborn silence," Emma informed the family during their afternoon dinner. Nat glanced at his father, surprised at his mother's change of heart. Nathan remained silent, answering with a shrug, and continued with his meal.

Debby, eager to express mutual agreement, quickly replied before Lizzy spoke her mind. "He thinks we're his servants." She nodded her head in all seriousness. "He never says thank you for his food."

"He raises his chin as if he's the son of a prince," Lizzy said. "Maybe he has royal blood."

Emma glanced at Dory, tormented by nearly killing the soldier, now tormented with placing her family and Stowe Ironworks in jeopardy. Her nightmares wouldn't allow her a full night's sleep, crying and screaming, imagining redcoat soldiers setting fire to the house and the forge. It broke Emma's heart to watch her daughter grieve over something she hardly had any control over. Dory excused herself from the table.

Dory's sad eyes wrenched John's heart. *She's much too young to bear such a burden*, he mused.

"John, will you saddle Dragon and Patience?" Emma asked. "Dory and I are riding to the meadow."

Nat stood by Aunt Mae's chair, offering his hand to escort her to her room. "Wonderful dinner as always. I'll help with the cleanup." He pecked his aunt's cheek.

The clinking of dishes and silver began as Lizzy and Debby assumed their responsibilities in the kitchen. Nathan grasped Emma's hand and pulled her close to him. "I'll miss our walk today, but Dory needs you now." He kissed her cheek. "I'll meet you in the barn. Captain and I are needed at the Black Rooster."

It was the first week of August, the dog days of summer. The hottest and unhealthiest days of summer. John woke from a restless night thinking of Private Winslow, wondering when he might demonstrate some initiative to discuss why he sought refuge on the mountain. From his calculation, he had camped there for two or more months. *Une grande catastrophe!*[46] He had never seen anyone so undeserving of the Stowe family's charitableness. *Something must be done today*, he decided.

While his cup of tea steeped, John dressed and cursed the soldier loudly, mostly in French, although he made an effort to voice his frustrations in English; it all meant the same. He had taken to heart the frustrations of each family member, especially Dory. *Each one has given their best effort to assist this invalid thief*, he riled. *Now, he uses them selfishly!* Unthinking, he swallowed a gulp of steaming tea, "*C'est chaud!*"[47] he yelled.

Nat and Nathan had been working at the foundry since before daylight, checking the work of the stonemason who had rebuilt two of the forges in the tower that produced the largest of the solid iron products: anchors and bells for schooners.

They headed to the house to eat a proper breakfast. A single mug of coffee with cream had done its job of supplying short-term nourishment. With empty bellies and watering mouths, they inhaled the inviting scents of fried sausages and hotcakes, walking at a quicker-than-normal pace while sweat poured from their brows as the day's heat intensified.

As John set out walking toward the schoolroom, he and his temper were soon to collide with Nat and Nathan as they walked to breakfast. The three men on a mission used better sense when they came to a halt. Their attention was aroused by the sound of the squeaky hinges emanating from the outhouse door.

John took off running toward the privy. The erstwhile patient, mindful of discharging himself from the privy in the quickest manner possible, caught a glimpse of John's angry countenance and took off running in the direction of the schoolhouse. John's gazelle-like speed was no match for the young soldier, who found himself swiftly tackled to the ground. The Stowe men watched the scene from a distance, curious to know John's intentions.

---

46. A great catastrophe!
47. It's hot!

Private Winslow was a good five inches shorter than John, slightly built with surprisingly muscular arms, and a fair runner, given all that his body had been through in the last month. He fought John's successful attempt to wrestle him to the ground. John seized the soldier's back shirt collar and pulled him to his feet.

"You're hurting me. I need my sling!" Private Winslow had never spoken so many words since his arrival at the Stowe property.

John held tight, knowing the man would run if he eased off. He pushed him up the steps and set him in a chair in the schoolroom away from the windows. Nathan and Nat followed, not wanting to miss all the action, and closed the only door in the building. They stood in front of the two open windows and folded their arms, assuming their position as guards. Both men patiently stood, regretting John's timing as hungry as they were, standing in attention while sweat trickled down their backs.

John looked at Nathan's face, receiving a nod for permission to proceed. "Tell me, Private Winslow, who is Francine?" John had listened to Winslow talk in his sleep, groaning and carrying on like a frightened and angry man.

No answer.

"I shall give you one more opportunity to answer my question. If you choose not to talk, then I shall hand you over to your Redcoat pursuers. The three of us shall escort you to the mountain or possibly to Massachusetts, where you will be forced to search for a bed and food. It is your decision. No more handouts!" John glared at the soldier's face, demanding an answer.

Private Winslow glanced at the door first, then his eyes darted between the two Stowe men, considering their height and their sinewy long arms, able to shackle and gag him with little difficulty. His mind flashed back to the cold nights on the mountain, wolves on the prowl, digging for roots and searching about for berries to stave off hunger. He weighed his alternatives and surrendered.

"Francine is my sister. She resides in the colony of South Carolina."

Nathan Stowe sat at the fireplace at the Black Rooster, the getaway he so needed during this intervening time of summer's dog days and the beginnings of autumn. Once he caught the sharp scents of vinegar and lemon juice diffused throughout the house, he dressed and left through the front door to search for Emma. He found her and Dory in the wash house, instructing the sufficiently recovered runaway soldier, George Winslow, in the fine art of washing bedding and kitchen linens.

He stuck his head through the top of the Dutch door opening, catching a glance of Emma, her golden hair tied back in a crude fashion such as he had seldom seen, busily teaching George how to mix lye soap and lavender crystals. The smell was as nauseating as the high-powered odors Aunt Mae had infused throughout the kitchen with her citrus canning process.

"Good morning," Emma said, standing on her tiptoes to receive a kiss from Nathan. "Wash day. Getting an early start with our new helper." She wiped her eyes with the corner of her damp apron. "Where are you off to?"

"Any place I can settle where the air doesn't make my eyes sting and cause my gut to go sour," Nathan answered with a sigh.

"Sounds like a morning to be spent at the Black Rooster. Aunt Mae and Debby are preserving lemons and limes, quite pungent for your tender olfactory senses, I suppose." Emma pursed her lips and shook her head in jest. Another tendril of hair fell loose from its comb.

"I'm off to finish some paperwork. I'll be home for dinner." Nathan took a step back, desiring not to inhale the lye concoction emanating from his wife. She laughed and waved him off.

The clock ticked on, during which Nathan drank several cups of coffee by the banked fireplace while he perused future orders, scheduling jobs for his workers, soon to begin on the first day of September. "I see the paperwork is never-ending for Stowe Ironworks," announced Clarence Tatum as he walked toward Nathan to shake his hand. "Just left the militia drilling in the capable hands of Charlie Talbot. Fine-looking group of potential soldiers. I daresay we will be thankful we're getting this early start."

"Expecting some action next spring?" asked Nathan, closing his ledger.

"The action has begun. Connecticut's delegates have been chosen, and they are assembling in Hartford as we speak, along with Massachusetts' delegates." Clarence took a long draw on his pipe, then continued, "They are all headed for New Haven."

Nathan stared into the fire. "Think they will accomplish anything?"

Clarence scoffed, "As long as they don't mention that particular word we're all thinking." He glanced at Nathan, then looked around the room for itchy ears, finally whispering, "Independence."

Nathan held his forefinger to his lips. "Shhh!"

Part V

BEAT THE DRUMS

Chapter 27

Travails of a Besieged Province

August 1774, Bradford Lane

Surprisingly, the late evening breeze felt somewhat cooler tonight, blowing through the gauze that covered the windows in my upstairs chamber, providing sufficient protection from *most* flying insects. Possibly, a sea breeze or an impending rainstorm accounted for the cool air. Anything to reduce the stuffiness of the stifling heat. Suddenly, I felt exhilarated by the thought that, should rain fall on Boston, the odious and never-ending din of drums and fifes might come to a halt, if for only a day.

At that moment, my eyes were drawn to a large moth firmly fastened to one of the window panes, feasting on any small insect that crept within its territory. I generally sat at my desk in the evening, my quill scratching along the paper, recording the events of my day, which lately was filled with sickness and destitute people. Some were long-time patients. Some were newcomers, possibly even Tories.

With the exception of the wealthy, Bostonians had, until recently, depended on work at the Boston port for their livelihood, whether you were a merchant or a dock worker. The business of importation and exportation had ceased, and ninety percent of Boston's inhabitants no longer earned a wage.

The closure of Boston's port officially began on the first day of June when the British government ordered their soldiers and Governor Gage to fulfill their mission of "bringing the province to its knees" until they surrendered the tea tax to London's bank.

Poverty was at an extreme level. With no money to pay rent or buy food from nearby farms, families made their pilgrimage to the countryside. Their hope was to exchange their labor for shelter, which was mostly clean hay under a lean-to and mostly vegetables and grains to cook over a campfire. Without a doubt, those driven from their Boston homes would have to come to terms with their survival during the harsh winter weather, beginning in late fall. At the moment, the daunting prospect of having to fill their children's bellies controlled their thoughts.

With the onset of cooler weather, hundreds of orchards would be in need of harvesting come September. An opportunity to exchange labor for food in these uncertain times. With the influx of friends and family members streaming into Lexington, Concord, Cambridge, and Worcester, among others. Dock workers soon became farmers and carpenters. Many joined the militia. Boston's population count of fifteen thousand had been dramatically reduced by thousands who were displaced across the Charles River to the countryside when the port closed on June 1st. An estimated four thousand British troops had now filled our tiny land mass, seizing control of the Common by the river and quartering troops in empty houses.

On the other hand, loyalists gave up their homes in the country and fled to Boston, seeking protection under Governor Gage. Tories had resolved that so-called patriots had crossed the line when they flung chests of expensive East India tea into the harbor, defying King George's authority. Such ruthlessness and treason convinced Tory farmers and craftsmen that residing in the country was not worth risking their lives. Threats of lynchings and tar-and-feathering were unnerving, to say the least.

In spite of it all, Father and I continued our business of doctoring, earning money as we could from those who could afford to pay out silver coins or barter certain provisions. Some exchanged their labor to mend and paint our fence, repair gutters, clean windows, or supply us with firewood. We were never sure whose trees surrendered their existence, but we asked no questions. In return, we provided the best medical care we could while educating patients about preventative care.

Food shortages were the most severe punishment to Bostonians. What little was left to purchase from merchants was priced so high that the unemployed could not possibly purchase adequate food. Help came in the form of bushels of grain and hundreds of sheep and cattle driven up by farmers from Connecticut, Rhode Island, and all coastal colonies, rallying their support of Massachusetts' Patriots.

Distribution of the provisions was organized by Boston's leaders—selectmen, they were called. Riots and thievery were rampant, mostly caused by unemployed dock workers. In exchange for cleaning docks and repairing streets, those men were paid with food and firewood. Of course, that didn't keep them from running up tabs at the taverns, which were always busy.

This plan served two purposes: angry workmen were kept busy during the daytime instead of rioting and harassing their neighbors, and their bellies were fed. We continued serving our patients with vegetables and fruits harvested from our garden. Thanks to Naomi and Lenora, an entire wall in our cellar housed an abundance of preserved foods: cabbage, apples, pickled peaches, peas, and carrots.

Providing food to those without resources had become a mission of the highest importance to ambitious and generous women such as Auntie and her quilting bee friends, who organized food for neighboring families who could not even afford a cord of firewood.

Mrs. Pierpoint and some of her Beacon Hill friends were equally generous, lending a hand by delivering vegetables and fruits from their massive gardens to homes located in the North Square area of town, providing aid where they could.

It was sad to see many of my favorite shops boarded up, especially Folgers Bookstore, which I had visited habitually once a week for new reading materials. We continued purchasing dairy, meats, eggs, and milled grain from the Harmon Farm, as did many others, including taverns that could afford the convenience of food deliveries. Limes and lemons, which we had purchased for many years from the street vendors, were sorely missed, for Auntie used them in preserving foods and making punch. An outbreak of scurvy was a constant concern, given a lack of fresh citrus. We accepted all this, knowing there were many whose pantries were bare and had nary a pence to their name.

At the moment, I worried about the Bignall family and their three children and decided I must walk by their home to learn of their current situation. Where were they to live, and how would the children be educated? Father and I planned to visit them under the guise of tending to Mr. Bignall's burn scars, naturally providing him special ointment and medical advice for his burned flesh.

Fletcher's Livery was another victim of this hideous siege. The majority of the horses, mainly old plugs remaining at the stables, were for pulling carriages, leaving a half dozen to be used for riding purposes. Finer steeds were delivered to Lexington to be maintained by a family member who owned a large farm, providing ample space and accommodations for thirty of Mr. Fletcher's finest horses. This was also an attempt to keep his steeds out of the hands of British officers.

Miles and his brother Amos had not forgotten the callous behavior of certain British officers the last time they crowded into Boston, believing they had the authority to subdue the owners by demanding their needs be met before or in place of local customers.

"I refuse to allow these ill-mannered clodhoppers the right to my horses. They beat them to break their spirits, and they never groom them properly. I will not have it!" Mr. Fletcher had his backup when he spoke to Father, completely justified in his decision. "They should ship their own mounts across the sea or bring them down from Canada. I'm not making it easy for them!"

All these wretched changes, along with fears that the British were preparing an attack in the countryside, hung like a constant gray cloud over our beloved province. When and how would it end? We were living in precarious times while secluded in our house on Bradford Lane.

I glanced at the yellow flowers Nat Stowe had delivered to me on the final day of his Boston trip. They were dried, and some of the petals had fallen. That enchanting night remained in my memory, as well as the summer scent of the arbor's yellow roses. It served as a remembrance of our time together. With the glow from the candle, my mind recalled certain images of the dinner party at the Pierpoints that evening when Nat so confidently introduced himself to me. A complete stranger that I was. He absolutely dropped in out of nowhere while I stood within the arbor enamored by hundreds of tiny yellow roses. *Hmm*, I pondered, *Dr. Pierpoint would have certainly known that I was the daughter of his former apprentice, my father!* That certainly cast a different light on the outcome of the party. A note of discord suddenly struck a deafening note within! I shook my head to scatter those thoughts.

"It's been a long day, Josie. Are you staying up until your father returns home?" Auntie stepped into my room on the way to her bedchamber. Her face was scrubbed clean, emitting a pleasant lavender scent. We were both in the habit of bathing more frequently. It was not because of the scorching hot summer days that caused us to sweat profusely but more so because we remained in close contact with patients and strangers. We were inclined to scrub away dried blood and pus and the foul smells of unclean bodies. Even Father took to bathing more often.

"Father looked especially handsome when he left tonight, don't you think? Someone special attending the Pierpoints' dinner party? If so, I would like to know who," I prodded Auntie.

Father and Dr. Pierpoint had renewed their professional friendship after all these years. They had met often during the summer months to discuss all matters of new medical findings in the form of printed medical journals, recently released from Edinburgh and the Netherlands.

"He said Dr. Church would be attending and, of course, Elise Beaumont. Beyond that, I do not know. I question Dr. Church's alliance with Patriots, including his Freemason and Sons of Liberty status," she said matter-of-factly. "I have never trusted his face nor his wandering eyes. He seems too agreeable, too quick to please everyone." Auntie's assessment of Dr. Church was warranted. Once her sixth sense of foresight kicked in, caution ruled, and there was no going back.

"I didn't know that about him. He seems so popular. Oh, I see what you mean. He wants to be a friend to all, or at least appear so. Correct?" I asked Auntie. I wanted to say "spy," but I scrapped that.

She smirked and nodded her head. "But your father is well aware of the doctor's guileful manner." Auntie turned to leave but stopped in her tracks when I brought up Elise Beaumont's name.

"I'm keeping a watch on that mystery woman for the time being. Josiah deserves to mingle with different people. S*he's* odd." Auntie was noticeably tired, yawning more than talking. "I'm turning in."

I turned my journal writing pages back to the end of May when I first encountered Nat on the Pierpoints' flower-laden terrace, recalling his easygoing manner and his handsome face with that enduring smile. I wondered about the young ladies residing near the Stowe's farm in Suffield. At that, I held the candle holder up to my face and moved closer to the mirror. I opened my mouth to examine my front teeth, deciding they needed a good cleaning. I promptly took care of that with my brush and toothpowder, rinsed, and went at it one more time.

I returned to my dresser mirror and held up the candle once again, making sure I had thoroughly rinsed off any excess powder. I glanced down at the dried roses, then smiled. *What's in a name? That which we call a rose by any other name would smell as sweet.* I treasured Shakespeare's words Nat had spoken to me at the yellow rose arbor. They came to me naturally during the day. I sighed.

I rose from my seat when I heard the front door close—Father, I hoped. Of course, it was. We had begun locking the outside doors since the encounter with the Big Englishman and the British siege. I leaned against the casement at the door of my room to greet Father, not because I was suspicious but just wanting to sniff Father's waistcoat for hints of perfume, recalling the mystery woman.

He gave me a quick kiss on my forehead, almost in passing and certainly not long enough to inhale the sort of perfume a beautiful, mysterious woman might wear. "Good night, Josie." So much for that!

British soldiers began their drills in the early morning, lasting until late afternoon, all day, every day. The drums beat, and the fifes shrilled their tattoo, and in between, church bells tolled the hour. Soldiers marched on the common and on the streets while drillmasters shouted their commands. Boston was the noisiest place in the world, and I wanted to move to the countryside, I said aloud, sipping my tea.

The following morning, Auntie and I sat at the breakfast table enjoying our breakfast of eggs and corn cakes with honey, sipping our homemade tea, entranced with the orange and reds splashed across the horizon, the sun predictably on the rise. "If the soldiers don't chop down the apple and pear trees for firewood, we could stir up some preserves for the winter months." Auntie offered.

"What about conserves? Do we have the currants and spices for that?" I asked. Auntie had set a bowl of peeled pears on the table for us to sample, solid and dense, which made them perfect for preserves. "Do you hear that noise? It's a clanking sound." We jumped up from the table and raced to the drawing room. Each of us chose a window and threw back the shutters.

The canvas-covered wagon pulled by two horses stopped in front of the stone walkway leading to our front door. "Who in the world could that be?" Auntie asked with a snappish face. Pots and pans hanging from a metal frame arranged over the top of the canvas clanged together when the horses came to a solid stop.

"Why, that's... Uh, uh, I don't remember his name, but he looks familiar," Auntie said, her brain working overtime to come up with the driver's name.

Several moments passed when we heard Father walking hastily down the stairs while stuffing his shirttails in his trousers. He then opened the front door, obviously anticipating a visit from the man driving the wagon with the clanging pots. "Good morning. May I help you?" asked Dr. Randolph as the two men met halfway on the stone path at the front door.

"Good morning," the man bowed. "Would you be needing your knives sharpened or your pots repaired, sir? I do my work on-site. Got all my tools situated in the back of the wagon." Father and the repairman looked at each other as if there was another purpose on their minds.

"Why yes, I believe we might. I'll just ask the lady of the house if you care to wait." Josiah looked the wagon over for a sign or a name. Nothing.

Father walked into the house while the man waited. "Minnie, I noticed our kitchen knives could stand to be sharpened, and what about your shears? The repairman can manage the work in his wagon."

"But I…" she caught a piercing look on her brother's face that demanded a yes for her answer. "Yes, I'll gather them in a basket. I will bring them outside." She started toward the kitchen. I turned around and caught a familiar furtive reaction from Father—his tongue took a swipe across his upper lip, followed by a sigh. He waited in the hallway at the stairs until she returned. Auntie spoke not a word.

Father grasped the basket and returned to the man who now stood at the rear of the wagon. The repairman stepped up into the back and began pedaling his grinding stone, forging an edge to the dull knives. He carefully rubbed a folded napkin across the knives to remove any residue, then casually dropped it into Auntie's basket.

Less than a half hour later, I saw the repairman step from the wagon and pass the basket to Father, who dropped four pence into the man's hand in view of anyone who happened to be watching from nearby. The driver settled himself on the wagon's seat and gently voiced a "walk on" to the horses. Clanking pot sounds resumed as the outfit jostled along the cobblestoned Main Street.

Auntie and I stood to the side of the same window and watched the entire scene play out on Main Street without saying a word. We gazed at each other, agog, as if we expected the obscure chariot to return to its place in the nether world.

Father walked to the kitchen, and we followed. "Have a seat, please," he said strongly. He held out his arm and directed us to the two brocade-covered settles positioned at the sunny windows.

His pale face and his dark eyes showed a glint of danger, making Auntie and me uneasy. We seated ourselves, prepared to listen to more harsh news. We desperately hoped he would entertain us with the details of last night's dinner party at the Pierpoint home. We were itching to hear local gossip and a description of Mrs. Pierpoint's French cuisine. But it was not to be at this juncture. Auntie and I were growing weary of our confinement at home all summer, not exactly our *métier*.[48]

"As you know, our printer friend and neighbor, Ezra Phillips, walked into the surgery last week with a cut finger. Not very serious, but it was bleeding and required several stitches. The matter of securing weapons has long been a demanding task for those of us, including Mr. Phillips, having been assigned that responsibility as a member of the Committee of Safety.

"We smuggle weapons into Concord after dark to the most inconceivable locations, believing they are secure. As it happens, the word soon gets around the taverns of what we had thought were safe locations. Then, we have to dig them from their cache and secure them in a different area. The governor has his soldiers searching for weapons in all the fields in Lexington, Lincoln, Essex, you name it."

"How does Mr. Phillips fit into this predicament?" asked Auntie.

"He set up the arrangements for the mender of pots and pans to stop by our house this morning to sharpen our knives." Father retrieved the folded napkin from his waistcoat and dropped it on the tea table. Auntie laid the cloth out flat, catching her breath when she recognized the locations drawn with black chalk. "This is the map we will use when the time comes," Father advised, eyes piercing.

"Why, these are all labeled as storage areas for cow manure," observed Auntie, now grinning at the brilliant strategy. "Look, there's the Ledbetters' and the Crafts' farms."

Father explained how a deep hole was dug inside the corners of each end of the pasture, large enough to contain boxes of muskets and gunpowder. The hole was then covered with dirt, and a wagon of cow manure or hay was parked over the hole. This gave the false appearance of a typical space for by-products a farmer would need to store and use in the future.

"Will the knife-sharpening man return with more maps? I don't recall his name." This entire clandestine operation sent chills up my spine and gave me a sickly feeling of the danger we were up against.

---

48. ...occupation.

"The man is called a tinker—never gave me his name, nor was there a name printed on his wagon. I assume the less we know about the carriers, the better," Father replied as a matter of fact.

"I must give both of you some advice." Father was seated on the opposite settle, leaning forward with his eyes fixed upon our faces. "Never discuss this information with your friends or any of our neighbors." He looked at us, showing a contrary grin. "If you are ever tempted to share confidential information, rebuke it by imagining the other person is Medusa. By looking at her hideous face, you would turn to stone!" Father's droll imagery eased some tension, but we caught the seriousness of it all.

We had been extremely busy since the beginning of June with the burn patients whom we had doctored and nursed for weeks, all of which took place during the closing of Boston's port. It was painful to watch parents and their children trudge along Boston's streets carrying what few possessions they had strapped to their backs or dragging clothes and necessities along behind them, giving up the only home they probably had since birth. At present, we were more concerned that our patients had a decent place to sleep and enough food and water to keep them alive.

In light of all the travails we experienced, we regretted that, as a family, we were unable to experience the celebration of Eli's return to Stoughton. The explanations were sketchy and fragmented, as Nat Stowe shared them, but I saw it as a miracle. This was a moment in time where, somehow by chance, certain people converged in the same place at the same time. Auntie called it an act of God. There were more details to the story, but I had no idea when they would be revealed to us.

We were advised by Mr. Adams to refrain from sending mail anywhere, especially to Uncle Jacob and family. Owing to the threats and, finally, the dreadful skirmish caused by the Big Englishman, we thought it best to avoid drawing attention to Mulberry Farm. The notoriety of the famous beer had distinguished itself more than we realized, and now, it became necessary to ensure its protection.

The British prided themselves on asserting their power to confiscate certain properties, particularly properties belonging to wealthy colonists. Father was dead set against sending notes by a messenger on horseback.

There was a genuine prospect that said person could be imprisoned on a British ship or that our families could be identified as conspirators. Tory eyes and ears pervaded Boston's streets.

As we got to know about Nat Stowe's family and he got to know about ours, it dawned on him that the Randolphs in Boston were related to the Randolphs in Stoughton. That's when we learned about Whales' Tale tavern—the Penrose brothers, their *shipping* business, and how Eli's bout with malaria brought him in contact with Nat Stowe, who happened to be visiting friends in New Haven, Connecticut.

I was mostly interested in how Eli was adjusting to his new life at Mulberry Farm and where he was imprisoned for the last twelve years, I explained to Father. He assured me that only Eli could supply those answers. "The British will not take up space in Boston forever," he said. "Keep reminding yourself that someday you will be riding with great speed atop Gertie. In the meantime, have patience." I knew from past experience that his answer would have to satisfy me for the time being. My distress for our current entrapment did not lessen.

I remained seated at the sunny windows, enjoying the orange and yellow marigolds and lettuce planted in the flower garden. I was finishing my lukewarm tea, experiencing a tiny sense of bliss mixed with overwhelming confusion with the ever-changing events totally out of our control. My little voice whispered that some days are filled with drama. After listening to Father's explanation of covert activities happening right under our noses, I couldn't help but anguish over his involvement with the Sons of Liberty; something life-changing was bound to be on the horizon.

I heard the surgery bell ring. Father answered the call by stepping onto the surgery stoop to welcome our friend Thomas Crafts. This had become common practice for Father to discuss a patient's ailment outside to allay suspicions where a Tory spy might be within ear reach.

"Good morning, Mr. Crafts. Having a problem with your arm? Come inside, and I'll take a look." Father gazed at the bandage wrapped around the man's left forearm. His shirt was limp, soaked with sweat, and stuck to his wet skin.

Thomas removed the loose bandage to reveal a nasty-looking boil filled with pus, surrounded by puffy, inflamed flesh. I stood viewing the scene from a distance. I quickly tied an apron over my dress and washed my hands in a solution of alcohol and water. I poured hot water over a large blunt-tipped needle, knowing Father would need to use it as a probe to release the yellowish secretion. From there, I assembled the beginnings of a poultice.

Thomas seated himself on a stool and began talking while Father examined his arm, cleaned the surrounding area with alcohol, and then probed the wound. Talking was a distraction for Thomas, which we were accustomed to. "I suppose you know about the delegates who are meeting in Philadelphia. I'm not sure what good it will do, but something is better than nothing, I reckon."

"Let me see. I'm sure of John Adams and Sam and possibly Elbridge Gerry. Who else would be brave enough to travel south in this scorching heat to a place hotter than Boston?" Father asked while pressing gently around the core of the boil.

Thomas mouthed a profane word and winced, "Right, and Robert Treat Paine and Thomas Cushing." He scowled and tried to remain calm. For a big, burly man, he certainly had a low resistance to pain, I thought, watching his eyes water. Boils could be very painful. "Do you think they will write a letter to Parliament to try to reconcile our differences?" he asked Father.

"They might, but the king won't accept it. According to Sam Adams, Parliament believes colonists have crossed the mark and are in open revolt against England. Speaking of which, if it had not been for Sam, there would never be this unity that has brought the colonies to meet in one central location to discuss their grievances. In my opinion, the best that can come of this congress would be to elect a commander to organize an army to fight the redcoats. The sooner, the better," Father declared.

Thomas blew out a breath, knowing deep down that Father was right. He bit down on his lower lip when Father pressed his thumbs down on the purplish sore, intending to start the ooze of fluid captured underneath the patient's tough skin. "That's what happened in '61 when we drove out the French. I've got the scar to prove it." Thomas looked in my direction. "Your father saved my leg, in case you didn't know." I raised my brow and nodded.

"Gazing upon Main Street, I see red in every direction." I retorted in disgust. "Sickening."

"They've anchored their warships and transports in the harbor around Dorchester peninsula and Castle Island. I would say they have us surrounded," Father maintained.

Thomas was more than a friend to our family. More like an extension of our family. He and Father had served in the British army fighting the French and their Indian allies. Father had recruited Thomas as a surgeon's assistant, removing bullets and tending to soldiers' needs, from frozen toes to "soldier's fever." Watching him at this moment, he didn't look like he could stomach the sight of blood.

He was a genius carpenter, truly a craftsman, who understood how barns and buildings were assembled to survive the extreme weather conditions in New England. For all his workmanship on our Bradford Lane home, we were happy to compensate him and his family with medical aid.

With my back turned toward the two men, I sterilized a lancet and covered it with a clean cloth while Father probed and Thomas talked. I had learned from past experiences not to expose sharp surgical instruments for patients to view in plain sight, sometimes causing them to have a change of heart and excuse themselves from the premises.

Thomas ceased talking when he saw Father eyeing the boil and shaking his head. I stood poised at Father's side as he took hold of the shiny lancet. "Thomas, look towards the windows, take a deep breath, and release it slowly." Poor man didn't have a chance to think. He trusted the doctor. Father held the sharp tip of the instrument at a slant. Without pause, he placed the perfect degree of pressure needed to slice into the tip of the core. The yellowish fluid flowed, and a gush of blood followed.

"Dare I look?" Thomas asked reluctantly. Definitely squeamish at the sight of blood. "What's next?"

"Let's give it a few minutes for the sore to ooze and air itself. Then we will apply a poultice," Father instructed. He suggested Thomas take a seat in the leather armchair at the side windows to catch a pleasant view of the line of fruit-laden trees along Bradford Lane. The same apples and pears Auntie and I planned to pluck off before the end of the day.

Thomas sat unusually expressionless as Father and I began sterilizing our instruments and tidying the surgery for the next patient, making small talk all along. Auntie entered the room with a tray holding a pot of ginger and honey tea and slices of seed cake, permeating the front room's atmosphere with sweet and tart aromas as she swept through, drawing Thomas' attention.

Always a thoughtful hostess, Auntie was aware their visitor anticipated some sustenance after driving his wagon the long distance from Lexington. More than that, she was looking for answers about the current state of affairs on the other side of the Charles River. It was unsettling enough just to have them encamped on this side of the river.

There was no need in bribing Thomas to extract secrets. He was more than willing to lay out the facts as he knew them, for he felt he had nothing to hide in our company. After all, he and Father were Freemasons and partners in the Sons of Liberty, working together in the colonies' defense.

"How is Lexington coping with this talk of revolution?" Auntie asked bluntly. She rarely minced words. She sought the facts, knowing that Thomas was the man to discharge them.

Thomas sipped his hot tea, proceeding to communicate what he knew was the truth, knowing Auntie would accept no less. "The militia is growing by leaps and bounds; more Whigs than Tories these days. The clergy are preaching the revolutionary spirit to their congregations, hoping to scare off those loyal to the king. Doing a good job of that. I guess you would know since so many are taking up residence in Boston. The issue with Tories is they're often seen talking to redcoat soldiers in the taverns and such, publicly giving themselves away. They're shunned by Patriots, so, out of fear for their lives, they high tail it out of the countryside to Boston. There's no place for them in Lexington.

"To the point, Tories showed their colors during our town meetings by letting it be known that they were not opposed to Parliament raising taxes. They have publicly slammed Sam Adams' efforts to unify the colonies, believing the only thing he's good for is causing insurrection and starting fights and riots.

"As for the redcoat soldiers, they remain in pursuit of our stashed weapons and gunpowder, regularly nosing around taverns, asking questions, and offering threats to patrons if they do not consent to their demands. I daresay every man, woman, and youngster has been trained in using a musket. A farmer doesn't give up his property so easily. He will fight for it.

"It's right noisy along Main Street. How do you bear it?" Thomas inquired with a degree of noticeable contempt in his observation.

"Whatever do you mean?" Auntie chimed in a facetious response. "You have militia drills in Lexington. Don't they create the same mind-numbing racket?"

"We do have hundreds upwards to a thousand, and they do produce an aggravating racket. Nothing as ear-splitting as these parading regulars. Drilling in wide open spaces may be the difference," Thomas concluded.

"Have another cup of tea, Thomas. It solves all that ails you!" Auntie offered. "I'm more concerned with how you arrived here and how you plan to return home. What about the guards over your way?"

"With the help of an old acquaintance," he replied with a wry grin. Auntie gave him an odd look.

"You remember Elias Denton, don't you, Josiah?" Father nodded. "I took the long route from Lexington and never encountered a redcoat until I got to the Neck. Elias is the head guard there. He's a Whig, you know. He asked about you."

"I stitched him up a few times," remembered Father.

"I'd say you saved his life a few times, and he has not forgotten it. The man kept shaking his head, saying how sorry he was that the king had ordered so many troops over here to invade Boston. Don't understand it, he said. Thousands in England are rooting for you Patriots, even some in Parliament," Thomas declared matter-of-factly.

While Thomas and Father entertained one another with war stories, Auntie and I gathered our wooden pails and headed outside to pick apples and pears. "I never thought to question Thomas where he stored our silver and good china on Mulberry Farm. You think we should ask him?" Auntie reminded me as her long arms reached high up the apple tree.

Three months ago, when our family was in the throes of dealing with the Big Englishman and his relentless chicanery, Mr. Adams wisely suggested that Thomas give Uncle Jacob some assistance at the farm concerning security matters. The pressure of completing the new malting house before the arrival of fall weather was another concern. Thomas, as big as he was and given that carpentry had been his line of work since he was a youngster, worked three times as fast as Ethan and Harry. He welcomed the opportunity for the visit, knowing that our family needed protection from the murderous villain. Thomas was well aware of the rare cuisine my aunt Lenora served up daily.

Before Thomas left for Stoughton and before British soldiers had filled our streets, he stopped by Bradford Lane to inform us he was departing for Mulberry Farm, wondering if we had any messages for our family there. He happened to mention that any of our treasured and valuable possessions would be best secured at the farm, not placing any trust in curious soldiers who would eventually station themselves along Main Street.

Auntie jumped at that suggestion and began filling burlap sacks with two silver tea services, our good china, Delftware from Holland, which was part of my mother's dowry, along with her jewelry and silk gowns. Father and I hurriedly gathered personal items that we valued. We parked our possessions on the scullery floor and began loading Thomas' wagon.

"Well, good thing I asked!" he commented with raised eyebrows. Before he left Bradford Lane with his packed wagon, Auntie paid him for his kindness with a corked jug of cider and a bag of corn cakes and cheese. He was smiling with contentment when he pulled onto Main Street.

After filling four wooden pails with fruit, the thought occurred to me that Lenora, caring about our family treasures as if they were her own, would likely have Ethan and Harry dig out a six-foot hole in the cemetery and safely store our possessions in a spot that looked like a grave.

I pulled a handkerchief from my sleeve to wipe the sweat off my face and neck until I could return indoors to wash. Auntie and I had resolved weeks before when the July heat became so unbearable that tying a scarf over our head was one way to keep our hair moderately clean and reduce the threat of flying insects to our scalp. Today, Auntie and I donned such a head covering and were proud of it. If there's anything I hate, it is a bee swarming about my head while I'm working.

When Auntie demonstrated how she tightly stretched the muslin headpiece from the top of her forehead, over and around her ears, and securely knotted at the base of her neck, I commented that she looked like a nun in a French hospital. After a few attempts, I picked up on her skill and realized the purpose it served, well-suited for outside work.

I recalled the first time Father encountered our scarved heads. He stood bent over the kitchen fireplace, stoking the embers under the big copper kettle, when Auntie and I entered through the scullery after we had pulled weeds and hung wet linens on the clothesline. "Reviving your years as a voyager?" He looked up at Auntie with raised eyebrows. "I do believe an eyepatch would complete your costume as a pirate." We snickered. He gently chided us as looking churlish and unprofessional, requesting we remove said scarf when attending patients.

We had picked apples and pears for an hour and were spent, eager to get out of the unforgiving heat. As I proceeded toward the scullery, I heard a familiar voice coming from across Bradford Lane and set down the heavy pails of fruit.

Ezra Phillips walked across the narrow dirt lane, his left arm bound in a sling and his cut finger bandaged, as Father had mentioned this morning. "Good morning, ladies," he bowed, revealing his sunburned pate, sparsely covered with thinning strands of golden hair. "I'd like the doctor to change the bandage on my finger."

He held up the index finger on his left hand, noticing my eyes focused on the sling. "Oh, this," he said as he touched the side of the roughly installed cloth around his arm and neck. "There's no problem here—merely for show." He cast his eyes sideways at the soldiers across the street.

"There is a particular soldier who parks himself across the street each morning outside of what was once Nettle's Dry Goods store. Don't look, just smile. A plainclothes man, probably a Tory informer, stops and speaks to him at intervals, writing notes as the soldier gives an account of activities on this section of Main Street."

Auntie and I immediately caught on to his disguise and jointly decided that we could play the undercover game as well. We turned Mr. Phillips' attention to our apple and pear picking by pointing to the trees, making cursory comments related to our plans to transform the fruit into conserves this afternoon.

"Allow us to escort you to the surgery, Mr. Phillips." Auntie took the lead, followed by the patient, toward the surgery entrance and rang the bell. Father stepped outside on the small stoop to greet Mr. Phillips, running his eyes over his slinged arm and making comments about a new bandage for the printer's finger. It was obvious to Father that the rudimentary sling was more of a ruse for the soldier's benefit.

"Let's go inside and have a look, Mr. Phillips." Father graciously helped his patient inside and closed the door. Auntie and I set the heavy pails of fruit on the scullery floor, relieved to take a break from impromptu visitors sharing secret information.

The week before, Ezra Phillips sought help at the surgery with a nasty cut on his forefinger. He had inadvertently slashed it with a sharp knife while cutting into a ream of printing paper. After Father stitched the cut, I sponged the inflamed area with an astringent and waited a few moments before dressing the wound. "How has Mrs. Phillips and the children managed during these troubling times?" I asked him.

"They're in a safe place away from Boston. Miranda and the children are residing in Braintree, where her parents work a farm. She was very troubled with all the activity in May when British regiments pulled into our harbor carrying thousands of soldiers and horses and supplies on their armed warships. She was distraught when she learned Boston's port would be closed, putting men out of work, thereby causing the likelihood of riots and crime. That did it for her. 'I cannot raise two children in a hostile environment.'

"The following day, we loaded a wagon with trunks and set off for the country." He grimaced and shook his head. "Most nights, I sleep on a pallet in my shop with a loaded pistol by my side."

I asked about the family home in North Square with it being vacated. "Mr. Revere and his oldest daughter look after it. With all his children, they sometimes stay overnight, allowing his wife, Deborah, some relief from managing the house and the children, giving the appearance that it is occupied."

It was true. Governor Gage allowed British officers quartering rights in empty houses in Boston by a decree signed by Parliament, part of their Intolerable Acts.

Auntie and I shed our scarves and set to work peeling apples and pears, leaving Father to deal with Ezra and Thomas. "Where did you find the lemons? I thought we were out," I asked Auntie.

"We were out. I walked to Eleanor Foster's house while you helped Josiah. She had plenty of lemons and limes. She's been such a good neighbor all these years," Auntie answered.

"Uh, we're making the conserves today?" I asked. "Seems like a big job to do all in the same day."

"It is a big job. Do you have other plans for the day? If not, there's no time like the present!"

"These apples seem underripe, don't you think?" It sounded like I was making excuses. I had hoped to start a new book today and retreat to my favorite reading spot. My mind needed a break, but Auntie was too practical-minded to allow the fresh pickings to sit unattended. A quote from B. Franklin via Aunt Minnie floated through my mind: *Be always employed in something useful.* I guess that means me.

"They're not underripe, Josie. You'll see what I mean when the fruit is cooked. The juices within make the perfect gel for conserves. I see you found the walnuts and the cinnamon. Let's get started."

"I'm more eager to see how it all transforms into a delicious spread for fresh hot bread. The end result, so to speak." I began peeling fruit.

I thought back to just three months before when we visited Mulberry Farm, all the delicious smells of pies and confections flowing from Aunt Lenora's kitchen. She and Naomi sent us home with all sorts of flower and vegetable seeds, which, without delay, we planted in our backyard. Now harvested and shared with our patients and neighbors.

On the trip back to Boston, we had overfilled the carriage with canvas bags and stacked boxes holding more than enough food supplies for the three of us. Auntie sat in her small corner on the bumpy ride home, folding her long legs in an uncomfortable position while holding seedlings of beans, radishes, pumpkin, and melon. All these vegetables kept our bellies fed during these summer months while so many people were doing without. The only vegetable we were lacking was corn.

"Did I hear someone mention fresh corn?" Heavy footsteps belonging to Thomas Crafts approached the kitchen where Auntie and I stood chopping the fruit, covering it generously with lemon juice.

I laughed. "Yes, we hope to get some fresh corn from the Harmon Farm in the next week or so." I was fearful the summer heat may have dried it out, thus giving it up to the hogs. "How does your corn look this year? Ripe for picking?" I hoped. Nothing better than hot, buttered corn.

"I depend on my cousin Leonard for corn and beans and such. He's the farmer in the family. Albeit, I do help him with the haying. It's a tradeoff. I repair his barn and outbuildings, and he keeps me eating well enough."

While Thomas drank a cup of tea and talked, we continued stirring the bubbling fruit and juices in an oversized roasting pan positioned over a low-burning fire. With my skirts tucked up for safety purposes, I relieved Auntie and pulled a chair to sit inside the fireplace to continue stirring the sugar into the apples and pears, miraculously mixing with the fruit juices to form a gel. While I stirred, Auntie emptied a jar of currants into the mix, along with more lemon juice, walnuts, and cinnamon. With great relief and a cramped right arm, I set the steaming pan on the table. Auntie skimmed the pinkish foam off the top, followed by expertly spooning the jellied mixture into the small crocks, promptly sealing them with heavy paper and cording.

"Not bad for a day's work. Let's take what's left in the pan and spread it on some fresh bread," I suggested, noticing Thomas' eyes getting big and happy with the prospect of such a treat becoming a reality.

Auntie looked up from her work when Father and Mr. Phillips walked into the kitchen, pursuing the flavorful scents of fresh bread and spices. "Why not make a party of it?" She laughed, inviting everyone around the table.

I set out the yellow mugs and poured the tea. "I haven't experienced an occasion such as this in ages," Mr. Phillips stated, lifting his cup in appreciation. "Good neighbors are hard to come by these days." We all laughed at the irony of that statement.

While our visitors enjoyed freshly baked bread and freshly made conserves, we listened to Thomas Crafts' monologue describing life in his neck of the woods in Lexington. "I believe it is safe to say that we have done an adequate job of frustrating the governor. I'm not saying that he's going to turn tail back to London, nor am I saying that British soldiers won't draw arms on us at any given time."

"Exactly, what are you saying, Mr. Crafts?" Auntie asked the man, knowing full well they would be listening to his tale until all the tea and bread had been consumed by three hungry men.

"We've outwitted him on the General Court by administering our own justice instead of recognizing the king's appointed judges. We've withdrawn two hundred barrels of gunpowder and various ammunition belonging to the militia from the powder house on Quarry Hill. We've threatened resistance by arming our militia. We've fed and housed thousands of Bostonians who otherwise would have starved.

"Boston's selectmen have voted five delegates to join with over fifty delegates to assemble in Philadelphia to meet with representatives from the colonies to create a united government." Thomas stopped long enough to drink his tea and slather on a healthy spoonful of conserves on another slice of bread. Mr. Phillips listened intently, nodding his head occasionally as he chewed.

I rather enjoyed Thomas' account of hard-headed Massachusetts leaders who refused to surrender their farms and their prospects for future business. It dawned on me that Parliament was toying with people's lives in the colonies by manipulating established charters and alliances as they felt so inclined. I looked across the table at Father and Thomas Crafts, two former soldiers who had risked their lives so England, not France, could hold claim to coastal colonies, the Appalachian Mountains, and far beyond the Mississippi River territories. Now, they have the nerve to attempt acquisition of settled lands that were once nothing but dark and bloody wilderness, transformed by ambitious colonials into something civilized with burgeoning towns and farmlands. There was no way these uncompromising Patriots would give an inch to these blue-blooded loons.

I took my handkerchief from my sleeve to wipe the sweat from my face and neck, evidence that I had worked myself into a frenzy, bursting inside with animosity towards greedy, high-handed patricians who believed they possessed absolute power to incarcerate us along with other colonies they had conquered around the world, many of them living in mud houses and trying to plow depleted farmland.

"Josie, are you quite alright?" Father asked me while fireworks exploded inside me, shooting off beams of hostility. Apparently, it showed in my demeanor. "Perhaps you should take some air."

With our visiting patients on their way home, each in possession of a jar of conserves and fresh bandages for their wounds, we wished Thomas well on his journey home and assured Ezra he was welcome anytime to a hot meal.

Purposely taking my mind off the everlasting drum and fife sounds, and with Auntie safely ensconced in the garden, I sipped my raspberry and peppermint tea and seated myself in my cozy reading spot in the keeping room. As always happens, my eyes swept across the long wall where the cupboard was set, pausing to stare at what remained of crockery and chinaware and a small tea service that gave definition to my mother's refined taste. The moment wilted when I realized that the shelves had been gradually emptied. Another reminder of British cruelty, robbing me of precious moments to meditate on my mother.

I was only several pages into my book where Robinson Crusoe was deep in discussion with his father that an adventure at sea was more to his liking than making a life for himself in the county of York, England. I continued reading until the character endured his first storm at sea. Right then, the surgery bell rang, and I called for Father. The bell rang again, and I jumped up from my cozy spot to see Father outside conversing with Auntie. I knocked on the window and motioned him inside.

Tying on an apron, I joined Father in the surgery. He had seated a man who was holding a blood-soaked handkerchief to his nostrils, clearly an unstoppable nosebleed. I laid out some clean linens and handed Father a small bowl from the cabinet. "Lean forward slightly, breathe through your mouth, and pinch both nostrils firmly. Allow the blood to drip into the bowl," he instructed the patient. "I'll tell you when to let go. Prop your elbow on this table if your arm gets tired."

I looked about the floor for any blood drippings. None that I could see. The afternoon sun shone brightly through the front windows facing Main Street, giving a clear view of a soldier pacing slowly in front of the deserted stores, looking occasionally at our house. I wondered about the identity of the new patient. Could he be a newly settled Tory? If so, he was putting on a good act with his bloody nose.

Father suggested I start a cup of yarrow tea for our patient. We use the plant as a cure-all, and it has proved to be an effective medicine for healing wounds. It's a good thing, too. Auntie and I brought home a massive quantity of yarrow from Mulberry Farm and more from Eloise Pierpoint's garden. We were overstocked, to say the least.

"How do you feel, Mister… I'm sorry, I never caught your name. I would like to record it in my patient journal." Father looked at the man, catching a strained demeanor and red-rimmed eyes, waiting for an answer.

"Of course. It's Ebenezer Crichton. I recently moved from the country to a house on Salt Street." The man's face was pale and sickly looking after losing so much blood, but he was genial under the circumstances. "In the process of cleaning the house, blood began pouring uncontrollably. There was no stopping it. I noticed a soldier walking down the street and inquired about the nearest doctor. He suggested your surgery, Dr. Randolph. Can you give me a reason for this copious bleeding?"

"Most likely caused by dust and dirt accumulated in your nostrils while you were cleaning, causing irritation. You will find the caustic air in Boston menacing to your breathing compared with the fresh air in the countryside. We're a bit more restricted with our houses and businesses built closely together in this small landmass, spreading contagions amongst its inhabitants. You will adjust, but you must take precautions by drinking medicinal teas and eating fruits and vegetables.

"Pinching your nostrils as you did encourages the blood to clot, which will seal the damaged blood vessels inside your nose. Now that the bleeding has stopped, don't blow your nose for several hours." Father wrote notes in the bulging black journal while I assisted Mr. Crichton.

It dawned on me that the Bignall family lived in a small house on Salt Street. I tried to envision the placement of their house in relation to neighboring houses, but the remembrance wasn't coming through clearly. That brought back to me the task I had set for myself to find out if the Bignalls had moved to the country. I could have asked Thomas Crafts if I had a mind to think of it before he departed earlier.

I could ask Mr. Crichton, sitting not three feet away from me, but I knew Father would give me a cross look, asking a total stranger such direct questions. *I'll attend it later*, I thought.

"Hello, I'm Josie Randolph. Would you like a wet cloth to clean up?" The patient stood when I introduced myself. He had a businessman look to him, wearing smart clothing and shoes and a recent shave. I noted when he accepted the wet cloth that he had clean fingernails and smooth palms, indicating he was not a tradesman or a farmer.

When he returned the slightly bloody cloth, he smiled, showing a mouth full of teeth, at least for all I could tell, proof that he was not the type of man who got into fights. All these signs led me to wonder why a man would move from the countryside in western Massachusetts to a three-room house in a province besieged by British soldiers. Naturally, I decided he must be a Tory escaping the bloodthirsty Patriots in Lexington. Oh well, I'm sure his identity will be revealed in due course.

"I made you an herb tea with yarrow to stanch the nosebleed." I set the tea on the table, which he began drinking immediately, not sure if he was just thirsty or anxious for a cure. I hope it was the latter.

Mr. Crichton stood looking around the room. His eyes stopped when he spotted Father's medical degree, framed and mounted on the side of one of the bookshelves. "I'm most appreciative of your help. Studied in Edinburgh, I see. May I say this is the cleanest surgery I have ever seen?"

Father looked at the patient and smiled in response. "We appreciate your business. Try not to push yourself cleaning your house. Do you have a family member helping you, perchance?"

"My son Eben is working on that at the moment. It's only the two of us in the small house," he answered. "What do I owe ye fer your services?"

"That will be four shillings. If you need my services again, you may stop in for a visit or send word, and I will come to your place." Mr. Crichton paid Father with silver coins, and before taking his leave, I gave him a package of yarrow tea.

Father and I walked to the front windows to see which direction he was walking. "I guess he truly lives on Salt Street," I surmised. I'm sure Father recognized Mr. Crichton's accent as did I, ever so slight when he spoke of his son, probably from the Scottish Lowlands but definitely not as heavy as Ozzie MacClure's heavy brogue and burr.

Still wearing my apron, I mixed a pan of alcohol and water and began washing down the surgery table and the wooden chairs used by today's patients. I found I was able to settle myself and collect my scattered thoughts. The mundane work of cleaning compelled me to reflect on the day's events and conversations, allowing me to consider the unexpected patients who had dropped in today. "This is the cleanest surgery I have ever seen," I recalled Mr. Crichton's comment. If he noticed Father's proclivity for cleanliness, I'm sure others had as well. I scrubbed with more enthusiasm.

Standing next to the back windows, I gazed across the street at Mr. Phillips' print shop. He said he sometimes slept on a pallet on the floor. He probably never gets a full night's sleep—concerned about his wife and children and contemplating narratives for future issues of *The Recorder*.

Newspaper writers are much like spies, sometimes called *sources*, I had read. They doggedly follow leads, by instinct, that could turn into big story headlines, keeping their eyes and ears open like a dog on the hunt. Local provincial notices such as Lost and Found, church meetings, or quilting bees may fill the blank spaces of a newspaper, but it's the headline that draws a reader's attention and sells newspapers.

Mr. Phillips depended on his spies—maids, butlers, cooks, gardeners, and footmen who served their Tory lords and masters in Boston's wealthy homes. Bits and pieces of information surreptitiously reached the ears of Ezra Phillips and, from there, combined what was already public knowledge along with confidential snippets meant for print in his weekly newspaper. Anything to goad Governor Gage and, of course, sell newspapers.

Political cartoons depicting London's ministers and Parliament members were especially popular. In one special edition of *The Recorder*, Ezra, or more than likely his wife, Miranda, had sketched a caricature of King George as a giant walking across the ocean wearing a coonskin hat atop his white wig and pointing a musket in Boston's direction. Written on the sole of his extraordinarily large boot were the words, "fifty pounds a head for Adams and Hancock."

Some articles contained quotes from the *London Times* of Englanders who were sympathetic to the cause of Patriots struggling to survive the gloomy conditions of besieged Boston. Members of Parliament who called themselves Whigs, Edmund Burke, for one, appealed repeatedly to his fellow lords that the use of force in the colonies was not the answer. Instead, seeking conciliation versus conquest made more sense. By printing such speeches in *The Recorder*, Ezra's aim was directed at the fence sitters, colonists who sympathized with Tories *and* Patriots but were hesitant to pledge their allegiance to either side.

Bostonians React Under Intolerable Acts was the headline in a recent edition printed the first week in August. "No truer words than those," I told Auntie. These new laws passed by Parliament bolstered Governor Gage's power when the word came from London that the Massachusetts colonial government was annulled. Now, the governor set to work replacing the colonial judges, sheriffs, and justices of the peace with royal appointees. Town meetings were abolished—now considered unlawful, as far as Gage and Parliament were concerned.

Sam Adams and the selectmen were incensed but continued their meetings anyway. Since their meetings could not be held in Boston, they leaped from one county to another—Worcester, Milton, Essex, Plymouth, and Bristol—to avoid interference by British soldiers and militant Tories, but always protected by armed colonial militia.

Beyond keeping Provincials from starving, there were additional matters within the province that required urgent decision-making. Dr. Warren's Committee of Safety stepped in with a show of force when several thousand rebels surrounded the county seat in Worcester, forbidding the new royal judges the opportunity to take the bench.

All the while, Sam Adams provided his most recent correspondence with New York and other New England colonies with dispatches from newspapers, including his personal accounts of all the goings on of the siege and Governor Gage's demands. He called for unity among the colonies to stop the consumption of British imports.

Paul Revere was one of several express riders who hit the roads weekly to deliver the latest news to taverns along the Boston Post Road, whipping up resistance as he traveled.

Father maintained that Parliament had propelled colonists to take defensive action. For the past ten years, with all their taxing requirements and complicated import and export rules, "rebellion is our only course of action without losing everything."

It was after eating a late afternoon meal of salad with fresh radishes and pickled onions that Father opened up to us with new information from Ezra Phillips. We were drinking our tea when he handed us each a copy of this week's newspaper with the headline:

A Game of Cat and Mouse
By Ezra Phillips, Editor, Boston Recorder
The Eve of September 5, 1774

The absolute power of the Tories' savior, the king's finest general, and the Big Cat. This describes the Honorable Thomas Gage, who arrived on Boston's shore three months prior with high hopes of bringing order and peace to the Province of Massachusetts Bay. He envisioned throttling those defiant colonists into submission by turning the Patriot's world upside down, including those incendiary leaders. Radical colonists who preached rebellion against forced illegal revenues, an established church, restricted trade on imports and exports with European countries, and British officials placed in charge of local governments.

The governor's royal orders: close the port of Boston, enforce the closure by filling the Province with four thousand British soldiers, confiscate all weapons and ammunition from the Provincials, cessation of town meetings and the General Court, break the backs of merchants, warehouse workers, longshoremen, and craftsmen. These are all men and women who earned a wage stemming from their labor and products, which occurred when privately owned ships flowed in and out of Boston's harbor.

I would venture to say that this very night, as I print this newspaper, the honorable governor is sitting alone in his grand accommodations at Province House, sipping his glass of sherry, pondering how to respond to King George and his lords. All his efforts to subdue thousands of radical colonists have resulted in naught. Likely scheming the next step he will take to "conquer" these revolutionaries.

Governor Gage, may I inform you that all the mice have scattered to the countryside. They are armed, as you well know, and will continue to make laws for the Massachusetts colony, elect judges, and keep the peace despite your fabricated government that holds no power and endurance. Chase us if you will, but we are cunning and resourceful, dedicated to preserving our liberties.

Five elected representatives from Massachusetts have traveled to Philadelphia to join with delegates from other coastal colonies to make decisions about our very existence in these colonies. You must understand that tens of *thousands of colonists have been fighting a personal war with Britain for the past fourteen years by weighing the options of holding onto their property or submitting to the Crown by paying taxes to fill London's coffers. Poor farmers cannot afford both. Our resistance is deep-seated. Your Intolerable Acts are fading out of sight.*

Take heed, Governor Gage. These self-reliant colonists would rather do without than submit to the wishes of your king!

"It's a wonder that the poor soul hasn't been arrested for treason. How does he get away with publishing such an assault on the governor?" Auntie asked, shaking her head in dismay.

He will continue printing such assaults because it's his right to speak his mind, I theorized silently. The predictability of our lives continuing as they had for so many years was nothing more than a distorted illusion that Boston could possibly come back from this catastrophe. These destructive changes happening right before our eyes were nightmarish for me. Father glanced at me and winked, naturally reading my thoughts.

"I suppose you're planning to read while there's still light," Auntie naturally assumed. The *Robinson Crusoe* book lay where I left it on the settle when Mr. Crichton arrived with a bloody nose.

"Perhaps so. Truly, I've had about all the excitement I can bear today. I believe a bath is in order, and it could take a while." I smiled and rose from the table to heat a kettle of water.

Chapter 28

Philadelphia

September 5, 1774, Carpenter's Hall in Philadelphia

Colonial settlers came to the New World for varied reasons. Some came to get rich; some came to become landowners; most came because religious reasons were as strong as economic ones. Such was the case with William Penn, who founded the colony of Pennsylvania in 1682 as a refuge for Quakers and persecuted religious minorities. In exchange for an unpaid loan made by his father, from Sir William Penn to King Charles II, Penn asked for a charter granting him lands to start a colony across the sea. Almost a hundred years later, the land that lay between the Schuylkill and the Delaware Rivers was the most prosperous and modern within the thirteen colonies.

The name Benjamin Franklin was synonymous with Philadelphia, Pennsylvania. The sociable, self-taught, community-minded, free-thinking young apprentice learned the printing business by the age of seventeen. He was too clever-minded to stand at a printing press for the balance of his life. It would seem that Franklin's career choices advanced him on an industrious mission toward that of a professional tradesman. Stemming from that successful and ambitious spirit, he evolved into an inventor, author, philosopher, and diplomat. His arcane nature set him apart from his peers, promoting him to use his wits and common sense to attack the challenges faced by the thirteen colonies during a time when independence was on the minds of self-determined Patriots.

Benjamin Franklin wholeheartedly sought to defend the rights of the colonies.

It was Monday morning when delegates from twelve of the thirteen colonies gathered outside Carpenter's Hall, under shady chestnut trees, to chat and make acquaintances. They were anxious to meet the popular men from Boston: John Adams, the famous lawyer who argued for British soldiers and their captain four years prior, and Sam Adams, author and driver of *communiqués* alerting the colonies that the original charter made with Britain was now in peril—betrayed by Parliament's Lords to suit the Crown.

Delegates were expecting to shake the hand of the enterprising John Hancock, the merchant king, as he was known. He had devoted his professional life to building businesses and ships and employing thousands of men to keep the province of Boston thriving. His supporters were disappointed to learn that he elected to stay home and keep a watchful eye on newly appointed Governor Gage, for he aimed to protect all that he and his uncle had built for the past fifty years. Under those circumstances, delegates understood his position.

As these fifty-four visitors stood in the largest and wealthiest province in the colonies, they could not help but see the fingerprints of the famous Benjamin Franklin—the hospital and medical college, numerous bookstores and print shops, libraries, street lamps, and stately buildings.

The mission of the delegates was clear. They must come to terms with the reckless Intolerable Acts imposed on the colonies by Parliament. In addition, an important high point on the minds of these men who had traveled for days and weeks to the city of brotherly love was, "When do we meet Dr. Franklin?"

In actuality, Benjamin Franklin temporarily resided in London. He had become a somewhat off-and-on fixture in this venue. On this, his third journey across the seas, which began in 1764, he was predisposed as a representative of the colonies. It was his mission to make the case to Parliament that colonists' refusal to pay their excessive taxes was believable. He maintained their tough spirit and would adamantly oppose any and all tyrannical oppression the Crown hurled in their direction.

Today, Philadelphia was a proud sight to behold for its leaders, welcoming delegates who had left their businesses to journey from New England and the middle and southern colonies. They stood in awe of the stately mansions, immense buildings, and broad streets that seemed never-ending, which undoubtedly culminated at the docks of the Delaware River, which was within walking distance.

Merchants and shopkeepers had planned for months to take advantage of this occasion to boost their profits by enticing delegates to shop and purchase items that may or may not be available in their own colony. Schooners full of merchandise had been docked at Philadelphia's port for weeks, unloading crates from the West Indies, France, and Holland.

The city's streets created a logical pattern: the vertical streets were numbered, and the horizontal streets were named for fruit and hardwood trees. William Penn, founder and designer of Philadelphia, envisioned paved streets lined with brick buildings for shops and churches and offices, complete with sidewalks and street lamps, beautified with all sorts of trees.

Bookstores and print shops offered the colonies' latest titles of pamphlets and tracts and novels from Europe. Taverns were plentiful and offered lodging and fine food. Depending on the proprietor, he aimed to provide a most excellent cuisine that would appeal to the various tastes of delegates. Such establishments were well stocked with Madeira, claret, wines, and beer, promising to meet the desires of the delegate's particular tastes. The bill of fare was designed to satisfy and delight the out-of-town customers by serving either rich gourmet cuisine or provincial food choices.

Horace Pelare nervously picked up one sheet of parchment after another, searching his desk for a list of printed names and backgrounds of the representatives from the colony of Virginia. "It's gone. It was just here last night. Sam! Where are you?" The man's plump red face poured sweat as he skirted around the noisy printing machine to the tall order desk stationed at the front entrance.

His eyes caught a movement outside on Market Street, where his seemingly inattentive apprentice stood chatting and smiling with an unrecognizable man dressed in a new suit of clothes, judging from his clean white stockings and polished shoes. "Another delegate," Horace barked, followed by a deep breath, then shaking his fist at the ceiling as he exhaled loudly. With a degree of composure, he opened the print shop door, attempting to alert his young employee. Hearing the bell ring, Sam concluded his conversation, satisfied that he had the beginnings of what would turn into his opinion piece for tonight's newspaper. He smiled confidently as he walked through to greet his boss.

"Good morning, Uncle Horace. I was just…" the young man, Samuel P. Crichton, the "P" stood for Pelare, his Swedish mother's maiden name. Sam had turned twenty on his last birthday and believed it was time to craftily edge away from the humdrum of setting fonts and printing newspapers and party invitations. This day, this historical day in his way of thinking, was his time to seize the opportunity to make a name for himself in a remarkable way as a newspaperman, a journalist, and perhaps a future writer for the *Philadelphia Enquirer* produced by Drake's News and Prints.

Sam owed his squarish facial lines and handsome bronzed coloring to his father, Samuel Crichton. A high forehead and dark blue eyes moved in sync when he spoke and listened, a fresh impression that instantly invited a hint of connection with his audience. A trait that could be a positive for a future newspaperman. His striking looks and appealing smile could not be misinterpreted, except by his uncle Horace, who looked past his nephew's appealing demeanor, being more concerned about receiving an honest day's work from the young man.

"Explain to me what you were doing out there, thinking you could flatter every plantation owner and Yankee you stopped in the street. No, I'd say you were making a fool of yourself, pretending to be somebody you're not! I have a paper to print tonight, and so far, I've written all the stories. Where's yours?" Horace bellowed. He looked into his nephew's keen eyes, searching for a plausible answer.

"I would say, Uncle Horace, some cool, refreshing water is just what you need." Sam held the half-filled cup to his uncle as a peace offering. Surprisingly, Horace took a sip, forcing a smile.

"It *is* cool and sweet," admitted Horace. Sam led him to take a seat on the tall stool at the desk, looking past his uncle's violent outburst. "Where did you find it, uh, the water?" he asked.

"Right outside Carpenter's Hall, where delegates were gathering before entering their meeting," he answered Horace tersely. Experience proved that providing his uncle with more facts than necessary sometimes caused *confusion* between the two. At that moment, Sam's attention was diverted to an oversized parchment attached to the wall by a nail. He walked over and pointed to the names of the three delegates he had spoken to earlier, committed them to memory, and left the room.

Horace watched this scene with interest and growled, "Who nailed this list to the wall?"

"You did, Uncle Horace. I'm finding it very useful," Sam answered. He walked up the steps to the writer's room and picked up a stick of chalk to begin sketching the faces of the three delegates from memory, their names and represented colonies, and their thoughts of what they might accomplish as a body of colonial representatives.

Before the noon bells pealed, Sam met his mother at the wagon parked near the side doors of Carpenter's Hall, where he began ladling cool water from the pails he had filled from the well earlier that morning. His mother set a collection of ceramic cups on wooden trays lined with white linen in anticipation of delegates thirsty for a cool drink. Arranged behind the cups, baskets of pastry sat tempting the visitors. "Refreshments for the hardworking delegates," she informed her son.

Sam had misgivings about his mother's business venture, believing the delegates would ignore her, thinking she could be a British spy. *A perfectly normal assumption*, he thought. Parliament and every Tory in Philadelphia were eager to pick up treasonous tidbits to report in their loyalist newspapers or at least to spread around taverns. He promptly rejected the idea when delegates made a beeline to Susannah's wagon. "Phff, what do I know? I'm just a reporter filling cups of water for thirsty Whigs!"

She charged two pence for each roll. An idea she had concocted as a means to earn ready cash to feed and house her son and mother. Gretchen Pelare, known as Gemma to her daughter and son, had worked hours preparing pastry before the first rooster crowed. Two bites of an unforgettable buttery delicacy stuffed with jam that could possibly mean repeat business for the duration of the congress. There was no way of knowing how long it would last. In Susannah's mind, it would not hurt to make a good first impression.

Who could turn their back on the gracious Susannah Crichton? Her heart-shaped face, with its fair complexion highlighting her pale blue eyes and yellowish braided hair pulled around in a bun, revealed a friendly nature. Something brave in her spirit arose since becoming a widow. Always a diligent, orderly, and energetic woman when her husband was in the best of health. After his sudden death, her resourcefulness had inched upwards for survival purposes. On a whim, she had gone to the trouble to provide tasty morsels and refreshing water to the Philadelphia visitors while they stretched their legs and mingled with fellow delegates.

It occurred to Sam that it might be an opportunity to learn about the goings on inside Carpenter's Hall while he aided his mother. *Hard work and a willing spirit never hurt anybody*, he thought. "A bite to tie you over until your afternoon meal," he listened to her cordial way with the crowd of thirsty men.

Naturally, Uncle Horace would rebuke his sister Susannah's efforts for participating in such a provincial scheme. *How would he know?* Sam asked himself. He stayed locked up in that stifling print shop from dawn until midnight, busily putting out the *Philadelphia Enquirer*. Frankly, his uncle would be surprised and embarrassed to learn what he and his mother did to make ends meet since his father's demise last year.

As the day wore on, Sam walked the horse away from the tree where she was tethered, nibbling grass and staring at passersby during the delegate's short break. Susannah stacked empty water cups in baskets, preparing the wagon for the trip home in the middle of a hot day. The chestnut bay naturally cooperated while Sam harnessed her to the wagon. "A lighter load when you travel home, Daisy," he said, rubbing her muzzle. He noticed the empty trays and baskets in the wagon's bed, marveling at his mother's industrious spirit. "Looks like she sold the whole lot."

She had smiled and made small talk as she filled cups with cool water and sold pastries to the delegates, some paying more than the two pence she had advertised. The men obliged her with compliments for her trouble in arranging the unexpected refreshments before they returned to the hall. "This is what I admire about Philadelphia: friendly people who see to the needs of others." One of the delegates from New Jersey spoke boldly. "Now, if only we could persuade Mrs. Crichton to honor us with more of that refreshing water for the balance of the week!" Other delegates cheered, prompting her to take a quick bob and flash a giddy smile.

"Go home, Mother, and take some rest. It will take me several hours to get my story set to print."

"I noticed you mingling with some of the delegates. They seemed agreeable to expressing their ideas. I'm proud of you, son." She fixed her water-filled eyes on his face and squeezed his hand. "Your Gemma is making meat pies for our afternoon meal; don't be late." She held the reins and made a clicking sound, prompting Daisy to walk on.

Susannah Crichton drove the wagon to her home on Apple Street, leaving behind the noise of the city, satisfied and relieved that the morning's work had met her expectations. She pulled into the dirt-packed drive and stopped at the covered porch outside the kitchen to unload the trays holding the clinking cups, intending to clean them in the wash tub later. *Guess I will need them for tomorrow morning*, she decided. She waved to her neighbor, Alfred Simpson, walking toward the back of his house, carrying two buckets of apples. He returned the greeting with a quick nod of his head in Susannah's direction.

Daisy stamped her right hoof and snorted, proclaiming her impatience to stretch her body and gallop at will. "I'm coming," Susannah assured the horse as she climbed up onto the seat of the wagon. "A bucket of oats and molasses is waiting for you." She drove the empty wagon through the doors of the barn, opened the back doors, and then led Daisy to the small fenced paddock and her trough of water.

Returning inside the barn, she noticed flyspecks flitting within a bar of brilliant light streaming through a crack in the roof, illuminating the stall where the milk cow once stood. A tear rolled down her face, reminding her that Samuel's absence remained at the surface of her emotions.

Selling the cow was a sacrifice, but it freed up time and effort that she could devote to the family business. It worked out well. Mr. Simpson offered to bring over a pail of milk after he milked his cows, charging her a meager two pence a pail, sometimes accompanied with a round of homemade cheese. Her mind turned to the afternoon of work awaiting her inside the house.

No small surprise when she walked into the kitchen saturated with the savory smells of onion and rosemary, suddenly aware she had skipped breakfast. Gretchen stood on the hearth, bent over, stirring the flavorful pot of goodness in one corner of the fireplace. "I'm starved, Gemma!" She sat at the table by the sunny window and poured out a cup of warm raspberry leaf tea. With closed eyes, the swallow of tea instantly took effect, restoring her spirits.

She needed a diversion. She had struggled all morning to hold back the deluge of tears that happens when important events occur, such as the meeting of delegates at Carpenter's Hall. *Samuel would have loved being by my side to serve such men who chanced their reputations as being treasonous*, she thought. He agreed that separation from England was part of the colonies' future, although it would be a struggle.

"Mr. Simpson brought over some apples." Gretchen tipped her head toward two pails of red and yellow fruit sitting in front of the big wooden cupboard, where each open shelf overflowed with yellow pottery—plates, cups, platters, and serving bowls. The base was filled with drawers containing odd collections of pewter utensils, knives, small tools, linens, and towels. Fruit and berry baskets sat haphazardly atop the cabinet, giving the impression someone tossed each basket upwards from a short distance, intending to secure it amongst the others.

Susannah stooped down to survey the colorful fruit. The sweet, tangy smell reached her nose. Spying what she judged to be a juicy, ready-to-eat apple, she turned it over in her hand to inspect it for wormholes, cleaned it with a handy towel, and began slicing it for her breakfast. Gretchen smiled at her daughter's cleverness. "I made a pan of flatbread after you left this morning if you're still hungry."

She looked across the long kitchen, past the cupboard, to the attached room. Her eyes lingered on the small fireplace where two lonely fire dogs stood amongst the cold, gray ashes. Two matched wooden chairs and a small round table in between adorned the gray slate hearth, all built with her father's hands as a wedding gift for Susannah and Samuel. The dark red cushioned seats were stuffed with horsehair, embellished with a lively contrast of bright yellow, orange, and green flowers and leaves embroidered by Gretchen, making the three-piece set an inviting centerpiece in the snug room.

A too familiar setting for the widow, where she and Samuel had sat together in the evenings drinking tea while he discussed details of his business, recounting transactions with his customers who resided in the Pennsylvania countryside, west of Philadelphia. Susannah listened attentively.

She walked guardedly into the room, never sure how her emotions would react to his silent presence in the room where he had spent so much of their married life. She walked to the windows, pushing the curtains aside to receive the morning light, exposing the stack of letters addressed to *Crichton Services of Pennsylvania* and two pieces with her name written across the front. Her heart jumped as she anxiously opened the letter from her cousin, Lenora Randolph.

Dearest cousin,

By the time you receive this missive, your town will by all accounts be in the throes of a most unusual convention of delegates, aiming to deliberate the entanglement our colony is presently enduring with Britain. Although we maintain our Mulberry Farm miles away from the troubles of Boston, we are feeling the effects of the siege, knowing our precious Josiah, Minerva, and Josie are trapped within the island as British soldiers have command of the waterways. The redcoat soldiers are preparing their encampment in Roxbury at this moment.

Our world changed for the better when, with the assistance of a young friend from Suffield, Connecticut, we rescued our beloved Eli Asher. He arrived home after living twelve years as a prisoner and slave of his former captain during that war fought so many years ago. We rightfully thought he was dead, but like Lazarus, he was brought back to life and in one piece. Naomi and Ethan are a complete family once again. As Naomi says so often, only "a miracle by God" protected her Eli.

I must express some concern for your husband's brother, Ebenezer, and his son while they make their living in Lexington. As you are aware, out-of-work merchants and longshoremen have fled Boston province, aiming to eke out a living in the countryside, bringing more chaos to the place. I fear for your brother-in-law's livelihood and the hazards that may ensue at the hands of the new Governor. I pray for Ebenezer's health and express my sympathy for the loss of his good wife, Lois.

I am convinced of your sound mind and capable hands to manage the occupation that your Samuel so diligently performed to support you, Gretchen and Sam. Your circumstances may seem overwhelming at times, but you have risen to the occasion as you naturally have a mind to do.

Jacob remains ready to assist legally if you encounter further foul play from your brother, Horace.

Your loving cousin,

Lenora

Susannah sorted through the stack addressed to *Crichton Services of Pennsylvania*, giving priority to the most urgent requests. Her husband, Samuel, and his brother, Ebenezer, had learned the business of *notaire*[49] from his father, the senior Samuel Crichton, an emigrant from Edinburgh in the 1690s. As a free man, a landowner, and having dutifully served as a selectman for two terms, he met the qualifications to launch his venture of drafting legal documents and evaluating estates for owners intending to sell, mostly after the death of family members.

He schooled and trained his two sons to work as future agents, preparing them to meet the challenges of the world as business owners. He educated them on how to assess properties according to the mandates of the province. They traveled with him to acquire knowledge of working with clients and evaluating the property's value. Eventually, they became certified and licensed just as their father had done forty years prior.

When Samuel Crichton senior died, his son was more than qualified to take the helm of the established business and property on Apple Street to his eldest son Samuel. The second son, Ebenezer, fared nearly as well by inheriting money to create his own business and settle himself with property in Lexington, Massachusetts, where his fiancée resided with her parents.

As the years passed and his son grew, Samuel perceived Susannah's keen mind and ambitious spirit as they spent their evenings together in front of the fireplace. He offered her an opportunity, which she eagerly accepted, to assist him in his work as a *notaire*, copying court orders and drafting documents while he traveled to western Pennsylvania to appraise property.

This had been Samuel's work for his entire adult life. As he traveled, he discerned that should he die suddenly, Susannah and Sam would need a remunerative occupation to support themselves. To this end, he devoted many hours to instructing them in the particulars of Crichton Services in the same room and at the same desk where he learned the trade from his father.

---

49. ...notary...

"Life is uncertain," he told Susannah. "If I should die, I want you to be skilled and prepared in this business, able to make a living for yourself and Sam." He had experienced his father-in-law's sudden death. One day, he was a healthy man. The next day, he collapsed in the pasture. Without the help of Samuel and Susannah, his mother-in-law Gretchen would have become a pauper.

She sipped her tea and browsed through Samuel's files until she found a similar document that described the details of an estate handled a year before in Harrisburg. She studied the size and similarities of the main house, outbuildings, property size, crops, pastures, livestock, and taxes, making comparisons and notes as she went to begin forming an evaluation of this customer's request.

She took down a book listing current taxes charged for various elements of the estate. She thought it time-consuming and confusing, wishing she could consult Samuel, but instead soldiered on. She preferred to bake pastry, which suited her more than evaluating property but was not as profitable.

I'll put this one in Germantown aside until Sam arrives. Sometimes, he offers a different perspective. She resumed her work. Between the dull routine of deeds and titles floated the handsome face of Samuel. She silently thanked him for his wise judgment in teaching her how to manage a business. Alive or dead, he was devoted to meeting his family's needs.

Last December, Susannah's brother, Horace, had shown compassion toward her little family since Samuel's death. He had thoughtfully contracted the delivery of firewood to their home on Apple Street during the coldest of months. A butcher regularly supplied shanks of lamb, a shoulder of beef or pork, a slab of bacon, hens, and turkey for roasting. Horace sent his mother Gretchen yards of linen, muslin, and broadcloth to sew for the family.

With such an abundance of meat and poultry than a family of three could consume, they yielded to their natural sense of benevolence and shared it with families they knew were in need. Gretchen eagerly began cutting up the linen into tunic pieces to sew together for Sam, and bodices for Susannah were stitched from the broadcloth, enhanced by embroidered flowers and pleated trim.

Not forgetting his sister's birthday, Horace picked up a box of lemons and oranges and spices at the Wednesday market along with a written note sent home by Sam. Susannah thought this was totally out of character for her brother to recognize her birthday. She and Gretchen remained quiet on the matter, believing any hint of suspicion on her part might jeopardize Sam's working relationship with his uncle.

Sam was a natural for the newspaper business and never faltered in meeting his afternoon deadline. Horace paid him a paltry wage as he did with all his employees. It fell absurdly short of paying for a rented room and sustenance, but his uncle knew that Susannah would never allow her son to go without the necessities.

As the months passed and winter turned to spring, Susannah noticed her brother's generosity begin to taper off when the weekly butcher delivery consisted of a dressed chicken and a few links of sausage. She had wondered how long Horace's charade would continue. But she kept her opinions to herself and expressed her thanks to her brother by sending a note through Sam.

She remembered Horace's words to her after Samuel's body had been lowered to the ground on that cold December morning. He stood in her warm kitchen at the big fireplace, pouring himself another rum punch. "You will need help until you can stand on your own two feet. I will see that you're cared for."

She shuddered now at his words and gagged when he kissed her hand. It had been only a week before when a messenger from a law firm had delivered a letter to her door. The contents were unnerving. Her brother proposed that her house and property on Apple Street legally belonged to him, being the oldest male in the family. She and Sam studied the twisted words and complicated phrases, finally realizing they required the aid of a lawyer to conquer the trickery Horace had incited.

"Ja," she muttered, "he will help me alright, with a shove out the door and a knife in my back."

Tyrus Drake was a self-made man who had received two years of education in philosophy, rhetoric, and literature at Harvard College in Cambridge, Massachusetts. His tuition was paid out of his own pocket, made the hard way by delivering newspapers and pamphlets. He studied as much as his time and attention allowed, but his job changed over forty years time, from newspaper delivery to apprentice to editor of the *Boston Chronicle*.

This change in responsibility turned from less time spent studying to more time running the printing machines and filling in the blank spaces of the newspaper. He turned his back on his education and continued his newspaper work in Philadelphia as publisher of the *Philadelphia Enquirer* and owner of Drake's News and Print for forty years until his death.

Horace Pelare thought he had struck gold twenty years ago when he married into the affluent Drake family. Resentful of his meager upbringing, twelve-year-old Horace was embarrassed to speak because of his Swedish inflections and enunciations. By speaking slowly and intentionally, just as his teachers had instructed him, he was now beginning to sound more like his former classmates in Philadelphia, something akin to British and colonial speak. Whatever it took to put a chasm between his Swedish speech and ancestry and the newly preferred gentleman he had conjured in his mind. He invented his own style by listening to important men who traveled in carriages and in conversations at the state building on Market Street.

He sought work, preferably not on a farm, to earn a wage and begin work toward his gentlemanly status. He willingly mixed the ink and trimmed the quills for Drake's newspaper writers. There were times when he stayed late to run errands for food and coffee, to sweep the floor or clean the windows at the shop, anything to accommodate Mr. Drake and his writers. Horace assumed the lowest position and was paid the lowest wage, but it did not matter. He patiently and loyally put in his time to acquire his dreamed-of stature. His alacrity awarded him with occasional nods from Tyrus Drake.

Months passed. One day, he sat under a shade tree on Market Street eating an apple. He sat deep in thought, gazing at Mr. Drake's print shop situated across the street, compelling him to read the latest edition of the newspaper, the same one he would soon be delivering to subscribers across Philadelphia.

To Horace's surprise, he found some of the news items actually appealed to him, particularly those concerning public opinions and local politics and government. He began to scrutinize certain articles, deciding the more disagreements and rivalry spouted amongst opposing sides, the more interested he was in reading further. *The reason why some newspapers sell better than others*, he determined. He set himself a course of becoming indispensable to Mr. Drake, confirming his decision that the newspaper business was a goal worth his time and work to achieve. The next step was learning how to write news that appealed to his boss. *That could be a long way into the future*, he brooded. Not to be defeated, he studied the methods used by writers to word public events and opinion pieces.

Delivering newspapers to taverns and homes was tedious work for Horace, plodding along dusty streets in the hot summer sun and rushing through the same streets in the freezing winter storms. Mr. Drake called him into his office one Saturday afternoon to pay him his weekly wage. To Horace's surprise, he complimented him on his speedy newspaper deliveries. He also mentioned that the subscription fees he collected from customers added up perfectly with the number of copies he delivered, which had never happened as long as Mr. Drake had been in the business. "I'm impressed with your honesty," said the owner.

"If you ever take an interest in writing for the paper, I can recommend several books that could put you on the right path," Mr. Drake spoke to Horace in a serious manner, pointing to the library to his right, which held a hundred or more books. "You think about it, and we'll discuss it further." New talent was hard to come by, but Tyrus Drake saw hard work and a willingness to learn in Horace's disposition.

"Yes, sir, I am interested and have been since I began reading your newspaper," Horace confessed.

"Well, let's get you started." Mr. Drake walked a few steps to the bookshelves and took down a leather-bound book of back copies of the newspapers and *Paradise Lost*. "You begin reading these in your spare time, and we will meet again next Saturday."

Dazed and confused that his employer had noticed his endeavors, Horace acquiesced. He accepted the books. Speechlessness overtook him, but he managed to squeak out an "I will, sir."

An understanding had developed between Mr. Drake and Horace. As each Saturday afternoon came, Horace was first paid his wages, and afterward, Mr. Drake quizzed and educated the young worker on his assigned studies, giving him opportunities to ask questions and make declarations. Finally, he allowed Horace to express his own ideas and opinions. "Do you understand why it is important to publish the news by contrasting either side of an event, a law, or perhaps an idea or one's motive?" Mr. Drake studied the young man's face, anticipating an answer.

"Yes, sir," Horace answered confidently. "Firstly, to sell newspapers. Secondly, even though I should personally embrace a certain opinion, it is not my job to prevail upon the reader to accept my ideas. I must examine it from all angles, challenging the reader to determine his or her own resolution."

Mr. Drake nodded and smiled. He held out his hand for Horace to shake. "Now we can begin in earnest."

The celebration began in a small banquet room at City Tavern on Walnut Street. Guests enjoyed duck and beef and custards, and the Madeira flowed generously. The guest of honor sat at the head of the table while city officials, staff writers, and Tyrus Drake toasted the new senior writer, Horace Pelare. It had been five years since he stood in Mr. Drake's office and accepted the challenge to begin his journey, producing articles for the *Philadelphia Enquirer*. Even more life-changing, one year later, he stood before a minister in Christ Church, stating his marriage vows before guests and his new in-laws, Tyrus Drake and his wife, Felicia. More importantly, Horace's new bride, Agnes Drake.

Sam Crichton had waited anxiously all morning for this moment to arrive. The hectic, uncertain activities of the morning had been like a whirlwind, pushing him in one direction and then another. Not that his brief *tête-à-tête*[50] with the delegates and Uncle Horace had not supplied him with sufficient material for his newspaper article, but the information was secured safely in his head. He would not rest until he could see it in writing. He dipped his quill in the inkstand, writing speedily, his mental capacity making more headway than his fingers.

His mind leaped back to the pails of water in the back of the wagon, causing his spirit to amplify since his mother's little impromptu gathering. Seeing the delegates up close and hearing them parley in their various colonial accents, huddled as they were under shady chestnut trees, had awakened his senses to what was truly happening. This spirit of unity among the colonies was the *key* to separating ourselves from Britain's hold on our divine and natural rights as men and women. This event was more like a gift that inspired him to sprint up the stairs to the writing room to quickly record his thoughts.

It was of no importance that the delegates could not speak of their discussions behind closed doors. It was all preliminary, anyway. Their debates and arguments would trickle out slowly as the days wore on at Carpenter's Hall, supplying him with information for future writings in the *Philadelphia Enquirer*.

He paused to gaze out the windows, looking like an oblong picture of High Street, generally referred to as Market Street, the busiest street in Philadelphia. Nothing in particular caught his eye. In his mind was a vision of Benjamin Franklin stepping out of a boat docked at the Market Street wharf, strolling along the dirt-packed Market Street as an independent seventeen-year-old runaway, not sure what he would eat or where he would sleep, but greatly relieved his former life spent in Boston was history.

---

50. …face-to-face…

Tribute to Philadelphia's Working Class by Samuel Crichton

What sort of person has in their mind to make their world, their environs, a better place to live?

Consider the farmer who grows our food. He rises before dawn to plow the fields and tend his livestock, finally retiring to bed before the moon and stars fill the sky. The blacksmith fires his forges to fashion hardware and harnesses. The weaver grows the flax, converts it into fiber to spin, resulting in durable cloth.

Is it any wonder that Pennsylvania lays claim to those very people who strive to make their community a representation of their skills and labor, evident in the persistent industry possessed by the men and women in this province.

The printer must survive in a complex workplace where interactions with the public are necessary and constant. Collecting the news, searching for advertisers, writing news articles, printing newspapers, publishing books— all done to inform the public. His work schedule is no different from the farmer or the tradesman, rising early and staying late to meet deadlines, asleep on their feet at times.

This was Benjamin Franklin's ambition, and it became his world, which, through years of work, culminated in a disciplined lifestyle. The sort of discipline that promotes thriftiness in spending, managing one's time, a continuance of education, and contributing to society,

One may ask, why make so much ado about Dr. Franklin? Amongst many honorable achievements, he is a proponent of the working man and woman— our talented citizens who regard work as honorable and create exceptional products through their accomplishments. He believes work is good for the soul and necessary for a fulfilling life with dignity and meaning.

Benjamin Franklin's thirst for knowledge and his apprenticeship in his brother's print shop long ago influenced his chosen profession, consistently raising the bar to become the intellectual scholar he is today. He attempted the unusual when he fabricated characters for the purpose of allowing common sense to rule in a person's habits, hence attracting a variety of readers from New England to the southern colonies. He kept his ear to the ground, recognizing the key players in government and Parliament, using his charm and debating skills to establish relationships.

Envious as I am of Dr. Franklin, I presume he frequents London's coffee houses for the purpose of acquainting himself with journalists and intellectuals, shifting the conversation toward his theories of how electricity is conducted and why the oceans contain salt.

He would most certainly edge in his philosophical ideas to his peers, reasoning that colonists desire and expect the cooperation of the king and his men to remove the burdensome constraints of the Intolerable Acts to allow colonists the opportunities to create and manufacture. This is an industry in the New World that requires protection and praise from the mountaintops, man's natural inclination to work and profit.

In answer to the delegates who wish to shake the hand of our city's treasure, Benjamin Franklin, he remains across the Atlantic in London working to secure the futures of millions of industrious colonists. Let's pray his diplomacy skills prove effective.

Sam read through and examined his article. "Uncle Horace will cringe when he reads this, but he always does and prints it anyway." Nephew and Uncle's relationship had existed under a veil of obscurity since Samuel Crichton died the previous December. Horace's sympathy was mixed with embarrassment at the outset since he never visited his mother and sister nor saw to their needs.

Gretchen and Susannah had met Horace's wife, Agnes, on one occasion and had never laid eyes on their two daughters, both now under the age of sixteen. Mother and daughter lamented they did not meet the necessary standards to be seen visiting Belleview, the stately mansion Horace Pelare had inherited as part of Tyrus Drake's estate.

After his father's death, Horace took charge of the family's farm in Germantown, collected the profits, delivered his mother to Apple Street, and never returned until the morning he stood at Susannah's living room fireplace following Samuel's burial. Gretchen and her son's eyes never met, nor did they have reason to speak. They both knew Horace had swindled his mother out of her part of the farm's profits.

Sam confided to his mother about this unusual working relationship with his uncle Horace, indicating the man was always in a foul mood not only with Sam but all the writers. "He's never pleased with his employee's work. He just growls and signs his initials, giving the go-ahead to print. I'm worried that he is ill or has money problems. Could it be possible?"

"You don't have to force yourself to work at Drake's. There's plenty of printers in this city," Susannah said. She hated seeing her son anguish over bigger problems than he could solve.

"Has he always been such a tyrant?" he asked.

"A tyrant, you say?" She laughed. "More like hungry for more money and recognition. Regretfully, as he got older, he was very sensitive about his appearance and his accent. I recall his school friends making fun of his speech and calling him Farmer Swede. He seemed to overcome that and later on apprenticed under Mr. Drake. Your father offered his help by giving him odd chores to do with the business, but he lost interest. He made it very clear to his papa that he did not like farm work, giving him cause to strike out on his own."

Three weeks into the congregation of delegates at Carpenter's Hall, Susannah's refreshments remained popular and appreciated by the hardworking men, likely providing a needed break from the hall's stuffy rooms and the boredom of long-winded speakers. Susannah noticed the strain in the men's faces and their habit of huddling with the same delegates at noontime, appearing frustrated as they whispered their words of disgust.

During this last week of September, autumn was in full display, showing gold and orange colors amongst the plentiful fruit trees lining the streets of Philadelphia. The cool air was like a balm, given that the hot summer months were finally exhausted, cycling in a new season, refreshing the spirits of shopkeepers, vendors of the outdoor markets, and Sam Crichton.

He strolled down the cobbled sidewalk on colorful Market Street, lined with whale oil lamps, observing the stately brick buildings and the majestic churches with their spirals touching the puffy white clouds.

The streets were busy with women shopping, men pushing carts, and gentlemen riding in carriages and sedans.

A pang of grief struck him when he realized that at this time last year, he had sat with his father at the Bunch of Grapes tavern drinking ale while discussing the particulars of a client's deed. Less than three months later, Samuel was struck down with a fever that ended his life.

Sam felt invigorated by the coolness of the autumn morning, even more so by the response he had heard from readers regarding the series of articles he had written about the "middling class," as it was called by some. Newspaper sales were up, not that it put a smile on Uncle Horace's face, and Sam was gaining more confidence in his capacity for writing. He enjoyed the challenge of arranging his thoughts on paper, deciding what would interest the public. His inspiration came from the greatest authors, in his opinion—Milton, Swift, and Socrates.

He had finished the outline for his afternoon article and read through his competitor's newspapers, the *Chronicle* and *Observer*. Now, he anticipated a walk to the library. Months ago, he had seen in one of Philadelphia's several bookstores a book of interest by Daniel Defoe called *Essay on Projects*. He progressed toward the closest library, hoping to borrow a copy.

Sam observed from a distance three women. *Likely a mother and her daughters*, he thought, stepping out of a large, shiny black carriage parked alongside the sidewalk just beyond the entry to the library. He decided to keep his distance from the women. Once they were settled inside, he would take his turn to enter. He had a vague feeling that the carriage belonged to Horace Pelare, having once seen him and another gentleman riding along Market Street, remembering the seats were covered in purple velvet. The thought struck him: with all the mansions in Philadelphia, it could belong to anybody.

The woman was tall and handsome with dark brown hair and a sharp nose, a serious, proud face that screamed self-importance. Agnes Pelare motioned her daughters to follow her to a section of shelves containing travel books about France, Italy, and Spain. The tallest daughter, the oldest, Sam decided, had her mother's coloring, dark eyes, and a strong chin. He overheard the daughter's words, remarking she preferred a novel over boring books about European culture and geography.

The younger daughter left the two arguing while she walked to a different section. Her yellow hair was pulled back in a braid, allowing a full view of her petite facial features and her pale blue eyes. She reached for a particular book and then smiled when she read the author's name, Jonathan Swift. She sat down at a table and began thumbing through the pages. Observing this scene from a distance, Sam thought how different the two sisters appeared. "Assuming they are who I think they are," he muttered. He moved on to search for the DeFoe book.

His attention was drawn to the mother and her daughters walking to the front to sign out their books. Mrs. Pelare leading the way in possession of the travel books. The tallest daughter followed behind, empty-handed, revealing a disinterest in the excursion to the library. The youngest daughter clutched her *Gulliver's Travels* and a copy of *Poor Richard's Almanack* by Franklin.

With the little time he had left, Sam sat at a table and anxiously read the introduction in Defoe's book. The clerk showed him where to sign his name for identification purposes and assigned to him the return date. His eyes widened when he saw the Pelare name written above his. *Wonder of wonders, after all these years, I've been informally introduced to my relatives, the Pelare women*, he mused.

On a cool morning in mid-October, the yard on Apple Street dotted with varying degrees of leafless trees, Sam stood at the well, located close to the side of the house and visible to the street, drawing pails of water to load into the wagon. He was quite overcome with the aromas of bread baking in one of the outdoor ovens and a sweet apple pastry baking in the second oven. Susannah and Gretchen had begun mixing dough before he dressed and walked downstairs. His mouth watered, struggling with temptation at the moment, anxious for hot coffee with cream and fresh buttered bread. His empty, growling stomach screamed, "Feed me!"

Sam counted six pails of water arranged in the wagon. *Four more to go*, he figured. He stepped away from the well when in the distance came the sounds of horse hooves pounding the dirt road, headed toward his house. Nothing visible as yet in the gray morning light. Either the rider noticed Sam standing at the well or smelled the outdoor cooking. Now, he could see the outline of a man wearing a tricorn hat and a cloak flying out at the sides. The rider slowed the horse to a walk when he noticed Sam and shouted, "Good morning, sir!"

The man dismounted the gray stallion covered in lather, holding the horses' reins as he walked into the yard toward the well. "May I trouble you for a cup of water and a rest for my mount?" The red-faced man uttered his request between staggered breaths, apparently having ridden a long distance. On closer inspection, Sam noticed his cloak was wet with morning dew, and the soles and tops of his boots were covered with mud.

Observing the condition of the horse, Sam invited the man to remove its saddle. "There's a trough of fresh water inside the fence." The horse ambled over to a patch of grass, then looked around at his owner as if he needed permission to begin nibbling.

The rider removed his hat and leaned against the well, sipping his water as he looked around the property. He was built small and stout and stood a good four inches shorter than Sam. He pushed his wet, dark hair from his face, finally setting his cup aside to use both hands to secure the loose strands of hair with a leather thong at the nape of his neck.

"I've never been to this part of Philadelphia. Can you direct me to Carpenter's Hall, where the delegates are meeting?" the man asked. "Pardon my manners. I'm Paul Revere from Boston."

Sam smiled and extended his hand. "I'm honored to meet you. Now that your horse is settled, would you like to come inside to refresh yourself? The delegates won't begin their discussions until nine bells."

"Uh, the necessary, if you don't mind?" Sam pointed the visitor in the direction of the privy.

Sam walked through to the warm kitchen, looking baffled and gray-faced. Susannah glanced at him and grinned as she sat at the table sipping her coffee. "Did you see a ghost or a wild animal?"

"No," he whispered, "something even better." He moved in close to his mother, breathing in the coffee's richness, speaking softly. "Someone I want you to meet—after he washes."

Susannah nodded. "Are you whispering to keep it a secret from Gemma?" his mother asked softly. She examined his face with wary eyes. "Is this good news or bad news?"

Sam remained *sotto voce*. "Mama, a visitor whom I just met, has been riding all night to deliver a message to Sam Adams at Carpenter's Hall this morning. He's played-out and travel-worn, so I offered him breakfast. Wait, that's him now, knocking at the scullery door."

Susannah could not help but see the amusement in her son's reaction to the spontaneous visit of the Boston rider. His uncle Ebenezer had kept the family informed about Boston's Patriot leaders who, for ten years, had organized resistance against Parliament and King George. Sam Adams had roused the colonies of Parliament's demands to directly tax colonists, as well as their abuse of individual rights. Paul Revere had traveled by horseback thousands of miles since 1765 to spread the word in towns and taverns across New England and the Middle Colonies, from there, trickling down to the South.

Susannah opened the door to meet the bedraggled man holding his hat. "Good morning, Mr. Revere. Will you join us for breakfast?" Susannah pointed him to a chair at the table set with a plate of eggs, bread and butter, and a cup of steaming coffee.

He offered no objection, as tired as he was. Once settled, he dove into the steaming food.

"I imagine it takes a week or more to travel to Philadelphia?" Susannah asked.

Paul nodded and sipped his coffee. "I've been on the road for twelve days. My horse needs shoeing. Is there a livery nearby?" He sat slumped over his plate like he was too exhausted to lift his fork to his mouth.

"Mr. Revere, are you awake?" Sam jumped up from his chair, thinking the worst. He shook the man's shoulder. Paul Revere answered with a groan, prompting Sam to pull him from his chair and walk him to the drawing room, gently lowering him onto the rug. Susannah settled a pillow under his head.

Sam drew close to his mother's side. "I'll give the horse some oats and molasses and see about his hooves. The man's been asleep on his feet for no telling how long."

Susannah and Gretchen looked on as Mr. Revere lay curled up on his side, sound asleep in the dark room. "Must be an important message to come this far," Gretchen said, shaking her head.

Two hours later, Susannah heard the man coughing. "Here, drink some water. You've been in a deep sleep." Paul drank all the water, then shook his head and yawned.

"Pardon me, madame, I couldn't go on." He scanned the room and spotted the handsome tea service set up on a table with tea cups. "This respite has restored my strength. I should be on my way. I don't know if your son told you, but I'm here to speak to Sam Adams and his cousin, John. Likely, you have never heard of them. They live in Boston."

Susannah laughed. "Mr. Revere, I can name nearly every Patriot up your way. We have followed the events of the siege and well before. Mr. Adams' newsletters are very straightforward. We have had the advantage of learning many details by way of my brother-in-law, who lives in Lexington."

"I know many people living in that direction. What is his name?" he asked in a hoarse voice.

"Ebenezer Crichton. He works as a *notaire*. Of course, all communication has ceased since the spring. I do, on occasion, receive mail from my cousin who lives on a farm in Stoughton. Perhaps you're familiar with the Randolph family?"

"I am familiar with Stoughton. The redcoats have not set up their base as yet in that area, although I did hear tell they're setting up an encampment in Roxbury." He offered that information but no more, being cautious about sharing more information than necessary. British spies were everywhere.

Sam walked through, happy to find Mr. Revere on his feet and some color in his face. "Your horse is shoed, rubbed down, tacked, and fed. I prepared a sack of oats and apples for when you're further up the road, at the least when you reach your first ordinary."

Gretchen met him in the kitchen with a burlap bag holding a bottle of cider and bread. "A refreshment for when you take a rest. May God go with you." She backed away shyly and returned to filling the trays with pastry for the delegates.

Susannah returned from her office with a note. "If you should happen to ride through Stoughton, will you give this note to my cousin?" She saw that Paul was hesitant. "I purposely left off your and Lenora's names for safety reasons. She will recognize my handwriting. If you need a rest, the Randolphs are very accommodating and will serve you a delicious beer. Thank you for all you do in the name of freedom."

"We should go." Sam led the way to the paddock. "I would like to walk with you a ways if you don't mind, sir. With so many streets crisscrossing, it can be confusing." The morning air remained cool as Sam guided Paul Revere and his horse toward Second Street, giving the Bostonian a view of the handsome brick buildings and acquainting himself with the streets and landmarks.

They stopped in front of City Tavern. "Just across the street is where Mr. Adams is lodging. With it being the breakfast hour, he could be dining there at this moment. I will step inside to inquire." Sam touched the brim of his hat and took his leave. A cool breeze from the docks at the Delaware brought the stench of sewage in Paul's direction, causing him to gag.

During his stay as a delegate, Mr. Adams and Sam engaged in light conversation during the daily noontime breaks; they were not strangers by any means. Now, as luck would have it, Sam escorted Mr. Adams outside to meet with Paul Revere.

Sam walked several yards away while the two men met privately to discuss a turn of events occurring in Boston at this very moment. He surveyed the streets, being on the lookout for British agents. There was no one in earshot, but there were two men across the street standing at opposite ends of a string of buildings reading their newspapers. If he could get a look at their faces, he would sketch them from memory when he returned home. Finally, one lowered his paper to turn the page.

Their discussion ended when Mr. Adams returned inside to his breakfast. Sam walked to where Paul stood. "We should return to Apple Street." Sam scanned the upper portion of the street. "In order to disorient two suspected agents, you should take the same route from my house, then follow the river toward Perth Amboy. I will give you the details while we ride."

Paul Revere remained fatigued, but he stepped up on his horse and bid Sam farewell. "I am grateful for your accommodations, and I will remain vigilant." He was wary of the Crichtons and their eagerness to aid him. *Can't be too sure*, he thought. "They could be part of a British spy ring. What do you think, Lucas?" he asked his horse while leaning forward to stroke his neck. The horse shook his head sideways and snorted, stirring up dust as he galloped up the road.

Chapter 29

Either Way, It's Treason

Mid-October 1774, Philadelphia

As much as Paul Revere was an experienced and competent rider, the thought of British agents watching the transaction between him and Sam Adams outside City Tavern caused him some consternation. *A lesson learned*, he thought. Perhaps out of his weariness, he had not considered the risk he was taking by meeting outside with a delegate in broad daylight, especially the notable firebrand Sam Adams. British spies could be anywhere. On the other hand, these men could be nothing more than Tory sympathizers taking note of delegates' activities to pass on to their British leaders or perhaps to tavern keepers, who stored such information until it became necessary to reveal it. Naturally, at a price.

After he left Apple Street and departed Philadelphia, putting some ten miles behind him, no evidence revealed he was being trailed. This alone took a load off his mind. He set out confidently, galloping toward the northeast for Perth Amboy in Jersey, which led him to the Staten Island ferry and on to New York. Once he was safely across the bay, the Night Owl tavern was within reach.

The ride to New York was long and boring, but the roads were passable, hard, and packed down, and the creeks and rivers were navigable. At times, he thought Lucas had a better grasp of the direction to follow than he did, but there were certain landmarks Paul used to guarantee he was traveling eastward toward New Haven. He was familiar with all the taverns along his route, and he had his favorites. Some he learned to avoid. Decent food and drink and a good night's sleep was all that mattered to him while his belly was empty and nighttime was imminent.

Paul Revere was born into the hardiest rank of New England's privateers, sea captains, and Indian Fighters. The abundance of irascible great-uncles and great-grandfathers on Paul's mother's side of the family tended to make their own rules in society. They found it more to their benefit if they ignored the law and settled matters to their way of thinking. They often ended up in court defending themselves and paying fines or spending time behind bars, but they sought to master their own life.

As a youngster, he listened to adventurous tales of his rough and tough ancestors, establishing themselves with a genuine strain of self-assurance and an independent spirit. His father, Apollos Rivoire, played a vital role in his son's natural appetite for independence. His Huguenot parents lived in southern France in the early 1700s—a perilous time for Protestants when Catholics were in the majority. At the age of twelve, Apollos' parents arranged for him to escape persecution by sailing to the English Channel and then to Boston. He apprenticed as a silversmith for ten years, giving him the experience to set up his own business. A worldwide system that had worked for centuries, affording boys ages twelve to fourteen to learn a craft—an occupation that would sustain them as adults. Many were equipped to advance to a higher education level, thus becoming ministers, lawyers, physicians, and teachers.

Perhaps Revere's passion for liberty stemmed from his father's family, who were doomed to face brutal consequences if they practiced their Protestant religion in France. It was for the same reason that Puritans persevered in the New World to escape the Church of England.

In the late 1750s, Revere went on to march with the Massachusetts militia to defend the colonies against the French, believing the freedom and democracy he had experienced in Boston during his nineteen years was worth the fight.

Paul Revere returned to his home to resume his deceased father's business as a master silversmith, tenaciously building a business that would eventually secure his position as one of the elite artisans in Boston. As with any business owner, profit remained the first priority for Revere. The costs for the workplace and the essential materials for constructing products were constant but achievable if managed properly, as his father had taught him. When Parliament asserted that directly taxing colonists was necessary to pay off their war debts, business owners began to rebel, causing political unrest in Boston to grow unrestrained. The chasm between Britain and Boston widened throughout the next few years, requiring Britain to dispatch soldiers to regulate order within the colony.

Many of Boston's opposition leaders were Freemasons. This private group of carefully selected, skilled craftsmen met independently as a charitable organization but also to discuss prominent matters of the province. Particularly, the slow revolution taking place in the minds of Boston's populace that was becoming more evident each day. The freedom to control their future was now under attack by the British government, which was pushing for heavy taxes and damaging regulations.

Being civic-minded, this secretive society fit Paul Revere like a glove—an independent thinker working to earn a living that required sweat and physical effort to meet the demands of his customers. Boston was bursting with such virtuous men and women, trained and disciplined to meet the challenges of a thriving province. Resistance to the restraints of royal governors and appointees was discussed within the bounds of Masonic meetings, brothers who were of the same mind, knowing a day of reckoning was on the horizon.

Sam Adams was a master at inventing new forms of political resistance. He had studied law at Harvard and understood the relevance of the Massachusetts Charter, a document that protected the rights of the colony's citizens against the Crown's abuse of power. He spoke out against Parliament when their attempts at collecting revenue from the colonists caused riots amongst the thirteen colonies along the eastern seaboard. His Committees of Correspondence was born out of London's failure to recognize that forced taxation would never succeed in the colonies. Adams' war of words manifested itself in the form of circulars delivered by express riders to New York and Philadelphia.

The fact that Sam Adams had never ridden a horse did not prevent him from searching for men who were capable and fast riders. Trusted Patriots who were ready to separate themselves from England's clutches and could speak intelligently with anyone with no hesitation or fear. Men of Boston who fought to cut off ties with England by boycotting their manufactured goods. Business owners who were living through political and economic stress, resulting in employee layoffs and forced to diversify their talents to make a living. Sam looked no further than his Sons of Liberty associates. The most dependable and qualified in Adams' mind was Paul Revere.

A seasoned express rider, Paul knew instinctively when the need to slow his horse to a walk revealed itself. After several hours of hard riding, it was time to stop and stretch his legs. His horse was thirsty and was anxious to munch on whatever ground cover appealed to the stallion. Catching a whiff of the earthy, wet scent of a creek bed, he dismounted and led Lucas off the beaten path to the stream of water. Revere's body was fatigued. Puffy dark circles under his eyes showed a lack of sleep, but over three hundred miles remained between him and his home on North Square in Boston.

With his horse settled, his mind turned to his own appetite. He reached into the leather bag for the bottle of cider and bread Gretchen had prepared this morning for his trip. He was ravenous enough to finish the refreshments, but tempted as he was, he left the half of it in the event he arrived at the tavern at too late an hour. Depending on the tavern keeper working the night shift, a supply of hot food could be depleted, leaving the scraps of a meager dinner.

A sense of anxiousness seized his thoughts when he quickly noted the position of the sun and the afternoon ticking away like the sound of a loud clock. He clucked to his horse, spurring Lucas his way. Their short respite was concluded, and they headed through the leafy orange and yellow trees toward the Night Owl on the west side of the Hudson River.

Traveling fifty miles each day toward his destination was Paul's limit if he and his horse were to survive the more than three-hundred-mile trip. He set his mind on Philadelphia, the width of the neat cobbled streets filled with expensive carriages and horse-drawn wagons driving in from the countryside with their produce for Wednesday's market. Germans and Swedes going about their business, talking amongst each other, arguing over where to park their wagons. So different from Boston's narrow winding streets and squawking gulls, inundated with soldiers marching to noisy tattoos on the Boston Common.

He shook his head at the turmoil happening throughout the countryside, Boston, Salem, and Worcester, with John Hancock snubbing Governor Gage and his redcoat soldiers by creating an autonomous colonial government. He recalled Sam Adams' face, white as a sheet when he read John Hancock's note—over two hundred Massachusetts delegates had met in Concord to form the first provincial congress and had elected Hancock as governor.

All this was taking place while fifty-four delegates representing twelve colonies were confined to Carpenter's Hall in Philadelphia. Paul wasn't sure if Sam Adams felt betrayed by Hancock's actions or if Hancock reacted quickly to kick Gage out of the way, preventing him from taking charge of the affairs of the colony. *Somebody has to hold the province together*, Paul decided. *If this doesn't start a war, nothing will.*

A breeze lifted the leaves of sycamores and elms, loosened and spent from their springtime home, fluttering to the ground. Paul breathed a sigh of relief when he caught the spicy scent of a grove of cedar trees, indicating the first leg of his journey was now behind him.

He walked into the Night Owl tavern, his stiff body moving slowly toward the proprietor standing behind the bar holding a rag in hand, wiping the remaining ale from the inside of tankards. "Abel Conrad, how is business this evening? I could use a hot meal."

Abel pushed a mug of ale before him. "We've got ham, cabbage, and apples, and plenty of bread and fresh butter." He offered Paul a seat near the fireplace. "If ye'll be needin' a room, you've got your choice, one looks over the stables, t'other looks over the creek. No need to bunk up this evening. Business is always light on Wednesday."

"The creekside is fine. Food smells good." Paul had left Lucas at the barn behind the tavern in the care of the stable hand. Relieved that only five other horses were stabled in their own stalls, they stood eating their meal from the feed bags covering their muzzles. Donnie welcomed the worn-out horse by taking hold of the reins and speaking in a low voice, gently patting Lucas' neck. He remembered the horse and its owner from more than a week before. "You could use a good brushing before you settle in." He cut into an apple and fed Lucas from his hand.

Paul held up a lantern as he climbed the stairs to his chamber. His leather bag of clothes and a loaded pistol were slung over his shoulder. The room smelled of wood burning in a small fireplace, giving off adequate heat to break the chill in the room. He had a bedstead all for himself, no pallets on the floor, no snoring strangers to disturb his sleep. He threw cold water from the washbowl on his face and neck, then toweled off the water and black dirt. As tired as he was, he tried again, using soap this time. "Phff, best I can do this evening. I'll give it another swipe come morning."

He removed his dusty waistcoat, revealing a smelly tunic and a paper that fell to the floor. "Hmm, the note from Susannah Crichton." He set it beside his bag of clothes. "Maybe I should stop by the Randolph farm. One more day getting home won't matter that much. He groaned at the work ahead of him in Boston." He fell into bed. "All this riding is making an old man out of me."

Mulberry Farm

Eli Asher and Chief Randolph, known as Poppi to his grandchildren, sat across from each other, feeling the warmth flowing through the sunny window in the library at Mulberry Farm while hunched over the chess board. More than twelve years had passed since the competitive twosome had used their own powers of concentration to assess tactical positions to their advantage or disadvantage. For the moment, Chief Randolph was the predicted winner—again.

"What will it take to defeat you, Chief?" Eli asked laughingly. He knew the answer, but he was reluctant to give away any part of his disgusting past that might upset the honorable man sitting before him.

There were many particulars about the past twelve years of his life as a kidnapped soldier that were cruel and inhuman. Eli was not prepared to share the dreadful details, not even with his wife, Naomi.

Chief Randolph looked at Eli, making every effort not to show sympathy towards the war veteran he had raised as his own son since he was a boy of eight years. "Practice, along with concentration, is what it takes. You're out of practice."

The Chief paused and gazed into Eli's hurting eyes. "It will come, I assure you, my son. It took a lot of courage to push through the hard times, but you never gave up. You were determined to escape and travel back to your home and your family. You're here for a reason." The Chief grinned. "Just so you know, I refuse to purposely lose a game so you can win. Ready to give it another go?" he asked. Eli reset the board, remaining hopeful.

For over four months now, during the hot summer months, he had lived under the care and protection of Naomi in the small farmhouse where the spacious kitchen and dining room remained the main living area. She started the fireplace before dawn, preparing coffee and porridge, flapjacks, and eggs—if her hens were laying. If not, she fried salted pork in a skillet, which brought all her men out of their slumber to begin a new day.

Tall Spruce and Gray Wolf were consigned to the front porch to make their sleeping space. Gray Wolf claimed he preferred to sleep outside in the cool night air. Three months of sleeping in a wooden box was plainly "confining and smothering," as he identified it. Ethan was happy to once again occupy the front room, confessing that the outdoors was noisy at nighttime, and he was uneasy that an opossum would come nosing around his pallet looking for food.

Eli sat at the table drinking coffee while Naomi cleared the dishes and began chopping onions, garlic, and a bowlful of herbs for a pot of chicken stew. From the window, he watched Ethan and Gray Wolf haul bags of barley to unload inside the malting shed, scatter, and then rake it gently to make it as smooth as a pancake. Harry and Tall Spruce were cutting boards of wood laid across two sawhorses to attach as a skirt around the bottom of the shed.

Talking and laughing as they worked, Eli commented, "They seem to work well together. I guess Tall Spruce and Gray Wolf will leave soon." He stared out the window, observing the autumn day of leafless trees and a bright blue sky, never turning his head as he talked to Naomi. *He's not being disrespectful*, she reminded herself. *He's afraid of what his eyes will reveal.*

"Yes, they must return to their winter homes and make ready the longhouses and chop firewood. The women and children will return from the shore with baskets of salted fish and shells for wampum."

Naomi knew her husband was struggling. For years, his life had been filled with hurt and suffering. His body had been tortured; the stripes on his back proved that. British discipline. He was unsure of how to be the Eli he once was. *This will take time and patience*, she agonized. She knew her son was worried too and embarrassed that his father was different now, not as Ethan remembered him.

She was content that, after twelve years, Eli had returned to her bed, desiring her closeness but not sure how to manage his feelings for her. The loneliness for her husband was now brought to an end, but his nightmares and distraught spirit brought her other worries. *How can I break through the shell of this man I once knew?* she thought wearily. The man who sat by the window most of the day with that faraway look in his eyes and responded to her questions with a nod or a shrug. She saw him walk to the porch a dozen times a day to stand and watch the trees and the sky, only to return to his chair in the kitchen. *When will my husband truly return to me?* she wondered. She decided to look to Jacob for help.

"The only way for you to move forward is to talk about your past experiences in England with Naomi. She's well aware that you've been through a kind of hell that none of us has endured. She's a sensible and discerning person with eyes like a hawk and ears like a deer." Jacob and Eli rode their horses, both tall geldings equally familiar with the vistas around the base of the Blue Hills, pausing for a drink from streams, inhaling the tangy hemlocks, standing salient amongst their bare counterparts. The horses showed no interest in the foraging nuthatches who moved to the tree's highest branches.

Eli looked out among the forest, gazing upwards toward the mountains. "For twelve years, I was denied the freedom to travel at will, always under the watchful eye of a brute shouting orders and cracking a whip. I wasn't alone. There were other soldiers abducted just as I was. Ten of us caged like animals while crossing the seas to the most degrading, devilish place imaginable. Trapped within a stone wall ten feet tall to slave for a man, Captain Cyrus, who demanded free labor from us from dawn until twilight. If I had only kept my mouth shut about my work here at the farm. All the knowledge I learned from your father about brewing beer."

"So, you were placed in charge of the brewery on this captain's estate?" Jacob's curious mind as a lawyer kicked in, searching for the facts.

"Yes. It was my job to teach the other soldiers, or slaves like me, I should say, to grow the barley and the hops, build a malting house, rake the barley, build the kiln, everything involved, as you well know. But it didn't end there. This captain, this slave driver, sought many ways to ensnare us.

"We slept in a stone building, bolted at nighttime, and as we got to know one another, we whispered of ways to escape. Little did we know that among us was an informant, a colonist who soldiered during the war. I did not know him personally, but he was a prisoner on the same ship I sailed.

"It was his job to record our schemes of escape and disclose the name of the main leader of such talk. His name was Jethro; he had a family and a farm in Vermont. The last time I saw him, his back was torn to shreds. Two of the slaves were forced to throw his body in a cart and dump him in the woods behind the stone wall." Eli shakily stepped down from his horse and gazed up at the hemlocks, the twittering nuthatches moving in their safe little world of miniature pine cones and thick branches.

"Did you learn the identity of the informer?" Jacob was chilled to the bone at the sight of Eli's face, white as a sheet. His vacant eyes stared toward the mountains.

"We knew him very well. The remaining soldiers and I killed him. We murdered the man. Crazed men such as myself who didn't give a whit that the man was human. While he slept, we smothered him with a pillow. He struggled and moaned. His legs stopped kicking, and his arms fell limp. I laid on my pallet and closed my eyes. I woke up when the guard unbolted the door, and I went about my business."

"Eli, you were desperate. The desire to survive the torture you endured was more important than the life of a deceitful man doing you harm. It was his life or yours. Did you kill French soldiers and Indians during the war to survive? Explain the difference." Jacob stared into Eli's hurtful eyes. "I'm sure there's more that you haven't told me, but you must be the judge of your conscience and defend yourself and your family."

They left the serenity of the wilderness, riding in silence, both knowing there was nothing more to be said at this juncture. Eli had emptied his mind to his trusted friend Jacob. It was a beginning, at least. He had been reluctant for four months to talk about his captivity in England, knowing questions would come. Emotionally, he was not prepared for that. He did not want his family members to be burdened with the nightmares he was withstanding. *Somehow, it's different with Jacob*, he thought.

He felt the tightening in his throat when he spoke. "Someone I met while in New Haven said the only way to restore my relationship with my family is to talk through my struggles with a person who cares about me. I'm afraid that person is you, Jacob."

"I'm honored to listen and help if I can. I'll warn you, though. I'm a lawyer. I've been trained to make people face the realities of life. I can be tough, and I won't let you off easy. Do you think you might have regrets?" Jacob watched his friend and brother warily, his both eyebrows raised.

Eli took a deep breath, then scoffed, nodding his head. "No, indeed."

He left his mount with Ozzie and walked to the porch steps to greet Naomi perched in a cushioned chair in the bright light. As she was engrossed in her knitting work, her fingers held long needles, stitching and looping the yarn, creating row after row of something small and unfamiliar to Eli. Naomi did not look up at her husband, but she knew it was him by the sound of his boots on the steps and the strong, gamy, sour smell rising from his wet skin. "You were gone for a while. Did you enjoy your ride?" she asked.

"The ride was invigorating and very worthwhile," Eli answered. This change of inflection in his voice prompted Naomi to break her concentration on knitting and look into his light blue eyes, which looked more vibrant than she had seen since his return. The strained lines in his face had lessened, and he sounded more like Eli. She stared at him and smiled. They both recognized the difference without comment. "If that's a sweater you're stitching for Ethan, don't you think it rather small?"

She smiled in her mind and laid her work in her lap, reaching for his dirty hand. "It's not intended for our son. I'm making it for Lenora's new baby." She paused to wait for his comment.

He nodded. "Uh, does Jacob know about this?"

"I should think so. She's four months gone." Naomi grinned and waited on her husband for further comment.

"Where have I been? Thinking I was the only person in the world who mattered. What an imbecile! Will you ever forgive me?" Eli sat down on the porch floor, looking into Naomi's dark eyes and her pretty face. "You are so beautiful." He exhaled deeply.

"There's nothing to forgive. We have to start over again. Would you like that?" A tear rolled down her face because she knew his answer would be yes. Eli nodded. He choked up and could not speak.

They came out of their trance when they heard hoofbeats pounding up the drive. Eli squeezed her hand and let it go. He walked toward the barn, and Naomi followed, wondering who would come visiting at this time of day. Her young men were at work at the brewery. They saw Jacob walk out of the house. Everybody on the farm seemed to be on high alert these days.

The visitor dismounted the gray horse. "Your sign at the gate, Mulberry Farm. Is this the Randolph home?"

So far, the day had delivered to Eli an epiphany, the realization that the clouds in his life had parted, now replaced with sunshine and the hope that his life was going to be different—if he had the resolve to see it through. He was willing and ready to return to the human race. Naomi knew all along that he would. *She's as long-suffering as Job*, he mused. He fully comprehended this genuine renewal of his mind and spirit in the seconds it took for him to walk from his front porch to greet the grimy, soaking-wet visitor, Paul Revere.

"From where have you traveled, Mr. Revere? Here, let's move out of the sun to the porch." Jacob pointed him in the direction of the farmhouse. Naomi and Eli followed. The weary, rough-looking man walked slowly, compelling Jacob and Eli to moderate their stride. Naomi branched off towards the well, returning with a cup of water.

"Philadelphia." He sipped the water and exhaled heavily. "Mr. Hancock was anxious for the Massachusetts delegates to learn about the change in the government before they returned to their homes. Mighty sweet water, Madame." Paul nodded a thank you to Naomi. Chief Randolph and Lenora approached the porch to receive the news, recognizing the rider's stature. They knew, without a doubt, he was the popular silversmith and express rider.

Lenora walked to Jacob's side, and the Chief pulled out a chair to sit, reasoning that the impending conversation might take a while. It wasn't every day that a famed resistance leader and select courier showed up on one's doorstep. "Like I said, I've been twelve days on the road from Philadelphia delivering news to Sam Adams before he returns to Boston. In the process of locating him, it was my good fortune to stop by the Crichton home for directions and to rest my horse." Hearing that news, Lenora looked up at her husband and smiled.

"The young man, Sam was his name, took care of my mount and gave me an uncommon breakfast and a place to rest. Afterward, he tracked down Mr. Adams at the tavern. Before I ventured north, Mrs. Crichton scribbled a note for you, Mrs. Randolph." He examined her friendly face. "I assume you are Lenora." He dug inside his waistcoat for the parchment and passed it to her. She pressed it against her bosom and nodded her gratitude. He bowed graciously to her.

"She spoke highly of you, Mrs. Randolph, and your fine cooking. Not that I didn't partake of more than adequate victuals at the Crichton home. Her mother filled a sack with the finest morsels a rider could fancy whilst traveling between one haven to the next."

"If that's the case, Mr. Revere, according to Susannah Crichton's note, you are to join us for our mid-day meal, which will be served in an hour, and she wrote 'to get a good night's rest before you travel to Boston tomorrow.'" Lenora brandished the note as proof for everyone to view, finally glancing at Paul Revere, with eyebrows raised. Never mind the note, Paul had learned during his rough travels to never turn down life's creature comforts when they're offered—a good meal, a stout beer, and a soft mattress.

"I'm in agreement," piped in Naomi. "Let's go make it ready."

"No need to challenge these hard-headed women on that count, Mr. Revere," Jacob advised.

"I know when I'm overruled. I live in a house full of females." Paul laughed. "Before I sit down at your table, I must wash off the road dirt."

"Eli, let's take him down to the swimming hole," Jacob suggested. With him and Eli towering over him, Paul figured it best to follow their lead. He took in the farm's surroundings as he tried to keep up with the tall men taking long strides, noticing the forest of oak trees on the mountain beyond.

He had not had a thorough washing or change of clothes since he had left Boston a month prior. The stench of sweat and filth rising from his body smelled putrid. If he could smell himself, he knew others could.

The men left Paul at the creek where they had swam and bathed for the last forty years. Once he maneuvered around the screen of prickly holly bushes, he stepped gingerly across the slippery rocks. Lying just beyond was a deep, swirling pool of water, the sun's rays casting down its warmth. He dove in. Jacob laid towels across the bushes, then yelled, "You forgot the soap!" The bar sailed through the air and landed with a splash in front of Paul.

"I guess I really do stink," he laughed. The sun shone over the top of the chilly pond water. He dunked himself repeatedly, then lifted his arms and upper body to capture the sun's warmth. Giving the rough rider more mental and physical refreshment than he had had in years.

He walked across the lawn toward the big house feeling renewed—a scrubbed body and clean clothes. Paul shook his head in disbelief, considering this a rare day in his life. The savory smells of roasted meat and hot bread wafted from Lenora's kitchen. He was famished.

"Mr. Revere, Mr. Revere!" a man's voice called. He looked to his left, encountering four very tall young men walking in his direction. He looked closely, shading his squinting eyes. Two were Indians for sure, one maybe half-Indian, and the other broad-shouldered man with reddish hair had to be a Randolph. The four of them smelled strongly of hops and beer mash and smoke. "We wanted to make your acquaintance," Harry smiled widely, taking a lengthy stride forward and extending his hand toward Paul. "Mother and Naomi won't give us a bite to eat until we wash off this dirt and malting smells." Harry pulled at his homespun tunic, shaking off the dust, then shrugged.

"I left the soap on top of the bushes," Paul smiled, pointing his thumb in the direction of the pond. He continued walking toward the food smells, intrigued with the vastness of Mulberry Farm, peering beyond trees, searching for the malting house. The smell of beer permeated the air—in a good way. He had drunk Mulberry beer at various taverns as he traveled, even at Dr. Randolph's kitchen table. There was no finer beer to be found.

"The wet heads have arrived!" Chief Randolph announced when Gray Wolf, Tall Spruce, Ethan, and Harry entered the dining room, each carrying a serving bowl generously filled with roasted sweet potatoes, green beans with ham, squash fritters with cream sauce, and stewed apples with cinnamon and raisins. Steam circled upwards; the essence of flavors filled the room. Eli and Jacob walked behind them with platters of roasted chicken and ham arranged at either end of the long table.

Paul's eyes widened, and his anxious face filled with delight at the abundance of simple food spread before him. The usual fare at most taverns of cold mutton and buttered bread with an occasional baked apple was considered a plentiful meal, and he was glad to get it. He would have kicked himself if he had turned down this dinner invitation.

Lenora took her place at the table's head with Jacob to her left. Between the two of them, they poured wine into glasses and passed them around the table to each guest. The young men waited until all guests were served, and then Jacob proposed a toast. "To our steadfast and Patriot friend, Paul Revere!" Each family member raised their glass to the special guest and took a sip. Now, the chaos began, with passing bowls in two different directions, making sure Chief Randolph and Paul had a serving from each bowl.

Paul had never sat at a formal dinner table with Indians, quickly noticing the effortless camaraderie between guests. Harry and Ethan evoking facetious remarks of Gray Wolf and Tall Spruce's carpentry skills, or lack thereof. Jacob raised his glass to the family's Indian friends. "What would we have done without you this summer?" Apparently, that statement struck a nerve amongst the young men as they all burst out laughing.

Gray Wolf spoke up. "As near as I can tell, your smokehouse would be overflowing with hams and salt pork if it were not for Tall Spruce and me. As it stands, rabbit stew will have to be served on cold winter days. That is if Ethan teaches Harry how to set a snare." He jabbed Ethan's arm with his elbow.

"Haha, and what will warm your bellies when snow covers the ground?" Eli asked, enjoying the sport with his friends across the bounty-filled table.

"Likely, smoked cod and mush. If we're lucky, rabbit stew!" Tall Spruce jested. "Perhaps nettle soup if my ancient cousin Shining Moon has her way." Naomi posed a frown at her nephew and snickered.

"I don't suppose we will be any better off in Boston. The manner in which we're cut off from the countryside leaves no prospect for smoked meat and grain," Paul opined, adding in his two cents worth.

"Perhaps the Almighty will bless us with a mild winter. I'm certain our friends from Connecticut and Rhode Island will continue their gracious spirit, providing Bostonians with ample provisions." The senior Randolph looked at Paul and smiled. "Even so, the outlook is grim and unpredictable."

"Mr. Revere, what of the conditions in Boston? Mr. Hancock and his newly elected provincial congress seem to be running circles around the new governor," Lenora inquired, pausing with a gracious smile, awaiting his answer.

Paul set down his fork. He was taken with Lenora's resemblance to her cousin, Susannah. Charmed by their similarities: fair complexion and yellow hair and a friendly smile. "Mr. Hancock seems to have it in hand, proceeding with the business of the colony—as he should. Governor Gage is a soldier who is learning the hard way that the towns across Massachusetts have great political power. He takes his orders from Parliament because he doesn't know how to run a government."

"It's called an autonomous government—independent, self-governing, and *illegal*," said Jacob. "That is, in the eyes of the Crown, who will mark us as defiant and insolent. Such independence will most definitely move us closer to war. Thomas Gage came in with the mind that he could sweep our town meetings, our General Court, our legislature, out the door, meaning to appoint an all-Tory government to manage our colony. London should know that after more than a hundred years of governing ourselves, we would never submit to their takeover. But they did it anyway, and so far, it has failed. Colonists are too strong and protective of their property to lose it so easily. For goodness sake, every town in the thirteen colonies has its own militia and is growing every day!"

Jacob and Josiah were alike in this respect. They saw the practicality of war through the eyes of a king who aimed to wield his power and authority to gain his own ends, disregarding the millions of lives that could potentially be destroyed.

"Is it true there was a showdown in Worcester of late between the Tories and the militia? I heard there were over three thousand Provincials there to overrun the British regulars sent by the governor." Harry had heard bits and pieces and conflicting stories of the imbroglio. Might as well get the facts firsthand; Paul Revere was sitting right across the table from him.

Paul began recounting the events as he heard them from Sam Adams and Thomas Crafts, two very reliable sources in his mind. "It was two thousand. As you know, all town meetings within each county have been forbidden to meet—prohibited by a new decree from Parliament. On the same day that a big meeting of selectmen was taking place in Boston with Sam Adams and Governor Gage and his lawyers, the town of Worcester's Committees of Correspondence was holding a meeting. Their delegates voted to deny the right of Parliament to create new laws without the consent of the colony.

"The delegates spread the word around to the other counties that the judges they personally had voted in were now to be replaced with new judges appointed by Governor Gage. Now, the county was in an uproar. As it turned out, two thousand armed provincial soldiers led by their militia officers had marched into Worcester, aimed at intimidating the new judges. Which they no doubt accomplished.

"When the Provincials determined that Gage planned to continue allowing his Crown-appointed judges to sit in Worcester and other towns, their aggression grew. Admittedly, there was distorted news that spread across the countryside. Enough so that during the first week in September, that news brought six thousand armed militia back to Worcester to show their strength, demanding that the newly appointed Tory judges return to their homes. At that, the governor received notes from these judges urging him to *not* send the British regulars due to the size of the armed Provincials. To avoid conflict and prevent harm to the judges, the governor called off his army. The county assembly remained in control."

"I should think this lack of governing would put Mr. Gage at odds with the king and Parliament," Ethan declared. "Perhaps the governor had at one time shown strength on the battlefield, but since his arrival on Boston's shores, I believe he has lost all credibility amongst Provincials, something akin to a fraud." While he listened to Paul's account, Ethan was struck that thousands of citizen soldiers had been galvanized to stand together as a unit to vehemently guard their liberties in the face of a British governor desperately seeking to follow the demands of his king. Eli and Naomi glanced at each other and smiled proudly, realizing their son understood what was at stake.

"Either way, it's treason. Here is the congress in Philadelphia: mostly rich, educated, and powerful men combing through these Intolerable Acts and finding ways to work around them, thereby revoking Parliament's demands. John Hancock: elected governor of Massachusetts by an illegal congress, running circles around Governor Gage, making him look foolish and incompetent. Worcester town legislators: kicking out the royal judges before they have a chance to sit in court.

"In essence, this has caused Britain to appear weak, and their plan to bring Boston to her knees has turned disastrous. They've been outdone, and they are furious!" Ethan continued his rant, thoroughly enjoying his moment.

"You are right, Ethan. It is treason. Every one of these Patriots could be tried and hanged." Jacob did not like throwing cold water on Ethan's declarations or the grand accomplishments of leaders in the thirteen colonies, but anything was possible in this incendiary environment.

Later in the day, when the sun lowered and the once brilliant blue sky was fading, Paul Revere sat outside with the Randolph men, including Ozzie MacClure, smoking their pipes and enjoying the peace and quiet of a fall day, sharing stories about the political scene in the colony and in New York. Jacob was full of questions to Paul about how Boston would survive under two governors: one appointed by Parliament, the other voted in by Provincials.

"Mr. Hancock will naturally outwit Mr. Gage, and Boston will remain in a state of confusion. We do have the protection of the militia in the countryside and the surrounding colonies. Not giving too many details; resistance has been in the making for ten years now. Our leaders are prepared. We know it's treasonous, and we could all hang." Paul spoke with candidness. The other men nodded in approval.

"No one can deny that John Hancock is fully capable of managing this colony. If it had not been for his industrious uncle, Boston would never have achieved the trade status that has benefited us all. It's as if he brought the world to our colony through his penchant for merchandising. He paved the way for others to use the resources in these colonies to promote business and stimulate economies."

Chief Randolph nodded at the truth his son Jacob spoke. He glanced around at the landscape—creeks and mountains, orchards, fields of barley and hops, the farmhouse where he grew up, and the big house he had built with his own two hands. His father had an idea to make a suitable beer for his drinking pleasure that took years to perfect. Never realizing that taverns across New England would be interested in buying his product.

A cooling breeze sent the whiffs of mash brewing at this very moment, proof that hard work and patience had provided the means of wealth for the Randolph family.

Always an interesting topic for discussion was the sagacious persona of John Hancock and his mentor and uncle. The House of Hancock was founded by the ambitious Thomas Hancock, who began his career as a bookbinder in 1724. A career of retailing, then wholesaling, making available to Boston resources from all over the world. He built an empire that set Boston apart from the other colonies. Such a rise from mediocrity to untold wealth, the uncle and nephew proved that in the proper environment, the common man had the tools needed to expand the business and provide work for thousands. Such a legacy was sunk deep into the souls of stout-hearted colonists.

The young Mulberry Men were engaged in their assigned kitchen duty—cleaning pots and dishes, sweeping the floor, shoveling out the fireplace ashes, and starting a fresh fire for the next morning. Doing their part in payment for a hearty meal and the labors of Naomi and Lenora. Snacking on tempting leftovers as they talked and worked. Harry caught Gray Wolf's eye and nodded his head at the backyard, unnoticed by Ethan and Tall Spruce as they continued scrubbing.

They walked through the grass and around the apple trees in the direction of the swimming hole, having in mind to pursue their favorite activity of late: wrestling. Something the foursome began after their trip to Captain Zeke's Whales' Tale tavern. A subject that was never discussed in Jacob and Lenora's presence. The Mulberry Men feared questions that could arise regarding the once-threatening presence of Big Shark and Little Minnow. Questions they were too ashamed to answer.

The young men knew Naomi had figured out the odd events of the day, so they kept their distance from her. She had a peculiar way of reading a person's mind. Ethan believed his mother was gifted with a certain mystical divine quality, intuitively aware when things were not on the up and up.

Gray Wolf and Harry walked to a level spot in the yard, giving themselves plenty of space to move, pulled off their tunics over their head, removed their shoes and socks, breathed out a deep breath, and stretched their back and arms. They assumed their position by crouching downwards at their knees, lifting their arms and hands, like the stance of a bear, more or less, then staring into each other's eyes to determine their first move.

Chief Randolph was the first to notice the actions of the two men. "Look yonder," removing his pipe and nodding his head in the direction of the two wrestlers. The men stopped their goings on about politics and revolution and moved their benches closer to the scene.

Gray Wolf made the first move, lunging toward Harry's left side, to which Harry stepped to the right, causing Gray Wolf to hit the ground behind him.

Gray Wolf swiftly got his footing, surprising his opponent by wrapping his arm around Harry's neck, placing him in a hold from behind, pulling Harry to the ground, and ending the first round.

Harry was too familiar with this move. He grabbed Gray Wolf's muscled arms, bent his knees, then slung his opponent over his head, slamming him to the ground.

The older men bent closer in, jerking their upper bodies and fists, moving their heads like a big nervous bird in response to the wrestlers' moves. Harry stood a distance from Gray Wolf, allowing him to get back on his feet, tracking his opponent's face and body for his next move.

Paul stood to get a closer look, holding his pipe in one hand, jabbing his arms in the air each time the wrestlers tried their darndest to make a move against the other, sweat rolling down their faces.

Circling one another, Harry's eyes widened at a booming sound in the distance, throwing off his concentration. Gray Wolf made a push toward him, grabbed his hands, and forced him to walk backward until Harry lost control and landed on his back. Laughing, he knew he was beaten when Gray Wolf stumbled sideways and landed across his opponent's middle. A few seconds later, the winner stood shaking both fists in the air, claiming victory, while Harry remained in a supine position on the grass. Another boom shook the air, bringing Harry to a seated position. "What the devil was that?" Harry shouted.

Tall Spruce spoke up first. "It's the redcoat soldiers. They have set up camp to the west of the mudflats."

"How do you know? Have you seen them?" Paul asked Tall Spruce, suddenly concerned about the direction to take when returning to Boston.

"I have seen them. Two days ago. I used your spyglass, Uncle Jacob, to watch them unload their wagons of tents and cannons," Tall Spruce answered.

"How close were you when you discovered them? Sounds to me like they've set up in Roxbury." Jacob knew it was only a matter of time before soldiers would move south to set up a drilling camp.

"If you climb up yon sycamore on the other side of the malting house, there's a place to sit and spy as long as you like, sir." Tall Spruce was tall and lanky. Climbing a tree was like kid's play for him, not so much for Jacob.

From the back of the house strolled Naomi and Lenora, searching the property for the source of the curiously loud boom. Leisure time was hard to come by, with seven hungry men wondering about their next meal. Lenora turned to Naomi, "What is going on with these youngsters, red-faced, bare chests, sweaty hair, walking around each other crouched like a bear on the attack?" She rolled her eyes at such foolishness. "I do not understand men. What more proof does one need that men and women are from different worlds? I sure hope this baby is a girl!" Without thinking, her hand immediately went to her bulging middle.

Naomi laughed. "Truth spoken." She paused in wonder at the sudden twitch in her belly.

Chapter 30

LEXINGTON, MASSACHUSETTS

April 16, 1775

It was rather unsettling when, one January morning, Father announced plans of moving our family of three to a safer location—temporarily. The tense atmosphere that prevailed in Boston after colonial delegates had met in Philadelphia consumed everyone's thoughts. We were unsure, from one day to the next, if General Gage aimed to give us a few hours' notice to evacuate or a gracious few days to pack our necessities. The thought of leaving the only home I had ever known chilled me to the bone, but we had no choice. As long as Boston remained inundated with British soldiers, it could never again be my home. My little voice reminded me: *Never say never*. We would leave Bradford Lane for Lexington.

Auntie saw things differently. "We should have used good sense and remained at Mulberry Farm last May. Gage may be slow in making his move to evacuate all rebels to the country, but the time will come when we will be forced to move. Here we are scrambling at the last moment to save our hides."

I had been resistant to Father's ideas of moving us to Thomas Crafts' home in Lexington. Waiting until the last minute to retreat to the countryside was not an option for Father. "Imagine the excitable crowds of Bostonians rushing to board the ferry to cross the Charles River, bells pealing and children crying. Your aunt Minnie would be tied up in knots for weeks! For our neighbors and friends who lean toward independence, they can leave of their own accord." That was it. We packed.

The unusually mild winter had played into making his decision. Snowflakes had whirled and swirled on the coldest of days but never accumulated as they typically do during the most bitterly cold months of the year. A positive sign as any to Father, prompting us to leave Boston to travel the ten or so miles to Lexington to set up a surgery and hospital in Thomas Crafts' spacious house.

With the numerous trips Mr. Crafts had made to our house during November and December, he had obligingly packed his mule-driven wagon with boxes of medical supplies and transported them to his house, where we were to live and work. According to Father, it was larger than our Bradford Lane house. We began packing our most essential and personal items.

Mr. Crafts had warned us, "Governor Gage will be pressed by the Crown to take action against us radicals. Springtime would be the most likely time for military action."

Auntie and I had spent the last six months preparing medicines and teas and rolling linen strips for bandages. Through his friendly connections with the British guard, Elias Denton, Thomas had been allowed to transport boxes and bags of medical supplies in his wagon, taking the long way to his home by traveling down through the Neck past Roxbury, then north through Concord to Lexington. The lieutenant's decision was swayed when he learned "the Doc" planned to set up his practice in the country. "He's saved my life more than once. I owe him."

My morale was very low, indeed, as I began packing a bag of everyday wear: muslin gowns, bodices, stockings, toiletries, and such. I filled a satchel with favorite books, parchment, my journal, and a box of writing quills. We locked the door to the surgery. I stood at the big window sipping the last of my tea, staring at the lonely leafless elms and oaks and Auntie's sparse winter garden. *When would we return?* I wondered.

I bid farewell to the empty house on Bradford Lane. I glanced at Ezra Phillips' print shop, lifeless with its boarded windows and doors. He wasn't the type to give up and pack away his printing press. Instead, he rented an empty barn in the small town of Acton near Concord, where he set up his print shop, catching the news in neighboring towns. Ebenezer Crichton joined us as we trudged up Main Street, pushing a cart laden with baggage to the ferry bound for Charlestown, where Thomas would be waiting in his wagon to drive us to his home.

Once the most prosperous town and port in the thirteen colonies, Boston was now barren and spiritless, so much so that as we walked up the cobblestoned street to the North end of town, our repetitive footsteps echoed as we drew nearer to the Charles River. The splashing sound of waves beating against the wharf, with no gulls squawking. The mile-long walk offered an eerie prospect. Most of the shops and markets had closed by the end of August last year, with a few exceptions. One being the bookshop owned and managed by Henry Knox, a Whig whose fascination with the arts of war and artillery attracted British officers who considered the shop to be a haven for military discourse.

I smiled at Father when we caught sight of the familiar published booklet *Analyzing Epidemics and Its Causes*, co-authored by Dr. Jerome Pierpoint and Dr. Josiah Randolph, handsomely displayed on an easel in the paned window front. Father leaned in close to my ear. "This gentleman," referring to Mr. Knox, "has imparted more valuable information to the rebel cause than I can allude to at the moment. I'll explain later." I scrutinized Father's face, vaguely nodding in response.

Father regarded Mr. Crichton as the obvious choice as caretaker for our Boston property, maintaining that British officers would certainly seize the empty house for their living quarters. A shrewd thinker, if there ever was one, when it came to property and finances. Ebenezer realized an opportunity when Father entrusted him with the management of Bradford Lane in our absence.

Mr. Crichton was neither a rebel nor a Tory. He was a businessman who looked beyond Boston's present situation to the potential circumstances in the foreseeable future, with the intent to realize a profit. Father accepted that sort of reasoning, and I trusted him.

Auntie and I were elated that the day before we were to board the ferry for Charlestown, Mr. Crichton produced a rental contract signed by a resident of Lexington, Mr. DeFore. With his wife and four children, they would take occupancy of our home as soon as we left Boston for the countryside. When Father inquired as to the man's hurried reasoning, Ebenezer Crichton explained that Mr. DeFore would rather live under the protection of the British governor than worry that his family's home might go up in flames when the rebels and redcoats got around to battling it out in Lexington or Concord.

When Thomas navigated Flip onto the gravel drive of the property, a handsome Georgian-style house painted a light green stood before us. I responded to the unexpected view with bulging eyes and a jab of my elbow into Auntie's side, mouthing, "What?" She laughed, knowing I would be surprised. It was a picture of simplicity encased within a white picket fence. The sun casts shadows of surrounding trees on the thick winter grass.

Before we left Boston, she had given me odd bits about Thomas' family. He had lost his wife and two children to smallpox during the plague that swept through Boston, Lexington, and Cambridge in the mid-1760s. Perhaps the reason why he and Father have a close bond, having lost their mates early in their marriage.

We walked inside through a long hallway with large rooms on either side and a paneled staircase built next to the drawing room side with five steps going up one way, switching to eight steps rising sideways to a hallway and three bedrooms. Windows in the bedchambers provided views northward and to the east. "Josiah said Thomas built all the bedsteads and dressers." Auntie ran her hand over the tops of the furniture, admiring the man's workmanship.

While the men unloaded our bags, we walked to the kitchen, fascinated by the distinctive shape of the sloping room attached to the back width of the lower level like a lean-to, housing a monstrous fireplace with more tools than I could name attached to its brick facade. "This house is called a saltbox. It's the shape of a saltbox used during Medieval times. Such a rare structure." *Auntie's compliments were rare*, I mused.

There were three small rooms along the way to the kitchen, which I had not yet investigated. We walked out the back door through the scullery, discovering the well and several outbuildings, including a barn where wagons were stored. "I don't see a garden," Annie commented. I breathed in the earthy country smells, so different from the briny Boston air.

"I've heard Thomas mention that he eats his meals at his cousin Leonard's house and sometimes at the tavern." From the looks of the fireplace, which was swept neat as a pin, there was naught but a low burning fire for heating the room and a lonely kettle for heating water. "Has it occurred to you that we have no provisions for a meal? Can you fathom the gall of that British officer not allowing us to bring a round of cheese or a loaf of bread? It's been a long while since breakfast. What shall we do?" I asked.

"Not to worry, ladies." In walked the jovial Thomas, flashing a toothy grin, carrying two baskets on each arm loaded with bread, ham, eggs, onions, teas, and jams. "Josiah will be delayed. Deliverin' Lucinda's baby. You'll not have met Leonard's lovely wife. I was helping her pack these baskets fer yer lauder, and not a minute passed before she slumped to the floor. Great with child, she was. The doc and I put her to bed." He stood at the work table, unpacking the baskets, and glanced around. "I'll stoke the fire and slice the ham."

While Father was out seeing to the ills of Lexington, Auntie and I assumed the task of installing a surgery in the dining room. We accepted Thomas Crafts' words as truth when he stated that General Gage would not engage his soldiers in military action until the spring. Now, we had a timeline from which to gauge our work. For it was our responsibility to design and stock the surgery. We chose the dining room due to its size and the large trestle table situated in the middle of the room. Another factor being the unrestricted natural light that shone in throughout the day.

From one of the barns, we found an assortment of cupboards with shelves, perfect for storing surgical tools, ceramic bottles filled with alcohol, medicines, teas, linens, and bandages. Thomas and Leo hauled the furniture into the designated room and arranged them as Auntie and I directed. We aimed to duplicate the Bradford Lane Surgery.

Upon Father's inspection, he praised our efforts and indicated that, without a doubt, it would prove to serve our needs and the small community of Lexington. We were grateful that Thomas Crafts had the skills and the tools to construct such furnishings. Why he was the proprietor of such an array of cabinets, I cannot say. Perhaps he had in mind to open a shop one day.

"Thomas, do you recall the day you brought your cousin Leonard to Bradford Lane when his arm was slashed with a knife?" Auntie asked our friend, hoping to paint a picture in his mind of what was forthcoming.

"I believe you're referring to those two English ruffians who assaulted me and Leonard on the bridge," Thomas answered, shaking his head as he remembered that harrowing night.

"Yes, and do you recall the small cots where you rested in our drawing room because of the sleep you and Leonard missed the night before?" Auntie was making her point. "We're going to need more of those cots for our minutemen whom we expect to doctor. Can you help us?"

Thomas sighed deeply. "I better sharpen my saws and get to work. What do you say, Leo?" Thomas raised his eyebrows at his cousin, expecting an answer.

"Sounds like we're assembling a hospital this week. Let's get a pint at Buckman's first," Leo suggested. The two giant men lumbered toward the front door, headed for the tavern.

"I guess we'll be sewing mattresses this week," Auntie decided. "It's approaching afternoon tea. Perhaps we should pull the cork on a bottle of elderberry wine."

"Only if Father doesn't return before we snatch a bottle from the cellar."

February came in with barely freezing weather, no icy lawns and roads, just spitting snow, then a blue sky appeared, bringing the sunshine. The front door bell rang early every morning, and patients gathered in the vestibule with common, treatable ailments and injuries. With a smile and my patient book in hand, I greeted a new and different type of patient in Lexington—busted fingers, strained back muscles and shoulders, broken collar bones, and burnt body parts from the misuse of forge tongs and hammers.

With the unusually mild winter, farmers worked outside repairing plows, pulling dead tree stumps, rebuilding their barns, and any work they had previously set aside for a more suitable time, which scarcely came for farmers. Their work lasted from dawn to dusk—every day. Markedly different from our Boston patients limping daily into our Bradford Lane Surgery with broken noses, cuts, and head injuries sustained by drunken longshoremen during a street fight.

Thomas and Leo had outfitted the drawing room turned hospital with a dozen wooden beds and small bedside tables for a bowl and ewer. I commented how practical it would be for each patient to have their own personal wash water and linens, but that convenience was not likely.

One afternoon, while tidying up the surgery, I heard a sound of jingling bells urging me to open the front door, thinking there might be a patient riding in on a horse. Standing at the entrance to the walkway in the dooryard stood a shiny chestnut harnessed to a wagon driven by two people I had never seen. Two slightly built young women were seated on the bench of the wagon. The back filled to the top with hay. I walked toward the visitors and introduced myself.

"Uhm, we're the Ledbetters. We've come to deliver some crockery we made at the request of Thomas Crafts," one of the girls spoke. I walked closer to see that the young ladies were identical twins, with absolutely no difference in their facial and bodily features. "Would you like for us to assist you in hauling them inside the house?" the same girl asked, staring at me, expecting a reply.

By this time, Auntie presented herself outside and walked to the wagon, eager to meet our visitors and curiously examining the wagon bed filled with hay. "Are you delivering hay for the paddock? We only have the mule."

Girl number two jumped down from the wagon seat, smiling hesitantly as she reached under the hay and pulled out a yellow pitcher with a bright green leaf design painted around its base. "Here's the matching bowl for that ewer, Sissy." Her sister accepted the bowl and set the ewer inside, holding it out for display to Auntie so she could understand the purpose of their visit.

"Do you mean to say that you ladies made all this crockery?" Auntie gazed at the cheery yellow set, shaking her head in disbelief. "I suppose there must be more under all this straw?" her eyebrows raised at the two girls. "Let's take them inside."

We looked around at all the yellows, greens, and blues we had sat atop the dull brown tables. "I'd say this room would lift anybody's spirits! You ladies look spent. I can offer you some cider if you have the time." I retrieved a jar from the springhouse and met Auntie and the twins in the kitchen.

When they held their cups and chatted with us, I got a close look at their dry hands, muddied and stained along the inside of their fingers and nails. Muscular hands and arms identified them as potterers. I decided at that moment to offer them a jar of Naomi's hand cream made from Burdock tops, really a salve to soothe dry skin. They accepted it graciously.

"I wasn't aware that anybody in these parts made pottery. I suppose you own a kiln, but where do you get the clay?" Auntie stopped short. "Perhaps that's a trade secret you would prefer not to share."

The twins looked at one another and grinned. Twin number one spoke up. "That's alright. We're proud that we can play a small role in helping our soldiers. We're thankful you're making this hospital available. When Thomas asked for our help, we began right away with the design and colors. I reckon we should be getting home. Patience likes to settle in early."

We walked the girls outside, and there stood Patience, staring at Flip in the paddock, the gentle wind catching her mane. Taking delight in the cool breeze and clean air I have enjoyed for almost two months, I noticed both twins squinted their red-rimmed eyes, whether they were inside the house or outside in the bright light. I decided their eyes might be inflamed because of the nature of working with clay. I glanced sideways at Auntie.

She read my mind and positioned herself to get a good look at their faces. "Both of you have inflamed eyes. Do they burn and itch?" The twins stared at each other, teary-eyed, then squinted as they nodded in

Auntie's direction, shading their eyes with their hands. "I can show you a way to treat your eyes so they won't continue to be irritated. If you can come back this way tomorrow, I will show you how to make a poultice. When you get home, wash your eyes with cool water and a clean cloth to remove the clay dust." Auntie gave a reassuring smile and stepped back, allowing the girls to continue their journey home.

We watched them drive away. "I caught the horse's name. Do you recall the names of the twins?"

"I guess we can ask tomorrow if they come to the surgery. Here it is, the end of February, and I haven't seen hide nor hair of Thomas for weeks," Auntie wondered out loud. "I hope he's not in any trouble. Listen, I hear somebody riding in on horseback. Let's get in the house."

Never far from access to a weapon in Thomas' house, we each grabbed a pistol and stood behind a doorway on opposite sides of the vestibule. My heart raced, and my eyes glued to the front door. When the door eased open, all I saw was a white handkerchief dangling from a big hand. "I surrender!" It was Father's voice. I hid my pistol behind my skirt. "You forgot to bolt the front door!"

"Can you blame us for protecting ourselves? We ran inside when we heard a horse pounding down the road, preparing for the worst." Father grinned at Auntie's unorthodox response. By nature, she was unruffled under most conditions. During these precarious times, we remained cautious.

"I didn't mean to cause you alarm. Anyway, come outside and meet our, uh, new friend." Father held the door open, and I walked out first, squealing at the site of the most beautiful dapple gray tethered to the hitching post, right where Patience had stood only minutes before.

"Where? How? Can we keep him?" I walked to his side and rubbed his mottled neck, talking softly to the contented horse. "We'll need some oats and carrots. Where will we board him?"

"His name is Dandy, and you'll understand what I mean when you get to know him. I assume you've not stepped foot into the barn lately?" I shook my head. "Thomas and Leo have shifted the wagons around and opened up the stalls. You'll see." Auntie and I followed Father and

Dandy to the barn, excited about the horse, country life, and the surprise wagon load of pottery, everything so new and different, the opposite of Bradford Lane. All three of us privately ached with the prospects of our unpredictable future, fearing that, in a few weeks, Gage would make his move to the countryside.

Auntie and I carried buckets of water from the well to Dandy's trough set up in the paddock beside Flip's. We thought a gesture of goodwill toward the mule might reduce any hard feelings by treating him with chunks of carrot and fresh hay. We weren't sure how he would react to Dandy being installed next door. Mules can be feisty and short-tempered, but for all that, Flip put in his share of work when it was deemed necessary. The mule surprised us with a hee-haw, but I'm not sure whether that meant "Thank you for the treat" or "Why is this handsome steed and I breathing the same air?" It was a wait-and-see experiment.

After a day of surprises, we washed up and settled down to our meal an hour later than usual. Auntie had stirred together a savory winter vegetable soup, she called it, with mushrooms, turnips, and leeks in a creamy chicken broth. Since our move to the Crafts' farm, we had received rounds of yeast bread, currant cakes, and gooseberry cakes from Sadie Cowpens, our neighbor who lived on the next farm in the direction of Concord. "Any friend of Thomas Crafts is a friend of mine," she repeated every time she made a delivery, which was twice a week. We appreciated the bread, but it was too much for us, so we shared it with patients. Bread baking was one tedious job that Auntie was thrilled to be relieved of, allowing her more time to start a garden and begin cultivating a collection of herbs.

"Josiah, I'm concerned about Thomas. He hasn't been around in a while." Auntie had a suspicious notion that Thomas was swept up in the spy ring headed by Paul Revere and Dr. Warren.

Father hesitated to reveal what he knew, but this was his sister, who he knew would dig out the truth from somebody, eventually. "The last I heard, Thomas was in jail on Castle Island. So were Paul Revere and other, erm, notables."

Auntie and I sat stunned, too frozen to comment. Our intrepid friend, defeated by that coward, Governor Gage. His own soldiers called him "granny" behind his back because he moved so slowly in his decision-making. He definitely showed no spine in restraining the rebels.

"It seems Revere, Crafts, Edes, and some others were scouting Castle Island where they had rowed on Saturday afternoon, keeping an eye on Colonel Leslie's sixty-fourth regiment. They had received word that the colonel was headed to Salem to confiscate our weapons supply. Once the scouts were spotted, they were arrested and put behind bars. Now, there was no way they could warn the Salem Provincials that the regulars were marching in their direction."

"By Sunday afternoon, one hundred fifty regulars were transported to Marblehead, three miles south of Salem. Most people were at church when the redcoats set out marching on Salem Road, likely searching for the town's store of weapons. The bells began tolling, alerting the militia and the townspeople to arm themselves and hurry to the bridge."

"The main issue for the regulars was the drawbridge. Once it was drawn up, the marching ceased, and nobody was crossing to the other side. Colonel Leslie went back and forth arguing with militia officers for several hours, finally caving to the wishes of the increased number of armed townspeople demanding the redcoat soldiers return to their garrison on Castle Island."

"What became of poor old Thomas and the others? Does anyone know?" Auntie asked.

"Whoo, it smells good in here. Anybody home?" A loud voice roared from the front of the house, and the door slammed. Thomas trudged into the kitchen, looking somewhat bedraggled and hungry.

We all laughed, more from the knowledge that he actually escaped from the clutches of the British army but because we missed our friend. We gave him a hearty welcome and invited him to join us at the table. He proceeded quickly to the scullery to wash off the visible grime before settling down to attack a loaf of bread with butter and a pot of fresh coffee. He wolfed down the remains of the winter soup while talking and describing the particulars until his brain and body ceased to work in tandem.

He had clearly exhausted himself answering our questions. His bulky frame slumped in the chair, and he noticeably fought sleep, catching himself as his head nodded. A long soak in the bathtub would have been the surest way to eliminate his disgusting body odors, but not before he slept for the next twelve hours. Auntie closed his chamber door, silently promising that removing his head lice would take priority after the next morning's breakfast. *Best done outside in the bright light*, she thought.

Josiah stood at the fence watching Dandy and Flip, pondering their behavior within the same pasture, sharing the same water and hay. *Might not work*, he thought. He examined the workmanship of the fence: three rails, held in place one above the other, at each joining, by four crossed sticks. He turned around to face Thomas walking his way. "Mighty strong fence you built, Thomas."

"Yup. Called a triple-rail fence—horse-high, bull-proof, and pig-tight. That's a fine-looking stallion, Doc. Where did you find him?" Thomas was in middling spirits when he met Josiah, who was feeding Dandy a breakfast of oats and molasses.

"I was walking by the Ludlow farm on my way to Buckman's when I noticed this horse in the front pasture unattended—no water in the trough, no hay in the bin. I walked to the house to inquire about the horse and looked in the front window. There lay a woman on the floor in apparent distress. I got her attention and told her I was a doctor. I showed her my medical bag so she wouldn't think I was a thief. Turns out she had a broken radius. She fell somewhere between the pasture and the house and collapsed inside."

"A broken radius, you say? Where? What?" Thomas fell short of Josiah's anatomical vocabulary.

The left sleeve of Josiah's tunic was rolled up to his elbow. He indicated the location of the radius that lay along the top inside of his forearm. "She broke it here," pointing at the halfway mark between his elbow and wrist. "She's fine now that I secured it with a splint. Josie visited her early this morning to help her get out of bed. Uh, we were discussing the horse. In payment for my doctoring, she gave me Dandy along with his tack." He shrugged. "I doubt she could manage the horse's upkeep."

Thomas stared at the horse, hearing Josiah talk but not absorbing the details of the story. Josiah could tell he was put out by the Salem disaster. "If there's anything I learned from this sortie, I'm never speaking to Dr. Church again. I'm avoiding him like the plague. He's the leak, I'm sure of it. Every time we find a new location to meet, Gage's men find us," Thomas lamented, downhearted as he was.

"All these months, we've met in secret at the inn, planning strategies, discussing the movement of Gage's troops, tracking them as they patrolled the streets, waiting in the woods to learn where they hid their boats. Who did we report our findings to? Adams, Hancock, Warren, and…" He couldn't say Dr. Benjamin Church's name. It made his gorge rise. He spat on the ground instead.

Josiah nodded, considering in retrospect the congratulatory dinner party at Dr. Pierpoint's home where Elise Beaumont and Dr. Church gave guests the impression they were entwined in an affair of the heart. Now, he was certain the two worked together as spies for the British, conveying information to Governor Gage.

Boston's Green Dragon Inn had been headquarters for the Masons and the thirty or so men who made up Boston's radical web of spies, contriving to thwart any attempts by Gage to seize and destroy military stores hidden by the rebels. This was their only defense against the Crown.

"Pull yourself together, Thomas, and be thankful the people of Salem had the good sense to devise a system that warned their militia and townspeople of advancing British troops, same as we have here. The people are angry now that they realize how far Parliament will go to take away their property and weapons. I hear it from every patient who enters the surgery, and they have no qualms about wearing a pistol and carrying a rifle everywhere they go. I mean to say, men and women are on the offensive." Josiah knew the time for standing against the world's most well-trained and organized army was approaching.

The ringleaders of the resistance movement were John Hancock, Samuel Adams, Joseph Warren, and the delegates to the Second Continental Congress in Philadelphia. Adams and Hancock were stowed away at various homes in the countryside, preparing for their journey to Philadelphia. Dr. Warren was stationed in Cambridge. It was risky business being the point man for the Committee of Safety, but this is where news was covertly received, and plans were formulated by the hour.

Paul Revere and his band of spies had watched the comings and goings of General Gage's officers since they had set up their headquarters at Province House last August. They recognized the same costumes worn by the cantiest of redcoat soldiers, disguising themselves as mechanics and farmers, rowing to the countryside with the intent to procure information about the whereabouts of hidden military stores. This network of British spies had *worked* Lexington and Concord for months, mapping the roads and bridges, learning the tempers of its citizens, visiting taverns to collect bits of local gossip. Once Gage was satisfied he had received adequate intelligence, a sortie was planned for mid-April.

At midnight on April 15th, Revere's spies witnessed boats launched from British transports. The grenadiers and light infantry were taken off duty. Clear signs that British regulars planned to cross the Charles River to Lexington and hunt down and arrest the prime suspects of the traitorous rebellion, Hancock and Adams. Secondly, proceed to Concord and Worcester to confiscate and destroy weapons hidden by militant colonists.

Hancock and Adams had traveled from Boston to Concord several days earlier to attend the Provincial Congress. Most of its members traveled back to their homes in nearby towns, but Hancock and Adams remained in Lexington on the advice of the Committee of Safety. The two "traitors to the Crown" were safely ensconced at the home of Reverend Jonas Clark. His household was immediately put under the protection of minutemen, constantly on alert to receive news from rebel riders who tracked the whereabouts of British regulars. When and if Hancock and Adams received the all-clear, they would travel to Philadelphia along with their clerk to join with delegates from all the colonies to continue the second debates at Carpenter's Hall.

At last, General Gage felt confident he could implement his orders from London: transport the Tenth Regiment under the command of Lieutenant Colonel Francis Smith to Lexington, arrest the two main resistance leaders, and seize the citizen's stores of weapons hidden in Concord. Parliament believed this was the surest way to put down Boston's rebellion. Gage's plans came as no surprise to the Provincials. They had welcomed such an engagement for the last ten months. Easier said than done.

Thomas Crafts stood anxiously nursing a tankard of ale while gazing out the window of Buckman's Tavern, a two-story Georgian-style structure that lay in walking distance of Thomas' house and ten miles west of Boston. The ordinary had served patrons for over sixty years. Thomas knew in his bones that something was afoot with Gage and his British regulars. Rumors had been flying for weeks.

Thomas looked around the room. Every man sitting at tables or pacing the floor had a pistol in his belt and a musket at his side, ready to take action if necessary. His mind was spinning. The ale gave him a sour stomach.

Over and over, he pondered the events of the past year—the Provincial's rejection of Gage's plans to turn the Massachusetts General Court system upside down to pack it with British appointees, the inflated Provincial militia that had grown by the thousands, the stockpile of weapons that had been transported mostly from Connecticut and New Hampshire to Lexington, Concord, Worcester, Acton, and Stow. "We've done all we can do," he muttered. "No backing down now."

Massachusetts citizen soldiers, inspired by the combat veterans of the French and Indian War, understood the strict discipline and training of British soldiers, having fought and trained beside them. Thomas Crafts being one of those veterans whose anecdotal stories and accounts of combat were invaluable to new recruits. In time, natural leaders would rise to the occasion. Such militia soldiers were well-trained and well-equipped. A ready force who were assigned to troops engaged in defensive battle. Minutemen were prepared to do battle in one minute at the sound of an alarm.

Thomas felt confident they had the manpower and the artillery to defeat the regulars. He was certain rebels would face off with redcoat soldiers if their arsenal of weapons were discovered, so valued and protected over the past months. Rebels would defend their property, and blood would be shed. He continued his gaze up the road toward Boston, ears pricked to the familiar cadence of fife and drum. The day of reckoning for the North American colonies was coming—April 19, 1775.

Take a peek at Book Two of the *Bradford Lane Chronicles*:

TRAITORS TO THE CORE

ON SALE SOON

Concord, Massachusetts
Morning of April 17, 1775

For three days, we were cooped up in the house, feeling like prisoners in our own home. Actually, it was not our home. Thomas Crafts invited us to live in his house so we could leave Boston to avoid harassment and possible eviction by the powers that be—Governor Gage and his officers.

Heavy rains had poured at our Lexington house, receiving very few sickly people brave or desperate enough to walk or drive their wagon to our surgery. Without the constant opening and closing of the front door and chattering patients sitting in wait for the doctor, the house felt more like Folger's Bookstore, where patrons communicated just above a whisper and shuffled from one section to another to read in solitude.

Auntie and I carried on with our daily routines, preparing meals for the three of us and tidying the surgery as necessary. Thomas felt more at home at Buckman's Tavern, confident that British regulars would make their appearance on our side of the Charles River any day to collect the townspeople's weapons and to generally oppress us by patrolling villages. Frankly making a nuisance of themselves.

I assumed the care of Dandy and Flip by providing a clean and roomy environment. Mucking out the stalls, feeding them twice a day, and giving them outside exercise—all part of the necessary chores required for a contented horse and mule. This took the burden off Father, giving him time to study his medical journals and visit patients in their homes. Auntie felt more at home digging in the vegetable garden and drying herbs for teas and medicines.

Both animals enjoyed watching me as I cleaned their stalls and replaced their straw and tended to their hooves and grooming. I would sing and recite Shakespeare as I worked, and when I stopped, Dandy would shake his head up and down, signaling that more vocal activity from me was to his liking. Unlike taciturn Flip, who was not prone to conveying any social connection to me or Dandy. He certainly didn't mind the brushing I gave him twice a day. All in all, the work kept me occupied and my body exercised.

Standing at the barn doorway to catch a breath of fresh air, I heard hooves in the distance pounding the road, advancing in the direction of our house. Perhaps my grim thoughts were coming true. I glanced across the road at the Sullivan farm, where the front yard was covered with fallen apple blossoms. The heavy downpours had subsided, giving way to occasional misting rains, creating a haze that made it impossible to determine the identity of the riders.

I swallowed hard and turned my eyes toward the dark walls of the barn, hoping to find a musket or pistol. I spotted the pitchfork and placed it in a standing position by my side.

Sure enough, one of the riders had slowed his mount before turning into the drive. The outline of horse and rider appeared more like a specter in the foggy mist. If I couldn't recognize the riders, I'm sure they could not determine my identity. I plopped a straw hat on my head and stepped into the misting rain. Dandy and Flip stood with their necks stretched over their stable gates, staring as mystified as I was at the snorts and neighs of oncoming horses on an unfitting day.

Oh fie, here comes one of the riders. Looking for shelter, I expect. When the tall man dismounted, I could have sworn he looked like one of my cousins. I moved cautiously closer.

"Josie Randolph. Is that you wearing breeches and boots?" To my surprise, cousin Jake stood before me covered in an oiled cape and a slouch hat not quite performing its job of keeping his head dry, with water running down its sides and his boots soaked. His horse looked wretched.

"What are you doing in this part of the country? Shouldn't you be at school in Cambridge?" We stepped under the wide eave on the back porch. "Who are those men traveling with you?"

"They're Harvard students like me. We're on our way to Concord to join the militia, hoping to run these redcoats out of the colony—if we can shoot enough of them. We've had a time traveling in this nasty storm. We'd appreciate something hot to drink if you can spare it." Without waiting for me to answer, he waved his hand, motioning his companions to join him.

We got the horses settled in the barn and made our way to the kitchen fire. "Well, cat and the moon, look who's gallivanting around Lexington on such a day?" Auntie had the coffee cooking, filling the room with its welcoming aroma. She looked at the three young men. "Make yourselves at home and get out of those wet shoes."

Jake moved first to pull a straight chair from the table to the fireplace, proceeding to remove his boots and wool stockings. He settled himself by arranging his feet as close to the fire as possible without burning himself on the grate. I attempted a demonstrative cough, forcing Jake to take notice of his questionable decorum. "Oh, pardon me, Auntie and Josie. My friends standing here with chattering teeth are Colin Barrett and Grayson Herndon. We call him Gray." The men removed their hats and nodded their heads as they stood just within the kitchen doorway, water dripping from their capes and boots. Lest he be scolded by his aunt Minnie for presuming he was the only man in the room with cold, wet feet, Jake dutifully arranged two more chairs at the fireplace for Gray and Colin.

"May I take your capes, gentlemen?" Auntie smiled and accepted the men's heavy wool outerwear, soaking wet on the outside and warm as toast on the inside. The men seated themselves at the fireplace and, in like manner, removed their footwear. Jake glanced up at Auntie and me, making an attempt to redeem himself by pouring each of his friends a mug of steaming coffee.

I turned toward our guests. "By the bye, gentlemen, you may eat as much as you like and pay no attention to my cousin. When he's in the presence of women, he imagines himself a lord to be waited on hand and foot." Gray and Colin looked at each other and laughed as if they were well acquainted with Jake's egregious behavior.

Gray and Colin sat listening to our back and forth but were mainly engrossed in the small banquet served before them." Jake chuckled. "You'll have to excuse these two pigs disguised as humans. They haven't eaten anything in two days. The school's dining room closed unexpectedly when the cook threw in the towel and left the property, fearing for his life. So I've heard. He perceived the rebels and redcoats were soon to clash. Another Tory seeking the governor's protection."

Jake's Harvard friends glanced at each other and burst out laughing. Auntie was quick to examine the sly grin and wide eyes on her nephew's face. "And what do you know about the cook's departure, Jake? Any roguish tricks you would like to confess to?" Auntie's narrowed eyes pierced through Jake until he was forced to shrug his shoulders and shake his head in confirmation."

"His cooking would turn your stomach, Auntie. I'm positive he chops dead rats disguised as stew meat." The two Harvard Men nodded. "He deserved what he had coming, and we're better off."

I chuckled at Auntie's coercing methods to learn the truth. "What was the final straw?" I asked.

Jake looked sideways at Gray and Colin. "We sewed his small clothes together at the legs and ran them up on the flagpole. And his stockings." At that, Jake barely managed to keep a straight face. His Harvard friends held their snickering as long as they could and exited the kitchen to the backyard.

"Such unmerciful shenanigans! Is that the reason you left school in a hurry? Surely, there will be discipline for your behavior." Auntie was well aware of Jake's propensity to prank, even as a child. It followed his character of a know-it-all. "Just like your father." She retorted.

After consuming two mugs of strong coffee and half an apple tart, Jake appeared fettled enough to ask questions about our survival in

Boston over the past months and any general knowledge of how rebels and Tories are surviving under King George's man, meaning Governor Gage.

"Are you aware that Tories have deserted the countryside to Boston for the protection of British soldiers? All the while, Rebels have escaped Boston to make their homes, albeit temporary, across the Charles River. At least we have access to fresh food." I shrugged and paused to allow Jake to respond.

Surprisingly, he merely nodded at the obvious truth, knowing full well all the reasons why. "Where is Uncle Josiah? Did you purchase this house? Have you installed a surgery?"

"Your uncle Josiah is out on this raw day attending patients, and no, we do not own this house." Auntie waved her hand through the air, indicating it was more of a sanctuary for the time being. "A friend of your uncle offered this place to us until the wind blows in a different direction, so to speak. They should be arriving any moment as hungry as bears, as usual."

"I heard a wagon come through. Perhaps they're here. Won't they be surprised to find the stables filled with strange horses?" Jake's face scowled, pulling a worrisome expression. The first sign of emotion he had shown for others, slight as it was, since he walked through the kitchen.

The back door slammed when Father and Thomas entered through the scullery, draping their sur-outs across the crowded coat rack. *Two more huge bodies to add to the kitchen fireplace and two more bellies to feed*, I fretted. Our three guests stood when Father and Thomas entered the room. Father was surprised and elated to encounter Jake—tall, dark-haired, and healthy-looking, very much favoring his father, Jacob.

He shook hands with Colin—dark brown eyes and hair, olive-skinned and slim as Jake, a handsome face with a welcoming smile. "Pleased to meet you, sir. Will you take my chair? You're in need of a warm drink, I'm sure." Father eyed Colin's bare feet and grinned. "It's a nasty wet day, sir."

"A student at Harvard, I gather." Father extended his hand to Gray, shorter and of smaller stature than his traveling companions, his tawny hair falling naturally from a part, tended to cover his left brow. "Do you live in Worcester, by chance? I served with a man named Herndon in the previous war."

"Indeed, sir, some of my people on my mother's side live in Worcester. However, my family works a farm in Lincoln." His greenish eyes expressed his gratitude. "These ladies have been most generous with fine food and drink, and we're thankful." Father smiled and nodded.

"I'm more than acquainted with this big creature. So they let you out of your cage?" Father gave Jake a hug, making him feel at home. "Shoeless as well?" Father laughed and invited Thomas to come and join the Harvard Men. Auntie and I glanced at each other with the same thought in mind. We started an extra-large pot of stew for our afternoon meal.

The men drained another pot of coffee and polished off a loaf of bread, a sweet potato pie, and a raisin cake while discussing the prospects for conflict with the regulars in the next day or so. "We've had our sights set on the Boston Common now for the last week—I mean, literally." Jake had filled his belly and was ready to discuss the reason for his stopover in Lexington.

"You could say we have our own team of spies who have been watching the flurry of activity on the Charles River. We climb to the top of the tower with our spyglass and can see for miles, making notes and observing how the soldiers' routines have changed. We have to be cautious of students who favor the Tory cause, but we stick to our strategies. That's when we, meaning the three of us, decided to leave school and ride to Lexington. We weren't expecting the rain to come down in buckets, which slowed us down significantly." Josiah grinned and nodded at his nephew's attempts to join the cause.

"So I suppose you're headed to Concord this afternoon. At least the rain has passed. You do realize that's a hard twenty miles to Wright's Tavern from this place. Mind you, the roads are narrow and winding, and today, they are soaked. Where do you plan to stay?" Thomas was full of questions, suspicious of every stranger he met, even if they were members of Josiah's family.

"We'll stay at my family's place. We hope to join with the militia and do what we can to frustrate the regulars from seizing weapons. The townspeople have worked non-stop collecting weapons from all over the colonies. It's our only means of defending what we own. We could not sit idly by in Cambridge, knowing all we've seen and doing nothing about it," Colin Barrett spoke without reservation.

"Did you travel with weapons? A musket and ammunition is required." Josiah was ready with his advice to the three students.

"My family has their own arsenal. I'm sure they will equip us sufficiently. Everyone is on high alert."

Father turned to Gray. "How do you fit into the picture since you live in Lincoln?"

"I'm of the same mind. With you and your family being forced to move from your home, there's more reason why we have a responsibility to protect our property. It proves to me that the British government is not concerned with our lives. Look at what they have done to their own people. I've learned that England's farms are used up, leaving people no choice but to move to London. If they want our property, they will have to take it by force. We've traveled here to do our part. If it turns into a revolution, then bring it on, and let's get this settled by asserting our independence."

"Let's make them reds turn tail and run. You're right. Concord is the strategic location, knowing the lay of the land and all." Thomas was mindful of the spirit of these young men. In fact, the majority of his militia was made up of young men eighteen years and older, many of them farmers.

Auntie and I stood at the work table, chopping vegetables for a sizable pot of stew. Not knowing the immediate plans of our guests, we opted for a meal that would feed ten people with big appetites. Auntie and I stood in the scullery, tending to the kitchen cleanup while we listened to the Harvard Men going on about their reasons for skipping classes. Auntie leaned close to my ear while scrubbing dishes and utensils. "They've eaten up everything in the kitchen." She was right, but I know she was as happy as I was that our visitors were consumed by the cause for defense.

I listened to their talk of Concord as being the targeted location where soldiers would begin their search for weapons, "strategically located along the main routes to the west," I heard Father say.

When I was younger, Father would hire a wagon from Fletcher's Livery to travel down Boston Neck, then west to Concord and Sudbury, where we would pick peaches in the late summer. We would cross the bridge over Concord River and make conversation about the surrounding hills, hoping to see a deer. The thought struck me just now that those woods would be a perfect place for our militia men to hide in wait as the regulars crossed the bridge.

"It's hardly a secret that the weapons are stored in Concord. Gage has his spies, and the Provincials have theirs. For months now, Gage has hired particular soldiers to hang about the taverns, offering to buy locals a pint in exchange for information. Sometimes, it works in their favor; sometimes, it doesn't. Some are better actors than others." Father finished his coffee and offered our guests beds in our hospital quarters if they desired to take a rest before traveling West, which they didn't, of course. Colin and Gray announced they should see about their horses, which probably meant a chance to retreat to the privy after all the coffee they consumed. Thomas made his move to leave for Buckman's Tavern. I was concerned about Thomas. His stooped shoulders and worried face marked his own misgivings of the face-off with British regulars. He refused the food and drink we offered him. In his words, "I not concerned that provincials will be defeated, for they are armed and ready. Regrettably, this is where the war with England will begin."

The rain had cleared away, and the sun shone brightly. Steam rose from the ground. Jake lingered in the kitchen to catch us up on Mulberry Farm news. "Yes, Mother gave birth to a girl, and they are healthy. Harry joined the Stoughton militia, but I've not heard if they are marching in this direction. Ethan and his Indian cousins are safeguarding the malthouse and have produced a sizable number of kegs for distribution. Tavern sales have risen since the redcoats arrived last spring.

"I assume you know Eli's story and the man from Suffield who doctored him. Naomi is with child, although I'm not sure when her baby is due. Poppi seems well enough, although he's quite concerned about the security of Mulberry Farm and the colonies in general. Everyone expressed their regrets that you all seem to have been pushed out of your house and surgery. Better than being held hostage in a town of redcoats!"

My heart jumped when Jake mentioned Suffield, which could only mean Nat Stowe to me. If I had probed for details about any part of Eli's story, Jake's suspicious brain would have put two and two together, formulating the idea that Nat Stowe and I were more than acquaintances. He would try out his lawyer tricks of pressing me for information, which I had no intention of sharing with him. My relationship with Nat, brief as it was, was so personal that I could not speak of it with anyone. I needed assurance that he felt about me the same as I felt about him. Then, there was the note he had delivered to me when he left Boston. But that was a while ago—almost a year. I tucked my feelings down deep. My world was soon to be shaken by outside forces, and I had no intention of losing my head.

Jake and his friends left for Concord, unusually excited that they could possibly be joining in a conflict against the most powerful army in the world. Earlier, while I listened to them talk about British plans and strategies, it caused me to evaluate things from a more practical standpoint. How long would it take for a regiment, which I learned amounted to about six hundred soldiers, to embark from Boston Common and row across the Charles River? Certainly, in the dead of night, to avoid discovery, they would land somewhere near Cambridge. How many boats did the British have, and how many back-and-forth trips would it take to assemble hundreds of soldiers to march through Cambridge during the night to Lexington and then on to Concord? After all, there was only one way in and one way out once the regiments reached land, except for Bay Road. Everything in between was wilderness. That was a mathematical problem that I pondered during what was left of the day.

I could see Auntie was agitated. She wasn't content to remain stationary long enough to knit a pair of socks. She stepped outside to her garden, muddy as it was, to weed and tend her sprouting herbs.

She knew more than I how fragile life became when faced with the formidable circumstances that war brings. We considered the lives of the three Harvard Men who, once they settled themselves in Concord, would convert from scholars in a classroom to citizen soldiers facing off with the enemy. They needed their wits about them. May the Lord protect them.

Concord, Massachusetts

Jake, Gray, and Colin arrived in Concord, grateful for the quarter moon casting a snippet of light when the clouds moved past. The roads were muddy in some areas, but with Colin's familiarity with the winding roads, he confidently took the lead. The two trailing riders pushed hard to keep up, hoping to outrun the consuming darkness. The intense smells of freshly dug earth mixed with cow manure hung heavily in the humid night air as they rode in closer. Without comment, they exhaled through their mouths and tried desperately not to breathe in the fetid air.

The closer they moved to Colin Barrett's home, the Harvard Men realized they were not the only ones foolish enough to travel the countryside on a dark, virtually moonless night. They slowed their horses to a walk as they closed in on the sounds of creaking wagons pulled by teams of groaning oxen driven by shouting farmers who had rigged lighted lanterns to the wagon sides.

"Jumping Jehoshaphat, those wagons are packed with cannon, ammunition, and muskets." Colin strained his eyes to get a more exact look. "There must be fifty wagons lined up on the road. Look yonder in the field. That man is digging up something in a box. Must be muskets." Colin looked over at Jake and Gray. "Unbelievable!"

"Hey, you, college boy. What are you doing in these parts? You better be here to help," Brent Barrett hollered to Colin. "Welcome home."

"We *did* come to help." Colin glanced toward his worn-out friends, pretending to smile. "Looks like you're digging up an arsenal. Where are you headed with it?"

Brent reined in his horse alongside Colin. "Acton, Bedford, and Stow. Planning to outwit the regulars by moving the weapons away from

Concord to certain farms, dispersing most of them to militiamen in surrounding towns. We got word from Dr. Warren that the regulars are on the move to Concord to demand our weapons. Anything to confuse Gage will be to our advantage."

Jake piped in, "Any idea when they will cross the Charles?"

"I'm hearing it will happen late tomorrow afternoon and into the evening. I can't say the exact number, but the captain believes five to seven hundred." The Harvard Men gasped loudly in unison. "Not to worry, gentlemen. Militia regiments have begun to gather all over Concord. The alarm has spread throughout Middlesex County. Remember, our kind of fighting is unique to the Redcoats. We fight Indian style..."

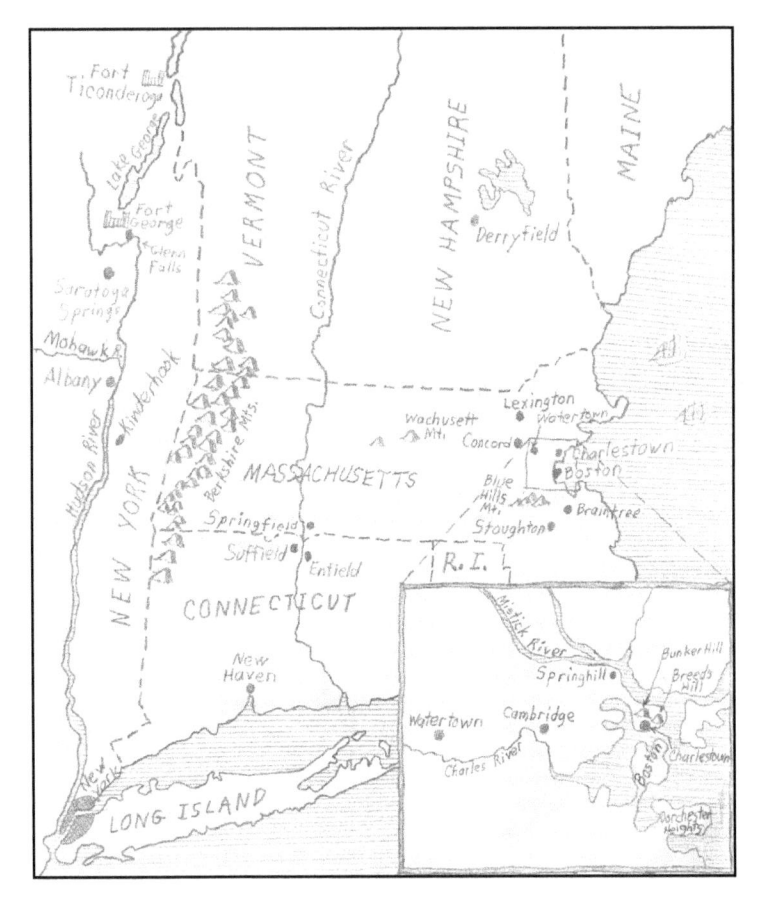

MAP OF COLONIAL NEW ENGLAND AND NEW YORK